EVERVILLE

CLIVE BARKER

EVERVILLE

The Second Book of the Art

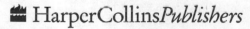 HarperCollins*Publishers*

HarperCollins books may be purchased for educational, business, or sales promotional use. For information please write: Special Markets Department, HarperCollins Publishers, Inc., 10 East 53rd Street, New York, NY 10022.

FIRST EDITION

Library of Congress Cataloging-in-Publication Data

Baker, Clive, 1952-
   Everville : the second book of the art / Clive Barker. — 1st ed.
       p. cm.
   ISBN 0-06-017716-0
   I. Title.
PR6052.A6475E94 1994
823'.914—dc20   94-27296

94 95 96 97 98 ❖/HC 10 9 8 7 6 5 4 3 2 1

CONTENTS

Memory, prophecy and fantasy—
the past, the future and
the dreaming moment between—
are all in one country,
living one immortal day.

To know that is Wisdom.

To use it is the Art.

PART ONE

Was, Is, and Will Be

I

*I*t was hope undid them. Hope, and the certainty that Providence had made them suffer enough for their dreams. They'd lost so much already along the trail—children, healers, leaders, all taken—surely, they reasoned, God would preserve them from further loss, and reward their griefs and hardships with deliverance into a place of plenty.

When the first signs of the blizzard had appeared—clouds that had dwarfed the thunderheads of Wyoming rising behind the peaks ahead, slivers of ice in the wind—they had said to each other: This is the final test. If we turn back now, intimidated by cloud and ice, then all those we buried along the way will have died for nothing; their suffering and ours will have been for nothing. We must go on. Now more than ever we must have faith in the dream of the West. After all, they told each other, it's only the first week of October. Maybe we'll see a flurry or two as we climb, but by the time the winter sets in we'll be over the mountains and down the other side, in the midst of sweet meadows.

On then; on, for the sake of the dream.

Now it was too late to turn back. Even if the snows that had descended in the last week had not scaled the pass behind the pioneers, the horses were too malnourished and too weakened by the climb to haul the wagons back through the mountains. The travelers had no choice but to go forward, though they had long since lost any sense of their whereabouts and were journeying blind in a whiteness as utter as any black midnight.

Sometimes the wind would shred the clouds for a moment, but there was no sign of sky or sun. Only another pitiless peak rising between them and the promised land, snow driven from its summit in a slow plume, then drooping, and descending upon the slopes where they would have to venture if they were to survive.

Hope was small now; and smaller by the day. Of the eighty-three optimistic souls who had departed Independence, Missouri, in the spring of 1848 (this sum swelled by six births along the way), thirty-one remained alive. During the first three months of the journey, through Kansas, into Nebraska, then across 487 miles of Wyoming, there had been only six fatalities. Three lost in a drowning accident; two wandered off and believed killed by Indians; one hanged by her own hand from a tree. But with the heat of summer, sicknesses abounded, and the trials of the journey began to take their toll. The very young and the very old had perished first, sickened by bad water or bad meat. Men and women who had been in the prime of their lives five or six months before, hardy, brave, and ripe, became withered and wretched as the food stocks dwindled, and the land, which they had been told would supply them with all manner of game and fruit, failed to provide the promised bounty. Men would leave the wagon train for days at a time in search of food, only to return hollow-eyed and empty-handed. It was therefore in an already much weakened state that the travelers faced the cold, and its effect had proved calamitous. Forty-seven individuals had perished in the space of three weeks, dispatched by frost, snow, exhaustion, starvation, and hopelessness.

It had fallen to Herman Deale, who was the closest the survivors had to a physician since the death of Doc Hodder, to keep an account of these deaths. When they reached Oregon, the glad land in the West, he had told the survivors they would together pray for the departed, and pay due respects to each and every soul whose passing he had set down in his journal. Until that happy time, the living were not to concern themselves overmuch with the dead. They had gone into the warmth and comfort of God's Bosom and would not blame those who buried them for the shallowness of their graves, or the brevity of the prayers said over them.

"We will speak of them lovingly," Deale had declared, "when we have a little breath to spare."

The day after making this promise to the deceased, he had joined their number, his body giving out as they ploughed through a snowfield. His corpse remained unburied, at least by human hand. The snow was coming down so thickly that by the time his few provisions had been divided up among the remaining travelers, his body had disappeared from sight.

That night, Evan Babcock and his wife, Alice, both perished in their sleep, and Mary Willcocks, who had outlived all five of her children, and seen her husband wither and die from grief, succumbed with a sob that was still ringing off the mountain-face after the tired heart that had issued it was stilled.

Daylight came, but it brought no solace. The snowfall was as heavy as ever. Nor was there now a single crack in the clouds to show the pioneers what lay ahead. They went with heads bowed, too weary to speak, much less sing, as they had sung in the blithe months of May and June, raising hosannas to the heavens for the glory of this adventure.

A few of them prayed in silence, asking God for the strength to survive. And some, perhaps, made promises in their prayers, that if they were granted that strength, and came through this white wilderness to a green place, their gratitude would be unbounded, and they would testify to the end of their lives that for all the sorrows of this life, no man should turn from God, for God was hope, and Everlasting.

*   *   *

ii

At the beginning of the journey west there had been a total of thirty-two children in the caravan. Now there was only one. Her name was Maeve O'Connell; a plain twelve-year-old whose thin body belied a fortitude which would have astonished those who'd shaken their heads in the spring and told her widowed father she would never survive the journey. She was stick and bones, they'd said, weak in the legs, weak in the belly. Weak in the head too, most likely, they whispered behind their hands, just like her father Harmon, who while the parties had been assembling in Missouri, had talked most elaborately of his ambitions for the West. Oregon might well be Eden, he'd said, but it was not the forests and the mountains that would distinguish it as a place of human triumph: It was the glorious, shining city that he intended to build there.

Idiotic talk, it was privately opined, especially from an Irishman who'd seen only Dublin and the backstreets of Liverpool and Boston. What could he know of towers and palaces?

Once the journey was underway, those who scorned Harmon among themselves became a good deal less discreet, and he soon learned to keep talk of his ambitions as a founder of cities between himself and his daughter. His fellow travelers had more modest hopes for the land that lay ahead. A stand of timber from which to build a cabin; good earth; sweet water. They were suspicious of anyone with a grander vision.

Not that the modesty of their requirements had subsequently spared them from death. Many of the men and women who'd been most voluble in their contempt for Harmon were dead now, buried far from good earth or sweet water, while the crazy man and his stick and bones daughter lived on. Sometimes, even in these last desperate days, Maeve and Harmon would whisper as they walked together beside their skeletal nag. And if the wind shifted for a moment it would carry their words away to the ears of those nearby. Exhausted though they were, father and daughter were still talking of the city they would build when this travail was over and done; a wonder that would live long after every cabin in Oregon had rotted, and the memories of those who'd built them gone to dust.

They even had a name for this time-defying metropolis.

It would be called Everville.

Ah, Everville!

How many nights had Maeve listened to her father talk of the place, his eyes on the crackling fire, but his gaze on another sight entirely: the streets, the squares, and the noble houses of that miracle to be.

"Sometimes it's like you've already been there," Maeve had remarked to him one evening in late May.

"Oh but I have, my sweet girl," he had said, staring across the open land towards the last of the sun. He was a shabby, pinched man, even in those months of plenty, but the breadth of his vision made up for the narrowness of his brow and lips. She loved him without qualification, as her mother had before her, and never more than when he spoke of Everville.

"When have you seen it, then?" she challenged him.

"Oh, in dreams," he replied. He lowered his voice to a whisper. "Do you remember Owen Buddenbaum?"

"Oh yes."

How could anybody forget the extraordinary Mr. Buddenbaum, who had befriended them for a little time in Independence? A ginger beard, going to gray; waxed moustaches that pointed to his zenith; the most luxurious fur coat Maeve had ever seen, and such music in his voice that the most opaque things he said (which was the bulk of his conversation as far as Maeve was concerned) sounded like celestial wisdom.

"He was wonderful," she said.

"You know why he sought us out? Because he heard me calling your name, and he knew what it meant."

"You said it meant joy."

"So it does," Harmon replied, leaning a little closer to his daughter, "but it's also the name of an Irish spirit, who came to men in their dreams."

She'd never heard this before. Her eyes grew huge. "Is that true?"

"I could never tell you a lie," he replied, "not even in fun. Yes, child, it's true. And hearing me call for you, he took me by the arm and said: *Dreams are doorways, Mr. O'Connell.* Those were the very first words he said to me."

"What then?"

"Then he said: *If we but have the courage to step over the threshold. . . .*"

"Go on."

"Well, the rest's for another day."

"Papa!" Maeve protested.

"You be proud, child. If not for you, we'd never have met Mr. Buddenbaum, and I believe our fortune changed the moment we did."

He had refused to be further drawn on the subject, but had instead turned the conversation to the matter of what trees might be planted on Everville's Main Street. Maeve knew better than to press him, but she thought much about dreams thereafter. She would wake sometimes in the middle of the night with the ragged scraps of a dream floating around her head, and lie watching the stars, thinking: *Was I at the door then? And was there something wonderful on the other side, that I've already forgotten?*

She became determined to keep these fragments from escaping her, and with a little practice she learned to snatch hold of them upon waking and describe them aloud to herself. Words held them, she found, however rudimentary. A few syllables were all that was needed to keep a dream from slipping away.

She kept the skill to herself (she didn't even mention it to her father), and it was a pleasant distraction for the long, dusty days of summer to sit in the wagon and sew pieces of remembered dreams together so that they made stories stranger than any to be found in her books.

As for the mellifluous Mr. Buddenbaum, his name was not mentioned again for some considerable time. When it *was* finally mentioned, however, it was in circumstances so strange Maeve would not forget them until the day she died.

They had been entering Idaho, and by the calculations of Dr. Hodder (who assembled the company every third evening and told them of their progress), there was a good prospect that they would be over the Blue Mountains and in sight of the fertile valleys of Oregon before the autumn had properly nipped the air. Though supplies were low, spirits were high, and in the exuberance of the moment, Maeve's father had said something about Everville: A chance remark that might have passed unnoticed but that one of the travelers, a shrewish man by the name of Goodhue, was the worse for whiskey, and in need of some bone of contention. He had it here, and seized upon it with appetite.

"This damned town of yours will never be built," he said to Harmon. "None of us want it." He spoke loudly, and a number of the men—sensing a fight and eager to be diverted—sauntered over to watch the dispute.

"Never mind him, Papa," Maeve had murmured to her father, reaching to take his hand. But she knew by his knitted brows and clenched jaw this was not a challenge he was about to turn his back on.

"Why do you say that?" he asked Goodhue.

"Because it's *stupid*," the drunkard replied. "And you're a fool."

His words were slurred, but there was no doubting the depth of his contempt.

"We didn't come out here to live in your little *cage*."

"It won't be a cage," Harmon replied. "It will be a new Alexandria, a new Byzantium."

"Never heard of either of 'em," came a third voice.

The speaker was a bull of a man called Pottruck. Even in the shelter of her father's shoulder, Maeve trembled at the sight of him. Goodhue was a loudmouth, little more. But Pottruck was a thug who had once beaten his wife so badly she had sickened and almost died.

"They were great cities," Harmon said, still preserving his equilibrium, "where men lived in peace and prosperity."

"Where'd you learn all this shit?" Pottruck spat. "I see you readin' a lot of books. Where'd you keep 'em?" He strode towards the O'Connells' wagon. "Goin' to bring 'em out or shall I bring 'em out fer ya?"

"Just keep out of our belongings!" Harmon said, stepping into the bull's path.

Without breaking his stride, Pottruck swiped at Harmon, knocking him to the ground. Then, with Goodhue on his heels, he hoisted himself up onto the tail of the wagon, and pulled back the canvas.

"Keep out of there!" Harmon said, getting to his feet and stumbling towards the wagon.

As he came within a couple of strides, Goodhue wheeled around, knife in hand. He gave Harmon a whiskey-rotted smile. "Uh-uh," he said.

"Papa . . . " Maeve said, tears in her voice, ". . . please don't."

Harmon glanced back at his daughter. "I'm all right," he said. He advanced no further, but simply stood and watched while Goodhue clambered up into the wagon and joined Pottruck in turning over the interior.

The din of their search had further swelled the crowd, but none of the spectators stepped forward in support of Harmon and his daughter. Few liked Pottruck any more than they liked the O'Connells, but they knew which could do them the greater harm.

There was a grunt of satisfaction from inside the wagon now, and Pottruck emerged with a dark teak chest, finely polished, which he unceremoniously threw down onto the ground. Leaping down ahead of his cohort, Goodhue set to opening the chest with his knife. It defied him, and in his frustration he started to stab at the lid.

"Don't destroy it," Harmon sighed. "I'll open it for you."

He took a key from around his neck and knelt to unlock the box. Pottruck was down from the wagon now, and, pushing Harmon aside, kicked open the lid.

Maeve had seen what lay in that box many times. It wasn't much to the uneducated—just a few rolls of paper tied with leather thongs—but to her, and to her father, these were treasures. The city of Everville lay waiting to be born upon those sheets of parchment: its crossroads and its squares, its parks and boulevards and municipal buildings.

"What did I say?" Pottruck spat.

"You said books," Goodhue replied.

"I said *shit*, is what I said," Pottruck said, rummaging through the rolls of paper and tossing them hither and thither as he searched for something he recognized as valuable.

Maeve caught her father's eye. He was trembling from head to foot, his face ashen. His anger, it seemed, had been overtaken by fatalism, for which she was glad. Papers could be replaced. *He* could not.

Pottruck had given up on his digging now, and by the bored expression on his face, he was ready to go back to his wife-beating. He might have done so too had Goodhue not caught sight of something lying at the bottom of the box.

"What's this?" he said, stooping and reaching into its depths. A grin spread over his unshaven face. "This doesn't look like shit to me."

He brought his discovery out to meet the light, sliding it out of the parcel of paper in which it had been slid and holding it up for the assembly to see. Here was something even Maeve had not set eyes on before, and she squinted at it in puzzlement. It looked like a cross of some kind, but not, she could see, one that any Christian would wear.

She approached her father's side and whispered, "What is it, Papa?"

"It was a gift . . . " he replied, ". . . from Mr. Buddenbaum."

One of the women, Marsha Winthrop, who was one of the few who had ever shown anything approaching kindness to Maeve, now stepped from the knot of spectators to take a closer look at Goodhue's find. She was a large woman with a sharp tongue, and when she spoke, the throng ceased muttering a moment.

"Looks like a piece of jewelry to me," she said, turning to Harmon. "Was it your wife's?"

Maeve would often wonder in times to come what had possessed her father at that moment; whether it was stubbornness or perversity that kept him from telling a painless lie. Whichever it was, he refused the ease of deception.

"No," he said. "It did not belong to my wife."

"What is it then?" Goodhue wanted to know.

The answer came not from Harmon's lips but from the crowd.

"One of the Devil's signs," said a strident voice.

Heads turned, and smiles disappeared as Enoch Whitney emerged from the back of the crowd. He was not a man of the cloth, but he was by his own description the most God-fearing among them; a soul commanded by the Lord to watch over his fellows and remind them constantly of how the Enemy moved and worked his works in their midst. It was a painful task, and he seldom let an opportunity slip by to remind his charges how much he suffered for their impurities. But the responsibility lay with him to castigate in public forum any who strayed from the commandments in deed, word, or intention—the lecher, of course, the adulterer, the cheat. And tonight, the worshipper of godless things.

He strode in front of the erring father and daughter now, bristling with denunciations. He was a tall, narrow man, with eyes too busy about their duty ever to settle on anything for more than a moment.

"You have always carried yourself like a guilty man, O'Connell," he said, his gaze going from the accused, to Maeve, to the object in Goodhue's fingers. "But I could never get to the root of your guilt. Now I see it." He extended his hand. Goodhue dropped the cross into it, and retreated.

"I'm guilty of nothing," Harmon said.

"This is *nothing*?" Whitney said, his volume rising. He had a powerful voice, which he never tired of exercising. "*This is nothing?*"

"I said I was guilty of—"

"Tell me, O'Connell, what service did you do the Devil, that he rewarded you with this unholy thing?"

There were gasps among the assembly. To speak of the Evil One so openly was rare; they kept such talk to whispers, for fear that it drew the attention of its subject. Whitney had no such anxieties. He spoke of the Devil with something close to appetite.

"I did no service," Harmon replied.

"Then it was a gift."

"Yes." More gasps. "But not from the Devil."

"This is Satan's work!" Whitney bellowed.

"It is not!" Harmon yelled back at him. "I have no dealings with the Devil. It's you who talk about Hell all the time, Whitney! It's you who sees the Devil in every corner! I don't believe the Devil cares much about us. I think he's off somewhere fancy—"

"The Devil's *everywhere!*" Whitney replied. "Waiting for us to make a mistake and *fall.*" This was not directed at Harmon, but at the assembly, which had thinned somewhat since Whitney's appearance. "There's no place, even to the wildernesses of the world, where his eyes are not upon us."

"You speak of the Devil the way true Christians speak of God Almighty," Harmon observed. "I wonder sometimes where your allegiances lie!"

The response threw Whitney into a frenzy. "How dare you question my righteousness," he foamed, "when I have proof, proof here in my hand, of your unholy dealings!" He turned to address the crowd. "We must not suffer this man in our midst!" he said. "He'll bring disaster upon us, as a service to his infernal masters!" He proffered the medallion, passing before his congregation. "What more proof do you need than *this?* It carries a parody of our Lord upon the cross!" He turned back upon Harmon, stabbing his finger at the accused. "I ask you again: What service did you do for this?"

"And I'll tell you, *one last time,* that until you stop finding the Devil's hand in our lives, you will be his greatest ally." He spoke softly now, as to a frightened child. "Your ignorance is the Devil's bliss, Whitney. Every time you scorn what confounds you, he smiles. Every time you sow the fear of him where there was none, he laughs. It's *you* he loves, Whitney, not me. It's you he thanks in his evening prayers." The tables had been turned so simply and so eloquently that for a moment Whitney did not fully comprehend his defeat. He stared at his opponent with a frown upon his face, while Harmon turned and addressed the crowd. "If you don't wish me and my daughter to travel with you any further," he said, "if you believe the slanders you've heard, then say so now, and we'll go another way. But be certain, all of you be certain, there is nothing in my heart or head but that the Lord God put it there. . . ."

There were tears in his voice as he came to the end of his speech, and Maeve slipped her hand into his to comfort him. Side by side they stood in front of the company, awaiting judgment. There was a short silence. It was broken not by Whitney but by Marsha Winthrop.

"I don't see no good reason to make you go your own way," she said. "We all started this journey together. Seems to me we should end it that way."

The plain good sense of this came as a relief to the crowd after all that talk of God and the Devil. There were murmurs of approval here and there, and several people began to depart. The drama was over. They had work to do: wheels to fix, stew to stir. But the righteous Whitney was not about to lose his congregation without one last warning.

"This is a dangerous man!" he growled. He threw the medallion to the dirt, and ground his heel upon it. "He'll drag us down into Hell with him."

"He ain't goin' to drag us anyplace, Enoch," Marsha said. "Now ya just go cool off, huh?"

Whitney cast a sour glance in Harmon's direction. "I'll be watchin' you," he said.

"I'm comforted," Harmon replied, which won a little laugh from Marsha.

As if the sound of laughter appalled him, Whitney hurried away, pushing through the crowd, muttering as he went.

"You'd better be careful," Marsha said to Harmon as she too departed. "You've got a tongue could do you harm one of these days."

"You did us a great kindness tonight," he replied. "Thank you."

"Did it for the child," Marsha replied. "Don't want her thinkin' the whole world's crazy."

Then she went away, leaving Harmon to gather up the scattered papers and return them to the chest. With her father's back turned, Maeve went in search of the medallion, picking it up and examining it closely. All of the descriptions she'd heard in the last few minutes seemed to her plausible. It was a pretty thing, no doubt of that. Shining like silver, but with flecks of color—scarlet and sky blue—in its luster. Any lady, wife or no, would be happy to wear it. But it was clearly more than a piece of decoration. There was a figure in the middle of it, outspread like Jesus on the cross, except that this savior was quite naked, and had something of both man and woman in its attributes. It was surely not a representation of the Devil. There was nothing fearsome in its aspect: no cloven hooves, no horns. Shapes flowed from its hands and head, and down between its legs, some of which she recognized (a monkey; lightning; two eyes, one above, one below), some of which were beyond her. But none were vile or unholy.

"Best not to look at it too long," she heard her father say.

"Why not?" she asked, staring still. "Will it bewitch me?"

"I don't know what it'll do, to tell the truth," her father said.

"Did Mr. Buddenbaum not tell you?"

Her father reached over her shoulder and gently pried the medallion from her fingers.

"Oh he told me, sure enough," Harmon said, returning to the box and placing the medallion inside, "only I didn't altogether understand him." With the contents now gathered up, he closed the lid and started to lug the box back to the wagon. "And I think maybe we should not speak that man's name aloud again."

"Why not?" Maeve said, determined to vex some answers out of her father. "Is he a bad man?"

Harmon set the box down on the tail of the wagon. "I don't know what kind of man he is," he replied, his voice low. "Truth is, I don't rightly know that he's a man at all. Maybe . . . " he sighed.

"What, Papa?"

"Maybe I dreamt him."

"But I saw him too."

"Then maybe we both dreamt him. Maybe that's all Everville is or will be. Just a dream we had, the two of us."

Her father had told Maeve he wouldn't lie to her, and she believed him, even now. But what kind of dream produced objects and real as the medallion she'd just held in her fingers?

"I don't understand," she said.

"We'll talk about this another time," Harmon said, passing his hand over his furrowed brow. "Let's have no more of it for now."

"Just tell me when," Maeve said.

"We'll know when the time's right," Harmon said, pushing the box back through the canvas and out of sight. "That's the way of these things."

II

i

These things, these things: what exactly *were* these things? For the next several weeks, as the wagon train wound its way through Idaho, following a trail forged by half a decade's westering, Maeve had puzzled over the mystery of all she'd seen and heard that day. In truth the puzzlement was a distraction—like the sewing together of dream-scraps—a distraction from the monotony of the trail. The weather through late June and July was mostly sweltering, and nobody had much energy for games. Adults had it easy, Maeve thought. They had maps to consult and feuds to fume over. And they had that business between men and women that her twelve-year-old mind did not entirely grasp, but that she yearned to comprehend. It was plain, from her observations, that young men would do much for a girl who knew how to charm them. They would follow her around like dogs, eager to supply any comfort; make fools of themselves if necessary. She understood these rituals imperfectly, but she was a good student, and this—unlike the enigmatic Mr. Buddenbaum—was a mystery she knew she would eventually solve.

As for her father, he was much subdued after the clash with Whitney, mixing with the rest of the travelers less than he had, and when he did so exchanging only the blandest of pleasantries. In the safety and secrecy of the wagon, however, he continued to pore over the plans for the building of Everville, scrutinizing them with greater intensity than ever. Only once did she attempt to coax him from his study. He told her sternly to let him be. It was his intention, he said, to have Everville by heart, so that if Pottruck or Goodhue or their like attempted and succeeded in destroying the plans, he could raise the shining city from memory.

"Be patient, sweet," he told her, then, his sternness mellowing. "Just a few more weeks and we'll be over the mountains. Then we'll find a valley and begin."

In this, as in all else, she trusted him, and left him to pore over the plans. What was a few weeks? She would content herself in the meanwhile with the triple mystery of dreams, things unsaid, and the business between men and women.

In a tiny time they would be in Oregon. Nothing was more certain.

ii

But the heat went out of the world even before August was over, and by the end of the third week, with the Blue Mountains not yet visible even to the keenest eye, and food so severely rationed that some were too weak to walk, the word had spread around the campfires that according to friendly natives, storms of unseasonal severity were already descending from the heights. Sheldon Sturgis, who had led the train thus far with a loose hand (some said that was his style; others that he was simply weak and prone to drink), now began to hasten along those who were slowing progress. But with a growing number of frail and sickened pioneers, mistakes and accidents proliferated, adding to the delays that were an inevitable part of such journeys: wheels lost, animals injured, trails blocked.

Death became a fellow traveler sometime in early September, that was Maeve's belief. She did not see him at first, but she was certain of his presence. He was in the land around them, killing living things with his touch or his breath. Trees that should have been fruitful in this season had already given up their leaves and were going naked. Animals large and small could be seen dead or dying beside the trail. Only carcass-flies were getting fat this September; but then Death was a friend to flies, wasn't he?

At night, waiting for sleep to come, she could hear people praying in the wagons nearby, begging God to keep Death at bay.

It did no good. He came anyway. To Marsha Winthrop's baby son, William, who had been born in Missouri just two weeks before the trek began. To Jack Pottruck's father, a beast of a man like his son, who suddenly weakened and perished in the middle of the night (not quietly, like the Winthrop child, but with terrible cries and imprecations). To the sisters Brenda and Meriel Schonberg, spinsters both, whose passing was only discovered when the train stopped at dusk and their wagon went unhalted, the women being dead at the reins.

Maeve could not help wonder why Death had chosen these particular souls. She could understand why he had taken her mother: She had been very beautiful and gracious and loving. He had wanted to make the world the poorer by removing her, and himself the richer. But what did he want with a baby and an old man and two withered sisters?

She didn't bother her father with such questions; he was fretful and beset enough. Though their wagon showed no sign of failing, and their horse was as healthy as any in the train, it was clear from the look in his sunken eyes that he too knew Death was an unwelcome outrider these days. She began to watch for the horseman more clearly, hoping to reassure her father by identifying the enemy; to say, I know the color of his horse and of his hat, and if he comes near us I'll know him and frighten him off with a prayer or a song. More than once she thought she caught sight of him, weaving between the wagons up ahead, dark in the dust. But she was never certain of any sighting, so she kept her silence rather than give her father an unverified report.

And the days passed, and the cold deepened, and when finally the Blue Mountains came into view, their slopes were white down below the tree line, and the clouds behind them black and bruised by their burden of ice.

And Abilene Welsh and Billy Baxter, whose antics in the summer had been the subject of much gossip (and clucking from Martha Winthrop), were found frozen in each other's arms one morning, touched by death as they enjoyed each other's company away from the warmth of the fires. Even as they were being buried, and Doc Hodder was speaking of how they would be eternally united in the Kingdom of the Lord, and those sins they might have committed in the name of love forgiven, Maeve looked up at the gray heavens and saw the first flakes of snow spiraling down. And that was the beginning of the end.

iii

She gave up looking for Death the Outrider after that. If he had ever accompanied the wagons on horseback, as she'd suspected, he had now put off that shape. He had become simpler. He was ice.

It killed many of the travelers quickly, and those it did not kill it tormented with intimations of the state ahead. It slowed the brain and the blood; it made the fingers fumble and the feet numb; it stiffened the sinews; it lined the lungs with a dusting of frost.

Sometimes, even now, with so many people dead and the rest dying, Maeve would hear her father say: "It wasn't supposed to be this way," as though some promise had been made to him that was presently being broken. She did not doubt the identity of the promise-maker. Mr. Buddenbaum. It was he who had filled her father's heart with ambition, who had given him gifts and told him to go West and build. It was he who had first whispered the word *Everville*. Perhaps, she began to think, Whitney had been right. Perhaps the Devil *had* come to tempt her father in the form of Mr. Buddenbaum, and filled his trusting heart with dreams for the pleasure of watching that heart broken. The problem vexed her night and day—never more so than when her father, in the midst of the storm—leaned over to her and said: "We must be strong, sweet. We mustn't die, or Everville dies with us!"

Hunger and exhaustion had her teetering on delirium now—sometimes she would imagine herself on the ship coming from Liverpool, clinging to the icy deck with her fingertips; sometimes she was back in Ireland, eating grass and roots to keep her belly from aching—but in times of lucidity she wondered if perhaps this was some kind of test; Buddenbaum's way of seeing whether the man to whom he'd given the dream of Everville was strong enough to survive. The notion seemed so plausible she could not keep it to herself.

"Papa?" she said, grabbing hold of his coat.

Her father looked round at her, his face barely visible beneath his hood. She could only see one of his eyes, but it looked at her as lovingly as ever.

"What, child?" he said.

"I think maybe—maybe it *was* meant to be this way."

"What are you saying?"

"Maybe Mr. Buddenbaum's watching us, to see if we deserve to build his city. Maybe just when we think we can't go on any longer he'll appear, and tell us it was a test, and show us the way to the valley."

"This isn't a test, child. It's just what happens in the world. Dreams die. The cold comes out of nowhere and kills them." He put his arm around his daughter, and hugged her to him, though there was precious little strength left in him.

"I'm not afraid, Papa," she said.

"Are you not?"

"No I'm not. We've come a long way together."

"That we have."

"Remember how it was back at home? How we thought we'd die of starvation? But we didn't. Then on the ship. Waves washing people overboard to right and left of us, and we thought we'd drown for certain. But the waves passed us by. Didn't they?"

His cracked, white lips managed a tiny smile. "Yes, child, they did."

"Mr. Buddenbaum knew what we'd come through," Maeve said. "He knew there were angels watching over us. And Mama too—"

She felt her father shudder at her side. "I dreamed of her last night—" he said.

"Was she beautiful?"

"Always. We were floating, side by side, in this calm, calm sea. And I swear, if I'd not known you were here, child, waiting for me—"

He didn't finish the thought. A sound like a single blast of a trumpet came out of the blind whiteness ahead; a note of triumph that instantly raised a chorus of shouts from the wagons in front and behind.

"Did ya hear that?"

"There's somebody up here with us!"

Another blast now, and another, and another, each rising from the echo of the last till the whole white world was filled with brazen harmonies.

The Sturgis' wagon, which was ahead of the O'Connells', had come to a halt, and Sheldon was calling back down the line, summoning a party of men to his side.

"Stratton! Whitney! O'Connell! Get your guns!"

"Guns?" said Maeve. "Papa, why does he want guns?"

"Just climb up into the wagon, child," Harmon said, "and stay there till I come back."

The din of trumpets had died away for a moment, but now it came again, more magnificent than ever. As she climbed up onto the wagon, Maeve's skinny frame ran with little tremors at the sound, as though the music was shaking her muscles and marrow. She started to weep, seeing her father disappear, rifle in hand. Not because she feared for him but because she wanted to go out into the snow herself and see what manner of trumpet made the sound that moved in her so strangely, and what manner of man played upon it. Perhaps they were not men at all, her spinning head decided. Perhaps the angels she'd been gabbing about minutes before had come to earth, and these blasts were their proclamations.

She started out into the snow, suddenly and uncontrollably certain that this was true. Their heavenly guardians had come to save them, and Mama too, more than likely. If she looked hard she would see them soon, gold and blue and purple. She stood up on the seat, clinging to the canvas, to get a better view, scanning the blank snow in every direction. Her study was rewarded. Just as the trumpets began their third hallelujah, the snow parted for a few moments. She saw the mountains rising to left and right like the teeth of a trap, and ahead of her a single titanic peak, its lower slopes forested. The perimeter of the trees lay no more than a hundred yards from the wagon, and the music she heard was coming from that direction, she was certain of it. Of her father, and of the men accompanying him, there was no sign, but they had surely disappeared among the trees. It would be quite safe to follow them, and wonderful to be there at her father's side when he was reunited with Mama. Wouldn't that be a blissful time, kissing her mother in a circle of angels, while Whitney and all the men who had scorned her father looked on agog?

The opening in the veil of snow was closing again, but before it did so she jumped down from the wagon and started off in the direction of the trees. Within moments, snow had obliterated the wagons behind her, just as it had covered the forest ahead, and she was following her nose through a blank world, stumbling with every other step. The drifts lay perilously deep in places, and she several times dropped into drifts so deep she was almost buried alive. But just as her frozen limbs threatened to give up on her, the trumpets came again, and the music put life back into her sinews and filled her head with bliss. There was a piece of paradise up ahead. Angels and Mama and her loving father, with whom she would build a city that would be the wonder of the world.

She would not die, of that she was certain. Not today, not for many years to come. She had great work to do, and the angels would not see her perish in the snow, knowing how far she had traveled to perform that labor.

And now she saw the trees, pines higher than any house, like a wall of sentinels in front of her. Calling for her father she ran towards them, careless of the cold and the bruises and her spinning head.

The trumpets were close, and there were bursts of color in the corner of her eye, as though some of the angelic throng, who had not yet picked their instruments, were clustered about her, the tips of their beating wings all that she was allowed to glimpse.

Borne by invisible hands, she was ushered beneath the canopy of trees and there, where the snow could not come, and the ground was soft with pine needles, she sank down onto her knees and drew a dozen heaving breaths while the sound of trumpets touched her in every part.

III

It was not music that finally picked her up, nor the hands of the invisible throng. It was a shout, which rose above the trumpet echoes, and filled her with alarm.

"*Damn you, O'Connell!*" She knew the voice. It was Whitney. "God in Heaven! What have you done?" he yelled.

She got to her feet and started towards his din. Her eyes were not yet accustomed to the gloom after the brightness of the blizzard, and the further from the edge of the forest she ventured, the darker it became, but the rage in Whitney's voice spurred her on, careless of what lay in her path. The trumpets had fallen silent. Perhaps the angels had heard his rants, she thought, and would not float their harmonies on tainted air, or perhaps they were simply watching to see what human rage was like.

"You knew!" Whitney was yelling. "You brought us into Hell!"

Maeve could see him now, moving between the trees, calling after his quarry into the shadows.

"O'Connell? O'Connell! You'll burn in a lake of fire for this. Burn and burn and—"

He stopped; swung round, his eyes finding Maeve with terrible speed. Before she could retreat, he yelled: "I see you! Come out, you little bitch!"

Maeve had no choice. He had her in the sights of his rifle. And now, as she approached him between the trees, she saw that he was not alone. Sheldon Sturgis and Pottruck were just a few yards from him. Sturgis was crouched against a tree, terrified of something in the branches above him, where his rifle was pointed. Pottruck was watching Whitney's antics with a bemused expression on his oafish face.

"O'Connell?" Whitney yelled. "I got your little girl here." He adjusted his aim, squinting for accuracy. "I got her right between the eyes if I pull the trigger. An' I'm going to do it. Hear me, O'Connell?"

"Don't shoot," Sturgis said. "You'll bring it back."

"It'll come anyway," Whitney said. "O'Connell sent it to fetch our souls."

"Oh Jesus Christ in Heaven—" Sturgis sobbed.

"Stand right there," Whitney said to Maeve. "And you call to your Daddy and you tell him to keep his demon away from us or I'll kill you."

"He hasn't—hasn't got any demons," Maeve said. She didn't want Whitney to know that she was afraid, but she couldn't help herself. Tears came anyway.

"You just tell him," Whitney said, "you just call." He pushed the rifle in Maeve's direction, so that it was a foot from her face. "If you don't I'll kill you. You're the Devil's child's what you are. Ain't no crime killing muck like you. Go on. *Call him.*"

"Papa?"

"*Louder!*"

"Papa?"

There was no reply from the shadows. "He doesn't hear me."

"I hear you, child," said her father. She looked towards his voice and there he was, coming towards her out of the murk.

"Drop your rifle!" Pottruck yelled to him.

Even as he did, the trumpets began again, louder than ever. The music clutched at Maeve's heart with such force she started to gasp for breath.

"What's wrong?" she heard her father say, and glanced back in his direction to see him start towards her.

"Stay where you are!" Whitney yelled, but her father kept running.

There was no second warning. Whitney simply fired, not once but twice. One bullet struck him in the shoulder, the other in the stomach. He stumbled on towards her, but before he could take two strides, his legs gave out beneath him, and he fell down.

"Papa!" she yelled, and would have gone to him, but then the trumpets began another volley, and as their music rose up in her, bursts of white light blotted out the world, and she dropped to the ground in a swoon.

"I hear it coming—"

"Shut up, Sturgis."

"*It is! It's coming again. Whitney! What do we do?*"

Sturgis's shrill shouts pricked Maeve awake. She opened her eyes to see her father lying where he had fallen. He was still moving, she saw, his hands clutching rhythmically at his belly, his legs twitching.

"*Whitney!*" Sturgis was screaming. "It's coming back."

She could not see him from where she lay, but she could hear the thrashing of the branches, as though the wind had suddenly risen. Whitney was praying.

"Our Lord, who art in Heaven—"

Maeve moved her head a little, in the hope of glimpsing the trio without drawing attention to herself. Whitney was on his knees, Sturgis was cowering against the tree, and Pottruck was staring up into the canopy waving wildly: "Come on, you fucking shit! Come on!"

Certain she was forgotten, Maeve got to her feet cautiously, reaching out to grab hold of the nearest tree trunk for support. She looked back to her father, who had raised his head a couple of inches off the ground and was staring at Pottruck as he fired up into the thrashing branches.

Sturgis yelled, "*Christ, no!,*" Whitney started to rise from his kneel, and in that same moment, a form that Maeve's bewildered eyes could not quite distinguish from the branches—it had their sweep and their darkness—swooped upon Pottruck.

Whatever it was, it was no angel. There were no feathers here. There was no gold or scarlet or blue. The beast was naked, of that she was reasonably certain, and its flesh gleamed. That was all she had time to grasp before it picked Pottruck up and carried him off, up into the canopy.

He screamed and screamed, and Maeve, though she hated the man with a passion, wished he might be saved from his torment, if only to stop his din. She covered her ears but his cries found their way between her fingers, mounting in volume as a terrible rain fell from the branches. First came the rifle, then blood, pattering down. Then one of Pottruck's arms, followed by a piece of flesh she could not distinguish; and another. And still he screamed, though the pat-ter of the blood had become a downpour, and the snaking part of his innards dropped from the tree in a glistening loop.

Suddenly, Sturgis was rising from his hiding place, and began to fire into the tree. Perhaps he put Pottruck from his misery, perhaps the beast simply took out the man's throat. Whichever, the terrible sound ceased, and a moment later Pottruck's body, so mangled it looked barely human, fell from the branches and lay steaming on the ground.

The canopy stilled. Sturgis backed away into the shadows, sti-fling his sobs. Maeve froze, praying that Whitney would go with him. But he did not. Instead he started towards her father.

"See what you did, calling the Evil One?" he said.

"I—didn't—call anybody," Harmon gasped.

"You tell it to go back to the pit, O'Connell. *You tell it!*"

Maeve looked back in Sturgis's direction. The man had fled. But her gaze fell on Pottruck's rifle, which lay beneath the dripping branches a yard from his corpse.

"You *repent*," Whitney was saying to Harmon. "You send that devil back where it came from, or I'm going to blow off your hands, then your pecker, till you're begging to repent."

With Sturgis gone and Whitney's back turned, Maeve didn't

need much caution. Eyes cast up towards the branches, where she was certain the beasts still squatted, she started towards the rifle. She could see no sign of the creature—the mesh of branches was too thick—but she could feel its gaze on her.

"Please . . . " she whispered to it, the syllables too soft to attract Whitney's attention, "don't hurt . . . me."

The squatter made no move. Not a twig shook; not a needle fell.

She glanced down at the ground. Pottruck's body lay sprawled in front of her, a nonsense now. She'd seen corpses before. Dead in Irish ditches, dead in Liverpool gutters, dead along the trail to the promised land. This one was bloodier than most, but it didn't move her. She stepped over it and stooped to pick up the rifle.

As she did so she heard the thing above her expel a sighing breath. She froze, heart thumping, waiting for the claws to come and pluck her up. But no. Just another sigh, almost sorrowful. She knew it wasn't wise to linger here a moment longer than she needed, but she couldn't keep her curiosity in check. She rose with the rifle, and looked back up into the knot of branches. As she did so a drop of blood hit her cheek, and a second fell between her parted lips. It was not Pottruck's blood, she knew that the moment it hit her tongue. The drop was not salty, but sweet, like honey, and though she knew it was coming from the beast (Pottruck's aim had not been so wild after all, it seemed), her hunger overcame any niceties. She opened her mouth a little wider, hoping another drop would come her way, and she was not disappointed. A little shower of drops struck her upturned face, some of them finding her mouth. Her throat ran with spittle, and she could not help but sigh with pleasure at the taste.

The creature in the tree moved now, and she briefly glimpsed its form. Its wings were open wide, as though it was ready to swoop upon her; its head—if she read the shadows right—cocked a little.

And still the blood came, the drops no longer missing her mouth but falling directly upon her tongue. This was no accident, she knew. The beast was feeding her; squeezing its wounded flesh above her face like a honey-soaked sponge.

It was a moan from her father that stirred her from the strange reverie that had overtaken her. She looked away from her nourisher, and back through the trees. Whitney was crouching beside Harmon's body, his rifle at her father's head.

She started towards them, lighter and fleeter than she'd been in weeks. Her belly no longer ached. Her head no longer spun.

Whitney did not see her until she was six or seven yards away, Pottruck's bloodied rifle pointing directly at him. She had never used a weapon like this before, but at such a distance, it would be difficult to discharge it without doing *some* harm. Plainly the tormentor made the same calculation, because his face grew fretful at the sight of her.

"You should be careful with that, child," he said.

"You leave Papa alone."

"I wasn't touching him."

"Liar."

"I wasn't. I swear."

"Maeve, my sweet—" Harmon murmured, raising his head with no little difficulty, "go back to the wagon. Please. There's something—something terrible here."

"No, there isn't," Maeve replied, the blood of the beast still sweet on her tongue. "It's not going to hurt us." She looked back at Whitney. "We've got to get my Papa fixed up, before he dies. You put down your rifle." Whitney did so, and Maeve approached, keeping her own weapon pointed in his direction while she looked upon her father. He was a pitiful sight, his jacket and shirt dark with blood from collar to belt.

"Help him up," she told Whitney. "Which way is it back to the wagons?"

"You go, child," Harmon said softly. "I got no life left in me."

"That's not true. We'll get you to the wagons and Mrs. Winthrop can bandage you up—"

"No," Harmon said. "It's too late."

Maeve came to her father's side, and looked directly down into his eyes. "You've got to get well," she said, "or what'll happen to Everville?"

"It was a fine dream I dreamed," he murmured, raising his trembling hand towards her. She took it. "But you're finer, child," he said. "You're the finest dream I ever had. And it's not so hard to die, knowing you're in the world."

Then his eyes flickered closed.

"Papa?" she said. "Papa?"

"He's gone to Hell—" Whitney murmured.

She looked up at him. He was smiling. The tears she'd held back now came in a bitter flood—of sorrow, and of rage—and she went down on her knees beside her father, pressing her face against his cold cheek. "Listen to me—" she said to him.

Did she feel a tremor in his body, as though he were still holding on to a tiny piece of life, listening to his child's voice in the darkness?

"I'm going to build it, Papa," she whispered. "I am. I promise. It won't be just a dream—"

As she finished speaking she felt a feather breath against her cheek, and she knew he had heard her. And having heard, had let go.

The joy of that knowledge was short-lived.

"You're not going to build *anything*," Whitney said.

She looked up at him. He had reclaimed his weapon, and was pointing it at her heart.

"Stand up," he said. As she did so he knocked Pottruck's rifle from her hand. "Your tears don't impress me none," he went on. "You're goin' the way of your Daddy."

She raised her arms in front of her as though her palms might deflect his bullets.

"Please—" she murmured, stumbling backwards.

"Stand still," he yelled, and as he yelled he fired, the bullet striking the ground inches from her feet. "You're coming with me, in case that devil your Daddy raised comes calling again."

He had no sooner spoken that there was a disturbance in the branches a few yards behind him.

"Oh Lord in Heaven—" Whitney breathed, and rushed at Maeve, spinning her around and pulling her back against his body.

She sobbed for him not to hurt her, but he grabbed a fistful of her hair and hauled her on to her tiptoes. Then he started to back away from the spot where the canopy was shaking, with Maeve obliged to match him step for step.

They had taken maybe six paces when the shaking stopped. The wounded beast was not prepared to risk another bullet, it seemed. Whitney's panicked breaths became a little more regular. "It's going to be all right," he said. "I got the Lord watching over me."

He'd no sooner spoken than the beast erupted, moving through the trees overhead with such speed and violence that entire boughs came crashing down. Maeve took her chance. She reached up and stabbed her nails into Whitney's hand, twisting her body as she did so. Her greasy hair slipped from his fist, and before he could catch hold of her again she was away, seeking the shelter of the nearest tree.

She'd taken three strides, no more, when what she took to be two branches dropped in front of her. As she raised her arms to cover her face, she realized her error. The limbs grabbed hold of her, their fingers long enough to meet around her waist. Her breath went out of her in a rush, and she was hauled off the ground and up into the shelter of the trees.

Whitney fired, and fired again, but her wounded savior was as quick in his retreat as he'd been to snatch her away.

"*Hold on,*" he told her, his hands hot against her, and even before she'd even found proper purchase went off through the canopy, his wings slicing the branches like twin scythes as they labored to carry the beast and his burden skyward.

IV

She had forgotten the trumpets. But now, as her savior bore her up through the trees, the music came again, more splendid than ever.

"The Lady comes," the creature said, alarm in his voice, and without warning began to descend again with such speed she almost lost her hold on him and was spilled from his arms.

"What lady?" she asked him, studying the shadows that hid his face from her.

"Better you not know," he said. The ground was in sight now. "Don't look at me," he warned her as they cleared the lower branches, "or I'll have to put out your eyes."

"You wouldn't do that."

"Oh wouldn't I?" he replied, his hand coming up over her face so swiftly she didn't have time to catch her breath before mouth, nose, and eyes were sealed. She drew what little air was trapped between her face and his palm. It smelled like his blood had tasted: sweet and appetizing. Opening her mouth, she pressed her tongue against his skin.

"I think you'd eat me alive if you could," he said. By his tone, it was plain the thought amused him.

She felt solid earth beneath her feet, and again he spoke, his mouth so close to her ear his beard or his moustache tickled her lobe.

"You're right, child. I can't blind you. But I beg you, when I take my hand from your face, close your eyes and keep them closed, and I will go from you whistling. When you can no longer hear me, open your eyes. But for your heart's sake—then and only then. Do you understand?"

She nodded, and he took his hand from her face. Her eyes were closed and stayed that way while he spoke again. "Go back to your family," he told her.

"My Papa's dead."

"Your Mama, then?"

"She's dead too. And Whitney'll kill me as soon as he sees me. He thinks I'm the Devil's child. He thinks you're a demon that my father conjured up."

The creature laughed at this out loud.

"You're not from Hell, are you?" she said.

"No, I'm not."

"Are you an angel then?"

"No, not that either."

"What then?"

"I told you: Better you not know." The trumpets were sounding again. "There. The ceremony's about to begin. I have to go. I wish I could do more for you, child, but I cannot." He laid his fingers lightly upon her eyelids. "Eyes closed until I'm gone."

"Yes."

"You promise me?"

"I promise."

His fingers were removed, and he began to whistle some pretty little tune, breaking it only to say: "Say nothing of this, to anyone," then picking up the melody again to mask his departure.

A promise made with fingers crossed was no promise at all; Maeve had known this from the age of five. Uncrossing her fingers now, she waited until the sound of whistling retreated just a little, then opened her eyes. Their flight had apparently taken them some considerable way up the mountain, because the ground around the rock on which he'd set her was steeply sloped. Far fewer trees grew here; and there was consequently far more light. She could see the sky overhead—the snow had stopped, the parting clouds tinged a delicate pink by the setting sun—and when she cast her eyes up the mountainside in pursuit of the whistler she found him readily enough. At this distance, she could make out almost no detail of his appearance, but she was determined not to be denied it long. Climbing down off the boulder, she started after him.

It was hard going. The dirt and rotted needles slid away beneath her feet and hands as she climbed, and several times she had to scrabble for a root or a stone to keep herself from sliding back down the slope. The distance between herself and the beast grew steadily wider, and just as she began to fear losing sight of him altogether the same roseate light that had tinged the clouds overhead came between the trees, and with it a balmy air the like of which she'd not felt on her face in a month or more. The trees were more widely spread than ever, and between them she could see something of the slope beyond. It rose in a snowy sweep up to the top of the mountain, where the clouds had cleared completely, so that the peak stood against a sky pricked with the first of the stars. Their glimmer, however, could not compete with the lights shed on the snowfield below, the source of which Maeve did not discover until she was a few yards from the edge of the trees.

Several forms of misty light hovered over the slope, shedding their gentle luminescence on a scene of such beauty she stood among the trees rooted with wonder. Though her rescuer had denied he was an angel, surely heaven was here. From what other place could the creatures that inhabited this place have come? Though few of them had wings, all were in some way miraculous. A dozen or more that better resembled birds than men—beaked and shiny-eyed—stood communing beneath one of the spheres of light. Another clan, this at first glance dressed in scarlet silks, descended the slope with much ostentation, only to suddenly draw their brilliance into their bodies and hang in the air like skinned snakes. Yet another group had torsos like fans that opened lavishly, exposing vast, pulsing hearts.

Not every member of this assembly was so strange. Some were near enough men and women but for a color that passed through their skin, or a tail they trailed behind. Others were so tenuous that they were nearly phantoms, their passage leaving no mark upon the snow, while others still—these surely the cousins of her savior—seemed almost too solid in this place of spirit, brooding in the shadows of their wings, reluctant, it seemed, to even keep company with their fellows.

As to the creature that had unwittingly led her here, he was limping his way through the congregation towards a place at the top of the slope where a tent the color of the darkening sky had been pitched. She was of course instantly curious as to what wonder it contained. Did she dare leave the cover of the trees and follow him to find out? Why not? she reasoned. She had nothing to lose. Even if she were able to find her way back down the mountain to the wagons, Whitney would be there, with his rifle and his righteousness. Better to go where the creature and her curiosity led.

And now, another astonishment. Though she took her way out from the trees and up through the hundred or so gathered here, none made a move to question her or block her way. A few heads were turned in her direction, it was true, a few whispers exchanged of which she was surely the subject. But that was all. Among such strangenesses, her size and sickliness were apparently taken to be a glamor of their own.

As she climbed the thought occurred to her that perhaps this was a dream: that she had swooned on her father's chest, and would wake soon with his body cold beneath her. There were simple proofs against such doubts, however. First she pinched her arm, then she poked her tongue in the bad tooth at the back of her mouth. Both hurt, more than a little. She wasn't dreaming. Had she maybe lost her mind then, and was inventing these wonders the way travelers in the desert invented wells and fruit trees? No, that made no sense either. If these were comforts she'd created, where were her mother and her father; where were the tables laden with cake and milk?

Extraordinary as all these visions were, they were real. The lights, the families, the shimmering tent; all as real as Whitney and the wagons and the dead in their graves.

Thinking of what she'd left behind, she paused for a moment and looked back down the mountain. Night was drawing on swiftly, and the forest had receded into a misty darkness. She could see no sign of the wagons, nor were there any fires burning below. Either the snow had buried them all, or—more likely—they had moved on towards the mountain while the blizzard's fury subsided, assuming she was lost.

So she was. Orphaned and wandering among strangers, countless miles from the place where she was born, she was as lost as any soul could be. But she felt no sadness at that thought (a prick, perhaps, knowing her father lay in the dark below, but no more). Instead she felt a kind of joy. She was of a tribe of one here; and if she was ever asked what manner of magic she carried to this sacred place, she would sit these miraculous folk down and tell them about Everville, street by street, square by square, and they would be astonished. Nor would she be lost, when she'd told her tale, because Everville was her true home, and she was as safe in its heart as it was in hers.

V

i

*I*t wasn't difficult for Whitney to convince those waiting back at the wagons that they should give up the O'Connell girl as lost and move on. Darkness was falling and Sturgis had already returned from the forest with babbled tales of a terror that had brutally dispatched Pottruck. It was still here, Whitney warned, and though its conjurer was dead, the creature's appetite for blood and souls would only become stronger as the night deepened. Besides, the storm had abated a little. This was God's way of thanking them for their part in O'Connell's dispatch; they should not scorn it.

Nobody—not even Marsha Winthrop—put up any argument against their departure. Whitney had graphically described the girl's abduction. It was unlikely she had survived.

Even though the snowfall had given way to mist, and the moon when it rose was round and bright, progress was exhausting, and after an hour of travel—with the fringes of forest a safe distance behind them—they made camp for the remainder of the night.

Whitney sang hymns as he lit the fire, raising his unmelodious voice to the glory of God, praising Him for leading them from Hell's dominion. "The Lord has us in his hands," Whitney told the company between verses. "Our journey is almost done."

At his suggestion, Everett Immendorf's widow, Ninnie, was charged to make a stew, its ingredients culled from the last of everyone's supply of vittles.

"It will be the last supper we will take along this dark road," Whitney said, "for tomorrow God will bring us into our promised land."

The stew was little more than gruel, but it warmed them as they sat huddled about the fire. Drinking it, they dared talk quietly of deliverance. And it was in the midst of this talk they had proof that Whitney had been right. As the flames began to die down, there came a sound from beyond the throw of the light: that of someone politely clearing their throat.

Sturgis—who had not stopped trembling since his return—was first to his feet, his gun drawn.

"No need of that," came a floating voice. "I'm here as a friend."

Whitney rose to his feet. "Then show yourself, *friend*," he said.

The stranger did as he was invited, and sauntered into view. He was shorter than any man around the fire, but he carried himself with the easy gait of one who was seldom, if ever, crossed. The high collar of his fur coat was turned up, and he smiled out from its luxury as though the faces before him were those of well-fed friends, and he was coming to join them at a feast. Apart from the snow on his boots, there was no sign that he had exerted himself to reach this spot. Every detail was in place and bespoke a man of cultivation: waxed moustache, clipped beard, calf-skin gloves, silver-tipped cane.

There was not one among the group around the fire unmoved by his presence. Sheldon Sturgis felt a deep shame for his cowardice, certain that this man had never shat his pants in his life. Alvin Goodhue's stomach rebelled at the powerful perfume the man wore, and he summarily threw up his portion of gruel. Its cook, Ninnie Immendorf, didn't even notice. She was too busy feeling thankful for her widowhood.

"Where'd you come from?" Marsha wanted to know.

"Up the pass," the stranger replied.

"Where's your wagon?"

The man was amused by this. "I came on foot," he said. "It's no more than a mile or two down into the valley."

There were murmurs of joy and disbelief around the fire.

"We're saved!" Cynthia Fisher sobbed. "Oh Lord in Heaven, we're saved!"

"You were right" Goodhue said to Whitney, "we *were* in God's hands tonight."

Whitney caught the twitch of a smile on the stranger's face. "This is indeed welcome news," he said. "May we know who you are?"

"No secret there," the man replied. "My name's Owen Buddenbaum. I came to meet with some friends of mine, but I don't see them among your company. I hope no harm has befallen them."

"We've lost a lot of good people," Sturgis said. "Who're you looking for?"

"Harmon O'Connell and his daughter," Buddenbaum replied. "Were they not with you?"

The smiles around the fire died. There were several seconds of uneasy silence, then Goodhue simply said: "They're dead."

Buddenbaum teased the glove off his left hand as he spoke, his voice betraying nothing. "Is that so?" he said.

"Yes it's so," Sturgis replied. "O'Connell—got lost on the mountain."

"And the child?"

"She went after him. It's like he says, they're both dead."

Buddenbaum's bare hand went up to his mouth, and he nibbled on the nail of his thumb. There was at least one ring on every finger. On the middle digit, three. "I'm surprised—" he said.

"At what?" Whitney replied.

"At God-fearing men and women leaving an innocent child to freeze to death," Buddenbaum replied. He shrugged. "Well, we do what we must do." He pulled his glove back on. "I'll take my leave of you."

"Wait," said Ninnie, "won't you have something to eat? We ain't got much, but—"

"Thank you, no."

"I got a little coffee tucked away," Sheldon said. "We could brew a cup."

"You're very kind," Buddenbaum said.

"So *stay*," said Sheldon.

"Another time perhaps," Buddenbaum replied. He scanned the group as he spoke. "I'm sure our paths will cross in the future," he said. "We go our many ways but the roads lead back and back, don't they? And of course we follow them. We have no choice."

"You could ride back down with us," Sheldon said.

"I'm not *going* back," came the reply. "I'm going up the mountain."

"You're out of you're mind," Marsha said with her customary plainness. "You'll freeze up there."

"I have my coat and gloves," Buddenbaum replied, "And if a little child can survive the cold, I surely can."

"How many times—?" Goodhue began, but Whitney, who had taken a seat on the far side of the fire from Buddenbaum, and was studying the man through the smoke, hushed him.

"If he wants to go, let him," he said.

"Quite so," Buddenbaum replied. "Well—goodnight."

As he turned from the fire, however, Ninnie blurted out: "Trumpets."

Buddenbaum looked back. "I beg your pardon?"

"We heard trumpets, up on the mountain—" She looked to her fellow travelers for support, but none offered a word. "At least, *I* did," she went on hesitantly, "I heard—"

"Trumpets."

"Yes."

"Strange."

"Yes." She had lost all confidence in her story now. "Of course, it could have been . . . I don't know—"

"Thunder," said Whitney.

"Thunder that sounds like trumpets? Well, there's a thing. I'll listen out for it." He directed a little smile at Ninnie. "I'm much obliged," he said, with such courtesy she thought she'd swoon.

Then, without a further word, he turned his back upon the assembly and strode out of the firelight, and the darkness swallowed him whole.

ii

All those gathered around the fire that night would survive the rest of the journey, and all in their fashion prosper. It was a brave time in the West, and in the years to come they would build and profit and procreate heroically, putting behind them the harm they'd suffered getting there. They would not speak of the dead, despite the promises they'd made. They would not seek out the bones of those ill-buried and see them laid to rest with better care. They would not mourn. They would not regret.

But they would remember. And of the incidents they'd conjure in the privacy of their parlors, this night, and the man who'd come visiting, would prove the most enduring.

Every time Sheldon Sturgis brewed a pot of coffee, he would think of Buddenbaum, and recall his shame. Every time Ninnie Immendorf had a suitor come knocking (and several did, for wives were hard to come by in those years, and Ninnie could cook a mean stew) she would go to the door praying it would not be Franklin or Charlie or Buck but Buddenbaum. Buddenbaum.

And every time the Reverend Whitney mounted his pulpit, and spoke to his parishioners about the workings of the Devil in the world, he would bring the man with the cane to mind, and his voice would fill with feeling and the congregation would shudder in their pews. It was as though the preacher had seen the Evil One face to face, people would say as they filed out, for he spoke not of a monster with the horns of a goat, but of a man fallen on hard times, stripped of his horses and his retinue, and wandering the world in search of children that had strayed from the fold.

VI

By the time Maeve reached the top of the slope she had lost sight of her savior, and as there were no lights around the tent, it was hard to make out much about those who lingered in its vicinity. Part of her hoped not to encounter him, given that she'd cheated on her promise and followed him into the midst of this ceremony, but another part, the part nourished by his honey-blood, was willing to risk his ire if she could know him better. Surely he wouldn't hurt her, she told herself, however angry he was. What was done was done. She'd seen the secrets.

All except for what lay inside the tent, of course, and she would soon put that to rights. There was a door a few yards from where she stood, but it was sealed, so she headed around to the side of the tent, where there was nobody to see, and pulled the fabric up out of the snow so that she could shimmy underneath.

Inside there was a silence so deep she almost feared to draw breath, and a darkness so profound it seemed to press against her face, like the hands of a blind man reading her flesh. She let it do so, fearing that she'd be removed if she rejected it, and after a few moments of scrutiny its touch became lighter, almost playful, and she felt the darkness coaxing her up from the ground and away from the wall. She was obliged to trust to it, but that was no great hardship. There was no peril here, of that she was certain, and as if in reward for her faith the darkness began to flower before her, bloom upon bloom opening as she approached. The darkness grew no lighter, but as she walked her eyes understood its subtleties better; saw forms and figures that she'd been blind to before. She was one of hundreds here, she realized, members of the families she'd seen in the snow outside, lucky or worthy enough to come into this sacred place. There were tears of bliss on some of their faces; smiles and reverence on others. A few even looked her way as she was led through the throng, but most were watching some sight the black blossoms had not yet shown her. Eager to know what wonder this was, she focused her attentions upon the mysterious air.

And now she began to see. There was a form appearing ahead of her, like the fruit of this blossoming darkness. It resembled nothing she could name, but it had the sinuousness of a serpent, or rather of many serpents, turned upon themselves over and over, a knot of sliding shapes in constant motion. It entered itself, this knot, and emerged remade. It divided and sealed, opened like an eye and broke like water on a rock. Sometimes, in the midst of its cavortings, a spray of darkness would spurt between its surfaces. Oftentimes it would slough off a skin of shadows, which would instantly fly apart, the fragments rising like seeds from a field of dandelions, sowing themselves in the fertile gloom.

She was watching one such seeding when her gaze fell upon the figures sitting beneath this display. A man and a woman, face to face, hand to hand, their heads bowed as if in prayer. Seeing the two of them so close she thought of Abilene Welsh and Billy Baxter, though she did not entirely comprehend the reason. Surely those two had not frozen to death looking for a place to hold hands and bow heads, but to perform that labor she'd witnessed countless times among beasts. And yet, was the getting of children not the purpose of that labor? And did the form hovering above this couple not seem to come from their mingled essences, which rose from their lips like coiling smoke and intertwined between their brows?

"It's a baby," she said aloud.

Either the darkness was negligent, and failed to catch her words before they flew, or else the sound her tongue made was too slippery to be seized. Whichever, she saw the words go from her lips like a turquoise and orange flame, the colors strident in such muted circumstances. They instantly flew towards the dark child, and were drawn into its workings, their brilliance streaking its every part.

The woman opened her eyes and raised her head with a look of pain upon her face, and her husband rose from his chair expelling a throatful of ether, then looked up at the creature he had fathered.

It was in turmoil now, its configurations changing even more rapidly, as if Maeve's colors had given it new fuel for its inventions. Too much, perhaps. In an ecstasy of change, its forms became even more erratic, feeding upon their own invention as they multiplied.

Maeve was in sudden terror. She retreated a couple of stumbling steps then turned and pelted away through the crowd. There was turmoil all around her, the darkness too traumatized to silence the voices of the throng, so that shouts of panic and alarm erupted on every side. She darted this way and that to keep anyone from catching hold of her, though it seemed few understood what had happened, much less recognized the culprit, and she reached the wall of the tent without a hand being laid upon her. As she stooped to duck under the fabric, she glanced back. The child was in decay, she saw, its forms ripened to bursting and rotting in the air. Its parents had separated, and lay in the arms of their respective families, stricken and sickened. Even as Maeve watched, the woman went into a fit so violent it was all her comforters could do to restrain her.

Clamping her hand over her mouth to subdue her sobs, Maeve dug under the tent wall and out into the snow. News of the calamity had already spread among those waiting outside and chaos had ensued. A fight had broken out towards the bottom of the slope, and someone was already sprawled on the ground with a spike in his heart. Elsewhere, people were running towards the tent, even as those within emerged, yelling at the tops of their voices.

Maeve sat down on the snow and pressed the heels of her hands against her eyes, which burned with all she'd seen, and with the tears that were about to come.

"Child."

She raised her head, and started to look around.

"What did you promise?"

She looked no further.

"It wasn't my fault," she said, wiping her nose with the back of her hand. "I just said—"

"It was *you?*" the beast replied, cutting her short. "Oh Lord, oh Lord, what have I done?"

She felt the beast's hands on her body, and without warning she was spun around. She finally saw his features plainly—his long, patient face, his golden eyes, his fur, thickening to a mane in the middle of his skull, sleek as a beaver's pelt on his brow and cheek and chin. His teeth were chattering slightly.

"Are you cold?"

"*No, damn you!*"

She started to weep softly.

"All right, I'm cold," he said, "I'm cold."

"No you're not. You're afraid."

The gold in his eyes flickered. "What's your name?" he said.

"Maeve O'Connell."

"I should have killed you, Maeve O'Connell."

"I'm glad you didn't," she said. "Who are you?"

"Coker Ammiano. Soon to be infamous. If I'd killed you, you wouldn't have done this terrible thing."

"What was so terrible?"

"You spoke at the marriage. That was forbidden. Now there'll be war. The families'll blame each other. There'll be bloodshed. Then when they realize it wasn't them, they'll come looking for the culprit, and they'll kill us. You for what you did in there, me for bringing you here."

Maeve pondered this chain of disaster for a moment.

"They can't kill us if they can't *find* us," she said finally. She glanced back down the slope. Just as Coker had predicted, the fighting had indeed escalated. If it was not yet war it would be very soon. "Is there another way?" she said.

"One," he replied.

She scrabbled to her feet. "Take us there," she said.

ii

Over the decades, Buddenbaum had assembled a comprehensive list of fictional works in which he appeared. To date he had knowledge of twenty-three characters he had directly inspired (that is to say a reader of the book in question, or a viewer of the play, if they knew him, instantly recognized the source), along with another ten or eleven characters that drew upon aspects of his nature for comic or tragic effect. It was testament to the many facets of his personality that he could step onto the stage as a judge in one piece and as a procurer in another and have both portraits judged accurate.

He took no offense at being exploited in this fashion, however scandalous the work or scurrilous the part. It was flattering to be a seed for so many creations, especially for one as certain to remain childless as he. And it amused him mightily that when these artists, in their cups, confessed to their homage, they invariably spoke of how much raw human truth they had discovered in him. He suspected otherwise. Know it or not (and in his experience artists knew very little) they were inspired by the very opposite of what they claimed. He was not raw. He was not true. And one day, if he was cautious and wise, he would not even be human. He was a fake through and through, a man who had traveled the trails of America in a dozen different guises, and would wear another dozen before his business was done.

He did not blame them for their credulity. Every art but one was a game of delusions. But oh, the road to that Art was hard, and he was glad to have his list of alter egos to divert him as he made his way along it. He even had some of the fruitier dialogue ascribed to him in these works by heart, and it pleased him to recite it aloud when there was nobody within earshot.

As now, for instance, trudging up the forested flank of this damnable mountain. A speech from a pseudo-historical tragedy called *Serenissima*: "I have nothing but you, my sweet Serenissima. You are my sense, my sanity and my soul. Go from me now, and I am lost in the great dark between the stars, and cannot even perish there, for I must live until you still my heart. Still it now! I beg thee, still it now, and let my suffering cease."

He stopped in mid-declaration. There was another sound competing for his audience of trees, this far less musical. He held his breath, to hear it better. It was coming from the summit of the mountain, or thereabouts: sufficient voices to suggest a cast of some substantial size was assembled there. No need to wonder what kind of drama was underway. The keening told all. It was a tragedy.

With his own voice now hushed, he started to climb again, the sounds more horrid the louder they became. It was only in fiction that pain made the dying poetic. In life, they sobbed and begged and ran with tears and snot. He had seen such spectacles countless times and did not relish seeing another. But he had no choice. The child might very well be up there somewhere—a child named for a goddess who brought dreams—and back in the balmy spring, in Missouri, his instincts had told him there was some significance in that naming. He'd lodged a little piece of his own dreams with the O'Connells as a consequence, which with hindsight had probably been an error. How much of an error the next hour or so would tell.

Meanwhile, there was the mystery of the voices to vex him. Was this the dying cries of pioneers, lost on the heights? He didn't think so. There were sounds amid the cacophony he had never heard from a human throat; nor indeed from any animal that lived in this corner of reality, which fact had made him sweat, despite the cold. A sweat of anticipation, that perhaps the impulsive gift he'd made to Harmon O'Connell had not after all been so unwise, and that the Irishman's daughter had led him, all unknowing, to the borders of his own promised land.

VII

There was a crack in the sky; that was Maeve's first thought. A crack in the sky, and on the other side of it another sky, brighter than the night in which she stood. She had seen the heavens produce many marvels: lightning, whirlwinds, hail, and rainbows—but nothing like the waves of color, vaster than the vastest thunderhead, that rolled across that sky beyond the crack. A breeze came out to find her. It was warm and carried on its back a deep, rhythmical boom.

"That's the sea!" she said, starting towards the crack.

It was not wide, nor was it stable. It wavered in the air, as jittery as the flame of a lamp in a high wind. She didn't care about the how and why of it; she'd seen too much tonight to begin asking questions now. All she wanted to do was cross this threshold, not because she feared the consequences of what she'd done earlier, but because there was a sky and a sea she'd never seen before waiting on the other side.

"There'll be no way back," Coker warned her.

"Why not?"

"It took a great Blessedm'n to make this door, and when it closes again it won't be easily opened." He glanced back down towards the battlefield, and moaned at what he saw. "Lord, look at that. You go if you want to. I can't live with this." He raised his hand in front of his face and a single razor claw appeared from his middle finger, gleaming.

"What are you doing?"

He put the claw to his throat. "No!" she yelled, and grabbed his hand. "All this dying, just because I said something I shouldn't. It's *stupid*."

"You don't understand the reasons," he said bitterly, though he made no further attempt to harm himself.

"And you do?" Maeve replied.

"Not exactly. I know there's some great argument between the families that's so bad they've been slaughtering one another for generations. This wedding was supposed to be a seal of peace between them. And the child was the proof of that."

"What's the argument?" she said.

He shrugged. "Nobody knows, outside the families. And after this—" he looked at the corpse-strewn slope, "there'll be fewer who know than ever."

"Well it's still stupid," she said again, "killing each other over an argument when there's so many things worth living for." She still had hold of his hand. As she spoke he retracted the claw. "I lost my Papa tonight," she said solemnly. "I don't want to lose you too."

"I've known Blessedm'ns less persuasive than you," Coker remarked softly. His voice was tinged with awe. "What kind of child are you?"

"Irish," Maeve replied. "Are we going then?"

She looked back towards the crack. The ground at its base was shifting, the stones and trampled snow softened in the heat of whatever power had opened this door, drawn through the threshold then pouring back again. She started towards it fearlessly but as she did so Coker laid his hand on her shoulder. "Do you understand what you're doing?" he said.

"Yes," she said, a little impatiently. She wanted to walk on that ebbing dirt. She wanted to know how it felt. But Coker hadn't done with his warnings.

"Quiddity's a dream-sea," he said, "and the countries there are strange."

"So's America," she said.

"Stranger than America. They're born from what's in here." He tapped her temple with his finger.

"People *dream* countries?"

"More than countries. They dream animals and birds and cities and books and moons and stars."

"They all dream the same books and birds?" she said.

"The shapes are different," Coker replied somewhat hesitantly, "But—the *souls* of things are the same."

She looked at him in befuddlement. "Whatever you say," she replied.

"No, it's important you understand," he insisted. He paused for a moment, frowning as he dug for enlightenment. Then it came. "My father used to say: *Every bird is one bird, and every book is one book, and every bird and every book is one thing too, under the words and the feathers.*" He finished with a flourish, as though the meaning of this was self-evident. But Maeve simply shook her head, more confounded than ever. "Does this mean *you're* somebody's *dream?*" she said.

"No," Coker told her. "I'm the child of a *trespasser!*"

Here at least was something she grasped.

"Quiddity wasn't meant to be a place of flesh and blood," he went on.

"But people get through?"

"A few. Tricksters, poets, magicians. Some of them die. Some of them go crazy. And some of them fall in love with the things they find, and children come, who are part human and part not." He spread his arms and his wings. "Like me."

"I do," she said with a sly little smile. "I like you a lot."

But he was deadly serious. "I want you to know what you're doing when you step through that crack."

"I don't mind being a trespasser."

"You'll be living in a place where your people can only come in dreams, and then only three times. The night they're born. The night they fall in love. And the night they die."

She thought of her Papa then, who'd spoken of floating in a calm sea with her Mama beside him. Had that sea been Quiddity?

"I want to go," she said, more eager than ever.

"As long as you understand," he said.

"I do," she told him. "Now, can we go?"

He nodded, and she was away in a heartbeat, stepping lightly over the shifting ground.

If Buddenbaum had learned anything in his years of wandering, it was that things mundane and things miraculous were not, as reason had it, irrevocably divided. Quite the reverse. Though the continent was everywhere being measured and possessed by unmagical minds, its sacred places overrun, and their guardians driven to drink and despair, the land was too deeply seeded with the strange to ever be made safe for the pioneer.

The proof was spread before him on the mountain slope. Creatures from the far side of sleep, breathing the same air as the brave souls who'd come to conquer this land, dying with the same stars overhead.

Walking among the corpses, he felt the itch to hike back down the trail and fetch a few of the pioneers back, to show to them that they were not the only travelers here, and that no law nor God nor well-laid pavement would keep beasts like these from coming again. He might have done so too, but for the girl. She was here somewhere, his instinct told him, and alive. Whatever mischief had brought this massacre about, she had survived it. But where?

Up the slope he climbed, pausing now and again when a particular bizarrity caught his eye. He had been a student of the occult for too long to doubt the origin of these species. They came from the Metacosm, the world of Quiddity. He had never been able to find his way into that place himself, but he had collected over the last many decades several unique works on its geography and zoology, most of which he knew by heart. He had even sought out and interrogated men and women—most of them in Europe, and most magicians—who claimed to have found their way over the divide between this world, the Helter Incendo, and into that other. Some of them had proved to be living in a state of self-delusion, but there had been three who had convinced him beyond reasonable doubt that they had indeed ventured onto the shores of the dream-sea. One had even voyaged across it, and had lived among the islands of the Ephemeris a life of sybaritic excess, before his mistress had conspired to strip him of his powers and return him to the Cosm.

None of these travelers had profited from their journeys however; they had returned wounded and melancholy. The sweet simplicities of God and goodness no longer made sense to them, and human intercourse gave them no comfort. Life was meaningless, they had all then concluded, whether in this world or that.

Buddenbaum had listened carefully, learned what he could, then left them to their wretchedness. If ever he swam with spirits, he told himself, or walked upon a shore where dreams took living form, he would not whine about the absence of God. He would lead those spirits and shape those dreams, and gain in power and comprehension until time and place folded up before him.

He was perhaps closer to realizing that ambition than he'd thought. A door had opened to let these creatures through; and if it was still ajar, then he would take his chances and step through it, unprepared though he was.

He went down on his hands beside some pitifully wounded creature and whispered softly to her.

"Can you hear me?"

Her speckled eyes flickered in his direction. "Yes," she said.

"How did you get here?"

"The ships—" she replied.

"After the ships. How did you get into the Cosm?"

"The Blessedm'n opened a way for us."

"And where *is* this way?"

"Who are you?"

"Just tell me—"

"Are you with the child?" she said.

Something about the way she asked this question cautioned Buddenbaum.

"No," he said, "I'm not with the child. In fact—" he studied the woman's face as he spoke, looking for clues, "in fact I'm here . . . to *kill* the child."

The woman grimaced through the pain. "Yes," she said. "Yes, yes, do that. Slaughter the little bitch and give her heart to the Blessedm'n."

"I have to find the bitch first," Buddenbaum said calmly.

"The way. That's where she'll be." The dying woman turned her head and stared up the slope. "Do you see the tent?"

"Yes."

"Beyond it, to the right, there are rocks, yes? Black rocks."

"I see them."

"On the other side."

"Thank you." Buddenbaum started to rise.

"The Blessedm'n," the woman said, as he did so. "Tell him to say a prayer for me."

"I will," Buddenbaum replied. "What's your name?"

The woman opened her mouth to reply, but death was too quick for her. Unnamed, she died. Buddenbaum paused to close her eyes— the stare of the dead had always distressed him—then he headed on up the slope towards the rocks, and the way that lay concealed between.

As she stepped over the threshold, Maeve took one last look back at the world she had been born into. If Coker was right, she would not see it again. Another hour and it would be day. The weaker stars had already flickered out, and the bright ones were dimming. There was a faint light in the east, and by it she could see a man between the rocks, climbing with the gait of one who could barely keep from breaking into a dash. Though he was still some distance away, she recognized him by his coat and cane.

"Mr. Buddenbaum," she murmured.

"You know him?"

"Yes. Of course." She took a step back the way she'd come, but Coker caught hold of her arm.

"He's attracted some attention," he said.

It was true. Two of the survivors of the bloodshed were following—one a dozen paces behind Buddenbaum, the second twice that—and by the state of their robes and blades it was plain they'd claimed more than their share of lives. In his haste, Buddenbaum was unaware of them, though they were closing on him fast. Alarmed, Maeve pulled away from Coker and stepped back over the threshold. The unstable ground, excited by her agitation, splashed up against her shins.

Coker called out to her again, but she ignored him and started down between the rocks, shouting to Buddenbaum as she went. He saw her now, and a smile crossed his face.

"Child!" Coker was behind her, yelling. "Quickly! Quickly!"

She glanced over her shoulder at the flame of the crack. It was wavering wildly, as though it might extinguish itself at any moment. Coker was standing as close to the crack as he could get without crossing over, beckoning to her. But she couldn't go; not without hearing from Buddenbaum some words of explanation. Her father had suffered and perished because of a dream this man Buddenbaum had sown in his heart. She wanted to know why. Wanted to know what the shining city of Everville had meant to Buddenbaum, that he had gone to such trouble to inspire its creation.

There was only half a dozen yards between them now.

"Maeve—" he began.

"Behind you!" she yelled, and he glanced back to see the assassins racing up between the rocks. With but a moment before the first of them was upon him, he took the offensive and struck out with his cane, bringing it down on the man's blade and dashing it from his hand. The blow splintered his cane, but he didn't cast it away. As his attacker bent to snatch up the fallen sword, Buddenbaum drove the broken cane into his face. He reeled backwards, shrieking, and before the other assailant could push past his companion and catch his now weaponless quarry, Buddenbaum was off again towards the crack.

"Stand aside, child!" he yelled to Maeve, who was frozen now, unable to advance or retreat. "Aside!" he said as he came upon her.

Coker let out an angered yell, and she looked up to see him stepping back through the crack, whether to aid her or to block Buddenbaum she didn't know. For a moment, picturing the look of hunger on Buddenbaum's face as he'd shoved her aside, she feared for Coker's safety. Buddenbaum knew what the door opened onto, that was plain, and equally plainly he'd not be denied whatever wonders lay there. He struck Coker four or five times, the blows powerful enough to crack Coker's nose and open his brow. Coker roared in fury, and seized hold of Buddenbaum by the throat, pitching him back the way he'd come.

Maeve had started to get to her feet, but as she did so a tremor ran through the ground, and she raised her head in time to see the crack convulse from one end to the other. Shaken by the violence in its midst, the flame was flickering out. "Coker!" she yelled, fearful he'd be trapped in the closing door.

He looked her way, his face all sorrow, and then retreated a step or two until he was safe from the threshold. The sliver of Quiddity visible through the crack was narrower by the moment, but her thoughts weren't of the voyages she'd never take there. They were of Coker, whom she'd known only half a night, but who'd been in that little time her savior and her tutor and her friend. He stared through the closing door like a beaten dog, so forlorn she couldn't bear to look at him.

Eyes stinging, she averted her gaze and Buddenbaum rose into her sight, his face spattered with Coker's blood.

"Never!" he was yelling, *"Never! Never!"* and raising his fists he stumbled back towards the narrowing crack as if to beat it open again.

In his passion he had forgotten the second assassin. He had clambered over his sprawled companion, and now, as Buddenbaum stepped onto the contested ground between slope and shore, the assassin lunged and drove his weapon into the enemy's back.

The wounding stopped Buddenbaum in his tracks. He let out a sob, more of frustration than of pain it seemed, and reached behind him, grabbing at the weapon and hauling it out of his flesh. As he did so he swung round, moving with such speed that his wounder had no time to avoid his own blade. It opened his belly from flank to flank in a single slice, and without a sound the man fell forward, his guts preceding him to the ground.

Maeve didn't watch his final moments. Her gaze went back to the crack, unable to keep from looking Coker's way one final time, and to her astonishment she saw him stepping forward and reaching through the gap, jamming his arms in the door before it could seal itself. Then he pressed forward and began to elbow the crack open a little way, pushing first his head, then his thickly muscled neck, then a shoulder, through the fissure.

It caused him no little pain, but the sensation seemed only to fuel his frenzy. Thrashing as he went, he dragged his body through the opening, inch by agonizing inch, until his wings met the crack. Though they were folded behind him as tight to his body as they'd go, they were too bulky to be pulled through. He let out a pitiful cry, and turned his eyes in Maeve's direction.

She started towards him, but he waved her away. "Just . . . be . . . ready—" he gasped.

Then, drawing a single, tremendous breath, he pressed every sinew into service and began to push again.

There was a terrible tearing sound, and blood began to flow from his back, running down over his shoulders. Maeve shuddered in horror, but she could not look away. His eyes were locked with hers, as though she was his only anchor in his suffering. He rocked back and forth, the muscle that joined wings to torso torn wide open, his body shuddering as he visited this terrible violence upon it.

The horror seemed to go on an age—the thrashing, rocking, and tearing—but his tenacity was repaid. With one final twisting motion he separated his body from its means of flight, pressed his mutilated form through the crack and fell, his honey blood flowing copiously, on the other side.

Maeve knew now what he'd meant by *just be ready*. He needed her help to stem the flow from his wounds before he bled to death. She went to the body of Buddenbaum's attacker and tore at his robes. They were thick and copious, precisely to her purpose. Returning to Coker, who was lying face-down where he'd fallen, she pressed the fabric gently, but firmly, against his wounds, which ran from his shoulder blades to waist, telling him softly as she did so that this was the bravest thing she'd ever seen. She would make him well, she said, and watch over him for as long as he wished her to do so.

He sobbed against the snow—the crack closed above him—and in the midst of his tears he answered her.

"Always," he said.

Buddenbaum had been wounded before, though only once as badly as this. The stabbing would not kill him—his patrons had rendered his constitution inhumanly strong in return for his services—but it would take a little time to heal, and this mountain was no place to do it. He lingered in the vicinity of the two rocks long enough to see the door close, then he stumbled away from the slope, leaving the O'Connell child and her miserable consort to bleed and weep together at the top. Discovering how innocent little Maeve had come to cause such mayhem he would leave for another day. Not all the witnesses to the night's events were dead; he'd seen a handful fleeing the field when he'd arrived. In due course, he'd trace them and quiz them till he better understood how his fate and that of Maeve O'Connell were connected.

One thing he knew for certain: connected they were. The instinct that had made him prick his ears that April day, hearing the name of a goddess called in a place of dust and dirt and unwashed flesh, had been good. The miraculous and the mundane lived side by side in this newfound land, and, in the person of Maeve O'Connell, were indivisible.

VIII

C oker and Maeve lay in the shelter of the two rocks for several
hours, resting bones, flesh, and spirits traumatized by all
that the previous night had brought. Sometimes she would
make little compresses of fabric soaked in melted snow, and systematically clean his wounds, while he lay with his head upon her lap,
moaning softly. Sometimes they would simply doze together, sobbing sometimes in their sleep.

There was no snow that morning. The wind was strong, and
brought convoys of puffy white clouds up from the southwest, shred
ding them against the peaks. Between them, sun, too frail to warm
them much but reassuring nevertheless.

The supplies of carrion lying on the slope had not gone unnoticed. An hour or two after sunrise the first birds began to circle and
descend, looking for morsels on the battlefield. Their numbers
steadily increased, and Maeve, fearful that she or Coker would have
an eye pecked out while they slept, insisted they move a few yards
into the cleft between the rocks, where the birds would be less likely
to come.

Then, sometime towards noon, she woke with her heart hammering to the sound of growls. She got up and peered over the rock.

A pack of wolves had nosed the dead on the wind, and were now either tearing at the bodies, or fighting over the tenderest scraps.

Their presence was not the only grim news. The clouds were getting heavier, threatening further snow. "We have to go," she told Coker.

He looked up at her through a haze of pain. "Go where?" he said.

"Back down the mountain," she told him, "before we freeze or starve. We don't have that much daylight left."

"What's the noise?"

"Wolves."

"Many of them?"

"Maybe fifteen. They won't come after us while they've got so much food just lying there." She went down on her haunches beside him. "I know you're hurting and I wish I could make it better. But if we can get back to the wagon I know there's clean bandages and—"

"Yes—" he muttered, "and what then?"

"I told you: We go on down the mountain."

"And what happens after that?" he said, his voice pitifully weak. "Even if we could find the rest of your people, they'd kill us soon as look at us. They think you're a child of the Devil, and I'm—I don't know *what* I am any more."

"We don't need them," she said. "We'll find our own place to live. Somewhere we can build."

"Build?"

"Not right now, but when you're well. Maybe we'll have to live in a hole for a while, steal food, do whatever we have to do, but we're not going to die."

"You're very certain."

"Yes," she said quietly. "We're going to build a shining city. You and me."

He looked at her almost pityingly. "What are you talking about?" he said.

"I'll tell you as we go," she said to him, pulling on his arm to raise him up.

*   *   *

She was right about the wolves: They had more than enough food to keep them occupied. Only one of the pack, a scarred, runty animal missing an ear, came sniffing after them. Maeve had armed herself with a short sword plucked from one of the corpses, and rushed at the animal with a blood-curdling shout. It fled, its tail between its legs, and did not venture near them again.

The first flakes of snow began to fall just as they reached the forest, but once beneath the canopy of branches it was no concern to them. Getting lost, however, was. Though the gradient of the ground plainly pointed the way down, the forest covered most of the lower slope, and without Coker's preternatural sense of direction, Maeve would have most assuredly lost her way between the trees, and never have emerged again.

They spoke very little as they went, but Coker—who despite his wounds showed amazing fortitude—did broach *one* subject: that of Buddenbaum. Was he a Blessedm'n, Coker asked?

"I don't know what a Blessedm'n is."

"One who works with the spirit—"

"Like a priest?"

"And does miracles."

"Priests don't do miracles."

"What do they do then?"

"They say prayers. They break bread. They tell people what to do and what not to do."

"But no miracles?"

"No miracles."

Coker thought about that for a time. "Then I mean something different," he said.

"Are Blessedm'n good or bad?"

"Neither. They're explorers, is what they are."

That sounded like Buddenbaum, she said.

"Well whatever he is," Coker went on, "he has more power in him than most. That wound should have killed him on the spot."

She pictured Buddenbaum as he spoke, pulling the blade out of his own back.

"It was extraordinary," Coker replied. Though she had not said a word she knew without question he was speaking of the same sight.

"How did you do that?" she said.

He looked at her guiltily. "I'm sorry," he said, "that was impolite. It's just that it was so clear."

"You saw what I saw?" He nodded. "What else have you seen?"

"Not much," he said.

"What?" she insisted.

"When you talked about building," he said. "I saw a city."

She named it for him. "That's Everville. My Papa was going to build it—" She paused a moment, then said: "What did it look like?"

"It was shining," he replied simply.

"Good," she said.

It was dark by the time they reached the wagon, but the snow that had blanketed the heights was falling only fitfully below. While Coker made a bed for himself, Maeve rooted around for what crumbs and scraps of food remained, and they ate together. Then they slept again, while the wind buffeted the wagon; fitful sleep, filled with dreams, the strangest of which Maeve woke from with such a start Coker stirred beside her.

"What is it?" he asked her.

She sat up. "I was back in Liverpool," she said. "And there were wolves in the streets, walking upright in fancy clothes."

"You heard them howling in your sleep," Coker said. The wind was still carrying the howls down the mountainside. "That's all." He raised his hand to her face and stroked it gently.

"I wasn't afraid," she said. "I was happy." She rose and lit the lamp. "I was walking in the streets," she went on, turning the blankets aside as she spoke, "and the wolves were bowing to me when I went by." She had uncovered the teak chest, and now threw open the lid.

"What are you looking for?"

She didn't answer, but delved through the papers in the chest until she found a piece of folded paper. She closed the chest and unfolded the paper on top of it. Though the light from the lamp was paltry, the object wrapped in the paper gleamed as it was uncovered.

"What is it?" Coker wanted to know.

"Papa never told me properly," she said. "But it was—" she faltered, and lifted the paper up towards the light so she could study it better. There were eight words upon it, in perfect copper-plate.

Bury this at the crossroads, where Everville begins.

"Now we know," she said.

ii

The snow continued to fall the following day, but lightly. They made two small bundles of supplies, wrapped up as warmly as they could, and began the last portion of their journey. The tracks left by the rest of the wagons were still visible, and they followed them for half a mile or so, their route steadily taking them further from the mountain.

"We've followed them far enough," Maeve announced after a time.

"We've got no choice," Coker replied.

"Yes we do," she said, leading him to the side of the trail, where a tree lined slope fell away steeply into a misty gorge. "They couldn't go that way 'cause of the wagons, but we can."

"I can hear rushing down there," Coker said.

"A river!" Maeve said with a grin. "It's a river!"

Without further debate they started down. It wasn't easy. Though the snow turned to a light dusting and then disappeared entirely as they descended, the rocks were slick with vivid green moss, which also grew in abundance on the trees, whether dead or alive. Twice they came to places where the slope became too steep to be negotiated, and they were obliged to retrace their steps to find an easier way, but for all their exhaustion they didn't stop to rest. They had the sound—and now the glittering sight—of the river to tempt them on; and everywhere, signs of life: ferns and berry bushes and birdsong.

At last, as they reached level ground, and began to beat a trail to the river, a breeze came up out of nowhere, and the mist that had kept them from seeing any great distance was rolled away.

They said nothing to one another, but stood a few yards from the white waters and looked in astonishment at the scene beyond. The dark evergreens now gave way to trees in all their autumnal glory, orange and red and brown, their branches busy with birds, the thicket beneath quickened by creatures pelting away at the scent of these interlopers. There would be food aplenty here: fruit and honey and fish and fowl.

And beyond the trees, where the river took its glittering way, there was green land.

A place to begin.

On the mountain that would come to be known as Harmon's Heights, the elements were beginning the slow process of erasing the dead and their artifacts. They stripped from the bodies what little flesh the wolves and carrion birds had left. They pounded the bones till they splintered, then pounded the splinters to dust. They shredded the tents and the fine robes; they rusted the blades and the buckles. They removed from the sight of any who might chance upon the battlefield in decades to come, all but the minutest signs of what had happened there.

But there was one sign the elements could not remove; a sign that would have certainly disappeared had there not been a last living soul upon the mountainside to preserve it.

His names were numerous, for he was the son of a great family, but to all who had loved him—and there had been many—he was called by the name of a legendary ancestor: Noah.

He had come to the mountain with such hopes in his heart he had several times wished aloud for the words to express them better. Now he half-believed he'd called disaster down, wishing for words.

After all, hadn't it been words spoken by a child that had undone the ceremony and brought the truce to such a bloody end?

He had fled the signs of that battle half-insane, fled into the forest where he had sat and sobbed for the wife he'd seen perish in front of him, her heart too tender to survive the trauma of having her spirit-child unknitted. He, on the other hand, was beyond such frailties, coming as he did from a line of incorruptibles. His mind was part of a greater scheme, and though nothing would have pleased him more than to cease thinking, cease living, he could not violate his family's laws against self-slaughter. Nor would his body perish for want of sustenance. He could fatten himself on moonlight if he so chose.

So at last, when he'd wept himself out, he returned to the sight of the tragedy. The beasts had already done their disfiguring work, for which he was grateful. He could not distinguish one corpse from another; they were all simply meat for this devouring world.

He climbed the slope and slipped between the rocks, up to the place where the door that had led on to the shores of Quiddity had burned. It was gone, of course; sealed up. Nor could he expect it to be opened again any time soon—if at all—given that most all of the people who had known about the ceremony were on this side of the divide, and dead.

Blessedm'n Filigree, who had opened the crack in the first place, was a notable exception (was he a conspirator in this, perhaps?), but given that his opening of the door was a crime punishable by servitude and confinement, he was likely to have fled to the Ephemeris since the tragedy and found a place to lie low until the investigations were over. But as Noah stood on the spot where the threshold between Cosm and Metacosm had been laid, he saw something flickering close to the ground. He went down on his haunches and peered at it more closely. The door, it seemed, had not entirely closed. A narrow gap, perhaps four or five inches long, remained in place. He touched it, and it wavered, as though it might at any moment flicker out. Then, moving very cautiously, he went down on his belly and put his eye close to the gap.

He could see the beach, and the sea, but there were no ships. Apparently their captains had sensed disaster and sailed away to some harbor where they could count their profits and swear their crews to silence.

All was lost.

He got to his feet, and stared up at the snow-laden sky. What now? Should he leave the mountain, and make his way in the world of Sapas Humana? What purpose was there in that? It was a place of fictions and delusions. Better to stay here, where at least he could smell the air of Quiddity, and watch the light shifting on the shore. He would find some way to protect the flame, so that it wasn't extinguished. And then he would wait, and pray that somebody ventured along the beach one day, and saw the crack, and came to it. He'd tell them the whole sorry story; persuade them to find a Blessedm'n who'd come and open the way afresh. Then he'd return to his world. That was the theory, at least. There was but a tiny chance that it could ever be more than that, he knew. The shore had been chosen for its remoteness; he could not expect many beachcombers there. But patience was easy if it was all you had; and it was. He would wait, and while he waited, name the stars in this new heaven after the dead, so he would have someone to confide in as time went by.

As things went, there was more to see below than above, for after a little while people began visiting the valley that lay in the shadow of the peak. Noah knew their lives were trivial things, but he studied them nevertheless, his gaze so sharp he could pick out the color of a woman's eyes from his lookout on the mountain. There were many women in the valley in those early days, all of them robust and well-made, a few even beautiful. And seeing that this stretch of earth was as good a place as any other to settle, their admirers built houses, and courted, and married and raised families.

And in time there grew and prospered in the valley a proud little city called Everville.

PART TWO

Congregation

I

"*Forgive me, Everville.*"

The words were written in fading sepia ink on paper the color of unwashed bed sheets, but Erwin had read texts far less legible in the sixteen years he'd been dealing with the will and testaments of Everville's citizens. Evelyn Morris's final instructions for instance ('Put the dogs to sleep, and bury them with me'), written in iodine on a table lamp beside her deathbed; or Dwight Hanson's codicil, scrawled in the margin of a book on duck decoys.

Erwin had read somewhere that Oregon had a larger percentage of heretical thinkers per capita than any other state. More activists, more flat-earthists, more survivalists; all happy to have three thousand miles between them and the seat of government. Out of sight, in a state that was still comparatively empty, they went their own sweet way; and what better place to leave a statement about their individuality than their last words to the world?

But even by the high standard of eccentricity he'd encountered in his time as an attorney, the testament he was now studying was a benchmark. It was not so much a will as a confession; a confession which had gone unread in the thirty or so years since it had been written in March of 1965. Its author was one Lyle McPherson, whose goods and chattels had apparently been so negligible upon his passing that nobody had cared to look for any indication as to how he had wanted them divided. Either that, or his only son, Frank, whose sudden demise had brought the confession into Erwin's hands, had discovered it, read it, and decided that it was best kept hidden. Why he had not destroyed it completely only the dead man knew for certain, but perhaps somewhere in his soul McPherson the Younger had been perversely proud of the claims his father made in this document, and had toyed with the possibility of one day making it public.

True or not, the contents would have certainly claimed the cover of the *Everville Tribune* for a couple of weeks and perhaps brought McPherson—who had lived a blameless but dull life running the city's only Drain Rooter and Septic Service—a welcome touch of notoriety.

If that had indeed been his plan, death had foiled it. McPherson the Younger had passed from the world with only a seven-line obituary in the *Tribune* (five lines of which bemoaned the lack of a replacement Drain Rooter and Septic Service now that good ol' Frank was gone) to mark his exit. The life and crimes of McPherson the Elder, however, were waiting to be discovered, and now, sitting by the window in the heat of the late August sun, their discoverer pondered how best to show them to the world.

It was certainly a good time to find himself an audience. Every year, at the last weekend of August, Everville had a festival, and for three days its otherwise quiet streets became thronged, its population (which had stood at 7403 at the previous November's census) swelling to half that size again. Every hotel, inn, motel, and lodging house in that region of the Willamette Valley, from Aurora and Molina in the north to Sublimity and Aumsville in the south was occupied, and there was scarcely a store in town that didn't do more business over Festival Weekend than it did in the three months preceding it. The actual substance of the festival was of variable quality. The town band, which in fact drew players from as far afield as Wilsonville, was very capable, and Saturday's parade, featuring the band, floats, and a troupe of drum majorettes, was usually counted the highlight of the weekend. At the other end of the scale were the

pig races and the frisbee-throwing contests, which were ineptly orga-
nized, and had several years ended in fistfights.

But the crowds who came to Everville in their hundreds every
August didn't come for the music, or the pig racing. They came
because it was a fine excuse to drink, dance, and enjoy the last of
summer before the leaves started to turn. Only once in the years
Erwin had been a resident of the town had it rained on Festival
Weekend. This year, if the weather reports were to be trusted, the
entire week ahead would be balmy, with temperatures climbing to the
low eighties by Friday. Perfect Festival weather. Dorothy Bullard, who
ran the offices of the Chamber of Commerce when she wasn't
accepting cash for water bills, fronting the Tourist Board, or flirting
with Jed Gilholly, the city's police captain, had announced in last
week's *Tribune* that the Chamber of Commerce expected this year's
Festival to be the most popular yet. If a man wanted to drop a bomb-
shell, there could scarcely be a better time to do it.

With that in mind, Erwin went back to the pages on his lap, and
studied them for the fourth time.

Forgive me, Everville, McPherson the Elder had begun.

I don't much like having to write these things that I'm going to write,
but I got to put down the truth while I still can, being as I'm the only one left
to tell it.

The fact is, everyone in town knew what we did that night, and they all
was happy we did it. But there was only me, Verl Nordhoff, and Richie
Dolan who knew the whole story, and now Verl's dead and I guess Richie
got so crazy he killed himself, so that leaves me.

I ain't writing this to save my soul. I don't believe in Heaven and Hell.
They're just words. I ain't going anywhere when I'm dead except into the
dirt. I just want to say all of it straight, just once, though it don't show
Everville up real pretty.

What happened was this. On the night of August 27, 1929, me and
Nordhoff and Dolan hung three people from a tree on the mountain. One
of them we hung was a cripple, and I feel more ashamed for that than I do
about the other two. But they was all in it together, and the only reason he
was crippled was he had bad blood in him . . .

The phone rang, and Erwin, wrapped up in his study, jumped. He waited for his answering machine to pick up the call, but it had been on the blink for weeks, and failed to do so. He let the phone go on ringing till the caller got bored, then returned to the confession. Where was he? Oh yes, the bit about the bad blood.

. . . and the way he jerked around on that rope, and hollered even though he couldn't breathe, I believe all the things folks were saying about him and his wife and that animal child of his.

We didn't find no human bones in the house, like we thought we might, but there was other weird stuff, like the pictures painted on the walls, and these carvings the cripple had made. That's why we set fire to the house, so's nobody would have to see any of that shit. And I don't regret none of that, because the son was definitely going after innocent children, and the mother was a whore from way back. Everybody knew that. She'd had a whorehouse right here in town, only it had been closed down in the twenties, and that's when she'd lost her mind and gone to live in the house by the creek with her crazy family.

So then when Rebecca Jenkins disappeared and her body was found in the reservoir, there wasn't nobody doubted what had happened. They'd kidnapped her on her way from school and done whatever they'd done to her then thrown her body in the creek, and it had been washed down into the reservoir. Only there was no proof. People was talking about it, and they were saying it was pitiful that the police couldn't pin it on the whore and her son and her damn husband, because everyone knew they'd been seen with kids before, kids they'd found in Portland, and brought back to the house at night, and if they got away with it again, with a kid from right here in Everville, nobody's kids were going to be safe.

So that's when the three of us decided to do something about it. Dolan had known the Jenkins girl because she'd used to come by his store, and when he'd think about what had happened to her he'd get choked up and he'd be ready to go hang the whore right there and then. Richie had a little girl of his own, who was right about Rebecca's age, and he kept saying if we can't keep the children safe we weren't worth a damn. So that's what we did. We went out to the creek, we burned the house, and then we took the three of them up the mountain and hanged them.

And everyone knew what we'd done. The house burned almost to the ground and nobody came to put out the fire. They just stayed out of sight till we'd done what we'd done and we'd come back down again.

But that wasn't the end of it. The following year, the police caught a man from Scotts Mills who'd killed a girl in Sublimity and he told them he'd murdered Rebecca too, and dumped her in the creek.

The day I heard that I got crazy drunk, and I stayed drunk for a week. People looked at me different after that, like I'd been a hero because of what we'd done and now I was just a killer.

Dolan took it even worse, and he started getting real angry, saying it was everybody's fault cause everybody knew, and that was true in a way. Everville was as much to blame as we were, and I hope if this ever gets read people forgive me for writing it down, but it's the truth, I swear on my mother's grave.

And then, in the same abrupt manner it had begun, McPherson's testimony ended, begging more questions than it answered and all the more intriguing for that.

Reading it over again left Erwin more excited than ever. He got up and paced around his office, chewing over the options available to him. It was his duty to bring this secret to light, that was not in doubt. But if he did so in Festival Week, when the city was polishing itself to perfection, he would gain a much larger audience while making enemies of his friends and clients.

Part of him replied: So what? Hadn't he been telling himself it was time to move on while he was still young enough to relocate? And what better calling card could he have than to be the man who had uncovered the McPherson Conspiracy? The other part of him, the part that had grown comfortable in this corner of the world, said: Have a little care for people's feelings. Let this news out in Festival Week and you'll be a pariah.

He paced, and he chewed, and finally he decided not to decide, at least not yet. First he'd check his facts to be certain the confession wasn't just McPherson's invention. Find out if a child called Rebecca Jenkins had indeed been dredged from the reservoir, if there had ever been a house by the creek, and if so, what had happened to those who'd occupied it.

He made a photocopy of McPherson's confession in Bettijane's office (he'd given her the day off so she could drive into Portland and pick up her mother), then sealed the original in an envelope and locked it up in the safe. That done, he folded up the copy, slipped it into his jacket pocket, and went out for lunch at Kitty's Diner. He wasn't by nature a self-analytical man, but as he wandered down Main Street he couldn't help but be struck by the paradox of his present mood. Murder, suicide, and the dispatch of innocents filled his head, but he could not remember when he'd last felt so utterly content with his lot in life.

II

---

i

There were those among Dr. Powell's patients that late morning who had seen looks like this on Phoebe Cobb's face before, and they knew from experience that caution was the byword. Woe betide the patient who reported to reception five minutes late, or worse still attempted to justify their tardiness with some lame excuse. Being carted into the waiting room in six pieces would not have won a sympathetic smile from Phoebe in her present mood.

There were even one or two of the doctor's regulars—Mrs. Converse, here for a fresh supply of blood pressure pills, and Arnold Heacock, in need of suppositories—who were familiar enough with Phoebe to have guessed the reason for her demeanor, and would have been correct in their assumptions.

Five and a half pounds. How was that possible? She'd not touched a candy or a doughnut in three weeks. She hadn't allowed herself even to inhale near a plate of fried chicken. How was it possible to eat so frugally, to deny her body everything it craved, and still put on five and a half pounds? Was the air in Everville fattening these days?

Audrey Laidlaw had just stalked in, holding her belly.

"I *have* to see Dr. Powell," she said, before she'd even reached the counter.

77

"Is it an emergency?" Phoebe wanted to know, floating the question so as not to betray the trap beneath.

"Yes! Absolutely!"

"Then you should have someone drive you over to Silverton," Phoebe replied. "They deal with emergencies there."

"It's not *that* much of an emergency," the Laidlaw woman snapped.

"Then you'll have to make an appointment." Phoebe consulted her diary. "Tomorrow at ten forty-five?"

Audrey Laidlaw narrowed her eyes. "Tomorrow?" she said. Phoebe kept smiling, which was a reliable irritant, and was pleased to see the woman grinding her teeth. Only two months before, under circumstances not unlike these, the thin and neurotic Miss Laidlaw had marched out of the waiting room muttering *fat bitch* just loudly enough to be heard. Phoebe had thought there and then: *You wait.*

"Will you just tell Dr. Powell I'm here?" Audrey said. "I'm sure he'll see me."

"He's with a patient," Phoebe said. "If you want to take a seat—"

"This is intolerable," the woman replied, but she had little choice in the matter. The round lost, she retired to a chair by the window, and fumed. Phoebe didn't stare, in case she looked triumphant, but went back to sorting the mail.

"Where have you been all my life?"

She looked up, and Joe was leaning over the counter, his words little more than a whisper. She glanced past his broad frame to see that everyone in the waiting room was looking their way, the same question in every gaze: What is a black man in paint-spattered overalls doing whispering to a married woman like Phoebe Cobb?

"What time are you finished here?" he asked her softly.

"You've got paint in your hair."

"I'll shower. What time?"

"You shouldn't be here."

He shrugged and smiled. Oh, how he smiled.

"Around three," she said.

"You got a date."

With that he was gone, and she was left meeting half a dozen stares from around the room. She knew better than to look away. It would instantly be construed as guilt. Instead, she gave her audience a gracious little smile and stared back, hard, until they had all dropped their gazes. Then, and only then, did she return to the mail, though her hands were trembling so badly she was butterfingered for the next hour, and her mood so much sweetened, she even found a few minutes for Audrey Laidlaw to be given something for her dyspepsia.

---

ii

Joe could do that to her: Come in and change her way of being in a matter of moments. It was wonderful of course, but it was also dangerous. Sooner or later, Morton would look up at her from his meatloaf and ask her why she was sparkling tonight and she wouldn't be able to keep the truth from her lips.

"Joe," she'd say. "Joe Flicker. You know who he is. You can't miss him."

"What about him?" Morton would reply, his tight little mouth getting tighter as he spoke. He didn't like blacks.

"I'm spending a lot of time with him," she'd say.

"What the hell *for*?" he'd say, and she'd look up at the face she'd married, the face she'd loved, and while she was wondering when it had become so sour and sad, he'd start yelling, "I don't want you talking with a nigger!"

And she'd say, "I don't just *talk* to him, Morton." Oh yes, she'd love to say that. "We kiss, Morton, and we get naked, and we do—"

"Phoebe?"

She snapped out of her reverie to find Dr. Powell at her side with the morning's files.

"Oh—I'm sorry."

"We're all done. Are you all right? You look a little flushed."

"I'm fine." She relieved him of the files and he started to pick through his mail. "Don't forget you've got a Festival meeting."

He glanced up at the clock. "I'll grab a sandwich and go straight over. Damn Festival. I'll be glad when it's—oh, I've referred Audrey Laidlaw to a specialist in Salem."

"Is it something serious?"

He tossed the letters back onto the desk. "Maybe cancer," he said.

"Oh Lord."

"Will you lock up?"

That happened, over and over. People came in to see the doctor with a headache or a backache or a bellyache and it turned out to be something terminal. They'd fight it, of course: pills, scans, injections. And once in a while they'd win. But more often than not she'd watch them deteriorate, week in, week out, and it was still hard after seven years, seeing that happen; seeing people's strength and hope and faith in things slip away. There was always such emptiness towards the end; such bitter looks on their faces, as though they'd been cheated of something and they couldn't quite figure out what. Even the church-goers, the ones she'd see in front of the tree in the square at Christmas singing hallelujahs, had that look. God wanted them in his bosom, but they didn't want to go; not until they'd made sense of things here.

But suppose there was no sense to be made? That was what she had come to believe more and more: that things happened, and there was no real reason why. You weren't being tested, you weren't being rewarded, you were just *being*. And so was everybody and everything else, including tumors and bad hearts: all just being.

She had found the simplicity of this strangely comforting, and she'd made her own little religion of it.

Then Joe Flicker had been hired to paint the hallway outside the surgery, and her homemade temple had cracked. It wasn't love, she'd told herself from the start. In fact, it wasn't anything important at all. He was an opportunist who'd taken a passing fancy to her, and she'd played along because she was flattered and she always felt sexier in the summer months, so why not flirt with him a little? But the flirting got serious, and secret, and before very long she was ready to scream if he didn't kiss her. Then, he did, and she was ready to scream if they didn't go all the way. Then they had, and she'd gone home with paint marks on her breasts and her belly, and sat in the bath and cried for a solid hour, because it felt like this was a reward and a test and a punishment all in one.

It still did. She was thirty-six years old, twenty pounds over-weight (her estimation, not Joe's), with small features on a moonish face, pale skin that freckled in the sun, ginger hair (with a few strands of gray already), and a mean streak she had from her mother. Not, she had long ago decided, a particularly attractive package. In Morton, she'd found a husband who didn't know or care what he'd married, for better or worse, as long as he was fed and the television worked. A man who'd decided at thirty that the best was over and only a fool would look beyond tomorrow, who increasingly defined himself by his bigotries, and who had not touched her between her legs in thirteen months.

So how then—how, how?—had she come to her present state of grace? How was it possible that this man from North Carolina, this Joe, who'd had a life of adventuring—he'd been stationed in Germany while he was in the army, he'd lived in Washington, D.C., for a while, Kentucky for a while, California for a while—how was it possible that this man had become so devoted to her?

When they talked, and they talked a lot, she wondered some-times if he was quizzing her about her life the way he did because the same question vexed him; as though he was digging around for some clue as to what it was in her that drew him. Then again, per-haps he was simply curious.

"I can't get enough of you," he'd say over and over, and kiss her in ways and places that would have appalled Morton.

She thought of those kisses now, as she let herself into the house. It was six minutes to three. He was always on time (army training, he'd said once); six minutes and he'd be here. She'd read in a maga-zine a couple of weeks ago that scientists were saying time was like putty; it could be pulled and pushed, and she'd thought *I could have told them that*. Six minutes was six hours waiting on the back doorstep (Joe never used the front, it was too conspicuous, but the house was the last on the row and there was just wooded land beyond, so it was easy to come in from that direction unseen); waiting for a glimpse of him between the trees, knowing that once he arrived time would be squeezed in the other direction, and an hour, or an hour and a half, would fly by in a matter of moments.

There he was, pushing his way through the thicket, his eyes already upon her and never leaving her, not for a stride, not for a glance. And the clock in the living room that had belonged to Morton's mother and had never kept good time until she died, was sounding three o'clock. And all was well with the world.

They climbed the stairs unbuttoning as they went. By the time they reached the spare bedroom (they'd never made love in the marital bed) her breasts were bare, and he had his arms around her from behind, toying as they went. He loved nothing better than to pleasure her this way, his face against the nape of her neck, his chest hard against her back, his embrace absolute. She reached back to unzip him. As ever, she found her hands full.

"I've missed this!" she said, sliding her hand along his dick.

"It's been three days," he said. "I've been going crazy." He turned and sat on the edge of the bed, pulling her down so she perched on his knees, then opening her legs by opening his own. His hand went into her with unerring ease.

"Oh *baby*," he said, "that's what I need." He played with her, in and out. "That's the hottest pussy, baby. You got the hottest fucking pussy—"

She loved to hear him say the words out loud, the dirty words she only wanted to hear or say when she was with him, the words that made her new, and ready.

"I'm going to fuck you till you're crazy. You want that?"

"Yes—"

"Tell me."

"I want you to fuck me—" She was starting to gasp.

"Now?"

"Till I'm—"

"Yeah."

"Till I'm *crazy*."

She fumbled with his belt buckle, but he shoved her hands away and rolled her over, face to the quilt, hoisting up her dress and tearing down her panties. Backside in the air, legs apart, she reached behind her, the words always easier than she'd thought they'd be.

"Give me your cock."

And it was in her hands as though she'd summoned it, slick and hot-headed. She pressed it against her pussy. He held back for a few seconds, then slid it all inside, down to the zipper from which it still poked.

iii

In the tiny committee room above the Chamber of Commerce, Larry Powell watched while Ken Hagenaner went through a full list of the weekend's activities and heard not a word, preoccupied as he was with his return home to Montana the weekend after next.

And in the offices below, Erwin Toothaker waited while Dorothy Bullard called around to see if anyone could let the attorney into the old schoolhouse, where the Historical Society kept its collection, because he needed to do some urgent research. And while he waited Erwin eyed the yellowed tape at the top of the window frames, still holding down an inch of Christmas tinsel, and the faded photographs of the mayor before last with his arms around the Bethany twins on their sixteenth birthdays, and he thought: I hate this place. I never realized till now. I hate it.

And outside, on Main Street, a youth called Seth Lundy—just turned seventeen and never been kissed—halted in the middle of the sidewalk outside the Pizza Place and listened to a sound he had not heard since Easter Sunday: the din of hammers knocking on the sky from Heaven's side.

He looked up, straight up above his head, because that was where the cracks usually began, but the blue was flawless. Puzzled, he studied the sky for maybe fifteen minutes, during which time the meeting in the committee room was brought to a tidy conclusion, and Erwin decided to tell the truth to the largest audience he could find, and somewhere behind closed drapes in a house on the edge of town, Phoebe Cobb began to quietly weep.

"What's wrong?"

"Don't stop."

"You're crying, baby—"

"It's all right. I'll be all right." She reached behind her; put her hand on his buttocks, pressing him home, and as she did, the three words she'd kept under lock and key escaped.

"I love you."

Oh Lord, what had she said? Now he'd leave her. Run away and find some other desperate woman, who didn't tell him she loved him when all he wanted was a fuck in the afternoon. A younger woman; a slimmer woman. "I'm sorry," she said.

"So am I," he replied.

There! He was going to pull out and leave right now.

"It's going to cause a lot of trouble, what's happening with you and me."

He kept fucking her while he talked, not missing a stroke, and it was such bliss she was sure she'd missed the sense of what he'd said. He couldn't have meant—

"I love you back. Oh baby, I love you so much. I can't think straight sometimes. It's like I'm in a daze till I'm here. Right here."

It would be too cruel of him to lie, and he wasn't cruel, she knew that, which meant he was telling the truth.

Oh Lord, he loved her, he loved her, and if all the trouble in the world would come down on their heads because of it, she didn't care.

She started to turn in his arms so that she could be face to face with him. It was a difficult manuever, but her body was different in his arms, lusher and more malleable. Now came those kisses she could feel the day after; the kisses that made her lips burn and her tongue ache; the kisses that brought the tremors that had her shaking and hollering as though possessed. Only today there were words between them, promises of his undying devotion. And the tremors, when they came, rose from some place that was not in any anatomy book on the doctor's shelf. An invisible, unnameable place that neither God nor tumors could touch.

"Oh, I almost forgot—" he said while they were dressing, and fumbled around in the top pocket of his overalls. "I wanted you to have this. And after this afternoon—well, it's more important than ever."

He pulled out a photograph and handed it to her.

"That's my Mom, that's my brother Ron, he's the baby of the family, and that's my sister Noreen. Oh yeah, and that's me." He was in uniform, and shining with pride. "I look good, huh?"

"When was this taken?"

"The week after I came out of basic training," he said.

"Why didn't you stay in the army?"

"It's a long story," he said, his smile fading.

"You don't have to—" The phone interrupted her. "Oh shit! I'm not going to answer that."

"It could be important."

"Yeah, and it could be Morton," she said. "And I don't want to talk to him right now."

"We don't want him getting suspicious," Joe said, "at least till we've made up our minds how we're going to handle all this."

She sighed, nodded, and hurried down to the phone, calling back as she went: "We have to talk about this *soon*."

"How 'bout tomorrow? Same time?" She told him yes, then picked up the receiver. It wasn't Morton, it was Emmeline Harper, who ran the Historical Society, an overwrought woman with a puffed up view of her own importance.

"Phoebe—"

"Emmeline?"

"Phoebe, I need a favor. Dorothy just called, and apparently somebody needs to get into the schoolhouse to look through the records. I can't get over there, and I was wondering would you be a sweetheart?" No was on the tip of Phoebe's tongue. Then Emmeline said: "It's that nice Mr. Toothaker, the attorney? Have you met him?"

"Yes. A couple of years back." A bit of a cold fish, as she remembered. But maybe this wouldn't be such a bad time to talk to a man who knew the law. She could quietly quiz him about divorce, and maybe she'd learn something to her advantage.

"I mean I'm sure he's very trustworthy—I don't think for a moment he'd tamper with the collection, but I think somebody should be there to let him in and show him what's what."

"Fine."

"He's over at the Chamber of Commerce. Can I call over and say you'll be twenty minutes?"

III

Since its foundation in 1972, the Everville Historical Society had been a repository for all manner of items relating to the city's past. One of the first and most valuable bequests came from Hubert Nordhoff, whose family had owned and run the mill that now stood deserted on the Molina road, three-quarters of a mile out of town. In the three and a half decades between 1880 and 1915, the Nordhoff Mill had provided employment for a good portion of Everville's citizens, while helping to amass a considerable fortune for the Nordhoffs. They had built a mansion in Salem, and another in Oregon City, before withdrawing from the blanket- and fabric-making business and putting their money into lumber, real estate (most of it in Portland), and even, it was rumored, armaments. Hubert Nordhoff's bequest of some thousand photographs of life at the mill, along with several other pieces of memorabilia, had been widely interpreted as a belated act of contrition for his ancestor's sudden desertion; the years immediately following the closure of the mill had been Everville's darkest hour, economically speaking.

The Nordhoff bequest had begun a small avalanche of gifts. Seventeen watercolors of local scenes, prettily if somewhat blandly painted by the wife of Everville's first dentist, were now framed and hung in the walls of the schoolhouse (the renovation of which had

87

been paid for by H. Nordhoff). A collection of walking sticks topped with the heads of fantastical animals, carved by one of the city's great eccentrics, Milius Biggs, was displayed in a glass case in what had been the principal's office.

But far outnumbering these aesthetic bequests were more mundane offerings, most of them from ordinary Evervillians. School reports, wedding announcements, obituaries, family albums, a collection of cuttings from *The Oregonian*, all of which mentioned the town (this assembled by the librarian Stanley Tharp, who had stammered traumatically for sixty-one years but on his deathbed had recited Milton's *Paradise Lost* without a stumble), and of course family letters in their hundreds.

The labor of organizing such a large body of material was slow, given that all the Society's workers were volunteers. Two of the schoolhouse's five rooms were still piled high with boxes of unsorted gifts, but for those visitors interested in Everville's past, the remaining three rooms offered a pleasant, if somewhat over-tidy, glimpse of the early days.

It was highly selective of course, but then so were most history lessons. There was no place in this celebration of the Evervillian spirit for the darker side; for images of destitution, or suicide, or worse. No room, either, for any individual who didn't fit the official version of how things had come to be. There were pictures of the city in its infancy, and accounts of how its roads were laid and its fine houses built. But of Maeve O'Connell, who had ventured to the shores of another world, and returned to make her father's dream real, there was no sign. And in that disinheritance lay the seeds of Everville's undoing.

ii

Phoebe was a little late coming for Erwin, but he was all politeness. He was sorry to be inconveniencing her this way, he said, but it really was urgent business. No, he couldn't really tell her what it was about, but it would be public knowledge before very long, and he'd be certain to thank her for her kindness in print. There was no need, she insisted; but she'd be very grateful if after the weekend she could come and pick his brains in a legal matter. He readily agreed. Was she planning to make a will?

No, she said, I'm planning to divorce my husband. To which he replied divorce was not really his area of expertise but he'd be happy to chat with her about it. In confidence, she said. Of course, he told her. She should drop by his offices on Monday morning.

The schoolhouse was still baking hot, even though it was now close to six, and while Phoebe went around raising the blinds and opening the windows, Erwin wandered from room to stifling room, peering at the pictures.

"Can you tell me what you're looking for?" Phoebe asked him. "I mean, vaguely."

"Back issues of the *Tribune*, for one thing," Erwin said. "Apparently they don't have room to keep them at their offices, so they're here."

"And what else?"

"Well, I'm not familiar with the collection. Is it arranged chronologically?"

"I'm not sure. I think so." She led Erwin through to the back room, where six tables were piled with files. "I used to come and help sort through things," she said. "But this last year's been so hectic—" She flicked through one of the piles. "These are all marked nineteen forty to forty-five." She moved on to the next pile. "And these are forty-five to fifty."

"So it's in increments of half-decades."

"Right."

"Well that's a start. And the newspapers?"

Phoebe pointed through the adjacent door. "They *are* in order. I know, 'cause I was the one did it."

"Wonderful. I'll get started then."

"Do you want me to wait till you're finished?"

"It depends how patient you're feeling."

"Not very," she said with a little laugh. "Maybe I should just jot down my telephone number, and when you're done—"

"I'll call you and you can come over and lock up."

"Right."

"That's a deal then." She went to the front desk, wrote her number on one of the Society brochures, and took it back to him. He was already plundering the contents of one of the files.

"You will put everything *back*, won't you?" Phoebe said, in her best forbidding manner.

"Oh yes. I'll be careful," Erwin replied. He took the brochure from her. "I'll call you when I'm done," he said. "I hope it won't be too late."

As she got into the car she thought: What would happen if I never went home again? If I just drove to Joe's place now and left town tonight? It was a tempting idea—not to have to go back to the house and cook dinner and listen to Morton bitching about every damn thing—but she resisted it. If her future with Joe was to have a chance then she had to plan it: carefully, systematically. They weren't teenagers, eloping in the first flush of love. If they were going to leave Everville permanently (and she couldn't imagine their staying, once the truth was out) then they had responsibilities to turn over and farewells to take. She'd be happy never to see the house or Morton or the stinking ashtrays he left behind him ever again, but she'd miss Dr. Powell, along with a handful of his regulars. She'd need to take the time to explain herself to the people she valued most, so that they knew she was going for love's sake, not because she was fickle or cruel.

So, she'd stay, and enjoy her last Festival in Everville. Indeed, thinking of it that way gave her a taste for the celebrations she'd not had in years. This weekend she'd get out and party, knowing that next year, come August, she'd be in another part of the world.

Hunger always made Morton bad-tempered, so rather than have him wait while she cooked, she went by Kitty's Diner to pick up a burger and fries. It was now three years since the death of Kitty Cowhick, and despite hard economic times her son-in-law Bosley had turned the place from a shabby little establishment into a thriving business. He was Born Again, and brought his strict moral viewpoint to bear in managing the diner. He forbade, for instance, the reading of any literature he deemed indecent in the booths or at the counter, and if a breath of profanity was exhaled he personally requested that the guilty party leave. She'd seen him do it too. *I want this to be a place the Lord himself could come to*, he'd told her once, *if He wanted a piece of pie.*

Morton's burger purchased, she set off home, only to find the house deserted. Morton had been back—his work jacket was on the kitchen table, along with a couple of empty beer cans—but he'd apparently tired of waiting for her to come home, and gone out in search of something to eat. She was pleased: It gave her a little more time to think.

She sat at the kitchen table picking over the soggy fries, and used the pad she usually made her shopping lists on to jot down the things she wanted to take with her when she left. There wasn't much. Just a few bits and pieces that had some sentimental significance: a chair she'd inherited from her mother; some needlepoint her grandmother had made; the quilt in the spare bedroom.

Thinking of the quilt, she left off her list-making and turned her mind back to the deeds of the afternoon. Or rather, to the deed performed in that room. It would not always be so wonderful, she counseled herself; the heat between them would be bound to mellow over the years. But if and when that happened, there would be a weight of feeling that remained. And there would be memories of events like this afternoon, that would spring to mind every time she pressed her face to the quilt.

iii

A little after eight-thirty, with his stomach growling for want of dinner, Erwin's search through the woefully disorganized files turned up an odd little pamphlet, penned by one Raymond Merkle. He knew the name, vaguely. The man had made himself a minor reputation as a chronicler of small-town Oregon. Erwin had seen companion volumes to this in the bookstore in Wilsonville. The text was a curious compendium of facts about Everville, written in the belabored style of a man who had aspirations to being a writer but precious little ear for language.

It was entitled *These Dreaming Hills*, which turned out to be a quote from a piece printed (without the name of the poet, so Erwin assumed it to be Merkle) of doggerel at the front of the pamphlet. And there, halfway through this little labor of love, Erwin encountered the following:

That the forces of heinous and unrepentant evil make their barbaric mark in a city as sweetly favored as Everville should come as no surprise to those of us who have seen something of the larger world. I, your author, ventured from the fertile climes of our glorious state in the forty-third year of this century to perform my duties as an American in the South Pacific, and will carry to my grave the scenes of cruelty and human degradation I witnessed there, in surroundings as paradisaical as any this globe can offer.

It surprised me then not at all to discover, in the course of preparing this volume, rumors of diabolical deeds performed within the precincts of Everville's comely community.

The sad story of the death of Rebecca Jenkins is well known. She was a daughter of that fair city, much prized and adored, who was murdered in her eighth year, her body deposited in the reservoir. Her murderer was a man out of Sublimity who later died in prison while serving a life sentence. But the mystery surrounding the tragedy of poor Rebecca does not end there.

While gathering stories about the stranger incidents associated with Everville, the quizzical demise of one Richard Dolan was whispered to me. He had owned a candy store, I was told, and little Rebecca Jenkins had been a regular customer of his, so he had taken the death of the child particularly hard. The capture and subsequent incarceration of her unrepentant murderer had done nothing to subjugate his great uneasiness. He had become more and more melancholy, and on the night of September 19, 1975, he had told his wife he was hearing voices from Harmon's Heights. Somebody was calling to him, he said. When she asked him who, he refused to say, but took himself off into the night. He did not return, and the next day a party ascended the Heights to look for him.

After two days of searching they found the delirious Richie Dolan, wedged in a crevice of rock on the northeast slope of the mountain. He was very horribly harmed by his fall, but he was not dead. Such was the state of his face and torso that his wife fell into a swoon at the sight of him and was never of sound mind again.

He died in Silverton Hospital three days later, but he did not die silent. In that seventy-two hours he raved like a bedlamite, unsubdued by the tranquilizers his doctors gave him.

What did he speak of in his final, agonizing hours? I could find no firsthand testament on this, but there is sufficient consensus among the rumors to suppose them broadly true. He raved, I was told, about dead men calling to him from Harmon's Heights. Over and over, even at the very end, when the doctors stood astonished at how he was clinging to life, he was begging forgiveness—

The account maundered on for a couple more paragraphs, but Erwin merely skimmed them. He had what he needed here: Evidence, albeit rudimentary, that there was some truth in what McPherson had written. And if one part was truthful, then why not the rest?

Content that his pursuit of verification was not a folly, he left off the search for the night, and called Phoebe Cobb. Would she come over and look up? he asked. She would, of course. If he would just be kind enough to close the windows, she'd pop over in a while to secure the front door.

Her voice sounded a little slurred, he thought, but maybe it was his imagination. The day had been long, and he was weary. Time to get home, and try and put the McPherson confession out of his head until he resumed his inquiries tomorrow.

He knew where he'd begin those inquiries: down by the creek. Though it was three decades since the events McPherson had described, if the house he claimed the trio had burned down had in truth existed, then there would be some sign of it remaining. And if

there was, then that would be another part of the confession veri-
fied, and he would be tempted to bring the whole story into the
open air, where the whole state could smell how much it stank.

iv

Phoebe had opened the brandy bottle around a quarter to eight,
telling herself she wanted to toast her coming liberation, but in truth
to dull the unease she was feeling. On the few occasions Morton
went out to get some dinner for himself, he was usually back within
the hour, ready to deposit himself in front of the television. Where
had he gone to tonight? And more: Why did she care?

She drowned her confusion in a brandy; then in another. That
did the trick just fine, especially on an almost empty stomach. By
the time the attorney called, she was feeling very mellow; too mellow
to drive. No matter. She'd walk to the Old Schoolhouse she decided.

The night was balmy, the air fragrant with pine, and the walk
proved more pleasant than she'd expected. At any other time of the
year, even at the height of summer, the streets would have been
pretty quiet in the middle of the evening, but tonight the lights were
still burning in many of the stores along Main Street, their owners
working on Festival window displays or stocking the shelves for the
profitable days ahead. There were even a few visitors around, come
early to enjoy the quiet of the valley.

At the corner of Main and Watson she halted for a moment or
two. A right turn took her up towards the schoolhouse, a left led
down past the market and the park to Donovan Street, and a little
way along Donovan Street was the apartment house where Joe lived.
It would be just a slip of the foot to turn left rather than right. But
she fought the urge. Better to let all that they'd felt and said this
afternoon settle for a few hours, rather than get hot and flustered
again. Besides, brandy always made her a little tearful, and her face
got puffy when she cried. She'd see him tomorrow, and dream about
him in the meantime.

Turning right, she headed on up the gentle gradient of Watson, past the new supermarket, which was still open and doing brisk business, to the schoolhouse. It took her five minutes to check all the windows, pull down the blinds, and lock up. Then she began the return journey.

About fifty yards from Main Street, somebody on the opposite sidewalk stepped out into the road, looking up at the night sky. She knew him vaguely. He was the youngest of the Lundy clan, Sam or Steve or—

"Seth."

Though she'd only murmured the syllable he heard her. Without moving from the middle of the street he looked round at her, his eyes glittering, and she remembered how she'd first encountered him. His mother had brought him in to see Dr. Powell, five or six years ago, and the child had stood in the waiting room with a look of such remoteness on his pinched little face, Phoebe had assumed he was mentally retarded. There was no remoteness now. He was fiercely focused.

"Do you hear it?" he said to her.

He didn't approach, but something about him intimidated her. Rather than get any closer, she halted, glancing back up the street towards the lights of the supermarket. There'd been plenty of cars in the lot when she'd passed, one of them would be bound to emerge soon, and she would use its passing as cover to continue on her way.

"You don't, do you?" he said, his voice singsong.

"Don't what?"

"You don't hear the hammering."

"Hammering?" She listened a moment. "No I don't."

"Hmm." He returned his gaze to the starry heavens. "You used to work at the doctor's," he said.

"I still do."

"Not for long," he replied.

She felt a shiver pass down her body from scalp to sole.

"How do you know?"

He smiled at the sky. "It's so loud," he said. "Are you sure you can't hear it?"

"I told you—" she began.

"It's okay," he said softly. "Only sometimes at night, other people hear it too. It never happens in the day. In the day it's only me—"

"I'm sorry—"

"Don't be sorry," he said; and then his smile went to her instead of the stars. "I'm used to it."

She suddenly felt absurd for fearing him. He was a lonely, bewildered kid. A little crazy in the head maybe, but harmless enough.

"What did you mean about me not working at the doctor's for long?" she asked him.

He shrugged. "Don't know," he said. "These things come out sometimes, without me really knowing what they mean." He paused for a moment. "Probably nothing," he said, and returned his gaze to the sky.

She didn't wait for a car to emerge from the lot, but continued on her way to Main Street. "Enjoy yourself," she said as she passed him by.

"Yeah," he murmured, "I do."

The incident lingered with her as she wandered home, and she made a mental note to look up the Lundy file when she got into work tomorrow, to see what had brought mother and child to the doctor's that day, and why they'd never returned. When she got back to the house, Morton was in his chair in front of the television, sound asleep, a beer can in his lap, and four more between his feet. She didn't bother to wake him. Instead she went into the kitchen and made herself a ham and cheese sandwich, which she ate leaning on the sink gazing out into the darkened yard. Clouds were coming in to cover the stars, but she didn't suppose it much mattered to the Lundy boy. If he could hear hammerings in Heaven, a few clouds wouldn't dull it much.

Sandwich eaten, she retired to bed, hoping that she'd be between the sheets and asleep before Morton roused himself. She needn't have worried. When finally a breath of cool air on her back stirred her from slumber and she felt him slide into bed beside her, the luminous face of the clock read ten past three. Grunting to himself, he pulled the sheets in his direction, rolled over and instantly began to snore.

It took her a little time to get back to sleep, and when she did it was fitful. In the morning, sitting alone at the kitchen table (Morton had already gone to work when she woke), she tried to sort through the dream fragments circling in her head and remembered that in one Joe had been introducing her to the people in the photograph he'd shown her. All five of them had been in a car for some reason, and Joe's brother kept saying: *Where are we? Hell and damn, where are we?* It wasn't the most reassuring of dreams. What was she thinking? That they were all lost together now? She took three aspirin with a cup of black coffee and headed out to work, putting the dream out of her mind. Which was a pity. Had she dwelt on it a little longer, she might have puzzled over the whereabouts of the photograph that had inspired it, and acted to spare herself, Joe, and Morton more grief than any of them expected or deserved.

IV

_T_he woman on the motorcycle looked like a seasoned traveler: her leathers dusty and beaten-up, her hair, when she eased off her helmet, cropped short and bleached by desert sun; her face, which had probably never been pretty, worn and raw. She had a bruise on her jaw, and lines deeply etched around her eyes and mouth; none of them laugh lines.

Her name was Tesla Bombeck, and today she was coming home. Not back to her literal birthplace (that was Philadelphia) nor even to the city where she'd been raised (which was Detroit) but to the town where the reconfiguring that had made her the raw, bruised, etched wanderer she was had begun.

Or rather, to the remains of that town. At the height of its mediocrity, this place—Palomo Grove—had been a nominee for the perfect California haven. Unlike Everville, which had grown organically over a century and a half, the Grove had sprung into being in three years, created by planners and real-estate magnates with sheaves of demographics for inspiration. And it had quietly prospered for a time, hidden in the folds of the Simi Valley a couple of miles from the highway that speeded its wage earners to Los Angeles every morning and speeded them home again every night.

The traffic on that highway was busier than ever now, but the off-ramp that served the Grove was seldom used. Occasionally a tourist who wanted to add the Town That Died Overnight to his list of Californian curiosities would come to look at the desolation, but such visits were increasingly rare. Nor was any attempt being made to rebuild the Grove, despite vast losses sustained by both landowners and individuals. Tesla wasn't surprised. These were recessionary times; people no longer believed in real estate as a solid investment, much less real estate that had proven unstable in the past.

For Palomo Grove hadn't simply died, it had buried itself, its streets gaping like graves for its fine houses. Many of those streets were still barricaded off to keep the sightseers from coming to harm, but Tesla had been hearing *yes* when she was told *no* from childhood, and it was up over the barricades she first went, to wander where the damage was worst.

She had thought about coming back here many times in her five-year journey through what she liked to call the Americas, by which she meant the mainland states. They were not, she had many times insisted to Grillo, one country; not remotely. Just because they served the same Coke in Louisiana as they served in Idaho, and the same sitcoms were playing in New Mexico as were playing in Massachusetts, didn't mean there was such a thing as America. When presidents and pundits spoke of the voice and will of the American people, she rolled her eyes. That was a fiction; she'd been told so plainly by a yellow dog that had followed her around Arizona for a week and a half during her hallucination period, turning up in diners and motel rooms to chat with her in such a friendly fashion she'd missed him when he disappeared.

If she remembered rightly (and she'd never know) it was the dog that had first mentioned going back to the Grove.

"You gotta bury your nose in your own shit sooner or later," he'd advised, leaning back in a threadbare armchair. "It's the only way to get in touch."

"With what?" she'd wanted to know.

"With what? With what?" he'd said, coming to perch at the bottom of the bed. "I'm not your analyst! Find out for yourself."

"Suppose there's nothing *to* find out?" she'd countered.

"Don't talk crap," he'd said. "You're not afraid of finding there's nothing to find. You're afraid of finding so much it'll drive you crazy." He wandered down the bed and straddled her, so they were nose to nose. "Well guess what, Miss Bombeck? You're *already* crazy. So what's to lose?"

She couldn't remember if she'd worked up some pithy reply to this or simply passed out. Probably the latter. She'd passed out in a lot of motel rooms during that phase. Anyway, the yellow dog had sown the seed. And the months had passed, and she'd gradually regained a semblance of sanity, and on and off, when she was consulting a map or looking at a sign-post, she'd think: maybe I should do it today. Maybe I should go back to the Grove.

But whenever she'd come close to doing so, another voice had spoken up; the voice of the personality who had shared her skull with her for the past half-decade.

His name was Raul, and he'd been born an ape. He'd not stayed that way for long, however. At the age of four he'd been evolved from his simian state to manhood, the agent of that miracle fluid which its discoverer had dubbed the Nuncio, the messenger. The fluid was not the fruit of pure science, but of a mingling of disci plines part biogenetics, part alchemy—and it had gone on to touch and transform others, including (briefly) Tesla, coaxing forth the natural propensities of those it influenced, and creating in the process the two warring forces who had made Palomo Grove their battleground.

One was the Nuncio's maker, a mescaline-addicted visionary by the name of Fletcher, who had become a force for transcendence under the messenger's tutelage. The other was his patron, Randolph Jaffe, who had funded the discovery in the hope of attaining access to a condition of flesh and spirit that was tantamount to divinity. The Nuncio had done nothing to dull that ambition, but it *had* shaped from the Jaff a creature so consumed by his dreams of power that his spirit had atrophied. By the time he'd won the war with Fletcher (destroying the Grove in the process), and was ready to claim his prize, his psyche was too frail to bear the triumph. He had forfeited his reason in pursuit of godhood. Soon after, he'd forfeited his life.

It was little wonder then, that Raul had protested so vigorously her desire to return to the Grove.

I hate California, he'd told her any number of times. *If we never go back there it'll be too soon.*

She hadn't fought with him over it. Though she had full control of her body, and could have driven West without his being able to do a thing to stop her, his presence had been comforting during the many terrible times that followed the demise of Palomo Grove, and given that she fully expected such times to come again, more terrible than ever, she wanted to keep relations sweet.

The paradox of this, that her dubious sanity was preserved by one of the things that drove people crazy (voices in the head) was not lost on her. Nor did she forget that her tenant, who was usually scrupulous in respecting the boundaries between his thoughts and hers, suffered from crises of his own, at which times she became the comforter. She would wake sometimes to hear him sobbing in her head, bemoaning the fact that he had given up his body in the war, and would never again have an anatomy to call his own. She would soothe him then as best she could; tell him they would find some way to free him one of these days, and until then wasn't it better this way, because at least they had each other?

And it was. When she doubted all that she'd seen, he was there to say: *It's true.* When she feared the burden of all she'd come to comprehend he was there to say: *We'll carry it together, till we can be done with it.*

Ah! To be done with it. That was the trick. To find some way to off-load the revelation onto strong and trustworthy shoulders, and go her way back to the life she'd been living before she'd ever heard of Palomo Grove.

She'd been a screenwriter by trade, with the scar tissue to prove it, and though it was a long time since she'd sat down to write, her cinematic instinct remained acute. Even in the bad times, a week would not go by without her thinking: *There's a scene here.* The way that sky looks, the way those dogs are fighting, the way I'm sobbing— it could be the beginning of something wonderful and strange.

But of late it had come to seem that all she had was beginnings— always setting off an unknown highway or opening a conversation with a stranger—and never getting to the second act. If the painful farce of her life to date was to have any resolution, then she was going to have to move the story on. And that could not happen, she knew, until she went back to the Grove and confronted its ghosts.

Later, she would see synchronicity at work, and come to believe that the timing of that journey was no accident. That either her subconscious, or powers operating upon it in the dream-state, had so haunted her with memories of the Grove that her only hope of deliverance was to return that particular week in August, when so much else was waiting to happen.

Even Raul, who had so forcibly rejected the notion over the years, accepted the inevitability of the journey when she put it to him.

Let's get it over with, he said, *though God knows what you think you're going to find there.*

Now she knew. Here she was in the middle of what had once been Palomo Grove's mall, its geographical and emotional hub. People had come to meet here, to gossip, to fall in love, and (almost incidentally) to shop. Now all but a few of the stores were heaps of rubble, and those that were left standing were reduced to shells, the merchandise they'd housed smashed, looted or rotted away.

Tesla? Raul murmured in her head.

She answered him, as always, not with her tongue and lips, but with her mind. "What?"

We're not alone.

She looked around. She could see no signs of life, but that didn't mean anything. Raul was closer to his animal roots than she; more alert to countless tiny signs her senses were receiving but that she no longer knew how to interpret. If he said they had company, they did.

"Where?" she thought.

Left of us, he replied. *Over that mound of rubble.*

She started towards it, orienting herself as she did so. The remains of the pet store lay off to her right, which meant that the heaps of plaster clotted steel and timbers in front of her was all that was left of the supermarket. She scrambled up over the debris, the sun bright against her face, but before she reached the top somebody appeared to block the way: a long-haired young man, dressed in T-shirt and jeans, with the greenest eyes she'd ever seen. "You're not allowed here," he said, his voice too soft to carry much authority.

"Oh, and you are?" Tesla said.

From the other side of the mound came a woman's voice. "Who is it, Lucien?"

Lucien directed the question at Tesla, "Who are you?"

By way of reply, Tesla started to climb again, until she could see the questioner on the other side. Only then did she say, "My name's Tesla Bombeck. Not that it's any of your business."

The woman was sitting on the ground, in a circle of incense-filled bowls, their smoke sickly sweet. At the sight of Tesla she started to rise, astonishment on her face.

"My God—" she said, glancing back at her second associate, an overweight middle-aged man, who was lounging in a battered chair. "Edward," she said. "Look who it is."

The man stared at Tesla with plain suspicion. "We heard you were dead," he remarked.

"Do I know you?" Tesla asked him.

The man shook his head.

"But *I* know you," the woman said, stepping out of the circle of smoke. Tesla was now halfway down the other side of the rubble, and close enough to see how frail and drawn this woman was. "I'm Kathleen Farrell," she said. "I used to live here in the Grove."

The name didn't ring a bell, but that was no surprise. Maybe it was having Raul using up some of her brain capacity for his own memories (and maybe it was just old age) but names and faces slipped away all the time these days.

"What brought you back?" Tesla wanted to know.

"We were—"

She was interrupted by Edward, who now rose from his chair. "Kate," he cautioned. "Be careful."

"But she—"

"We can't trust *anybody*," he said. "Not even her."

"But she wouldn't even *be* here—" Kate said. She looked at Tesla. "*Would* you?" Back at Edward now. "She knows what's going on." Again, at Tesla. "You do, don't you?"

"Of course," Tesla lied.

"Have you actually seen him?" said Lucien, approaching her from behind.

"Not—not in the last couple of months," Tesla replied, her mind racing. Who the hell were they talking about?

"But you *have* seen him?" Kate said.

"Yes," she replied. "Absolutely."

A smile appeared on Kate's weary face. "I *knew*," she said.

"Nobody doubts he's alive," Edward now said, his gaze still fixed upon Tesla. "But why the hell would he show himself to *her?*"

"Isn't it obvious?" said Kate. "Tell him, Tesla."

Tesla put on a pained look, as though the subject was too delicate to be spoken about. "It's difficult," she said.

"I can see that," Kate said. "After all, you started the fire—"

In her head, Tesla heard Raul let out a low moan. She didn't need to ask him why. There was only one fire of any consequence Tesla had started, and she'd started it here in the mall, perhaps on the very spot where Kate Farrell had been sitting.

"Were you here?"

"No. But Lucien was," Kate said.

Lucien stepped into Tesla's line of sight, taking up the thread of the story as he did so. "It's still so clear," he said. "Him covering himself in gasoline, then you firing the gun. I thought you were trying to kill him. We all did, I'm sure—"

This doesn't make any sense, Raul murmured in her head. *They're talking about—*

"Fletcher," she thought back. "I know."

But it's as though they think he's still alive.

"I didn't understand what you were doing," Lucien was saying.

"But you do now?" Tesla asked him.

"Of course. You killed him so that he could live again."

As Lucien spoke, Fletcher's last moments played out on the screen in her skull, as they had hundreds of times in the intervening years. His body, doused in gasoline from head to foot. Her aiming the gun at the ground close to his feet, praying for a spark. She'd fired once. Nothing. He'd looked at her with despair in his eyes, a warrior who had fought his enemy until he had nothing left to fight with but the spirit trapped in his wounded flesh. *Release me,* that look had said, *or the battle is lost.*

She'd fired again, and this time her prayers had been answered. A spark had ignited the air, and a column of flame leapt up to consume the Nunciate Fletcher.

"He died right here?" she said, staring down at the circle.

Kate nodded, and stepped aside so that Tesla could approach the spot. After five years of sun and rain, the asphalt was still darker there where he'd perished; stained with fat and fire. She shuddered.

"Isn't it wonderful?" Kate said.

"Huh?"

"Wonderful. That he's back among us."

"It means the end can't be far off," Lucien said.

Tesla turned her back on the stained asphalt. "The end of what?" she said.

He gave her a tender smile. "The end to our cruelties and our trivialities," he said. That didn't sound too bad, Tesla thought. "The time's come for us to *move on*, up the ladder. But you know this already. You were touched by the Nuncio, right?"

"Much good it did me," she said.

"There's pain at the beginning," Kate said softly. "We speak to shamans across the country—"

Once again, Edward interrupted. "I think Ms. Bombeck's already heard too much," he said. "We don't know enough about her allegiances—"

"I don't have any," Tesla replied plainly.

"Is that supposed to reassure me?" Edward said.

"No—"

"Good. Because it doesn't."

"Edward," Kate said, "we're not at war here."

"Slow down," Tesla said. "A minute ago he—" she jabbed a thumb over her shoulder in Lucien's direction, "was saying we were heading for paradise, and now you're talking about war. Make up your minds."

"I already made mine up," Edward said. He turned to Kate. "Let's leave this till later," he said, glaring down at the circle. "When she's gone."

"I'm not going anywhere," Tesla said, taking a seat on the rubble. "I can hang out all day."

Edward smiled. "See?" he said, his voice becoming frayed. "She's a troublemaker. She wants to keep us from the work—"

"What work?" Tesla said.

"Finding Fletcher," Kate said.

"Shut up, will you?" Edward snapped.

"Why?" said Kate, her equilibrium undisturbed. "If she's here to stop us, she already knows what we're doing. And if she isn't, then maybe she can help."

The argument silenced Edward for a few seconds. Time enough for Tesla to say, "If you think Fletcher's some kind of messiah, you're going to be disappointed. Believe me."

"I'm talking as though he's alive," she thought as she spoke, to which Raul murmured: *Maybe he is.*

"I don't believe he's a messiah," Lucien was saying, "we've had too many messiahs as it is. We don't need another guy telling us what to be. Or what happens to us if we fail." Tesla liked the sound of that, which Lucien clearly saw, because he went down on his haunches in front of her, and continued to speak, face to face. "Fletcher's come back because he wants to be here when we rise, all of us, all rise up together and become something new."

"What—exactly?"

Lucien shrugged. "If I knew that I'd have to kill myself."

"Why?"

"Because I'd be a messiah." He laughed, as did she. Then he rose, shrugging. "That's all I know," he said.

She looked up at him guiltily. There was a sweet simplicity to him she found charming. More than charming in fact, almost sexual.

"Look," she said, "I lied when I said I'd seen Fletcher. I haven't."

"I knew it," Edward sneered.

"No you didn't," Tesla replied a little wearily. "You didn't have a fucking clue." She looked back at Lucien. "Anyway, why's it so important you find him, if he's only here as a sightseer?"

"Because we have to protect ourselves from our enemies," Kate said, "And he can help us."

"Just so you know," Tesla replied, "I'm *not* one of your enemies. I know Eddie over there doesn't believe me, but it's true. I'm on nobody's side but my own. And if that sounds selfish, it's because it is." She got to her feet. "Do you have any solid evidence that Fletcher's alive?" she asked Lucien.

"Some," he said.

"But you don't want to tell me?"

He look at his sandaled feet. "I don't think that'd be particularly useful right now," he replied.

"Fair enough," she said, starting back up the slope of rubble, "I'll leave you to it then. If you see him, give him regards, will you?"

"This isn't a joke," Edward called after her.

It was probably the one remark which she couldn't let slide by. She stopped climbing, and looked back at him. "Oh yes it is," she said. "That's exactly what it is. One big fucking joke."

V

i

*T*hat encounter aside, Tesla's return to the Grove was a bust. There were no moments of revelation; no confrontations with ghosts (real or imagined) to help her better understand the past. She left in the same state of confusion she'd arrived in.

She didn't run for the state line, but drove back into L.A., to the apartment in West Hollywood she'd kept through her years on the road. She'd actually slept there perhaps two dozen times in the last five years, but the rent was peanuts, and the landlord a burnout case who liked the idea of having a real screenwriter as a tenant, however much of an absentee she was, so she'd kept it as a place to laughingly call home. In truth, it had grim associations, but tonight, as she lounged in front of the TV to eat her curried tofu-burger and watch the news, she was glad of its familiarity. It was several weeks since she'd paid any attention to events around the planet, but nothing of significance had changed. A war here, a famine there; death on the highway, death on the subway. And always, people shaking their heads, witnesses and warlords alike, protesting that this tragedy should never have happened. She sickened of it after ten minutes and turned it off.

Would it be so bad . . . ? Raul murmured.

"Would *what* be so bad?" she said, staring at the blank screen.

To have a messiah.

"You really think Fletcher's been resurrected?"

I think maybe he was never dead.

Now *there* was a possibility: that Fletcher's death-scene in Palomo Grove had merely been a part of some greater scheme, a way to slip out of sight for a few years until he was better equipped to deal with the Nuncio and its consequences.

"Why now?" she wondered aloud.

Ask Grillo, Raul suggested.

"Must I?" Grillo had been strange the last couple of times she'd called him: remote and short-tempered. When they'd spoken five or six weeks before, she'd come off the phone thinking maybe he was on serious drugs, he sounded so damn strange. She almost headed over to Nebraska to check on him, but she'd been feeling spooked enough without going into that apartment of his. Raul was right, however: If anyone knew what was happening in the places that never found their way onto the evening news, it was Grillo.

Less than happily, she called him. He was in a better mood than the last occasion, though he sounded tired. She got straight to the point; told him about returning to the Grove, and her encounter with the trio.

"Kate Farrell, eh?" Grillo said.

"Do you know her?"

"She was the mother of one of the League of Virgins. Arleen Farrell. She went crazy."

"Mother or daughter?"

"Daughter. She died in an institution. Starved herself to death."

This was more like the Nathan Grillo Tesla was used to. A clean, clipped summary of the facts, presented with the minimum of sentiment. In his pre-Grove days he'd been a journalist. He'd never lost his nose for a good story.

"What the hell was Kate Farrell doing in Palomo Grove?" he asked.

She explained, as best she could. The circle of incense bowls, set around the place where Fletcher had perished (or at least done a damned good impersonation of perishing); the talk of sightings; the exchange about messiahdom.

"Have you heard anything about this?" she finished up by asking him.

There was a moment's silence. Then he said, "Sure."

"You *have?*"

"Listen, if it's there to be heard, I hear it."

This was not an idle boast. There in Omaha—a city built at the Crossroads of America—Grillo had established himself as a clearing-house for any and all information that related, however remotely, to events in Palomo Grove. Within a year he had won the trust and respect of a vast circle of individuals, from molecular physicists to beat cops, to politicians, to priests, all of whom had one thing in common: Their lives had somehow been brushed by mysterious, even terrifying, forces, the details of which they felt they could not share, either for personal or professional reasons, with their peers.

Word had quickly spread through the thicket where those marginalized by their experiences and beliefs and terrors had taken cover; word of this man Grillo who had seen the way things really were and wanted to hear from others who'd seen the same; who was putting the pieces together, one by one, until he had the whole story.

It was that ambition—whether practical or not—that had kept Tesla and Grillo talking to each other in the years since the Grove. Though she had gone wandering, and he seldom left his apartment, they were both engaged in the same search for *connections*. She had failed to find them in the Americas—it was chaos out there—and doubted Grillo had been any more lucky; but they still had the search in common.

And she never failed to marvel at his ability to put two appar-ently disparate fragments of information together to suggest a third more provocative possibility. How a rumor from Boca Raton con-firmed a hint from a suicide note found in Denver which in turn supported a thesis spoken in tongues by a prodigy in New Jersey.

"So what have you heard?"

"People have been sighting Fletcher on and off for the last five years, Tes," he said. "He's like Bigfoot, or Elvis. There's not a month goes by I don't get somebody sending me his picture."

"Any of them the real thing?"

"Shit, I don't know. I used to think . . . " His words trailed away for a moment, as though he'd lost track of his thought.

"Grillo?"

"Yeah."

"What did you used to think?"

"It doesn't matter," he said a little wearily.

"Yes it does."

He drew a long, ragged breath. "I used to think it mattered whether or not things were real. I'm not so sure any more. . . ." Again he faltered. This time she didn't prompt him, but waited until he had his thoughts in order. "Maybe the messiahs we *imagine* are more important than the real thing. At least they don't bleed when you crucify 'em."

For some reason he found this extremely funny, and Tesla was obliged to wait while he got over his bout of laughter.

"Is that it then?" she said, faintly irritated now. "You don't think it matters whether things are real or not, so I should just give up caring?"

"Oh I care," he said. "I care more than you know." He was suddenly icy.

"What the hell's wrong with you, Grillo?"

"Leave it alone, Tes."

"Maybe I should come see you—"

"*No!*"

"Why the hell not?"

"I just—leave it alone." He sighed. "I gotta go," he said. "Call me tomorrow. I'll see if I can dig up anything useful about Fletcher. But, you know Tes, I think it's time we grew up and stopped looking for fucking *explanations*."

She drew breath to reply, but the line was already dead. In the old days, they'd had a routine of cutting each other off in mid-farewell; an asinine game, but diverting. He wasn't playing now, however. He'd cut her off because he wanted to be away from her. Back to his grapevine, or to the doubts rotting on it.

Well it was worth a try, Raul said.

"I'm going to go see him," Tesla thought.

We only just got here. Can't we stay in one place for a few days. Kick back? Relax?

She opened the sliding door and stepped out onto the balcony. It was a voyeur's paradise. She could see into half a dozen living rooms and bedrooms from where she stood. The windows of the apartment directly across the yard from her were open wide; people were partying there, music and laughter floating her way. She didn't know the hosts: They'd moved in a year or so ago, after the death of Ross, who'd been in residence a decade when she'd moved in. The plague had taken him, the way it had taken so many others in the vicinity, even before she'd left for her travels. But the parties went on, the laughter went on.

"Maybe you're right," she thought to Raul, "maybe it is time I—"

There was a knock on the door. Had somebody seen her listening alone on the balcony, and come to invite her over?

"What is it?" she called as she crossed the living room.

The voice from the far side of the door was little more than a whisper.

"Lucien," it said.

ii

He had come without Kate Farrell or her sidekick Eddie knowing; told them he wanted to look up some friends in L.A. before he rejoined the pursuit of Fletcher.

"Where's Kate gone?" Tesla wanted to know.

"Up to Oregon."

"What's in Oregon?"

Lucien sipped the neat vodka Tesla had poured for him, and

looked a little guilty. "I don't know if I should be telling you this," he said, "but I think there's more going on than Kate realizes. She talks about Fletcher as though he's got all these answers—"

"Fletcher's in Oregon?" Lucien nodded. "How do you know?"

"Kate has a spirit-guide. Her name's Friederika. She came through after Kate lost her daughter. Kate was channeling her when you arrived. And she picked up the scent."

"I see."

"A lot of people still find it difficult to believe—"

"I've believed a lot weirder," Tesla replied. "Was, uh, was Friederika specific about this, or was it just somewhere in Oregon?"

"Oh no, she's very specific."

"So they've gone looking for him?"

"Right." He drew a deep breath, swallowed the last of his vodka, then said: "And I came after you." He gazed up at her with those submarine eyes. "Was I wrong to do that?" She was very seldom dumbfounded, but this silenced her. "Shit," he said, grimacing, "I thought—maybe something was going on . . . " The words became shrugs.

"Have another vodka," she said.

"No, I think I'd better go."

"Stay," she said, catching hold of his arm with a little more urgency than she'd intended. "I want you to know what you're getting into."

"I'm ready."

"And drink up. You'll need it."

She told him everything. Or at least everything her increasingly vodka-sodden brain could remember. How she'd first gone to Palomo Grove because Grillo was there writing a story, and how circumstances had elected her—much against her will—as Fletcher's cremator, or liberator, or both. How after his death she'd traveled down to his laboratory in the Misión de Santa Catrina to destroy whatever remained of the Nuncio, only to be shot in the attempt by the Jaff's son, Tommy-Ray. How she had been saved, and changed, by the very fluid she'd come to destroy, and then returned to the Grove with Raul—via the apartment they were sitting in—to find it close to destruction.

Here she stopped. Getting this far had taken the better part of three hours, and she still had to speak of the most problematic part of the whole story. The party in the apartment opposite had quieted down considerably, the various rock-and-roll of earlier forsaken in favor of ballads for slow-dancing. It was scarcely the most appropriate music to accompany what she had to say.

"You know about Quiddity of course," she said.

"I know what Friederika's said."

"And what's that?"

"That it's some kind of dream-sea, and we go there three times in our lives. Edward says it's a metaphor for—"

"Fuck metaphors," Tesla said. "It's real."

"Have you been there?"

"No. But I know people who have. I saw the Jaff tear a hole between this world and Quiddity—tear it open with his bare hands." This was not strictly true. She'd not been in the room when the Jaff had done the deed. But the story played so much better telling it as though she had.

"What was it like?"

"I don't want to live through it again, put it that way."

Lucien poured himself another vodka. He'd started to look distinctly queasy in the last few minutes—his face pasty and moist—but if he needed the liquor to deal with what he was hearing, who was she to argue? "So who closed the door?" he asked her.

"That doesn't matter," she said. "Doors open, doors close. It's what's on the other side you need to know about."

"You already told me. Quiddity."

"Beyond Quiddity," she said, aware that the very words carried a palpable menace. He looked at her with his green eyes now bloodshot, breathing rather too fast through his open mouth. "Maybe you don't want to know," she said.

"I want to know," he replied, without a trace of inflection.

"They're called the Iad Uroboros."

"Uroboros," he said, speaking the word almost dreamily. "Have you seen these things?"

"From a distance," she said.

"Are they like us?" he asked her.

"Not remotely."

"What then?"

She remembered as clearly as her own name the words Jaffe had used to describe the Iad, and repeated them now, for Lucien's benefit, though Lord knows it didn't help much.

"*Mountains and fleas,*" she said. "*Fleas and mountains.*"

Lucien rose suddenly. "Excuse me—"

"Are you—?"

"I'm going to—" He turned towards the bathroom, raising his hand to his mouth. She went to help him, but he waved her away and lurched through the door, closing it behind him. There was a moment's hush, then the sound of retching, and of vomit splashing into the toilet. She kept her distance. Her own belly, which was pretty strong, weakened at the smell of puke.

She look down at her vodka glass, decided she'd had more than enough, and walked out onto the balcony. She didn't wear a watch (the yellow dog had told her to bury her imitation Rolex in the desert) so she could only guess at the time. Certainly way after midnight; perhaps one-thirty, perhaps two. The air was a little chilly, but fragrant with night-blooming jasmine. She inhaled deeply. Tomorrow she was going to have a splitting headache, but what the hell? She'd actually enjoyed telling her story, laying it out as much for her own benefit as Lucien's.

He has the hots for you, Raul said.

"I thought you'd gone to sleep."

I was afraid you'd do something stupid.

"Like try to fuck him?" She glanced back into the apartment. The bathroom door was still closed. "I don't think there's much chance of that tonight—"

Or any night.

"Don't be so sure."

We had an agreement, Raul reminded her. *As long as I'm in here with you: no sex. That's what we agreed. I don't have a homosexual bone in my body.*

"*My* body," Tesla reminded him.

Of course, if you wanted to sleep with a woman, I could probably stretch the point—

"Well you might just have to look the other way," Tesla said, "I think my celibate phase is coming to an end."

Don't do this.

"Oh for God's sake, Raul, it's just a fuck."

I mean it.

"If you screw this up," she said, "you'll be sorry you ever got inside my head. I swear."

Raul was silent.

"Better," Tesla said, and went back inside. The shower was running in the bathroom. "Are you okay in there?" she called, but he couldn't hear her over the water, so she left him to his cleaning up and went through to the kitchen to look for something to fill her growling stomach. All she could find was a box of year-old Shredded Wheat, but it was better than nothing. She munched, and waited, and munched some more. The shower continued to run. After a couple of minutes she went back to the bathroom door, knocked and yelled: "Lucien? Are you all right?"

There was still no reply. She tried the handle. The door was unlocked; the room so filled with steam she could barely see across it. His clothes were scattered on the floor, and the shower curtain closed.

She called his name again, and again there was no answer. Concerned now—he must have heard her, even over the water—she grabbed the curtain and pulled it back. He was sprawled naked in the tub, the water beating on his belly, eyes closed, mouth open.

Some lover, Raul said.

"Shut the fuck up," she told him, going down on her haunches beside the tub and lifting Lucien into a sitting position. He coughed up a throatful of watered down puke.

Very pretty.

"I'm warning you, *monkey*—"

That was the forbidden word: *monkey*—the word that always threw him into a fit.

Don't call me that! he yelled.

She didn't give him the satisfaction of a response, so he shut up. It worked like a charm every time.

She turned off the shower, then gently slapped Lucien into opening his eyes. He looked at her dozily, mumbling something about feeling stupid.

"Have you finished throwing up?" she asked him.

He nodded, so she fetched a clean bath towel and did what she could to dry him off while he was lying in the tub. He wasn't in bad shape. A little skinny perhaps, but meaty where it counted most. Even though he was near as damnit comatose, his dick swelled as she dried him, and she couldn't help but stroke it a little, which brought it to full erection. It was pretty. If he had the wit to use it well he might be fun in bed.

He was as dry as she was going to be able to get him, so rather than try to lift him out of the tub, she decided to let him sleep where he lay. She fetched a pillow and a blanket, and made him as comfortable as she could, given the cramped conditions. As she tucked the blanket around him, he murmured, "What about tomorrow?"

"What about it?" she said.

"Can we . . . do it . . . tomorrow?"

"Well, that depends," she said. "I was thinking of heading up to Oregon—"

"Oregon . . . " he mumbled.

"That's right."

"Fletcher . . . "

"That's right." She leaned a little closer to him, until she was almost whispering in his ear. "He's up there, right? In . . . in—"

"Everville."

"Everville," she said softly.

Have you no shame? Raul muttered.

She laughed, and for a moment Lucien's eyes fluttered open.

"You sleep," she said to him. "We're going to take a trip tomorrow."

The notion seemed to please him, even in his stupor. He was still wearing a little smile when she put the light out and left him to his slumbers.

VI

*G*rillo called the body of knowledge he'd gathered over the last five years the Reef, in part because, like coral, it had grown through countless minute accretions (more often than not of dead matter) and in part because a marine image seemed appropriate for information that pertained to the secrets of the dream-sea. But of late the name mocked him. He no longer felt like the Reef's keeper, but its prisoner.

It was housed, this Reef, in the memory-banks of four linked computers, donated to Grillo's strange cause by a man in Boston, who'd asked only one thing in return for his generosity: that when Grillo finally persuaded the computers to collate all the information and spit out the answer to the mysteries of America, he'd be the one to spread the news. Grillo had agreed. He'd even believed, when the gift had first been mooted, that such a moment might one day come.

He believed that no longer. The husks and shreddings he'd gathered so studiously over the years did not contain the secrets of the universe. They were worthless trash, lost to sense and meaning, and he would join them in their senselessness, very soon.

His body, which had done him good service for forty-three years, had in the last six months begun a calamitous decline. At first he'd ignored the signs; put the dropped coffee cups and aching spine and blurred vision down to overwork. But the pain had been too much after a time, and he'd gone to the doctor for something to control it. He'd got his painkillers, and a lot more besides: visits to specialists, mounting paranoia, and finally, the bad news. "You've got multiple sclerosis, Nathan."

He'd closed his eyes for a moment, not wanting to look at the sympathetic face in front of him, but the darkness behind his lids was worse. It was a cell, that darkness; it stank of himself.

"This isn't a death sentence," the doctor had explained. "A lot of people live long, fruitful lives with this disease, and there's no reason why you shouldn't be one of them."

"*How* long?" he wanted to know.

"I couldn't even hazard a guess. The disease moves in different ways from person to person. It could take thirty years—"

He'd known, sitting there in that bland little office, that he didn't have three decades of life ahead of him. Nothing like. The disease had him in its teeth, and it was going to shake him until he was dead.

His appetite for information had not deserted him, however, even in these grim circumstances. He researched the nature of his devourer meticulously, not out of any hope that he would defeat it, but simply to know what was going on inside his body. The coverings of his nerve fibers were being stripped, it seemed, in his brain and in his spine. Though many fine minds were working to discover why, there were no definitive answers. His disease was a mystery as profound as anything in the Reef, and a good deal more palpable. Sometimes, while he was sitting in front of the monitors watching messages come in, he imagined he could feel the beast Sclerosis moving through his body, unmaking him cell by cell, nerve by nerve, and the words appearing on the screens, tales of sightings and visitations, began to seem like just another manifestation of disease. The healthy psyche had no need of such fantasies. It lived in the world of the possible, and was content.

Sometimes, in a fury of despair, he would switch off the screen and toy with the notion of unplugging the whole system; leaving the tale-tellers to babble on in silence and darkness. But he would always return to his chair after a time, addict that he was, guiltily turn the screens back on to study whatever bizarrities the Reef had accrued in his absence.

In early spring, the beast Sclerosis had suddenly become ambitious; within the space of a month he felt twenty years of frailties overtake him. He was prescribed heavier medications, which he diligently took, and the doctor offered advice about planning for disability, which he just as diligently ignored. He would never go into a wheelchair; that much he'd decided. He'd take an overdose one night, and slip away; it would be easier that way. He had no wife to hold on for; no children to watch grow just another day. He had only the screens, and the tales they told; and they would go until the end of the world, with or without him.

And then, in early June, a strange thing: There was a sudden escalation in the number of reports, the systems besieged every hour of the day and night with people wanting to share their secrets. There was no coherent pattern in this onslaught, but the sheer scale of it made him wonder if the madness was not reaching critical mass.

Around that time Tesla had checked in from New Mexico, and he'd told her what was going on. She'd been in one of her fatalistic moods (too much peyote, he suspected) and not much interested. When he'd called Harry D'Amour in New York, however, the response had been entirely different. D'Amour, the sometime detective whose cases had invariably turned into metaphysical excursions, was eager for information. They had spoken at least twice daily over a three-week period, with D'Amour demanding chapter and verse of any report that smacked of the Satanic, particularly if it originated in New York. Grillo found D'Amour's faith in the vocabulary of Catholicism absurd, but he played along. And yes, there were a number of reports that fitted the description. Two mutilation-murders in the Bronx, involving nails through the hands and feet, and a triple suicide at a convent in Brooklyn (all of which D'Amour had already investigated); then a host of other more minor oddities which he was not aware of, some of which clearly supported some thesis or other.

D'Amour had declined to be explicit, even on a safe line, as to the precise nature of that thesis, until their last conversation. Then he'd solemnly told Grillo he had good reason to believe that the return of the Anti-Christ was being plotted in New York City. Grillo had not been entirely able to disguise how laughable he thought the notion.

"Oh you don't like the *words*, is that it?" D'Amour had replied. "We'll find something different, if you prefer. Call it the Iad. Call it the Enemy. It's all the Devil by another name."

They hadn't spoken after that, though Grillo had several times attempted to make further contact. There were new reports from the five boroughs almost every day, it seemed, many of them involving acts of sickening brutality. Several times Grillo had wondered if perhaps one of the bodies found rotting on the city's wastelands that summer was not that of Harry D'Amour. And wondered too what name he might call the Devil if it came looking for D'Amour's informer, here in Omaha.

Sclerosis, perhaps.

ii

And then there'd come this recent call from Tesla, asking about sightings of Fletcher, and he'd finished the exchange with such an emptiness inside him, he was almost ready to take the overdose there and then. Why could he not bear the notion of her coming to see him? Because he looked too much like his father now; legs like sticks, hair gray and brittle? Because he was afraid she'd turn away, unable to see him like this? She'd never do that. Even in her crazy times (and she'd had more than her share) she never lost her grip on the feelings between them.

No, what he feared was regret. What he feared was her seeing him in decline, and saying: Why didn't we do better with what we feel for each other? Why didn't we enjoy what was in our hearts, instead of hiding it away? What he feared was being told it was too late, even though he already knew it.

Once again, the Reef had saved him from utter despair. After her call he'd brooded for a while—thinking of the pills, thinking of his stupidities—and then, too weary to think any more but too stirred up to sleep, he'd gone back to his place in front of the monitors, to see if he could find any convincing reports of the Fletcher's presence.

It was not Fletcher he found, however. Sifting through the reports logged in the last couple of weeks, he came across a tale that had previously gone unread. It came from a regular and, he thought, reliable source: a woman in Illinois who printed up crime-scene photographs for a local county sheriff's department. She had a horrible account to make. A young couple had been attacked in late July, the female victim, who was seven months pregnant, killed outright and then opened up by the attacker, who had taken his leisurely time to examine her in front of her wounded lover, then removed the fetus and absconded with it. The father had died a day later, but not before he passed a strange description along to the police, which had been kept out of the newspapers because of its bizarrity, but which Grillo's informer felt needed relating. The killer had not been alone, the dying man had said. He'd been surrounded by a cloud of dust "full of screams and faces."

"I begged him," he'd gone on to say, "begged him not to mess up Louise, but he kept saying he had to, he had to. He was the Death-Boy, he said, and that's what Death-Boys did."

That, in essence, had been the report. Having read it Grillo sat for half an hour in front of the screen, as confounded as he was intrigued. What was happening out there in the real world? Fletcher had died in the mall at Palomo Grove. Cremated; gone to flame and spirit. Tommy-Ray McGuire, the son of the Jaff, the Death-Boy, had died a few days later, at a spot in New Mexico called Trinity. He too had been cremated, but in a more terrible fire than had consumed Fletcher.

They were both *dead*, their parts in the tangled tale of humanity and the dream-sea over. Or so everyone had supposed.

Was it possible everyone had been wrong? That somehow they'd defied oblivion and each returned to pick up the threads of their ambition? If so, there was only one explanation as to how. Both had been touched by the Nuncio during their lives. Perhaps evolution's message was more extraordinary than anyone had guessed, and it had put them beyond the reach of death.

He shuddered, daring to think that. *Beyond the reach of death.* Now there was a promise worth living for.

He called California. A bleary Tesla answered the phone.

"Tes, it's me."

"What time is it?"

"Never mind the time. I've been going through the Reef, looking for stuff about Fletcher."

"I know where he's headed," Tesla said. "At least I think I know."

"Where?"

"This town in Oregon, called Everville. Has it ever turned up in the Reef?"

"It doesn't ring a bell, but that doesn't mean much."

"So why are you calling? It's the middle of the fucking night."

"Tommy-Ray."

"Huh?"

"What do you hear about Tommy-Ray?"

"Nothing. He died in the Loop."

"Did he?"

There was a hush from the other end. Then Tesla said, "Yeah."

"*You* got out. So did Jo-Beth and Howie—"

"What are you saying?"

"I've found a report in the Reef about a killer calling himself the Death-Boy—"

"Grillo," Tesla said. "You wake me up—"

"And he's surrounded by a cloud of dust. And the dust's *screaming.*"

Tesla drew a long breath, and expelled it slowly. "When was this?" she said softly.

"Less than a month ago."

"What did he do?"

"Killed a couple in Illinois. Ripped a baby out of the woman. Left the guy for dead."

"Careless. Is that the only report?"

"It's the only one I've found so far, but I'll keep looking."

"I'll check in on my way up to Oregon—"

"I was thinking—" Grillo began.

"You should talk to Howie and Jo-Beth."

"Yeah, I will. I was thinking about Fletcher."

"When did you last talk to them?"

"A couple of weeks ago."

"And?" Tesla pressed.

"They were fine," Grillo replied.

"Tommy-Ray had the hots for her, you know. They're twins—"

"I know—"

"One egg, one soul. I swear, he was *crazy* about her—"

"Fletcher," Grillo said.

"What about him?"

"If he's there in Everville I'm going to come meet him."

"What for?"

There was a short pause. Then Grillo said, "For the Nuncio."

"What are you talking about? There *is* no Nuncio. I destroyed the last of it."

"He's got to have kept some for himself."

"He was the one that asked me to *destroy* it, for God's sake."

"No. He kept some."

"What the hell's all this about?"

"I'll tell you some other time. You find Fletcher, and I'll try tracing Tommy-Ray."

"Try sleeping first, Grillo. You sound like shit."

"I don't sleep much these days, Tes. It's a waste of time."

VII

*H*owie had started working on the car just after eight, intending to get his tinkering over and done with before the sun
got too hot. This was the fifth blistering summer they'd
lived in Illinois, and he was determined it would be the last. He'd
thought returning to the state where he'd been born and raised
would be reassuring in a time of uncertainty. Not so. All it had done
was remind him of how radically his life had changed in the last half-
decade, and how few of those changes had been for the better.

But whenever his spirits were down—which was often since he'd
lost his job in March—he only had to look at Jo-Beth cradling Amy
and he would feel them rise again.

It was five years since he'd first laid eyes on Jo-Beth in Palomo
Grove; five years since their fathers had waged war on the streets to
keep them apart. Years in which they'd lived under an assumed
name in a suburb where nobody cared about your life because they'd
given up caring about their own. Where the sidewalks were littered
and the cars dirty and smiles hard to come by.

It wasn't the life he'd wanted to give his wife and his daughter,
but D'Amour had put it to them this way: If they lived in plain sight
as Mr. and Mrs. Howard Katz, they would be found within months
and murdered. They knew too much about the secret life of the

world to be allowed to survive. Forces sworn to protect that life would silence them, and call themselves heroes for doing so. This was certain.

So they had hidden themselves away in Illinois, and only called each other Howie and Jo-Beth when the doors were bolted and the windows locked. And so far the trick had kept them alive. But it had taken its toll. It was hard, living in shadow, not daring to plan too much, to hope too hard. Once every couple of months Howie would talk to D'Amour, and ask him for some sense of how things were going. How long, he'd say, before they've forgotten who the hell we are, and we can get out into the light again? D'Amour was no great diplomat, but time after time Howie could hear him doing his best to prettify the truth a little; to find some way of keeping them from despair.

But Howie was out of patience. This was the last summer they'd be in this God forsaken hole of a place, he told himself as he sweated under the hood; the last summer he'd pretend he was somebody he wasn't to satisfy D'Amour's paranoia. Maybe once he and Jo-Beth had some part to play in the drama they'd glimpsed half a decade before; but that time had surely passed. The forces D'Amour had evoked to intimidate them—the murderous heroes who would slaughter them in their beds—had more urgent matters on their minds than pursuing two people who'd chanced to swim in Quiddity once upon a time.

The phone was ringing in the house. Howie stopped work, and picked up a rag to clean his hands. He'd skinned his knuckles, and they were stinging. He was sucking at the bloodiest when Jo-Beth appeared on the step, squinting in the sun just long enough to say, "It's for you," then disappearing into the darkness of the house.

It was Grillo.

"What's up?" Howie said.

"Nothing much," came the reply. "I was calling to see if you were okay."

"Amy's keeping us up most nights, but otherwise—"

"Still no job?"

"No job. I keep looking, but—"

"It's tough."

"We're going to have to move, Nathan. Just get out there and start a proper life."

"This . . . may not be the best time to do it."

"Things are going to look up."

"I'm not talking economics."

"What then?" Silence. "Nathan?"

"I don't want to alarm you—"

"But?"

"It's probably nothing—"

"Will you spit it out, for God's sake?"

"It's Tommy-Ray."

"He's dead, Grillo."

"I know that's what we've *assumed*—"

Howie lowered his voice to a fierce whisper. "What the hell are you telling me?"

"We're not exactly sure."

"We?"

"Tesla and me."

"I thought she'd disappeared."

"She did for a time. Now she's on her way up to Oregon—"

"Go on."

"She says your father's up there." Howie was a heartbeat from slamming the phone down. "I know how this sounds—" Grillo said quickly.

"It sounds like shit is what it sounds like," Howie said.

"I wasn't ready to believe it either. But these are strange times, Howie."

"Not for us they're not," Howie replied. "They're just a fucking waste, okay? We're wasting our fucking lives waiting for somebody to tell us something that makes sense and all you can do—" He wasn't whispering any longer, he was shouting, "all you can do is tell me my father—who's dead, Grillo, he's *dead*—is wandering around Oregon, and Tommy-Ray—" He heard Jo-Beth let out a sob behind him. "Shit!" he said. "Just stay out of our lives from now on, Grillo. And tell D'Amour to do the same, okay? We've had it with this *crap!*" He slammed down the phone, and turned to look at Jo-Beth. She was standing in the doorway, with that woebegone look on her face she wore so often these days. "What do they fucking take us for?" he said, covering his eyes with his hand. They were burning.

"You said *Tommy-Ray*."

"It was just—"

"What *about* Tommy-Ray?"

"Shit. That's all it was. Grillo's fucking shit." He glanced up at her. "It's nothing, sweetie," he said.

"I want to know what Grillo told you," Jo-Beth said doggedly.

She would worry more if he didn't tell, he suspected. So he gave a précis of what Grillo had said.

"That's it?" she asked him when he was done.

"That's it," he said. "I told you it was nothing." She nodded, shrugged, and turned away. "It's all going to change, sweetie," he said. "I swear."

He wanted to get up and go to her. Wrap her in his arms and rock her till she melted against him. So many times in the past they'd ended up entwined after hard words. But no longer. Now when she turned from him he kept his distance, afraid she'd refuse him. He didn't know why or where this doubt had originated—was he reading some subtle signal in her eyes that told him to keep his distance?—but it was too strong to be overcome; or else he was too weak.

"So fucked up," he murmured to himself, his hands returning to cover his face.

Grillo's words circled in the darkness.

These are strange times. . .

Howie had refuted it at the time, but it was true. Whether Fletcher was in Oregon or not, whether Tommy-Ray was alive or not, when a man could no longer put his arms around his wife, they were indeed strange times.

*   *   *

Before returning to work on the car he headed upstairs to take a peek at Amy. She'd been sick the last couple of days—her first summer on the planet she'd caught a cold—and she lay exhausted in her cot, arms splayed, head to one side. He took a tissue from the box beside the bed and wiped a little gloss of spit from her chin, his touch too gentle to wake her. But somewhere in sleep, she knew her daddy was there, or so he believed. A barely perceptible smile appeared on her bow-lips, and her cheeks dimpled.

He leaned on the railing of the cot and gazed down at her in unalloyed bliss. Fatherhood had been unexpected—though they'd talked about children many times, they'd decided to wait until their situation had improved—but he didn't regret for a moment the accident that had brought Amy into their lives. She was a gift; a simple sign of the goodness in Creation. All the magic in the world, whether wielded by his father, or the Jaff, or any of the secret powers D'Amour talked about—weren't worth a damn in the face of this simple miracle.

The little time spent with his sleeping beauty thoroughly invigorated him. When he stepped out into the heat again, the problems of a sickly car seemed piffling, and he set to solving them with a will.

After a few minutes of work a light wind started to get up; cooling gusts against his sweaty face. He stood clear of the hood for a moment and drew a deep breath. The wind smelt of the green beyond these gray streets. They would escape there soon, he told himself, and life would be good.

Standing chopping carrots in the kitchen, Jo-Beth paused to watch the wind shaking the unkempt thicket that choked the yard, thought of another yard in another year, and heard Tommy-Ray's voice calling her name out of the past. It had been dark that night in the Grove, but she remembered things having an exquisite luminosity: dirt, trees, reeling stars all filled with meaning.

"*Jo-Beth!*" Tommy-Ray was yelling, "*Something wonderful!*"

"*What?*" she'd said.

"Outside. Come with me."

She'd resisted him at first. Tommy-Ray was wild sometimes, and the way he was shaking had made her afraid.

"I'm not going to do anything to hurt you," he'd said. *"You know that."*

And she had. Unpredictable though he was, he had never shown her anything but love.

"We feel things together," he'd said to her. That was true; they had shared feelings from the beginning. *"So come on,"* he'd said, taking hold of her hand.

And she'd gone, down the yard to where the trees churned against a pinwheel sky. And in her head she'd heard a whispering voice, a voice she'd been waiting to hear for seventeen years without realizing it.

Jo-Beth, it had said. *I'm the Jaff. Your Father.*

He had appeared then, out of the trees, and she remembered him looking like a picture from Mama's Bible. An Old Testament prophet, bearded and absolute. No doubt he had been wise, in his terrible fashion. No doubt if she'd been able to speak with him, and learn from him, she would not now be living in the grave, drawing only the tiniest breaths for fear of depleting what little supply of sanity remained to her.

But she had been parted from him, the way she'd been parted from Tommy-Ray, and she'd fallen into the arms of the enemy.

He was a good man, this enemy, this Howie Katz; a good and loving man. And when they'd slept together for the first time, they had each dreamed of Quiddity, which meant that he was the love of her life. There would be none better. But there were affections that went deeper than found love. There were powers that shaped the soul before it was even born into the world, and they could not be gainsaid. However loving the enemy was, and however good, he would always be the enemy.

She hadn't realized this at first. She'd assumed her unease would disappear as the traumas of the Grove receded, and she learned a new normality. But instead it grew. She started to have dreams about

Tommy-Ray, light pouring over his golden face like syrup. And sometimes in the middle of the afternoon, when she was at her most
weary, she'd seem to hear her father speaking to her, and she'd ask
him under her breath the question she'd asked in Mama's backyard.

"Why are you here now? After all this time?"

"Come closer," he would say, "I'll tell you . . . "

But she hadn't known how to get closer, how to cross the abyss of
death and time that lay between them.

And then, out of nowhere, hope. Sometimes she remembered
how it had come to her very clearly, and on those days she would
have to hide herself away from Howie, in case he saw the knowledge
on her face. Other times—like now—when she knew he was in pain,
and her heart opened to him the way it had at the beginning, the
memory became confounded. Her thoughts lost focus, and she
would spend hours staring out of the window, or at the sky, trying to
catch hold of some elusive possibility.

No matter, she told herself. It would come back. Meanwhile, she
would chop the carrots and wash the dishes and tend the baby and—

The wind threw a scrap of litter against the window and pinned
it there for a moment, flapping like a one-winged bird. Then a second gust carried it away.

She would go soon, with the same ease. That was part of the
promise. She would be carried off, and away, to a place where the
secrets her father had almost told her were waiting to be whispered,
and her loving enemy would never find her.

VIII

i

*E*verville rose early that Thursday morning, even though it had gone to bed later than usual the night before. There were banners to hang and windows to polish, grass to be cut, and streets to be swept. No idle hands today.

At the Chamber of Commerce, Dorothy Bullard fretted about the clouds that had blown in overnight. The weatherman had promised sun, sun, sun, and here it was, eleven twenty-two, and so far she'd not seen a glimmer. Masking her anxiety with a beam of her own, she got about the business of the day, organizing the distribution of the Festival brochures, which had arrived that morning, to the list of sites that always carried them. Dorothy was a great believer in lists. Without them, all was chaos.

Just before noon, at the intersection of Whittier and Main, Frank Carlsen ploughed his station wagon into the back of a stationary truck, the collision bringing traffic on Main Street to a virtual halt for the better part of an hour. Carlsen was taken off to the police station, where he admitted to having started celebrating a little early this year; just a few beers to get into the spirit of things. There was no great damage done to the truck, so Ed Olson, who'd brought him in, sent him out again with a simple reprimand. "I'm bending the law for you, Frank," he told Carlsen, "so stay sober and don't make me look like an asshole."

Main Street was running freely again by twelve-fifteen, at which time Dorothy looked out of her office window to see that the clouds had started to thin, and the sun was breaking through.

---

ii

Erwin had set out for the creek a little after ten, stopping off at Kitty's Diner for some apple pancakes and coffee to fortify himself. Bosley was his usual ebullient self, which on some days Erwin found grating but today merely amused him.

Appetite satisfied, Erwin set off for the creek, parking his car beside the Masonic Lodge on First Street and walking from there. He was glad he'd put on sturdy boots and an old sweater. The warmth of the late summer days, along with the rains of a week or so ago, had made the thicket lusher than ever, and by the time he reached the creek he had scratches on his neck, face, and hands, and enough twigs in his sweater to fuel a small fire.

Over the centuries the creek itself had carved itself a deep trench to run in, its shallow, speeding waters overcast with antediluvian ferns. He had not ventured here in six or seven years, and he was surprised afresh at how remote it felt. Though Main Street lay no more than three-quarters of a mile behind him, the whine of gnats around his head was louder than the murmur of traffic, while in front of him, on the other side of the creek, the thickly wooded slope rose up towards the Heights undeveloped and, he supposed, untenanted. He was alone, and that was by no means an unpleasant feeling. He'd take his time looking for the house by the creek, and chew over his future while he did so.

---

iii

Joe called Phoebe at the doctor's in the middle of the morning and asked her if she'd be available to meet him at lunchtime rather than in the afternoon. She warned him it'd only give them a few minutes together; it was a ten-minute drive in both directions between the office and home. Longer, most likely, with the streets so busy. He had anticipated this. Come to the apartment, he suggested, it's just a couple of minutes away. She told him she would. Expect me just after twelve-thirty, she told him.

"I'll be waiting," he said, and she got goosebumps from the heat in his voice.

She spent the rest of the morning with a twitchy little smile on her face, and at twelve twenty-eight she was gone. She'd visited him at the apartment only twice before, once when Morton had been sick in bed with the flu, and once during his vacation. It was riskier than the house, because there was no way into his building without being seen. Especially today, with so many people out and about. She didn't care. She parked on the street right outside the building, and defiantly marched up the side steps that led to Joe's front door almost hoping she was being seen.

Her knuckles had barely touched the door when it was opened. He was wearing just his shorts, and was running with sweat.

"The fan's broken," he said, ushering her inside. "But you don't mind sweatin', right?"

The place was a mess, as usual, and baking hot. He cleared a place for her on the sofa, but instead of sitting she followed him through to the kitchen, where he poured a glass of ice water for her. There they stayed, with the noise of the street coming in through the open window.

"I've been thinkin'," he said. "The sooner we come clean about this, the better."

"I'm going to see an attorney on Monday."

He grinned. "Good girl." He laid his arms on her shoulders, clasping hands to wrist behind her head. "You want me to come with you?"

"No. I'll do it."

"Then we'll just get out of here. As far away as possible."

"Any place you like."

"Somewhere warm," he said. "I like the heat."

"Suits me," she said. She put her thumb to his cheek and rubbed. "Paint," she said.

"Kiss," he said back.

"We have to talk."

"We'll talk while we fuck."

"Joe—"

"Okay, we'll fuck while we talk, how's that?" He drew a little closer to her. "It's too hot to say no." There was sweat trickling down between her breasts; sweat between her buttocks, sweat between her thighs. She was almost dizzy with the heat.

"Yes?" he said.

"Yes," she said, and stood there, head spinning, while button by button, clasp by clasp, he bared her to the air.

---

iv

Erwin had first followed the creek downstream, thinking that the house was more likely to be situated on the flatter land than on the uneven terrain of the Heights' lower slopes. Either he was wrong in that assumption, he discovered, or else this part of McPherson's confession was a lie. After an hour he gave up trailing the creek's southeasterly course and turned round, following his own tracks back to the place where he'd begun. There he halted for a couple of minutes to smoke a cigarette and plot his next move. Bosley's pancakes would sustain him for another hour and a half at least, but he had quite a thirst after clambering over boulders and thrashing his way through the thicket. Maybe a respite was in order. A cup of coffee back at Kitty's; then back to the trek refreshed. After a few moments, he decided to forgo the break and continue his search. Once he'd found the house the coffee would taste all the better anyway.

The terrain rapidly became more problematic as he moved upstream, however, and after a quarter of an hour of fighting his way through the dense undergrowth, his hands stained green with moss, his knees skinned from slipping on rocks, he was about ready to retreat. He paused to pull off his sweater—in which he was now cooking—and as it cleared his face he caught sight of a mysterious shape between the trees up ahead. He started towards it, tugging his arms from the sweater as he went, little sounds of pleasure escaping him the closer he got.

"Oh . . . oh . . . that's it! That's it!"

There it was, right in front of him. Fire and rot had claimed most of the boards, but the framework and the brick chimneys were still standing.

He hung his sweater in a branch, then thrust his way through the thicket until he reached the front of the house—though it scarcely deserved the word—shack, more like—and stepped over the threshold.

There were a few pitiful signs of the life that had been lived here underfoot: sticks of charred furniture, a piece of decayed rug, fragments of some plates, a battered pail. The scene was pitiful, of course, but Erwin was elated. There was now no doubt in his mind that McPherson's confession was substantially true. He had evidence enough to make public what he knew without fear of contradiction. All he had to do now was work out how to get maximum mileage out of the announcement.

He went down on his haunches and pulled a shard of crockery out from the tangle of undergrowth, touched for the first time by a tremor of unease. He didn't believe in ghosts—the dead were the dead, and they stayed that way—but the dripping hush of the place gnawed at him nevertheless. It was time to go back; time to get that cup of coffee, and maybe a celebratory slice of carrot cake to go with it.

Wiping the dirt from the plate shard, he got to his feet. As he did so he caught a motion in the trees on the other side of the creek. He looked towards it, and his stomach leapt. Somebody was standing there, watching him. The plate shard slipped from his fingers. The hairs at his nape prickled.

The shadows between the pines were too dense to make out much detail of the watcher's appearance, but it was plain he was no hiker. He was wearing something dark and full, almost like robes, his face half-hidden by a substantial beard, his pallid hands clasped in front of him.

He inclined his head in Erwin's direction now, as if to say: *I see that you see me*. Then he raised his left hand and beckoned Erwin towards him. The creek lay between them, of course, the humble gorge it had cut for itself deeper here, closer to its source, than further downstream. It afforded sufficient protection should the stranger prove to be a lunatic that Erwin felt safe to obey the man's instruction, and come a little nearer.

As he reached the edge of the bank, which fell away steeply four or five feet, the man spoke. His voice was low, but it carried over the rush of water.

"What place is this?" he said.

"This is Unger's Creek."

"I meant the town."

"It's not a town, it's a city. It's called Everville."

"Everville—"

"Are you lost?"

The man started down the incline between the trees. He was barefoot, Erwin saw, and with every stride the strangeness of his garb and features became more apparent. As Erwin had guessed, he was indeed wearing robes, of a blue so deep it was almost black. As for his face, it was a curious mingling of severity and ease: the brow knitted, the eyes lively, the mouth narrow, but carrying a little smile.

"I thought I was lost," he said, "but now I see I'm not. What's your name?"

"Erwin Toothaker."

"Erwin, I have a favor to ask of you."

"First tell me who you are."

"Oh, by all means." The stranger had reached the opposite bank now, and opened his arms to Erwin. "My name," he said, "is Richard Wesley Fletcher. And I am come to save you from banality."

v

"Joe. There's somebody coming up the stairs."

He unglued his lips from her breast, and listened. There were children yelling in the street outside and a radio playing in the apartment below. But no footfall, no creak. He went back to licking her nipple.

"I swear," she whispered, her eyes turned towards the door.

"Okay," he said, snatching his shorts off the floor and pulling them on, pressing his ever-buoyant erection against his belly in order to do so.

She ran her fingers over the breast he'd so conscientiously licked, then plucked the nipple between middle finger and thumb.

"Let me see what you got, baby," he said, looking back at her from the doorway.

She let one leg drop off the sofa on which she was sprawled and raised her hips a little. He stared at her cunt.

"Oh baby."

"You like that?" she whispered.

"You're going to see how much I like that."

She almost called him back to her there and then, but before she could do so he was gone into the hallway. She looked down at her body, grabbing hold of the excess flesh around her waist. He said he loved her this way; but *she* didn't. She would shed twenty pounds, she swore to herself, twenty pounds before Thanksgiving. That was—

"Nigger!" she heard Morton yell. The door smashed against the wall. Joe stumbled back along the hallway, clutching his bare belly.

She reached for the back of the sofa to haul herself up, but before she could do so Morton was in the doorway, staring down where Joe had stared moments before, disgust on his face.

"Christ!" he yelled. "Christ, look at you!" and came at her across the room, arms outstretched. He grabbed her splayed legs, and pulled her off the sofa with such violence she screamed.

"Don't!"

But he was past hearing anything. She'd never seen such an expression on his face: teeth bared, lips flecked, veins, sweat, and eyes popping. He wasn't red, despite his exertion: he was the color of somebody about to puke or pass out.

He reached down and hauled her up onto her knees.

"You fucking whore!" he yelled, slapping her face. "Does he like these?" He slapped her breasts this time, back and forth. "I bet he does!" Harder now, back and forth, stinging blows. "I bet he fucking eats your fucking tits!"

She tried to cover herself, but he was into the sport of it now.

"Nice tits!" Slapping, slapping so hard tears came. "Nice tits! Nice, nice tits!"

She hadn't seen Joe get up, she was too busy begging Morton to stop. But suddenly he was there, grabbing hold of her tormentor's collar and flinging him back across the room. Morton was a good three or four inches taller, and easily fifty pounds heavier, but Joe was after him in a heartbeat, fists driving him against the wall.

Wiping the tears from her eyes, Phoebe reached for some article of clothing to cover her nakedness. As she did so Morton—his nose pouring blood—let out a roar and lunged forward again, the mass of his body thrown against Joe with such force they were carried across the room. Joe landed on the television, which toppled off the low table on which it was set, and Joe went down with it, the table cracking beneath him. Morton fell on top of him, but he was up a moment later, returning Joe's punches with kicks. They were aimed between Joe's legs, and landed solidly, five, six, seven times, while Joe lay winded and dazed on a bed of splinters and glass.

Forsaking her attempts at modesty Phoebe got to her feet and tried to pull Morton off him, but he put his hand over her face, pinching her cheeks.

"You wait your turn!" he said, stomping on Joe's groin now. "I'll get to you."

Then he pushed her away, almost casually, so as to concentrate on his brutalities. She looked down at Joe—at his body sprawled over the debris, at the bloody patch spreading in his shorts—and realized with a kind of giddiness that Morton would not be done till Joe was dead.

She had to do something, *anything*. She looked around the room for a weapon, but there was nothing she could lift that would fell Morton. In desperation she raced through to the kitchen, hearing as she went the terrible dull thud of boot against body, and the moans of Joe, weaker by the moment.

She pulled the kitchen drawers open one after the other, looking for a steak knife or a bread knife; something to threaten Morton with. But there was only a collection of battered cutlery.

"You're fucked, nigger—" Morton was saying. Joe's moans had stopped altogether.

In desperation she snatched up an ordinary knife and fork and raced back into the living room, in time to see Morton reach down and pull Joe's shorts away from his body to inspect his handiwork. The sickening intimacy of this fueled her rage, and she threw herself at Morton, weapon raised. He swung round as she did so, and more by chance than intention dashed the knife from her hand. The fork, however, found its mark, her momentum sufficient to thrust it into the flesh of his upper chest.

He looked down at it, more puzzled than pained, then struck her a backhanded swipe that had her stumbling back towards the door. Blood was running from the wound, but he didn't waste time pulling the fork out.

"You fucking *slut!*" he said, coming at her like a driverless truck.

She backed out into the hallway. The front door was still open. If she made a dash she might still outrun him. But that meant leaving Joe here while she found somebody to help her, and God alone knew what Morton would do to him in the meantime.

"Stand still," he said to her, his voice dropping now to a pained rasp. "You've got this coming." He almost sounded reasonable. "You *know* you got this coming."

She glanced down the narrow hallway towards the bathroom, and as he lunged at her she threw herself through the door, turning to close it before he reached her. Too late. His arm shot through the gap; grabbed hold of her hair. She threw her weight against the door, slamming it on his arm. This time he yelled, a stream of obscenities rising into a howl of rage and pain. He started to push against the door, pulling his bloodied arm out again and wedging his leg in the gap when it was wide enough.

Her bare feet slid on the tiles; it was only a matter of moments before he had the door open. Then he would kill her, she was certain of it. She started to scream at the top of her voice, her din filling the tiny bathroom. Somebody had to come quickly, or it would be too late.

His face appeared at the opening now, white and clammy as the tiles.

"*Open up*," he said, pushing harder. "You know how to do that." And with a final shove he threw the door wide. She had nowhere to run and he knew it. He stood in the doorway, bleeding and gasping, looking her up and down.

"You're a whore," he said. "A fat, fucking whore. I'm going to rip your fuckin' tits off."

"Hey!" Joe shouted.

Morton looked down the hallway. Joe was up and hanging onto the frame of the living room door.

"You not dead yet?" Morton said, and strode back towards Joe.

To the end of her days, Phoebe would never be exactly sure what happened next. She went after Morton to hold him back, or at least delay him long enough for Joe to get to the front door—that much was sure—but as she grabbed his shoulder, Joe stepped or slipped into his path. Perhaps he struck Morton; perhaps Morton stumbled, weak from blood loss; perhaps her weight was enough to topple him. Whichever it was, he fell forward, reaching to snatch hold of Joe even as he did so. As he struck the ground there was a snapping sound, followed by something like a sob from Morton. He didn't get up. His legs twitched for a moment. Then he lay still.

"Oh . . . my . . . God . . ." Joe said, and turning from Phoebe started to vomit violently.

Still afraid Morton could get up again, she approached him cautiously. There was blood seeping from beneath his chest. The fork! She'd forgotten the fork!

She started to roll him over. He was still breathing, but his breaths were like spasms, shaking him from head to toe. As for the fork, it had snapped halfway down its length. The rest, maybe three inches of it, was buried in his chest.

Joe was getting to his feet now, wiping his mouth with the back of his hand.

"Gotta get a doctor here," he said, and disappeared into the living room.

Phoebe went after him. "Wait, wait," she said. "What are we going to say?"

"Tell 'em the truth," he said. He pulled the phone out of the debris. It had been dragged out of the wall. Grimacing with every move he made, he stopped to plug it back in, while Phoebe pulled on her underwear. "They're going to put me away for this, baby."

"It was an accident," she said.

He shook his head. "That's not the way it works," he went on. "I've had trouble before."

"What do you mean?"

"I mean I've got a record," he said. "I would've told you—"

"I don't care," she said.

"Well, you should," he snapped, "because that screws everything." He had found the end of the phone line, but it ended in sheared wires. "It's no good," he said, tossing the phone down amid the trashed furniture. Then he got to his feet, tears filling his eyes. "I'm so sorry . . . " he said, "I'm so . . . sorry."

"You'd better go," she said.

"No."

"I can take care of Morton. You just go." She'd pulled on her skirt, and was buttoning up her blouse. "I'll explain everything, he'll be looked after, then we'll just get out together." There was faulty logic here, she knew, but it was the best she could do. "I mean it," she said. "Get dressed and go!"

She went back to the door. Morton was muttering now, which

was an improvement on the spasms: obscenities mingled with non-sense, like baby talk, except that there was blood coming from between his lips instead of milk and spit.

"He's going to be all right," she said to Joe, who was still standing in the middle of the wrecked room looking desolate. "Will you please *go?* I'll be fine."

Then she was out into the sunlight, and down the stairs. The kids had stopped playing in the street, and were watching from the opposite sidewalk.

"What are you looking at?" she said to them in the tone she took to latecomers at the surgery. The group dispersed in seconds, and she hurried along to the phone at the corner of the street, not daring to look back for fear she'd see Joe slipping away.

IX

I bet you thought this was a quiet little town, right?" Will Hamrick said, sliding another glass of brandy the way of his sobersuited customer.

"Is it not?" the fellow said.

He had the look of money about him, Will thought; an ease that only came when people had dollars in their pocket. Hopefully, he'd spend a few of them on brandies before he moved on.

"There's been some kind of bloodshed across town this afternoon."

"Is that so?"

"A guy comes in all the time, Morton Cobb, sits at the table by the wall there," Will pointed to it, "been carted off to the hospital with a fork in his heart."

"A fork?" said the man, plucking at his perfect moustaches.

"That's what I said, I said *a fork*, just like that, *a fork*, I said. Big man too."

"Hmm," said the man, pushing the glass back in Will's direction. "Another?"

"Why not? We should celebrate."

"What are we celebrating?"

"How about bloodshed?" the fellow replied. This struck Will as tasteless, which fact must have registered on his long, dolorous features, because the drinker said, "I'm sorry. I misunderstood. Is this fellow Cobb a friend of yours?"

"Not exactly."

"So this attempt upon his life, by the wife, or her lover, her black lover—"

"You've heard."

"Of course I've heard. This bloody, scandalous deed is really just something to be . . . savored, isn't it?" He sipped his brandy. "No?"

Will didn't reply. The fellow was spooking him a little, truth to tell.

"Have I offended you?" he asked Will.

"No."

"You are a *professional* bartender, am I right?"

"I own this place," Will said.

"All the better. You see a man like yourself is in a very influential position. This is a place where people congregate, and when people congregate, what do they do?"

Will shrugged.

"They *tell tales*," came the reply.

"I really don't—"

"Please, Mr.—"

"Hamrick."

"Mr. Hamrick, I've been in bars in cities across the world— Shanghai, St. Petersburg, Constantinople—and the great bars, the ones that become *legendary*, they have one thing in common, and it isn't the perfect vodka martini. It's a fellow like you. A disseminator."

"A what?"

"One who sows seeds."

"You got me wrong, mister," Will said with a little grin. "You want Doug Kenny at Farm Supplies."

The brandy drinker didn't bother to laugh. "Personally," he said, "I hope Morton Cobb dies. It'll make a much better story." Will pursed his lips. "Go on, admit it," the man said, leaning forward, "if

Morton Cobb dies of a fork wound to the chest will it not be a far better story for you to tell?"

"Well . . . " Will said, "I guess maybe it would."

"There. That wasn't so difficult was it?" The drinker drained his glass. "How much do I owe you?"

"Nine bucks."

The man brought out an alligator-skin wallet, and from it drew not one but two crisp ten-dollar bills. He laid them down on the counter. "Keep the change," he said. "I may pop back in, to see if you've got any juicy details about the Cobb affair. The depth of the wound, the size of the lover's apparatus—that sort of thing." The brandy drinker smirked. "Now don't tell me it didn't cross your mind. If there's one thing a good disseminator knows it's that every detail counts. Especially the ones nobody'll confess they're interested in. Tell them shameful stuff and they'll love you for it." Now he laughed, and his laughter was as musical as his voice. "I speak," he said, "as a man who has been well-loved."

And with that he was gone, leaving Will to stare down at the twenty bucks not certain whether he should be grateful for the man's generosity or burning the bills in the nearest ashtray.

ii

Phoebe stared at the face on the pillow and thought: *Morton's got more bristles than a hog.* Bristles from his nose; bristles from his ears; bristles erupting from his eyebrows and from under his chin where he'd missed them shaving.

Did I love him before *the bristles?* she asked herself. Then: *Did I ever love him?*

Her musings were curiously detached, which fact she put down to the tranquilizers she'd been given a couple of hours before. Without them, she doubted she would have got through the humiliations and interrogations without collapsing. She'd had her body examined (her breasts were bruised and her face puffy, but there was no serious damage); she'd had Jed Gilholly, Everville's police chief, asking her questions about her relationship with Joe (who he was; why she'd done it); she'd been ferried back from the hospital in Silverton to the apartment, and quizzed about what, precisely, had happened where. And finally, having told all she'd could tell, she was brought back to the bedside where she now sat, to sit and meditate on the mystery of Morton's bristles.

Though the doctor had pronounced his condition stable, she knew the patient's vices by rote. He smoked, he drank, he ate too much red meat and too many fried eggs. His body, for all its bulk, was not strong. When he got the flu—which he did most winters—he'd be sick for weeks. But he had to live. She hated him down to every last wiry bristle, but he had to live.

Jed Gilholly came by a little before five, and called her out into the hallway. He and his family (two girls, now both in their early teens) were all patients of Dr. Powell's, and while his wife and children were pretty healthy, Jed himself was severely dyspeptic, and—if memory served—had the first mumbling of a prostate problem. It made him rather less forbidding, knowing these little things.

"I got some news," he said to her. "About your . . . er . . . boyfriend."

They've caught him, she thought.

"He's a felon, Phoebe."

No, maybe they hadn't.

"He was involved in a wounding incident in Kentucky, four or five years ago. Got probation. If you know where he is . . . "

They *hadn't* got him, thank the Lord.

"I suggest you tell me right now, 'cause this whole mess is looking pretty bad for him."

"I told you," she said, "Morton was the one started it."

"And Morton's also the one lying in there," Jed replied. "He could have died, Phoebe."

"It was an accident. *I* was the one stuck the fork in him, not Joe. If you're going to arrest anybody, it should be me."

"I saw what he did to you," Jed said, a little embarrassed, "knocking you around like that. I reckon what we got here is some wife beating, some assault, *and*," he looked Phoebe in the eyes, "a man who's been in trouble with the law before, and who's maybe a danger to the community."

"That's ridiculous."

"I'll be the judge of what's ridiculous and what's not," Jed said. "Now I'm asking you again: do you know where Flicker is?"

"And I'm telling you straight," Phoebe replied, "no I don't."

Jed nodded, his true feelings unreadable. "I'm going to tell you something, Phoebe, that I wouldn't maybe say if I didn't know you."

"Yes?"

"It's simple really. I don't know what the story was between you and this guy Flicker. I do know Morton isn't the friendliest of guys the way he beat you around this afternoon," he shook his head, "that's a crime all of its own. But I have to consider your boyfriend dangerous, and if there's a choice between his safety and the safety of my officers—"

"He's not going to hurt anybody."

"That's what I'm telling you, Phoebe. He isn't going to get the chance."

iii

Without a vehicle, Joe had been presented with a limited number of options. He could steal a car and drive somewhere isolated then come back for Phoebe after dark. He could find somewhere to hide within the city limits, and bide his time there. Or he could climb.

He chose the latter. The stealing of a vehicle would only add to his sum of crimes, and the city was too small and too white for him to pass unnoticed in its streets. Up the mountain he would go, he decided; at least far enough to be safe from pursuers.

He'd left the apartment with the barest minimum of supplies: some food, a jacket for later on, and, most important, given the condition he was in, the first-aid box. He'd only had time for a perfunctory self-examination (just enough to check that he wasn't going to bleed to death) before making his escape, but the pain was excruciating, and he only got as far as the creek before he had to stop. There, he slithered down into the ditch where the creek ran, and, out of sight of all but the fishes, washed his bruised and bloodied groin as tenderly as he could. It was a slow, agonizing business. He could barely suppress his cries when the icy water ran over his lacerated flesh, and several times had to stop completely before the pain made him pass out. At last, against his better judgment, he resorted to chewing two painkillers he'd stored with the kit, the last (but one) of ten Percodan he'd been prescribed for a back injury. It was powerful stuff; and had induced in him a kind of blissful stupor which was not to his present advantage. But without it he doubted he'd be able to get much further than the creek.

He sat on the bank for a while and waited for them to kick in before he finished with his ministrations, his trousers and blood-crusted underwear around his ankles. The blaze of the day was over, but the sun still found its way through the ferns and gilded the sliding water. He watched it go while the pain subsided. If this was what death was like, he thought—pain receding, languor spreading—it would be worth the wait.

After a few minutes, with his thoughts fuzzier than they'd been and his fingers more clumsy, he returned to washing his wounds. His balls had ballooned to twice their normal size in the last half-hour, the sac purplish in places and raw-red in others. He felt the testicles gently, rolling them in between his fingers. Even through the haze of Percodan they were painful, but he felt nothing separated or clotted. He might yet have children, one of these distant days. As to his cock, it was badly torn in three places, where Morton had ground his heel upon it. Joe finished cleaning the cuts with creek water and then applied liberal dollops of antiseptic cream.

Once, during this delicate procedure, a wave of nausea rose up in him—less at the sight of his wounds than at the memory of how he'd come by them—and he had no choice but to stop and watch the sun on the water until the feeling subsided. His mind wandered as he waited. Twenty-nine years on the planet (thirty in a month's time) and he had nothing to show for it but this pitiful condition. That would have to change if he was to get through another twenty-nine. His body had taken enough punishment for one lifetime. From now on, he would chart his course, instead of letting circumstances take him where they would. He'd put the past behind him, not by denying it but by allowing it to be part of him, pain and all. He was lucky, wasn't he? Love had found him, in the form of a woman who would have died for him this afternoon. Most people never had that in their lives. They lived with compromise where love was concerned; with a mate who was better than nothing but less than everything. Phoebe was so much more than that.

She wasn't the first woman to have said she loved him, nor even the first he'd replied to in kind. But she was the first he was afraid to lose, the first he knew his life would be empty without; the first he thought he might love after the fierce heat was gone, after the time when she'd cared to spread her cunt for him, or he to see it spread.

A sharp pain in his groin reminded him of his present state, and he looked down to see that all was not lost. His cock had risen to respectable erection while he'd pictured Phoebe's display, and he had to concentrate on counting flies until it had subsided. Then he finished putting on ointment, and bandaged himself up, albeit roughly It was time to move on, before the search spread as far as the creek; and before the effect of the painkillers wore off.

He pulled up his pants, buried the litter from his salvings, and wandering a little way up the bank found a place where the creek was narrow enough to be crossed in a hobbled leap. Then he clambered up the opposite bank and headed off up the slope between the trees.

iv

At six-seventeen, while Phoebe was at the hot drink machine getting a cup of coffee, Morton opened his eyes. When she got back to the room, he was babbling to the nurse about how he'd been on a boat, and fallen overboard.

"I coulda drowned," he kept saying, clutching at the sheets as though they were lifelines. "I coulda. I coulda drowned."

"No, Mr. Cobb. You're in a hospital—"

"Hospital?" he said, raising his head off the pillow an inch or two, though the nurse did her best to restrain him. "I was floating—"

"You were dreaming, Morton," Phoebe said, stepping into his line of vision.

At the sight of her the memory of what had brought him here seemed to come back. "Oh Christ," he said through clenched teeth, "Christ in Heaven," and sank back onto the pillow. "You bitch," he muttered now. "You fucking bitch."

"Calm down, Mr. Cobb," the nurse insisted, but fueled by a sudden spurt of rage, Morton sat bolt upright, tearing at the drip tube in his arm as he did so.

"I *knew!*" he screamed, jabbing his finger in Phoebe's direction.

"Do as the nurse says, Morton."

"Please, give me a hand, Mrs. Cobb," the beleaguered woman said.

Phoebe put down her coffee and went to assist, but the proximity of his wife threw Morton into a frenzy.

"Don't you fucking touch me! Don't you—"

He stopped in mid-sentence, and uttered a tiny sound, almost like a hiccup. Then all the venom went out of him at once—his arms dropped to his sides, his knotted face slackened and went blank—and the nurse, unable to support the weight of his upper body, had no choice but to let him sink back onto the pillow. It did not end there. Even as the nurse raced to the door calling for help, Morton began to draw a series of agonizing breaths, each more panicked and desperate than the one before.

She couldn't watch him suffer without trying to do something to calm him.

"It's all right," she said, going back to the bedside and laying her hand on his cold brow. "Morton. Listen to me. It's all right."

His eyes were roving back and forth behind his lids. His gasps were horrible.

"Hold on, Morton," she said, as his suffering continued to mount. "You'll bust something."

If he heard her, he didn't listen. But then when had he ever listened? He went on gasping, until his body was out of power. Then he simply stopped.

"Morton," she murmured to him. "Don't you dare—"

There were nurses back at the bedside now, and a doctor spewing agitated orders, but Phoebe registered none of them. Her focus was upon Morton's stricken face. There were flecks of spittle on his chin, and his eyes were still wide open. He looked the way he'd looked at the bathroom door—raging; raging even as the sea he'd been dreaming about closed over his head.

One of the nurses took hold of her hand and now gently escorted her away from the bed.

"I'm afraid his heart's given out," she murmured consolingly.

But Phoebe knew better. The damn fool had drowned.

---
v

There was always a moment at the close of day when the blue gloom of dusk had settled on the city, but the sun was still in glory on Harmon's Heights. The effect was to make Everville seem like a ghost town, sitting in the shadow of a living mountain. What had seemed unequivocal a minute ago had now become ethereal. Folks who'd been able to read their neighbors' smiles across the street could no longer do so; children who'd known for certain there was nothing darting behind the fence, or snaking between the garbage cans, were no longer secure in their belief.

In that uncertain time before the sun left the Heights entirely, and the streetlamps and porch lights of Everville asserted their authority, the city bathed in doubt, and insolid souls in insolid streets entertained the notion that this life was just a candle-flame dream, and likely to flicker out with the next gust of wind.

*   *   *

It was Seth Lundy's favorite time of day. Better even than midnight, or that time before dawn when the moon had sunk, and the sun was no more than a gray hope in the east. Better than those, that minute.

He was standing in the town square, looking up at the last of the light on the mountaintop and listening for the hammering, which was often loud at this uncertain hour, when a man he hoped at one glance he would come to know better stepped out of the murk towards him and said, "What can you hear?"

He had only ever been asked that question by doctors. This was no doctor.

"I can hear angels hammering on the sky from Heaven's side," he replied, seeing no reason to lie.

"My name's Owen Buddenbaum," the man said, coming so close that Seth could smell the brandy on his breath. "May I ask yours?"

"Seth Lundy."

Owen Buddenbaum came a little closer still. Then, while the city waited in doubt around them, he kissed Seth on the lips. Seth had never been kissed on the lips by a man before, but he knew the rightness of it, to his heart, soul, and groin.

"Shall we listen to the hammering together?" Owen Buddenbaum said, "or shall we make some for ourselves?"

"For ourselves," Seth replied.

"Good," said Owen Buddenbaum. "Ourselves it will be."

PART THREE

Vessels

I

*T*esla had woken early, despite the late-night call with Grillo and the pukings from Lucien; early enough to enjoy the birdsong before the sound of traffic from Melrose and Santa Monica drowned it out. With the kitchen cupboards empty she ambled up to the cafe below the Health Club on Santa Monica, which had been open since five for the benefit of masochists, and bought coffee, fruits, and bran muffins for herself and her guest.

I don't want you screwing him, Raul reminded her as she walked back to the apartment. *We agreed: No sex till we're separated.*

"That may never happen, Raul," she pointed out, "and I'm damned if I'm going to live like a nun for the rest of my life. Which might be, by the way, *a very short time.*"

My, we are feeling chipper this morning.

"Anyway, monkeys like sex. It's all they ever do at the zoo."

Go fuck yourself, Bombeck.

"That's all I've been doing. Which you haven't been complaining about, by the way. Did you get off on me diddlin' myself?"

No comment.

"I'm going to fuck Lucien, Raul. So you'd better get used to the idea."

Slut.

"Monkey."

Lucien was showered and sitting on the balcony in the sun by the time she got back to the apartment. He had found some of Tesla's old clothes in the closet: patchwork jeans circa 1968 and a leather vest which fitted his skinny torso better than it had ever fitted her. Ah, the resilience of youth, she thought, seeing how quickly he'd recovered from the excesses of the previous night. Face flushed, smile lavish, he rose to help her unpack the breakfast and partook with no little appetite.

"I feel so stupid about throwing up," he said. "I never do that. Mind you, I never drink vodka." He gave her a sidelong glance. "You're teaching me bad habits," he said. "Kate says you have to purify the body if you want to be a vessel for the infinite."

"Now *there's* a phrase," Tesla said. "*Vessel for the infinite*. What does that mean—*exactly?*"

"Well . . . it means . . . you know, we're made from the same stuff stars are made of . . . and . . . all we have to do is open our souls up . . . and the infinite, I mean, you know . . . everything becomes one, and everything flows through us."

"*The past, the future, and the dreaming moment between are all one country living one immortal day.*"

The quote had Lucien agog. "Where'd that come from?" he said.

"You never heard it before? I learned it from—" She paused to think about this. "Fletcher maybe," she said, "maybe Kissoon."

"Who's Kissoon?" Lucien said.

"Somebody I don't want to talk about," she said. There were few experiences in her life she still kept filed away under *untouchable*, but Kissoon was definitely one of them.

"I want you to tell me, when you're in a good space to do it," Lucien said. "I mean, I want to share all the wisdom in you."

"You'll be disappointed," Tesla said.

He laid his hand over hers. "Please. I mean it."

She heard the monkey make a retching sound in her head, and could not keep a smile from her lips.

"What's so funny?" Lucien said, looking a little hurt.

"Nothing," she said. "Don't be sensitive. If there's one thing I can't bear it's sensitive men."

ii

They were heading north by seven-thirty, and made good time up the coast. Either Tesla, or Raul, or perhaps a combination of them both, had developed an uncanny instinct when it came to the presence of cops, and she gunned the cycle to a hundred, a hundred and ten when they were certain they were unwatched. By Thursday evening they were across the state line, and about ten at night decided they'd come far enough for one day. They found a motel and checked in. One room, one bed. What this meant went undiscussed.

While Lucien headed out for food, Tesla called Grillo. He sounded glad to hear from her. The conversation with Howie had not gone well, he told her, and suggested she might have to put a call in to the couple herself, to offer some support for his warning.

"What the hell happened to D'Amour?" Tesla wanted to know. "I thought he was supposed to be watching over them?"

"Want my best guess?" Grillo said.

"Yeah."

"He's dead."

"What?"

"He was closing on something big—he wouldn't tell me what—then he just ceased communication."

The news shook Tesla. While her relationship with D'Amour had never been that close—she'd met with him one time only since the Grove, when her trek through the Americas had taken her up to New York—she'd vaguely thought of him as both a backstop and a source of esoterica, as someone who would always be in the picture. Now it seemed that this was not the case. And if D'Amour, who'd been fighting this fight for fifteen years and had defenses against the enemy in every corner (including several tattooed on his person), had lost the battle, then what hope did she have? Little or none.

Lucien had not taken her hint about sensitivity, thank God; he knew the moment he saw her face that she wasn't as blithe as she'd been. He gently inquired as to why, and she told him. He reassured her as best he could with words, but she quickly made their inadequacy plain, and he turned instead to touches, and kisses, and before long they were getting naked and he was warning her that he was no great lover and that she shouldn't expect too much.

She found his modesty disarming, and, as it turned out, unnecessary. He was no great experimenter, to be sure, but what he lacked in range he made up for in depth, which wasn't to be despised. They coupled with the kind of fervor she'd not experienced since her college days, all of twenty years before, the bed squeaking under them, the headboard deepening a groove in the wall made by those who'd loved here before.

Raul kept his silence for the first bout. She heard not a peep from him. But when, after she and Lucien had eaten a couple of slices of cold pizza, the nuzzling began again, he piped up.

He's not going to do it again.

"He can do it all night," she thought, "if he's up for it." She put her hands down between their legs, and guided him inside her. "And it looks like he is."

Christ! Raul sobbed. *How can you bear this? Make him pull it out!*

"Shut up," she said, staring down at her and Lucien's locked groins.

At least close your eyes, Raul said.

She was far too intrigued to do that. "Look at that," she thought, raising her hips to welcome his length. "Him meeting me meeting him—"

Damn you—

"Like crossroads."

You're raving, woman.

She looked up into Lucien's face. He had his eyes half closed and his brows knitted.

"Are you . . . all right?" he gasped.

"Never better," she said.

The ape continued to sob in her head, the words expelled upon Lucien's thrusts. *It's like—he's stabbing—us. I can't—take any— more!*

As he spoke she felt his will impinging on hers, crossing the divide they'd established at the beginning of their co-tenanting. It hurt, and she let out a moan, which Lucien took for a sigh of appreciation. His embrace became tighter, his jabs more frenzied.

"Oh yes," he started to chant, "yes! yes! yes!"

No! Raul hollered, and before Tesla could demand her body back he took control of it.

Her arms, which had been languishing on the pillow, suddenly flew at Lucien, her nails raking his naked back. From out of her throat came a bestial din she'd never known she was capable of making, and as he recoiled in mute shock her legs rose behind him, hooking beneath his armpits and pulling him back. All this in such a blur of noise and motion Tesla wasn't even certain what had happened until it was over, and Lucien was sprawled on the floor beside the bed.

"What the hell was that all about?" he said, finding his voice now.

Satisfied with its efforts, the monkey's hold relaxed enough for her to say, "It . . . it wasn't me."

"What do you mean, it wasn't you?" Lucien said.

"I swear— " she said, getting up from the bed. But he wasn't going to allow her near him again. He was up on his feet in a flash, retreating to the chair where he'd thrown his clothes.

"Wait," she said, not making any further attempt to approach him. "I can explain this."

Watching her warily he said, "I'm listening."

"I'm not alone in here," she told him, knowing as she spoke there was no easy way to say what she was about to say. "There's somebody else in my skull." Still, she thought, he should be able to understand the principle. Hadn't he been talking about being a vessel for the infinite that very morning? "His name's Raul."

He looked at her as though she were speaking in an alien language. "What *are* you talking about?" he said, plainly incredulous.

"I'm talking about the spirit of a man called Raul being here in my head with me. He's been here for five years. And he doesn't want us to do what we've been doing."

"Why not?"

"Well . . . why don't I let him speak for himself?"

What? she heard Raul say.

"Go on," she said aloud, "you've done the damage. Now explain it."

I can't.

"You owe it to mé, damn you!"

Lucien listened to the side of the argument he could hear with disbelief all over his face. She waited, leaving her tongue slack in her mouth.

"You *snarled*," she reminded Raul, "now you can damn well talk."

Before she'd finished the thought she felt her tongue start to flap and sounds emerged, crude at first, but quickly turning into syllables. Lucien watched and listened to this bizarre performance without moving a muscle. She suspected he thought he was in the presence of a lunatic, but she had no way of reassuring him until this was over.

"What she's just told you . . . " Raul began, Tesla's voice now in his possession, "is true. I'm the spirit of a man who . . . gave up my body to a great evil called Kissoon." She'd not expected him to offer Lucien a guide to body-hopping, but it ameliorated her fury somewhat to hear him do so. This was difficult territory for him to discuss, she knew. Kissoon and his persuasions were a bitter memory for them both, but how much more so for him, who had lost his very flesh to the shaman's tricks?

"She . . . did me a great . . . kindness," he went on hesitantly.

"One which I will . . . always be thankful for." He licked her lips, back and forth a couple of times. His nervousness had made her mouth arid. "But . . . this thing you do to me with *men* . . . " He shook her head, "It *sickens* me."

As Raul spoke, Lucien instinctively dropped his hand between his legs, covering his sex.

"I'm sure you mean to give her pleasure," Raul cautioned. "But *her* pleasure is *my* pain. Do you understand?"

Lucien said nothing.

"I *want* you to understand," he pressed. "I don't want you to think this is any failing on your part. It isn't. Truly it isn't."

At this juncture Lucien plucked his briefs off the floor and began to pull them on.

"I've said all I can say," Raul concluded. "I'll leave you two to—" Tesla leapt on his words before they were finished. "*Lucien*," she said. "What are you doing?"

"Which of you is it now?"

"It's me. Tesla." She got up from the bed, pulling the sheet around her as she did so, and squatted on the ground in front of him. He continued to dress as she spoke. "I know this is probably the strangest thing you've heard—"

"You're right."

"What about Kate and Friederika?"

"I wasn't fucking with Kate. Or Friederika," he said, his voice tremulous. "Why didn't you tell me?"

"I didn't think you needed to know."

"I'm making it with a guy—and you don't think I *need to know?*"

"Wait. Is that what this is about?" She got up from the floor, and stared down at him imperiously. "Where's your sense of adventure?"

"I guess I'm all out of it," he said, hauling on her patchwork jeans.

"You're leaving?"

"I'm leaving."

"And where will you go?"

"I don't know. I'll get a ride somewhere."

"Look, at least stay the night. We don't have to do anything." She heard the desperation in her voice, and despised herself for it. What was this? One and a half fucks and suddenly she couldn't face sleeping alone? "Strike that remark," she said. "If you want to go find a ride, go find a ride. You're acting like an adolescent, but that's your problem."

With that she retired to the bathroom and showered, singing loudly enough to herself so that he knew she didn't care if he left or not.

Ten minutes later, when she emerged, he'd gone. She sat down on the edge of the bed, her skin still wet from the shower, and called Raul out from hiding.

"So . . . I guess it's just you and me."

You're taking this better than I thought.

"If we survive the next few days," she said, "we're going to have to part. You realize that?"

I realize that.

There was a silence between them, while she wondered what it would be like living alone.

"By the way, was it really so terrible?"

Abominable.

"Well at least you know what you're missing," she said.

So strike me blind.

"What?"

Tiresias, he said.

She was none the wiser.

You don't know that story?

It was one of the paradoxes of their relationship that he, the sometime ape, had been educated in the great myths of the world by Fletcher, while she, the professional storyteller, had only the sketchiest knowledge of the subject.

"Tell me," she said, lying back on the bed.

Now?

"Well, you scared off my entertainment." She closed her eyes. "Go on," she said, "tell me."

He'd several times regaled her with his versions of classical tales, usually when she'd questioned some reference of his. The philanderings of Aphrodite; the voyages of Odysseus; the fall of Troy. But this story was so much more appropriate to their present situation than any he'd shared with her, and she slipped into sleep with images of the Theban seer Tiresias (who according to legend had known sex as both a man and a woman, and declaring the woman's pleasures ten times finer had been struck blind by a goddess, irritated that the secret was out) wandering through the wilds of the Americas in search of Tesla, until he found her in the rubble of Palomo Grove, where they made love, at last, with the ground cracking open around them.

II

i

At about the same time Tesla was falling asleep in a motel somewhere south of Salem, Oregon, Erwin was stirring from a strange slumber to find himself lying on the floor of his own living room. Somebody had lit a fire in the grate—he could see it flickering from the corner of his eye—and he was glad of the fact, because for some reason he was incredibly cold; colder than he could ever remember being in his life before.

He had to work hard to recall the return journey from the creek. He had not come alone; of that he was certain. Fletcher had come too. They'd waited until dusk, hadn't they? Waited in the ruins of the house until the first stars showed, and then wound their way through the least populated streets. Had he left the car down by the Masonic Hall? Presumably so. He vaguely remembered Fletcher saying that he despised engines, but that sounded so absurd Erwin dismissed it as delirium. What was there to hate in an engine?

He started to raise his head off the ground, but lifting it an inch was enough to induce nausea, so he lay down again. The motion, however, brought a voice out of the shadows. Fletcher was here in the room with him.

"You're awake," he said.

"I think I must have the flu," Erwin replied. "I feel terrible."

"It'll pass," Fletcher replied. "Just lie still."

"I need some water. Maybe some aspirin. My head—"

"Your needs are of no importance," Fletcher said. "They too will pass."

A little irritated by this, Erwin rolled his head to one side to see if he could get a glimpse of Fletcher, but it was the remains of a chair his eyes found: one of a quartet of Colonial pieces which had cost him several thousand, now reduced to scrap wood. He let out a groan.

"What happened to my lovely furniture?"

"I fed the fire with it," Fletcher replied.

This was more than Erwin could take. Defying his giddiness, he sat up, only to discover that the other chairs had also gone for tinderwood, and that the rest of the room—which he had kept as meticulously as his files—was in total disarray. His prints gone from the walls, his collection of stuffed birds swept from the shelves.

"What happened?" he said. "Did somebody break in?"

"It was your doing, not mine," Fletcher replied.

"Out of the question." Erwin's gaze sought Fletcher as he spoke and found him sitting in the one chair that wasn't tinder, his back to Erwin. In front of him, the window. Beyond the window, darkness.

"Believe me, you're responsible," Fletcher said. "If you had just been a little more *compliant*."

"What are you talking about?" Erwin said. He was getting angry, which was in turn making his head thump.

"Just lie down," Fletcher said. "All of this will pass, by and by."

"Stop saying that," Erwin replied. "I want some explanations, damn it."

"Explanations?" said Fletcher. "Oh, those are always so difficult." He turned from the window, and by some trick Erwin didn't comprehend, the whole chair swiveled with him, though he put no effort into realigning it. The firelight flattered him. His skin looked healthier than Erwin remembered it looking, his eyes brighter. "I told you I'd come here with a purpose," he said.

Erwin recalled that claim more clearly than any other detail of recent events. "You came to save me from banality," he replied.

"And how do you suppose I'll do that?" Fletcher said.

"I don't know and right now I don't care."

"What more do you have to care *about?*" Fletcher asked him. "Your furniture? It's a little late for that. Your frailty? Too late for that too, I'm afraid—"

Erwin didn't like the way this conversation was going; not at all. He reached for the mantelpiece, caught hold of it, and started to haul himself to his feet.

"What are you doing?" Fletcher wanted to know.

"I'm going to get myself some medication," he said. It would not be wise, he suspected, simply to announce that he was going to call the police. "Can I get you anything?" he added lightly.

"Such as?"

"Something to eat or drink? I've got juice, soda water—" His legs were weak, but the door was just a few strides away. He tottered towards it.

"Nothing for me," Fletcher replied. "I have everything I need here."

Erwin reached for the door handle, barely listening to Fletcher now. He wanted to get out of this room, out of this house in fact, even if it meant shivering in the street until the police arrived.

As his fist closed around the handle, the firelight—which had been so kind to Fletcher—showed him the state of his flesh. The news was not good. His skin was hanging loosely at his wrist, as though the sinew had withered. He pulled the sleeve of his shirt back from his arm, and the sight made him cry out. No wonder he was weak. He was emaciated; his forearm down to little more than nerve and bone.

Only now did the significance of Fletcher's last remark sink in.

Nothing for me—

"Oh God no," Erwin said, and started to pull on the door. It was locked, of course, and the key gone.

I have everything I need here.

He threw himself against the door and beat on it, unleashing a yell. As it died in his throat for want of wind he heard a motion behind him, and glanced over his shoulder to see Fletcher—still seated on the last Colonial chair—moving towards him. He turned to face his devourer, back hard against the door.

"You promised you were going to save me," he said.

"And is your life not banality?" Fletcher said. "And will death not save you from it?"

Erwin opened his mouth to say: No, my life isn't banal. I've got a secret, *such a secret.*

But before he could utter a word Fletcher reached out and caught hold of his hands—cold flesh on cold flesh—and he felt the last of his life rushing out of him, as if eager to be gone into a body that would use it more wisely.

He started to sob, as much in rage at its desertion as in fear, and he went on sobbing as the substance of him was sucked away and sucked away, until there was not enough of him left even to sob.

ii

It had not been Joe's intention to venture far up the mountain. He'd intended to stay among the trees on the lower slope until the last of the late-night traffic had died away in the streets below. Then he'd descend and make his way to Phoebe's house. That had been the plan. But sometime in the middle of the evening—he'd no way of telling exactly when—he'd decided to walk a little way to relieve the boredom, and once he'd started, his dreamy thoughts had counseled him to keep on climbing until he was clear of the trees. It was a fine night. There would be such a view from the Heights: The city, the valley, and more important than either, a glimpse of the world beyond, the world where he and Phoebe would be headed after tonight. So he'd climbed and climbed, but the trees, instead of thinning, grew so dense for a time he could barely see the stars between their branches. And still he climbed, the narcotic side-effects of the drug leaving him indifferent to the fact that its painkilling properties were steadily wearing off. It almost added to the pleasure of the ascent that some part of his mind and body was suffering: a touch of bitterness to sharpen his bliss.

And after a time out of time, the trees did indeed begin to thin, and repeated backward glances as he cleared the canopy confirmed that the journey had been worth taking. The city looked like a little box of jewels nestling below, and finding himself a rocky promontory, he sat down to enjoy the sight a while. His eyes had always been sharp and even at this distance he could see people walking on Main Street. Tourists, he supposed, out to taste the charms of Everville by night.

As he studied them he felt something tugging at his floating thoughts. Without quite knowing why, he looked back towards the mountaintop. Then he got to his feet and studied it. Were his eyes deceiving him, or was there a light up there, brightening and diminishing in waves? He watched it for fully a minute, and then, seduced by its gentle fluctuations, started up the mountainside again, keeping his eyes fixed upon it as he went.

He could not make out its source—it was hidden behind rocks—but he had no doubt now that the phenomenon was real. Nor was the light its only manifestation. There was a sound, albeit so remote he felt it rather than heard it: a rhythmical boom, as of some vast drum being beaten in another state. And, almost as subtle, a tang in the air that made his mouth water.

He was within fifty yards of the twin rocks now, his eyes fixed on the cleft between them. His cock and balls were aching furiously, their throbs matched to booms of the drum; his sinuses, pricked by the air, were stinging; his eyes were wet, his throat running with spittle.

And now, with every step he took, the sensations grew. The throbbing spread from his groin, up to his scalp and down to his soles, until it seemed every nerve in his body was twitching to the rhythm of the boom. His eyes ran with tears; his nose with mucus. Spittle spilled from his gaping mouth. But he stumbled on, determined to know what mystery this was, and as he came so close to the rocks he would have touched them had he fallen, he saw that he was not the first to have done so. There was a body lying in the gap between the rocks, washed by the waves of light. Though it was the size of an adult, its proportions were more like those of a fetus: its head overlarge, its limbs, which it had wrapped around it in extremis, wasted; almost vestigial.

The sight distressed Joe, and had there been another route to the light available he would have gladly taken it. But the rocks were too smooth to climb, and he was too impatient for answers to try and find his way around them, so he simply strode up to the cleft and stepped past the body.

As he did so, one of those frail, dead limbs reached out and caught hold of his leg.

Joe let out a yelp and fell back against the rock. The creature did not let him go, however. Raising its unwieldy head off the hard ground, it opened its eyes, and even through the haze of tears, Joe could see that its gaze was not that of a dying soul. It was crystalline, as was the voice that issued from the lipless mouth.

"I am Noah," it said. "Have you come to carry me home?"

iii

Phoebe had stayed at the hospital until after midnight, going through all the paperwork that came with Morton's passing. Gilholly had reappeared, as she knew he would once he got the news.

"This makes things a lot more serious for you and loverboy," he told Phoebe. "You realize that?"

"Morton had a heart attack," Phoebe pointed out.

"We'll wait for the autopsy reports on that. In the meantime, I want you to holler the moment you get word from Flicker, you understand me?" He wagged his finger at Phoebe, which under normal circumstances would have earned him a choice retort. But she kept her temper under control, and did her best to play the grieving wife.

"I understand," she said quietly.

The show seemed to convince Gilholly. He softened a little. "Why'd you do it, Phoebe?" he said. "I mean, you know me, I'm no racist, but if you were going to spread a little love around, why'd you go with him?"

"Why do any of us do anything?" she replied, unable to look him in his sorry face for fear she'd lose control and slap him.

He apparently read her downcast gaze as further proof of contrition, because he laid his hand on her shoulder and murmured, "I know it's hard to believe right now, but there's always a light at the end of the tunnel."

"Is there?" she said.

"Trust me," he replied. "Now you go home and try to sleep. We'll talk in the morning."

I won't be here in the morning, bozo, she thought as she padded away. *I'll be someplace you'll never find me, with the man I love.*

She couldn't sleep, of course, even though she was aching to her bones, and the rest would have been welcome. There was packing to do, for one thing, which she interspersed with trips to the refrigerator for a slice of pie or a frankfurter—yellow mustard dripping on her underwear as she sorted through the stuff she wanted Joe to see her in, and the stuff she would leave in the garbage—and then, with the clothes packed, a quick trip through the photograph albums, in search of a few memories to take with her. A picture of this house, when she and Morton had first moved in, all shiny with hope. A couple of pictures from childhood. Ma, Pa, Murray, and herself; her looking pudgy, even at the age of six.

She'd always hated the wedding photographs—even the ones without Morton in them—but she took the group photograph, for sentiment's sake, along with a couple of shots of the 1988 Festival Parade, when the doctor had decided to pay for a float of his own and she'd made a witty costume for herself as a human pill bottle, which had proved quite a hit.

By the time she'd finished her packing, her photo selection, her pie, and her frankfurters, it was almost three o'clock in the morning, and she began to wonder if maybe Gilholly hadn't caught up with Joe already. She dismissed the thought. If he had, he'd have called her to crow about it. Either than, or Joe would have used his call to tell her he wouldn't be coming for her and she should get him a lawyer.

No, her loverboy was still out there somewhere; he just hadn't reached her yet. Maybe he'd slipped back into his apartment once the streets were completely deserted to do some packing of his own; or gone to find them a getaway car that would be difficult to trace. Or maybe he was simply taking his time, the way he did when they had some hours to spare in the afternoon, idling here and there, just for the pleasure of it.

As long as they were away before dawn, everything would be fine; so they still had two or three hours. She went to the back door, and stood on the step watching the dark trees for some sign of him. He'd come. Later perhaps than sooner, but he'd come.

iv

"Where *is* your home?" Joe had asked Noah, and the creature had raised its left hand—keeping fierce hold of Joe's leg with his right—and pointed up the slope between the rocks. Up towards the source of light and tang and boom, which he could not yet see.

"What is it?" Joe had said.

"You truly don't know?"

"No I don't."

"The shores of Quiddity lie ten strides from here," the creature replied. "But I'm too weak to get there."

Joe went down on his haunches beside Noah. "Not *that* weak," he said, wrenching his trouser leg from Noah's fist.

"I've tried three times," Noah replied, "but there's too much power at the threshold. It blinds me. It cracks my bones."

"And it won't crack mine?"

"Maybe it will. Maybe it will. But listen to me when I tell you I am a great man on the other side. Whatever you lack here I will provide there—"

"Whatever I lack, eh?" Joe mused, half to himself. The list was long. "So if I carry you over this threshold . . . " he went on, wondering as he spoke if perhaps he hadn't slipped from the promontory and was lying somewhere conjuring this as he bled to death, "what happens?"

"If you carry me over, you can put every fear you harbor in this world aside, for power awaits you there, that I promise you. Power that would seem to you unlimited, for your skull docs not contain ambition enough to exhaust it."

The syntax was fancier than Joe was used to, and that—along with the distractions of tears and throbs—prevented him from entirely grasping what he was being told. But the broad strokes were plain enough. All he had to do was carry this creature ten, eleven, maybe twelve strides *over* the threshold and he'd be rewarded for the service.

He looked back at the light, trying to distinguish some detail in its midst, and as he did so, his opiated thoughts began to make sense of this mystery.

"That's your *ship*, isn't it?" he murmured. "It's a fucking UFO."

"My ship?"

"My God . . . " He looked down at the creature with awe on his face, "Are there more of you?"

"Of course."

"How many?"

"I don't know. I haven't been home in more than a century."

"Well who's in the ship—"

"Why do you keep talking about a ship?"

"That!" Joe said, pointing towards the light. "What did you call it? Quiddity?"

"Quiddity's not a ship. It's a sea."

"But you came here in it?"

"I sailed on it, yes, to reach this place. And I wish I'd not."

"Why?"

"Because I found only sorrow here, and loneliness. I was in my prime when I first set foot here. Now look at me. Please, in the name of compassion, carry me over the threshold. . . ." Noah's face began to sweat beads of dark fluid as he spoke, which gathered at the bridge of his nose and in the corners of his mouth. "Forgive my emotion," he said, "I have not dared hope until now. . . ."

The sentiment found an echo in Joe; one he could not be deaf to. "I'll do what I can," he said to Noah.

"You're a good man."

Joe put his hands under Noah's body. "Just so you know," he said, "I'm not in such great shape myself. I'll do my best, but I'm not guaranteeing anything. Put your arm around my shoulder. Yeah, that's it. Here we go." He started to stand. "You're heavier than you look," he said, and teetered for a moment before he got his balance. Then he straightened up.

"I want to know what planet you come from," he said as he proceeded towards the threshold.

"What planet?"

"Yeah. And what galaxy it's in. All that shit. 'Cause when you're gone, the only way I'm going to have a hope of convincing people of this is if I've got details."

"I don't believe I understand you."

"I want to know . . . " Joe began, but the question went unfinished, as he stepped clear of the cleft between the rocks, and finally grasped something of what lay ahead. There was no starship here; at least none that was visible. There was only the sky, and a crack in that sky, and a light through the crack in that sky that touched him like a loving gaze. Feeling it upon him he wanted nothing more than to step beneath whatever sun shed this light, and meet it eye to eye.

Noah was trembling in his arms. His brittle fingers dug deep into Joe's shoulder.

"Do you see?" he murmured now. "Do you see?"

Joe saw. Another heaven; and under it a shore. And beyond the shore a sea, the boom of whose waves had become as familiar as his heartbeat, the spice of whose air had made him shed waters of his own, as if in tribute.

"Quiddity . . . " Noah breathed.

Oh Lord, Joe thought, *wouldn't it be fine to have Phoebe beside me right now, to share this wonder?* Awed by the sight, Joe was scarcely aware that the ground underfoot was in flux until he was ankle-deep in liquid dirt; dirt that was flowing back and forth over the threshold. There was strength in it, and in order not to be thrown off his feet he had to halt a moment and better distribute the weight of his burden. He was no more than two strides from the crack itself, and the energies loose here were considerable. He felt his joints creaking, his guts churning, his blood thumping in his head as if it would burst out and flow into Quiddity of its own accord if he didn't pick up speed.

He took the hint, clasped Noah close to him and ducked down, like a man walking into a high wind. Then he strode forward again, the first stride hard, the second harder still, the third less a stride than a lunge. His eyes were closed tight against the onslaught of energies, but it wasn't black behind his lids. It was blue, a velvet blue, and through the roar of his ambitious blood he heard birds, their voices like streaks of scarlet in the blue, somewhere overhead.

"I don't know your name," somebody whispered to him, "but I hope you hear me."

"Yes . . . " he imagined he said, "I hear you."

"Then open your eyes," the voice went on. It was Noah, he realized. "And let's be on our way."

"Where are we going?" Joe asked. Though he had instructed his eyes to open, the blue behind his lids was so serene he wasn't all that eager to desert it.

"We're going to Liverpool," Noah said.

"Liverpool?" said Joe. The few images he had of that city were gray and prosaic. "We've come all this way to visit Liverpool?"

"It's the ships we want. I can see them from here."

"What kind of ships?" Joe wanted to know. His lids still refused to open.

"See for yourself."

Why not? Joe thought. The blue will always be there, the moment I close my eyes. And so thinking, he opened them.

III

i

Friday morning, and it was too late for excuses. If the shelves weren't stocked, if the windows weren't polished, if the door wasn't painted, if the street wasn't swept, if the dog wasn't clipped, if the swing wasn't fixed, if the linen wasn't pressed, if the pies weren't ordered, well, it was too damn late. Folks were here, ready to spend some money and have some fun, so whatever had been left unfinished would have to stay that way.

"No doubt about it," Dorothy Bullard had announced to her husband as she rose to see the sun at the windowsill, "this is going to be the best year yet."

She didn't need to look far for confirmation. When she drove down Main Street a little shy of eight, it was already busier than an ordinary Saturday noon, and among the faces on the sidewalk there were gratifyingly few she knew. These were visitors; folks who'd checked into their motels and boarding houses the night before, and had driven or walked into town to begin their weekend with ham, eggs and a slice of Evervillian hospitality.

As soon as she got to the Chamber of Commerce she checked in with Gilholly, whose offices were just across the hall, to see if there was any news on the Phoebe Cobb business. Gilholly wasn't in yet, but Dorothy's favorite among the officers, Ned Bantam, was sitting behind his desk with a copy of the Festival Weekend edition of the *Tribune* and a carton of milk.

"Looks like it's going to be a fine weekend, Dottie baby," he grinned. This nickname was one she'd several times forbidden him to use, but he defied her with such charm she'd given up trying to enforce the ban.

"Did you arrest Joe Flicker?"

"Gotta find him first."

"You didn't find him?"

"If we'd found him we'd have arrested him, Dottie," Ned replied. "Don't look so grim. We'll get him."

"You think he's dangerous?"

"Ask Morton Cobb," Ned said. "I guess it's a bit late for that."

"What?"

"You didn't know?" Ned said. "Poor bastard died last night."

"Oh my Lord." Dorothy felt sick. "So we've got a murder-hunt going on in the middle of Festival Weekend?"

"It should spice things up a bit, huh?"

"That's not funny," Dorothy said. "We work all year—"

"Don't worry," Ned said. "Flicker's probably in Idaho by now."

"And what about *her*?" Dorothy said. She knew Phoebe by sight only; the woman had airs and graces, was her impression.

"What about her?"

"Is she going to be arrested or what?"

"Jed had Barney watching her house all night, in case Flicker came back, but he's not going to do that. I mean, why'd he do that?"

Dorothy didn't reply, though there was an answer on the tip of her tongue. Love, of course. He'd come back for love.

"So there was no sign of him?"

Ned shook his head. Dorothy couldn't help but feel a little spurt of satisfaction that the Cobb woman's lover had not returned to find her. She'd had all the secret trysts she was going to get. Now she'd have to pay the price.

Her anxieties salved somewhat, she asked Ned if he'd keep her up to date on the manhunt, and then went to work, content that even if the felon wasn't in Idaho, he was too far away to spoil the next seventy-two hours.

<hr>

ii

He hadn't come for her. That was the thought Phoebe had woken with. She'd waited and waited at the back door, until the day had driven every star from sight, and he hadn't come for her.

She sat at the kitchen table now, with the remains of a plateful of pancakes between her elbows, trying to work out what she should do next. Part of her said just go; go now, while you can. If you stay you'll be stuck playing the grieving widow for every damn person you meet. And then there'll be all the funeral arrangements to make, and the insurance policies to dig through. And don't forget Gilholly. He'll be back with more questions.

But then there was another voice, with conflicting advice. Leave town now and he'll never find you, the voice said. Maybe he got lost in the dark, maybe Morton did him more harm than she'd thought, maybe he was lying bleeding somewhere.

What it comes down to is this, the voice said: Do you trust him enough to believe he'll come for you? If you don't, go now. If you do, then put a brave face on things, and stay.

When it was made simple like that, she knew there was no question. Of course she trusted him. Of course, of course.

She brewed herself a pot of very strong coffee to help her get over her fatigue, then took a brisk shower, fixed her hair, and dressed. At eight forty-five, just as she was about to get out for the doctor's office, the telephone rang. She raced to it and snatched up the receiver, her heart crazed, only to be greeted by Gilholly's drear tones.

"Just checking on your whereabouts," he said.

"I'm just going to work," Phoebe said. "If that's all right with you, that is."

"I guess I'll know where to find you."

"I guess you will."

"Your boyfriend didn't come home last night."

She was about to say *no*, when she realized that he wasn't asking her a question, he was telling her. He already knew that Joe hadn't come back to the house. Which meant that he'd had one of his men patroling around all night; which in turn meant that there was every chance Joe had seen the man, and had kept his distance for fear of being caught. All this flashed through her mind in a matter of moments, but not so quickly that her stunned silence wasn't noted.

"Are you still there?" Gilholly said.

She was glad this was a telephone conversation, so that she didn't have to hide the smile that was spreading across her face.

"Yes," she said, doing her best to keep the relief from her voice. "Yes, I'm still here."

"If he makes any attempt to contact you—"

"I know, I know. I'll call you, Jed. I promise."

"Don't call me Jed, Mrs. Cobb," he replied sniffily. "We've got a professional relationship here. Let's keep it that way."

With that he was gone. She put the phone down, and sat on the stairs for a moment, trembling. Then, without warning tears of relief and happiness came, and it was fully ten minutes before she could get them sufficiently under control to go up and wash her face.

iii

Despite the exertions of the night before, Buddenbaum had woken, as always, a few minutes before dawn, stirred by a body-clock so perfectly calibrated he'd not missed a sunrise in the better part of eighty years. His business was the epic, after all, and he knew of no drama as primal as that which was played out every dawn and dusk. The victory of light over darkness, however, had carried a particular poignancy this morning, illuminating as it did the arena for a narrative that would, he hoped, be deemed as memorable as any in the human canon.

It was a century and a half since he'd sown the seed that had become Everville; a century and a half in which he had sown many such seeds in hope of apotheosis. Lonely and frustrating years, most of them, wandering from state to state, always a visitor, always an outsider. Of course there were advantages to his condition: not least a useful detachment from the crimes and torments and tragedies that had so quickly soured the pioneers' dream of Eden. There was little left, even in a town like Everville, of the fierce, pure vision of those souls with whom he'd mingled in Independence, Missouri. It had been a vision fueled by desperation, and nourished by ignorance, but whatever its frailties and its absurdities, it had moved him, after its fashion. It moved him still, in memory.

There had been something to die for in those hard hearts, and that was a greater gift than those blessed with it knew; a gift not granted those who'd come after. They were a prosaic lot, in Owen's estimations, the builders of suburbs and the founders of committees: men and women who had lost all sense of the tender, terrible holiness of things.

There were always exceptions, of course, like the kid lying asleep in the bed behind him. He and little Maeve O'Connell would have understood each other very well, Owen suspected. And after years of honing his instincts he was usually able to find one such as Seth within a few hours of coming to a new town. Every community had one or two youths who saw visions or heard hammerings or spoke in tongues. Regrettably, many of them had taken refuge in addiction, he found, particularly in the larger cities. He discovered them on seedy street corners dealing drugs with one eye on Heaven, and gently escorted them away to a room like this (how many like this had he been in? tens of thousands) where they would trade visions for sodomy, back and forth.

"Owen?"

The boy's hair was spread on the pillow as though he were floating.

"Good morning," Owen had replied.

"Are you going to come back to bed?"

"What time is it?"

"Just before seven," Seth had said. "We don't have to get up yet." He stretched, sliding down the bed as he did so.

Owen looked at the spiral of hair beneath the boy's arms and wondered at the workings of desire. "I have to go exploring today," he'd replied. "Do you want to come with me?"

"It depends what you're going to explore," Seth said, shamelessly fingering himself beneath the sheet.

Owen smiled, and crossed to the bottom of the bed. The youth had turned from waif to coquette in the space of one night. He was lifting the sheet up between his knees now, just high enough to give Owen a glimpse of his butthole.

"I suppose we could stay here an hour or so," Owen conceded, slipping the belt of his robe so that the boy could see what trouble he was inviting. Seth had flushed—his face, neck, and chest reddening in two heartbeats.

"I had a dream about that," he said.

"Liar."

"I did," Seth protested.

The sheet was still tented over his raised knees. Owen made no attempt to pull it off, but simply knelt between Seth's feet, and stared down at him, his prick peeping out from his robe.

"Tell me—" he said.

"Tell you what?"

"What you dreamed." Seth looked a little uncomfortable now. "Go on," Owen said, "or I'm going to cover it up again."

"Well," said Seth, "I dreamed—oh Jeez, this sounds so dumb—"

"Spit it out."

"I dreamed that," he pointed to Owen's dick "was a hammer."

"A hammer?"

"Yeah. I dreamed it was separate from you, you know, and I had it in my hand, and it was a hammer."

Odd as the image was, it didn't strike Owen as utterly outlandish, given the conversation they'd had on the street the night before. But there was more.

"I was using it to build a house."

"Are you making this up?"

"No. I swear. I was up on the roof of this house, it was just a wooden frame but it was a big house, somewhere up on the mountain, and there were nails that were like little spikes of fire, and your dick—" He half sat up and reached to touch the head of Owen's hard-on "your dick was driving the nails in. Helping me build my house." He looked up at Owen's face, and shrugged. "I said it was dumb."

"Where was the rest of me?" Owen wanted to know.

"I don't remember," Seth said.

"Huh."

"Don't be pissed off."

"I'm not pissed off."

"It was just a dumb dream. I was thinking about hammering and—can we stop talking about it now?" He slid his hand around Owen's sex, which had lost size and solidity while its dream-self was discussed, and attempted to stroke it back to its previous state. But it wouldn't be coaxed, much to Seth's disappointment.

"We'll have some time this afternoon," Owen said to him.

"Okay," said Seth, dropping back onto the bed and snatching the sheet off his lower torso. "But this is going to make walking around a little uncomfortable."

Owen gazed at the nearly hairless groin before him with a vague sense of unease. Not at the sight itself—the boy's equipment was pretty in its lopsided way—but at the thought of his manhood being used to hammer in spikes of fire, while the rest of him went unremembered.

Most of the time, of course, dreams were worthless. Bubbles in the stew of a sleeping mind, bursting once they surfaced. But sometimes they were revelations about the past; sometimes prophecies, sometimes ways to shape the present. And sometimes—oh, this was rare, but he'd known it happen—they were signs that the promise of the Art was not a hollow promise; that the human mind could know the past, present, and future as one eternal moment. He didn't believe that Seth's dream of house and hammer fell into this category, but something about it made his palms clammy and his nape itch. There was meaning here, if he could only decode it.

"What are you thinking?"

Seth was looking up at him with a troubled expression on his long, pale face.

"Crossroads," Owen replied.

"What about them?"

"That's what we're going to look for this morning." He got off the bed, and went through to the bathroom to piss. "I want to find the first crossroads in the city."

"Why?" Seth wanted to know.

He contemplated lying to the boy, but why? The answer was a paradox anyway.

"Because my journey ends where the roads cross," he said.

"What does that mean?"

"It means—I'm not going to be here for very much longer," Owen said, addressing Seth from the bathroom door, "so we may as well enjoy ourselves."

The boy looked downcast. "What will I do when you've gone?" he said.

Owen ruminated for a moment. Then he said, "Build a house, maybe?"

IV

*T*esla got lost just north of Salem, and had traveled thirty-five miles along the Willamina road before she realized her error and turned round. By the time she reached the Everville city limits it was past one, and she was hungry. She drove around for ten minutes, orienting herself while she looked for a suitable eatery, and eventually settled on a place called Kitty's Diner. It was busy, and she was politely told there'd be a ten-minute wait.

"No problem," she said, and went to sit out in the sun. There was plenty to divert her while she waited. The diner was situated at the intersection of the city's Main Street and a second, equally bustling thoroughfare. People and vehicles flowed by ceaselessly in both directions.

"This place is busy," she thought.

There's some kind of festival going on, Raul replied.

"How do you know?"

It's right in front of you, he said.

"Where, damn it?" she said, scanning the intersection in all four directions.

Up a couple of feet, Raul said.

Tesla looked up. There was a banner strung across the street, announcing WELCOME TO THE EVERVILLE FESTIVAL WEEKEND in blue letters three feet high.

"How come I didn't see that?" she thought, confounded (as ever) by the fact that she and Raul could look through the same eyes and see the world so differently.

You were concentrating on your stomach, Raul replied.

She ignored the remark. "This isn't an accident," she said.

What isn't?

"Us being here the weekend they're having a festival. It's some kind of synchronicity."

If you say so.

She watched the traffic in silence for a time. Then she asked Raul, "Do you feel anything?"

Like what?

"I don't know. Anything out of the ordinary?"

What am I, a bloodhound?

"All right," she said, "forget I spoke."

There was another silence. Then, very softly, Raul said, *Above the banner.*

She lifted her gaze, past the blue letters, past the roofs. "The mountain?" she said.

Yes . . .

"What about it?" she said.

Something, he replied. *I don't know, but something . . .*

She studied the peak for a little time. There wasn't that much to see; the summit was wreathed in mist. "I give up," she said, "I'm too hungry to think."

She glanced back at the diner. Two of its customers were up from their table, chatting to the waitress.

"About time," she muttered, and getting to her feet, headed inside.

"Just for one is it?" the waitress said, leading her to the vacated table and handing her a menu. "Everything's good, but the chicken livers are *really* good. So's the peach cobbler. Enjoy."

Tesla watched her pass between the tables, bestowing a word here and a smile there.

Happy little soul, Raul remarked dryly.

"Looks like Jesus is cookin' today," Tesla replied, eyeing the simple wooden cross hung above the serving hatch.

Better go for the fish then, Raul said, at which Tesla laughed out loud.

A few querulous glances came her way, but nobody seemed to much mind that this woman was so entertained by her own company she was weeping with laughter.

"Something funny?" the waitress wanted to know.

"Just a private moment," Tesla said, and ordered the fish.

ii

Erwin could not remember what terrible thing had happened in his house; he only knew that he wanted to be out of it and away.

He stood at the unopened front door with his thoughts in confusion, knowing there was something he had to take with him before he left, but unable to remember what. He turned and looked back down the hallway, hoping something would jog his memory.

Of course! The confession. He couldn't leave the house without the confession. He started back down the hallway, wondering where he'd set it down. As he came to the living room, however, his desire to have the papers suddenly evaporated, and without quite knowing how he got there he found himself standing outside his house again with the sun beating down on him. It was altogether too bright, and he dug in his pockets, looking for his sunglasses, only to discover that he was wearing an old tweed jacket that he thought he'd given away to charity years before. The gift had been spontaneous (which was rare for him) and he'd almost instantly regretted it. All the more wonderful then to have chanced upon it again, however mystifying the circumstances.

He found no sunglasses, but he did find a host of mementoes in the various pockets: ticket stubs for concerts he'd attended in Boston two decades before; the much-chewed remains of a cigar he'd smoked to celebrate passing the bar exam; a little piece of wedding cake, wrapped up in a napkin; the stiletto heel of a scarlet shoe; the little bottle of holy water his mother had been clutching when she died. Every pocket contained not one but four or five such keepsakes and tokens, each one unleashing a deluge of memories—scents, sounds, faces, feelings—all of which might have moved him more had the mystery of the jacket not continued to trouble him. He was certain he'd given it away. And even if he hadn't, even if it had languished unseen at the back of his wardrobe for a decade, and by chance he'd plucked it out of exile this morning without realizing he'd done so, that still didn't solve the problem of where the memorabilia in its pockets had appeared from.

Something strange was going on; something damned strange.

Next door, Ken Margosian emerged from his house whistling, and sauntered among his rose bushes with a pair of scissors, selecting blooms.

"The roses are better than ever this year," Erwin remarked to him.

Margosian, who was usually a neighborly sort, didn't even look up.

Erwin crossed to the fence. "Are you okay, Ken?" he asked.

Margosian had found a choice rose, and was carefully selecting a place to snip it. There was not the slightest sign that he'd heard a syllable.

"Why the silent treatment?" Erwin demanded. "If you've got some bitch with me—"

At this juncture, Mrs. Semevikov came along, a woman whom under normal circumstances Erwin would have happily avoided. She was a voluble woman, who took it upon herself to organize a small auction every Festival Saturday, selling items donated by various stores to benefit children's charities. Last year she had attempted to persuade Erwin to donate a few hours of his services as a prize. He had promised to think about it, and then not returned her calls. Now here she was again, after the same thing, no doubt. She said hello to Ken Margosian, but didn't so much as cast a glance in Erwin's direction, though he was standing five yards from her.

"Is Erwin in?" she asked Ken.

"I don't think so," Ken replied.

"Joke over," Erwin piped up, but Ken hadn't finished.

"I heard some odd noises in the night," he told Mrs. Semevikov, "like he was having a brawl in there."

"That doesn't sound like him at all," she replied.

"I knocked on his door this morning, just to see that he was okay, but nobody answered."

"Stop this," Erwin protested.

"Maybe he's at his office," Mrs. Semevikov went on.

"I said *stop it!*" Erwin yelled. It was distressing him now, hearing himself talked about as though he were invisible. And what was this nonsense about a brawl? He'd had a perfectly peaceable—

The thought faltered, and he looked back towards the house, as a name rose from the murk of his memory.

Fletcher. Oh my God, how could he have forgotten Fletcher?

"Maybe I'll try him at his office," Mrs. Semevikov was saying, "because he promised me last year—"

"Listen to me," Erwin begged.

"He'd donate a few hours—"

"I don't know why you're doing this, but you've got to listen."

"To the auction."

"There's somebody in my house."

"Those are beautiful roses, by the way. Are you entering them in the flower competition?"

Erwin could take no more of this. He strode towards the fence, yelling at Ken, "*He tried to kill me!*" Then he reached over and caught hold of Ken's shirt. Or at least he tried to. His fingers passed through the fabric, his fist closing on itself. He tried again. The same thing happened.

"I'm going crazy," he thought. He reached up to Ken's face and prodded his cheek, hard, but he got not so much as a blink for his efforts. "Fletcher's been playing with my head."

A wave of panic rose in him. He had to get the meddler to fix his handiwork, now, before there was some serious damage done. Leaving Ken and Mrs. Semevikov to their chatter about roses, Erwin headed back up the path to the front door. It looked to be closed, but his senses were utterly unreliable, it seemed, because two strides carried him over the threshold and into the hallway.

He called out for Fletcher. There was no reply, but the meddler was somewhere in the house, Erwin was certain of it. Every angle in the hallway was a little askew, and the halls had a yellowish tinge. What was that, if not Fletcher's influence?

He knew where the man lay in wait: in the living room, where he'd held Erwin prisoner in order to toy with his sanity. His fury mounting—how dare this man invade his house and his head?—he marched down the hallway to the living room door. It stood ajar. Erwin didn't hesitate. He stepped inside.

The drapes were drawn to keep out the day, the only source of light the fire that was now dying in the grate. Even so, Erwin found his tormentor at a glance. He was sitting cross-legged in the middle of the floor, his clothes shed. His body was broad, hirsute, and covered with scars, some of them fully six inches long. His pupils were rolled up beneath his eyelids. In front of him was a mound of excrement.

"You filthy animal," Erwin raged. His words drew no response from Fletcher. "I don't know what kind of mind-tricks you've been playing," Erwin went on, "but I want you to undo them. Right now. Hear me? *Right now!*" Fletcher's pupils slipped back into view, much to Erwin's satisfaction. He was tired of being ignored. "And then I want you—"

He stopped to let out a groan of disgust as Fletcher reached out and took a handful of his own shit, then mashed it into his groin. Erwin averted his eyes, but what his gaze found in the shadows was infinitely worse than Fletcher's scatological games.

There was a body there, lying with its face to the wall. A body he recognized.

There were no words to express the horror of that moment; nor its terrible clarity. He could only let out a sob, a wracking sob, that went unheard by the masturbator.

He knew why now. He was dead. His wizened body was lying in

the corner of the room, drained of life by Fletcher. Whatever consciousness he still possessed, it was clinging to the memory of the flesh, but it had no influence in the living world. He could not be seen or heard or felt. He was a phantom.

He sank down in front of Fletcher and studied his face. It was brutish beneath the beard, the brow louring, the mouth grotesquely wide.

"What *are* you?" he murmured to himself.

Fletcher's manipulations were apparently bringing him close to crisis. His breathing was fast and shallow, and punctuated with little grunts. Erwin couldn't bring himself to watch the act concluded. As the grunts grew louder he rose and made for the door, passing through it, down the hall and out into the sunlight.

Mrs. Semevikov had gone on her way, and Ken was heading back into his house with an armful of roses, but there was a thin, high-pitched whining sound coming from nearby. Something is in pain, Erwin thought, which fact curiously comforted him, to know that he was not the only soul suffering right now. He went in search of the sufferer, and didn't have to look far. It was the rose bushes that were giving off the whine; a sound he assumed only the dead could hear.

It was a poor compensation. Tears, or rather the memory of tears, fell from his remembered eyes, and he quietly swore an oath that even if he had to do a deal with the Devil to possess the means, he would somehow revenge himself on the beast that had taken his life. Nor would it be quick. He'd make the bastard suffer so loudly the grief of a million roses could not drown out his screams.

iii

The Friday of Festival Weekend was always a slack day at the doctor's. Early next week there'd be a waiting room full of folks who'd put off a visit because they had too much to do, their fingers turned septic, their constipation chronic. But today only those in extreme discomfort, or so lonely a trip to see Dr. Powell was a treat, came in.

None of the patients made any mention of recent events to Phoebe, though she didn't doubt that every man, woman, and child in Everville was by now steeped in the scandal. Even Dr. Powell kept his remarks to a minimum. He was sorry to hear about Morton's death, he said, and would perfectly understand if she needed to take a few days off. She thanked him, and asked if she might perhaps leave around two, so she could drive over to Silverton and meet the funeral director. The answer, of course, was yes.

In fact, that wasn't the only meeting she had planned. She needed more urgently than ever the guidance of a legal mind; someone who could give her a clear picture of just how bad a position she was in. She would try to see Erwin this afternoon she'd decided, rather than wait until Monday. A lot could happen in seventy-two hours, as the turmoil of the last twenty-four proved. Better that she knew the bad news and planned accordingly.

iv

The fish was good. Tesla took her leisurely time eating, and listened while she ate, tuning in to conversations going on at five tables in her vicinity. It was a trick she'd first learned as a screenwriter (quickly finding that ordinary conversation was littered with remarks no producer would believe) and had gone on to hone it during her travels, when it had allowed her to keep track of the way the world was going without benefit of media or social skills.

Today, much to her surprise, she found that three of the five conversations were about the same thing: the life and crimes of a local woman called Phoebe, who was apparently implicated in the bizarre demise of her husband.

While she was listening to one of the tables debating the morals of adultery, a parched-looking fellow, whom she took to be the manager of the place, came through with hamburgers for the debaters, and on his way back to the counter gathered up her dishes and casually asked if she'd enjoyed the fish. She said she had. Then, hoping to squeeze a little more information from him said:

"I was wondering . . . do you happen to know a guy called Fletcher?"

The man, his name tag read *Bosley*, thought for a moment. "Fletcher . . . Fletcher . . . " he said.

While he mused, Raul said, *Tesla?*

"In a minute," she thought to Raul.

But there's something— Raul went on.

He got no further before Bosley said, "I don't believe I know of any Fletcher. Does he live in town?"

"No. He's a visitor."

"We're swamped with visitors," Bosley replied.

Clearly this wasn't going to prove a fruitful line of inquiry. But while she had the man in front of her she decided to quiz him about something else.

"Phoebe," she said. Bosley lost his smile. "Do you know her?"

"She came in now and again," Bosley conceded.

"What's she like?" By the expression on his face, Bosley was caught between the requirements of civility and his desire to ignore Tesla's question entirely. "Everybody's talking about her."

"Then I hope her story serves as a lesson," Bosley replied, chilly now. "The Lord sees her sin and judges her."

"Has she been accused of something?"

"In the Lord's eyes—"

"Forget the fucking Lord's eyes," Tesla said, irritated by the guy's cant. "I want to know what she's like."

Bosley set the dishes back on the table and quietly said, "I think you'd better leave."

"What for?"

"You're not welcome to break bread with us," he replied.

"Why the hell not?"

"Your language."

"What about it?" Tesla said.

The F word, Raul prompted.

She repeated it aloud, to test the thesis. "Fuck?" she said, "you don't like me saying *fuck?*"

Bosley flinched as though the syllables were stings. "Get out," he said.

"All I said was *fuck*," Tesla replied sweetly. "What's wrong with *fuck?*"

Bosley had taken hurts enough. "I want you out of here," he said, the volume of his voice rising. "Your foul tongue isn't welcome."

"I can't stay for the peach cobbler?" Tesla said.

"*Out!*" Bosley yelled. The gossiping patrons had fallen silent now. All eyes were turned in the direction of Tesla's table. "Take your abominations elsewhere. They're not welcome here."

Tesla lounged in her chair. "*Fuck* isn't an abomination," she said. "*Fuck*'s just a word, it's just a useful little word. Come on, Bosley, admit it. There are times when only *fuck* will do."

"I want you out of here."

"You see. *I want you the fuck out of here* would sound so much more forceful."

There were giggles from here and there, and a few nervous coughs.

"What do you say to your wife on a Saturday night? You want to fornicate, honey? No, you say I want a fuck."

"*Out!*" Bosley yelled. There were others coming to his aid now, among them a cook from the kitchen who looked like he might have seen the light in San Quentin. Tesla got to her feet.

"Okay, I'm going," she said. She gave the cook a dazzling grin. "Great fish," she said, and sauntered to the door. "Of course we shouldn't forget the most important use of *fuck*," she said as she went. "The exclamation. As in *oh fuck*, or *what a fuck up*." She'd reached the door, and halted there to look back at Bosley. "Or the ever-useful *fuck you*," she said, and, offering him a little smile, took her leave.

She was standing on the corner, wondering where she might next go in search of Fletcher, when Raul whispered, *Did you hear what I said in there?*

"I was just defending my constitutional rights," Tesla replied.

Before that, Raul murmured.

"What?" she said.

I don't know what, he replied. *I just felt some presence or other—*

"You sound nervous," Tesla replied, glancing around. The intersection was busier than ever. It was an unlikely place to be haunted, she thought, at least right now. At midnight, perhaps, it'd be a different story.

"Didn't they bury suicides at crossroads?" she said to Raul. There was no reply. "*Raul?*"

Listen.

"What am I—?"

Just listen, will you?

There was plenty to hear. Horns honking, tires squealing, folks laughing and chattering, music from an open window, shouting through an open door.

Not that, Raul said.

"What then?"

Somebody's whispering.

She listened again, trying to filter out the din of people and vehicles.

Close your eyes, Raul said, *it's easier in the dark.*

She did so. The din continued, but she felt a little more remote from it.

There, Raul murmured.

He was right. Somewhere between the traffic and the chatter, a tiny voice was trying to be heard. *No*, it seemed to be saying. And something about *ketchup*. Tesla concentrated, trying to tune her mind's ear into the voice, the way she'd tuned in to the conversations in the Diner. *No*, it said again, *no about, no about—*

"Know about," Tesla murmured. "It knows about something."

"Ketch . . . ketch . . . " the voice said.

Ketch?

"Ketch a—"

No, not ketch a: Fletcher.

"You hear that?" she said to Raul. "It knows about Fletcher.

That's what it's saying. It knows about Fletcher." She listened again, tuning into the frequency where the voice had been. The sound was still there, but barely. She held her breath, focusing every jot of her attention upon interpreting the signal. It wasn't words she was hearing now, it was a number. Two. Two. Six.

She said it aloud, so that the whisperer knew she'd understood.

"Two—two—six. Right?"

And now came further syllables. *Itch* or *witch*. Then *hell*, or something like it.

"Try again," she said softly. But either her powers of concentration or the whisperer's strength was giving out. *Itch*, she thought it said again. Then it was gone. She kept listening, hoping it would make further contact, but there was nothing. "Shit," she muttered.

What we need's a map, Raul said.

"What for?"

It was an address, Tesla. He was telling you where to find Fletcher.

She looked back towards the diner. Her waitress caught sight of her as she opened the door.

"Please—" the woman began.

"It's okay," Tesla said. "I just want one of these." She picked up a Festival brochure from the rack just inside the door. "Have a nice day."

When did you get to be so rabid about Jesus, by the way? Raul asked her as she sat astride the bike studying the map on the back of the brochure.

"I'm not," she said. "I love all that shit. I just think words are—" She stopped. Peered more closely at the map. "Mitchell Street," she said. "That's got to be it. *Mitchell.*"

She pocketed the map and started the bike. "Are you ready for this?" she said.

Precious, he replied.

"What?"

You were going to say words are precious.

"Was I?"

And no: I'm not ready.

V

i

E rwin had journeyed down to Kitty's Diner in search of the familiar; some face or voice he knew and liked, to settle the panic in him. Instead he'd heard a woman he'd never seen in his life before asking about his murderer, and he had almost gone crazy with frustration, haranguing her at a volume that would have torn his throat if he'd had a throat to tear, while she paraded her command of gutter-talk for Bosley.

She was neither as stupid or insensitive as that display might have suggested, however. Once she was outside she'd stopped to listen, and he'd pressed so close to her it would have been deemed molestation if he'd been flesh and blood, telling her over and over where Fletcher was. His tenacity had paid off. She'd gone back for the city map, and while she'd studied it, he had tried to warn her that Fletcher was dangerous.

This time, however, she hadn't heard. He wasn't quite sure why. Perhaps people couldn't map-read and hear the dead talk at the same time. Perhaps the fault lay with him, and he'd lost the knack of communication with the living moments after finding it. Whichever, what he had hoped would blossom into a fruitful exchange had been cut short, and the woman had been off on her motorcycle before he could tell her about Fletcher's murderous tendencies. He was not overly concerned for her well-being. If she was in search of Fletcher, he reasoned, then she surely knew what he was capable of, and to judge by her performance in the diner she was no milquetoast.

He watched her carving her way through the traffic on Main Street and envied her access to the combustion engine. Though he'd always been contemptuous of ghost stories (they'd belonged to the negligible realm of fable and fantasy), he knew phantoms had a reputation for defying gravity. They hovered, they flew; they perched in trees and steeples. Why then did he feel so *earthbound*, his body— which he knew damn well was notional; the real thing was lying in his living room—still behaving as though gravity had a claim on it?

Sighing, he started back towards his house. If the return journey took as long as the outward, then by the time he reached home the encounter he'd initiated would be over. But what was a lost soul to do? He would have to make his way as best he could, and hope that with time he'd better understand the state he'd died into.

ii

Phoebe went to Erwin's office unannounced and found it closed. On any other day but today she would have left the matter there. Gone home. Waited till Monday. But these were very special circumstances. She couldn't wait; not another hour. She would go by his house, she decided, and beg for just half an hour of his time. That wasn't much to ask, now was it? Especially since she'd inconvenienced herself for him the day before.

She popped into the drugstore two blocks down from the offices, and asked Maureen Scrimm, who had her hair tinted for the celebrations and looked like the local tart, if she could borrow the phone book. Maureen wanted to gossip, but the store was crowded. Armed with Erwin's home address, Phoebe left Maureen to make eyes at every able-bodied man under sixty-five, and headed for Mitchell Street.

✳   ✳   ✳

It was a quiet little thoroughfare lined with attractive, well-kept houses, the lawns and hedges trimmed, the fences and window frames painted. The kind of haven Tesla had fantasized about many times on her journey across the Americas; a place where people were good to each other, and lived, physically and spiritually, within their modest means. It didn't take much guesswork to figure out why Fletcher had chosen to lodge here. He had staged his own immolation back in the Grove in order to imagine from the dreams of its healthy, loving citizens, a legion of champions. *Hallucigenia*, he'd dubbed them, and left them to wage war in the streets of the Grove after his demise. If another battle was now in the offing, as Kate Farrell had predicted, then where better to seek out minds from which he could create new soldiers than in a haven like this, where people still had faith in a civilized life, and might conjure heroes to defend it?

Listen to you, Raul said as Tesla wandered along the street looking for Fletcher's hideaway.

"Was I thinking aloud or were you just eavesdropping?"

Eavesdropping, Raul replied. *And I'm amazed.*

"By what?"

By the way you're drooling over this place. You hated Palomo Grove.

"It was phoney."

This isn't?

"No. It looks . . . comfortable."

You've been on the road too long.

"That may have something to do with it," Tesla conceded. "I am a little saddle-weary. But this looks like a good place to settle down—"

Maybe raise some kids? You and Lucien? Wouldn't that be nice.

"Don't be snide."

All right, it wouldn't be nice. It'd be a living hell.

They had come, at last, to the whisperer's house, and very smart it was too.

Tesla—

"What?"

Fletcher was always a little crazy, remember that.

"How could I forget?"

So forgive him his trespasses—

"You're excited. I can feel you trembling."

I used to call him father *all the time. He used to tell me not to, but that's what he was. That's what he is. I want to see him again—*

"So do I," she said. It was the first time she'd actually admitted the fact in so many words. Yes, Fletcher was crazy, and yes, unpredictable. But he was also the man who'd created the Nuncio, the man who'd turned to light in front of her eyes, the man who'd had her half-believing in saints. If anyone deserved to have outwitted oblivion, it was him.

She started up the front path, studying the house for some sign of occupancy. There was none. The drapes were drawn at all but one of the windows, and there were two newspapers uncollected on the step.

She knocked. There was no response, but she wasn't that surprised. If Fletcher was indeed in residence, he was unlikely to be answering the door. She rapped again, just for good measure, then went to the one window without closed drapes and peered in. It was a dining room, furnished with antique furniture. Whoever lived here when Fletcher wasn't visiting had taste.

Something's wrong with the sewers, Raul said.

"The sewers?"

Don't you smell it?

She sniffed, and caught a whiff of something unpleasant.

"Is it from inside?" she asked Raul, but before he could reply she heard a footfall on the gravel path and somebody said, "Are you looking for Erwin?"

She turned. There was a woman standing a couple of yards from the front gate: large, pale, and overdressed.

"Erwin—" Tesla said, thinking fast, "yeah. I was just . . . is he around today?"

The woman studied Tesla with faint suspicion. "He should be," she said. "He's not at his office."

"Huh. I knocked, but there was no reply." The woman looked

distinctly disappointed. "I was going to try round the back," Tesla went on, "see if he's getting himself a tan."

"Did you try the bell?" the woman replied.

"No, I—"

The woman marched down the path and jabbed the bell. A saccharine jingle could be heard from inside. Tesla waited ten seconds. Then, when there was no sign of movement, she started round the side of the house, leaving the woman to try jabbing the bell again at the front.

"Ripe," she remarked to Raul as the smell of excrement intensified. She watched the ground as she went, half-expecting to find that a pipe had burst and the last flushings of Erwin's toilet were bubbling up from the ground. But there was nothing. No turds; and no Erwin either, sunning himself in the backyard.

"Maybe this isn't the house," she said to Raul. "Maybe there's another street that sounds like Mitchell."

She turned on her heel, only to find that bell-jabber was coming down the side of the house herself, with a look of slight agitation on her face.

"There's somebody inside," she said. "I looked through the letterbox and I saw somebody at the end of the hall."

"Was it Erwin?"

"I couldn't see. It was too dark."

"Huh." Tesla stared at the wall, as though she might pierce it with her sight if she looked hard enough.

"There was something weird about him—"

"What?"

"I don't know." She looked spooked.

"You want to call the cops?"

"No. No, I don't think we have to bother Jed with this. Maybe I'll just . . . you know . . . try another day."

This is one nervous lady, Raul said.

"If there's some problem in here . . . " Tesla said. "Maybe I'll just look round the other side." She started back towards the yard. "I'm Tesla by the way," she called over her shoulder.

"I'm Phoebe."

Well, well . . . said Raul, *the scarlet woman.*

It was all Tesla could do not to say: *Everybody's talking about you.*

"Are you a relative of Erwin's?" Phoebe asked her.

"No, why?"

"It's none of my business, but I know you're not from Everville—"

"So you're wondering what I'm doing here," Tesla replied, as she tried the back door. It was locked. Cupping her hands around her eyes she peered through the glass. There were a few signs of life. A carton of orange juice overturned on the table; a small pile of dishes beside the sink. "I'm not here to see Erwin," Tesla went on. "Truth is, I don't even *know* Erwin." She glanced round at Phoebe, who didn't seem overly concerned that she was talking to a potential house-breaker.

"I came to see a guy called Fletcher. Don't suppose the name means anything?"

Phoebe thought about this for a moment, then shook her head. "He's not a local man," she stated. "I'm sure I'd know him if he were."

"Small town, huh?"

"It's getting too small for me," Phoebe said, unable to disguise her sourness. "Everybody pretty much knows everybody else's business."

"I heard a few rumors myself."

"About me?" said Phoebe.

"You're *the* Phoebe Cobb, right?"

Phoebe pursed her lips. "I wish to God I wasn't right now," she said, "but yes. I'm Phoebe Cobb." She sighed, her robust façade cracking. "Whatever you heard—"

"I couldn't give a shit," Tesla said. "I know it can't be much fun—"

"I've had better days," Phoebe said, seeming to suddenly catch the defeat in her voice and pulling herself together. "Look, obviously Mr. Toothaker doesn't want to answer the door to either of us."

Tesla smiled. "Toothaker? That's his name? Erwin Toothaker?"

"What's so funny about that?"

"Nothing. I think it's perfect," Tesla said. "Erwin Toothaker." She peered through the window again, squinting.

The door that led into the rest of the house was a couple of inches ajar, and as she stared, a sinuous shadow seemed to move through the gap.

She recoiled from the back door six inches, startled.

"What is it?" Phoebe said.

Tesla blinked, licked her lips, and looked again. "Does our Erwin keep snakes?" she said.

"Snakes?"

"Yeah, snakes."

"Not that I know of. Why?"

"It's gone now, but I could swear I saw . . ."

Tesla? Raul murmured.

"What?"

Snakes and the smell of shit. What does that combination remind you of?

She didn't answer. Just backed away from the door, suddenly clammy. *No,* her mind said, *no, no, no. Not Lix. Not here. Not in this little backwater.*

Tesla, get hold of yourself.

She was suddenly trembling from head to foot.

"Is it there again?" Phoebe said, taking a step towards the door.

"*Don't,*" Tesla said.

"I'm not scared of snakes."

Tesla put her hand to block Phoebe's approach. "I mean it," she said.

Phoebe pushed her arm aside. "I want to look," she said forcibly, and put her face to the window. "I don't see anything."

"It came and went."

"Or it was never there," Phoebe replied. She looked back at Tesla. "You don't look so good," she said.

"I don't *feel* so good."

"Have you got a phobia?"

Tesla shook her head. "Not about snakes." She reached out and gently plucked at Phoebe's arm. "I really think we should get out of here."

Either the grim tone in her voice, or the look on her ashen face apparently was enough to convince Phoebe she was deadly serious, because now she too retreated from the back door.

"Maybe I was just imagining it," Tesla replied, hoping to any God who'd listen that this was true. She was ready for anything but Lix.

With Phoebe trailing after her she made her way back round to the front of the house, and up the path to the street.

"Happy now?" Phoebe said.

"Just walk with me, will you?" Tesla said, and set the pace until they'd put fifty yards between themselves and the Toothaker house. Only then did Tesla slow down.

"Happy now?" Phoebe said again, this time a little testily.

Tesla stood staring up at the sky, and drew several long, calming breaths before she said, "This is worse than I thought."

"What is? What are you talking about?"

Tesla drew another deep breath. "I think there's something evil in that house," she replied.

Phoebe glanced back down the street, which looked more serene than ever as the afternoon drew on.

"I know it's hard to believe—"

"Oh no," Phoebe said flatly. "I can believe it." When she looked back at Tesla she was wearing a small, tight smile. "This place is cruel," she said. "It doesn't look it, but it is."

Tesla began to think maybe there'd been a certain synchronicity in their meetings. "Do you want to talk about it?"

"No," she said.

"Okay. I'm not going to try and—"

"I mean yes," Phoebe said. "Yes, I do want to talk about it."

VI

*T*here's something wrong with the sea."

Joe sat up, and looked down the shore towards the booming surf. The waters were almost velvety, the waves large enough to tempt a surfer, but curling and breaking more slowly than those on any terrestrial shore. Flecks of iridescence rose in their lavish curl, and glittered on their crests.

"It's beautiful," he said.

Noah grunted. "Look out there," he said, and pointed out beyond the breakers, to the place where the horizon should have been. Black and gray and green pillars of clouds were apparently rising from the sea as though some titanic heat was turning the waters to steam. The heavens, meanwhile, were falling in floods and fires. It was a spectacle the scale of which Joe had never conceived before, like a scene from the making of the world, or its unmaking.

"What's causing all that?"

"I don't want to speak the words until I'm certain," Noah said. "But I begin to think we should be careful, even here."

"Careful about what?"

"About waiting for the likes of that to come our way," he said, and pointed along the shore.

Three or four miles from where they stood he could see the roofs and spires of a city. Liverpool, he presumed. In between, perhaps a quarter of that distance away, was an approaching procession.

"That's a Blessedm'n," Noah said, "I think we're better away, Joe."

"Why?" Joe wanted to know. "What's a Blessedm'n?"

"One who conjures," Noah said. "Perhaps the one who opened this door."

"Don't you want to wait and *thank* him?" Joe said, still studying the procession. There were perhaps thirty in the line, some of them on horseback; one, it seemed, on a camel.

"The door wasn't opened for me," Noah replied.

"Who was it opened *for?*" There was no answer. Joe looked round to see that Noah was once again staring out towards the apocalyptic storm that blocked the horizon. "Something out there?" he said.

"Maybe," Noah replied.

Half a dozen questions appeared in Joe's head at the same time. If what was out *there* was coming *here*, what would happen to the shore? And to the city? And if it passed over the threshold, would the storm it brought go with it? Down the mountain, to Everville? To Phoebe?

Oh my God, *to Phoebe?*

"I have to go back," he said.

"You can't."

"I can and I will," Joe said, turning and starting back towards the crack. It was not hidden here, as it was on the mountain. It crackled like a rod of black lightning against the shifting sky. Was it his imagination, or was it wider and taller than it had been?

"I promised you power, Joe," Noah called after him. "And I still have it to give."

Joe turned on his heel. "So give it to me and let me go," he said.

Noah stared at the ground. "It's not as easy as that, my friend."

"What do you mean?"

"I can't grant you power here."

"On the other side, you said."

"Yes, I did. I know I did. But that wasn't quite the truth." He looked up at Joe now, his oversized head seeming to teeter on his frail neck. "I'd hoped that once you got here and saw the glories of the dream-sea, you'd want to travel with me a little way. I can give you power. Truly I can. But only in my own country."

"How far?" Joe said.

There was no answer forthcoming. Infuriated, Joe went back to Noah, moving at such speed the creature raised its arms to ward off a blow. "I'm not going to hit you," Joe said. Noah lowered his guard six inches. "I just want an honest answer."

Noah sighed. "My country is the Ephemeris," he said.

"And where's the Ephemeris?" Joe wanted to know.

Noah looked at him for perhaps ten seconds, and then pointed out to sea.

"No shit," Joe said, deadpan. "You really put one over on me."

"Put one over?" Noah said.

"Tricked me, asshole." He pushed his face at Noah, until they were almost nose to nose. "You tricked me."

"I believed you'd been sent to take me home," Noah said.

"Don't be pathetic."

"It's true, I did. I still do." He looked up at Joe. "You think that's ridiculous, that our lives could be intertwined that way?"

"Yes," said Joe.

Noah nodded. "So you must go back," he said. "And I'll stay. I feel stronger here, under my own sky. No doubt you'll feel stronger under yours."

Joe didn't miss the irony. "You know damn well what I'll be when I get back there."

"Yes," said Noah, getting to his feet. "Powerless." With that he started to hobble away down the beach. "Goodbye, Joe," he called after him.

"Asshole," Joe said, staring back up the shore at the sliver of night sky visible in the crack. What use would he be to himself or to Phoebe if he returned home now? He was a wounded fugitive. And just as Noah had pointed out, he was utterly powerless.

He turned again to scan the strange world into which he'd

stepped. The distant city, the approaching procession, the storm raging over Quiddity's tumultuous waters: none of it looked particularly promising. But perhaps—just perhaps—there was hope for him here. A means to get power of some kind, *any* kind, that would make him a man to be reckoned with when he got back to his own world. Perhaps he'd have to sweat for it, but he'd sweated in the Cosm, hadn't he, and what had he got for his efforts? Broken balls.

"All right," he said, going down the shore after Noah. "I'll stay. But I'm not carrying you, understand?"

Noah smiled back at him. "May I . . . put my arm around your shoulder, until I get some nourishment in me, and my legs are stronger?"

"I guess," said Joe.

Noah hooked his arm around Joe's neck. "There's a beached boat down there," he said, "we'll take refuge until the procession's gone."

"What's so bad about these Blessedm'n?" Joe asked him as they made their hobbling way down to the vessel.

"No one ever knows what's in a Blessedm'n's heart. They have secret reasons and purposes for everything. Perhaps this one is benign, but we've no way of knowing."

They walked on in silence, until they reached the vessel. It was two-masted, perhaps twenty-five feet long, its boards and wheelhouse painted scarlet and blue, though its voyages had taken their toll on both paintwork and boards. Its name, *The Fanacapan*, had been neatly lettered on its bow.

Hunger was beginning to gnaw at Joe, so he left Noah squatting in the lee of the vessel, and clambered on board to look for some sustenance. The narcotic effect of the painkillers was finally wearing off, and as he went about the boat, looking above and below for a loaf of bread or a bottle of beer, he felt a mingling of negative feelings creep upon him. One of them was unease, another trepidation, a third, disappointment. He had found his way into another world, only to discover that things here weren't so very different. Perhaps Quiddity was indeed a dream-sea as Noah had claimed, but this boat, that had apparently crossed it, showed no sign of having been built or occupied by creatures of vision. Its two cabins were squalid, its galley unspeakable, the woodwork of its wheelhouse crudely etched with drawings of the obscenest kind.

As for nourishment, there was none to be found. There were a few scraps of food left in the galley, but nothing remotely edible, and though Joe searched through the strewn clothes and filthy blankets in the cabins in the hope of finding a bar of chocolate or a piece of fruit, he came up empty-handed. Frustrated, and hungrier than ever after his exertions, he clambered back down onto the shore to find that Noah was sitting cross-legged on the ground, staring up the shore with tears on his face.

"What's wrong?"

"It just reminds me . . . " Noah said, nodding towards the procession. Its destination was the crack, no doubt of that. Five or six celebrants, who looked to be children, and nearly naked, had broken from the front of the procession and were strewing a path of leaves or petals between their lord and the threshold.

"Reminds you of what?"

"Of my wedding day," Noah said. "And of my beloved. We had a procession three, four times that one. You never saw such finery. You never heard such music. It was to be the end of an age of war, and the beginning . . . " He faltered, shuddering. "I want to see my country again, Joe," he said after a time. "If it's only to be buried there."

"You haven't waited all this time just to die."

"It won't be so bad," Noah murmured. "I've had the love of my life. There could never be another like her, nor do I want there to be. I couldn't bear to even think such a thought until now, but it's the truth, Joe. So it won't be so bad, if I die in my own country, and I'm laid in the dirt from which I came. You understand that, don't you?" Joe didn't reply. Noah looked round at him. "No?"

"No," he said, "I don't have a country, Noah. I hate America."

"Africa then."

"I was never there. I don't think I'd much like that either." He drew a long, slow breath. "So I don't give a fuck where I'm buried." There was another long silence. Then he said: "I'm hungry. There's nothing on the boat. I'm going to have to eat soon or I'm going to start falling down."

"Then you must catch yourself something," Noah said, and getting to his feet, led Joe down to the water's edge. The waves were not breaking as violently as they had been, Joe thought. "See the fish?" Noah said, pointing into curling waves.

The streaks of iridescence Joe had seen from the threshold were in fact living things: fishes and eels, bright as lightning, leaping in the water in their thousands.

"I see them."

"Take your fill."

"You mean, just catch them in my hands?"

"And swallow them down," Noah said. He smiled, seeing the disgusted look on Joe's face. "They're best alive," he said. "Trust me."

The ache in Joe's stomach was now competing with that in his balls. This was, he knew, no time to be persnickety about his options. He shrugged and strode out into the water. It was balmy warm, which came as a pleasant surprise, and if he hadn't known better he'd have said it was eager to have him in its midst, the way it curled around his shins, and leapt up towards his groin. The fish were *everywhere*, he saw; and they came in a number of shapes and sizes, some as large as salmon, which surprised him given the shallowness of the waters, others tiny as hummingbirds and almost as defiant of gravity, leaping around him in their glittering thousands. He had to exert almost no effort at all to catch hold of one. He simply closed his hand in their midst, and opening it again found he'd caught not one but three—two a reddish silver, the third blue—all flapping wildly in his palm. They didn't look remotely appetizing, with their black, black eyes and their gasping flanks. But as long as he and Noah were trapped here he had little choice. He either ate the fish, or went hungry.

He plucked one of the reddish variety off the plate of his palm, and without giving himself time to regret what he was doing, threw back his head and dropped it into his mouth. There was a moment of disgust when he thought he'd vomit, then the fish was gone down his gullet. He'd tasted nothing, but what the hell. This wasn't a gourmet meal; it was eating at its most primal. He took one more look at his palm, then he popped both the remaining fish into his mouth at the same time, throwing back his head so as to knock them back. One slipped down his throat as efficiently as the first, but the other flapped against his tonsils, and found its way back onto his tongue. He spat it out.

"Bad taste?" Noah said, wading into the surf beside Joe.

"It just didn't want to get eaten," Joe replied.

"You can't blame it," Noah replied, and strode on until he was hip deep in the waters.

"You're feeling stronger," Joe yelled to him over the crash of surf.

"All the time," Noah replied. "The air nourishes me." He plunged his hands into the water and came up not with a fish, but something that resembled a squid, its huge eyes a vivid gold.

"Don't tell me to eat *that*," Joe said.

"No. No, never," Noah replied. "This is a Zehrapushu; a spirit-pilot. See how it looks at you?"

Joe saw. There was an eerie curiosity in the creature's unblinking gaze, as though it were studying him.

"It's not used to seeing your species in flesh and blood," Noah said. "If you could speak its language it would surely tell you to go home. Perhaps you want to touch it?"

"Not much."

"It would please the Zehrapushu," Noah said, proffering the creature. "And if you please one you please many."

Joe waded out towards Noah, watching the animal watch him.

"You mean this thing's connected to other . . . what'd you call them . . . Zehra-what?"

"People call them 'shu, it's easier." He pressed the creature into Joe's arms. "It's not going to bite," he said.

Joe took hold of it, gingerly. It lay quite passively in his hands, its gaze turned up towards Joe's face.

"The oldest temples on the twelve continents were raised to the 'shu," Noah went on, "and it's still worshipped in some places."

"But not by your people?"

Noah shook his head. "My wife was a Catholic," he said. "And I'm . . . I'm a nonbeliever. You'd better put it back before it perishes. I think it'd happily die just watching you."

Joe stooped and set the 'shu back in the water. It lingered between his palms several seconds, the gleam of its eye still bright, then with one twitch of its boneless body it was away, out into deeper waters. Watching it go, Joe could not help but wonder if even now it was telling tales of the black man to its fellows.

"There are some people," Noah said, "who believe that the 'shu are all parts of the Creator, who split into a billion pieces so as to pilot human souls in Quiddity, and has forgotten how to put the pieces back together again."

"So I just had a piece of God in my hands?"

"Yes." Noah reached down into the water again, and this time brought up a foot-long fish. "Too big?" he said.

"Too big!"

"The little ones slip down more easily, is that it?"

"Much easier," Joe said, and reaching into the waters plucked out two handfuls of the tiny fish. His encounter with the 'shu had taken the edge off his pickiness. Plainly these blank-eyed minnows were of a much lower order of being than the creature that had studied him so carefully. He could swallow them without concerning himself about the niceties of it. He downed two handfuls in as many seconds and then found himself something a little larger, which he bit into as though it were a sandwich. The meat of it was bright orange, and sweetly tender, and he chewed on it careless of how the thing thrashed in his grip, tossing it back only when one of its bones caught between his teeth.

"I'm done for now," he announced to Noah, working to ease the bone out.

"You won't drink?" Noah said.

"It's salty," Joe said, "isn't it?"

"Not to my palate," Noah said, lifting a cupped handful of Quiddity's waters to his lips and sucking it up noisily. "I think it's good."

Joe did the same and was not disappointed. The water had a pleasant pungency about it. He swallowed several mouthfuls and then waded back to the shore, feeling more replete than he'd imagined possible given the fare.

In the time he and Noah had been discussing fish and God, the entire procession had arrived at the crack—which was indeed growing larger: It was half as tall again as it had been when he'd stepped through it—the members of the procession now gathered at the threshold.

"Are they going through?" he said.

"It looks that way," Noah replied. He glanced up at the sky, which though it had no sun in it was darker than it had been. "If some of them remain," he said, "we may find our crew among them."

"For what ship?"

"What other ship do we have but *this?*" Noah said, slamming his palm against *The Fanacapan*.

"There are others in the harbor," Joe said, pointing along the shore towards the city. "Big ships. This thing doesn't even look seaworthy. And even if it is, how the hell are we going to persuade anyone to come with us?"

"That's my problem," Noah said. "Why don't you rest a while? Sleep if you can. We've a busy night ahead of us."

"Sleep?" Joe said. "You've gotta be kidding."

He thought about getting a blanket and a pillow out of one of the cabins, but decided it wasn't worth being lice-ridden for the little snugness they'd afford, and instead made himself as comfortable as he could on the bare stones. It was undoubtedly the most uncomfortable bed he'd ever attempted to lie upon, but the serenity of the sky made a powerful soporific, and though he never fell into a deep enough sleep to dream, he drifted for a while.

VII

*A*round four on Friday afternoon, while Tesla and Phoebe were getting to know each other in Everville, and Joe was lying under a darkening sky on Quiddity's shores, Howie Katz was sitting on the doorstep with Amy in his arms, watching a storm coming in from the northeast. A good rainstorm, he thought, maybe some thunder, and the heat would break.

The baby had not slept well the night before and had been fractious for most of the day, but now she lay contentedly in his arms, more asleep than awake. Jo-Beth had gone up to bed half an hour before, complaining of an upset stomach. The house was completely quiet. So was the street, except for the neighborhood dogs, who were busier than ever right now, racing around with their noses high and their ears pricked, all anticipation. When he'd found a better place for them all to live, they'd get a mutt, he decided. It would be good for Amy to have an animal around as she grew up, as a protector and a playmate.

"And he'll love you," Howie whispered to her. "Because everybody loves you." She grew a little restless in his arms. "Want to go lie down, honey?" he said, lifting her up and kissing her face. "Let's take you upstairs."

He tiptoed up, and laid Amy down in the spare room, so as not to disturb Jo-Beth. Then he went to take a quick shower.

It felt good to put his head under the cool water and soap off the sweat and grime of the day; so good that he sprung a hard-on without touching himself. He ignored it as best he could—shampooed his hair, scrubbed his back—but the water kept beating on it, and eventually he took himself in hand. The last time he'd made love to Jo-Beth she'd been four months pregnant, and the attempt had ended with her crying and saying she didn't want him touching her. It was the first indication of how problematic the pregnancy was to prove. During the next few months it sometimes seemed to him he was living with two women, a loving twin and her bitch-sister. The loving Jo-Beth didn't want sex but she wanted his arms around her, and his comfort when she wept. The bitch-sister wanted nothing from him: not kisses, not company, nothing. The bitch-sister would say: I wish I'd never met you, and say it with such conviction he was certain she meant it. Then the old Jo-Beth would surface again—usually through tears—and tell him she was sorry, so sorry, and she didn't know what she'd do without him.

He'd learned to curb and conceal his libido pretty well during this time. Kept a stash of skin magazines in the garage; found a soft-core channel to watch late at night; even had a couple of wet dreams. But Jo-Beth was never far from his imagination. Even in the last two weeks of her term, when she was enormous, the sight of her remained intensely arousing. She'd known it too, and seemed to resent his interest in her: locked the bathroom door when she was washing or showering, turned her back on him when she prepared for bed. She'd reduced him to a state of trembling adolescence, watching her from the corner of his eye in the hope of glimpsing the forbidden anatomy; picturing it later when he was jerking off.

He'd had enough of that. It was time they were man and wife again, instead of shy strangers who happened to share the same bed. He turned off the shower, roughly dried himself, then wrapped the towel around his waist and went into the bedroom.

Thunder was rolling in, low and cracked, but it hadn't woken Jo-

Beth. She lay fully dressed on top of the bed, her pale face silvery with sweat in the gloom. He went to the window, and opened it a crack. The clouds were bruised and fat with rain; it would only be minutes before they loosed their waters on the dusty yard and the dusty roof.

Behind him, Jo-Beth murmured in her sleep. He went back to the bed, and gently sat down beside her. Again, she murmured something—he couldn't make out what—and raised her hand from her side, grazing his shoulder with her fingers as she did so. Her hand moved on to touch her mouth, and then, as though her sleeping self had realized somebody was sitting beside her, returned to his arm.

He was certain she'd awaken, but she didn't. The faintest of smiles appeared on her face, and her hand went from his arm to his chest. Her touch was feather-light but intensely erotic. All the more so, perhaps, because her unconscious was allowing her to do what her waking self could, or would not. He let her hand dally on his chest, and while it did so he gingerly pulled at the tuck of his towel. His erection had raised its head, eager to be touched. He didn't move; didn't breathe. Just watched while her hand wandered down his hard belly until it found his dick.

He exhaled as quietly as he could, luxuriating in her attention. She didn't linger at his sex any longer than she had at chest and belly, but by the time her fingers had moved over his balls and on down his thigh he was so aroused he feared if she returned there he'd lose control. He looked away from her fingers to her face, but the sight of her troubled beauty only heated him further. He closed his eyes, tight, and tried to picture the street outside, the storm clouds, the engine he'd been working on yesterday, but her face kept finding him in his refuge.

And now he heard her murmuring again, the words still incomprehensible, and without planning to do so he opened his eyes to watch her lips.

It was too much. He gasped out loud, and as if in response the murmurs grew a little more urgent, and her hand, which had been trailing on his leg, began to move back up towards his groin. He felt the first spasm behind his balls, and reached down to take tight hold of his dick in the hope of delaying the inevitable a moment longer. But it seemed she sensed the motion, because her hand went to his sex, reaching it before he could stop her, and at her touch he overflowed.

"Oh God," he gasped, and threw back his head. He could hear her words for the first time—

"It's all right," she was saying. He could only gasp. "It's all right, Tommy. It is. It is. It's all right—"

"Tommy?"

He kept spurting, as her slickened hand worked his dick, but the pleasure was already gone.

"No," he said. "*Stop.*"

She didn't obey him because she didn't hear him. She was gabbling deliriously: "ItisitisitisallrightTommyallrightitis."

He pulled his hand off her, sick to his stomach, and started to get up off the bed. But she caught hold of his hand as he rose, her aim good despite her closed eyes. The gabbling ceased.

"Wait," she said.

His dick dribbled on, mindlessly. He was sorely tempted to straddle her right now; let her open her eyes and see it there, raw and wet. To say: It's me, *Howie.* Remember me? You *married* me.

But he was too ashamed of his vulnerability, of his sweat, and of the fear in him, tickling away in his belly even now. The fear that Tommy-Ray McGuire was close, and getting closer. Before reason could stop him he scanned the murky room, looking for some sign, any sign, of the Death-Boy. There was none, of course. He wasn't here in the flesh. At least not yet. He was in Jo-Beth's mind. And that in its way was a far more terrible place for him to be.

Snatching up his towel to cover his nakedness, Howie pulled his hand away and retreated to the door, the rage in him gone already, become ash and nausea.

Before he could reach for the handle Jo-Beth opened her eyes.

"Howie?" she said.

"Who were you expecting?"

She raised her sticky hand, sitting up as she did so. "What's been going on?" she said, her tone accusatory.

He wasn't going to let her turn this around. "You were dreaming of Tommy-Ray," he said.

She swung her legs off the bed, scraping his semen off her fingers onto the sheet as she did so. "What are you talking about?" she said. There were red blotches on her neck and upper chest; sure signs that she too had been aroused. Still was, probably.

"You kept saying his name," Howie replied.

"No, I didn't."

"You think I'd make a thing like that up?" he said, his volume rising.

"Yeah, *probably!*" she yelled.

He knew by the way she came back at him she was fully aware that he was telling the truth (she was only ever this vehement if she was concealing something), which meant she had some waking knowledge of her brother. The thought made Howie want to weep, or puke, or both. He hauled open the door and stumbled out onto the landing. As he did so the rain began—a sudden tattoo against the window. He looked up: saw the purple black clouds through the streaming glass, felt thunder rattle the house.

Amy had woken and was sobbing in the spare room. He wanted to go to her, but heard Jo-Beth at the bedroom door, and couldn't bear to be seen in the light the way he was now, with fear on his face. She'd tell Tommy-Ray, for certain, next time she saw him in her dreams. She'd say: *Come get me. You've got no opposition here.*

He stepped into the bathroom, and slammed the door behind him. After a time, Amy's crying subsided. And a little while after that, the storm passed, but it left the air uncleansed, and the heat as smothering as ever.

ii

"Grillo? It's Howie."

"I didn't expect to hear—"

"Have you heard anything m-m-m-more about Tommy-Ray?"

"Something happened?"

"Sort of."

"Want to tell me what?"

"Not right now, no, I j-j-just have to k-k-know where he is. He's coming f-f-for her—"

"Calm down, Howie."

"I k-k-*know* he's coming for her."

"He doesn't know where you live, Howie."

"He's inside her head, Grillo. He was right. I—f-f-*fuck!*—haven't stuttered in f-five years." He paused to draw a ragged breath. "I thought it was over. At least w-w-with him."

"We all did."

"I th-th-thought he was gone and it was over. But he's s-s-still there, inside her. So d-d-don't tell me he doesn't know where w-w-we live. He knows *exactly*."

"Where are you right now?"

"At a gas station half a mile from the house. I didn't want to c-c-call from there."

"You'd better get back there. Have you got any weapons?"

"I got a handgun. But what the fuck use is th-th-th-that g-g-going, going to be? I mean, if he's alive—"

"He's cheated death."

"And a handgun ain't goin' to be a h-h-hell of a lot of good."

"Shit."

"Yeah, man, right. Shit. Right. That's what it, what it, what it is. It's *fucking shit!*" Grillo heard him slam his fist against the phone. Then there was a muffled sound. It took him a moment to realize Katz was weeping.

"Listen, Howie—" The muffled sound went on. He'd put his hand over the phone, to keep Grillo from hearing. I know that feeling, Grillo thought to himself. If I cry and nobody hears, maybe I didn't cry at all. Except that it didn't work that way. "Howie? Are you there?" There was a moment or two of silence, then Howie came back on the line. The tears had calmed him a little.

"I'm here," he said.

"I'm going to drive up there. We'll work this out, somehow."

"Yeah?"

"Meantime, I want you to stay put. Understand me?"

"What if he . . . I mean, what if h-h-he comes for her?"

"Do what you have to do. Move if you have to move. But I'll keep checking in, okay?"

"Yeah."

"Anything else?"

"He's not going to get her, Grillo."

"I know that."

"Whatever the f-f-fuck it takes, he's not going to get her."

What have I done? That was all Grillo could think when he'd put the phone down: What have I done volunteering for this? He couldn't help Howie. Jesus, he could barely help himself.

He sat in front of the screens—which were filling up like barrels in a cloudburst: news coming in from every state, all of it bad—and tried to work out some way to withdraw the offer, but he knew he'd not be able to live with himself if he turned his back and something happened.

The fact was, something *would* happen. If not tonight, tomorrow night. If not tomorrow night, the night after. The world was losing its wits. The evidence was right there on the screens in front of him. What better time for the resurrected to settle their scores? He had to do what he could, however little, however meaningless, or else never meet his gaze in the mirror again.

He turned off the screens and went up to pack an overnight bag. He was just about finished, when the telephone rang. This time it was Tesla, calling from Everville.

"I'm going to be staying with a woman I met here. She needs some company right now. Have you got a pen?" Grillo took the number, then gave her a brief update on the Katz situation. She didn't sound all that surprised. "There's a lot of endgames going to get played this weekend," she said. He told her he was going to drive up to Howie's. Then the conversation turned to the subject of D'Amour.

"I always thought his totems and his tattoos were so much shit," Grillo said, "but right now—"

"You wish you had one of them?"

"I wish I had something I *believed* in," Grillo said. "Something that'd actually do some good if Tommy-Ray is on the loose."

"Oh he's probably loose," Tesla said grimly. "Just about everything that *could* be loose is loose right now."

Grillo chewed on this for a moment. Then he said, "What the fuck did we do to deserve this, Tes?"

"Just lucky, I guess."

iii

The storm that had broken over the Katzes' house moved steadily southwest, unloading its burden of rain as it went. There were a number of collisions on the slickened streets and highways, all but one of them inconsequential. The exception occurred one hundred and fifty-five miles from the house, on Interstate 84. An RV carrying a family of six, on their way home from a vacation in Cedar City, swerved on the treacherous asphalt, struck a car in the adjacent lane, and crossed the divide, taking out half a dozen vehicles traveling south before it plunged off the side of the highway.

The police, medics, and fire crews were at the scene with remarkable speed given that the highway was blocked in both directions, and the rain so torrential it reduced visibility to fifteen yards, but by the time they arrived, five lives had already ebbed away, and another three people—including the driver of the RV—were dead before they could be cut from the wreckage.

Almost as though it was intrigued by the chaos it had wrought, the storm slowed its progress and lingered over the accident scene for the better part of half an hour, its deluge weighing down the smoke that poured from the burning vehicles. In a bitter, blinding soup of smoke and rain, rescued and rescuers alike moved like phantoms, stinking and stained with blood and gasoline. Some of the survivors were lucky enough to weep; most simply stumbled from fire to fire, body to body, as if looking for their wits.

But there was one phantom here who was neither a rescuer nor in need of rescue; who moved through the hellish confusion with an ease that would inspire nightmares in all who saw him.

He was young, this phantom, and by all accounts indecently handsome: blond, tanned and smiling a wide, white smile. And he was singing. It was this, more than his easy saunter, more than his easy smile, that distressed those who spoke of him later. That he went from wreck to wreck with this bland, nameless jingle on his lips was nothing short of demoniacal.

He did not go unchallenged, however. A police officer found him reaching into the backseat of one of the wrecked vehicles and demanded he instantly desist. The phantom ignored the order and smashed the back window, reaching in for something he'd seen on the seat. Again, the officer ordered that he stop, and drew his gun to enforce his order. By way of response the phantom ceased his singing long enough to say, "I got business here."

Then, resuming the melody where he'd left off, he pulled the body of a child, her pitiful corpse overlooked in the chaos, out through the broken window. The officer leveled his weapon at the thief's heart, and ordered him to put the child down, but this, like the rest of the orders, was ignored. Slinging the body around his shoulders like a shepherd carrying a lamb, the phantom made to depart.

What followed was witnessed by five individuals, including the officer, all of them in highly agitated states, but none so traumatized as to be hallucinating. Their testimonies, however, were outlandish. Turning his back on the officer, the corpse-stealer started to amble off towards the embankment, and as he did so a convulsion ran through the smoke around him, and for a moment or two it seemed to the witnesses there were human forms in the billows—their faces long and wretched, their bodies sinewy but softened, as though they'd had their bones sucked out of them—forms that were plainly in the thief's employ, because they closed around him in a moaning cloud which no one, not even the officer, was willing to breach.

Five hours later, the body of the child—a three year old called Lorena Hernandez—was discovered less than a mile from the highway, in a small copse of birch trees. She had been stripped of her blood-stained clothing and her body carefully, even lovingly, washed in rain water. Then her little corpse had been arranged on the wet ground in a fetal position: legs tucked up snug against her belly, chin against her chest. There was no sign of any sexual molestation. The eyes, however, had gone from her head.

Of the singing beauty who'd taken her, and gone to considerable trouble to lay her out this way, there was no sign. Literally none. No foot marks in the grass, no fingerprints on her body, nothing. It was as though the abductor had *floated* as he'd gone about his grim and inexplicable ritual.

A report of these events was added to the Reef that very night, but there was nobody there to read it. Grillo was on his way to Idaho, leaving the reports to accrue behind him at an unprecedented rate. Strange, terrible stories.

In Minnesota, a man undergoing heart surgery had woken on the operating table and despite the anaesthetists' desperate attempts to return him to a comatose state, had warned his surgeons that the tail-eaters were coming, the tail-eaters were coming, and nothing could stop them. Then he'd died.

On the campus of Austin College in Texas, a woman in white, accompanied by what witnesses described as six large albino dogs, was seen disappearing into the ground as though descending a flight of stairs. There was sobbing heard from the earth, so sorrowful one of those who heard it attempted suicide an hour later.

In Atlanta, the Reverend Donald Merrill, midway through a sermon of particular ferocity, suddenly veered from his subject—*There is one love, God's love*—and began to speak about Imminence. His words were being broadcast across the nation live, and the cameras stayed on him as he pounded and paraded, his vocabulary becoming more obscure with every sentence. Then the subject veered again, on to the subject of human anatomy. The answer is *here*, he said, starting to undress in front of his astonished flock: in the breast, in the belly, in the groin. By the time he was down to his underwear and socks, the broadcast had been blacked out, but he continued to harangue his assembly anyway, instructing his appalled and fascinated congregation to go home, find a large mirror, and study themselves naked, until—as he put it—Imminence was over, and time stood still.

There was one report among those swelling the Reef that would have been of particular interest to Tesla, had she known about it; indeed might have changed the course of events to come significantly.

It came from the Baja. Two visitors from England, parapsychologists writing a book on the mysteries of mind and matter, had gone in search of a nearly mythical spot where rumor had it great and terrible events had taken place some years before. This had of course brought them to the spot where Fletcher had first created the Nuncio, the Misión de Santa Catrina. There, on a headland overlooking the blue Pacific, they'd been in the midst of photographing the ruins when one of the number who still tended the little shrine that nestled in the rubble came running up to them, tears streaming down her face, and told them that a fire had walked in the misión the night before, a fire in the form of a man.

Fletcher, she said, *Fletcher, Fletcher* . . .

But this tale, like so many others, was soon buried beneath the hundreds that were flooding in every hour from every state. Tales of the freakish and the unfathomable, of the grotesque, the filthy, and the frankly ludicrous. Unminded, unwatched, and now uncared for, the Reef grew in ignorance of itself, a body of knowledge without a head wise to its nature.

VIII

i

Finding the crossroads where Maeve O'Connell had buried the medallion had proved more difficult than Buddenbaum had anticipated. With Seth in tow, he'd spent two hours following Main Street north-northwest and south-southeast from the square, assuming (mistakenly, as it turned out) that the intersection he was seeking—that crossroads where his journey would end—would be close to the center of town. He found it eventually, two-thirds of a mile from the square; a relatively insignificant spot on Everville's map. There was a modest establishment called Kitty's Diner on one corner, opposite it a small market, and on the other two a rundown garage and what had apparently been a clothing store, its naked mannequins and EVERYTHING MUST GO signs all that remained of its final days.

"What exactly are you looking for?" Seth asked him as they stood surveying the crossroads.

"Nothing now," Buddenbaum replied.

"How do you know this is the right crossroads?"

"I can feel it. It's in the ground. You look up. I look down. We're complementaries." He locked his fingers together "Like that." He pulled, to demonstrate their adhesion.

"Can we go back to bed soon?" Seth said.

"In a while. First I'd like to take a look up there." He nodded towards the windows above the empty store. "We're going to need a vantage point."

"For the parade?" Seth asked.

Buddenbaum laughed. "No. Not for the parade."

"What for then?"

"How do I best explain?"

"Any way you like."

"There are places in the world where things are bound to happen," Buddenbaum said. "Places where powers come, where . . . " He fumbled for the words a moment, "Where *avatars* come."

"What's an avatar?"

"Well, it's a kind of face. The face of something divine."

"Like an angel?"

"More than an angel."

"More?" Seth breathed.

"More."

Seth pondered this a moment. Then he said, "These things—"

"Avatars."

"Avatars. They're coming here?"

"Some of them."

"How do you know?"

Buddenbaum stared down at the ground. "I suppose the simplest answer is that they're coming because I asked them to."

"You did?" Seth said with a little laugh. It clearly delighted him that he was chatting on a street corner with a man who made invitations to divinities. "And they just said yes?"

"It isn't the first time," Buddenbaum replied. "I've supplied many—how shall I put this?—many *entertainments* for them over the years."

"What kind of things?"

"All kinds. But mostly things that ordinary people would shudder at."

"They like those the best, do they?"

Buddenbaum regarded the youth with frank amazement. "You

grasp things very quickly," he said. "Yes. They like those the best. The more bloodshed the better. The more tears, the more grief, the better."

"That's not so different from us, is it?" Seth said, "We like that stuff too."

"Except that this isn't make-believe," Buddenbaum said. "This isn't fake blood and glycerine tears. They want the real thing. And it's my job to deliver it." He paused, watching the flow of traffic on street and sidewalk. "It isn't always the most pleasant of occupations," he said.

"So why do you do it?"

"I couldn't begin to answer that. Not here. Not now. But if you stay by my side, the answer will become apparent. Trust me."

"I do."

"Good. Well, shall we go?"

Seth nodded, and together they headed across the street towards the untenanted building.

Only when they were on the opposite side of the street, standing in the doorway of the clothing store, did Seth ask Buddenbaum, "Are you afraid?"

"Why would I be afraid?"

Seth shrugged. "I would be. Meeting avatars."

"They're just like people, only more *evolved*," Buddenbaum replied. "I'm an ape to them. We're *all* apes to them."

"So when they watch us, it's like us going to the zoo?"

"More like a safari," Buddenbaum replied, amused by the aptness of this.

"So maybe *they're* the nervous ones," Seth remarked. "Coming into the wild."

Buddenbaum stared hard at the kid. "Keep that to yourself," he said forcibly.

"It was only—"

Buddenbaum cut him short. "I shouldn't even have told you," he said.

"I won't say anything," Seth replied. "I mean, who would I tell?"

Buddenbaum looked unamused. "I won't say anything, to anybody," Seth said. "I swear." He drew a little closer to Buddenbaum, put his hand on Buddenbaum's arm. "I want to do whatever makes you happy with me," he said, staring into Buddenbaum's face. "You just tell me."

"Yes, I know. I'm sorry I snapped. I guess I *am* a little nervous." He leaned closer to the youth, his lips inches from his ears and whispered. "I want to fuck you. Right now." And with one apparently effortless motion he forced the lock on the door and led Seth inside.

This little scene had not gone unnoticed. Since his encounter with the foul-mouthed virago, Bosley had been on the alert for any further sign of Godless behavior, and had witnessed the curious intimacy between the Lundy boy, whom he'd known was crazy for years, and the stranger in the well-cut suit. He said nothing about it to Della, Doug, or Harriet. He simply told them he was going to take a short walk and slipped out, keeping his eyes locked on the empty store as he crossed the street.

The subject of sex had never been of much interest to Bosley. Three or four months might pass without him and Leticia being moved to perform the act, and when they did it was over within a quarter of an hour. But sex kept finding him, however much he attempted to purify his little corner of the world. It came in on the radio and television, it came in magazines and newspapers, dirtying what he tried so hard to keep clean.

Why, when the Lord had raised man from dust, and given him dominion over the beasts of the field, did people have such an urge to *act* like beasts, to go naked like beasts, to rut and roll in dirt like beasts?

It distressed him. Angered him sometimes too, but mostly distressed him, seeing the young people of Everville, denied the guiding principles of faith, stumbling and succumbing to the basest appetites. For some reason, perhaps because of the boy's mental disturbance, he'd thought Seth Lundy a bystander to these debaucheries. Now he suspected otherwise. Now he suspected the Lundy boy was doing something worse than his peers, far worse.

He pushed open the front door and stepped into the store. It was cooler inside than out, for which he was grateful. He paused a moment a yard over the threshold, listening for the whereabouts of the boy and his companion. There were footsteps above, and murmured voices. Weaving between the debris left by the Gingerichs, he made his way to the door out the back of the store, moving lightly and quietly. The door led in to a small storage room, beyond which lay a steep, murky flight of stairs. He crossed the room and started his ascent. As he did so, he realized the voices had stopped. He froze on the stairs, fearful his presence had been discovered. He was taking his life in his hands, spying on creatures that lived in defiance of morality. They were capable of anything, including, he didn't doubt, murder.

There was no footfall, however, and after a short pause he started up the stairs again, until he reached the door at the top. It stood an inch or two ajar. He pushed it a little wider, and listened.

Now he heard them. If dirt and depravity had a sound, then what he heard was it. Panting and slobbering and the slap of flesh on flesh. It made his skin itch to hear it, as though the air was filthy with their noise. He wanted to turn and go but he knew that was cowardice. He had to call the wrongdoers on their wrongs, the way he had the virago, or else wouldn't the world just become filthier and filthier, until people were buried in their own ordure?

The door creaked as he pushed it open, but the beasts were making too much din to hear it. The room was so configured he could not yet see them; he had to edge his way along a wall before he came to a corner around which to peep. Drawing breath in preparation, he did so.

They were there, coupling on the bare boards in a patch of sunlight, the Lundy boy naked but for his socks, his sodomizer with his trousers around his ankles. He had his eyes closed, as did the boy— how could he feel pleasure at this act, delving into a place of excrement?—but within two thrusts the sodomite opened his eyes and stared at Bosley. There was no shame on his face, nor in his voice. Only outrage.

"How *dare* you?" he said. "Get out of here!"

Now Lundy opened his eyes. Unlike his violator, he had the good grace to blush, his hand going up between his legs to conceal his sex.

"I told you, get out!" the sodomite said. Bosley didn't retreat; nor did he advance. It was the boy who made the next move. Sliding forward until he'd disengaged himself he turned to his impaler and said, "*Make* him go."

The sodomite started to pull up his pants, and while he was doing so, and vulnerable, Bosley took the offensive.

"Animals!" he raged, coming at the sodomite with his raised arms.

"Owen!" the boy yelled, but the warning came too late. As the violator started to straighten up, Bosley's weight struck him, carrying him backwards in a flailing stumble.

The boy was getting to his feet now—Bosley saw him from the corner of his eye—a wordless cry of rage roaring from his throat. Bosley glanced round at him, saw the feral look on his sallow face, teeth bared, eyes wild, and started to step out of his path. But as he did so he heard the sound of breaking glass, and looked back to see that the sodomite had fallen against the window. He had a moment only to register the fact, then the Lundy boy was on him, naked and wet.

Panic erupted in him, and a shrill sound escaped him. He tried to thrust Lundy off him, but the boy was strong. He clung to Bosley as if he wanted kisses; pressed his body hard against Bosley's body, his breath hot on Bosley's face.

"No-no-no!" Bosley shrieked, thrashing to free himself of the embrace. He succeeded in detaching himself, and retreated, gasping, almost sobbing, towards the door.

Only then did he realize that the sodomite had gone.

"Oh Christ . . . " he murmured, meaning to begin a prayer. But further words failed him. All he could do was stumble back towards the broken window, murmuring the same words over and over. "Oh Christ. Oh Christ. Oh . . . "

Lundy ignored him now. "Owen!" he yelled and was at the window in three strides, slicing his body on the jagged glass as he leaned out. Bosley was beside him a moment later, his litany ceased, and there on the sidewalk below lay the sodomite, his trousers still halfway down his thighs. Traffic had come to a halt at the crossroads, and horns were already blaring in all directions.

Dizzy with vertigo and panic, Bosley retreated from the window.

"Fuckhead!" the Lundy kid yelled, and apparently thinking Bosley meant to escape, came after him afresh, blood running from his wounded flank.

Bosley tried to avoid the youth's fists, but his heel caught in a tangle of discarded clothes and he fell backwards, the breath knocked from him when he hit the ground. Lundy was on him in a second, setting his skinny butt on Bosley's chest and pinning Bosley's upper arms with his knees. That was how they were found, when the first witnesses came racing up the stairs: Bosley on his back, sobbing *Oh Christ, Oh Christ, Oh Christ* while the naked, wounded Seth Lundy kept him nailed to the boards.

11

Whatever speculations Erwin had entertained where death was concerned, he'd not expected the experience to be hard on the feet. But he'd walked further in the last six hours than in the previous two months. Out from the house, then back to the house, then down to Kitty's Diner, then back to the house again, and now, drawn by the sight of an ambulance careening down Cascade Street, back to the diner again. Or rather, to the opposite corner, in time to see a man who'd been pushed from an upper window being loaded into the back of an ambulance and taken off to Silverton. He hung around the crowd, picking up clues as to what had happened, and quickly pieced the story together. Apparently Bosley Cowhick had done the deed, having discovered the pushee in the middle of some liaison with a local boy. Erwin knew Bosley by reputation only: as a philanthropist at Christmas, when he and several good Christian souls made it their business to take a hot dinner to the elderly and the housebound, and as a rabid letter writer (barely a month would go by without a missive in the *Register* noting some fresh evidence of Godlessness in the community). He had never met the man, nor could even bring his face to mind. But if it was notoriety he was after, he'd plainly got it this afternoon.

"Damn strange," he heard somebody say, and scanning the dispersing crowd saw a man in his late fifties, early sixties, gray hair, gray eyes, badly fitting suit, looking straight at him.

"Are you talking to me?" Erwin said.

"Yeah," said the other, "I was saying, it's damn strange—"

"You can't be."

"Can't be what?"

"Can't be talking to me. I'm dead."

"That makes two of us," the other man replied, "I was saying, I've seen some damn strange things around here over the years."

"You're dead too?" Erwin said, amazed and relieved. Finally, somebody to talk to.

"Of course," the man said. "There's a few of us around town. Where did you come in from?"

"I didn't."

"You mean you're a local man?"

"Yeah. I only just, you know—"

"Died. You can say it."

"Died."

"Only some people come in for the Festival. They make a weekend of it."

"Dead people."

"Sure. Hey, why not? A parade's a parade, right? A few of us even tag along, you know, between the floats. Anything for a laugh. You gotta laugh, right, or you'd break your heart. Is that what happened? Heart attack?"

"No . . . " Erwin said, still too surprised by this turn of events to have his thoughts in order. "No, I . . . I was—"

"Recent, was it? It's cold in the beginning. But you get used to that. Hell, you can get used to anything, right? Long as you don't start looking back, regretting things, 'cause there's not a hell of a lot you can do about it."

"Is that right?"

"We're just hanging on awhile, that's all. What's your name, by the way?"

"Erwin Toothaker."

"I'm Richard Dolan."

"Dolan? The candy store owner?"

The man smiled. "That's me," he said. He jabbed his thumb over his shoulder at the empty building. "This was my store, back in the good old days. Actually, they weren't so good. It's just, you know, when you look back—"

"The past's always prettier."

"That's right. The past's always—" He halted, frowning. "Say, were you around when I owned the store?"

"No."

"So how the hell do you know about it?"

"I heard a confession by a friend of yours."

Dolan's easy smile faded. "Oh?" he said. "Who's that?"

"Lyle McPherson?"

"He wrote a confession?"

"Yep. And it got lost, till I found it."

"Sonofabitch."

"Is he, I mean McPherson, is he still . . . in the vicinity?"

"You mean is he like us? No. Some people hang around, some people don't," Dolan shrugged. "Maybe they move on, somewhere or other, maybe they just"—he clicked his fingers—"disappear. I guess I wanted to stay and he didn't."

"These aren't our real bodies, you know that?" Erwin said. "I mean, I've seen mine."

"Yeah, I got to see mine too. Not a pretty sight." He raised his hands in front of him, scrutinizing his palms. "But whatever we're made of," he said, "it's better than nothing. And you know it's no better or worse than living. You get good days, you get bad days . . . " He trailed away, his gaze going to the middle of the street. "'Cept I think maybe all that's comin' to an end."

"What makes you say that?"

Dolan drew a deep breath. "After a while you get to feel the rhythm of things, in a way you can't when you're living. Like smoke."

"What's like smoke?" he said.

"We are. Floatin' around, not quite solid, not quite not. And when there's something weird in the wind, smoke knows."

"Really?"

"You'll get the hang of it."

"Maybe I already did."

"What'd you mean?"

"Well if you want to see something weird, you don't have to look any further than my house. There's a guy there called Fletcher. He looks human, but I don't think he is."

Dolan was fascinated. "Why'd you invite him in?"

"I didn't. He . . . just came."

"Wait a minute . . . " Dolan said, beginning to comprehend. "This guy Fletcher, is he the reason you're here?"

"Yes . . . " Erwin said, his voice thickening. "He murdered me. Sucked out my life, right there in my own living room."

"You mean he's some kind of vampire?"

Erwin looked scornful. "Don't be absurd. This isn't a late-night movie, it's my life. *Was* my life. *Was! Was!*" He was suddenly awash in tears. "He didn't have any right—any right at all—to do this to me. I had thirty years in me, thirty good years, and he just—just takes them away. I mean, why me? What have I ever done to anybody?" He looked at Dolan. "You did something you shouldn't have done, and you paid the price. But I was a useful member of society."

"Hey, wait up," Dolan said testily. "I was as useful as you ever were."

"Come on now, Dolan. I was an attorney. I was dealing with matters of life and death. You sold cavities to kids."

Dolan jabbed his finger in Erwin's direction. "Now you take that back," he said.

"Why would I do that?" Erwin said. "It's the truth."

"I put some pleasure in people's lives. What did you ever do, besides get yourself murdered?"

"Now you take care."

"You think your customers will mourn you, Toothaker? No. They'll say: Thank God, there's one less lawyer in the world."

"I told you, take care!"

"I'm quaking, Toothaker." Dolan raised his hand. "Look at that, shaking like a leaf."

"If you're so damn strong why'd you put a bullet through your brain, huh? Gun slip, did it?"

"Shut up."

"Or were you just so full of guilt—"

"I said—"

"So full of guilt the only thing left to do was kill yourself?"

"I don't have to listen to this," Dolan said, turning his back and stalking away.

"If it's any comfort," Erwin called after him, "I'm sure you made a lot of people very happy."

"Asshole!" Dolan yelled back at him, and before Erwin had a chance to muster a reply, was gone, like smoke in a high wind.

IX

i

We have our crew, Joe."

Joe opened his eyes. Noah was standing a little way up the beach with six individuals standing a couple of yards behind him, two of them less than half Noah's height, one a foot taller, the other three broad as stevedores. He could make out little else. The brightness had almost gone out of the sky entirely. Now it simmered like a pot of dark pigments—purples and grays and blues—that shed a constantly shifting murk on the beach and sea.

"We should get moving," Noah went on. "There are currents to catch."

He turned to the six crew members, and spoke to them in a voice Joe had not heard from him before, low and monotonous. They moved to their tasks without so much as a murmur, one of the smaller pair clambering up into the wheelhouse while the other five went to the bow of *The Fanacapan* and began to push the vessel down the beach. It was a plainly backbreaking labor, even if they made no sound of complaint, and Joe went to lend a hand. But Noah intercepted him. "They can do it," he said, drawing Joe out of the way.

"How did you hire them?"

"They're volunteers."

"You must have promised them something."

"They're doing it for love," Noah said.

"I don't get it."

"Don't concern yourself," Noah said. "Let's just be away while we can." He turned to watch the volunteers pushing the boat out. The waves were breaking against the stern now, sending up fans of spray. "The news is worse than I'd imagined," Noah went on, now turning his gaze towards the invisible horizon. Lightning was moving through the clouds that coiled there, the bolts, if that was what they were, vast and serpentine. Some rose from sea to sky, describing vivid scrawls that burned in the eye after they'd gone. Some came at each other like locomotives, and, colliding, gave birth to showers of smaller bolts. Some simply fell in blazing sheets and seemed to sink into the sea, their brilliance barely dimmed by the fathoms, until they drowned.

"News about what?" Joe asked.

"About what's out there."

"And what *is* out there?"

"I suppose you should be told," Noah replied. "The Iad Uroboros is moving this way. The greatest evil in this world or yours."

"What is it?"

"Not *it*. Them. It's a nation. A people. Not remotely like us, but a people nevertheless, who've always harbored a hunger to be in your world."

"Why?"

"Does appetite need reasons?" Noah said. "They've tried before, and been stopped. But this time—"

"What's being done about it?"

"The volunteers don't know. I'm not sure they even care." He drew a little closer to Joe. "One thing," he said. "Don't engage them in conversation, however tempted you are. Their silence is part of my deal with them." Joe looked puzzled. "Don't ask," Noah said, "for fear you won't like the answer. Just believe me, this is for the best." The vessel was in the water now, rising and falling as the waves broke against it. "We'd better get aboard," Noah said, and with more strength in his limbs than Joe he strode out into the surf and was hauled up onto the deck by one of the volunteers, all of whom were now aboard. Joe followed, his mind a mass of confusions.

"We're out of our minds," he told Noah once he was aboard. The volunteers were at the oars and laboring to row the vessel out beyond the breakers. Joe had to yell above the noise of sea and creaking timbers. "You know that? We're out of our fucking minds!"

"Why's that?" Noah yelled back.

"Look what we're heading into!" Joe hollered, pointing out towards the maelstrom.

"You're right," Noah said, catching hold of a rope ladder to keep from being thrown off his feet. "This may be the end of us both." He laughed, and for a moment Joe considered throwing himself overboard and striking out for the shore while he was still within swimming distance. "But my friend," Noah went on, laying his hand on Joe's shoulder. "You've come so far. So very far. And why? Because you know in your heart this is *your* journey as much as it's mine. You *have* to take it, or you'll regret it for the rest of your life."

"Which would at least be *long*," Joe yelled.

"Not without power," Noah replied. "Without power it's over in a couple of breaths, and before you know it you're on your deathbed thinking: Why didn't I trust my instinct? Why didn't I *dare?*"

"You talk like you know me," Joe replied, irritated by Noah's presumption. "You don't."

"Isn't it a universal truth that men regret their lives?" Noah said. "And die wishing they could live again?" Joe had no reply to this. "If you want to make for shore," Noah went on, "best do it quickly."

Joe glanced back at the beach, and was astonished to see that in this short time the vessel had cleared the breakers and was in the grip of a current that was carrying it away from land at no little speed. He looked along the darkened shore towards the city, its harbor lights twinkling, then back to the crack, and the small encampment around it. Then, determined he would regret nothing, he turned his back on the sight, and his face towards the raging seas ahead.

ii

Tesla and Phoebe had little in common, beyond their womanhood. Tesla had traveled; Phoebe had not. Phoebe had been married; Tesla had not. Tesla had never been in love, not obsessively; Phoebe had, and still was.

It made her curiously open, Tesla soon discovered; as though anything was plausible in a world where passion held sway. And sway it held; no doubt of that. Though they knew each other scarcely at all, Phoebe seemed to sense an uncensorious soul in Tesla, and soon began to freely talk about the scandal in which she'd played so large a role. More particularly, she spoke of Joe Flicker—of his eyes, his kisses, his ways in bed—all of this with a sweet boastfulness, as if he were a prize she had been awarded for suffering a life with Morton. The world was strange, she said several times, apropos of how they'd met, or how quickly they'd discovered the depth of their feelings.

"I know," Tesla said, wondering as she listened how much this woman would accept if and when she asked for Tesla's story in return. That was put to the test when Tesla got off the phone from Grillo, and Phoebe, who'd been in the room throughout the call said, "What was that all about?"

"You really want to know?"

"I asked, didn't I?"

She began with the easy stuff: Grillo, and the Reef, and how she'd traveled the states in the last five years, discovering in the progress that things were damn weird out there.

"Like how?" Phoebe said.

"This is going to sound crazy."

"I don't care," said Phoebe. "I want to know."

"I think maybe we're coming to the end of being what we are. We're going to take an evolutionary jump. And that makes this a dangerous and wonderful time."

"Why dangerous?"

"Because there are things that don't want us to take the jump. Things that'd prefer us to stay just the way we are, wandering around blindly, afraid of our own shadows, afraid of being dead and afraid of being too much alive. They want to keep us that way. But then there's people everywhere saying: I'm not going to be blind. I'm not going to be afraid. I can see invisible roads. I can hear angel's voices. I know who I was before I was born and I know what I want to be when I'm dead."

"You've met people like this?"

"Oh yes."

"That's wonderful," said Phoebe. "I don't know if I believe any of those things, but it's still wonderful." She got to her feet and went to the refrigerator, talking on as she surveyed the contents. "What about the things that want to stop us?" she said. "I don't think I believe in the Devil, so maybe you're right about that, but if not the Devil then who are these people?"

"That's another conversation," Tesla said.

"Want to talk while we eat?" Phoebe said. "I'm getting hungry. How about you?"

"Getting that way."

"There's nothing worth having in there," she said, closing the fridge. "We'll have to go out. You want pizza? Chicken?"

"I don't care. Anywhere but that fucking diner."

"You mean Bosley's place?"

"What an asshole."

"The hamburgers are good."

"I had the fish."

They walked rather than taking the car, and while they walked Phoebe told Tesla how she'd come to gain a lover and lose a husband. The more she told, the more Tesla warmed to her. She was a curious mingling of small-town pretensions (she plainly thought her self better than most of her fellow Evervillians) and charming self-deprecation (especially on the subject of her weight); funny at times (she was wittily indiscreet about the medical problems of those who, upon seeing her on the sidewalk, played the Pharisee) and at other times (speaking about Joe, and how she'd almost given up believing she could be loved that way) sweetly touching.

"You've got no idea where he's gone, then?" Tesla said.

"No." Phoebe surveyed the thronged street ahead of them. "He can't hide in a crowd, that's for sure. When he comes back he'll have to be really careful."

"You're sure he'll come back?"

"Sure I'm sure. He promised." She cast Tesla a sideways glance. "You think I sound stupid."

"No, just trusting."

"We've all got to trust somebody, right?"

"Do we?"

"If you could feel what I feel," Phoebe said, "you wouldn't ask that question."

"All I know is, you're alone in the end. Always."

"Who's talking about the end?" Phoebe said.

Tesla stepped out of the stream of people into the street, taking Phoebe with her. "Listen to me," she said, "something terrible's going to happen here. I don't know exactly *what* and I don't know exactly *when*, but trust me: This place is finished."

Phoebe said nothing at first. She simply looked up and down the busy street. Then, after a moment to consider, she said, "It can't happen fast enough as far as I'm concerned."

"You mean that?"

"Just 'cause I live here doesn't mean I like it," Phoebe replied. "I'm not saying I believe you, I'm just saying if it happens you won't hear any complaints from me."

She's quite a piece of work, Raul said when they found a table at the pizza parlor, and Phoebe had gone off to relieve herself.

"I wondered where you'd got to."

I was just enjoying the girl-talk, Raul said. *She's one angry lady.*

"She's no lady," Tesla said, "that's what I like about her. Pity about her boyfriend."

You think he's gone for good, right?

"Don't you?"

Probably. Why are you wasting time with her? I mean she's very entertaining, but we came here to find Fletcher.

"I can't go back to Toothaker's house alone," Tesla replied. "I just can't. Soon as I smelled that smell—"

Maybe it was just a backed-up sewer.

"And maybe it was Lix," Tesla said. "And whoever raised them's already killed Fletcher."

But we have to get in to find out.

"Right."

And you think this woman's going to lend some moral support?

"If it's not her who's it going to be? I can't wait till Lucien comes crawling back."

I knew we'd get to him—

"I'm not blaming you, I'm just saying: I need help, and she's the only help available."

Suppose she comes to some serious harm?

"I don't want to think about that."

You have to.

"What are you, Jiminy Cricket? I'll be honest with her. I'll tell her what we're up against—"

So then you're not responsible, is that it? Tesla, she's just an ordinary woman.

"So was I," Tesla reminded him.

Whatever you were, Tesla, I don't think you were ever ordinary.

"Thank you."

My pleasure.

"She's coming back. I'm going to tell her, Raul. I have to."

It'll end in tears—

"Doesn't it always?"

*   *   *

It was a hell of a conversation to have over a pepperoni pizza, but Phoebe's appetite wasn't visibly curbed by anything that Tesla had to say. She listened without comment as Tesla went through her experiences in the Loop, detail by terrible detail, stopping every now and then to say: *I know this sounds ridiculous* or *You probably think this is crazy* until Phoebe told her not to bother, because yes, it was crazy, but she didn't care. Tesla took her at her word, and continued the account without further interruption, until she got to the matter of the Lix. Here she stopped.

"What's the problem?" Phoebe wanted to know.

"I'll leave this bit to later."

"Why?"

"It's disgusting, is why. And we're eating."

"If you can bear to tell it, it won't bother me. I've worked in a doctor's office for eight years, remember? I've seen everything."

"You never saw anything like a Lix," Tesla said, and went on to describe them and their conception, dropping her volume even lower than it had been. Phoebe was unfazed.

"And you think it was one of these Lix things you saw in Erwin's house?"

"I think it's possible, yes."

"This guy Fletcher made them?"

"I doubt it."

"Then what?"

"Somebody who meant Fletcher harm. Somebody who came after him, and found him there and—" She threw up her hands. "The fact is, I don't know. And the only way I'll find out—"

"Is by going in there."

"Right."

"Seems to me," Phoebe said, "if the Lix are real—I'm not saying they are, I'm saying *if* they are—and if they're made of what you say they're made of, they shouldn't be that hard to kill."

"Some they grow six, seven feet long," Tesla said.

"Huh. And you've actually seen these things?"

"Oh, I've seen them." She turned her gaze out through the window, in part so as not to look at the congealing pizza on her plate, in part so that Phoebe couldn't see the fear in her eyes. "They got into my apartment in L.A.—"

"What did they do: Come up through the toilet?"

Tesla didn't reply.

You're going to have to tell her, Raul murmured in her head.

"Well?" Phoebe said.

Tell her about Kissoon.

"She'll freak," Tesla thought.

She's doing pretty well so far.

Tesla glanced back at Phoebe, who was finishing off her pizza while she waited for a reply.

"Once I've started with Kissoon, where do I stop?" she said to Raul.

You should have thought of that before you mentioned the Lix. It's all part of the same story.

Silence from Tesla.

Isn't it? he prodded.

"I guess so."

So tell her. Tell her about Kissoon. Tell her about the Loop. Tell her about the Shoal. Tell her about Quiddity if she hasn't got up and left.

"Did you know your lips move when you're thinking?" Phoebe said.

"They do?"

"Just a little."

"Well—I was debating something."

"What?"

"Whether I could tell you the truth, the whole truth, and nothing but—"

"And have you decided?"

Tell her.

"Yes. I've decided," Tesla leaned forward, pushing her plate aside. "In answer to your question," she said, "no, the Lix didn't come up from the toilet. They came from a loop in time—"

This was the tale she'd never told. Not in its entirety. She'd given Grillo and D'Amour the bare outlines, of course, but she'd never been able to bring herself to fill in the details. They were too painful, too ugly. But she told it now, to this woman she barely knew, and once she'd begun it wasn't so difficult, not with the clatter of plates and the chatter of patrons all around them; a wall of normality to keep the past from catching hold of her heart.

"There was a man called Kissoon," she began, "and I think if we had to make a list of the worst people to have graced the planet he'd probably be somewhere near the top. He was a—what was he?—a shaman, he called himself, but that doesn't really get to it. He had power, a lot of power. He could play with time, he could get in and out of people's heads, he could make Lix—"

"So he was the one."

"It's an old trick, apparently. Sorcerers have been doing it for centuries. And when I say sorcerers I'm not talking about rabbits and hats, I'm talking about people who could change the world—who *have* changed the world, sometimes—in ways we'll never completely understand."

"Are they all men?" Phoebe wanted to know.

"Most of them."

"Hmm."

"So Kissoon was one of a group of these people, they were called the Shoal, and they were dedicated to keeping the rest of us from ever knowing about—" She paused here a moment.

"Go on," said Phoebe. "I'm listening."

"About a place called Quiddity."

"Quiddity?"

"That's right. It's a sea, where we go sometimes in dreams."

"And why aren't we supposed to know about it?" Phoebe asked. "If we go there in dreams, what's the big secret?"

Tesla chewed on this a moment. "You know, I don't know? I always assumed—what did I assume?—I guess I assumed that the Shoal were the wise ones, and if they lived and died keeping this secret it was because the secret needed to be kept. But now that you mention it, I don't really know why."

"But they're all dead now anyway."

"All dead. Kissoon murdered them."

"Why?"

"So that he could eventually have control over the greatest power in the world. A power called the Art."

"And what's that?"

"I don't think anyone really knows."

"Not even this guy Kissoon?"

Tesla pondered this a moment. "No," she said eventually, "not even Kissoon."

"So he committed these murders to get something when he didn't even know what the something was?" she said, her incredulity perfectly plain.

"Oh, he did more than murder. He hid the bodies in the past—"

"Oh come on."

"I swear. He'd killed some of the most important people in the world. More important than the pope or the president. He had to hide the bodies where they'd never be found. He chose a place called Trinity."

"What's that?"

"The *when*'s more important than the *where*," Tesla said. "Trinity's where the first A-bomb was detonated. Sixteenth of June, nineteen forty-five. In New Mexico."

"And you're telling me that's where he took the people he'd murdered."

"That's where he took 'em. Except—"

"What?"

"Once he was there, he made a mistake—a little mistake—and he got himself trapped."

"Trapped in the past?"

"Right. With the bomb ticking away. So—he made a loop of time, that went round and round on itself, always keeping that moment at bay." Phoebe smiled and shook her head. "What?" said Tesla.

"I don't whether you're crazy or what, but if you made all this up, you should be selling it. I mean, you could make a movie for TV—"

"It's not a movie. It's the truth. I know, because I was there three times. Three times, in and out of Kissoon's Loop."

"So you actually *met* this guy?" Phoebe said.

"Oh sure, I met him," Tesla replied.

"And—?"

"What was he like?" Phoebe nodded; Tesla shrugged. "Hard to find the words," she said.

"Try."

"I've spent five years trying not to think of him. But he's there all the time. Every day something—something dirty, something cruel, maybe just the smell of my own shit—reminds me of him. He wasn't much to look at, you know? He was this runt of a guy, old and dried up. But he could turn you inside out with a look. See inside your head. See inside your guts. Work you, fuck you." She rubbed her palms together, to warm them, but they wouldn't be warmed.

"What happened to him?"

"He couldn't hold the moment."

Phoebe looked vacant. "What?"

"The little loop of time that kept the bomb from being detonated," Tesla explained, "he couldn't hold it."

"So the bomb went off?"

"The bomb went off and he went with it."

"You were there?"

"Not right there, or I would have gone up with him. But I was the last out, I'm sure of that." She settled back in her chair. "That's it. Or as much of it as I can tell you right now."

"It's quite a story."

"And you don't believe a word of it."

"Some bits I *almost* believe. Some bits just sound ridiculous to me. And some bits—some bits I don't want to believe. They frighten me too much."

"So you won't be coming with me to Erwin's house?"

"I didn't say that," Phoebe replied.

Tesla smiled, and dug into the pocket of her leather jacket.

"What are you looking for?"

"Some cash," she said. "If you're willing to dare Lix with me, the least I can do is pay for the pizza."

X

i

*A*s the streets started to empty, Erwin began to regret his contretemps with Dolan. Though his feet ached, and he felt weary to his imagined marrow, he knew without putting it to the test that phantoms didn't sleep. He would be awake through the hours of darkness, while the living citizens of Everville, safe behind locked doors and bolted windows, took a trip to dreamland. He wandered down the middle of Main Street like a lonely drunk, wishing he could find the woman he'd whispered to outside Kitty's Diner. She at least had heard him, if only remotely, whereas nobody else with a heart beating in their chests even glanced his way, however loud he shouted. There'd been something special about that woman, he decided. Perhaps she'd been psychic.

He did not go entirely ignored. At the corner of Apple Street he encountered Bill and Maisie Waits, out walking their two chocolate labradors. As they approached Erwin the dogs seemed to sense his presence. Did they smell him or see him? He couldn't be sure. But they responded with raised hackles and growls, the bitch standing her ground, the male dashing away down Apple Street, trailing his leash. Bill—who was in his fifties and far from fit—went after him, yelling.

The animal's response distressed Erwin. He'd never owned a dog, but by and large he liked the species. Was being a phantom so profoundly unnatural a state that the nearest whiff of him was enough to make the beasts crazy?

He went down on his haunches, and softly called to the bitch.

"It's okay . . . it's okay . . . " he said, extending his hand, "I'm not going to hurt anybody—"

The animal barked on ferociously, while Maisie watched her husband pursue the other dog. Erwin crept a little closer, still murmuring words of reassurance, and the bitch showed signs of hearing him. She cocked her head, and her barking became more sporadic.

"That's it," Erwin said, "that's it. See, that's not so bad, now is it?" His open hand was now maybe two feet from her nose. Her din had lost all its ferocity, and was now reduced to little more than an occasional bark. Erwin reached a little further, and touched her head. She stopped barking entirely now, and lay down, rolling onto her back to have her stomach scratched.

Maisie Waits looked down at her. "Katy, what on earth are you doing?" she said. "Get up." She lugged on the leash, to raise the animal, but Katy was enjoying Erwin's attentions too much. She made a little growl as though vaguely remembering that her stroker had frightened her a minute or two before, and then gave up even on that.

"*Katy,*" Maisie Waits said, exasperated now, then, to her husband, "Did you find him?"

"Does it *look* like I found him?" Bill gasped. "He's headed off down towards the creek. He'll find his way home."

"But the traffic—"

"There *is* no traffic," Bill said. "Well, hardly any. And he's got lost before, for God's sake." Bill had reached the corner of the street now, and he stared at the recumbent Katy. "Look at you, you soft old thing," he said fondly, and went down on his haunches beside the dog. "I don't know what spooked him that way."

"Me," Erwin said, stroking the bitch's belly along with Bill. The dog heard. She pricked her ears and looked at Erwin. Bill, of course, heard nothing. Erwin kept talking anyway, the words tumbling out.

"*Listen*, will you, Waits? If a mutt can hear me you damn well can. Just listen. I'm Erwin Toothaker—"

"As long as you're sure," Maisie was saying.

"Erwin Toothaker."

"I'm sure," Bill replied. "He'll probably be home before us." He patted Katy's solid belly, and got to his feet. "Come on, old girl," he said. Then, with a sly glance at his wife: "You too, Katy."

Maisie Waits nudged him in the ribs. "William Waits," she said in a tone of mock outrage.

Bill leaned a little closer to her. "Want to fool around some?" he said to her.

"It's late—"

"It's Saturday tomorrow," Bill said, slipping his arm around his wife's waist. "It's either that or I *ravish* you in your sleep."

Maisie giggled, and with one quick jerk on the leash got Katy to her feet. Bill kissed Maisie's cheek, and then whispered something into his wife's ear. Erwin wasn't close enough to hear everything, but he caught *pillow* and *like always*. Whatever he said, Maisie returned his kiss, and they headed off down the street, with Katy casting a wistful glance back at her phantom admirer.

"Were you ever married, Erwin?"

It was Dolan. He was sitting in the doorway of Lively's Lighting and Furniture Store, picking his nose.

"No, I wasn't."

"Mine went off to Seattle after I passed over. Took her seven weeks and two days to uproot and go. Sold the house, sold most of the furniture, let the lease go on the store. I was so mad. I howled around this damn town for a month, weeping and wailing. I even tried to go after her."

"And?"

Dolan shook his head. "I don't advise it. The further I went from Everville the more . . . vague . . . I became."

"Any idea why?"

"Just guessing, but I suppose me and this place must be connected, after all these years. Maybe I can't imagine myself in any other place. Anyhow, I don't weep and wail any more. I know where I belong." He looked at Erwin. "Speaking of which, I came looking for you for a reason."

"What?"

"I was talking to a few friends of mine. Telling them about you and what happened outside my old store, and they wanted to see you."

"This is more—"

"Go on. You can say it."

"Ghosts?"

"We prefer revenants. But yeah, ghosts'll do it."

"Why do they want to see me?"

Dolan got up. "What the hell does it matter to you?" he hollered, suddenly exasperated, "got something better to be doing?"

"No," Erwin said after a moment.

"So are you coming or not? Makes no odds to me."

"I'm coming."

ii

Buddenbaum woke up in a white room, with a splitting headache. There was a sallow young man standing at the bottom of the bed, watching him.

"There you are," the young man said.

Clearly the youth knew him. But Buddenbaum couldn't put a name to his face. His puzzlement was apparently plain, because the kid said, "Owen? It's me. It's Seth."

"Seth." The name made a dozen images flicker in Buddenbaum's head, like single frames of film, each from a different scene, strung together on a loop. Round and round they went, ten, twenty times. He glimpsed bare skin, a raging face, sky, more faces, now looking down at him.

"I fell."

"Yes."

Buddenbaum ran his palms over his chest, neck, and stomach. "I'm intact."

"You broke some ribs, and cracked some vertebrae and fractured the base of your skull."

"I did?" Buddenbaum's hands went to his head. It was heavily bandaged. "How long have I been unconscious?"

"Coming up to eight hours."

"Eight hours?" He sat up in bed. "Oh my Lord."

"You have to lie down."

"No time. I've got things to do. Important things." He put his hand to his brow. "There's people coming. I've got to be . . . got to be . . . Jesus, it's gone out of my head." He looked up at Seth, with desperation on his face. "This is bad," he said, "this is very bad." He grabbed hold of Seth, and drew him closer. "There was some liaison, yes?" Seth didn't know the word. "You and I, we were coupling—"

"Oh. That. Yes. Yes, we were goin' at it, and this guy Bosley, he's a real Christian—"

"Never mind the Christians." Buddenbaum snarled. "Do you trust me?"

"Of course I trust you," Seth said, putting his hand to Buddenbaum's face. "You told me what's going to happen."

"I did, did I? And what did I say?"

"You said there's *avatars* coming." Seth pronounced the word haltingly. "They're more than angels, you said."

Comprehension replaced the despair on Buddenbaum's face. "The avatars," he said. "Of course." He started to swing his legs off the bed.

"You can't get up," Seth said, "you're hurt."

"I've survived worse than this, believe me," Buddenbaum said. "Now where are my clothes?" He stood up, and made for the small dresser in the corner of the room. "Are we still in Everville?"

"No, we're in Silverton."

"How far's that?"

"Thirty-five miles."

"So how did you get here?"

"I borrowed my mother's car. But Owen, you're not well—"

"There's more at risk here than a cracked skull," Buddenbaum replied, opening the dresser, and taking out his clothes. "A lot more."

"Like what?"

"It's too complicated—"

"I catch on quickly," Seth replied. "You know I do. You said I do."

"Help me dress."

"Is that all I'm good for?" Seth protested. "I'm not just some idiot kid you picked up."

"Then stop acting like one!" Buddenbaum snapped.

Seth immediately withdrew. "Well I guess that's plain enough," he said.

"I didn't mean it that way."

"You want somebody to dress you, ask the nurse. You want a ride back home, hire a cab."

"Seth—"

It was too late. The boy was already out of the door, slamming it behind him.

Owen didn't try to go after him. This was no time to waste energy arguing. The boy would come round, given time. And if he didn't, he didn't. In a few hours he would not need the aid—or the affection—of Seth or any other self-willed youth. He would be free of every frailty, including love; free to live out of time, out of place, out of every particular. He would be unmade, the way divinities were unmade, because divinities were without beginning and without end: a rare and wonderful condition.

As he was halfway through dressing, the doctor—a whey-faced young man with wispy blond hair—appeared.

"Mr. Buddenbaum, what are you doing?" he asked.

"I would have thought that perfectly obvious," Owen replied.

"You can't leave."

"On the contrary. I can't *stay*. I have work to do."

"I'm amazed you're even standing," the doctor said. "I insist you get back into bed."

He crossed to Owen, who raised his arms. "Leave me be," he said. "If you want to make yourself useful, call me a cab."

"If you attempt to leave," the doctor said, "I will not be responsible for the consequences."

"Fine by me," Owen replied. "Now will you please leave me to dress in peace?"

iii

For a city of such modest scale, Everville boasted an unusually large number of cemeteries. St. Mary's Catholic Cemetery lay two miles outside the city limits on the Mulino road, but the other three, the Pioneer Cemetery (the smallest and most historically significant), the Potter Cemetery (named for the family who had buried more people in the region than any other), and the plain old Everville Cemetery, were all within the bounds of the city. It was to the Potter Cemetery, which lay on Lambroll Drive, close to the Old Post Office building, that Dolan took Erwin.

He chatted in his lively fashion as they went, mostly about how much the city had changed in the last few years. None of it was for the better, in his opinion. So many of the things that had been part of Everville's history—the family businesses, the older buildings, even the streetlamps—were being uprooted or destroyed.

"I didn't think much about that kind of thing when I was breathing," Dolan remarked. "You don't, do you? You get on with your life as best you can. Hope the taxman doesn't come after you; hope you can still get it up on Saturday night; hope your hair doesn't fall out too quickly. You don't have time to think about the past, until you're part of it. And then—"

"Then?"

"Then you realize what's gone is gone forever, and that's a damn shame if it was something worth keeping." He pointed over at the Post Office building, which had been left to fall into dereliction since a larger and more centralized facility had opened in Salem. "I mean look at that," he said. "That could have been preserved, right? Turned into something for the community."

"What *community?*" said Erwin. "There isn't one. There's just a few thousand people who happen to live next door to one another, and hate the sight of each other eighty percent of the time. Believe me, I saw a lot of that in my business. People suing each other 'cause a fence was in the wrong place, or a tree had been cut down. Nice neighbors, you'd say, looking at them: regular folks with good hearts. But let me tell you, if the law allowed it, they'd murder each other at the drop of a hat."

This last remark was out of his mouth before he realized quite what he'd said. "I was just trying to protect the children," Dolan muttered.

"I wasn't talking about you," Erwin replied. "What you did—"

"Was wrong. I know that. We made a terrible error, and I'll regret it forever. But we did it because we thought we had to."

"And how did your precious community treat you when they realized you'd screwed up? Like pariahs, right?" The other man said nothing. "So much for the community," Erwin said.

They did not speak again until they reached the gates of Potter's Cemetery, when Dolan said, "Do you know who Hubert Nordhoff is?"

"Didn't his family own the mill?"

"A lot more than the mill. He was a great man hereabouts, for fifty years."

"So what about him?"

"He holds court on the last Friday of every month."

"Here?" Erwin said, peering through the ironwork gate into the cemetery. There was a thin veil of clouds covering the moon, but it was light enough to see the graves laid out ahead. Here and there a carved angel or an urn marked the resting place of a family with money to waste, but most of the tombs were simple stones.

"Yes, here," said Erwin, and led him inside.

There was an ancient, moss-covered oak at the far end of the cemetery, and there, under its titanic branches, was an assembly of six men and a woman. Some lounged on stones; one—a fellow who looked sickly even for a dead soul—sitting on the lowest of the branches. And standing close to the trunk of the tree, presently addressing the group, was a man in his seventies, his dress, his spectacles, and his somewhat formal manner suggesting he had lived and died in a earlier age. Erwin did not need Dolan whispering in his ear to know that this was the aforementioned Hubert Nordhoff. He was presently in full and rhetorical flight.

"Are we unloved? My friends, we are. Are we forgotten? By all but a few, I'm afraid so. And do we care? My friends, do we care?" He let his sharp blue gaze rest on every one of his congregation before he answered, "Oh my Lord, *yes*. To the bottom of our broken hearts, we care." He stopped here, looking past his audience towards Dolan and Erwin. He inclined his head.

"Mr. Dolan," he said.

"Mr. Nordhoff." Dolan turned towards Erwin. "This is the guy I was telling you about earlier. His name's—"

"Toothaker," Erwin said, determined not to enter this circle as Dolan's catch, but as a free-willed individual. "Erwin Toothaker."

"We're pleased to see you, Mr. Toothaker," the old man said, "I'm Hubert Nordhoff. And this . . . " he took Erwin round the group, introducing them all. Three of the names were familiar to Erwin. They were the members of families still prominent in Everville (one was a Gilholly; another the father of a former mayor). The others were new to him, though it was apparent by their post-mortem finery that none had been disenfranchised in life. Like Hubert, these were men who'd had some significant place in the community. There was only one surprise: that the single female in this group was not a woman at all, but one Cornelius Floyd, who had apparently been delivered into the afterlife in rather dowdy drag, and seemed quite happy with his lot. His features were too broad and his jaw too square to be called feminine, but he effected a light, breathy tone when telling Erwin that though his name was indeed Cornelius, everybody called him Connie.

With the introductions over, Hubert got down to business. "We heard what happened to you," he said. "You were murdered, we understand, in your own house."

"Yes, that's right."

"We're of course appalled." There were suitably sympathetic murmurs all around the circle. "But I regret to say not terribly surprised. This is increasingly the way of the world."

"It wasn't a normal murder," Erwin pointed out, "if any murder's normal."

"Dolan mentioned something about vampires," Gilholly the Elder said.

"His word, not mine," Erwin pointed out. "I got the life sucked out of me, but there was none of that neck-biting nonsense."

"Did you know the killer?" asked a portly fellow called Dickerson, who was presently recumbent on the top of a tomb.

"Not exactly."

"Meaning?"

"I met him down by Unger's Creek. His name was Fletcher. I think he fancies himself some kind of messiah."

"That's all we need," said the scrawny guy in the tree.

"What do we do about this, Nordhoff?" Gilholly wanted to know.

"There's nothing we *can* do," Erwin said.

"Don't be defeatist," Nordhoff snapped. "We have responsibilities."

"It's true," said Connie. "If we don't act, who will?"

"Act to do *what?*" said Erwin.

"To save our heritage," Nordhoff replied. "We're the men who made this city. We poured our sweat into taming this wilderness and our geniuses into building a decent place to raise our families. Now it's all coming apart. We've suspected it for months now. Seen little signs of it everywhere. And now you come along, murdered by something unnatural, and the Lundy boy, raped in Dolan's store by something else, equally unnatural—"

"Don't forget the bees," Dickerson put in.

"What bees?" Erwin said.

"Do you know Frank Tibbit?" Dickerson said, "Lives off Moon Lane?"

"No, I can't say—"

"He keeps bees. Or rather he did. They all took off ten days ago."

"Is that significant?" Erwin said.

"Not if it were a solitary case," Nordhoff said. "But it isn't. We watch, you see, and we listen. It's our business to preserve what we made, even if we've been forgotten. So we hear everything that goes on, sooner or later. And there are dozens of examples—"

"Hundreds," said Connie.

"Many dozens, certainly," Nordhoff said, "many dozens of examples of strange goings-on, none of them of any greater scale than Tibbit's bees—"

"Barring your murder," Dickerson put in.

"Is it possible I could finish a sentence without being interrupted?" Nordhoff said.

"Maybe if you weren't so long-winded about it," said Melvin Pollock, who looked to be at least Nordhoff's age, and had the long, drawn dour mouth of one who'd died an unrepentant curmudgeon. "What he's trying to say is this: We invested our lives in Everville. The signs tell us we're about to lose that investment forever."

"And when it's gone—" Dickerson said.

"We go with it," Pollock said. "Into oblivion."

"Just because we're dead," Nordhoff said, "it doesn't mean we have to take this lying down."

Dickerson chuckled. "Not bad, Hubert. We'll make a comedian of you yet."

"This isn't a laughing matter," Nordhoff said.

"Oh but it is," Dickerson said, heaving his bulk into a sitting position. "Here we are, the great and the good of Everville, a banker"—he nodded in Pollock's direction. "A real-estate broker." At Connie now. "A mill owner." Nordhoff, of course. "And the rest of us all movers and shakers. Here we are, holding on to our dignity as best we can, and thinking we've got a hope in hell of influencing what goes on out there"—he pointed through the gate, into the world of the living—"when it's perfectly obvious to anyone with eyes in his head that it's over."

"What's over?" said Connie.

"Our time. Everville's time. Maybe . . . " He paused, frowned. "Maybe *humanity*'s time," he murmured.

There was silence now, even from Nordhoff. Somewhere in the streets outside the cemetery, a dog barked, but even that most familiar of sounds carried no comfort.

At last, Erwin said, "Fletcher knows."

"Knows what?" said Nordhoff.

"What's going on. Maybe he's even the reason for it. Maybe if we could find some way to kill him—"

"It's a thought," said Connie.

"And even if it doesn't save the city," Dickerson said, clearly heartened by this prospect, "we'd have the sport of it."

"For God's sake, we can't even make people hear us," Dolan pointed out, "how the hell do we *kill somebody?*"

"He's not *somebody*," Erwin said. "He's a thing. He's not human."

"You sound very certain of that," Nordhoff said.

"Don't take my word for it," Erwin replied. "Come see for yourself."

XI

*T*esla had bought her first gun in Florida, four years ago, after narrowly escaping assault or worse at the hands of two drunken louts outside a bar in Fort Lauderdale, who'd decided they simply didn't like the look of her. Never again, she'd sworn, would she be without some means of self-defense. She'd bought a modest little .45, and had even taken a couple of lessons so she'd be able to handle it properly.

It was not the last of the armaments she came by, however. Six months later, during her first trip to Louisiana, she'd found a gun lying in the middle of an empty highway, and despite Raul's warnings that it had surely been discarded for a reason, and she'd be a damn fool to pick it up, she'd done so. It was older and heavier than her purchase, the barrel and butt nicked and scratched, but she liked the heft of it; liked too the sense of mystery that surrounded it.

The third gun had been a gift from a woman called Maria Lourdes Nazareno, whom she'd met on a streetcorner in Mammoth, Arizona. Lourdes, as she'd preferred to be called, had been waiting for Tesla on that corner for several days, or so she'd claimed. She had the sight, she'd said, and had been told in a dream that a woman of power would be passing by. Tesla had protested that she was not the one, but Lourdes had been equally certain she was. She had been waiting with gifts, she said, and would not be content until Tesla had accepted them. One of the gifts had been a clavicle bone, which Lourdes told her belonged to a St. Maxine. Another had been a brass compass—"for the voyage" she'd said. The third had been the gun, which was certainly the prettiest of the three weapons, its handle inlaid with mother-of-pearl. It had a secret name, Lourdes had told her, but she did not know what that name was. Tesla would discover it, however, when she needed to call it.

That occasion had not come along. She had traveled for a further two years after her encounter with Lourdes, and had never had need of any of the guns.

Until now.

"Which one do I get?" Phoebe said.

They had returned to the Cobb house from the pizza parlor for one purpose only: to arm themselves.

"Do you know how to use a gun?" Tesla asked her.

"I know how to point my finger," Phoebe said.

"Your finger isn't going to make a hole in somebody," Tesla said.

Phoebe picked up Lourdes' gun, and passed it from palm to palm. "It can't be that difficult, when you see the men who do it." She had a point.

"You want that one?" Tesla asked.

"Yeah," she said, smiling.

"We're only going to use them if we really have to."

"If something that looks like a snake and smells like shit comes sniffing around."

"You still don't believe me, do you?"

"Does it matter whether I do or I don't?" Phoebe said.

Tesla thought about this for a moment. "I guess not," she said. "I just want you to be ready for the worst."

"I've been ready for years," Phoebe said.

ii

The Toothaker house was in darkness, but they'd come prepared for that eventuality. Phoebe had a large flashlight, Tesla a slightly smaller one.

"Feel anything?" Tesla asked Raul as she and Phoebe headed down the path.

Not so far.

The smell of excrement still lingered in the air, however, and it grew stronger the closer they got to the front door. The temperature had dropped considerably since they'd left the restaurant almost an hour before, but Tesla felt clammy-hot, as though she was developing a bad bout of flu. Weak at the knees, too.

"What do we do?" Phoebe said once they reached the step. "Just knock?"

"It beats trying to break the door down," Tesla said. She still harbored the hope that this was a wild-goose chase: that the whisper she and Raul had heard outside the diner had been a trick of the wind, and the smell was just a backed-up sewer, as Phoebe had said. She knocked on the door, loudly. They waited. There was no answer. She knocked again, and while she did so asked Raul if he sensed the presence of an occupant. His answer was not the one she wanted.

Yes, he said. *I hear somebody.*

The beast that had been twitching in Tesla's belly since they'd set out convulsed. She caught hold of Phoebe's arm. "I can't do this," she said.

"It's all right," Phoebe replied. She was reaching for the door handle. "We've come this far." She turned the handle, and to Tesla's surprise the door opened. A wave of cold, sour air broke over the threshold.

Tesla retreated from the step, tugging on Phoebe's arm, but Phoebe made a little grunt between her teeth and jerked her arm free.

"I want to see," she said.

"We'll see tomorrow," Tesla replied. "When it's light."

"Tomorrow might be too late," Phoebe said, without glancing back at Tesla. "I want to see now. Right now." And so saying she stepped into the house. As she did so Tesla heard her murmur, "Where are you?"

Where are you? said Raul.

"Yeah, I heard it too."

Somebody's got into her head, Tes.

"Fuck!"

Phoebe had already taken half a dozen strides into the house, and the darkness had almost closed around her.

"Phoebe?" Tesla yelled. "Come out of there."

The other woman didn't falter however. She just kept walking, until Tesla was in danger of losing sight of her completely.

Get in there— Raul said.

"Shut up!"

Or you'll lose her completely.

He was right, of course, and she knew it. She pulled the found .45 out of her belt and stepped inside, following Phoebe down the darkened hallway. If she was quick she could maybe catch hold of her and haul her out into the street before—

The door slammed behind her. She spun round, the cold air pressing against her face like a stale, damp washcloth. It was a labor to draw breath, and she didn't waste air calling after Phoebe again. Plainly whatever had its hooks in her wasn't going to let go without a fight.

Tesla?

"I'm here."

She turned right. There's a door.

She could vaguely make out the door frame, and yes, there was Phoebe stepping through it. Picking up her pace Tesla hurried down the hallway, but she was too late to catch hold of her quarry, who had slipped through the door into the room beyond. There was a little more light there, Tesla was pleased to see; candles perhaps, flickering. Grateful for this small mercy at least, she followed Phoebe through the door. It was not candlelight illuminating the room, it was the remains of a fire, guttering in the grate. A number of blackened branches littered the hearth. The smell in the air was not woody, however, but meaty; almost appetizing after the sourness at the threshold. Somebody had cooked and eaten here, recently, though she could not yet see who. The room was large, and had been comprehensively trashed, the furniture almost all destroyed, the ornaments and bric-a-brac reduced to fragments underfoot. At the far end, fifteen feet or so from where she stood—and half that from Phoebe, who was standing in the middle of the room, her arms slack at her sides—the darkness was denser than elsewhere, and busier. She tried to study the place, certain that somebody was standing there, but when she rested her gaze on the spot her eyes flickered violently back and forth, as though they couldn't (or wouldn't) make sense of what they were seeing.

"Fletcher?" she said. "Is that you?"

As she spoke Phoebe glanced round at her. "Leave us alone," she said. "It's me he wants."

"Is that right?" Tesla said, approaching her gently. There were tremors and tics around Phoebe's mouth and eyes, as though she might well weep or shriek at any moment.

"That's right," she said.

"And is this person who wants you Fletcher?" Tesla said, trying—and once again failing—to fix her eyes on the shadows.

"It doesn't matter what his name is," Phoebe said.

"It matters to me," Tesla replied. "Maybe you can ask him. Would you do that for me?" Phoebe looked back towards the darkness. She seemed to have no difficulty focusing upon it.

"She wants to know who you are," she said.

"Is he Fletcher?" Tesla said.

"Are you—?" Phoebe didn't finish the question, but listened, head slightly cocked.

There was silence, but for the crackle and spit of the fire. Tesla glanced back down at the hearth. There were pools of melted wax or fat around the branches, and in the grate itself a stone or-

"If that's what you want," Phoebe said to the darkness.

Tesla looked back at her. She was reaching up to unbutton her blouse.

"What are you doing?" Tesla said.

"He wants to see me," Phoebe said simply.

Tesla crossed to her and pulled her hands from her blouse.

"No he doesn't."

"Yes he does," Phoebe said fiercely, her hands going back to her buttons. "He says . . . he says—"

"What's he saying?"

"He says . . . *we should fuck for the millennium.*"

Tesla had heard the phrase before. Spoken once, and dreamed a thousand times.

Now, at the sound of it, the floor seemed to pitch beneath her, as if to tip her into the darkness at the other end of the room.

It was five years since she'd first heard the words spoken; five years in which she had many times thanked God their speaker was dead. Her gratitude, it seemed, had been premature.

"Kissoon . . . " she murmured, and leaving her lips the syllables took on a life of their own. *Kissss-sssoooon. Kiiissssssoonn.* Shimmying around her.

She'd met him in countless nightmares—run from him, succumbed to him, been judged, murdered, raped, and eaten by him—but she'd always woken from those ordeals, even the most terrible, with the comfort that one day the memories of him could recede, and she'd be free.

Not so. Oh Lord in Heaven, not so.

Here he was, come again.

She reached down to her belt, pulled out her gun, and pointed it at the darkness.

It isn't Fletcher then—Raul murmured. He sounded close to tears.

"No."

You think it's Kissoon.

"I *know* it's Kissoon," she said, leveling the gun.

Suppose you're wrong.

"I'm not," she said, and fired, once, twice, three times. The din careened around the room, coming back an instant later, bruisingly loud. But there was no gratifying cry from the darkness; no spillage of blood, no death-rattle.

The only effect the shots seemed to have was upon Phoebe, who began to sob pitifully.

"What am I doing?" she gasped, and reeled away from Tesla's side, as if making for the door.

Tesla glanced after her in time to see Phoebe coming back with her arms outstretched. She struck the gun from Tesla's fist with one hand and caught hold of her neck with the other. Tesla's breath was summarily stopped. She reached up to wrench Phoebe's hand away but before she could do so the woman's sobs—which had gone on unabated through the assault—stopped dead.

"Go to him," she said, her voice monotonal. "Go to him and tell him you're sorry."

She started to push Tesla back towards the far end of the room, towards the darkness and whatever form of Kissoon it contained. Tesla kicked and flailed but Phoebe's weight, fueled by her possessor's will, was not easily resisted.

"Phoebe! Listen to me!" Tesla yelled. "He's going to kill us both!"

"No—"

"You can fight him. I know what it feels like, having him sitting on your head"—this was no lie. Kissoon had worked this same trick on Tesla in the Loop: pressed on the top of her head to subdue and control her—"but you can fight it, Phoebe, you can fight it."

The face in front of her showed no flicker of comprehension. The tears just continued to fall. Tesla reached down to her belt. The Florida gun was there. If Phoebe wouldn't listen to reason, maybe she'd respond to the business end of a .45.

As she grabbed the butt however, Phoebe let her go. Tesla drew a grateful breath, bending over as she did so, and as her gaze met the floor she saw a dark, serpentine form wiggle into view from behind her. She pulled her second gun from her belt, and was stepping out of the Lix's way to fire when she sensed that the darkness at her side seemed to be unfolding; she heard it shifting, and felt the air around her disturbed by its motion.

She looked down at the ground again. The Lix at her feet had been joined by several of its siblings; piffling little horrors, by comparison with some she'd seen, the biggest eighteen inches long or so, the smallest as fine as hair. But they kept coming, and coming, some of them no longer than a finger, as though one of their nests had been overturned at her feet. None of them seemed much interested in doing her harm. They squirmed off across the debris-strewn floor towards the last of the fire.

The only threat lay in the person of their maker, in whose direction Tesla now turned her gaze. This time, though her eyes remained incapable of fixing upon him, she caught a glimpse. He was sitting on a chair, it seemed, but the chair was hovering three or four feet off the ground. And though she could not look directly at him, he was not so restricted. She felt his gaze. It pricked her neck. It made her heart rattle.

"It'll pass . . . " he said, and with those words any last hope that she'd made a mistake, and that this was not Kissoon, vanished.

"What'll pass?" she said, fighting hard to look at him. Doubtless he had good reason to prevent her laying eyes on him, which was all the more reason to defy the edict. If she could just distract him for a few moments, perhaps he'd drop his guard long enough for her to get one good look at him. "What'll pass?" she asked him again.

"The shock."

"Why should I be shocked?"

"Because you thought I was dead and gone."

"Why would I think that?"

"Don't try this."

"Try what?"

"This stupid game you're playing."

"What game?"

"I said *stop it!*" As he yelled, she looked at him, and for perhaps the length of two heartbeats his irritation made him careless, and she had plain sight of him.

It was long enough to see why he'd kept her from looking at him. He was in transition, his skin and sinew drooping around him, gangrenous and fetid. Enough of his flesh remained for her to recognize his face. The post-simian brow, the wide nose, the jutting jaw: All had been Raul's, before Kissoon had stolen them.

Jesus . . . she heard Raul say, *look away. For pity's sake, look away* . . .

As it was, she had little chance. She'd no sooner registered the sight than Kissoon became aware of her scrutiny, and his will, sharp as a blow, slapped her sight aside. Tears of pain sprang into her eyes.

"You're too curious for your own good," Kissoon said.

"You're getting very vain in your old age," she replied, wiping the tears off her cheeks.

"Old? Me? No. I'll be new forever. You, on the other hand, look like shit. Were your travels worth it?"

"What do you know about my travels?"

"Just because I've been out of sight doesn't mean I've been out of touch," Kissoon replied. "I've been watching the world very closely. And I've reports of you from a lot of grubby little corners. What *were* you looking for? Fletcher?"

"No."

"He's gone, Tesla. So's the Jaff. That part of things is over. It was a simpler age, so I suppose you felt at home there, but it's over and done with."

"And what follows?" Tesla said.

"I think you know." Tesla said nothing. "Are you too afraid to say it?"

"Iad, you mean?"

"There. You knew all along."

"Haven't you seen enough of them?" Tesla said.

"We've seen more than most, you and I. Yet we've seen *nothing*. Nothing at all." There was excitement in his voice. "They will change the world out of all recognition."

"And you want that?"

"Don't *you?*" Kissoon said. She'd forgotten how strangely persuasive he could be; how well he comprehended the ambiguities in her heart. "This chaos is no good, Tesla. Everything severed. Everything broken. The world needs to be put back together again." Like all great liars, there was enough truth in what he said to make it sound perfectly plausible. "Unfortunately, the species can't heal itself without help," he went on. "But not to worry. Help's on its way."

"And when it comes?"

"I told you. It'll change things out of all recognition."

"But you—"

"What about me?"

"What will it do for you?"

"Oh—that."

"Yes, that."

"It'll make me king of the hill, of course."

"Plus ça change."

"And I'll have the Art." Ah, the Art! Sooner or later it always came back to that. "I'll live in one immortal day—"

"Sounds lovely. And what about the rest of us?"

"The Iad'll make their judgments. You'll abide by them. Simple as that. I think they have quite an appetite for the feminine. Ten years ago, they probably would have kept you for breeding. Now, of course, you'd be better used for fertilizer." He laughed. "Don't worry, I'll make sure you don't go to waste."

She felt something move against her ankle, and looked down. There was a Lix there, five or six times larger than any of those she'd seen here previously. It curled around her foot, raising its head as it did so. Its open mouth was lined with tiny scarlet teeth, row upon row of them, receding down its throat.

"Wait—" she said.

"No time," Kissoon said. "Maybe I'll see you in the past, tomorrow. Maybe I'll find you in the Loop and we'll talk about how you died today."

The Lix was climbing her leg, its hold on her already tightening.

She screamed and stumbled backwards, her legs caught in the creature's coils. There was a moment when she teetered, then she fell, fell hard, the debris biting into her back. For a moment the room went white, and if she'd not had Raul yelling in her head, telling her to *Hold on, hold on*, she'd certainly have lost consciousness.

When the whiteness receded, she was looking towards the hearth. The Lix that had ventured there before her dialogue with Kissoon had done with warming themselves, and had turned their heads in her direction. Now they came, in a squirming river.

She tried to sit up, but their monstrous sibling had wound itself around her, incapacitating her. Her only hope was Phoebe. She craned her head round, looking for the woman, yelling her name as she did so. It was a lost cause. The room was empty, but for Kissoon and her devourers.

She looked back towards the hearth, and as if this weren't nightmare enough, realized what the Lix had been doing there. Not warming themselves at all, but feeding. What she'd taken to be branches scattered around the fire were human bones, and the stone amidst the embers a skull. Erwin Toothaker hadn't left home after all, except as smoke.

She let out a sob of horror. Then the Lix were upon her.

XII

*I*s she alive?"

Erwin went down onto his haunches beside the woman sprawled on his doorstep. Her brow was bleeding, and there was a trail of puke running from her mouth, but she was still breathing.

"She's alive," he said. "Her name's Phoebe Cobb."

The front door stood open. The air from out of the house smelled like shit and meat. Though Erwin had little to lose in his present condition, he was as scared as he'd ever been in life. He glanced back at the trio that had accompanied him here—Nordhoff, Dolan, and Dickerson—and saw unease on their faces too.

"He can't do anything to us, right?" Erwin said. "Not now."

Nordhoff shrugged. "Who the hell knows?" he said.

"What if he can see us?" Dickerson replied.

"We're never going to find out if we stay here," Dolan said impatiently and, stepping over Phoebe Cobb, he entered.

Erwin suddenly felt proprietorial. This was still his house: If anyone was going to lead the way, it should be him.

"Wait," he said to Dolan, and hurried after him down the hallway.

*   *   *

The Lix were not interested in her flesh (perhaps it was too leathery after so many years in the sun). They sought out her mouth and her nostrils, they went to her ears and eyes, so as to gain access to the tender stuff inside her.

She thrashed and rolled, her mouth sealed against their probing and pushing, but her nose was stopped with them now, and in a few seconds she would be out of breath. As soon as she parted her lips they would into her, and that would be the end.

Tesla—

"Not now."

It's over, Tesla.

"No."

I want you to know—

"No, I said, no!"

She heard him keen in her head; the sound not quite human.

"Don't give up," she told him. "It's not . . . over . . . yet."

He stifled his moans, but she felt his terror in her marrow, as though at the last he was not merely sharing her mind but her body too.

And this *was* the last, despite her protestations. She had to draw breath: now, or else never. Though the Lix were at her lips, waiting, she had no choice. She opened her mouth, teeth clenched, drawing air between the gaps. But where breath could go, so could the finest of the Lix. She felt them sliding between the cracks, under her tongue and down her throat.

Her system revolted. She started to gag, and the reflex bettered her will. Her teeth parted. It was all the Lix needed. They were in her mouth in a moment, filling it up. She bit down on them, tasting their shit and rot, and spitting out what she could. But for every one she expelled, there were two hungry to eat her out from the inside, and willing to risk her teeth to do so.

Gagging, spitting, and thrashing she fought with every ounce of power in her, but the battle was beyond winning. Her throat was choked, her nostrils blocked, her body creaking in the coils of the giant Lix.

At the last, hanging on the slivers of consciousness, she thought she heard Raul say: *Listen.*

She listened. There were voices coming from somewhere in the room.

"Christ Almighty!" one of them said.

"Look there! In the fire!"

Then a cry of anguish, and at the sound she used her last drop of energy to turn her head in its direction. Death was almost on her, and her eyes—which had witnessed so many strangenesses in their time, but had always been wedded to the real—were now in extremis, wise to subtle presences. Four of them—all men, all aghast—approaching from the door.

One went to the fire. Two lingered a couple of yards from her. The fourth and oldest, God bless him, went down on his knees beside her, and reached to touch her face. No doubt he intended to soothe her passage from life to death, but his phantom touch did more than that. At his touch she felt the Lix writhe upon her face like cutworms, then soften and liquefy and pour off down her cheeks and neck. Down her throat too, as though their dissolution was contagious.

A look of astonishment crossed her liberator's face, but he plainly understood in a moment what power he possessed, because as soon as she drew a breath, he then turned his attention to the Lix that had her in its coils. She raised her head off the ground in time to see the creature rising off her body like a startled cobra, spitting a warning. The phantom was unmoved. He reached out and ran his hand over the Lix's head, almost as though he were stroking it. A shudder passed through its glossy length, and its head began to droop, its filthy anatomy collapsing on itself. The lower jaw softened and ran like molasses; the upper followed moments later, its collapse initiating the dissolution of the beast's entire length. She pulled herself free of its sticky grasp, and as she turned over her system revolted and she puked up the filth that had found its way down her throat. When she looked up, wiping her mouth with the back of her hand, the phantoms were already indistinct, and growing more so as she retreated from their condition.

She had moments, she knew, to make sense of this.

"Name yourselves."

The old man's voice, when it came, was feather-light. "Hubert Nordhoff," he said, "and him"—he pointed to the man at the hearth—"he's Erwin Toothaker."

She was looking in Erwin's direction when she heard another voice: this from behind her.

"When did you learn to raise spirits?"

She'd forgotten Kissoon, in the rush of deliverance. But he hadn't forgotten her. When she looked round at him, he was too astonished by what he'd seen to keep her gaze at bay, and she had a second opportunity to study him in the midst of transformation. He was more naked than he'd been minutes before; much more. All resemblance to Raul had disappeared. In fact, there was barely anything left that was human. The vague shape of a head, formed from a roiling darkness; the last remnants of a ribcage, and a few fragments of leg and arm bones; that was all. The rest—the sinew, the nerves, the veins and the blood that had pulsed in them—had corrupted away.

I think . . . maybe he's afraid of you, Raul said, his tone astonished.

She dared not believe it. Not Kissoon. He was too crazy to be afraid.

Look at him, Raul told her.

"What am I supposed to be seeing?"

Look past the particulars.

As she looked, Kissoon spoke again.

"You played with me," he said, his tone almost admiring. "You endured the Lix, to prove they were nothing to you."

"You've got the general idea," she said, still trying to do as Raul had instructed, and see what he was so eager she saw.

"Where did you learn to raise spirits?" Kissoon wanted to know.

"Detroit," she said.

"Are you mocking me?"

"No. I learned to raise spirits in the Motor City. Something wrong with that?"

As she spoke, the last portions of Kissoon's usurped anatomy fell away, and with their passing she glimpsed what Raul had already seen. In the center of Kissoon's shadow-self, there was another form, glimmering remotely. A spiral, receding from her like a tunnel, as its curves tightened. And at the far end, where her gaze was inexorably drawn, something glittering.

"You don't know what you've done," Kissoon murmured.

His voice shook her from her scrutiny, and she was glad of it. The spiral had claimed her gaze with no little authority. What Kissoon meant by the remark (was he warning her about raising spirits or staring into spirals?) she didn't know, nor was this any time to quiz him. As long as he believed she was a woman who could raise spirits, and might do him harm while he was vulnerable, she might yet escape this room alive.

"Take care—" Kissoon was saying.

"Why's that?" she said, glancing back towards the door. It was probably six, perhaps seven, strides away. If she was to preserve the illusion of authority, she would have to exit without falling flat on her face, which would be a challenge given her trembling limbs.

"If you make any assault upon me now"—he *is* vulnerable, she thought—"I will have every soul in this city slaughtered. Even for the tiniest harm you do me." So this was the way power treated with power. It was a lesson she might profit from if she had occasion to play bluff with him again.

She didn't reply, however, but pretended to chew the deal over.

"You know I can do it," Kissoon said.

This was true. She didn't doubt him capable of any atrocity. But suppose this was a bluff of his own? Suppose he was so susceptible in his present condition that she might reach into the dark spiral at his core right now, and squeeze the life from him?

Don't even think it, Raul said.

Wisdom, no doubt. But oh, she was sorely tempted to try.

Let's get out while we can, Raul was saying. *Tesla? Are you listening to me?*

"Yes . . . " she replied reluctantly. There would never be another opportunity like this, she knew. But Raul's defensive instincts were right. Get out now, and live to fight another day.

There was one last piece of theatrics before she departed, however. She went down on her trembling haunches, and whistled lightly, as if to invisible dogs. She waited a moment, then smiled to welcome her spirits back, and rose again.

"Consider this—" Kissoon said as she turned to go.

"What?"

"That we're not after all so far apart. You want revelation. So do I. You want to shake your species up. So do I. You want power—you already have a little, but a little's never enough—and so do I. We've taken different paths, but are we not coming to the same spot?"

"No."

"I think we are. Maybe it's too much for you to admit right now, but you'll see the sense in it. And when you do—"

"I won't."

"When you do I want you to know there's a place for you in my heart"—did he turn this phrase deliberately, she wondered, tempting her gaze back towards the spiral at his core?—"and I think a place for me in yours."

Say nothing, Raul murmured.

"I want to tell him to fuck off."

I know you do, but leave him guessing.

Biting back a retort, she headed for the door, her legs strong enough not to betray her.

"Let me say *something* snide," Tesla implored.

Don't even look at him, Raul replied.

She took his advice. Without word or glance she opened the door a little wider and slipped out into the cooler air of the hallway.

Phoebe was sitting on the step, her head in her hands. Tesla went to her, comforted her and persuaded her to her feet. Then they hobbled away up the path and down the street, under trees that were sighing in sweet breezes from the mountain.

XIII

*P*erhaps a mile out from the shore, *The Fanacapan* was caught
by a second current, this one of no little ferocity, which
threw the vessel around like a plaything before speeding it on
its way. The scale of the waves rapidly increased, much to Joe's distress, lifting the boat up twenty, thirty feet one moment, giving them
a precarious perch from which to see the awesome vista ahead, then
dropping it like a stone into a trough so deep and dark it seemed
with every descent this would be their last, and the foaming waves
would bury them. Not so. Each time they rose again, though every
board in the vessel creaked, and the decks were awash from bow to
stern.

It was impossible to speak under these conditions. All Joe could
do was cling to the frame of the wheelhouse door, and pray. It was a
long time since he'd begun a sentence with *Our Father*, but the
words came back readily enough, and their familiarity was comforting. Perhaps, he thought, there was even a remote chance that the
words were being heard. That notion—which would have seemed
naïve the day before—did not seem so idiotic now. He'd crossed a
threshold into another state of being; a state that was just like
another room in a house the size of the cosmos: literally, a step away.

If there was one such door to be entered, why not many? And why should one not be a door that led into Heaven?

All his adult life, he'd asked why. Why God? Why meaning? Why love? Now he realized his error. The question was not *why*; it was *why not?*

For the first time since childhood, since hearing his grandmother tell Bible stories like reminiscences, he dared to believe; and for all the darkness of the troughs and terrible turmoils that lay ahead, for all the fact that he was soaked to the skin and sickened to his stomach, he was strangely happy with his lot.

If I had Phoebe beside me now, he thought, I'd be lacking nothing.

ii

Tesla refused to answer any of Phoebe's questions until she'd stood under a hot shower for a quarter of an hour, and scrubbed every inch of her body from scalp to feet, sniffing water up her nose and snorting it out to clean the last of the shit from her nostrils and using half a tube of toothpaste and a full bottle of mouthwash to scour her mouth and throat.

That done, she stood in front of the mirror and surveyed her body from as many angles as anatomy allowed. She'd looked better, no doubt of that. There was scarcely six square inches of flesh unmarked by the yellow stain of an old bruise, or the livid purples and reds of a new one, but in its strange way the sight pleased her.

"You've lived some," she told her reflection. "I like that."

Let's be sure we live a little longer, Raul counseled.

"Any bright ideas?"

We need help, that's for sure. And don't start with me about Lucien. He'd be no use right now. We need somebody who can help us defend ourselves. And I'm not talking about guns.

"You're talking about magic."

Right.

"There's only D'Amour that I know of," Tesla said. "And Grillo thinks he's dead."

Maybe Grillo didn't look hard enough.

"Where the hell do you suggest we start?"

He worked with a psychic, remember?

"Vaguely."

Her name was Norma Paine.

"How'd you remember that?"

What else have I got to do with my time?

She found Phoebe in the kitchen, standing beside the dishwasher in a litter of twitching roaches with a can of Raid in her hand.

"Damn things," Phoebe said, brushing a couple that had expired on the countertop onto the floor. "They breed where it's warm. I open the machine sometimes and they're swarming everywhere."

"Looks like you pretty much finished them off," Tesla said.

"Nah. They'll be back. You feeling better?"

"Much. What about you?"

"I took some aspirin. My head feels like it's ready to burst. But I'm okay. I made some peppermint tea. You want some?"

"I'd prefer something stronger. Got a brandy?"

Phoebe picked up her cup and led the way through to the living room. It was chaotic: magazines everywhere and brimming ashtrays. The whole room stank of stale cigarettes.

"Morton," Phoebe remarked, as if that explained everything. Then, while she went through the array of liquor bottles on the dresser, told Tesla, "I don't really remember what happened in Erwin's house."

"Don't worry about it."

"I remember going down the hallway with you. Then the next thing I remember was waking up on the step. Did you find Fletcher?"

"No."

"I've only got bourbon. We had some brandy from last Christmas, but—"

"Bourbon's fine."

"But the house wasn't empty, was it?"

"No, it wasn't empty."

"Who was in there?"

"A man called Kissoon."

"Was he a friend of Fletcher's?" Phoebe asked. She'd poured an ample measure of bourbon, and now passed the glass to Tesla. She took a stinging mouthful before answering.

"Kissoon doesn't have friends," she said.

"That's sad."

"Believe me, he doesn't deserve them." The bourbon took an almost instant toll on her brain functions. She could practically feel its influence through her cortex, slowing her systems down. It was a pleasant sensation.

"Is the clock on the TV right?" she asked Phoebe. It read three-oh-five.

"Near enough."

"We'd better get some sleep," she said, her words faintly slurred.

"This man Kissoon—" Phoebe said.

"We'll talk about it tomorrow."

"No. I want to know now," she said. "He's not going to come after us, is he?"

"What the hell put that idea in your head?"

"The state of you when you came out of there," Phoebe said. "He messed you up. I thought maybe—"

"He wasn't done?"

"Right."

"No. I think we can sleep easy. He's got bigger fish to fry than me. But tomorrow morning, I think you should get the hell out of here."

"Why?"

"Because he's a malicious sonofabitch, and if things don't go the way he wants them to he'll trash this city from one end to the other."

"He could do that?"

"Very possibly."

"I can't leave," Phoebe said.

"Because of Joe?" Phoebe nodded. "He's not coming back any

time soon," Tesla said. "You've got to look after yourself for a while."

"But what if he *does* come back and I'm gone?"

"Then he'll go looking for you, and he'll find you."

"You believe that? Really?" Phoebe said, studying Tesla's face. "If we're meant to be together, then we will be?"

Tesla avoided her gaze for a few moments, but at last she had no choice but to meet Phoebe's eyes. When she did, she couldn't find it in her heart to lie.

"No," she said. "I don't believe that. I wish I did, but I don't."

There was little to say after that. Phoebe retired to her bed, and left Tesla to make herself comfortable on the sofa. It was ill-sprung and smelled of Morton's cigarettes, but these were minor details given how exhausted she was. She laid down her head, and was just wondering whether the bourbon in her head would keep her awake, when she stopped wondering, and slept.

Upstairs, in the double bed that seemed larger tonight than it had the night before, Phoebe wrapped herself up in her arms, and tried to put Tesla's words out of her head. But they wouldn't go. They stalked the hopes she'd worked so hard to keep alive the last forty-eight hours, sniffing their weakness, ready to pounce and devour them the moment Phoebe looked the other way.

"Oh God, Joe," she said, suddenly sobbing, "Joe, Joe, Joe, where *are* you?"

iii

Just as Joe was beginning to think the swell would never die down and the continued violence of its motion would shake *The Fanacapan* apart at the timbers, the towering waves began to diminish, and after a time the current delivered them into a region of much calmer waters.

Noah ordered the volunteers to check on the condition of the vessel's boards (it had fared better than Joe had expected; it was taking in water in one place only, and that no more than a trickle), then the torches were lit at stern and bow, and everyone took time to rest and catch their breaths. The volunteers all sat together at the stern, heads bowed.

"Are they praying?" Joe asked Noah.

"Not exactly."

"I'd like to thank them for what they did back there," Joe said.

"I wouldn't bother."

"No, I want to," Joe said, leaving Noah's side.

Noah caught hold of Joe's arm. "Please leave them be," he said.

Joe pulled himself free. "What's the big problem?" he said, and strode down the deck towards the half-dozen. None of them looked up at his approach.

"I just wanted to thank you—" Joe began, but he stopped as a dozen little details of their condition became apparent. Several of them had been hurt in the storm—gashed arms and flanks, bruised faces—but none of them were nursing their wounds. They bled freely onto the soaked deck, shuddering occasionally.

Unnerved now, Joe went down on his haunches beside them. This was the first opportunity he'd had to study their physiognomy closely. None of them looked entirely human. Each had some detail of skin or eye or skull that suggested they had come of mixed marriages: the blood of Homo sapiens mingled with that of creatures who either lived beside Quiddity or below it.

He looked from face to face. None of them showed the slightest sign of pain or even discomfort.

"You should get those cuts covered up," he said.

He got no response. They weren't deaf, he knew that. They'd heard Noah's instructions, even over the roar of surf. But they showed no sign of even knowing that Joe was beside them, much less understanding his words.

Then, a voice from behind him.

"I had no choice."

Joe looked back over his shoulder. Noah was standing a couple of yards down the deck from him.

"What did you do to them?"

"I simply put them in my service," Noah said.

"How?"

"I worked what I think you call a *conjuration* upon them."

"Magic?"

"Don't look so disdainful. It plainly works. We needed their service, and I had no other way of getting it."

"Would you have done the same thing to me, if I hadn't agreed to bring you here?"

"I didn't have the strength back there. And even if I had, you'd have resisted me better than they did."

"They've hurt themselves."

"So I see."

"Can't you wake them up? Get them to tend to themselves?"

"What for?"

"Because otherwise they're going to be scarred for life."

"Their lives are over, Joe."

"What do you mean?"

"I told you: They're in my service. Permanently. We'll use them to get us home, and then," he shrugged "they'll have no further purpose."

"So—what?"

"They'll lie down and die."

"Oh my God."

"I told you: I had no choice. How else were we going to get off the shore?"

"You're killing them."

"They don't feel anything. They don't even remember who they are."

"Is that supposed to make me feel *better?*" Joe said. "Look at me, Noah. I don't like this slave shit. *Wake them up!*"

"It's too late."

"Try, damn you!" Joe yelled, his fingers itching to wipe the sham of pity off Noah's face.

The man knew it. He retreated down the boards a few yards.

"We've done well together so far," he said to Joe. "Let's not fight now and spoil our fellowship."

"*Fellowship?*" Joe said. "I didn't notice any fellowship. You wanted something from me. I wanted something from you. Simple as that."

"Very well," Noah said. "I tell you what," he said, "I'll do what I can to reverse the conjuration—"

"Good."

"I don't believe they'll thank us for it, but I suppose you think freedom's preferable to their present state, even if it brings agony with it. Am I right?"

"Of course."

"And if I liberate them, we'll assume the bargain between us over."

"What?"

"You heard me."

"That wasn't what we agreed."

"But it's what I'm offering now," Noah calmly replied. "They can be free or you can have power. One or the other, but not both."

"You sonofabitch."

"Which is it to be, Joe?" Noah replied. "You seem very certain in your righteousness so I suppose it's an easy decision. You want to liberate the slaves, yes?" He watched and waited. "Yes, Joe?"

After several seconds of deliberation Joe shook his head. "No."

"But they're bound to my will, Joe. They're sitting there bleeding, bound to my will. You can't want that, can you?" He waited a beat. "Or can you?"

Joe looked back at the creatures sitting on the deck, his mind a maze. There'd been a clear path ahead of him moments before, but Noah had confounded it. And why? For the pleasure of seeing him squirm.

"I came here because you promised me something," Joe said.

"So I did."

"And I'm not going to have you talk me out of it."

"You talked yourself out of it, Joe."

"I didn't agree to anything."

"Do I take it then that the slaves will remain in thrall?"

"For now," Joe said. "Maybe I'll set them free myself, when I get what I'm due."

"A noble ambition," Noah replied. "Let's hope they survive that long." He wandered over to the starboard side. "Meanwhile," he said, "I have work for them to do." He glanced at Joe, as if expecting some objection. Getting none, he gave a little smile and went back to the stern of the vessel to make his instructions known.

Cursing under his breath, Joe looked over the side to see what the problem was, and found the water clogged in every direction with sinuous weed of some kind. Its fronds were the palest of yellows, and here and there it was knotted up into bundles, the smallest like footballs, the largest twenty times that size. Plainly the weed was slowing the vessel's progress, but the slaves were already at the bow, clambering over the sides and lowering themselves into the water to solve the problem. Digging their way through the floating thicket they started to hack at the weed, two with machetes, the others with pieces of broken timber. Watching them labor, making no sound of complaint, Joe could not help the shameful thought that perhaps it was better they felt nothing. The task before them was substantial— the weed field stretched at least two hundred yards ahead of the vessel—and would surely exhaust their wounded limbs. But at least the waters beyond the field looked calm and clear. Once the boat reached them the slaves would be able to rest. He might even try bargaining with Noah afresh, and get him to release the weakest of them from bondage, so they could tend themselves.

Meanwhile, he retired to the wheelhouse, stripping off his damp shirt and hanging it on the door before sitting down to ponder his situation. The air had grown balmier of late, and despite his recent agitation, he felt a kind of languor creep upon him. He let his head drop against the back of the cabin seat, and closed his eyes . . .

In her lonely bed in Everville, Phoebe had finally drifted to sleep on a pillow damp with her tears, and had begun to dream. Of Joe, of course. At least of his presence if not his flesh and blood. She drifted in a misty place, knowing he was not that far from her, but unable to see him. She tried to call to him, but her voice was smothered by the mist. She tried again, and again, and her efforts were rewarded after a time. The syllable seemed to divide the mist as it went from her, seeking him out in this pale nowhere.

She didn't let up. She kept calling, over and over.

"Joe . . . Joe . . . Joe . . ."

Sprawled asleep in the cabin of *The Fanacapan*, Joe heard somebody calling his name. He almost stirred, thinking the summons was coming from somewhere in the waking world, but as soon as he began to float up out of his slumbers, the call became more remote, so he let the weight of his fatigue carry him back down into dreams.

The voice came again and this time he recognized it.

Phoebe! It was Phoebe. She was trying to find him.

He started to reply to her, but before he could do so she called out to him again.

"Where are you, Joe?" she said.

"I'm here," he said. "I can hear you. Can you hear *me*?"

"Oh my God," she gasped, plainly astonished that this was actually happening. "Is that really you?"

"It's really me."

"Where are you?"

"I'm on a ship."

On a ship? she thought. What the hell was he doing on a ship? Had he fled to Portland and hopped the first cargo vessel out?

"You've left me," she said.

"No, I haven't. I swear."

"That's easy to say—" she murmured, her voice thickening with tears, "I'm on my own, Joe—"

"Don't cry."

"And I'm afraid—"

"Listen to me," he said softly. "Are you dreaming?"

She had to think about this for a moment. "Yes," she said. "I'm dreaming."

"Then maybe we're not that far apart," he said. "Maybe we can find each other."

"Where?"

"In the sea. In the dream-sea."

"I don't know what you're talking about."

"Hold on," he said. "Just hold on to my voice. I'll lead you here."

He didn't dare wake. If he woke, the contact between them would surely be broken, and she'd despair (she was already close to that; he could hear it in her voice) and perhaps give up on ever finding him again. He had to walk a very narrow path; the path that lay between the state of dreaming, which was one of forgetfulness, and the waking world, where he would lose contact with her. He had to somehow find his way across the solid boards of this solid boat without rising from slumber to do so, and plunge into the waters of Quiddity, where perhaps the paradox of dreaming with his eyes open would be countenanced and he could call her to him.

"Joe?"

"Just wait for me—" he murmured.

"I can't. I'm going crazy."

"No you're not. It's just that things are stranger than we ever thought."

"I'm afraid—"

"Don't be."

"I'm afraid I'm going to die and I'll never see you again."

"You'll see me. Just hold on, Phoebe. You'll see me."

He felt the cabin door brush against his arm; felt the steps up into the deck beneath his feet. At the top, he stumbled, and his eyes might have flickered open, but that by chance she called to him, and her voice anchored him; kept him in a sweet sleep.

He turned to his right. Walked two, three, four strides until he felt the side of the boat against his shins. Then he threw himself overboard.

The water was cold, the shock of it slapped him into wakefulness. He opened his eyes to see the weeds around him like a swaying thicket, its tangle rife with fish, most of them no larger than those he'd swallowed whole on the shore. Cursing his consciousness, he looked up towards the surface, and as he did so heard Phoebe again, calling him.

"Joe—?" she said, her voice no longer despairing, but light; almost excited.

He caught hold of the knotted weed around him, so as not to float to the surface. "I'm here," he thought. "Can you hear me?"

There was no answer at first, and he feared her call had been the remnants of their previous contact. But no. She spoke again, softly.

"I can hear you."

It was as though her voice was in the very water around him. The syllables seemed to caress his face.

"Stay where you are," she said.

"I'm not going anywhere," he replied. It seemed he had no need of breath; or rather that the waters were supplying him with air through his skin. He felt no ache in his chest; no panic. Simply exhilaration.

He turned himself around in the water, parting the strands of weed to look for her. The fish had no fear of him. They darted around his face, and brushed against his back and belly; they played between his legs. And then, out of the tangle to his right, a form he knew. Not Phoebe, but a Zehrapushu, a spirit pilot, its golden gaze fixed upon him. He gave up turning a moment, in order to let it see him properly. It scooted around him once, clockwise, then reversed its direction and did the same again, always coming to a perfect hovering halt in front of his face.

It knew him. He was certain of it. The way its huge eye tilted in its socket, scanning his face; the way it came close enough to brush his cheek with its tentacles, fearlessly; the way it flirted with his fingers, as though encouraging them to caress it: all were signs of familiarity. And if this was not the same 'shu he'd cradled on the shore (and how many billion to one was that chance?) then he had to assume that for all Noah's misrepresentations, he'd been telling the truth on the subject of 'shu. They had not many minds, but one, and this individual knew him because it had seen him through its brother or sister's eyes.

Suddenly, it darted away. He watched it go, weaving through the thicket of weeds, and as it disappeared from sight, the tangle around him convulsed, and he heard Phoebe say his name again, not remotely this time, but almost like a whisper in his ear. He turned his head to the left, and—

There he was, just a few feet from her, floating in the forested water, looking at her. Even now, she wasn't sure how she'd got here. One moment she'd been lost in a mist, hearing Joe's voice but unable to reach him; the next she'd been naked and tumbling down the bank of Unger's Creek. The creek was running high and fast, and in the grip of its water she was carried away. She'd been vaguely aware that this was her mind's prosaic creation; its way of supplying pictures to accompany the journey her spirit was taking. But even as she'd grasped that slippery notion, the landscape had receded around her, the sky overhead becoming vast and strange, and Unger's Creek had disappeared, delivering her into far deeper waters.

Down she went, down, down into the dream-sea. And though she felt its currents caress her and saw its shoals part like shimmering veils to let her pass, and so knew she wasn't imagining this, she didn't fear that she'd drown. The laws that bound her body in the world she'd left had no authority here. She moved with exquisite ease, passing over a landscape whose mysteries she could not begin to fathom, the most puzzling of which lay waiting for her at the end of the journey in the person of the man she'd last seen hobbling out of a door in Everville.

"It's really you," she said, opening her arms to him.

He swam to meet her, his voice in her head, the way it had been from the beginning of this strange journey. "Yes," he said, "it's really me," and held her tight.

"You said you were on a ship."

He directed her gaze up towards the dark shadow overhead.

"That's it," he said.

"Can I go with you?" she asked him, knowing as she spoke what the answer would be.

"You're dreaming this," he said. "When you wake up—"

"I'll be back in bed?"

"Yes."

She took fiercer hold of him. "Then I won't wake up," she said, "I'll stay with you until you wake up too."

"It's not as easy as that," he said. "I have a journey I have to take."

"Where to?"

"I don't know."

"Then why are you taking it? Why not just tell me where you're sleeping and I'll go find you?"

"I'm *not* sleeping, Phoebe."

"What do you mean?"

"This is me." He touched her face. "The real me. You're dreaming but I'm not. I'm here, mind and body."

She started to draw away from him, distressed. "That's not true," she said.

"It is. I walked through a door, and I was in another world."

"What door?" she demanded to know.

"On the mountain," he said.

Her face grew slack. She stared past him into the swaying fronds. "Then it's true," she said. "Quiddity's real."

"How do you know that name?"

"A woman I met . . . " Phoebe said, her tone and expression distracted.

"What woman?"

"Tesla . . . Tesla Bombeck. She's downstairs right now . . . I thought she was crazy—"

"Whoever she is," Joe said, "she isn't crazy. Things are weirder than either of us ever guessed, Phoebe."

She put her hands on his face, "I want to be with you," she said.

"You are."

"No. *Really* be with you."

"I'm going to come back," Joe said, "sooner or later." He kissed her face. "Things are going to be all right."

"Tell me about the door, Joe," she said.

Instead, he kissed her again, and again, and now she opened her mouth to let his tongue between her lips, still speaking her thoughts at him. "The door, Joe—"

"Don't go near it," he said, pressing his face against hers. "Just be here with me now. Be close with me. Oh God, Phoebe, I love you." He kissed her cheek and eyes, running his fingers up through her hair.

"I love you too," she said. "And I want us to be together more than anything. More than anything, Joe."

"We will be. We will be," he said. "I can't live without you, baby. I told you, didn't I?"

"Keep telling me. I need to know."

"I'll do better than tell you." He ran his hands down her shoulders, and round to touch her breasts. "Beautiful," he murmured. His left hand lingered there while his right slid on down over her belly, between her legs. She raised her knees little. He ran his fingers back and forth over her sex.

She sighed, and leaned forward to kiss him. "I want to stay here," she said. "I want to sleep forever and just stay here with you."

He slid down her body now, kissing her along the way, her neck, her breasts, her belly, until he had his lips where his fingers had been, his tongue darting between. She opened her legs a little wider, and he took the signal of her abandon, pressing his palms against her knees to spread her still wider and burying his face in her groin.

The weeds seemed to sense the passion in their midst, and were excited by it. Their sinuous stems stroked her body with an eagerness all of their own, their silky pods nuzzling her. Four or five of them dallied around her face, like suitors awaiting an invitation to her mouth, while others ran up her spine and down between the cleft of her buttocks.

She started to let out little gasps of bliss, and reached out to left and right of her to take handfuls of the weed. It responded to her attentions instantly, wrapping lengths of itself around her wrists and elbows to anchor her, and swaying against her body with fresh abandon, its strands, soft though they were, falling on her naked back like gentle whips, rousing her dreamed skin, her spirit skin, to new heights of sensation.

All the while Joe licked and probed below, and with each new wave of sensation that passed through her and over her, and spread out into the forest of weed around her, she felt the limits of her body dissolving, as though she and the waters and the weeds were no longer quite distinct. There was nothing unpleasant or distressing about this. Quite the reverse. The more she spread, the more of her there was to feel pleasure, her sensations flowing out into the stems and the pods and the swaying element in which she floated, then returning in waves to the soft vessel of her body, which in turn spread wider to accommodate the feelings, so that body and feelings kept on growing, each feeding off the other's advancement.

She looked up at the surface of the dream-sea, and at the dark shape of the boat above. There were figures working in the water up there, she saw, hacking at the weed to clear a path for the vessel. She wished she could coax them down to join the fun; to share what she was feeling and exuding; to watch them dissolve in the grip of bliss, and have them open to her.

She felt a sliver of shame at these thoughts—moments ago this had been the most intimate of encounters between herself and Joe, now here she was, wanting to invite everyone in sight to join the party—but she couldn't help it. Her pleasure didn't belong to her. It couldn't be boxed, it couldn't be banked, it couldn't be traded or trafficked. It moved through her and disappeared, existing for the length of a shudder or a sigh, or a loving afternoon.

It was part of being alive, like tears and hunger; and given that her being was connected with everything else with the water and the weeds and the men on the boat above—what right did she have to prevent pleasure radiating from her, giving itself freely?

With a great democracy of bliss founded in her head, she looked down at Joe through the swaying veil of stems that were caressing her face. Oh, but he was beautiful. The flesh of him, the bone of him; the bruise and blood of him.

He seemed to sense her scrutiny, and cast his gaze up towards her. She smiled down upon him, feeling at that moment like some sea goddess in her temple while he, her worshipper, rose up from the darkness to eat and drink from her.

The stems had caught hold of him as they had her, she saw. They were wrapped around his limbs, and pressed against his back and buttocks with the same shamelessness as they pressed against her. She no longer saw any reason to keep them out. She relaxed her body and on the instant they floated into her, down her throat, up into her bowels, even pressing between her labia and Joe's lips to come into her by that route.

The surge of sensations almost undid her, literally. For a moment her body seemed to lose its coherence, shredding itself in pleasured layers, opening at every pore and letting the waters and all they contained rush into her, dissolving her dreamed bones.

Oh, but it was wonderful. Her parameters spread to contain all that swayed and surged around her. She was present in the waters, and in the stems and in the pods; she was rising towards the boat, she was plunging towards the darkness. She was embracing Joe as she never embraced him before, her consciousness surrounding him from all sides. She nuzzled at his ass in the form of pods, eager to enter him as she was entered; she bound his legs and arms, round and round, so tight she could feel the throb of his veins; she flowed across his back and against his chest, and against his groin too, where the water was murky with blood. He was plainly wounded, but not so badly that he couldn't be aroused. She could see and feel his rod, hard in his pants, wanting liberty.

If not for the memory of their previous couplings—the particulars of which would never leave her—she might have let her body dissolve completely. But the promise of having that intimacy again, even if it was just one more time, kept her from embracing dissolution.

Tomorrow maybe, or the day after, she'd let *Phoebe* go, and be unmade into everything. But before that happened—before her body slipped from her and went into the world—she wanted to enjoy its particulars a little longer; wanted to take pleasure in knitting her substance with Joe's.

She pulled her arms free of the strands and reached down to take hold of his head. Again, he looked at her, but now his expression was so distracted she wasn't even certain he saw her. Then a smile appeared in his eyes and loosing himself from the eager weeds he climbed her body until they were face to face, mouth to mouth.

Did he know what had happened to her in the last few moments, she wondered? It seemed not, for when she heard his voice in her head again, murmuring his love to her, it was as if he was picking up where he'd left off.

"You can't stay," he said. "You'll wake up sooner or later, and when you do—"

"I'll come and find you."

He laid his forefinger against her lips, though she was not using them to speak. "Stay away from the door," he said, "it's dangerous. There's something terrible coming through it. Understand me? Please, Phoebe, tell me you understand me?"

"*What's* coming through it?" she said. "Tell me."

"Iad," he said, "Iad Uroboros."

His hand slipped from her mouth to the back of her head, and took firm hold of her. "I want you to promise me you'll stay away from the door," he said.

She pushed her tongue out between her lips. She wasn't going to promise anything.

"*Phoebe,*" he said, but before he could get beyond her name she mashed her face against his, distracting him with her fervor.

"I love you," she thought, "and I want you inside me."

He didn't need a second invitation. She felt him pulling his belt, then felt his dick pressing into her. It was easy; oh it was easy. But it pained him. He grimaced, and stopped moving; stopped kissing her even.

"Are you all right?" she breathed.

"Your damn husband," he said, his voice small, and punctuated with little gasps. "I don't know . . . I don't know if I can . . . do this—"

"It's okay."

"Christ, it hurts."

"I said it's okay."

"I want to finish what I started," he said, and began to push into her again. She looked down. The water between them was tinged red; he was plainly bleeding, and badly.

"We should stop," she said.

But he had a dogged look upon his face: teeth gritted, brow furrowed. "I want to finish," he gasped, "I want to—"

A shadow fell upon them both. Phoebe looked up, and saw that somebody was leaning over the side of the boat, pointing down into the water. Did she hear a voice, remotely? She thought so.

And now two of the weed-cleaners left off their labors and were diving down through the tangle of weeds. She didn't doubt their purpose. They were coming to rescue Joe.

He hadn't seen them. He was too intent on fucking, pressing into her over and over, despite the pain on his face.

"Joe . . . " she murmured.

"It's okay," he thought to her. "It's kinda raw but—"

"Open your eyes, Joe." He opened them. "They're coming for you." He looked up now, and tried to wave his rescuers away, but either they thought the gestures were pleas, or else they didn't care.

The latter, Phoebe guessed, glimpsing their features. They had a distinctly alien cast to them, but it wasn't their strangeness that chilled her, it was their total absence of expression. She didn't want Joe taken from her by these blank-faced creatures. She took tighter hold of him.

"Don't go," she said.

"No way," he murmured, "I'm here, baby, I'm here."

"They're going to take you."

"No they're not. I won't let them." He pulled out of her, almost all the way, then slid back up into her, slowly, slowly, as though they had all the time in the world. "We're staying together till we're done," he said.

He'd no sooner spoken than his rescuers laid their hands on him. Was she perhaps invisible to all but the man who had brought her here? It seemed so, for they made no attempt to detach her arms from around his body. They simply tugged on him; as though it was the weeds he'd fallen prey to.

Joe had no choice but to unhand Phoebe in order to beat them off. But the moment he did so, they claimed him. He was hauled up through her arms, a shocking burst of blood coming from his groin as he was detached from her. For a moment she lost sight of him in the stained water. All she could do was cry out to him, mind to mind.

"*Joe! Joe!*"

He answered her, but all the strength had gone from his voice.

"No. . . " he moaned, "I don't want . . . don't want to . . . "

She started to flail blindly, hoping to catch hold of his leg or ankle, and keep him from being taken, but the weeds resisted her motion, and by the time the water cleared enough for her to see his body, it was beyond her grasp.

"Can you hear me, Joe?" she sobbed.

The sound she heard in her head was not words, not even moans, but a hiss, like gas escaping a slit pipe.

"Oh God, Joe," she said, and began to struggle against the weeds afresh, desperate to rise and be with him. But their desire for her, which had been so arousing a couple of minutes before, had become nightmarish. They pressed at her orifices with the same insistence as ever, the pods swaying in her mouth and depositing a bitter fluid down her throat.

She started to shudder from head to foot, her whole body spasming. There were other sounds coming from somewhere: distant voices, children's laughter. Was it from the ship?

No. Not the ship. The world. It was coming from the world. It was morning, Festival morning, and folks were already up to meet the day.

"Don't panic," she told herself, and gave up thrashing in the weeds for a few moments, to regain control of her body. The spasms lessened. The sounds withdrew a little way. Very slowly, she looked for Joe. He and his rescuers had broken surface, she saw. Others were leaning over the side of the vessel to haul him out of the water. It didn't take her long to realize why he hadn't replied to her. He was a dead-weight, his arms hanging loosely at his sides.

A shudder of horror shook her.

"Not dead," she murmured. "Oh God, please; please, not dead."

Blood was running from between his legs, a spreading pool staining the surface.

"Joe," she said. "I don't know if you can hear me . . . " She listened, hoping for a reply, but none came. "I want you to know I'm going to come and find you. I know you told me not to, but I am. I'm going to find you and we're going to—"

She stopped, puzzled to see one of the creatures leaning over the side of the vessel, gesturing to Joe's rescuers. The mystery was solved a moment later. Without ceremony, they released the body, returning it to the elements they'd claimed it from.

"No!" she yelled, seeing her worst fears confirmed. "No, *please, no* "

There was no controlling the spasms this time. They convulsed her body from scalp to sole. And as they came, so did the day she had shunned, laughter, light, and all. She felt the lumpy mattress beneath her back; smelled the staleness of the room.

Even now, she fought to keep wakefulness at bay. If she could only catch hold of Joe's body—stop him from tumbling away down into the darkness—perhaps she could work some miracle upon him. Put her last dreaming breath into him, and keep him from oblivion.

She started to reach up towards his sinking form—the day was upon her; she had seconds at best— and her fingers caught hold of his trouser leg. She pulled him closer. His mouth was open and his eyes closed. He looked deader than Morton had looked. *"Don't, love,"* she said to him, meaning don't *give up*, don't *die*, don't *leave me*.

She let go of his trousers and took hold of his face, cupping it in her hands and drawing his mouth to hers. He came with horrible ease, but she refused to be discouraged. She laid her lips on his, and said his name, like a summons.

"Joe."

There was light in her eyes. She could not resist it any longer.

"Joe."

Her eyes opened. And as they did so, in the last moment before the sea and the weeds and her lover disappeared, she saw, or imagined she saw, his lids flicker, as though her summons had stirred some sliver of life in him.

Then she was awake, and there was no way of knowing.

She squinted up at the beam of sunlight slipping between the crack in the drapes. The sheets were as tangled around her as the weeds where she'd almost let her body go to joy; the pillow was damp with her sweat. She had dreamed all that she'd just experienced, but she knew without question this was no ordinary dream. While her body had tussled and sweated here, her spirit had been in another place, a place as real as the bed on which she lay.

It was probably wonderful that such a place existed. It would probably change the world, if the world were ever to find out. But she didn't care. All that concerned her right now was Joe. Without him, the world wasn't worth a damn.

She got up and pulled back the drapes. It was Festival Saturday, and the sky was a perfect, cloudless blue. An escaped helium balloon, shining silver, floated into view. She watched it as the breeze carried it up over the pinetops towards the Heights. She would be following soon, she thought. No matter that this was Everville's day of days. No matter that the valley would be ringing from end to end with the din of people making music and money and love. Somewhere on the mountain a door stood open, and she would be through it before noon, or be dead in the attempt.

PART FOUR

The Devil and D'Amour

I

*T*hat," said the man with the salmon-pink tie, gesturing towards the canvas on the gallery wall, "is an abomination. What the hell's it called?" He peered at his price sheet.

"*Bronx Apocalypse*," the man at his side said.

"*Bronx Apocalypse*," the critic snorted. "Jesus!"

He eyed the man who'd supplied the title. "You're not him, are you?" he said. "You're not this fellow Dusseldorf?"

The other man—a well-made fellow in his late thirties, with three days' growth of beard and the eyes of an insomniac—shook his head. "No I'm not."

"You *are* in one of the paintings though, aren't you?" said the Asian woman at Salmon Tie's side.

"Am I?"

She took the sheet from her companion's hand and scanned the twenty or so titles upon it. "There," she said. "*D'Amour in Wyckoff Street*. It's the big painting next door," she said to Salmon Tie, "with that bilious sky."

"Loathsome," the man remarked. "Dusseldorf should go back to pushing heroin or whatever the hell he was doing. He's got no business foisting this crap on people."

"Ted didn't push," D'Amour said. He spoke softly, but there was no doubting the warning in his voice.

"I was simply stating my opinion," the man said, somewhat defensively.

"Just don't spread lies," D'Amour said. "You'll put the Devil out of work."

It was July 8, a Friday, and the Devil was much on Harry's mind tonight. New York was a stew as ever, and, as ever, Harry wished he could be out of the pot and away, but there was nowhere to go; nowhere he wouldn't be followed and found. And here, at least, in the sweet-and-sour streets he knew so well, he had niches and hiding places; he had people who owed him, people who feared him. He even had a couple of friends.

One of whom was Ted Dusseldorf, reformed heroin addict, sometime performance artist, and now, remarkably, a painter of metropolitan apocalypses.

There he was, holding court in front of one of his rowdier pieces, all five foot nothing of him, dressed in a baggy plaid suit, and chewing on a contender for the largest damn cigar in Manhattan.

"Harry! Harry!" he said, laying eyes on D'Amour. "Thanks for coming." He deserted his little audience and hooked his arm over Harry's shoulder. "I know you hate crowds, but I wanted you to see I got myself some admirers."

"Any sales?"

"Yeah, would you believe it? Nice Jewish lady, big collector, lives on the park, fancy address, buys that"—he jabbed his cigar in the direction of *Slaughtered Lambs on the Brooklyn Bridge*—"for her dining room. I guess maybe she's a vegetarian," he added, with a catarrhal laugh. "Sold a couple of drawings too. I mean, I ain't gonna get rich, you know, but I proved something, right?"

"That you did."

"I want you to see the masterwork," Ted said, leading Harry through the throng, which was divided into three distinct camps. The inevitable fashion victims, here to be seen and noted in columns. A smattering of well-heeled collectors, slumming. And Ted's friends, several of whom had tattoos as colorful as anything on the walls.

"I had this guy come up to me," Ted said, "fancy shoes, designer haircut, he says: Fantasy's so *passé*. I said: What fantasy? He looks at me like I farted. He says: These works of yours. I said: This isn't fantasy. This is my life. He shakes his head, walks away." Ted leaned closer to Harry. "I think sometimes there's two different kinds of people in the world. The people who understand and the people who don't. And if they don't, it's no use trying to explain, 'cause it's just beyond them, and it always will be."

There was an eight-by-six foot canvas on the wall ahead, its colors more livid and its focus more strident than anything else in the exhibition.

"You know, it keeps me sane, doin' this shit. If I hadn't started lettin' all this out onto canvas, man, I'd have lost my fuckin' mind. I don't know how you keep your head straight, Harry. I really don't. I mean, knowing what you know, seeing what you see . . . "

The knot of people standing in front of the picture parted, seeing the artist and his model approach, giving them plain view of the masterpiece. Like most of the other works it too depicted a commonplace street. Only this was a street Harry could name. This was Wyckoff Street, in Brooklyn, where one sunny Easter Sunday almost a decade before Harry had first been brushed by infernal wings.

Ted had painted the street pretty much as it looked—drab and uncomfortable—and had placed the figure of D'Amour in the middle of the thoroughfare, regarding the viewer with a curious gaze, as if to say: Do you see what I see? At first glance it seemed there was nothing untoward about the scene, but further study gave the lie to that. Rather than simply accruing a host of disturbing details on the canvas, Ted had worked a subtler effect. He'd laid down a field of mushy scarlets and ochers, like the guts of an over-ripe pomegranate, and then stroked the details of Wyckoff Street over this seething backcloth, the grays and sepias of brick and iron and asphalt never completely concealing the rotted hues beneath, so that for all the carefully rendered detail, Wyckoff Street looked like a veil drawn over a more insistent and powerful reality.

"Good likeness, huh?" Ted said.

Harry assumed it was, given that he'd been recognized from it, but hell, it was less than comforting. He had good bones—Norma had told him so the first time she'd touched his face—but did they have to *protrude* quite so much? The way Ted had laid the paint down on Harry's face he'd practically *carved* the features: long nose, strong jaw, wide brow and all. As for the marks of age, he hadn't stinted. The gray hairs and the frown-lines were much in evidence. It wasn't a bad face to be wearing into his forties, Harry supposed. Sure, there was none of the serenity that was rumored to be compensation for losing the bloom and ease of youth—his stare was troubled, the smile on his lips tentative to say the least—but it was a picture of a sane man with all his limbs and faculties intact, and of the people who'd wrestled with the beasts of the abyss, that pretty much put Harry in a league of one.

"Do you see it?" Ted said.

"See what?"

Ted brought Harry a couple of steps closer to the canvas and pointed to the lower half.

"There." Harry looked. First at the sidewalk, then at the gutter. "Under your foot," Ted prompted.

There, squirming under Harry's right heel, was a thin black snake, with burning coals for eyes.

"The Devil Himself," Ted said.

"Got him where I want him, have I?" Harry said.

Ted grinned. "Hey, it's art. I'm allowed to lie a little."

At Ted's request, Harry hung around for an hour or so in the offices at the back of the gallery until the crowd had begun to thin. He put his feet up on the desk and flipped through a couple of old copies of the *Times* while he waited. It was good sometimes to remember how other people, ordinary people, lived their lives: entertained by political dog-fights and foreign misery; by scandal and frippery and murder. He envied them their ignorance, and the ease with which they idled their lives away. Right now, he would have given just about everything he had for a week of that bliss; a week going about trivial business for trivial reasons, forgetful of the presences that scurried beneath the surface of things.

They weren't figments, these presences. He'd met them face to face (those that had faces) in alleyways and tenements and elevator shafts. Found them squatting in hospital garbage, sucking on soiled bandages; seen them in the mud at the river, eviscerating dogs. They were everywhere, and more arrogant by the day. It was only a matter of time, Harry knew, before they took the streets at noon. And when they did, they would be unopposed.

At the beginning of his career—when his investigations as a private detective had first led him into the company of the inhuman—he had entertained the delusion that he might with time help turn the tide against these forces by alerting the populous to their presence. He soon learned his error. People didn't want to know. They had drawn the parameters of belief so as to exclude such horrors, and would not, *could* not, tolerate or comprehend anybody who sought to move the fences. Harry's stumbling attempts to articulate all that he knew or suspected were met with derision, with rage, and, on one or two occasions, with violence. He quickly gave up trying to make converts, and resigned himself to a lonely war.

He wasn't entirely without allies. In the course of the next few years he'd met a handful of people who had all in some fashion or other come to know what he knew. Of these few, none was more important to him than Norma Paine, the black blind medium who, though she never left her tiny two-room apartment on Seventy-fifth, had tales to tell from every corner of Manhattan, passed on to her by the spirits that came looking for guidance on their journey to the Hereafter. Then there'd been Father Hess, who had for a little time labored with Harry to discover the precise nature of the presences that haunted the city. Their work together had come to an abrupt halt that Easter Sunday in Wyckoff Street, when one of those presences had sprung a trap on them both, and Hess had perished on the stairs while the triumphant demon sat on the bed where it had been found, speaking the same riddle to Harry over and over:

"I am you, and you are love, and that's what makes the world go round. I am you, and . . . "

In the years since that appalling day, Harry had never found an individual whose judgment he'd trusted as he'd trusted Hess's judgment. Though Hess had been a fervent Catholic, he'd not let his faith narrow his vision. He'd been a keen student of all manner of religions, with a passion for life and its mysteries that had burned more brightly than in any soul Harry had encountered. A conversation with Hess had been like a trip on whitewater rapids: by turns dizzying and dangerous. One moment he was theorizing about black holes, the next extolling the virtues of peppered vodka, the next speaking in reverential tones about the mystery of the Virgin Birth. And somehow always making the connections seem inevitable, however unlikely they were at first glance.

There wasn't a day went by Harry didn't miss him.

"Congratulate me," Ted said, appearing at the office door with a broad grin on his face, "I sold another piece."

"Good for you."

Ted slipped inside and closed the door behind him. He had a bottle of white wine in his hand. Squatting down against the wall, he sipped from it.

"Jeez, what a night," he said, his voice quivering with emotion. "I almost canceled last week. I wasn't sure I wanted people looking at what's in my head." He leaned back against the wall, and closed his eyes, expelling a long, low breath. There was silence for perhaps half a minute. Then he said, "I got what you wanted, Harry."

"Yeah?"

"I still think you're out of your mind—"

"When's the ceremony?"

"Next Tuesday."

"Do you know where?"

"Of *course*," Ted said, giving Harry a mock-offended look.

"Where?"

"Down around Ninth and—"

"Ninth and what?"

"Maybe I should just take you."

"No, Ted. You're going to stay out of this."

"Why?" Ted said, passing the wine bottle to Harry.

"Because you swore off all that shit, remember? Heroin and magic, out of your life. That's what you said."

"They are. I swear. Are you going to drink or not?"

Harry took a mouthful of wine. It was sour and warm. "So keep it that way. You've got a career to protect."

Ted gave a little self-satisfied smile. "I like the sound of that," he said.

"You were about to tell me the address."

"Ninth, between Thirteenth and Fourteenth. It's a triangular building. Looks deserted." He claimed the wine bottle back from Harry's hand, dropping his voice to a near whisper. "I've dug some secrets out of people in my time, but shit, getting this address, Harry, was like getting blood from a stone. What's going on down there?"

"You don't want to know."

"The less you tell me," Ted warned, "the more damn curious I'm going to get."

Harry shook his head despairingly. "You don't let go, do you?"

"I can't help it," Ted replied with a shrug, "I've got an addictive personality." Harry said nothing. "Well?" Ted pressed. "What's the big deal?"

"Ever heard of the Order of the Zyem Carasophia?"

Ted stared hard at Harry. "You're kidding?" Harry shook his head. "This is a Concupigaea ceremony?"

"That's what I heard."

"Harry . . . do you know what you're messing with? They're supposed to be exiles."

"Are they?" Harry said.

"Don't bullshit me, Harry. You know fucking well."

"I hear rumors, sure."

"And what do you think?"

"About what?"

"About where the fuck they came from?" Ted said, his agitation increasing.

"Like I say, it's all rumors, but—"

"But?"

"I think they're probably from Quiddity."

Ted let out a low whistle. He needed no introduction to the notion of the dream-sea. He'd dabbled in occult practices for half a decade, until in the midst of a conjuration, high on heroin, he'd unwittingly unleashed something with psychopathic tendencies, which it had taken all of Harry's wits to beat. Ted had sworn off magic and signed on for a detox program the same day. But the vocabulary of the occult still carried its old, familiar power, and there were few words in that vocabulary as potent as *Quiddity*.

"What are they doing here?" Ted said.

Harry shrugged. "Who knows? I'm not even sure they're the real thing."

"But if they are—?"

"If they are, I got some questions I need answering."

"About what?"

"About that snake you put under my heel."

"The Anti-Christ."

"They call it the Iad."

Again, Ted needed no education in seminologies. "The Uroboros and the Anti-Christ are the same thing?" he said.

"It's all the Devil by another name," Harry replied.

"How can you be so sure?"

"I'm a believer."

---

ii

The next day Harry went downtown to take a look at the building Ted had pinpointed. It was utterly commonplace, a four-story tenement, now apparently deserted, its windows boarded blind, its doors either padlocked or bricked up altogether. Harry ambled around it twice, studying it as discreetly as possible, in case he was being watched from inside. Then he headed back up to Norma's apartment, to get some advice.

Conversation wasn't always easy at Norma's place. She had been since adolescence a beacon for lost and wandering souls (particularly the recently dead) and when she tired of their importunings she turned on the thirty-odd televisions she owned, the din of which drove the wanderers away for a spell, but rendered ordinary exchanges near impossible.

Today, however, the televisions were all mute. The screens flickered on, selling diets and cars and life everlasting. Norma didn't see them, of course. She'd been blind since birth.

Not that she ever spoke like someone who was sightless.

"Look at you," she said as soon as Harry opened the door. "Are you catching something?"

"No, I'm fine. I just didn't get very much sleep."

"More tattoos?" Norma said.

"Just one," Harry admitted.

"Let me see."

"Norma."

"*Let me see,*" Norma said, reaching out from the well-cushioned comfort of her armchair.

Harry tossed his jacket on top of one of the televisions, and went over to Norma, who was sitting by the open window. The sounds of voices and traffic drifted up from below.

"Why don't you turn on the air-conditioning?" Harry said as he rolled up his shirt sleeve. "You're just breathing fumes."

"I like to hear the world going by," Norma said. "It's reassuring. Now, let's see the damage." She took hold of Harry's wrist and drew him a little closer, running her fingers up his arm to the place close to his elbow where he'd been most recently marked. "You still go to that old fake Voight?" Norma said, pulling away the bandage the tattooist had applied and running her fingers over the tender skin. Harry winced. "It's nice work," Norma conceded. "Though Christ knows what good you think it's going to do you."

This was an old debate between them. Harry had gathered the better part of a dozen tattoos over the last half-decade, all but two of which had been the handiwork of Otis Voight, who specialized in what he called protective ink: talismans and sigils etched into his clients' skin to keep the bad at bay.

"I owe my life to some of these," Harry said.

"You owe your life to your wits and your bloody-mindedness, Harry; no more nor less. Show me a tattoo that can stop a bullet—"

"I can't."

"Right. And a demon's a damn sight worse than a bullet."

"Bullets don't have psyches," Harry countered.

"Oh, and demons do?" said Norma. "No, Harry. They're pieces of shit, that's all they are. Little slivers of heartless filth." She bared her fine teeth in a grimace. "Oh God," she said, "but I'd love to be out there with you."

"It's not much fun," Harry said. "Believe me."

"Anything's better than this," she said, slamming her hands down on the arms of the chair. The glasses on the table beside her clicked against the rum and brandy bottles. "Sometimes I think this is a punishment, Harry. Sitting here day after day hearing people coming through with their tales of woe. Sobbin' about this, sobbin' about that. Regrettin' this, regrettin' that. I want to yell to 'em sometimes, *It's too damn late!* You should've thought about regrettin' while you could still do something about it. Ah! What's the use? I'm stuck talking to the snotty dead while you have all the fun. You don't know you're born, boy. You really don't."

Harry wandered over to the window and looked down seven floors to Seventy-fifth. "One of these nights," he said.

"Yeah?"

"I'm going to come fetch you and we're going to ride around for a few hours. Check out a few of the bad places, the *really* bad places, and see how quickly you change your mind."

"You're on," Norma said. "In the meanwhile, to what do I owe the honor? You didn't come here to show me Voight's handiwork."

"No."

"And you didn't come bearing rum."

"I'm sorry."

She waved his apology away. "Don't be silly. I'm happy you're here. But why?"

"I need some advice. I'm going to a party Tuesday night."

"Go on, ask a blind woman what you should wear," Norma replied, much amused. "Who's throwing the party?"

"The Order of the Zyem Carasophia."

Norma's smile vanished. "That's not funny, Harry."

"It's not meant to be," Harry replied. "They're having some kind of ceremony, and I have to be there."

"Why?"

"Because if anyone knows where the Iad'll attempt another breach it's them."

"There's a good reason why nobody ever talks about them, Harry."

"Because everybody buys the rumors. The fact is, nobody knows who the hell they are."

"Or *what*," Norma said.

"So you believe the stories?"

"About them being exiles?" Norma shrugged. "Seems to me, we're all exiles."

"Now don't get metaphysical on me."

"It's not metaphysics, it's the truth. All life began in the dream-sea, Harry. And we've all been trying to get back there ever since."

"Why don't I find that very comforting?"

"Because you're afraid of what it means," Norma said, lightly. "You're afraid you'd have to throw away all the rules you live by, and then you'd go crazy."

"And you wouldn't?"

"Oh no, I'd probably join you," Norma replied. "The issue isn't my sanity or yours, Harry. It's what's true or not. And I think you, me, and the Zyem have a lot in common."

"What have I got to fear?" Harry said.

"They're probably as afraid of you as you are of them, and that means they'd prefer to have your head on a plate where they can see it. Or eat it."

"Ha fucking ha."

"You asked," Norma replied.

Harry turned his attention from the street to the television screens. Three dozen silent dramas were in progress before him, the cameras' eyes picking up every little triumph and agony, whether real or rehearsed.

"Do you ever think we're being watched?" Harry said, after a few moments of staring at the screens.

"I am, all the damn time," Norma replied.

"I don't mean by ghosts," Harry replied.

"What then?"

"Oh, I don't know—God?"

"No."

"You sound very sure."

"I am. Sitting here right now. Ask me tomorrow I might have a different answer. I doubt it, but you never know."

"You talk about demons—"

"So?"

"That means the Devil's in the mix somewhere."

"And if the Devil's on the planet God must be too?" She shook her head. "We've had this argument before, Harry. It's one of those useless subjects."

"I know."

"I don't know what your demons are—"

"They're *not mine*, for a start."

"You see, we're disagreeing already. I think they're very much yours."

"You mean what happened to Hess was *me?*" Harry said, his timbre darkening.

"You know that's not what I mean."

"What then?"

"The demons find you, because you need them. So did Hess. You need them for the world to make sense to you. Some people believe in—I don't know, what do people believe in? Politicians, movie stars . . . " she sighed, exasperated. "Why are you fretting about it anyway?"

"Time of year. Time of life. I don't know." He paused. "That's not true. I *do* know."

"Goin' to tell me?"

"I've got this constant feeling of *dread*."

"About the Order?"

"No."

"What then?"

"I still believe in Hell. It's *me* I don't believe in any longer."

"What the heck are you talkin' 'bout?" Norma said. She extended her arm in Harry's direction. "Come here," she said. "Harry? You hear me?" Harry extended his arm, and Norma unerringly seized hold of his wrist. "I want you to listen to me," she said. "An' I don't want you shushing me or tellin' me you don't want to hear, 'cause sometimes things don't get said that should be said and I'm goin' to say 'em now. Understand me?" She didn't wait for Harry to agree to her conditions, but went on, tugging on Harry's arm to bring him still closer to her chair. "You're a good man, Harry, an' that's rare. I mean *really* rare. I think something moves in you that doesn't move in most men, which is why you're always being tested this way. I don't know what it is testin' you—or me come to that—but I know we got no choice. Understand me? We got no choice but to just get on with things, day by day, and make our way as best we can."

"Okay, but—"

"*I haven't finished.*"

"Sorry."

She drew Harry down beside her. "How long we known each other?" she asked him.

"Eleven years."

Her free hand went to his face. Touched his brow, his cheek, his mouth. "Takes its toll, huh?" she said.

"Yep."

"If we knew why, Harry, we wouldn't be what we are. Maybe we wouldn't even be human."

"You think that, really?" Harry said softly. "You think we have to just stumble on because that's what being human is?"

"Part of it."

"And if we get *did* understand?" Harry said.

"We wouldn't be human," Norma said.

Harry let his head sink on Norma's arm. "Maybe that's it then," he murmured.

"What is?"

"Maybe I think it's time to stop being human."

iii

The new tattoo hurt more than any of the others. That night it itched furiously, and several times Harry woke from dreams of the design moving on his arm like a living thing, writhing to be out from under the dressing.

The next day he'd called Grillo and had what was to be his last conversation with the man, in the midst of which he'd spoken about the Anti-Christ. Grillo had made his contempt for the term perfectly plain (You're too damn Catholic for your own good, he'd said) after which the exchange had come to a chilly end. The Reef and its keeper had been Harry's last hope of useful information about the Order, and he had come up empty-handed. He would enter the building between Thirteenth and Fourteenth without any real sense of what he was facing. But then what else was new?

He took up his position across the street from the spot before noon the following day and waited. There was little sign of activity until the middle of the afternoon, when the first of the celebrants arrived, slipping out of a car, crossing the sidewalk fast, and disappearing down a flight of steps that led below ground level. Harry had no time even to glimpse his or her face. There were another ten or so appearances before dusk, all the visitors heading on down the same flight. Harry had checked it out when he'd first examined the building. There was an iron door at the bottom of the steps, which had looked to be rusted shut when he'd examined it. Plainly it was not.

He had expected things to speed up somewhat as darkness fell, but that was not the case. Another half dozen partygoers arrived, and disappeared down into the ground, but it began to seem as though the gathering would be considerably more intimate than he'd anticipated. This was both good news and bad. Good, because there would be fewer eyes to spot an interloper like himself; bad, in that it implied the ceremony was not mere ritual reunion; rather a meeting of a few authorities, bringing with them who knew what powers? Not a comfortable doubt.

Then, just a little before nine, with the last of the daylight gone from the sky, a cab drew up outside the liquor store at the corner of Thirteenth and Ted got out. The cab drove off, and he stood at the intersection a minute, pulling on a cigarette. Then he crossed towards the building. Harry had no choice but to break cover, and start towards him, hoping Ted would catch sight of him and retreat. But Ted had his eyes fixed on his destination, and before Harry could intercept him he'd disappeared around the back of the building. Slowing his pace somewhat so as not to attract undue attention (could he doubt somebody was watching from inside?) Harry gained the opposite side of the street and followed Ted around the block. But he had already gone. Harry doubled back, and turned the corner in time to see Ted starting down the flight of steps. Quietly cursing him, Harry picked up his pace. There was not sufficient traffic to cover the sound of his footfalls. Ted glanced back over his shoulder, flattening himself into the shadows of the stairs as he did so, only to emerge a moment later with a grin of welcome on his face.

"It's you—"

Harry hushed him with a gesture, and beckoned him out of the stairwell, but Ted shook his head, pointing down the stairs to the door. Grimacing, Harry hurried along the wall, and headed down into the shadows to Ted's side.

"You're not coming with me," he hissed.

"You think you're going to get through that door without help?" Ted replied, pulling a hammer and crowbar from inside his jacket.

"You're not getting involved with magic any more, remember?" Harry said.

"This is my farewell appearance," Ted replied. Then, his voice dropping to a near growl, "I'm not taking no for an answer, Harry. You wouldn't even *be* here if it weren't for me."

"I'm not going to be responsible for you," Harry warned him.

"I'm not asking—"

"I *mean* it. I got too much on my plate as it is."

"Deal," Ted said, with a little grin. "So are we going or what?"

So saying, he slipped down the flight of stairs to the door. Harry followed on.

"Got your lighter?" Ted asked.

Harry fished for it and flicked it on. The flame showed them a door, encrusted with rust. Ted pulled out his crowbar and pushed it between the door and the jamb. Then he leaned all his weight against it. A hail of rust particles flew against their faces and the hinges of the door creaked, but it didn't open.

"That's no damn use," Harry whispered.

"You got a better idea?" Ted hissed.

Harry snapped the cigarette lighter shut. In the darkness he said, "Yeah, I got a better idea. But you look the other way."

"What the hell for?"

"Just damn well do it," Harry said, and flicked the lighter back on to see that his instruction was being obeyed.

It wasn't. Ted was staring at him with a quizzical look on his face.

"You've got some *suit*, haven't you?" he said, his tone more admiring than accusatory.

"Maybe."

"*Jesus*, Harry—"

"Listen, Ted, if you don't like it get the fuck out of here."

"What you got?" Ted said. There was a gleam in his eyes as he spoke, like an addict in the presence of his preferred poison. "You got a hand of glory?"

"Christ, no."

"What then?"

"You're not seeing it, Ted," Harry insisted. "I told you: Look away."

Very reluctantly Ted averted his eyes and Harry brought from his pocket the *prodigile suit,* a minor magical device for which he'd paid Otis Voight four hundred bucks. It was a sliver of aluminum two inches long and one and a half inches wide, with a small sigil stamped at one end, and five narrow grooves radiating from the sign. Harry pressed it into the gap between the door and the frame, as close to the lock as he could get it.

Behind him he heard Ted say, "You got a *prodigile.* Where the fuck'd you get that?"

It was too late to tell him to look away, and no use lying. Ted knew magic's methods and implements too well to be deceived.

"It's none of your business," Harry told him. He didn't like dabbling in the craft (even the use of a *prodigile*, which was an extremely minor device on the thaumaturgic scale, brought with it the danger of contamination or addiction), but sometimes circumstances demanded that the enemy's weapons be used in the very labor of destroying them. Such was the sour reality of war.

He pressed his thumb against the exposed edge of the suit, and jerked it down. His flesh opened easily, and he felt the prodigile throb as it drew blood. This, he knew, was the most likely moment for addiction; when the suit was activated. He told himself to look away, but could not. He watched, never less than amazed, as his blood hissed against the metal and was sucked along the grooves and out of sight. He heard Ted draw a sharp breath behind him. Then there was a burst of luminescence from the crack between door and jamb, and the unmistakable sound of the lock mechanism snapping open. Before the light had quite died, Harry put his shoulder to the door. It opened without resistance. He glanced round at Ted, who despite his earlier bullishness, now looked a little fearful.

"Are you ready?" Harry said, and without waiting for an answer slipped inside, leaving Ted to come or stay as he wished.

II

i

The interior smelled of stale incense and week-old sushi—the odors, in short, of bad magic. It made Harry's heart hammer to smell those smells. How many times do I have to do this? he found himself wondering as he advanced into the murk. How many times into the maw, into the sickened body? How many times before I've done my penance?

Ted laid his hand on Harry's shoulder.

"There," he murmured, and directed Harry's gaze off to the right. Some ten yards from where they stood was a further flight of stairs, and from the bottom a wash of silvery light.

Ted's hand remained on Harry's shoulder as they crossed to the top of the flight and began the descent. It grew colder with every step, and the smell became steadily stronger: Signs that what they sought lay somewhere at the bottom. And, if any further evidence was required, Harry's tattoos supplied it. The new one itched more furiously than ever, while the old ones (at his ankles, at his navel, in the small of his back, and down his sternum) tingled.

Three steps from the bottom, Harry turned to Ted, and in the lowest of voices murmured, "I meant it: about not being responsible for you."

Ted nodded and took his hand off Harry's shoulder. There was nothing more to be said; no further excuse to delay the descent. Harry reached into his jacket and lightly patted the gun in its holster. Then he was down the last three steps and, turning a corner was delivered into a sizable brick chamber, the far wall of which was fifty feet or more from where he stood, the vaulted ceiling twenty feet above his head. In the midst of this was what at first glance resembled a column of translucent drapes, about half as wide as the chamber itself, which was the source of the silvery light that had drawn them down the stairs. Second glance, however, showed him that it was not fabric, but some kind of ether. It resembled the melting folds of a Borealis, draped over or spun from a cat's cradle of filaments that criss-crossed the chamber like the web of a vast, ambitious spider.

And amid the folds, figures: the celebrants he'd seen coming here through the afternoon. They no longer wore their coats and hats, but wandered in the midst of the light nearly naked.

And *such* nakedness! Though many of them were partially concealed by the drooping light, Harry had no doubt that all he'd heard about the Zyem Carasophia was true. These were exiles; no doubt of it. Some were plainly descended from a marriage of bird and man, their eyes set in the sides of their narrow heads, their mouths beakish, their backs feathered. Others gave credence to a rumor Harry'd heard that a few of Quiddity's infants were simply *dreamed* into being, creatures of pure imagination. How else to explain the pair whose heads were yellowish blurs, woven with what looked like bright blue fireflies, or the creature who had shrugged off the skin of her head in tiny ribbons, which attended her raw face in a fluttering dance.

Of the unholy paraphernalia Harry had expected to see, there was no sign. No sputtering candles of human fat, no ritual blades, no gutted children. The celebrants simply moved in the cradle of light as if drifting in some collective dream. Had it not been for the smell of incense and sushi he would have doubted there was even error here.

"What's going on?" Ted murmured in Harry's ear.

Harry shook his head. He had no clue. But he knew how to find out. He shrugged off his jacket and proceeded to unbutton his shirt.

"What are you doing?"

"I'm going to join them," he replied.

"They'll be on to you in a minute."

"I don't think so," Harry said, heeling off his shoes as he pulled his shirt out of his trousers. He watched the wanderers as he did so, looking for any trace of belligerence among them. But there was none. It was as if they were moving in a semi-mesmerized state, all aggression dulled.

There was every possibility they wouldn't even notice if he went among them clothed, he suspected. But some instinct told him he would be safer in this throng if he were as vulnerable as they.

"Stay here," he said to Ted.

"You're out of your mind, you know that?" Ted replied.

"I'll be fine," Harry said, glancing down at his near-naked body and patted his belly. "Maybe I need to lose a pound or two. . . ." Then he turned from Ted and walked towards the cradle.

He hadn't realized until now that either the light or the filaments was making a low, fluctuating whine, which grew louder as he approached. It throbbed in his skull, like the beginning of a headache, but uncomfortable as it was it could not persuade him to turn round. His skin was gooseflesh now, from head to foot, the tattoos tingling furiously.

He raised his left arm in front of him and pulled the dressing off his fresh ink. The tattoo looked livid in the silvery light, as though it had been pricked into his flesh moments before: a ruby parabola that suddenly seemed an utter redundancy. Norma had been right, he thought. What defense was a mere mark in a world so full of power?

He cast the dressing aside and continued to advance towards the cradle, expecting one of the celebrants to look his way at any moment. But nobody did. He stepped into the midst of the drapes without so much as a glance being cast in his direction and, weaving among the wanderers, made his way towards the center of the Borealis. He raised his arms as he did so, and his fingers brushed one of the filaments, sending a small charge of energy, too minor to be distressing, down to his shoulders and across his chest. The Borealis shook, and for a moment he feared that it intended to expel him, for the shimmering folds closed around him from all sides. Their touch was far from unpleasant, however, and whatever test they had put him to he apparently passed, for a moment later they retreated from him again, and returned to their gentle motion.

Harry glanced back, out into the chamber, in search of Ted, but everything beyond the light—the walls, the stairs, the roof—had become a blur. He didn't waste time looking, but turned his attention back to whatever mystery lay waiting in the center of the cradle.

The ache in his head grew more painful as he approached, but he bore it happily enough. There was something ahead of him, he saw: a sliver of darkness at the core of this cradle of light. It was taller than he was, this sliver, and it almost seemed to exercise some authority over him, because now that he had it in view he could not turn his eyes from it.

And with the sight, another sound, audible beneath the whine, like the repeated roll of muffled drums.

Mystified and mesmerized though he was, the identity of the sound was not lost on him. It was the sea he was hearing.

His heartbeat grew urgent. Tremors ran through his body. The sea! My God, the sea! He breathed its name like a blessing.

"Quiddity—"

The word was heard. He felt a breath upon his back and somebody said, "Hold back."

He glanced round, to find that one of the exiles, its face an eruption of color, was close to him.

"We must wait before the *neirica*," the creature said. "The blessing will come."

The blessing? Harry thought. Who were they expecting down here, the Pope?

"Will it be soon?" Harry said, certain that at any moment the creature would see him for the simple Homo sapiens he was.

"Very soon," came the reply, "he knows how impatient we are."

The creature's gaze went past Harry to the darkness. "He knows how we ache to return. But we must do it with the blessing, yes?"

"Yes," said Harry. "Of course. Yes."

"Wait . . ." the creature said, turning its head towards the outside world, "is that not him?"

There was a sudden flurry of activity in the vicinity as the creatures—including Harry's informant—moved off towards the edge of the Borealis. Harry was torn between the desire to see whoever this was, coming to bless them, and the urge to see Quiddity's shore. He chose the latter. Turning on his heel he took two quick strides towards the sliver of darkness, his momentum speeded by the force it exercised. He felt the ground grow uncertain beneath him, felt a gust of rainy wind against his face, fresh and cold. The darkness opened before him, as though the gust had blown open a door, and for an instant his sight seemed to race ahead of him, his lumpen flesh stumbling after, out, out across a benighted shore.

Above him the sky was spired with clouds, and creatures trailing dusty light swooped and soared in lieu of stars. On the stones below, crabs made war or love, claws locked as they clattered towards the surf. And in that surf, shoals leapt the waves as though aspiring to sky or stones, or both.

All this he saw in a single hungry glance.

Then he heard a cry behind him, and with the greatest reluctance looked back over his shoulder towards the chamber. There was some consternation there, he saw. The cradle was shaking, the veils that circled the crack, like bandages wrapped around a wound, torn here and there. He tried to focus his eyes to better see the cause, but they were slow to shake off the wonders they'd just witnessed, and while they did so screams erupted to right and left of him. Their din was sufficient to slap him from his reverie. Suddenly fearful for his life he took off from his place beside the sliver, though its claim on him was powerful, and it took all his strength to do so.

As he ran he caught sight of the creature who had so recently addressed him, stumbling through the veils with a wound in its chest the size of a fist. As it fell to its knees its glistening eyes fixed on

Harry for a moment, and it opened its bony mouth as to beg some explanation. Blood came instead, black as squid's ink, and the creature toppled forward, dead before it hit the ground. Harry searched for its killer among the shaking veils, but all he found were victims: creatures reeling and falling, their wounds atrocious. A lopped head rolled at his feet; a creature with half its body blown away took hold of him in its agony, and expired sobbing in his arms.

As to the cradle, which had so suddenly become a grave, it shook from one end to the other, the veils shaken down by the violence in their midst, and bringing the filaments with them. They spat and spasmed on the ground, the light they'd lent the veils dying now, and steadily delivering the chamber into darkness.

Shielding his head against the falling cradle, Harry gained the outer limit of the circle, and now—finally—had sight of the creature that had visited these horrors on the scene.

It was a man. No more, no less. He had the beard of a patriarch, and the robes of a prophet. Blue robes once, but now so stained with blood he looked like a butcher. As to his weapon, it was a short staff, from which spurts of pallid fire broke, going from it almost languidly. Harry saw one go, snaking through the air to catch a victim who had so far avoided harm. It struck the creature (one of the blur-and-firefly couple) above her buttocks and ran up her back, gouging out the flesh to either side of her spine. Despite the appalling scale of her wounding, she was not felled, but swung round to face her wounder.

"Why?" she sobbed, extending her flabby arms in his direction. "Why?"

He made no answer. Simply raised his staff a second time, and let another burst of energy go from it, striking his victim in the mouth. Her pleas ceased on the instant, and the fire climbed up over her skull, turning it to ruin in a heartbeat. Even then she didn't fall. Her body shook as it stood, her bowels and bladder voiding. Wearing a look close to amusement, the prophet stepped over the bloody litter that lay between them and with one backhanded swipe struck the seared face with the staff, the blow so hard her head was separated from her neck.

Harry let out an involuntary cry, more of rage than of horror. The killer, who was already striding past the beheaded woman towards the crack, stopped in mid-step, and stared through the blood-flecked air. Harry froze. The prophet stared on, a look of puzzlement on his face.

He doesn't see me, Harry thought.

That was perhaps overly optimistic. The man continued to look, as though he glimpsed some trace of a presence in the deepening darkness, but could not quite decide whether his eyes were deceiving him. He wasn't about to take any chances. Even as he stared on in puzzlement he raised his staff.

Harry didn't wait for the fire to come. He made a dash for the stairs, hoping to God that Ted had escaped ahead of him. The killing fire sighed past him, close enough for Harry to feel its sickly heat, then burst against the opposite wall, its energies tracing the cracks as it dispersed. Harry looked back towards the prophet, who had already forgotten about the phantom and had turned towards the dark crack that let on to Quiddity.

Harry's gaze went to the sliver. In the diminishing light of the chamber the shore and sea were more visible than they had been, and for a moment it was all he could do not to turn back; to race the prophet to the threshold and be out under that steepled sky.

Then, from the murk off to his left, a pained and weary voice.

"I'm sorry, Harry . . . please . . . I'm sorry—"

With a sickening lurch in his stomach Harry turned and sought out the source of the voice. Ted lay seven or eight yards from the bottom of the stairs, his arms open wide, his chest the same. Such a wound, wet and deep, it was a wonder he had life enough to breathe, much less to speak. Harry went down at his side.

"Grab my hand, will you?" Ted said.

"I've got it," Harry said.

"I can't feel anything."

"Maybe that's for the best," Harry said. "I'm going to have to pick you up."

"He came out of nowhere—"

"Don't worry about it."

"I was keepin' out of the way, like you said, but then he just came out of nowhere."

"Hush, will you?" Harry slid his arms under Ted's body. "Okay, now, are you ready for this?"

Ted only moaned. Harry drew a deep breath, stood up, and without pausing began to carry the wounded man towards the stairs. It was harder to see the flight by the moment, as the last of the light in the filaments died away. But he stumbled on towards it, while little spasms passed through Ted's body.

"Hold on," Harry said. "Hold on."

They had reached the bottom of the flight now, and Harry began to climb. He glanced back towards the center of the chamber just once, and saw that the prophet was standing at the threshold between Cosm and Metacosm. No doubt he would step through it presently. No doubt that was what he had come here to do. Why had it been necessary to slaughter so many souls in the process was a mystery Harry did not expect to solve any time soon.

ii

"It's late, Harry," Norma said. She was sitting in the same chair beside the window, with the televisions burbling around her. Hour-before-dawn shows.

"Can I get a drink?" Harry said.

"Help yourself."

His passage lit only by the flickering screens, Harry crossed to the table at Norma's side and poured himself a brandy.

"You've got blood on you," Norma said. Her nose was as keen as her eyes were blind.

"It's not mine. It's Ted Dusseldorf's."

"What happened?"

"He died about an hour ago."

Norma was silent for a few seconds. Then she said, "The Order?"

"Not exactly," Harry sat on the hard, plain chair set opposite Norma's cushioned throne, and told her what he'd witnessed.

"So the tattoos were a good investment after all," she said when he'd finished the account.

"Either that, or I was lucky."

"I don't believe in luck," Norma said. "I believe in destiny." She made the word sound almost sexy, the way she shaped it.

"So it was Ted's destiny to end up dead tonight?" Harry said. "I don't buy that."

"So don't," Norma said, without a trace of irritation. "It's a free country."

Harry sipped on the brandy. "Maybe it's time I got some serious help," he said.

"Are you talking therapy? 'Cause if you are, I'm telling you right now I've had Freud through here—least he said he was Freud—and that man was so *fucked up—*"

"I'm not talking about Freud. I'm talking about the Church, or maybe the FBI. I don't know. Somebody's got to be told what's going on."

"If they're inclined to believe you, then they've already been recruited by the enemy," Norma said. "You can be certain of that."

Harry sighed. He knew what she said was true. There were people out there wearing uniforms and cassocks and badges of office whose daily agenda was the suppressing of information about the miraculous. If he chose the wrong car in which to whisper what he knew he was dead.

"So we choose carefully," Harry said.

"Or we let it be."

"The door's not supposed to be open, Norma."

"Are you sure?"

"That's a damn stupid question," Harry replied. "Of *course* I'm sure."

"Well that's comforting," Norma said. "Do you remember when you first decided this?"

"I didn't decide it. I was told."

"By whom?"

"I don't know. Hess maybe. You."

"Me? Don't listen to me!"

"Then who the hell *should* I listen to?"

"You could start with yourself," Norma replied. "Remember what you said to me a few days ago?"

"No."

"You were talking about how maybe it was time to stop being human?"

"Oh that—"

"Yes, that."

"That was just talk."

"It's all just talk till we make it true, Harry."

"I'm not following this."

"Maybe the door's *supposed* to be open," Norma said. "Maybe we have to start looking at what's in our dreams, only with our eyes open."

"We're back to Freud."

"No we're not," she said softly. "Not remotely."

"Suppose you're wrong?" Harry said. "Suppose leaving the door open is some kind of catastrophe, and if I don't do something about it—"

"Then the world comes to an end?"

"Right."

"It won't. It can't. It can change, but it can't end."

"I have to take your word for that, I suppose?"

"No. You could ask your cells. They'd tell you."

"We don't talk much these days, me and my cells," Harry said.

"Maybe you're not listening carefully enough," Norma replied. "The point is: So what if the world changes? Is it so dandy the way it is?"

"It could be a damn sight worse."

"Says who?"

"Me! I say so!"

Norma raised her arm, reaching out for Harry. "Let's go up onto the roof," she said.

"Now?"

"Now. I need some air."

Up they went, Norma wrapped in her shawl, onto the roof nine floors above Seventy-fifth. Dawn was still a while away, but the city was already gearing up for another day. Norma looped her arm through Harry's, and they stood together in silence for perhaps five minutes, while the traffic murmured below, and sirens wailed, and the wind gusted off the river, grimy and cold. It was Norma who broke the silence.

"We're so powerful," Norma said, "and so frail."

"Us?"

"Everybody. *Powerful*."

"I don't think that's the way most people feel," Harry said.

"That's because they can't feel the connections. They think they're alone. In their heads. In the world. I hear them all the time. Spirits come through, carryin' on about how *alone* they feel, how terribly *alone*. And I say to them, let go of what you are—"

"And they don't want to do that?"

"Of course not."

"I don't like the sound of it either," Harry said. "I'm all I've got. I don't want to give it up."

"I said let go of it, not give it up," Norma said. "They're not the same thing."

"But when you're dead—"

"What's dead?" Norma shrugged. "Things change but they don't end. I told you."

"And I don't believe you. I want to, but I don't."

"Then I can't convince you," Norma said. "You'll have to find out for yourself, one way or another." She drew a little closer to Harry. "How long have we known each other?" she said.

"You asked me that."

"And what did you say?"

"Eleven years."

"That long, huh?" She lapsed into silence again, for a minute or so. Then she said, "Are you happy, Harry?"

"Christ, no. Are you?"

"You know what? I am," Norma said, her voice tinged with surprise. "I like your company, Harry. Another time, another place, we would have made quite a pair, you and me. Maybe we did." She laughed, softly. "Maybe *that's* why it feels like I've known you longer than eleven years." She shuddered. "I'm getting a little chilly," she said. "Will you take me back downstairs?"

"Of course."

"You sound so tired, Harry. You should sleep for a few hours. I've got a mattress in the spare room."

"It's okay, thanks. I'll go home. I just needed somebody to talk to."

"I wasn't much use, was I? You want plain answers and I don't have any."

"There was something I didn't tell you."

"What's that?"

"I almost stepped through."

"Through the door?"

"Yeah."

"And why didn't you?"

"I couldn't leave Ted, for one thing. And—I don't know—I guess I was afraid there'd be no way back."

"Oh, maybe the best journeys are the ones with no return ticket, Harry," Norma said, with yearning in her voice. "Tell me what it was like."

"The shore? It was beautiful." He conjured it in his mind's eye now and could not help but sigh.

"Go back, then," Norma said.

Harry didn't reply for a moment, but instead scanned the glittering panorama before him. It too was beautiful, after its fashion, but only from this angle, and only at night.

"Maybe I should," he said.

"If you're thinking about me, don't," Norma said. "I'll miss you, but I'll be fine. Who knows, maybe I'll come after you one of these days."

iii

He went back to his apartment to clean up (his shirt was glued to his chest with Ted's blood) and gather a few items for the journey. It was an absurd procedure, of course, given that he had no clue as to what lay on the other side, beyond sea, sky, and stones.

He pocketed his wallet, though he doubted they traded in dollars. He put on his watch, though surely time was redundant there. He slipped on his crucifix, despite the fact that he'd heard the tale of Christ had been fashioned to distract attention from the very mystery he was about to enter. Then, with the new day barely dawning, he made his way back to the building between Thirteenth and Fourteenth.

The door he'd opened using the *prodigile*, less than a dozen hours before, was open. With the steady beam of a flashlight to precede him he made his way to the top of the stairs. There he paused, listening for any sound from below. He'd escaped the prophet's murderous ways once; twice was tempting fate. There was no noise, however; not a moan. Extinguishing the flashlight, he made his way down the stairs by what little illumination came from the door above. It had given out by the time he reached the bottom of the flight, but there was a second source below, this far stronger. The blood of one of the murdered celebrants, spilled liberally from head and heart, threw up a lilac light from its pools, like the phosphorescence of something rotted.

Harry halted at the bottom of the step until his eyes had become properly accustomed to the illumination. After a time, it showed him a scene he had prepared himself for as best he could, but which still raised the hairs on the nape of his neck.

He'd seen death arrayed before, of course, all too many times, and seldom neatly. Bodies carved and corroded, their limbs broken, their faces erased. But here was something stranger than that; twice stranger. Here were creatures he'd thought unholy—worshippers of the Anti-Christ, he'd thought—whose flesh was not the stuff of any simple biology. He had a primal suspicion of things that looked as different from himself as these beasts had. Such forms had in his experience housed malice and lunacy. But surveying this scene he could not bring himself to rejoice at their dispatch. Perhaps they'd been innocents, perhaps not. He would never know. What he *did* know was that in the past week he'd spoken of moving beyond what he'd once assumed were the limits of his species. He could no longer afford to scorn any form, however unlikely, for fear in time it might turn out to be his own. Anything was possible. Perhaps, like a fetus which resembled a reptile and a bird before it came to its humanity, he would revisit those states as he moved on. In which case he had siblings here, in the darkness.

He looked beyond them now, towards the center of the chamber. Though the filaments had lost their light, a few scraps of the misty veils that had hung from them remained. But they could not conceal the absence at the heart. The opening that had led on to Quiddity's shore was gone.

Stumbling over corpses as he went, Harry crossed to the spot, hoping with every step that his eyes deceived him. It was a vain hope. The prophet had closed the door behind him when he'd stepped away into that other place, and left nothing to mark the place.

"Stupid," Harry told himself.

He'd been so close. He'd stood on the threshold of the miraculous, where perhaps the mysteries of being might be solved, and instead of taking the opportunity while he had it, he'd let himself be distracted. He'd turned his back, and lost his opportunity.

Was this the destiny Norma had spoken of? That he be left among the dead, while the miracle train moved off without him?

His legs—drained of the adrenaline that had fueled him thus far—were ready to give out. It was time to go, now; time to bury his frustration and his sorrow in sleep for a few hours. Later, maybe, when he had his thoughts in better order, he'd be able to make better sense of all this.

He made his way back across the slaughterhouse and up the stairs. As he came to the top of the flight, however, something lurched out of the shadows to block his path. The prophet's massacre had not been completely thorough, it appeared. Here was one who'd survived, though even in the paltry light of the passageway it was plain she could not be far from death. She wore a wound from the middle of her chest to her hip, its length gummy with dried blood. Her face was as flat as an iron, her eyes gleaming gold in her noseless, lipless face.

"I know you," she said, her voice low and sibilant. "You were at the ceremony."

"Yes I was."

"Why did you come back?"

"I wanted to get through the door."

"So did we all," she said, leaning in Harry's direction. Her eyes shone and fluttered eerily, as if she were reading his marrow. "You're not one of us," she said.

Harry saw no reason to lie. "No, I'm not."

"You came with *him*," she suddenly said. "Oh by the 'shu . . ." She flung herself back away from Harry, raising her arms to protect her face.

"It's all right," Harry said. "I wasn't with him. I swear."

He came up the last few steps and started towards her. Too weak to outrun him, the creature sank down against the wall, her broken body wracked with sobs. "Kill me," she said. "I don't care. There's nothing left."

Harry went down on his haunches in front of her. "Listen to me, will you? I didn't come with whoever it was— "

"Kissoon," she said.

"What?"

She peered at him through her webbed fingers. "You *do* know him."

"The Kissoon I know's dead," he said. "Or at least I thought he was."

"He murdered our Blessedm'n and came in to our ceremonies wearing his flesh. And why?"

Harry had an answer to that, at least. "To get into Quiddity."

The creature shook her head. "He didn't leave," she said. "He just sealed the door."

"Are you sure?"

"I saw it with my own eyes. That's how I know it was Kissoon."

"Explain that."

"When it closed, at the very last moment, there was a light went through everything—the brick, the flow, the dead—and I seemed to see their true nature, just for a little time. And I looked up at him—at the man we'd thought was our Blessedm'n—and I saw another man hidden in his flesh."

"How did you know it was Kissoon?"

"He had tried to join us, once. Said he was an exile, like us, and he wanted to come home with us, back to Quiddity." When she said the word, she shuddered, and more tears came down. "You know what's strange?" she said with a sour little laugh. "I was never there. Most of us were never there. We're the children of exiles, or their children's children. We lived and died for something we only ever knew in stories."

"Do you know where he went?"

"Kissoon?"

Harry nodded.

"Yes, I know. I went after him, to his hiding place."

"You wanted to kill him?"

"Of course. But once I got there I had no strength left. I knew if I faced him like this, he'd finish me. I came back here to prepare myself."

"Tell me where he is. Let me do the job for you."

"You don't know what he can do."

"I've heard," Harry replied. "Believe me. I've heard."

"And you think you can kill him?"

"I don't know," Harry said, picturing in his mind's eye the portrait Ted had produced. The heavens livid, the street reeling, and a black snake under his pointed heel. Kissoon was that snake, by another name. "I've beaten some demons in my time."

"He's not a demon," the creature said. "He's a man."

"Is that good news or bad?"

The creature eyed him gravely. "You know the answer to that," she said.

Bad, of course.

Demons were simple. They believed in prayer and the potency of holy water. Thus they fled from both. But men—what did men believe?

iv

The address the creature had given him was up in Morningside Heights, around 110th and Eighth Avenue: an undistinguished house in need of some cosmetic repair. There were no drapes at the lower windows. Harry peered inside. The room was empty: no pictures on the walls, no carpets on the floor, no furniture, nothing. He knew before he'd reached the front door, and found it an inch ajar, and stepped through it into the gray interior, that he'd come too late. The house was empty, or nearly so.

A few signs of Kissoon's occupancy remained. At the top of the stairs, lying in a pool of its own degenerating matter, was a modestly sized Lix. It raised its head at Harry's approach, but with its maker departed, it had lost what tiny wits it had, overreached itself, and slid down the stairs, depositing cobs of sewerage on each step as it descended. Harry followed the fetid trail it had left to the room that Kissoon had lately occupied. It resembled a derelict's hideaway. Newspapers laid in lieu of carpets; a filthy mattress under the grimy window; a heap of discarded cans and plates of rotted food, alongside a second pile, this of liquor bottles. In short, a squalid pit.

There was only one piece of evidence to mark the ambition of the man who had shat and sweated here. On the wall behind the door, a map of the continental United States, upon which Kissoon had inscribed all manner of marks and notations. Harry pulled the map off the wall and took it to the window to study. The man's hand was crabbed, and much of the vocabulary foreign to Harry's eye, like a mismatched marriage of Latin and Russian, but it was plain that over a dozen sites around the country had been of significance to Kissoon. New York City and its environs had attracted the densest concentration of marginalia, with a region in the southwest corner of North Dakota, and another in Arizona, of no little interest to him. Harry folded up the map and pocketed it. Then he made a quick but efficient search of the rest of the room, in the hope of turning up further clues to Kissoon's purpose and methodology. He found nothing of interest, however, excepting a pack of bizarre playing cards, plainly hand-made and much used. He flicked through them. There were perhaps twenty cards, each marked with a simple design: a circle, a fish, a hand, a window, an eye. These he also pocketed, as much for the taking as the wanting, and having done so slipped away past the decayed Lix and out into the warm, pale air.

It was only later, when he spread the cards out on the floor of his office, that he realized what the deck represented. Tesla Bombeck had first described these symbols to him, when speaking of the medallion she'd decoded in the caves beneath Palomo Grove. There had been a human figure at its center, she'd said: a form that Kissoon the card-maker had divided into two sides of a torso, each with an outstretched arm and two legs. The rest of the images were lifted from the medallion design unchanged. Rising above the head of the figure, if Harry remembered Tesla's account aright, had been four symbols apparently representing humanity's ascension to oneness. Below it, another four, representing its return to the simplicity of the single cell. On its left hand, which spurted energy, or blood, symbols that led to a cloud-eclipsed circle: the Cosm. On its right, which spurted like its fellow, symbols leading to an empty circle: the mystery, or perhaps the sacred absence, of the Metacosm.

Harry arranged the signs as Tesla had described, pondering as he did what purpose they'd served Kissoon. Was this a game he'd played? Metaphysical solitaire, to keep himself occupied while he planned his plans? Or was it something less frivolous? A way of predicting (or even *influencing*) the processes the deck described?

He was in the midst of turning these questions over when the telephone rang. It was Norma.

"Turn on the news," she said. He did so. Images of a fire-gutted building emerged along with a commentary from an on-site reporter. Several corpses had been discovered in the basement of the building, he said. Though the count was as yet unconfirmed, he personally had seen twenty-one victims removed from the building. There was no sign of any survivors, nor much hope now of finding any.

"Is that where I think it is?" Norma said.

"That's the place," Harry said. "Have they said anything about the state of the bodies?"

"Just that most of them are burned beyond recognition. They *were* exiles, I assume."

"Yes."

"Noticeably oo?"

"Very."

"That's going to raise a few questions," Norma remarked dryly.

"They'll file it away and pretend it never happened," Harry said. He'd seen the process at work countless times. Rational men dealing with the apparently irrational by turning blind eyes.

"There was something else, Norma. Or rather somebody."

"Who?"

"Kissoon."

"Impossible."

"I swear."

"You saw him? In the flesh?"

"Actually in somebody else's flesh," Harry replied, "but I'm pretty sure it was him."

"He was leading the Order?"

"No. He was the one slaughtering them," Harry said. "They had a door open to Quiddity. A *neirica*, one of them called it."

"It means passageway," Norma said. "A passageway to sacred wisdom."

"Well, he closed it," Harry replied.

There was a silence while Norma chewed this over. "Let me get this straight," she said. "They opened the *neirica*; he murdered them and left through it—"

"No."

"I thought you said—"

"I said he closed it. He didn't leave. He's still here in New York."

"You've found him?"

"No. But I will."

III

i

*H*arry returned to Morningside Heights later that day, and watched the house for seventy-two hours, in the hope of catching Kissoon. He had no particular plan as to how he would deal with him if he did, but took some comfort in the fact that he had the cards and the map. Both, he suspected, were of some value to Kissoon. Enough to have him stay his hand if killing Harry meant he'd never be able to find out where they were hidden. At least, that was the calculation.

As it turned out, both wait and calculation were wasted. After three days of almost constant surveillance, without so much as a glimpse of Kissoon, Harry went back into the house. The Lix at the bottom of the stairs was little more than a crusty stain on the boards. As for Kissoon's bedroom, it had been ransacked, presumably by its sometime occupant searching for the cards. He would not come back, Harry guessed. He'd done his work here. He was off on the road somewhere.

The next day Harry left for North Dakota, and the pursuit that would occupy the next seven weeks of his life began. The only person he informed was Norma and, despite her questions, he refused to furnish her with details for fear Kissoon had an agent among the dead listening in. The only other person he was tempted to tell was Grillo, but he decided against it. He'd never been certain of Grillo's agenda, or in truth of his allegiances. If Harry shared any part of what he knew in the hope of tracking Kissoon through the Reef, he risked the information finding its way back through the system to the enemy. Better to disappear silently, presumed incapacitated or dead.

Harry spent eleven days in North Dakota, first in Jamestown, then in Napoleon and Wishek, where by chance he picked up a trail that led him west, into the Badlands. There, during a spell of brutally hot weather at the end of July, he came within a day, perhaps two, of Kissoon, who had moved on, leaving another massacre behind. This time, there was no fire to conceal the bizarre nature of the corpses, and after a short time all reports of the incident were suppressed. But Harry had garnered enough information to be certain Kissoon had done here what he'd done in New York: located and destroyed a group of exiles from Quiddity. Whether they too had been in the process of opening a door back into the Metacosm he could not discover, but he assumed so. Why else would Kissoon go to the trouble of slaughtering them?

The assumption begged a question that had been itching at the base of his skull since he'd left New York. Why, after being exiled in the Cosm for so many years, were these people now gaining access to Quiddity? Had they discovered some conjuration previously unknown to them, which opened doors where there had only been solid walls? Or were those walls becoming thinner for some reason, the divide between this world and the Metacosm growing frail?

The heat did nothing for his equilibrium. Lingering in Wishek, hoping to discover where Kissoon had headed next, his fears grew gross in the swelter, and bred hallucinations. Twice in two days he thought he saw Kissoon out walking, and pursued him around corners only to find the streets empty. And at dusk, watching the solid world succumb to doubt, he seemed to see the shadows shift, as though darkness was the weakest place in the Cosm's wall, and there the cracks were beginning to show.

He looked for some comfort in the people around him, the tough, uncomplicated men and women who had chosen this joyless corner of the planet to call home. Surely there was some reserve of hard-won truth in them that would help him keep the delirium at arm's distance. He couldn't ask for evidence of it outright, of course (they already viewed his presence with suspicion enough), but he made a point of listening to their exchanges, hoping to find some plain wisdom there that could be used against the insanities he felt creeping upon him. But there was no solace in his study. They were as sad and cruel and lost as any people he'd encountered. By day they made their dull rounds with sullen faces, their feelings locked out of sight. By night, the men got drunk (and sometimes violent) while the women stayed home, watching the same chat shows and cop shows that softened wits from coast to coast.

He was glad to go, finally, into Minnesota, where he'd read of an incident of cult murder outside Duluth, and hoped to discover Kissoon's hand at work. He was disappointed. The day after his arrival, the cultists—two brothers and their shared mistress, all three in severely psychotic states—were arrested and admitted to the slaughter.

With the trail growing colder by the hour, he contemplated traveling down into Nebraska and hooking up with Grillo in Omaha. It was not his preference—the man's contempt still rankled—but he increasingly suspected he had no choice. He put off calling Grillo for a day. Then, finally, dulling his irritation with half a bottle of scotch, he made the call, only to discover that Grillo wasn't home. He declined to leave a message, fearful as ever that the wrong ears would be attending to it. Instead, he finished off the other half bottle, and went to bed drunker than he'd been in many a year.

And he dreamed; dreamed he was back in Wyckoff Street, up in that foul room with the demon that had slaughtered Father Hess, its flesh like embers in a gusty wind, dimming and brightening in the murky air.

It had called itself by many names during the long hours of their confrontation: the Hammermite, Peter the Nomad, Lazy Susan. But towards the end, either out of fatigue or boredom, it gave up all its personas but one.

"*I am D'Amour,*" it had said, over and over. "*I am you and you are love and that's what makes the world go round.*"

It must have repeated this nonsense two hundred, three hundred times, always finding some fresh way to deliver it—as wisdom from the pulpit, as an invitation to intercourse, as a skipping song—until it had imprinted the words on Harry's mind so forcibly he knew they'd be circling his skull forever.

He woke strangely calmed by the dream. It was as though his subconscious was making a connection his conscious mind could not, pointing him back to that terrible time as a source of wisdom.

His head thumping, he drove in search of a twenty-four hour coffee shop, and finding one out on the highway, sat there until dawn, puzzling over the words. It was not the first time he'd done so, of course. Far sweeter memories had died in his cortex, gone forever into whatever oblivion happiness is consigned, but the demon's words had never left his head.

I am you, it had proclaimed. Well, that was plain enough. What infernal seducer had not tried confounding its victim with the thought that this was all a game with mirrors?

And you are love, it had murmured. That didn't seem to demand much exegesis either. His name was D'Amour, after all.

And that's what makes the world go round, it had gasped. A cliché, of course, rendered virtually meaningless by repetition. It offered nothing by way of insight.

And yet, there was meaning here; he was certain of it. The words had been designed as a trap, baited with a sliver of significance. He had simply never understood what that significance was. Nor did pondering it over half a dozen cups of coffee, and—as dawn came up—Canadian bacon and three eggs over easy, give him the answer. He would just have to move on, and trust that fate would bring him to Kissoon.

Fortified, he returned to his motel, and again consulted the map he had taken from the hovel in Morningside Heights.

There were several other sites his quarry had deemed worthy of marking, though none of them had been as significant to him as New York or Jamestown. One was in Florida, one in Oregon, two in Arizona; plus another six or seven. Where was he to begin?

He decided on Arizona, for no better reason than he'd loved a woman once who'd been born and bred in Phoenix.

ii

The trip took him five days, and brought him at last to Mammoth, Arizona, and a street corner where a woman with a voice like water over rock called him by his name. She was tiny, her skin like brown paper that had been used and screwed up a dozen times, eyes so deeply set he was never quite certain if they were on him at all.

"I'm Maria Lourdes Nazareno," she told him. "I've been waiting for you sixteen days."

"I didn't realize I was expected," Harry replied.

"Always," the woman said. "How is Tesla, by the way?"

"You know Tesla?"

"I met her on this same corner, three years ago."

"Popular place," Harry remarked, "is there something special about it?"

"Yes," the woman replied, with a little laugh. "Me. How is she?"

"As crazy as ever, last time we spoke," Harry said.

"And you? Are you crazy too?"

"Very possibly."

The response seemed to please the woman. She lifted her head, and for the first time Harry saw her eyes. Her irises were flecked with gold.

"I gave Tesla a gun," the woman went on. "Does she still have it?" Harry didn't reply. "D'Amour?"

"Are you what I think you are?" Harry murmured.

"What do you mean?"

"You know damn well."

Again, the smile. "It was the eyes that gave it away, yes? Tesla didn't notice. But then I think she was high that day."

"Are there many of you?"

"A very few," Maria replied, "and the greater part of all of us is Sapas Humana. But there's a tiny piece"—she put thumb and fore-finger a quarter of an inch apart to demonstrate how little—"a tiny piece of me which Quiddity calls to. It makes me wise."

"How?"

"It lets me see you and Tesla coming."

"Is that all you see?"

"Why? Do you have something in mind?"

"Yes I do."

"What?"

"Kissoon."

The woman visibly shuddered. "So *he's* your business."

"Is he here?"

"No."

"Has he been here?"

"No. Why? Do you expect him?"

"I'm afraid so."

The woman looked distressed. "We thought we were safe here," she said. "We haven't tried to open a *neirica*. We don't have the power. So we thought he wouldn't notice us."

"I'm afraid he knows you're here."

"I must go. I must warn everyone." She took hold of Harry's hand, her palms clammy. "Thank you for this. I will find some way to repay you."

"There's no need."

"Oh, but there is," she said, and before Harry could protest fur-ther she'd gone, off across the street and out of sight.

He stayed in Mammoth overnight, though he was pretty certain that the Nazareno woman was telling the truth, and Kissoon was not in the vicinity. Weary after so many weeks of travel, he retired to bed early, only to be woken a little after one by a rapping on his door.

"Who is it?" he mumbled as he searched for the light.

The answer was not a name but an address. "One-two-one, Spiro Street," said a low sibilant voice.

"Maria?" he said, picking up his gun and crossing to the door. But by the time he had it open the speaker had disappeared from the hallway.

He dressed, and went down to the lobby, got the whereabouts of Spiro Street from the night manager, and headed out. The street he sought was on the very edge of town, many of its houses in such an advanced state of disrepair he was amazed to see signs of occupancy: rusty vehicles in the driveways, bags of trash heaped on the hard dirt where they'd once had lawns. One-two-one was in a better state than some, but was still a dispiriting sight. Comforted by the weight of his gun, Harry stepped up to the front door. It stood a couple of inches ajar.

"Maria?" he said. The silence was so deep he had no need to raise his voice.

There was no reply. Calling again, he pushed the door open, and it swung wide. There was a fat white candle—set on a dinner plate surrounded by beads—on the threadbare rug. Squatting in front of it, with her eyes downcast, was Maria.

"It's me," he said to her. "It's Harry. What do you want?"

"Nothing, now," said a voice behind him. He went for his gun, but before his fist had closed on it there was a cold palm gripping the back of his skull. "No," the voice said simply.

He showed his weaponless hands.

"I got a message—" Harry said.

Another voice now; this the message carrier. "She wanted to see you," he said.

"Fine. I'm here."

"Except you're too damn late," the first man said. "He found her already."

Harry's stomach turned. He looked hard at Maria. There was no sign of life.

"Oh Jesus."

"Such easy profanity," said the message carrier. "Maria said you were a holy man, but I don't think you are."

The palm tightened against the back of Harry's head, and for one sickening moment he thought he heard his skull creak. Then his tormentor spoke, very softly: "*I am you, and you are love—*"

"Stop that," Harry growled.

"I'm just reading your thoughts, D'Amour," the man replied. "Trying to find out whether you're our enemy or our friend."

"I'm neither."

"You're a death-bringer, you know that? First New York—"

"I'm looking for Kissoon."

"We know," came the reply. "She told us. That's why she sent her spirit out, to find him. So you could be a hero, and bring him down. That's what you dream of, isn't it?"

"Sometimes—"

"Pitiful."

"After all the harm he's done your people I'd have thought you'd be happy to help me."

"Maria died to help you," came the reply. "Her life is our contribution to the cause. She was our mother, D'Amour."

"Oh—I'm sorry. Believe me, I didn't want this."

"She knew what you wanted better than you did," the message carrier replied. "So she went out and found him for you. He came after her and sucked out her soul, but she found him."

"Did she have time to tell you where he is?"

"Yes."

"Are you going to tell *me*?"

"So eager," the skull holder said, leaning close to Harry's ear.

"He killed your mother, for Christ's sake," Harry said. "Don't you want him dead?"

"What we want is irrelevant," the other son replied, "we learned that a long time ago."

"Then let me want it for you," Harry said. "Let me find some way to kill the sonofabitch."

"Such a *murderous* heart," the man at his ear murmured. "Where are your metaphysics now?"

"What metaphysics?"

"*I am you, and you are love—*"

"That's not me," Harry said.

"Who is it, then?"

"If I knew that—"

"If you knew that?"

"Maybe I wouldn't be here, ready to do your dirty work."

There was a lengthy silence. Then the message carrier said: "Whatever happens after this—"

"Yes?"

"Whether *you* kill *him* or *he* kills *you*—"

"Let me guess. Don't come back."

"Right."

"You've got a deal."

Another silence. The candle in front of Maria flickered.

"Kissoon's in Oregon," the message carrier said. "A town called Everville."

"You're sure?" There was no reply. "I guess you are." The hand didn't move from the back of Harry's head, though there was no further response from either of the sons. "Have we got some further business?" Harry asked.

Again, silence.

"If we're done, I'd like to get going; get an early start in the morning."

And still, silence. Finally, Harry reached round and tentatively touched the back of his head. The hand had gone, leaving only the sensation of contact behind. He glanced round. Both of Maria's children had disappeared.

He blew out the candle in front of the dead woman, and said a quiet goodbye. Then he went back to his hotel, and plotted his route to Everville.

PART FIVE

Parade

I

Not for the first time in the dark years since the Loop, Tesla dreamed of fleas. A veritable tsunami of fleas, that rose over Harmon's Heights with the wreckage of America on its busy crest, and teetered there, ready to drop at a moment's notice. In its itching shadow, Everville had become a lagoon city. Main Street was a solid river of fleas, upon which makeshift rafts were paddled from house to house, rescuing people from the leaping surf.

A few folks seemed to know her, though she didn't recognize any of them.

"You! You!" they said, stabbing their fingers in her direction as she towed her own creaky little boat down the street, "You did this! You with the monkey!" (She had a monkey on her shoulder, complete with vest and red felt hat.) "Admit it! You did this!"

She protested her innocence. Yes, she'd known the wave was coming. And yes, maybe she'd wasted time with her wandering when she should have been warning the world. But it wasn't her fault. She was just a victim of circumstance, like all of them. It wasn't—

"Tesla? Wake up! Tesla? Listen to me. Wake up, will you?"

She unglued her eyes to find Phoebe staring down at her, grinning from ear to ear.

"I know where he is. *And* I know how he got there." Tesla sat up, shaking the last of the fleas from her head.

"Joe?"

"Of course Joe." Phoebe sat down on the edge of the sofa. She was trembling. "I was with him last night, Tesla."

"What are you talking about?"

"I thought it was a dream at first, but it wasn't. I know it wasn't. It's just as clear in my head now as it was when I was there."

"Where?"

"With Joe."

"Yes, but *where*, Phoebe?"

"Oh. In Quiddity."

Tesla was ready to dismiss the whole thing as wishful thinking at first, but the more Phoebe told, the more she began to think there was truth here.

Raul concurred. *Didn't I tell you?* he murmured in Tesla's ear when Phoebe came to the part about the door on Harmon's Heights. *Didn't I say there was something about the mountain?*

"If there is a door up there. . . " she thought.

It explains why this damn town's gone crazy.

"I have to go up there," Phoebe was saying. "Get through the door, so I can go find Joe." She grabbed hold of Tesla's hands. "You will help me, won't you? Say you will."

"Yes, but—"

"I knew. I said the moment I woke this is why Tesla came into my life, because she's going to help me find Joe."

"Where was he when you left him?"

Phoebe's face fell. "He was in the sea."

"What about his boat?"

"It went on without him. I think . . . I think they must have thought he was dead. But he isn't dead. I know he isn't. If he was dead I wouldn't be feeling what I'm feeling now. My heart'd be empty, you know?"

Tesla looked at the woman's elation, and heard her faith, and felt a pang of envy, that never in her life had love taken hold of her this way. Perhaps it was a lost cause, going in search of a man lost overboard in the dream-sea when it seemed the world was about to end, but she'd always had a taste for lost causes. And if she spent the last few hours of life trying to reunite these lovers, was that so petty an ambition?

"Did Joe tell you *where* the door was on the mountain?"

"Just somewhere near the top. But we'll find it. I know we'll find it."

ii

It was less than half an hour later when Tesla and Phoebe stepped out into the sun, but Everville was already in high gear. Main Street was fairly swarming with people: bleacher builders, banner hangers, balloon inflaters, barricade raisers. And where there was labor, of course, there were people around to watch and remark upon it: coffee drinkers and doughnut dippers, advice givers and troubleshooters.

"We shouldn't have come this way," Phoebe said as they waited in a line of a dozen vehicles for a truckload of chairs to be unloaded.

"Calm down," Tesla said. "We've got a long day ahead of us. Let's just take things as they come."

"If only they knew what we know," Phoebe said, watching the people on the sidewalk.

"Oh they know," Tesla said.

"About Quiddity?" Phoebe replied incredulously. "I don't think they've got the slightest idea."

"Maybe it's buried deep," Tesla said, studying the blithe faces as they passed. "But everybody gets to go to Quiddity three times, remember."

"I got to steal a visit," Phoebe said proudly.

"You had help on the other side. Everybody else gets their glimpses, then forgets them. They just get on about their lives, thinking they're real."

"Did you do a lot of drugs?" Phoebe said.

"I've had my moments," Tesla said. "Why?"

"Because some of the stuff you come out with—it doesn't make any sense to me." She looked across at Tesla. "Like what you just said, about people thinking they're real. They *are*. I'm real. You're real. Joe's real."

"How do you know?"

"That's a stupid question," Phoebe said.

"So give me a stupid answer."

"We *do* stuff. We make things happen. I'm not like . . . like—" she faltered, searching for some frame of reference, then pointed at one of the coffee sippers, who was sitting on the curb scanning the cartoon strips in the morning's *Oregonian*. "I'm not in the funny pages. Nobody invented me. I invented myself."

"Just remember that when we get to Quiddity."

"Why?"

"Because I think a lot of things got invented there."

"Go on."

"And where things are made, they can be unmade. So if something comes after you—"

"I'll tell it to go fuck itself," Phoebe said.

"You're learning," Tesla said.

Once they were off Main Street the traffic lightened up considerably, and disappeared completely once they reached the road that wove up the flank of Harmon's Heights. It didn't take them all that far. About a third of the way up the mountainside it came to an unceremonious halt, without so much as a sign or a barrier to mark the place.

"Damn," Phoebe said. "I thought it went further than this."

"Like all the way to the top?"

"Yeah."

"Looks like we've got quite a hike ahead of us," Tesla said, getting out of the car and staring up the forested slope.

"Are you up for it?"

"No."

"But we're here. We might as well give it a try."

And with that, they began their ascent.

_____ **iii** _____

In his long life, Buddenbaum had met many individuals who had tired of the human parade. People who had gone to their death with a shrug, content that they no longer had to witness the same old dramas played out over and over again. He had never understood the response. Though the general shapes of human exchange were unchanging, the particulars of this personality or that made each new example fascinating in and of itself. In his experience no two mothers ever educated their children with quite the same mingling of kisses and slaps. No two pairs of lovers ever trod quite the same path to the altar or to the grave.

In truth, he pitied the nay-sayers; the souls too stunted or too narcissistic to revel in the magnificent minutiae that the human drama had to offer. They were turning their backs on a show that divinities were not too proud to patronize and applaud. He'd heard them with these ears, many times.

Despite the fact that his body knitted together with extraordinary speed (in a week his defenestration would be an embarrassing memory), he was still in very considerable discomfort. Later, perhaps, when the avatars had arrived and he was certain everything was in hand, he'd take a little laudanum. In the meanwhile, his chest hurt like the Devil and he had a distinct limp, which gained him some unwarranted attention as he made his way out in search of a decent breakfast. It would be inappropriate, he decided, to go to the diner, so he found a little coffee shop two blocks from his hotel and sat by the window to eat and watch.

He ordered not one but two breakfasts, and consumed the better part of both in preparation for the exertions and last-minute panics ahead. His eyes scarcely strayed to his plates as he emptied them. He was too busy watching the faces and hands of the passersby, looking for some sign of his employers. It was by no means certain they would come in human garb, of course. Sometimes (he never knew when) they would descend out of the clouds wreathed in light: the wheels of Ezekiel rolling into view. Twice they'd come in the form of animals, amused, he supposed, by the conceit of watching the drama from the perspective of wild beasts or lap dogs. The one way they had never come was as themselves, and after years of doing them service he'd given up hope of ever seeing their true faces. Perhaps they had none. Perhaps the plethora of faces they put on, and their appetite for vicarious experience, were evidence that they had neither lives nor flesh of their own.

"Was everything okay?"

He looked round to see his waitress standing at his side. He had not taken too much notice of her until now, but she was a wonderful sight: hair raised in a vivid orange hive, breasts rampant, face daubed and drawn and dusted.

"You're looking forward to *something* today, I can see that," Buddenbaum remarked.

"Tonight," she said, with a flutter of her mascaraed lashes.

"Why do I think it's not a prayer meeting?" Buddenbaum replied.

"We always throw a little party Festival Weekend, me and some of my girlfriends."

"Well that's what festivals are for, isn't it?" Buddenbaum said. "Everybody has to let their hair down—or put it up—once in a while."

"Do you like it?" the woman said, patting the hive affectionately.

"I think it's *extraordinary*," Buddenbaum said, without a word of a lie.

"Well thank you," the woman beamed. She dug in the pocket of her apron, and pulled out a little sheet of paper. "If you feel like dropping in," she said, proffering the paper. On it was an address and a simple map. "We have these little invites made, just for the chosen few."

"I'm flattered," Buddenbaum said. "My name's Owen, by the way."

"I'm pleased to meet you. I'm June Davenport. Miss."

The addendum could not be ignored politely. "I can't believe you haven't had offers," Buddenbaum said.

"None worth accepting," June replied.

"Who knows? Maybe tonight'll be your lucky night," Owen said.

A lifetime of yearning crossed the woman's face. "It better be soon," she said, more lightly than it was felt, and moved off to ply the needy with coffee.

Was there anything more beautiful, Owen wondered as he left the coffee shop, than a sight of yearning on the human face? Not the night sky nor a boy's buttocks could compare with the glory of June Davenport (Miss) dolled up like a whore and hoping to meet the man of her dreams before time ran out. He'd seen tale enough for a thousand nights of telling there on her painted face. Roads taken, roads despised. Deeds undone, deeds regretted.

And tonight—and every moment between now and tonight— more roads to choose, more deeds to do. She might be turning her head even now, or now, or now, and seeing the face she had longed to love. Or, just as easily, looking the other way.

As he made his way down towards the intersection, where— despite the previous day's encounter—he still intended to keep watch, he chanced to look up towards Harmon's Heights. There was a mist cloud gathering on the summit, he saw, hiding it from view. The sight gave him pause. The sky, but for this mist, was flawless, which made him think it was not of natural origin.

Was this the way his employers would come: down out of a clouded mountaintop, like Olympians? He'd not seen them do so before, but there was a first time for everything. He only hoped they wouldn't be too baroque with their theatrics. If they came into Everville like blazing deities, they'd clear the streets.

Then who'd go to June Davenport's party?

_____ **iv** _____

The mist had not gone unnoticed in other quarters. Dorothy Bullard had called up Turf Thompson, whose meteorological opinion she'd long trusted, for some reassurance that the cloud wasn't going to dump rain on the day's festivities. He told her not to worry. The phenomenon was odd, to be sure, but he was certain there was no storm in the offing.

"In fact," he remarked, "if I didn't know better I'd say that was a sea mist up there."

Comforted by his observations, Dorothy went on with the business of the morning.

The first of the day's special events—a little pageant about how the first settlers came to Oregon, enacted by Mrs. Henderson's fourth-graders in the park, got underway ten minutes later than advertised, but drew a crowd of perhaps two hundred, which was very gratifying. And the kids were completely enchanting, with their little bonnets and their cardboard rifles, declaiming their lines as though their lives depended on it. There was a particularly affecting scene created around one Reverend Whitney (Dorothy had never heard of him, but she was certain Fiona Henderson had done her homework and the tale was true), who had apparently led a group of pioneers out of the winter snows to the safety of the Willamette Valley. Seeing Jed Gilholly's son Matthew, who was playing the good reverend, forging through a blizzard of paper scraps to plant a cross in the grass and give thanks for the deliverance of his flock quite misted Dorothy's eyes.

When the show was over, and the crowd dispersing, she found a proud Jed with his arm around his son, both beaming from ear to ear.

"Things are off to a damn good start," he said to Dorothy, and anyone else in listening range.

"You're not bothered about that other business, then?" Dorothy said.

"Flicker, you mean?" Jed shook his head. "He's gone and he's not coming back."

"Music to my ears," Dorothy said.

"And what about little Matty then?" Jed said.

"He was wonderful."

"He's been learning his lines for the past few weeks."

"I almost forgot them this morning," Matthew said. "Didn't I?"

"You just thought you had," Jed said, "but I knew you'd remember them."

"You did?"

"Sure I did." He ruffled his son's hair, lovingly.

"Can we get some ice cream, Dad?"

"Sounds like a plan," Jed said. "I'll see you later, Dorothy."

She'd seldom had occasion to see Jed this way, and it was a real pleasure.

"This is what the Festival's all about, isn't it?" she said to Fiona as they watched the kids deposit their props and hats in cardboard boxes, then peel off with their parents. "People enjoying themselves."

"It *was* fun, wasn't it?" Fiona said.

"Where did you find that bit about the reverend, by the way?"

"Well, I cheated a little," Fiona confessed, lowering her voice a tad. "He didn't actually have much to do with Everville."

"Oh."

"In fact, he had nothing at *all* to do with Everville. He founded his church in Silverton. But it was *such* a good story. And frankly, I couldn't find anything about *our* founding fathers that was appropriate for the children."

"What about the Nordhoff story?"

"That comes *much* later," Fiona said, in her best school-marmish tones.

"Yes, of course."

"No, when it comes to the early years I'm afraid we have some very murky waters. I was quite shocked at how licentious Everville was at the start. There was certainly nothing very Christian about some of the goings-on here."

"Are you quite sure?" Dorothy said, frankly surprised by what she was hearing.

"Quite," said Fiona.

Dorothy left the subject there, certain that the woman was misinformed. Everville had probably seen some robust behavior in its time (what city didn't have its share of drunkards and hedonists?), but its origins were nothing to be ashamed of. If there was to be a pageant next year, she said to herself, then it wouldn't be some phoney story, it would be the truth. And she would tell Fiona Henderson in no uncertain terms that it was her responsibility as a teacher *and* as a citizen not to be telling lies, however well intentioned, to her charges. As she left the park, she took a moment to study the mist on Harmon's Heights. Just as Turf had promised, it was showing little sign of spreading. It *was* denser than it had been three-quarters of an hour before, however. The actual peak, which had earlier been visible through the fog, was now lost to sight.

No matter, she thought. There was nothing much to see up there anyhow. Just some bare rocks and a lot of trees. She consulted her watch. It was ten after eleven. The Pancake Contest and All-You-Can-Eat Brunch would soon be underway at the Old Bakery Restaurant, and the Pet Parade lining up in the square. She was due to be one of the judges of the flower arranging at noon, but she had time to drop by and see how things were going at the Town Hall first, where people would already be assembling for the Grand Parade, even though it wouldn't start for another two hours. So much to see. So much to do. Smiling people spilling off the crowded sidewalks, banners and balloons snapping and glittering against the blue August sky. She wished it could go on forever: a festival that never stopped. Wouldn't that be wonderful?

II

I don't like this," Tesla said.

She wasn't speaking of the climb—though it had steadily become steeper, and now left her gasping between every other word—but of the mist that had been little more than shreds when they'd begun their ascent and was now a thick, white blanket.

"I'm not turning back," Phoebe said hurriedly.

"I didn't say we should," Tesla replied. "I was just saying—"

Yes. What are you saying? Raul murmured.

"That there's something weird about it."

"It's just mist," Phoebe said.

"I don't think so. And just for the record, neither does Raul."

Phoebe came to a halt, as much to catch her breath as to continue the debate. "We've got guns," she said.

"That didn't do us much good at Toothaker's place," Tesla reminded her.

"You think there's something *hiding* in there?" Phoebe said, studying the black wall that was now no more than three hundred yards from them.

"I'd bet my Harley on it."

Phoebe let out a shuddering sigh. "Maybe you *should* go back," she said. "I don't want anything to happen to you on my account."

"Don't be ridiculous," Tesla said.

"Good," said Phoebe. "So if we get parted in there—"

"Which is very possible—"

"We don't go looking for each other?"

"We just go on."

"Right."

"All the way to Quiddity."

"All the way to Joe."

Lord, but it was clammy cold in the mist. Within sixty seconds of entering it, both Tesla and Phoebe were shuddering from head to foot.

"Watch where you walk," Tesla warned Phoebe.

"Why?"

"Look there," she said, pointing to a six-inch wide crack in the ground. "And there. And there."

The fissures were everywhere, and recent. She was not all that surprised. The opening of a door between one reality and another was a violation of the physical by the metaphysical; a cataclysm that was bound to take its toll on matter that lacked mind. It had been the same at Buddy Vance's house as here: the solid world had cracked and melted and fallen apart when the door had opened in its midst. The difference however, and it was notable, was how quiet and still it was here. Even the mist hung almost motionless. Vance's house, by contrast, had been a maelstrom.

She could only assume that whoever had opened this door was both an expert in the procedure and a creature of great self-discipline; unlike the Jaff, who had been a mere novice, and utterly incapable of controlling the forces he had claimed as his own.

Kissoon? Raul suggested.

It was not at first thought an unlikely choice. She did not expect to meet a more powerful entity than Kissoon in the living world.

"But if he can open a door between here and the Cosm," Tesla thought, "that means he has the Art."

That would follow.

"In which case, why is he still playing in the shit down in Toothaker's house?"

Good question.

"He's got something to do with this—I don't doubt that—but I don't think he could open a door on his own."

Maybe he had help, Raul said.

"You're talking to the monkey, aren't you?" Phoebe said.

"I think we should keep our voices down."

"You are though, aren't you?"

"Am I moving my lips?" Tesla said.

"Yep."

"I never coul-d-" She stopped: talking, and in her tracks. She grabbed Phoebe's arm.

"What?" Phoebe said.

"Listen."

Anyone for carpentry lessons? Raul remarked. Somebody higher up the mountainside was *hammering.* The sound was muted by the mist, so it was difficult to know how far off the handyman was, but the din laid to rest what little hope Tesla had entertained of finding the door unguarded. She reached into her jacket and took out Lourdes. "We're going to go *very slowly,*" she whispered to Phoebe. "And keep your eyes peeled."

She led the way now, up the fissured slope, the hammering of her heart competing with that of the handyman. There were other sounds she heard, just audible between the blows. Somebody sobbing. Somebody else singing, the words incomprehensible.

"What the hell is going on up there?" Tesla murmured. There were lopped branches strewn on the ground, and a litter of twigs stripped from other branches, presumably those judged useful by the hammerer. Was he building a little house up there, or an altar, perhaps?

The mist ahead of them shifted, and for a moment Tesla caught a glimpse of somebody moving across her field of vision. It was too brief for her to quite grasp what she was seeing, but it *seemed* to be a child, its head too unwieldy for its emaciated body. It left a trail of laughter where it ran (at least she thought it was laughter; she couldn't even be certain of that), and the sound seemed to draw patterns in the mist, like ripples left by darting fish. It was a strange phenomenon, but in its way rather beguiling.

She looked round at Phoebe, who was wearing a tiny smile.

"There are children up here," she murmured.

"It looks that way."

She'd no sooner spoken that the child reappeared, capering and laughing as before. It was a girl, Tesla saw. Despite her almost infantile body, she had budding breasts, which were ruddier than the rest of her pale body, and a yard-long ponytail that sprouted from the middle of her otherwise shaved skull.

Nimble though she was, her foot caught in one of the cracks as she ran by, and she fell forward, her laughter ceasing.

Phoebe let out a little gasp of concern. Despite the hammerings and the sobs, the child heard her. She looked round, and her eyes, which were black and shiny, like polished stones, were briefly laid upon the two women. Then the child was on her feet and away, racing off up the slope.

"So much for secrecy," Tesla remarked. She could hear the child's shrill voice, raising the alarm. "Let's get out of their way," she said, catching hold of Phoebe's arm and hauling her off across the slope. The traumatized ground made speed virtually impossible, but they covered fifty stumbling yards before halting and listening again.

The hammering had stopped, and so had the singing. Only the sobbing went on.

That's not grief, Raul said.

"No?"

It's pain. It's somebody in terrible pain.

Tesla shuddered, and looked straight at Phoebe. "Listen to me—" she whispered.

"You want to go back."

"Don't you?"

Phoebe's face was pale and wet. "Yes," she breathed. "Part of me does." She looked over her shoulder, though there was nothing to see but mist. "But not as much . . . " she hesitated, full of little tremors, "not as much as I want to be with Joe."

"If you keep saying that," Tesla said, "I'm going to start believing it."

A burst of nervous laughter escaped Phoebe, but turned into tears the next moment. "If we get out of this alive," she said, doing her best to stifle her sobs, "I'll owe you so much."

"You'll owe me an invitation to the wedding is all you'll owe me," Tesla said. Phoebe put her arms around Tesla, and hugged her.

"We're not there yet," Tesla said.

"I know, I know," Phoebe replied. She stood back from Tesla, sniffed hard, and wiped the tears from under her eyes with the heel of her hand. "I'm ready."

"Good." Tesla looked back towards the spot where they'd been seen. There was neither sound nor sign of motion. It was not much comfort, given how hard it was to judge distance under these circumstances, but at least there was no horde of Lix or children bearing down upon them. "Let's climb," she said, and led the way up the slope again. It was impossible to judge their precise direction, of course, but as long as the ground continued to rise ahead of them, they knew they were still on their way to the summit.

After a few paces they had further evidence that they were headed in the right direction. The moaning sound was becoming louder with every yard they covered, and it was soon joined by the voice of the singer. She faltered at first, as though trying to pick up the threads of whatever piece she'd left off singing. Then she apparently despaired of doing so, and began another song: this more melancholy than the first. A lament, perhaps; or a lullaby for a dying child. Whatever it was, it made Tesla feel positively queasy, and she found herself wishing a nest of Lix would appear from the cracked ground, so she'd have something upon which to pin her trepidation. Anything rather than the sobs, and the song, and the image of the skipping child with its lifeless eyes.

And then, as the song came round for another dirging verse, the mist unveiled a horror even her most troubled imaginings had not conjured.

There, twenty yards up the slope, was the hammerer's handiwork. He hadn't built a house. He hadn't built an altar. He'd felled three trees, and stripped them, and dragged them up the slope to fashion crosses, ten, twelve feet high. Then somebody—perhaps the hammerer, perhaps his masters—had crucified three people upon them.

Tesla could not see much of the victims. She and Phoebe were approaching the site from behind the crosses. But she *could* see the hammerer. He was a small, broad fellow, his head wide and flat, with eyes like the laughing child's eyes, and he was gathering up his tools in the shadow of the crosses with the casual manner of someone who had just fixed a table leg. A little way beyond him, lounging in a chair, was the singer. She had her gaze turned up towards the crucified, her lament still maundering on.

Neither individual had seen Tesla and Phoebe. As the women watched, appalled, the hammerer finished collecting up his tools and went on his jaunty way, disappearing into the mist beyond the crosses without so much as a backwards glance. The singer threw back her head, almost languorously, and halted her song to draw on a thin cigarette.

"Why would anybody do something like this?" Phoebe said, her voice trembling.

"I don't give a shit," Tesla replied, pulling her gun from her jacket. "We're going to do something about it."

Like what? said Raul.

"Like getting those poor fuckers *down*," Tesla said aloud.

"Us?" said Phoebe.

"Yes, us."

Tesla, listen to me, Raul said. *This is horrible, I know. But it's too late to help them—*

"What's he saying?" Phoebe asked.

"He hasn't finished."

It was a damn fool thing to do in the first place, coming up here. But we've got this far.

"So what? Turn a blind eye?"

Yes! Absolutely!

"Christ . . ."

I know, Raul said. *This is a terrible thing and I wish we weren't here to see it. But let's find the door and get Phoebe through it. Then we can both get the fuck out of here.*

"You know what?" Phoebe said, nodding towards the singer. "She might know where the door is. I think we should ask her." She pointed to Tesla's gun. "With that."

"Good deal."

Just don't look at the crosses, okay? Raul said, as they started up the slope.

The singer had finally given up her lament and was simply slumped in her chair, eyes still closed, smoking her dope. The only sound was the sobbing of one of the crucified, and even that had dwindled as they advanced, until it was barely audible.

"Just look at the ground," Tesla told Phoebe. "It's no use breaking our hearts."

Eyes downcast, they continued to climb. Tesla was horribly tempted to look up at the victims, but she resisted. Raul was right. There was nothing they could do.

Up ahead, the singer was talking to herself in her blissed-out state.

"Hey, Laguna . . . ? You hear me? I got them, I got right there. *Right there.* White they are. So white. You wouldn't believe how—"

Tesla put the gun to the woman's temple. The stream of consciousness stopped abruptly, and the woman's eyes flickered open. She was by no means a beauty: her skin was leathery, her eyes tiny and surrounded with coarse bristles, her mouth—which was similarly ringed—was twice the width of any human mouth, her teeth tiny, pointed—perhaps sharpened—and innumerable. Despite her drugged condition, she plainly understood her jeopardy.

"I'll sing some more," she said.

"Don't bother," Tesla replied. "Just point us to the door."

"You're not one of the Blessedm'n's company?"

"No."

"Are you Sapas Humana?" she said.

"No. I'm just the lady with the gun," Tesla said.

"You *are*, aren't you?" the singer replied, her gaze going back and forth between the two women. "You're Sapas Humana! Oh, this is wonderful."

"Are you listening to me?" Tesla said.

"Yes. You want the door. It's there." Without looking round she pointed off into the mist.

"How far?"

"A little way. But why would you want to leave? There's nothing on the other side but more of this mist and a filthy sea. *Here*'s where the wonders are, in the Helter Incendo. Among Humana, like you."

"Wonders?" said Phoebe.

"Oh yes, oh yes," the woman enthused, ignoring the gun that was still pointed at her head. "We've lived a shadow-life in the Ephemeris, dreaming of being here, where things are pure and real."

My God, is she in for a disappointment, Raul remarked.

But there was more here than a misinformed tourist. "Isn't the Iad coming through this door?" Tesla asked her.

She smiled. "Oh yes," she said, almost dreamily.

"So why are you hanging around?"

"We're waiting to greet them."

"Then you'll never see the wonders of the Helter Incendo, will you?"

"Why not?"

"Because the Iad's coming to destroy it."

The woman laughed. Threw back her head and laughed. "Who told you that?" she said.

Tesla didn't answer though she had no difficulty remembering. The first person she'd heard that from had been Kissoon. Not perhaps the most reliable of sources. But then hadn't she had the theory supported on several occasions since? It was D'Amour's belief, for certain. According to him the Iad was the Enemy of Mankind, the Devil by another name. And hadn't Grillo told her of men and women across the continent who listed on the Reef the weapons they'd use to defend themselves if, or rather *when*, the holocaust occurred?

Still the woman laughed. "The Iad's coming here for the same reason that I came," she said. "They want to live among miracles."

"There aren't any," Phoebe piped up. "Not here."

The singer grew serious. "Perhaps you've lived with them for so long," she said, "you don't see them."

Ask her about the crucifixions, Raul prompted.

"Damn right," Tesla thought. "What about them?" she said, jabbing her thumb over her shoulder.

"The Blessedm'n wanted that. They're spies, he said; enemies of peace."

"Why kill them *that* way?" Phoebe said. "It's so horrible."

The singer looked genuinely confounded. "The Blessedm'n said it was best for them."

"*Best* for them?" Tesla said, appalled. "*That?*"

"Don't you have it in one of your holy books? A god dies that way—"

"Yes, but—"

"And he's reunited with his father, or his mother."

"Father," said Phoebe.

"Forgive my ignorance. I've no memory for stories. Songs; that's a different matter. I hear a song once, and I've got it for life. But a joke, or a piece of a gossip, or even a god-tale"—she snapped her fingers—"forgotten!"

Suppose she's telling the truth, Raul muttered.

"About crucifixions?"

About the Iad. Maybe we've had the whole thing wrong from the beginning.

"And they're just coming to see the sights?" Tesla replied. "I don't think so. Remember the Loop?" She brought her one and only glimpse of the Iad to mind now, in all its vastness and foulness. Even now, after five years, the memory made her queasy. Perhaps the Iad was not the Enemy of Mankind, the Evil One itself, but nor had it seemed to have love and peace on its collective mind.

"Will you join with me?" the singer was saying.

"Doing what?" Tesla said.

"She asked if she could smoke," Phoebe said. "Didn't you hear her?"

"I was thinking."

"About what?"

"About how fucking confused I am."

The singer was stroking the tip of her reefer with a match flame. Whatever she was smoking, it wasn't hashish. The smoke was almost sickly sweet, like cinnamon and sugar. She inhaled deeply.

"Again," Tesla said. "Inhale again." The woman looked mystified, but obeyed. "And again," Tesla said, nudging he gun against the woman's head for emphasis. The woman duly inhaled two more lungfuls. "That's it," Tesla said, as a soporific smile spread over the woman's face, and her eyelids began to flutter closed. "One more for luck."

The woman raised the reefer to her lips and inhaled a final time. Halfway through doing so the drug claimed her consciousness. Her hand dropped to her side, the cigarette falling from her fingers. Tesla picked it up, nipped off the burning weed, and pocketed the rest.

"You never know," she said to Phoebe. "Let's get going."

Only now, as they started off the slope again, did Tesla realize that the sound of sobbing had completely ceased. The last of the spies—crucified as an indulgence of their faith—had died. There was no harm now in looking.

Don't—Raul warned her, but it was too late. She was already turning, already seeing.

Kate Farrell was hanging on the middle cross, her belly bared and lacerated. On her left hand they'd nailed Edward. On her right—

"Lucien."

He was the most battered of the three, and the most nearly

naked, his thin white chest splashed with blood from a face thank-
fully almost hidden from her by his hair.

The breath went out of Tesla's body in a rush, and the strength
from her limbs. She dropped the gun. Put her hands over her mouth
to keep the sobs from coming.

"You know one of them?" said Phoebe.

"All of them," Tesla gasped. "All of them."

Phoebe had hold of her, tight. "We can't do anything for them
now."

"He was alive . . ." Tesla said, the thought like a skewer in her
heart, "he was alive, and I didn't look, and I could have saved him."

"You didn't know it was him," Phoebe said.

She started to coax Tesla away from the spot, turning her as she
did so. Tesla resisted however, unwilling to take her eyes off Lucien.
He looked so pitifully exposed up there, unable to defend himself
against the world. She needed to put him in the ground, at least. If
she left him here he'd be a spectacle: pecked and buffeted and
gnawed at. She couldn't bear it. She couldn't.

Somewhere in the turmoil, she heard Raul say: *Phoebe's right.*

"Leave me alone."

*You can't help him. And Tesla: You're not to blame. He made his
way. We made ours.*

"He was alive."

Maybe.

"He saw me."

If you want to believe that, believe it, Raul said. *I'm not going
to try and tell you he didn't. But if he did, then maybe that's why he
let go.*

"What?"

*He could have called your name, but he didn't. Maybe he just laid
eyes on you and thought: It's enough.*

Tears started to fill her eyes.

"It's enough?"

Yes. It doesn't have to be terrible always. Even this.

She'd never believe that, not to the end of her days.

What did he say we were? Vessels for something—

"For the infinite. Vessels for the infinite."

"What did you say?" Phoebe murmured.

"It's what he wanted to be," Tesla replied.

No, said Raul. *It's what he was all along.*

Tesla nodded. "You know," she said to Phoebe, "I have a very good soul in my head." She sniffed hard. "The pity of it is, it isn't mine."

Then she let Phoebe turn her around, and together they headed on, up towards the door.

III

i

The tide took Joe at last, claiming him from the darkness and bearing him away, the way it had borne *The Fanacapan* before him. For a while he was barely aware of his passage. Indeed he was barely aware of being alive. He drifted in and out of consciousness, his eyes fluttering open long enough for him to glimpse the heavens boiling overhead, as though sky and sea had exchanged places. Once, when he awoke this way, he saw what he thought were burning birds, falling out of the seething air like winged meteors. And once, seeing something glitter from the corner of his eye, he turned his head to catch sight of a 'shu, darting through the churning waters, its gaze gleaming. Seeing it, he remembered the conversation he'd had with Noah on the shore— "Please one 'shu and you please many"—and returned to his dreaming state comforted, thinking perhaps the creature knew him and was somehow guiding him through this maelstrom.

When he was not quite awake, which was often, he remembered Phoebe in the weeds; saw her body rising and falling in front of him, lush and pale. And tears came, even in his sleeping state, thinking she had gone from him, back into the living world, and all he would ever have of her from now on was memory.

* * *

Then even the dreams of Phoebe faded, and he floated on through a cloud of dirty smoke, his mind too weak to shape a thought. Ships passed him by, but he didn't see them. If he had—if he'd seen how they rocked and creaked, filled to the gunnels with people escaping the Ephemeris—he might have tried to catch hold of a trailing rope and haul himself aboard, rather than let the current they were fighting carry him on towards the archipelago. Or at very least—seeing the terror on the faces of the passengers—he might have prepared himself for what awaited him on the shore. But seeing nothing, knowing nothing, he was carried on, and on, through the remains of splintered vessels that had foundered for want of captains, through floating mortuaries of doomed travelers, through places where the sea was thick with yellow ash, and cobs of fire glittered around him like burning fleets.

Steadily the waters grew shallower and less tempestuous, and at last he was carried up onto the shores of an island that in its glory days had been called the island of Mem-é b'Kether Sabbat. There he lay, among the flotsam and jetsam, his balls bleeding, his mind confounded, while moment by moment the island he had been carried to was undone, and its undoer, the Iad Uroboros, came closer to the shore on which he slept.

ii

The distance between the shores of Mem-é b'Kether Sabbat and the mountainside where Tesla and Phoebe were climbing was not readily measured. Though generations of thinkers in both the Cosm and the Metacosm had attempted to evolve a theory of distance between the two worlds, there was little consensus on the subject. The only thing the various factions agreed upon was that this distance could not be measured with a rule and an abacus. After all, it was not simply the distance between two points: It was the distance between two *states*. Some said it was best viewed as an entirely symbolic space, like that between worshipper and deity, and proposed an entirely new system of measurement applicable to such cases. Others argued that a soul moving from the Helter Incendo into Quiddity underwent such a radical altering that the best way to describe and analyze the distance, if the word *distance* were still applicable (which they doubted), was to derive it from the vocabulary of spiritual reformation. The notion proved untenable, however, one man's reformation being another's heresy.

Finally, there were those who argued that the relationships between Sapas Humana and the dream-sea were all in the mind, and any attempt to measure distance was doomed to failure. Surely, they opined, the space between one thought and another was beyond the wit of any man to measure. They were accused of defeatism by some of their enemies; of shoddy metaphysics by others. Men and women only entered the dream-sea three times, they were reminded. For the rest of their lives Quiddity was a lot further than a thought away. Not so, the leader of this faction—a mystic from Joom called Carasophia—argued. The wall between the Cosm and the Metacosm was getting steadily thinner, and would—he predicted—soon disappear altogether, at which point the minds of Sapas Humana, which seemed so pathetically literal, would be revealed to be purveyors of the miraculous, even in their present, primal state.

Carasophia had died for his theories, assassinated in a field of sunflowers outside Eliphas, but he would have found comforting evidence for his beliefs had he wandered through the minds of the people gathered along the parade route in Everville. People were dreaming today, even though their eyes were wide open.

Parents dreaming of being free as their children; children dreaming of having their parents' power.

Lovers seeing the coming night in each other's eyes; old folks, staring at their hands, or at the sky, seeing the same.

Dreams of sex, dreams of oblivion; dreams of circus and bacchanalia.

And further down the parade route, sitting by the window from which he'd so recently fallen, a man dreaming of how it would be when he had the Art for himself, and time and distance disappeared forever.

"Owen?"

Buddenbaum had not expected to see the boy again; at least not this side of midnight. But here he was, looking as invitingly languorous as ever.

"Well, well—"

"How are you?" Seth said.

"Mending."

"Good. I brought some cold beers."

"That was thoughtful."

"I guess it's a peace offering."

"Consider it accepted," Buddenbaum said. "Come here and sit down." He patted the boards beside him. "You look weary."

"I didn't sleep well."

"Hammerings in heaven?"

"No. I was thinking about you."

"Oh dear."

"Good thoughts," Seth said, settling himself down beside Buddenbaum.

"Really?"

"Really. I want to come with you, Owen."

"Come with me where?"

"Wherever you're going after this."

"I'm not going anywhere," Owen said.

"You're going to live in Everville?"

"I'm not going to live *anywhere.*"

"Is that just some way of saying you don't want me around," Seth said, "'cause if it is, why don't you just come right out and say it and I'll go?"

"No, that's not what I'm saying at all," Owen replied.

"Then I don't understand."

Owen peered out of the window, chewing something over. "I know so little about you," he said. "And yet I feel—"

"What?"

"I've never really trusted anybody," Owen said. "That's the truth of it. I've wanted to many times, but I was always afraid of being disappointed." He looked at Seth. "I know I've cheated myself of a lot of feelings," he went on, his turmoil plain, "maybe even love. But it was what I chose, and it kept me from being hurt."

"You've never loved anybody?"

"Infatuations, yes. Daily. In Italy, hourly. All ridiculous, all of them. Humiliating and ridiculous. But love? No. I could never trust anyone enough to love them." He sighed heavily. "And now it's almost too late."

"Why?"

"Because sentimental love is a human affliction, and I won't be susceptible for very much longer. There. I've said it."

"You mean—you won't be *human?*"

"That's what I mean."

"This is because of the avatars?"

"In a manner of speaking."

"Explain it, will you?"

"Stand up," Owen said, coaxing Seth to his feet. "Now look out of the window." Seth did so. Owen stood behind him and laid his hands on Seth's shoulders. "Look down at the intersection."

There was no traffic below; the streets had been turned over to pedestrians until the parade was finished.

"What am I supposed to be looking at?" Seth wanted to know.

"You'll see," Owen said, his hands moving up to Seth's neck.

"Am I getting a massage?"

"Hush for a moment," Owen said. "Just—let the vision come."

Seth felt a tingling at the nape of his neck, which quickly spread up into the base of his skull. He let out a little sigh of pleasure. "That feels good."

"Keep your eyes on the road."

"I wish you'd just . . . " The remark fell away. He gasped, and grabbed hold of the windowsill. *"Oh. My. God."*

The intersection was melting; the streets turning into laval rivers, decorated with flickering bands of scarlet and gold. They were moving—all four of them—towards the center of the crossroads, their brilliance increasing and their breadth diminishing, so that by the time they met they were narrowed to blazing ribbons, so bright Seth could only bear to look at the place for a heartbeat.

"What is this?" he breathed.

"It's beautiful, isn't it?"

"Oh God, yes. Did you make it?"

"A thing like this isn't *made*, Seth. It doesn't come out of the air, like a poem. All I can do is *set it in motion.*"

"All right. Did you set it in motion?"

"Yes I did. A very long time ago."

"You still haven't told me what it is."

"It's an invitation to a dance," Owen said softly, his mouth close to Seth's ear.

"What kind of dance?"

"The dance of being and becoming," he said. "Look at it, and forget your angels, hammering in the sky from heaven's side. This is where the miracles come."

"Where things meet."

"Precisely."

"My journey ends at the crossroads. That's what you said."

"Remember that, later on," Owen said, his voice hardening. "Remember I never lied to you. I never told you I was here forever."

"No you didn't. I wish you had, but you didn't."

"As long as we understand each other, we can have some fun today."

Seth turned his gaze from the street now. "I don't think I can look at it any longer," he said. "It makes me feel sick."

Owen ran his hand lightly over Seth's skull. "There," he said. "It's gone."

Seth looked back at the intersection. The vision had indeed disappeared. "What's going to happen?" he said to Owen. "You just stand in the middle of the crossroads and something comes to take you away?"

"Nothing so simple," Owen replied.

"What then?"

"I'm not even sure myself."

"But you know what's going to happen to you, at the end of all this?"

"I know I'll be free from time. The past, the future and the dreaming moment between will be one immortal day . . . " His voice grew softer as he quoted the words, until by the end it was barely audible.

"What's the dreaming moment?" Seth said.

Owen drew the youth closer to him, and laid a kiss on his lips. "You don't need me to work that one out," he said.

"But I do," Seth said, "I don't want you to go, Owen."

"I have to," Buddenbaum said. "I'm afraid I have no choice in the matter."

"Yes you do. You could stay with me, for a while at least. Teach me some of what you know." He slid his hand down over Owen's chest. "And when you weren't teaching me"—his hand was at Owen's belt now, unbuckling it—"we could fuck."

"You have to understand how long I've waited," Owen said. "How much planning and plotting and manipulation I've had to do to get here. It hasn't been easy, believe me. I've almost given up countless times." Seth had unbuckled Owen's belt, and was now unbuttoning his trousers. Owen kept talking as though indifferent to the boy's manipulations. "But I held on to the vision," he said.

Seth's fingers had found Owen's sex. Plainly his indifference had been play-acting.

"Go on!" Seth said, clasping the thing.

"Are you always in heat like this?" Owen said.

"I don't remember," Seth said. "Everything that happened before I met you"—he shrugged—"is a blur."

"Don't be silly."

"I'm not. It's true. I was waiting for you to come. I knew you would. Maybe I didn't know what you'd look like—"

"Listen to me."

"I'm listening."

"I'm not the love of your life."

"How do you know?"

"Because I can't be what you want me to be. I can't stay and watch over you."

Seth kept stroking. "So?" he said.

"So you'll have to find somebody else to love."

"Not if you take me with you," Seth said, "into the dance." He looked out of the window, down at the hard, gray street. "I could bear the heat of it, if I was with you."

"I don't think so."

"I could! Just give me a chance." He dropped down onto his haunches in front of Owen, and applied his tongue to the man's half-hard prick. "Think what it'd be like," he said, between licks and kisses, "if we were together down there."

"You don't know what you're asking."

"So *tell* me. *Teach* me. I can be whatever you want. Believe me."

Owen stroked the boy's face. "I believe you," he said, idly toying with his prick. "I've told you before, you're remarkable."

Seth smiled up at him. Then he took the tumescent prick into his mouth, and sucked. He was no great technician, but he had an appetite for the act that could turn him into one very quickly. Owen ran his hands through the boy's hair, and let out a shuddering sigh. Usually, in the midst of being pleasured, he lost his grasp of any business but the one at hand, or mouth. Not so now. Perhaps it was the sense of finality that attended his every deed today (his last breakfast, his last noon, his last blow-job), perhaps it was simply the fact that the boy had a way with him, but the sensations running up his body from his groin made his thoughts almost crystalline.

What was the use, he wondered, living an immortal day if it was a solitary condition? Rare and wise and lonely was no way to live out eternity. Perhaps if he'd had his druthers he might have chosen someone closer to his physical ideal with whom to share the experience, but then accommodations could probably be made in the flux of possibilities that would presently appear in the street outside. When the powers of evolution were unleashed, it would be easy to fix the boy's profile and narrow his hips. He looked down at Seth, running his thumb over the wet rendezvous of lip and shaft.

"You *do* learn fast," he said. The boy grinned around his lollipop. "Keep going, keep going," Owen said, pushing his full length down Seth's throat. Seth gagged a little, but born cocksucker that he was, he didn't retreat from the challenge. "Good Lord," Owen said. "You're very persuasive, you know that?" He stroked Seth's face. The cheekbones were too low, the nose too lumpen. As for the hair, it was characterless: a mousy mop that he would need to re-create completely. Perhaps give him black ringlets to his shoulders, like something from Botticelli? Or maybe make him a sun-bleached blond, with a fringe that flopped over his eyes. He didn't have to decide now. Later would do. Just before the abolition of *nows* and *laters*.

He felt the familiar tingle in his groin.

"That's enough," he said gently. "I don't want to finish just yet."

If the boy heard him he didn't obey. Eyes closed, he was lost in an oral reverie, his drool so copious his motion had foamed it up at the root of Owen's cock.

My dick's Venus, Owen thought, *rising from the surf.*

The thought amused him, and while he was giggling at his own wit the boy's mouth brought him to crisis.

"No!" he yelled, and forcibly pulled himself from between Seth's lips, pinching it behind the head so hard it hurt. For a moment he thought he'd lost the battle. He grunted and convulsed, closing his eyes against the bewitching sight of Seth kneeling in front of him, his chin shiny. He pinched harder still, and by and by the crisis retreated.

"That was very close," he gasped.

"I thought you wanted me to finish."

Seth opened his eyes again. Sometime during the proceedings Seth had unzipped, and slickened his cock. He was still working it.

"I haven't time to kick back and recover," Owen replied, "Lord knows, I shouldn't have let you start, but—"

"You kissed me first," Seth said, a little petulantly.

"*Mea culpa*," Owen said, raising his hands in mock surrender. "I'll know better next time."

Seth looked despondent. "There's not going to *be* a next time, is there?" he said.

"Seth—"

"There's no need to lie to me," the boy replied, tucking his sex out of sight. "I'm not stupid."

"No, you're not," Owen said. "Get up, will you?" Seth got to his feet, wiping his lips and chin with the ball of his hand. "It's because you're not stupid I've told you all I have. I'm trusting you with secrets I haven't shared with any living soul."

"Why?"

"Honestly, I don't know. Maybe because I need your company more than I thought I did."

"But for how long?"

"Don't push me, Seth. There are consequences here. I have to be certain I won't lose everything I fought for if I bring you along."

"But you might?"

"I said: *Don't push me.*" Seth hung his head. "And don't do that, either. Look me in the eyes." Slowly Seth raised his head again. He was close to tears. "I can't be responsible for you, boy. Do you understand me?" Seth nodded. "I don't know what's going to happen out there myself. Not exactly. I only know that a lot of powerful minds have been wiped clean—gone, just like that—because they got to the dance, and found they didn't know the steps." He shrugged and sighed. "I don't know what I feel for you, Seth, but I know I don't want to leave you a vegetable. I couldn't forgive myself that. On the other hand"—he took hold of the boy's chin, his thumb in the cleft—"something about our destinies seems to be intermingled." Seth opened his mouth to speak, but Owen hushed him with a look. "I don't want another word on this subject," he said.

"I wasn't going to say a word."

"Yes you were."

"Not about that."

"What then?"

"I was just going to say: I hear the band. Listen."

He was right. The distant sound of brass and drum was drifting in through the broken window.

"The parade's started," Seth said.

"At last," Owen replied, his gaze going past Seth to the crossroads below. "Oh my boy, *now we shall see—*"

IV

I *suggest you stand still for a moment,* Raul said.

Tesla stopped in her tracks, bringing Phoebe to a halt beside her.

Very still.

There was movement in the mist ten or twelve yards ahead of them, Tesla saw. Four figures (one of them was the hammerer, she thought) moving across the slope. Phoebe had seen them too, and was holding her breath. If any of the quartet glanced in their direction, the game was up. With luck Tesla thought she might take out two of the four before they reached the spot where Phoebe and she were standing, but any one of the quartet looked fully capable of killing them both with a blow.

Not the prettiest things in creation, Raul remarked.

That was an understatement. Each displayed a particular foulness, which fact was emphasized by the way they hung upon each other's shoulders, like brothers in grotesquerie. One was surely the thinnest man alive, his black flesh pasted over his sharp bones like tissue paper, his gait mincing, his eyes fiery. At his side was a man as gross as the first was wasted, his robes, which were pale and mud- or blood-spattered, like his brother's, open to his navel. His breasts were pendulous, and covered in bruises, the source of which was a creature that resembled a cross between a lobster and a parrot—winged, clawed, and scarlet—that clung to his tits like a suckling child. The third member of this quartet was the hammerer. He was the most brutish of the four, with his iron shovel head and his bullish neck. But he whistled as he went, and the melody was sweetly lilting, like an Irish air. On his right, and closest to the woman, ran the runt of the litter, a full head shorter than the hammerer. His skin was the color of bile and had a clammy gleam to it, his scrawny form full of tics and stumbles. As for his features, they were testament to calamitous inbreeding, eyes bulging, chin receding, his nose no more than two slits that ran from between his eyes to just above his twisted mouth.

They didn't seem to be in any great hurry. They took their time, chattering and laughing as they went, sufficiently entertained by one another's company that they didn't even glance down the slope towards the women.

At last the mist closed around them and they were gone.

"Horrible," Phoebe said softly.

"I've seen worse," Tesla remarked, and started up the slope again, with Phoebe still clinging to her arm.

There was a subtle ebb and flow in the mist around them now, which became more pronounced the higher they climbed.

"Oh my Lord," Phoebe murmured, pointing to the ground. The same motion was visible underfoot: the grass, the dirt, even the rocks strewn around, being pulled by some force further up the mountain, and then released, only to be plucked up again seconds later. Some of the smaller pebbles were actually rolling uphill, which was odd enough, but odder still was the way the solid rock of the mountain responded to this summons. Here, close to the threshold, it hadn't cracked, it had *softened*, and was subject to the same motion as mist, dirt, and grass.

"I think we're getting warmer," Tesla said, seeing the phenomenon. This was the same extraordinary sight she'd witnessed at Buddy Vance's house: apparently solid objects losing faith in their solidity, and bending out of true. The Vance house had been a maelstrom. This was not. It was a gentle, rhythmic motion (*Tidal*, Raul quietly observed), the rocks being coaxed rather than bullied into surrendering their solidity. Tesla was still too traumatized by Lucien's death to be in any state to enjoy the spectacle, but she could not help but feel a twinge of anticipation. They were close to the door; she didn't doubt it. A few yards more, and she'd have sight of Quiddity. Even if the doped singer was right, and there were no wonders to be found on the shore, it would still be an event of consequence, to see the ocean where being was born.

Laughter erupted somewhere nearby. This time the women didn't stop climbing, but instead picked up their pace. The motion of mist and ground was more urgent with every yard they covered. It was like an undertow, tugging at their feet and ankles, and though it didn't have sufficient strength to overturn them yet, it would only be a matter of time, Tesla guessed, until it did.

I feel a little strange, Raul said.

"Like how?"

Like—I don't know—like I'm not quite secure in here, he replied.

Before she had a chance to quiz him further on this, a particularly powerful wave passed through ground and air, parting the mist in front of them. Tesla let out a gasp of astonishment. It was not the mountaintop unveiled before them, but another landscape entirely. A sky of roiling colors, and a shore upon which the waters of the dream-sea threw themselves, dark and foamy.

Phoebe let go of Tesla's arm. "I don't believe it," she said. "I see it, but I don't—"

Tesla—

"Amazing, huh?"

Hold on to me.

"What are you talking about?"

I'm losing my grip.

"So what else is new?"

Tesla! I mean it! He sounded panicky. *Don't get any closer.*

"I've got to," she said. Phoebe was already three strides ahead of her, her eyes fixed on the shore. "I'll be careful." She called out to

Phoebe. "Slow down!" But her request was ignored. Phoebe hurried on as though mesmerized by the spectacle ahead, until without warning the motion in the ground escalated, and she was thrown off her feet. She went down with a cry loud enough to rouse anyone within a twenty-yard radius and had difficulty getting back onto her feet.

Tesla stumbled to her aid, the earth and air increasingly agitated, as if stirred up by their very presence. She grabbed hold of Phoebe's arm and helped her to her feet, which was no minor task.

"I'm all right," Phoebe gasped, "really I am." She looked round at Tesla. "You can go back now," she said.

Listen to her, Raul said, his voice quivering.

"You've done everything you can," Phoebe went on. "I can make it from here." She threw her arms around Tesla. "Thank you," she said. "You're an amazing woman, you know that?"

"Take care of yourself," Tesla said.

"I will," Phoebe replied, breaking their embrace now, and turning her gaze and her body towards the shore.

"I meant what I said," Tesla called after Phoebe.

"What's that?"

"I wasn't—"

She didn't have time to finish, distracted as she was by a figure who appeared on the shore ahead of Phoebe. He was, of all the creatures she'd seen at work and play here, the most authoritative; a fleshy, imperious individual, with sly, hooded eyes and a dozen or so small gingerish beards sprouting from his cheeks and chins, each teased and twirled so they resembled horns. In one hand he carried a small staff. The other he was using to lift up his voluminous robes, allowing three children—identical to one another and to the laughing child Phoebe and Tesla had encountered on the slope below— room to play tag between his bare and spindly legs. He was not so diverted by their frolics, however, that he didn't see the women in his path, and by the look on his face it was plain he knew they were not part of his retinue. Instantly, he raised a shout, "Gamaliel! To me! Mutep! To me! Bartho! Swanky! To me! *To me!*"

Phoebe turned and looked back at Tesla, her face a picture of despair. The shore lay ten strides from her, at most, and now the way was blocked.

"Duck!" Tesla yelled, and pointed Lourdes at the man in the robes.

He raised his staff the same instant. There was energy skittering about it, she saw, gathering coherence—

It's a weapon! Raul yelled.

She didn't wait for proof. She simply fired. The bullet struck the man in the middle of his belly, lower than she'd aimed. He dropped his robes and his staff, and let out a cry of such shrillness she'd thought maybe she'd mis-sexed him. The children's giggles turned to shrieks, and they raced around him as he tottered forward, the cry still coming between his tiny teeth.

One of the children pushed past Phoebe, ignoring or indifferent to the gun, yelling, "Somebody help Blessedm'n Zury!"

"Go!" Tesla yelled to Phoebe, but the order got lost in the din of Zury's agony and the children's shrieks. The mist didn't mute the cacophony, it served as a roiling echo-chamber, the tumult gathering so much power it made the soft ground shudder.

By the panicked look on Phoebe's face it was plain she was too confused to take advantage of the chance while she had it. Yelling to her again, Tesla started through the shallows to press her on her way.

No farther! Raul was yelling in her head. *I can't hold on.*

He wasn't alone in this. The assault of noise and motion threw Tesla's senses into confusion. Her sight seemed to fly ahead of her, drummed from her skull, and for several sickening heartbeats she was looking back at herself from the very threshold between Cosm and shore. She might have been claimed completely, but that Phoebe reached out for her, and the contact brought her sight to heel.

"Get going!" she yelled to Phoebe, glancing towards Zury. He was in no condition to protest Phoebe's departure. He was bent double, puking up blood.

"Come with me!" Phoebe hollered.

"I can't."

"You can't go back that way!" Phoebe said. "They'll kill you."

"Not if I'm—"

Tesla—? Raul was yelling.

"Quick. Go on, for God's sake!"

Tessllaa—?

"All right!" she said to him, and pushed Phoebe from her, down towards the shore.

Phoebe went, wading through a swamp of softened rock.

Tesssllaaa—

"We're going!" Tesla said, and turning from Phoebe started back towards solid ground.

As she did so there was a moment of utter disorientation, as though her sanity suddenly fled her. She halted in mid-stride—her purpose, her will, her memory—gone from her in a blaze of white pain. There was a blank time when she felt nothing: no pain, no fear, no desire for self-preservation. She simply stood teetering in the midst of the tumult, Lourdes slipping out of her hands, and lost in the tidal ground. Then, as quickly as her wits left her, they returned. Her head ached as it had never ached in her life, and blood ran from her nose, but she had sufficient strength to continue her stumbling journey to safe ground.

There was bad news ahead, however, and it came in four appalling shapes: Gamaliel, Mutep, Bartho, and Swanky.

She had no strength left in her limbs to outrun them. The best she could hope now was that they not execute her on the spot for wounding Zury. As the hammerer closed upon her, she glanced back over her shoulder, looking for Phoebe, and was pleased to see that she had crossed the threshold, and was gone.

"That's something," she thought to Raul. He made no reply. "I'm sorry," she said. "I did my best."

The hammerer was within a stride of her, reaching to seize her arm.

"Don't touch her," somebody said.

She raised her spinning head. The somebody was striding out of the mist, carrying a shotgun. It was pointed past Tesla, towards the wounded Blessedm'n.

"Walk away, Tesla," the shotgun wielder said.

She narrowed her eyes, to better make out the face of her savior. "D'Amour?"

He gave her a wearily wolfish grin. "None other," he said. "Now, do you want to just walk this way?"

The hammerer still stood within striking distance of Tesla, plainly eager to do her damage. "Move him," D'Amour told Zury. "Or else."

"*Bartho,*" the Blessedm'n said. "Let her pass."

Whining like a frustrated dog, the hammerer stepped out of Tesla's path, and she stumbled down the slope to where D'Amour stood.

"Gamaliel?" Harry said. The black stick-man turned his seared head in D'Amour's direction. "You explain to the Brothers Grimm here that I've got sights on this gun that can see through fog. You understand what I'm telling you?" Gamaliel nodded. "And if any of you move in the next ten minutes I'm going to blow the old fuck's head off. You don't think I can?" He took a bead on Zury. Gamaliel whimpered. "Yeah, you get it," he said. "I can kill him from a long way down the hill with this. A long, long way. Okay?"

It wasn't Gamaliel who spoke, but his obese brother.

"O-key," he said, raising his fat-fingered hands. "No shoot, o-key? We not move. O-key? You not shoot. O-key?"

"O-key do-key," D'Amour said. He glanced round at Tesla. "You fit to run?" he whispered.

"I'll do my best."

"Go on then," D'Amour replied, slowly backing away.

Tesla started off down the slope, slowly enough to keep D'Amour in view while he retreated from Zury and the brothers. He kept retreating until he could no longer be seen, then he turned, and raced down to join Tesla.

"We got to make this quick," he said.

"Can you do it?"

"Can I do what?"

"Pick Zury off in the fog?"

"Hell no. But I'm betting they won't risk it. Now let's get going."

It was easier descending than climbing, even though Tesla's head felt as though it were splitting. Within ten minutes the fog ahead of them brightened, and a short while after they stumbled into the bright summer air.

"I don't think we're out of trouble yet," Harry said.

"You think they'll come after us?"

"I'm damn sure they will," he said quickly. "Bartho's probably making crosses for us right now."

The image of Lucien flashed into her head and a sob escaped her. She put her hand to her mouth, to stop another, but tears came anyway, pouring down.

"They're not going to get us," D'Amour said, "I won't let them."

"It's not that," Tesla said.

"What is it then?"

She shook her head. "Later," she said, and turning from him started on down the slope. The tears half-blinded her, and several times she stumbled, but she pushed her exhausted limbs to their limits, until she made the relative safety of the tree line. Even then she only slowed her pace a little, glancing back now and again to be certain she hadn't lost D'Amour.

At last, with both of them gasping so hard they could barely speak, the trees began to thin out, and a mingling of sounds came drifting up towards them. The rush of Unger's Creek was one. The murmuring roar of the crowd was another. And the thump and blare of the town band as it led the parade through the streets of Everville was a third.

"It's not quite Mozart," Tesla thought to Raul. "Sorry."

Her tenant didn't reply.

"Raul?" she said, this time aloud.

"Something wrong?" D'Amour wanted to know.

She hushed him with a look, and turned her attention inward again. "Raul—?" she said. Again, there was no answer.

Concerned now, she closed her eyes and went looking for him.

Two or three times during her travels he had hidden from her in this fashion, out of anger or anxiety, and she'd been obliged to coax him out. She took her thoughts to the divide between his territory and hers, calling his name as she went. There was still no response.

A sickening suspicion rose up in her.

"Answer me, Raul," she said. She was again met with silence, so she crossed over into the space he occupied.

She knew the instant she did so that he'd gone. When she'd trespassed here on previous occasions his presence had been all-pervasive, even when she hadn't been able to make him speak to her. She'd felt his essence, as something utterly unlike her, occupying a space which most people lived and died believing theirs and only theirs: Their minds. Now there was nothing. No challenge, no complaint, no wit, no sob.

"What's wrong?" D'Amour said, studying her face.

"Raul," she said. "He's gone."

She knew when it had happened. That moment of agony and temporary madness at the threshold had marked his departure, her mind convulsing as he was ripped out of it.

She opened her eyes. The world around her—the trees, the sky, D'Amour, the sound of creek and crowd and band—were almost overwhelming after the emptiness where Raul had been.

"Are you sure?" D'Amour said.

"I'm sure."

"Where the hell did he go?"

She shook her head. "He warned me, when we were close to the shore. He said he was losing his grip. I thought he meant—"

"He was going crazy?"

"Yes." She growled at her own stupidity. "Christ! I let him go. How could I have let that happen?"

"Don't beat yourself up because you didn't think of everything. Only God thinks of everything."

"Don't get Christian on me," Tesla said, her voice thick. "That's the last fucking thing I want right now."

"We're going to need help from somewhere," D'Amour said, casting his eyes back up the mountain. "You know what they're doing up there, don't you?"

"Waiting for the Iad."

"Right."

"And Kissoon's head of the welcoming committee."

"You know about Kissoon?" D'Amour said, plainly surprised.

So was Tesla. "You know about him too?"

"I've been following him across the country for the last two months."

"How did you find out he was here?"

"A woman you know. Maria Nazareno."

"How'd you come to find her?"

"She found me, the way she found you."

Tesla put her hand to her face, wiping away some of the sweat and dirt. "She's dead, isn't she?"

"I'm afraid she is. Kissoon traced her."

"We're a lethal pair, D'Amour. Everybody we touch—" She let the thought go unfinished. Simply turned from him and continued her descent through the trees.

"What are you going to do now?"

"Sit. Think."

"Mind if I come with you?"

"Have you got some last-minute maneuver up your sleeve?"

"No."

"Good. Because I'm sick of believing there's a damn thing we can do about any of this."

"I didn't say that."

"No, but I did," Tesla said, marching on down the slope. "They're coming, D'Amour, whether we like it or not. The door's open and they're coming through it. I think it's about time we made our peace with that."

Harry was about to argue the point, but before he could find the words he remembered the conversation he'd had with Norma. The world could change, she'd said, but it can't end. And where was the harm in change? Was it so dandy the way it was?

He looked up through the swaying branches at the gleaming blue sky, while the music of the town band came to him on a balmy breeze, and he had his answer.

"The world's just fine the way it is," he said, loud enough for Tesla to hear it. She didn't answer him. Just marched on down to the creek and waded over. "Just fine," he said to himself, asserting with that his inalienable right to defend it. "Just fine."

V

*A*fter her literal fashion, Phoebe had expected to find a door awaiting her at the end of her trek. It would more than likely be fancier than any door she'd seen, and she wasn't so naïve as to expect a bell and a welcome mat, but to all intents and purposes it would be a door. She would stand before it, turn the handle, and with a majestic sigh it would open before her.

How wrong she'd been. Passing between worlds had been like having ether at the dentist's in the bad old days: her mind fighting to hold on to consciousness, and losing, losing, losing—

She didn't remember falling, but when she opened her eyes again she was face-down on snow-dusted rocks. She lifted herself up, her body chilled to the bone. There were drops of blood among the snowflakes, and more falling from her face. She put her hand up and cautiously touched her mouth and nose. It was the latter that was bleeding, but there was very little pain, so she assumed she hadn't broken it.

She dug for a handkerchief in the pocket of her dress (which she'd chosen for its skimpiness, in expectation of Joe seeing her in it; a decision she now regretted) and found a balled-up tissue to clamp to her nose. Only then did she start to take much notice of her surroundings.

Off to her right was the crack through which she'd come, the day on the other side brighter (and warmer) than the purplish gloom in which she found herself. Off to her left, partially surrounded in mist, was the sea, its dark waves almost viscous. And on the shore between, squatting in countless numbers, were birds that vaguely resembled cormorants. The largest perhaps two feet tall, their bodies mottled and almost waxen, their heads—some of which were decorated with crests of green feathers, others of which were completely bald—tiny. The closest of them were perhaps two yards from her, but none showed the slightest interest in her. She got to her feet, her teeth chattering with the cold, and cast a glance back the way she'd come. Was it worth risking a return journey, just to find herself some more adequate clothing? Without something to cover her up she was going to be dead from the cold in a very short time.

She only contemplated this for a moment. Then she caught sight of one of the Blessedm'n's children on the other side, apparently staring in her direction, and the horror of all that she'd experienced to get here came flooding back. Better the cold than the crosses, she thought, and before the child could summon someone to come after her she retreated down the shore towards the water, the veil of mist between her and the doorway thickening with every step, until she could no longer see it; nor, she prayed, be seen.

It was still colder by the water's edge, a chilling spray rising off every breaking wave. But there was compensation. Off to her right the mist was patchy, and she caught sight of lights twinkling some distance along the shore, and the vague silhouettes of roofs and spires. Thank God, she thought, civilization. Without delay, she started towards it, staying within sight of the water at all times, so as not to get lost in the mist. As it turned out, it thinned and disappeared after she'd been walking for five minutes, and she finally had an uninterrupted view of the landscape before her. It was not a reassuring sight. The city lights seemed to be no nearer than they'd been when she'd first spotted them, and the rest of the scene—the shore, the rocky terrain beyond it, and the dream-sea itself—was desolation, or near enough. The only color was in the sky, and that was a fretful stew of bruisy purples and iron grays. There were no stars to light her way, nor any moon, but the spattering of snow upon the scene lent it an eerie luminescence, as though the ground had stolen what little light the sky had owned. As for life, there were the birds, whose numbers were now very considerably thinned, but were still dotted along the shore, like an army awaiting orders from some absentee general. A few had left their stations and were diving after fish in the shallows. It was not a difficult task. The waves were fairly brimming with tiny silver fish, and she saw a few of the divers emerging from the water with their beaks and gullets so stuffed with thrashing fish she wondered they didn't choke.

The sight reminded her of her own hunger. It was six hours or more since the breakfast she and Tesla had snatched before setting out. By now, even on a diet day, she'd have snacked twice and eaten lunch. Instead, she'd climbed a mountain, viewed a crucifixion, and crossed into another world. It was enough to make anybody's stomach grumble.

One of the birds waddled past her, and as it flung itself into the water in search of nourishment her gaze went up the beach a yard or two to the place where it had been squatting. Was that an egg, nestling between the stones? She strode to the spot and picked it up. It was indeed an egg, twice the size of a hen's egg, and subtly striped. The notion of eating it raw was less than appetizing, but she was too hungry to fret. She cracked it open and poured the contents into her mouth. It tasted more pungent than she'd anticipated; almost *meaty*, in fact, with the texture of phlegm. She swallowed it down, to the last drop, and was just casting her eyes around for another when she heard a vehement squawking sound and swung round to see the irate egg layer charging up the shore towards her, its head down, its ruff of feathers raised.

Phoebe was in no mood to indulge its tantrum.

"Shoo, birdie!" she told it. "Go on, damn you! Shoo!"

The bird was not so easily driven off. Its din rousing similar squawkings from all the birds in the vicinity, it kept coming at Phoebe, and its darting beak caught her shin. The wound stung. She yelped and hopped back from the bird to keep out of its range, her advice to it less gentle now.

"Piss off, will you?" she yelled at it. "Damn thing!" She glanced down at her stinging leg as she retreated, and her heel slipped on the snow-slickened stones. Down she went for the second time in half an hour, for once glad her buttocks were well padded. Her fall had landed her in more trouble, however, not just from the egg layer but from several of its fellows, who plainly viewed her fall and the howl of rage that accompanied it as a threat. Crests and ruffs erected on all sides, and two or three dozen throats gave up the same shrill squawk.

This was no longer a little inconvenience. Ludicrous though it seemed, she was in trouble. The birds were coming at her from all directions, their attacks capable of doing no little damage. She went on yelling in the hope of keeping them at bay while attempting to scramble to her feet. Twice she almost did so, but her heels slid over the rocks. The closest of the birds were in pecking distance now. Beaks stabbed at her arms and shoulders and at her back.

She started to flail wildly, catching birds with her hands and even knocking a few of them over, but there were too many to floor. Sooner or later, one of the beaks would puncture an artery, or stab her eye. She had to get to her feet, and quickly.

Shielding her face with her arms she got onto her knees. The birds didn't have much room in their skulls for brains, but they sensed her vulnerability, and escalated their assault, pecking at her back and buttocks and legs as she struggled to rise.

Suddenly, a shot. Then another, and a third, this accompanied by a hot spray against Phoebe's left arm. The tone of the squawking instantly changed from mob mania to panic, and parting her arms Phoebe saw the birds retreating in disarray, leaving three of their flock dead on the ground. Not just dead in fact, almost blown apart. One was missing its head, another half its torso, while the third—

which was the sprayer—still twitched beside her, with a hole the size of her fist in its abdomen.

She looked for their slaughterer.

"Over here," said a faintly bemused voice, and a little way along the shore stood a man wearing a coat of furs, his cap fashioned from an animal pelt, with the snout as a peak. In his arms, a rifle. It was still smoking.

"You're not one of Zury's mob," he observed.

"No, I'm not," Phoebe replied.

The man pushed back the peak of his hat. To judge by his features he was of the same tribe as the hammerer, his head flat and wide, his lower lip bulbous, his eyes tiny. But whereas the cross maker had been unadorned, this creature's face was decorated from brow to chin, his cheeks pierced with rings perhaps fifty times, from which tiny ornaments dangled, his eyes ringed with scarlet and yellow paint, his hair teased into ringlets, which softened his beetling brow.

"Where are you from?" he said.

"The other side," Phoebe said, the correct vocabulary momentarily deserting her.

"You mean the Cosm?"

"That's right."

The man shook his head, and his decorations danced. "Oh," he sighed, "I hope that's the truth."

"You think I'd dress this way if I was a local?" Phoebe said.

"No, I don't suppose you would," the man replied. "I'm Hoppo Musnakaff. And you?"

"Phoebe Cobb."

Musnakaff had unbuttoned his coat, and now shrugged it off. "We're well met, Phoebe Cobb," he said. "Here, put this on." He tossed the coat to Phoebe. "And let me escort you back to Liverpool."

"Liverpool?" That sounded like a mundane destination after such a journey.

"It's a glorious city," Musnakaff said, pointing towards the lights along the shore. "You'll see."

Phoebe put on his coat. It was warm, and smelled of a sweet perfume tinged with oranges. She plunged her hands into the deep, fur-lined pockets.

"You'll soon warm up," Musnakaff said. "I'll attend to those wounds of yours while we go. I want you to be presentable for the Mistress."

"The Mistress?"

"My—employer," he replied. "She sent me along here to see what Zury was up to, but I think she'd be happier if I forsook the spying, and brought you home instead. She'll be eager to hear what you have to tell her."

"About what?"

"About the Cosm, of course." Musnakaff replied. "Now will you let me give you a hand?"

"Please."

He came to her (the perfume on the coat was his, she discovered: He reeked of it) and putting his arm through hers escorted her over the slithery rocks.

"That's our transport," he said. There was a many-colored horse, as bright as a peacock's tail, a little way ahead of them, grazing on the coarse grass that spurted between the slabs of what had once been a fine road.

"King Texas had this highway laid, when he was wanting to impress the Mistress. Of course it's gone to ruin since."

"Who's King Texas?"

"He's the rock," Musnakaff replied, slamming his foot down. "Crazy now, since she left him. He loved her beyond love, you see; rock can do that."

"You know I don't have a clue what you're talking about, don't you?" Phoebe said.

"Let's get you up on the nag, eh?" Musnakaff said. "That's it. Right foot in the stirrup. And up! Good! Good!" He flipped the reins over the horse's head, so as to lead it. "Are you secure?" he asked.

"I think so."

"Take hold of her mane. Go on, she's not going to complain." Phoebe did as she was instructed. "Now," said Musnakaff, gently coaxing the animal into a walk. "Let me tell you about the Mistress and King Texas, so you'll understand her insanities better when you meet her face to face."

ii

It was the sound of panicked shouts that roused Joe from his stupor. He lifted his head up off the fine red sand of Mem-é b'Kether Sabbat's shore and turned it back towards the sea that had delivered him here. Two or three hundred yards from the beach was the good ship *Fanacapan*, loaded down with passengers. They squatted on the wheelhouse roof; they clung to the mast and ladders; one even hung on the anchor. But their weight and agitation was proving too much for the vessel. Even as Joe watched, *The Fanacapan* tipped over sideways, pitching two dozen of its passengers into the water, where their shouts were redoubled.

Joe got to his feet, watching the disaster unfold with sickened fascination. The people in the water were now scrabbling to climb back on the boat, their efforts assisted by some of their fellow passengers, and violently opposed by others. Whatever the intention, the effect was the same. *The Fanacapan* tipped over completely, clearing decks, wheelhouse, mast, and ladders in two seconds, and as it did so its timbers cracked and with startling suddenness it proceeded to sink.

It was a pitiful sight. Small though the vessel was, its descent threw the dream-sea into a fair frenzy. The waters churned and spumed, seeming to seize many of the people in the water and pluck them down. They went shrieking and cursing, as though to their deaths, though Joe supposed it could not be by drowning. After all, he'd lingered under water for several minutes with Phoebe, and had not lacked for air. Perhaps these panicky souls would discover the same; but he suspected not. Something about the way the waters circled these flailing souls made him think there was sentience there; that the dream-sea would be as cruel to these failed voyagers as it had been kind to him.

He turned his back on the sight, and scanned the shore. It was far from deserted. There were people along the beach in both directions as far as his eyes could see, which was a long way. The gloomy sky had given way to an exquisite luminescence, the source of which was not a heavenly body but objects themselves. Everything was shining with its own light, some of it steady, some of it glittering, but glorious in its sum.

Joe looked down at his body, at his blood-stained clothes and his wounded flesh, and saw that even he was shining here, as though every pore and crease and thread wanted to make itself known. The sight exhilarated him. He was not unmiraculous in this miraculous place, but came with glories of his own.

He started up the shore now, towards the groves of titanic trees that lined it, so vast he could see nothing of the island itself. This was, he was certain, Mem-é b'Kether Sabbat. On the voyage Noah had rhapsodized about the color of its sand. There was no shore so red, he'd boasted; nor any other island so fine. Beyond that Joe had little sense of what to expect. The Ephemeris was not one island but many, he knew that, an archipelago formed—so tradition had it—around pieces of debris from the Cosm. Some of that debris was *alive*: the tissue of trespassers, which the dream-sea had transformed and fantasticated, using the minds of those men and women as inspiration. Most of the debris was dead stuff, however, fragments of the Helter Incendo that had slipped through a crack. With time, and with Quiddity's attentions, these became the lesser, plainer islands in the group. Though they numbered in their thousands, Noah had said, most of them were deserted.

So, Joe had asked, what man or woman had founded the island that Noah had constantly referred to as "my country." Noah had replied that he didn't know, but there were those in the great city of b'Kether Sabbat who knew, and perhaps Joe would find favor with one of them, and be initiated into that mystery.

A frail hope, even then. Now it was not worth entertaining. The people on the shore were plainly refugees, most likely from that very city. If b'Kether Sabbat still stood, it probably stood deserted.

Joe intended to see it nevertheless. He'd come so far, and at such cost. Not to see the city which had been, according to Noah, the jewel of the Ephemeris—its Rome, its New York, its Babylon—would be defeatist. And even if he didn't make it, even if there was only a wasteland on the other side of the trees, anything was better than lingering here, among these desolate people.

So thinking, he started up the shore, the dream of power with which he had begun this journey entirely dashed, and in its place the simple desire to see what could be seen and know what could be known before he lost the power to do either.

VI

i

Though Liverpool had seemed charmless to Phoebe when she and Musnakaff first entered—its public buildings austere and grimy, its private houses either tenement rows or gloomy mansions—they soon encountered signs of an inner life that quite endeared the place to her. There were noisy parties going on in a number of residences they passed by, with parties spilling out onto the sidewalk. There were huge bonfires blazing in several of the squares, surrounded by dancing people. There was even a parade of children, singing as they went.

"What's the celebration?" she asked Musnakaff.

"There isn't one," he replied. "People are just making the most of what little time they think's left to them."

"Before the Iad comes?" He nodded. "Why don't they try and leave the city?"

"A lot of folks have. But then there's a lot more who think: What's the use? Why go and shiver in Trophetté or Plethoziac, where the Iad's going to find you anyway, when you could be at home drinking yourself stupid with your family around you?"

"Do you have a family?"

"The Mistress is my family," the fellow replied. "She's all I need. All I've ever needed."

"You said she was insane."

"I exaggerated," he replied fondly. "She's just a little loopy."

They came at last to a three-story house standing on its own, in a snow-dusted garden. There were lights burning in every room, but there were no partygoers here. The only sound was the din of seagulls, who sat on the roof and chimneys, staring out to sea. They had quite a view. Even from the street Phoebe was able to gaze down over a chilly but spectacular vista of roofs and spires, all snow-dusted, to the docks and the many dozens of sailing ships at anchor there. She knew very little about ships, but the sight of these vessels moved her, evoking as it did an age when the world had still possessed mystery. Now, perhaps, the only sea left to explore was the sea that stretched beyond the harbor, the dream-sea, and it seemed right to her that these sleek, elegant vessels be the ones to ply it.

"That's how the Mistress made herself," Musnakaff remarked, coming to Phoebe's shoulder to share the panorama.

"Ships?"

"Sailors," he replied. "She traded in dreams, and it made her rich beyond counting. Happy, too; till King Texas."

As he'd promised, Musnakaff had spoken about King Texas on the journey, and it was a sad tale. He had seduced the Mistress in her prime, so Musknakaff explained, and then, tiring of her, had left her for another woman. She had pined for him pitifully, and had several times attempted to kill herself, but life, it seemed, hadn't been done with her, because each time she'd survived to grieve another day.

And then, many years after his departure, he'd suddenly returned, begging her forgiveness, and asking to be allowed back into her arms and bed. Against all expectation, she had refused him. He had changed, she said. The man she had loved and lost, the man she still mourned, and always would, was gone.

"Had you been with me," she'd said, "we might have changed together; and found new reasons for love. But there's nothing left of you for me to want, except the memory."

The story seemed to Phoebe ineffably sad, as did the notion of trading in dreams, though she had no little difficulty imagining what that actually meant.

"Can dreams be bought and sold?" she asked Musnakaff.

"*Everything* can be bought and sold," he replied, looking at her quickly. "But you know that, coming from the Cosm."

"But dreams—?"

He raised his hand to ward off further questions and led her to the gates of the house—which he unlocked with a key hanging at his belt—then ushered her up to the front steps. Here he paused to offer one last piece of advice before they entered.

"She'll want to quiz you about the Cosm. Tell her it's a vale of tears, and she'll be happy."

"That's no lie," Phoebe said.

"Good," he replied, and started up the stairs. "Oh, one more thing," he said as he went. "You may want to tell her I saved you from certain death. Please feel free to lie a little about that, just to make it seem more—"

"Heroic?"

"Dramatic."

"Oh yes. Dramatic," Phoebe said with a little smile.

"Don't worry."

"Only I'm all she's got left now that the sailors don't come. And I want her to feel protected. You understand?"

"I understand," Phoebe said. "You love her as much as King Texas."

"I didn't say that."

"You didn't have to."

"It's not even . . . I mean . . . she doesn't . . . " All his confidence had suddenly drained from him. He was trembling.

"You're saying she doesn't know?"

"I'm saying . . . " he studied the steps, "I'm saying she wouldn't care even if she did." Then, not meeting Phoebe's eyes, he turned from her and hurried up the icy steps to the front door. It was open in an instant, and he went inside, where the lamps were turned to tiny glittering flames, and he could wrap his sorrow in the shadows.

Phoebe followed him up and in. He directed her down a narrow, high-ceilinged passage to the back of the house. "You'll find plenty of food in the kitchen. Help yourself." Then he headed up the lushly carpeted stairs, his ascent announced by a tinkling of tiny bells.

The kitchen, Phoebe discovered, had probably been modern in nineteen-twenty, but it was a reassuring place to sit and rest her heavy body. There was an open fire, which she fed with a few logs, there was an immense black iron stove, pots large enough to cook for fifty, and the raw materials for such an enterprise arrayed everywhere: shelves of canned goods, bowls and baskets of fruit and vegetables, bread and cheese, and coffee. Phoebe stood in front of the fire for a couple of minutes, to get some warmth back into her chilled limbs, then set to constructing herself a substantial sandwich. The beef was rare and soft as butter, the bread still warm from the oven, the cheese ripe and piquant. By the time she'd finished putting the sandwich together, her mouth was awash. She took a hearty bite—it was better than good—then poured herself a cup of fruit juice and settled down in front of the fire.

Her thoughts drifted as she ate and drank, back along the shore, through the crack and down the mountain to Everville. It seemed like days since she and Tesla had waited in the traffic on Main Street, and talked about whether people were real or not. The conversation struck her as even more nonsensical now than it had at the time. Here she was in a place where dreams were traded, eating rare beef in front of a warm fire; things were as real here as they'd been in the world she'd left, and that was a great comfort to her. It meant she understood the rules. She wouldn't fly here, but nor would she be chased by the Devil. This was just another country. Of course it had its share of strange customs and wild life, but so did Africa or China. She just had to get used to its peculiarities, and she'd be able to make her way here without difficulty.

"The Mistress wants to see you," Musnakaff announced from the doorway.

"Good," she said, and started to rise. She instantly felt lightheaded. "Boy, oh boy," she said, picking up her cup and peering into it. "That juice has got a kick to it."

Musnakaff allowed himself a smile. "It's mourningberry," he said. "Are you not familiar with it?"

She shook her head, which was a mistake. Her senses swam.

"Oh Lord," she said, and started to sit down again. "Maybe I should just *wait* a few minutes."

"No. She wants to see you now. Trust me, she's not going to give a shit if you're a little tipsy. She's scarcely ever sober herself." He came over to Phoebe, and persuaded her back to her feet. "Now remember what I told you—"

"King Texas ..." Phoebe mumbled, still trying to order her thoughts.

"No!" he yelped. "Don't you *dare* mention him."

"What then?" she said.

"The vale of tears," he reminded her.

"Oh yes. I remember. The Cosm's a vale of tears." She repeated it to herself, just for safety's sake.

"Have you got it?"

"I've got it," she said.

Musnakaff sighed. "Well then," he said, "I can think of no excuse to put this off any further," and duly escorted her out of the kitchen, along the passageway and up the stairs to meet with the Mistress of the strange house.

ii

Though the trees that bounded the shore of Ephemeris grew so close together their exposed roots knotted like the fingers of praying hands, and the canopy overhead was so dense the sky was blotted out altogether, there was not a leaf, twig, or patch of moss that didn't exude light, which eased Joe's progress considerably. Once in the midst of the forest, he had to rely upon his sense of direction to bring him out the other side, which indeed it did. After perhaps half an hour the trees began to thin, and he stumbled into the open air.

There, a scene lay before him of such scale he could have stood and studied it for a week and not taken in every detail. Stretching in front from his feet for perhaps twenty miles was a landscape of bright fields and water-meadows, the former blazing green and yellow and scarlet, the latter sheets of silver and gold. Rising overhead, like a vast wave that had climbed to titanic height and now threatened to break over the perfection below, was a wall of darkness, which surely concealed the Iad. It was not black, but a thousand shades of gray, tinged here and there with red and purple. It was impossible to judge the matter of which it was made. It had the texture of smoke in some places, in others it glistened like skinned muscle; in others still it divided in convulsions, and divided again, as though it were reproducing itself. Of the legion, or nation, that lurked behind it, there was no sign. The wave teetered, and teetered, and did not fall.

But there was another sight that was in its way more extraordinary still, and that was the city that stood in the shadow if this toppling sky: b'Kether Sabbat. The glory of the Ephemeris, Noah had called it and, had Joe's journey taken him not one step closer to the city's limits, he would have believed the boast.

It was shaped, this city, like an inverted pyramid, balanced on its tip. There was no sign of any structure supporting it in this position. Though there were myriad means of ascent from the ground to its underbelly, which was encrusted with what he assumed to be dwellings (though their occupants would have to have the attributes of bats to live there), the sum of these ladders and stairways was nowhere near sufficient to bear the city's weight. He had no way to judge its true scale, but he was certain Manhattan would have fitted upon the upper surface with room to spare, which meant that the dozen or so towers that rose there, each resembling a vast swathe of fabric, plucked up by one corner and falling in countless folds, were many hundreds of stories high.

Despite the lights that blazed from their countless windows, Joe doubted the towers were occupied. B'Kether Sabbat's citizens were choking the roads that led from the city, or rising from its streets and towers in wheeling flocks.

Such was the sheer immensity of this spectacle he was almost tempted to find himself a comfortable spot among the roots, and watch it until the wave broke, and it was obliterated. But the same curiosity that had brought him from the shore now pressed him on, down the slope and across a swampy field, where a crop of crystalline flowers sprouted, to the nearest of the roads. Despite the vast diversity of faces and forms in the throng upon that road, there was a certain desperation in their faces and in their forms a common dread. They shuddered and sweated as they went, their eyes—white, golden, blue, and black—cast over their shoulders now and again towards the city they'd deserted, and the teetering darkness that shadowed it

Few showed any interest in Joe. And those few that did looked at him pityingly, judging him crazy, he supposed, for being the only traveler on this highway who was not fleeing b'Kether Sabbat, but heading back towards it.

iii

Musnakaff's Mistress was sitting in a bed so large it could readily have slept ten, propped up on twenty lace pillows and surrounded by a litter of torn paper, which was so light that the merest breath of wind from window or hearth was enough to raise fifty of the scraps into the air and make the sheets rustle like leaves. The chamber itself was absurdly overwrought, the smoke-stained ceiling painted with naked deities cavorting, the walls lined with mirrors, some cracked, the rest in severe decay. The same might have been said for the Mistress herself. Decayed she was, and plainly cracked. For fully five minutes Phoebe and Musnakaff waited at the end of her bed while she tore up pieces of paper into yet smaller pieces, muttering to herself as she did so.

What light there was came from the oil-lamps on the various tables, which were—like those in the rest of the house—turned down so that they barely glimmered, lending the whole chamber a troubled air. Its ambiguity did little to flatter the woman. Even by this subdued light she was a grotesque, her sparse hair dyed a lush black (which only served to emphasize her parchment pallor), her cheeks furrowed, her neck like a fraying rope.

At last, without looking up from her litter-making, she spoke, her thin lips barely moving.

"I could have used a woman like you, in the old days. You've got some meat on your bones. Men like that." Phoebe didn't respond. Not only was she intimidated by this crone, she was afraid her lack of sobriety would be all too evident if she spoke. "Not that I care what men like or don't like," the Mistress went on. "I'm past that. And it feels fine, not to care." She looked up now. Her eyes were rheumy, and roved back and forth in Phoebe's general direction, but didn't come to rest. "If I cared," she said, "you know what I would do?" She paused. "Well, do you?" she demanded.

"No—"

"I would dream myself a beauty," she replied, chuckling at the notion. "I would make myself over as the most fetching woman in Creation, and I would go out in the streets and break every heart I could." The chuckled disappeared. "Do you think I could do that?" she said.

"I . . . I daresay you could."

"You *daresay*, do you?" the Mistress responded softly. "Well let me tell you: I could do it as easily as piss. Oh yes. No trouble. I dreamed this city, didn't I?"

"Did you?"

"I did! Tell her, my little Abré!"

"It's true!" Musnakaff replied. "She dreamed this place into being."

"So I could dream myself a fetching woman just as easily." Again, she paused. "But I choose not to. And you know why?"

"Because you don't care?" Phoebe ventured.

The paper the woman was in the middle of tearing fell from her fingers. "Exactly," she said, with great moment. "What's your name? Felicia?"

"Phoebe."

"Even worse."

"I like it," Phoebe replied, her tongue responding before she could check it.

"It's a vile name," the woman said.

"No it isn't."

"If I say it's a vile name, then vile it is. Come here." Phoebe didn't move. "Did you hear me?"

"Yes I heard you, but I don't care to come."

The woman rolled her eyes. "Oh for God's sake, woman, don't take offense at a little remark like that. I'm allowed to be objectionable. I'm old, ugly, and flatulent."

"You don't have to be," Phoebe said.

"Says who?"

"You," Phoebe reminded her, glad she'd had all those years of dealing with obstinate patients. She was damned if she'd allow the harridan to intimidate her. "Two minutes ago, you said—" She caught Musnakaff frantically gesturing to her, but she'd begun now and it was too late to stop. "You said you could just dream yourself beautiful. So dream yourself young and gasless at the same time."

There was a weighty silence, the Mistress's eyes roving maniacally. Then she began to chuckle again, the sound escalating into a full-throated laugh. "Oh you believed me, you believed me, you sweet thing," she said. "Do you truly think I would live with *this*"— she raised her skeletal hands in front of her—"if I had any *choice* in the matter?"

"So you can't dream yourself beautiful?"

"I might have been able to do it, when I first came here. I was barely a hundred back then. Oh I know it sounds old to you, but it's nothing, nothing. I had a husband whose kisses kept me young."

"This is King Texas?" Phoebe said.

The woman's hands dropped back into her lap, and she uttered a shuddering sigh. "No," she said. "This was in the Cosm, in my youth. A soul I loved far more than I ever loved Texas. And who loved me back, to distraction. . . ." An expression of utter loss crossed her face. "It never passes," she murmured. "The pain of losing love. It never truly passes. I'm afraid to sleep some nights—Abré knows; poor Abré—I'm afraid because when I sleep I dream he's returned into my arms, and I into his, and the hurt of waking is so great I can't bear to close my eyes, for fear the dream will come again." She was suddenly weeping, Phoebe saw. Tears pouring down her gouged cheeks. "Oh Lord, if I had my way I'd unmake love. Wouldn't that be fine?"

"No," Phoebe said softly. "I don't think that would be fine at all."

"You wait until you've outlived all those you care for, or lost them. You wait till all you've got left is a husk and some memories. You'll lie awake the way I do, and pray not to dream." She beckoned to Phoebe. "Come closer, will you?" she said. "Let me see you a little more clearly."

Phoebe duly moved to the side of the bed. "Abré, that lamp. Bring it closer. I want to see the face of this woman, who's so in love with love. Better, better." She lifted her hand as if to touch Phoebe's face, then withdrew from the contact. "Are there any new diseases in the Cosm?" she said.

"Yes there are."

"Are they terrible?"

"Some of them, yes," Phoebe said, "One of them's very terrible indeed." She remembered Abré's phrase. "The Cosm's a vale of tears," she said.

It did the trick. The Mistress smiled. "There," she said, turning to Abré. "Isn't that what I always say?"

"That's what you say," Musnakaff replied.

"No wonder you fled it," the woman said, turning her attention back to Phoebe.

"I didn't—"

"What?"

"Flee. I didn't flee. I came because there's somebody here I want to find."

"And who might that be?"

"My . . . lover."

The Mistress regarded her pityingly. "So you're here for love?" she said.

"Yes," Phoebe replied. "Before you ask, his name's Joe."

"I had no intention of asking," the Mistress rasped.

"Well I told you anyhow. He's somewhere out there at sea. And I've come to find him."

"You'll fail," the harridan said, making no attempt to disguise her satisfaction at the thought. "You know what's going on out there, I presume?"

"Vaguely."

"Then you surely know there's no chance of finding him. He's probably already dead."

"I know that's not true," Phoebe said.

"How can you *know*?" the Mistress said.

"Because I was here in a dream. I met him, out there in Quiddity." She dropped her voice a little, for dramatic effect. "We made love."

"In the sea?"

"In the sea."

"You actually *coupled* in Quiddity?" Musnakaff said.

"Yes."

The Mistress had picked up a sheet of paper from the bed—it was covered, Phoebe saw, with line upon line of spidery handwriting—and proceeded to tear it up. "Such a thing," she said, half to herself. "Such a thing."

"Is there any way you can help me?" Phoebe said.

It was Musnakaff who replied. "I'm afraid—"

He got no further. "Maybe," the Mistress said. "The sea doesn't speak. But there are those in it that do." She had reduced the first sheet of paper to litter, and now picked up a second. "What would I get in return?" she asked Phoebe.

"How about the truth?" Phoebe replied.

The Mistress cocked her head. "Have you lied to me?" she said.

"I said what I was told to say," Phoebe replied.

"About what?"

"About the Cosm being a vale of tears."

"Is that not so?" the Mistress said, somewhat testily.

"Some of the time. People live unhappy lives. But not all the time. And not all of the people." The Mistress grunted. "I guess maybe you don't want to hear the truth after all. Maybe you're happier just sitting tearing up love letters and thinking you're better off here than there."

"How did you know?"

"What, that they were love letters? By the look on your face."

"He's been writing to me every hour on the hour for six years. Tells me he'd let me have this whole damn continent, if I'd only grant him a kiss, a touch. I've never answered a single billet-doux. But still he writes 'em, reams and reams of sentimental nonsense. And every now and then I take a day or so to tear them up."

"If you hate him that much," Phoebe said, "you must have loved him—"

"I told you, I've loved one creature in my life. And he's dead."

"In the Cosm," Phoebe said. It was not a question, it was a statement, plain and simple.

The Mistress looked up at her. "Do you read minds?" she said, very softly. "Is that how you know my secrets?"

"It wasn't much of a leap," Phoebe replied. "You said you dreamed this city into being. You must have seen the original once."

"I did," the Mistress said. "A very long time ago. I was a mere child."

"Did you remember much?"

"More than I care to," the woman said, "far more. I had great ambitions, you see, and they came to nothing. Well, almost nothing . . ."

"What ambitions?"

"To build a new Alexandria. A city where people would live in peace and prosperity." She shrugged. "And what did I end up with?"

"What?"

"Everville."

Phoebe was flummoxed. "Everville?" she said. What on earth could this bizarre creature have to do with safe, smug little Everville?

The woman dropped the love letter she was tearing and stared into the flames. "Yes. You may as well know the whole truth, for what it's worth." She looked from the fire to Phoebe and made a tiny smile. "My name's Maeve O'Connell," she said, "and I'm the fool who founded Everville."

VII

*U*ntil the early eighties, the route of the Saturday Parade had been simple. It had started at Sears' Bakery on Poppy Lane and proceeded along Acres Street to Main, where it had moved—in about an hour—to its conclusion in the town square. But as the scale of both the parade and the crowd attending it had grown, a new route had to be devised that would allow breathing room for both. After several six-to-midnight meetings in their smoke-filled room above Dorothy Bullard's office, the Festival Committee had hit upon a simple but clever solution: The parade would describe an almost complete circle around the town, setting out from behind the Town Hall. This almost tripled the length of the route. Main Street and the town square would still remain the prime sites for viewing, of course, but the spectators there would be obliged to wait somewhat longer for the show to come their way. For the impatient then, or those with impatient kids, the streets closer to the starting-place were preferable, while for those folks who thrived on anticipation, and were happy to eat, drink, and swelter for an hour and a half while the music grew tantalizingly louder, there was still no better place to be than on the bleachers, fire escapes, and window-sills of Main Street.

*   *   *

"The band's never sounded better," Maisie Waits said to Dorothy as the two women stood in the sun outside Kitty's Diner, watching the parade slowly make its way towards the crossroads.

Dorothy beamed. She couldn't have been more proud, she thought to herself, if she'd given birth to every one of these musicians herself, and was about to say so when she checked herself. Wherever that notion had popped up from it was perhaps better left unspoken. Instead she said, "We all loved Arnold, of course," speaking of Arnold Langley, who had led the band for twenty-two years until his sudden death of a stroke the previous January, "but Larry's really worked on updating the repertoire."

"Oh Bill just thinks the sun shines out of Larry," Maisie remarked. Her husband had played the trombone in the band for a decade. "And he loves the new uniforms."

They'd cost a tidy sum, but there was no doubt the money had been well spent. Along with Larry Glodoski's recruiting drive, which had brought a number of new, younger players into the ranks (all but one of them from out of town), the uniforms had given the band a fresher, snappier appearance, which had in turn improved their marching and their playing. There'd even been talk of the band entering one of the big interstate competitions in the next couple of years. Even if it didn't win, the publicity would only help the Festival.

Not that it needed help, Dorothy thought, her gaze moving from band to crowd. There were about as many people here as the streets would bear; five or six deep in some places, their weight putting the barricades under considerable strain, their din so loud it drowned out all but the band's bass drum, which thumped away in Dorothy's lower belly like a second heart.

"You know I really should eat something," she said to Maisie. "I'm feeling a little floaty."

"Oh, well that's no good," Maisie said. "We'll have to get some food inside you."

"I'll just wait until the band gets here," Dorothy said.

"Are you sure?"

"Of course. I can't miss the band."

*   *   *

"I feel like a damn fool," Erwin said.

Dolan grinned. "Nobody can see us but us," he pointed out. "Oh come on, lighten up, Erwin. Didn't you always want to march in a parade?"

"Actually, no," Erwin replied.

They were all there—Nordhoff, Dickerson, even Connie, marching among the glittering ranks—all playing the fool.

Erwin couldn't see the joke. Not today, when plainly there was so much wrong with the world. Hadn't Nordhoff himself said that they had to somehow protect their investment in Everville? And here they were capering like children.

"I'm done with this!" he said sourly. "We should be after that bastard in my house."

"We will be," Dolan said. "Nordhoff told me he had a plan."

"Somebody taking my name in vain?" Nordhoff called over his shoulder.

"Erwin thinks we're wasting our time."

"Do you indeed?" Nordhoff said, swinging round, and marching backwards while he addressed the question. "It may seem like a pathetic little ritual to you, marching with the town band, but it's like that jacket you're wearing."

"This thing?" Erwin said. "I thought I'd given it away."

"But you found the pockets full of keepsakes, didn't you?" Nordhoff said. "Little pieces of the past?"

"Yes."

"It was the same for all of us," Nordhoff replied, plunging his hand into the pocket of his less-than-perfect tux and pulling out a handful of bric-a-brac. "Either our memories or some higher power supplied us with these comforts. And I'm grateful."

"What's your point?" Erwin pressed.

"That we have to stay connected to Everville the way we stay connected to *ourselves*. Whether it's an old shirt or an hour with the town band, it doesn't matter. They serve the same function. They help us remember what we loved."

"What we *still* love," Dolan said.

"You're right, Richard. What we *still* love. You see the point, Erwin?"

"I can think of better ways to do it than this," Erwin growled.

"Doesn't a band make your heart strike up?" Nordhoff said, raising his knees a little higher with each step. "Listen to those trumpets."

"Raucous!" Erwin said.

"Jesus, Toothaker!" Nordhoff said. "Where's your sense of celebration? This is what we're fighting to preserve."

"Then God help us," Erwin said, at which reply Nordhoff turned his back, and picking up his pace marched off through the brass section.

"Go after him," Dolan told Erwin. "Quickly. Tell him you're sorry."

"Go to Hell," Erwin said, peeling off from the ranks and heading for the choked sidewalk. Dolan went after him.

"Nordhoff's not a very forgiving man," Dolan said.

"I don't care," Erwin said. "I'm not going to abase myself." He stopped, his gaze fixed on somebody in the crowd.

"What is it?" Dolan wanted to know.

"There," Erwin said, pointing to the bedraggled woman moving through the crowd.

"You know her?"

"Oh yes."

Tesla was about a hundred yards from the crossroads when she realized where she was. She halted. It took Harry just a second or two to catch up with her.

"What's the problem?" he hollered to her.

"We shouldn't have come this way!" she yelled back.

"You know a better one?"

Tesla shook her head. Perhaps with Raul's aid she'd have been able to plot an alternative route to Phoebe's house, but from now on she'd have to start working these problems out for herself.

"So we just have to plough on," Harry said.

Tesla nodded, and did just that, plunging on into the press of bodies with the abandon of an orgiast. If only there were some way to harness the power of this communion, she thought; to turn it to practical purpose instead of letting it evaporate. What a waste that was; what a pitiful waste.

Caught in the grip of the crowd, unable to entirely control her route, nor entirely concerned to do so, she felt curiously comforted. The touch of flesh on flesh, the stench of sweat and candy-sweetened breath, the sight of oozing skin and glittering eye, all of it was fine, just fine. Yes, these people were vulnerable and ignorant; yes, they were probably crass, most of them, and bigoted and belligerent. But now, right now, they were laughing and cheering and holding their babies high to see the parade, and if she did not love them, she was at least happy to be of their species.

"Listen to me!" Erwin yelled at her.

The woman showed no sign of hearing, but the expression on her face gave Erwin hope that maybe she could be persuaded to hear. Her eyes had a lunatic gleam in them, and there was a twitching smile on her lips. He could not feel her temperature, but he was certain she was running a fever.

"Just *tune in, will you?*" he hollered.

"Why are you bothering?" Dolan wanted to know.

"Because she knows a damn sight more than we do," Erwin told him. "She knew that thing in my house by name. I heard her call it *Kissoon.*"

"What about him?" Tesla said to Harry, throwing the question over her shoulder.

"What about who?" Harry replied.

"You said *Kissoon.*"

"I didn't say a word."

"Well somebody did."

* * *

"She heard me!" Erwin whooped. "Good girl! Good girl."

Dolan was intrigued now. "Maybe she'd hear better if we said it together," he suggested.

"Not a bad idea. After three . . . "

This time Tesla stopped. "You didn't hear that either?" she said to Harry. He shook his head. "Okay," she said. "No big deal."

"What are you talking about?"

She pushed through the crowd to an empty doorway, with Harry following. The store—a florist's—was closed, but the scent of flowers was powerful.

"There's somebody talking to me, Harry. Besides you. His name's Toothaker."

"And . . . where is he?"

"I don't know," she said. "I mean, I know he's dead. I was in his house. That's where I saw Kissoon." She kept scanning the crowd while she spoke, hoping to catch a glimpse of the presence, or rather presences, she'd heard. "He's not alone this time. I heard two voices. They want to get through to me. I just don't know how to tune in."

"I'm no help, I'm afraid," Harry said. "I'm not saying they're not here—"

"It's okay," Tesla told him. "I just have to *listen*—"

"You want to find somewhere quieter?"

She shook her head. "I might lose them."

"You want me to step away?"

"Don't go far," she said, and closing her eyes, tried to shut out the din of the living and listen for the voices of the dead.

Dorothy caught hold of Maisie's arm, very tight.

"What's wrong?" Maisie said.

"I really don't . . . I don't feel too good at all . . . " Dorothy said. Her surroundings had started to throb in rhythm with the band, as though everything had a heart sewn inside it (even the sidewalk, even the sky), and the closer the band came, the harder those hearts beat, until it seemed they would surely burst, every one of them burst wide open, and tear a hole in the world.

"Shall I get you something to eat?" Maisie said. The drums were louder with every beat: booming and booming. "Maybe a tuna salad, or—"

Without warning, Dorothy bent double and puked. The knot of people in front of her parted—not quickly enough to keep themselves from being spattered, but fast—as she heaved up what little her stomach contained. Maisie waited until the spasms had stopped then tried to coax her out of the sun into the shade of the diner. But she wouldn't go, or couldn't.

"It's going to burst," she said, staring down at the ground.

"It's all right, Dottie—"

"No it isn't. It's going to burst!"

"What *are* you talking about?"

Dorothy shook off Maisie's grip. "We've got to clear the street," she said, stumbling forward. "*Quickly!*"

"What's going on down there?" Owen said, leaning out of the window. "Do you know that woman?"

"The one who just puked? Yeah. It's Mrs. Bullard. She's a real bitch."

"Extraordinary," Owen said.

Dorothy was pushing and shoving her way through the crowd. She was yelling something, but Owen couldn't catch it over the din of the approaching band.

"She looks really upset," Seth said.

"That she does," Owen said, leaving the window and heading for the stairs.

"Maybe she saw the avatars!" Seth yelled after him.

"The same thought occurred to me," Owen said. "The *very* same—"

* * *

Dorothy Bullard's warning had not gone unheard by the crowd around Kitty's Diner. As she strode forward they cleared a path for her, in case she intended to puke again. One girl, perhaps a little worse for drink, failed to get out of her way fast enough and was shoved aside as Dorothy charged the barricade. It fell before her, and she ran out into the middle of the crossroads, waving her hands wildly.

At the head of his shining ranks, Larry Glodoski saw the Bullard woman flailing in front of him, and was presented with a choice. Either he brought the band—and thus the parade—to a halt in the next ten seconds, or trusted that somebody would have the presence of mind to get the bitch out of his way before there was a collision. In truth, it was no dilemma at all. She was one; they were many. He lifted his baton a little higher, and marked the beats with sharper motions than ever, as if to erase the woman from the street in front of him.

"I'm listening," Tesla murmured, "I'm listening as hard as I can."

Every now and then she heard what might have been a murmur, but her mind was whining with hunger and heat. Even if it was the ghosts speaking she could make no sense of the sounds.

And now there was yet another distraction: some kind of brouhaha up at the crossroads. The crowd had become more frenzied than ever. She went up on her tiptoes in the hope of seeing what was happening, but her sight was blocked by heads and balloons and waving hands.

Harry had the scoop, however. "There's a woman in the middle of the street, yelling—"

"Yelling what?"

Harry listened for a moment. "I think she's telling people to get off the street—"

An instinct she would once have called Raul's had her out of the doorway in a moment, back into the swelter and stench of the crowd, pushing Harry ahead of her. "Clear the way!" she yelled to him.

"Why?"

"It's the crossroads! It's something to do with the fucking crossroads!"

"Do you see them?" Seth said, as he and Owen carved their way to the front of the crowd. Owen didn't answer him. He was afraid if he opened his mouth he'd cry out: in hope, in pain, in expectation. He ducked under the barricade and out into the open street.

This was the most dangerous of moments, he knew: when everything could be gained or lost. He hadn't expected it to come upon him so suddenly. Even now, he wasn't certain this was indeed the *moment of moments,* but he had to act as though it were. The sun suddenly seemed merciless, beating on his bare head, softening his thoughts, and on the bare street, softening that too. It would flow soon, the way it had in the vision he'd shared with Seth; flow into the place where flesh met flesh, and the Art ignited—

"Get away!" Dorothy yelled, turning to appeal to the crowd. "*Get away before it's too late!*"

"She *has* seen something," Owen thought.

There were people converging on the woman from all sides, intent on silencing her, but Owen put on a burst of speed to reach her first.

"It's all right!" he yelled as he went, "I'm a doctor!"

It was a trick he'd used before, and as before, it worked. He was given clear access to the crazed woman.

Larry saw the doctor wrap his arms around poor Dorothy, and offered up a little prayer of thanks. Now all the guy had to do was get the Bullard woman out of the way—but quickly, *quickly!*—and the rhythm of the band would not be broken. He heard somebody in the ranks calling, "Larry? We gotta stop!"

Larry ignored the cry. They still had another ten strides before they would reach the spot where the doctor was talking to Dorothy.

Nine, now. But nine was plenty. Eight—

*   *   *

"What are you seeing?" Owen demanded of the woman.

"It's all going to *burst*," she said to him. "Oh God, oh God, it's all going to burst!"

"What is?" he asked her.

She shook her head.

"Tell me!" he yelled at her.

"The world!" she said. "The world!"

Harry had no difficulty clearing a way through the crowd for Tesla. Now he lifted the barricade and she ducked under it, out into the open street, delivering her into the arena. There were perhaps a dozen players ahead of her—excluding the band—but only three were of significance. One was the woman at the very center of the crossroads, another the bearded man who was presently talking to her, the third the young man a few yards ahead of her, who was calling out:

"*Buddenbaum!*"

The bearded man glanced round at his companion, and Tesla had a clear look at his face. The expression he wore was grotesque; every muscle in his face churning and his eyes blazed.

"*Mine!*" he yelled, his voice shrill, and swung back towards the woman, who was in some delirious state of her own, her eyes rolling in her sockets. She started to pull herself free of Buddenbaum, and in doing so her blouse tore open from neck to belt, exposing bra and belly. She scarcely noticed, it seemed. But the crowd did. A roar rose from all sides—gasps, wolf-whistles, and applause all mingled. Flailing, the woman stumbled away from Buddenbaum—

Larry couldn't believe it. Just as he thought things were in hand Dorothy pulled away from the doctor—practically showing her all to the world in the process—and reeled round, straight in front of the band.

Larry yelled "*Halt!*" but it was too late to prevent catastrophe. The Bullard woman collided with him, and he staggered backwards into the trumpet section. Two of the band members went over like bowling pins, and Larry fell on top of them. There was another roar from the spectators.

Larry's spectacles had come off in the melee. Without them the world was a blur. Detaching himself from the knot of trumpeters he started to search the ground, patting the warm asphalt.

"Nobody move!" he yelled. "*Please!* Nobody move!"

His plea went unheard. People were moving all around him. He could see their blurry forms; he could hear their shouts and curses.

"We're all going to die," he heard somebody sob nearby. He was sure it was Dorothy, and good man that he was, forsook his search a moment to comfort her. But when he looked up from the street to seek out the blur that most resembled her, something else came into view. It was a woman, but she was not blurred; far from it. He could not have wished for a vision more perfectly in focus. She was not standing in the street, but hovering a little distance above it. No; not even hovering, *standing*; she was standing in the air, with a silk robe loosely knotted around her. Very loosely, in fact. He could see her breasts—they were glossy and full—and a hint of what lay between her legs. He called out to her, "Who are you?" But she didn't hear him. She just moved off, climbing the air as though ascending a flight of invisible stairs. He started to get to his feet, wishing he could follow, and as he did so she looked back, coquettishly, not at him, he knew, but at somebody whom she was coaxing to follow her.

Oh how she smiled at him, the lucky bastard, and plucked at her robe to tease him with a glimpse of her beautiful legs. Then she continued to climb, and a few steps up the flight, seemed to encounter another woman—this one descending—the contact briefly illuminating the second beauty.

"Larry—?"

What was he seeing?

"I got your spectacles."

"Huh?"

"Your spectacles, Larry." They were thrust in front of him, and he fumbled for them, not wanting to take his eyes off the woman.

"What the hell are you looking at?"

"Don't you see them?"

"See what?"

"The women."

"Put your damn spectacles on, Larry."

He did so. The world came into focus around him, in all its confusion. But the woman had gone.

"God, *no*—"

He pulled his spectacles off again, but the vision had escaped him into the bright summer sky.

In the midst of this confusion—Dorothy Bullard escaping, Buddenbaum going after her, the band falling down like tin soldiers—Tesla had made her way to the center of the crossroads. It had taken her perhaps five seconds to do so, but in those seconds she had been assailed by a legion of sensations, her spirits lifted one moment and dropped the next, her body wracked and caressed by turns, as though whatever lay at the heart of the crossroads was testing her wits to breaking point. Clearly the town woman had failed the test. She was bawling like an abandoned child. Buddenbaum, however, was made of sterner stuff. He was standing a couple of yards from Tesla, staring down at the ground.

"What the fuck's going on?" she yelled to him. He didn't look up. Didn't even speak. "Can you hear me?"

"Not. Another. Step," he said. Despite the cacophony, and the fact that he spoke in a near-whisper, she heard him as clearly as if he'd murmured in her ear.

A terrible suspicion rose in Tesla, which she instantly voiced.

"Are you Kissoon?" she said.

This certainly got his attention.

"Kissoon?" he said, his lip curling. "He's a piece of shit. What do you know about him?"

That answered her question plainly enough. But it begged another. If he wasn't Kissoon, but he knew who Kissoon was, then *who was he?*

"He's just some name I heard."

His face was quite a sight: a mass of bulges, about to burst. "*Some name?*" he said, reaching for her. "*Kissoon*'s not *some name!*" She dearly wanted to retreat from him, but a part of her was irrationally possessive of this contested ground. She stood it, though he took hold of her by the neck.

"Who are you?"

She was afraid for her life.

"Tesla Bombeck," she said.

"You're Tesla Bombeck?" he said, plainly amazed.

"Yes," she said, barely able to get the words out from under his thumbs. "Do you mind . . . letting go—"

He drew her closer to him. "Oh God," he said, with a twisted little smile on his face. "You're an ambitious little bitch, aren't you?"

"I don't know what you're talking about."

"Oh you don't, huh? You came to take away all I've worked for and—"

"I haven't come to take anything," Tesla gasped.

"*Liar!*" Buddenbaum said, tightening his hold on her neck.

She reached up to his face and jabbed her finger in his eye, but he wasn't about to let go.

"The Art's mine," he yelled. "You can't have it! *You can't.*"

She had no breath left to contest her innocence, not much strength to fight him off. The world began to throb to the rhythm of her pulse, pulsing with every heartbeat. She kicked at his legs, hoping she might knock him off his feet, but he seemed to feel nothing, to judge by his unchanging face. He just kept saying: "Mine . . . Mine . . . " though his voice, like the whole world, was growing paler and thinner, preparing to disappear completely.

"Don't we know that woman?" somebody said nearby.

"I believe we do," came the reply.

She couldn't turn to see the speakers, but she didn't need to. She knew them by their voices. The leader of the phantoms she'd met in Toothaker's house was here, and not alone.

Buddenbaum's face was barely visible now, but just before it flickered out completely she saw him raise his eyes, looking past her at something nearby. He spoke, but the words were white noise. Then there was burst of heat, and a red mark appeared above his right eye. She squinted hard, trying to make sense of it, but before she could do so his fingers relaxed, and she slipped from his grasp. Her legs were too weak to bear her up. They folded beneath her, and down she went. She drew a breath as she collapsed, and her grateful brain rewarded her with a sliver of comprehension. Buddenbaum had been shot. The mark on his face was a bullet hole.

She didn't have a chance to take satisfaction in the fact. When she struck the ground her thoughts flickered out.

One shot, and the crowd was in turmoil. Cheers turned to screams, laughter to panic. Suddenly people were running in every direction, except towards the gunman and his victim.

D'Amour slipped his gun into his jacket and started towards the middle of the street. The man he'd shot was still standing, despite the blood flooding from his brow, which fact supported the suspicion that there was magic here. Despite the sun, despite the crowds, a suit had been worked and was still *being* worked, in fact. The closer he got to the place where Tesla was lying, the more his ink itched.

There were other signs, too, that he did his best to keep at bay. The ground under his feet seemed to brighten and shift when he looked at it, as though it was trying to flow towards the middle of the crossroads. And there was a brightness in the air; gossamer shapes moving across his field of vision, shedding beads of light. There was more here than an invocation, he knew; far more. Reality was soft here, and getting softer. Things meeting, intersecting, trying—*perhaps*—to flow together.

If so, he had no doubt as to who was masterminding the affair. It was the man he'd just shot, who now, with consummate indifference, had actually turned his back on Harry and was studying the departing crowd.

Harry turned his gaze on Tesla, who was lying quite still.

Don't be dead, he said to himself, and almost closing his eyes completely to fend off the blandishments of sky and street he stumbled on towards her.

The avatars were here. Owen knew it. He could feel their eyes upon him, and it was a feeling like no other he knew. Like being spied on by God. Terrible and wonderful at the same time.

He wasn't the only one feeling such confusions, he knew. Though the crowd scattering around him did not possess the knowledge he possessed, they were all of them—even the dullest and the dumbest—sensing something untoward. The shot that had wounded him had wounded them too, in a different fashion: loosed a flood of adrenaline rather than blood, thus alerting their staled senses to signs they would have otherwise missed. He could see the recognition in their faces, wide with awe and terror; he could read it off their trembling lips. It wasn't the way he'd intended things, but he didn't care. Let them gape, he thought. Let them pray. Let them tremble. They'd have to do a lot more of that before this Day of Days was done.

He gave up on looking for the avatars—as long as they were there, what did it matter what shape they'd taken?—and went down on his haunches to touch the ground. Though there was blood running into his right eye, he could see better than he'd seen in his long life. The ground was turning to ether below him, the medallion buried far below him blazing in its bed. He pressed his hand against the ground, and let out a low moan of pleasure as he felt his fingers slip and slide down into the warm asphalt, towards the cross.

There were phenomena on every side. Voices speaking out of the ether (revenants, he thought; and why not? The more the merrier), vague, wispy forms riding on the air to left and right of him (too perfect for the past, surely; perhaps the future, coming to find the moment when it ceased to matter), agitations in the ground and sky (he would paint the heavens with stone, when he remade the world, and make the earth sprout lightning). So much happening, and all because of the object that lay inches from his fingers, the cross that had accrued the power to change the world, buried here at the cross-roads.

"You're beautiful," he murmured to it, the way he might have cooed to a pretty boy. "So, so beautiful."

His fingers were almost there. Another foot and a half, no more—

Erwin had followed Tesla as far as the edge of the crowd, but then—seeing the chaos in front of him—had held back. It was no use trying to speak to her in the midst of such tumult, he'd realized. Better to wait.

Dolan had not been so reluctant. Ever eager for fun, he'd slipped through the barricade and out across the melting ground. He'd been inches from Dorothy Bullard when her blouse tore (cause for much hilarity), and had actually stood in the path of the bullet that had struck Buddenbaum, amused to see it pass straight through him.

Suddenly, the clowning had ceased. From his place on the side-walk, Erwin saw Dolan's expression becoming troubled. He turned to Nordhoff, who was bending over the fallen Tesla, and let out a moaning word, "Whaaat—?"

Nordhoff didn't reply. He was staring down at the wounded man, who was plunging his hand into too solid ground. And as he stared, his face grew longer, as though he was about to be transformed into a dog or a camel. His nose lengthened, his cheeks puffed up, his eyes were sucked from his sockets.

"Oohhh Hellll . . . " Dolan moaned, and turning on his heel started back towards the sidewalk. It wasn't safe terrain. Though Erwin was a good deal farther from the source of this phenomenon, he too felt something plucking at his self-invented flesh. The pockets of his coat were torn off, and a number of the keepsakes carried away towards the epicenter; his fingers were growing longer; his face, he was sure, the same.

Dolan was in even worse condition. Though he was further from the hub than Nordhoff, Dickerson and the rest, the claim of what-ever force had been unleashed there was irresistible. He dropped to his knees and dug his nails into the ground, hollering at Erwin for help as he did so, but his matter had no purchase on the asphalt, and he was dragged back towards the hub, his body growing softer and longer, until he began to resemble a stream of melting flesh, coursing across the street.

Erwin covered his ears to shut out the din of his shrieks, and retreated back down the rapidly emptying street. It was hard going. The power at the hub of the crossroads was growing apace, and with every step he took it threatened to overwhelm him and drag him to his destruction. But he resisted its claim with all his will, and after twenty yards he began to outpace it. After thirty, its hold on him was dwindling rapidly. After forty, he felt sufficiently confident to slow a little and look for Dolan. He'd gone. So had Nordhoff, so had Dickerson, so had they all; all melted and run away into the ground.

The sound of sirens drew his gaze off down the street. Jed Gilholly was getting out of his car, along with two of his officers, Cliff Campbell and Floyd Weeks, neither of whom looked very happy with their lot.

Erwin didn't wait to see what the trio made of the forces awaiting them at the crossroads—or indeed what those forces made of *them*—but instead slipped away while the going was good. He had believed in the law once; valued it, served it, and trusted its power to regulate the world. But those certainties belonged to another life, and, like that life, had slipped away.

VIII

---

*W*hen Tesla opened her eyes, D'Amour was already hauling her to her feet.

"We've got more problems," he said, nodding down the street.

She started to follow his direction, but her gaze was distracted by the strange sights surrounding them. The band members, crawling away on all fours like beaten animals. The remnants of the crowd, many of them sobbing uncontrollably, others praying the same way, standing or kneeling in a litter of forsaken belongings: purses, hot dogs, baby carriages. And beyond all this, the police, approaching the crossroads with leveled guns.

"*Stand still!*" one of them yelled. "*All of you, stand still!*"

"We'd better do it," Tesla said, glancing back towards Buddenbaum. He had both hands in the ground, up to his elbows, and he was working them in and out, in and out, with a motion she could not help but think of as sexual; easing open this hole in the solid world. The air around them all was as hazy as ever, and its contents as incomprehensible.

"What the fuck is he doing?" D'Amour murmured to her.

"He's after the Art," Tesla said.

447

"You two, *shaddup!*" the lead officer yelled at them. Then, to Buddenbaum, "You! Get up! I want to see your hands!"

Buddenbaum showed no sign of even hearing the order, much less obeying it. The order came a second time, with little variation. Again, it was ignored.

"I'm going to count to three—" Jed warned.

"Go on," Tesla muttered. "Shoot the fucker."

"One—"

Jed continued his steady advance as he counted, his officers keeping place with him.

"Two—"

"Hey Jed?" Floyd Weeks said.

"Shaddup."

"I don't feel so good."

Jed glanced round at Weeks. The man had gone the color of a urinal, and his eyes were swiveling up into his sockets. "Don't do this!" Jed ordered him. This order was no more obeyed than that he'd given Buddenbaum. The gun fell from Weeks's trembling fingers and he let out a gasp that was as much pleasure as it was capitulation. Then he fell to his knees.

"I never knew . . . " he murmured. "Oh God, why didn't . . . why didn't anybody *tell me?*"

"Take no notice of him," Jed said to Cliff Campbell.

The man obeyed, but only because he had delusions of his own to deal with. "What's going on, Jed?" he murmured. "Where'd these *women* come from?"

"What women?" Jed said.

"They're all around us," Campbell babbled, turning as he spoke. "Don't you see them?"

Gilholly was about to shake his head when he let out a low moan. "Oh my Lord," he said.

"Are you ready?" D'Amour murmured to Tesla.

"As ready as I'll ever be."

Harry went back to watching Gilholly, who was fighting to keep a hold on his senses. "This isn't happening . . . " he murmured, glancing over at Campbell for support. He got none. His deputy had fallen to his knees and was laughing to himself like a crazy. In desperation, Jed pointed his gun at the forms drifting in front of him. "Stay out of my way!" he yelled at them. "I mean it! I'll use this if I have to."

"Let's go," Harry said, "while he's distracted," and he and Tesla started away from the middle of the street.

Jed saw their escape attempt.

"You! Stay—" He faltered in the middle of the order, as if he'd forgotten the words. "Oh Jesus," he said, his voice trembling now, "Jesus, Jesus, Jesus . . . "

Then, finally, he too dropped to his knees.

In the middle of the street, Buddenbaum let out a howl of frustration. Something was wrong here. One moment the crossroads had been melting beneath him, power flowing into its heart, the next the taste he'd had in his tongue had soured, and the dirt was hardening around his arm. He pulled it out. It was like extracting his hand from the bowels of something dead or dying. A shudder of revulsion coursed through him, and stinging tears sprang into his eyes.

"Owen—?"

The voice was Seth's of course. He was standing a yard or two away, looking fretful and afraid. "Has something gone wrong?" Buddenbaum nodded. "Do you know what?"

"Maybe this," Owen said, putting his hand up to his wounded head. "Maybe it simply distracted me—"

"Come away," Seth said.

Owen raised his wounded head and studied the air. "What do you see?" he said.

"The women, you mean?"

Owen squinted. "I just see bright shapes. Are they women?"

"Yes."

"You're sure?"

"Yes."

"Then it's some kind of conspiracy," he said. He reached up and grabbed hold of Seth's arm, pulling himself to his feet. "Somebody put them there to block the working."

"Who?"

"I don't know," Buddenbaum said. "Somebody who knows—" He halted, turning his gaze in Tesla's direction. "Bombeck," he murmured. Then shouted: "*Bombeck!*"

"What's *his* problem?" Harry said as Buddenbaum started towards them.

"He thinks I'm here to take the Art."

"Are you?"

Tesla shook her head. "I saw what it did to the Jaff," she said. "And he was ready for it. Or thought he was."

Buddenbaum was closing on them. Harry went for his gun, but Tesla said: "That's not going to stop him. Let's just get the hell out of his way."

She turned from Buddenbaum only to find that in the seconds she'd been looking back a little girl had stepped into their path and was studying them gravely. She was absurdly perfect: a petite blonde-ringleted five year old in a white dress, white socks, and white shoes. Her face was rose pink, her eyes huge and blue.

"Hello," she said, her voice sweet and cool. "You're Tesla, aren't you?"

Tesla wasn't in any mood to be chatting to kids, however perfect they were. "You should go find your Mommy and Daddy," she said.

"I was watching," the child said.

"This isn't a good thing to watch, honey," D'Amour said. "Where are your Mom and Dad?"

"They're not here."

"You're on your own?"

"No," she replied. "I've got Haheh with me, and Yie." She glanced back towards the ice cream parlor. There, sitting on the step, was a man with the face of a born comedian—jug-eared, wall-eyed, rubber-mouthed—who had six cones of ice cream in his hands, and was licking from one to another with a look of great concentration.

Beside him was another child, this a boy, who looked nearly moronic.

"Don't worry about me," the little girl said. "I'm fine." She studied Tesla carefully. "Are you dying?" she said.

Tesla looked at D'Amour. "This is not a conversation I want to have right now."

"But I do," Miss Perfection said. "It's important."

"Well, why don't you ask somebody else?"

"Because it's *you* we're interested in," the little girl replied gravely. She took a step towards Tesla, lifting her hand as she did so. "We saw your face, and we said: She knows about the story tree."

"About what?"

"The story tree," the child replied.

"What the fuck is she talking about?" Tesla said to D'Amour.

"Never mind," came another voice, this from behind them. Tesla didn't need to look round to know it was Buddenbaum. His voice was curiously hollow, as though he were speaking from an empty chamber. "You should have kept out of my business, woman."

"I've no interest in *your* business," Tesla said. Then, suddenly inquisitive, she turned to him. "But just for the record: What *is* your business?"

Buddenbaum looked terrible, his face more bloody than not, his body trembling. "That's for me to know," he said.

At this, the little girl piped up. "You can tell her, Owen," she said.

Buddenbaum looked past Tesla at the child. "I've no wish to share our secrets with this woman," he said stiffly.

"But we do," the child replied.

Tesla studied Buddenbaum's face through the odd exchange, trying to decode its signs. Plainly, he knew the girl well; and equally plainly was somewhat nervous of her. Perhaps wary rather than nervous. Once again, Tesla missed Raul's incisive grasp of such signals. Had he been with her she was certain he could have armed her with insights for whatever encounter lay ahead.

"You look sick," Buddenbaum said.

"You and me both," Tesla replied.

"Ah, but I'll mend," Buddenbaum went on. "You, on the other hand, are not long for this world." He spoke lightly enough, but she couldn't miss the threat in the words. He was not simply prophesying death, he was *promising* it. "I suggest you start making your farewells while you can."

"Is this all part of it?" the little girl said. Tesla glanced back at her. She was wearing a coy little smile. "Is it, Owen?"

"Yes," Buddenbaum said. "It's all part of it."

"Oh good, good." The child shifted her attention back to Tesla. "We'll see you later then," she said, stepping aside to let them pass.

"I don't think that's very likely," Tesla said.

"Oh, but we will," the girl said, "for sure. We're very interested in you and the story tree."

Tesla heard Buddenbaum mutter something behind her. She didn't hear what, and she was in no state of mind or body to make him repeat it. She simply returned the child's sweet smile and with Harry at her side left the crossroads, with the sound of the officers' bewildered worship floating after them on the summer breeze.

ii

Though it was next to impossible that news of what had happened at the crossroads had already reached the ears of every man, woman, and child in Everville, the streets Tesla and Harry walked to get back to Phoebe's house were preternaturally quiet, as though people had read the trembling air, and judged silence the safest response. Despite the heat, doors were closed and windows shuttered. There were no children playing on the lawns or in the street; not even dogs were showing their twitching noses.

It was doubly strange because the day was so perfect: the air candied with summer flowers, the sky flawless.

As they turned the corner onto Phoebe's street, out of the blue Harry said, "God, I love the world."

It was such a simple thing to say, and it was spoken with such easy faith, Tesla could only shake her head.

"You don't?" Harry said.

"There's so much shit," she said.

"Not right this minute. Right this minute it's as good as it gets."

"Look up the mountain," she said.

"I'm not up the mountain," Harry replied. "I'm here."

"Good for you," she said, unable to keep the edge from her voice.

He looked across at her. She looked, he thought, about as frail and weary as any living soul could look and still be living. He wanted to put his arm around her, just for a little while, but he supposed she wouldn't thank him for the gesture. She was in a space all of her own, sealed off from comfort.

It took her a little time fumbling with the spare keys Phoebe had given her before they gained access to the house. Once inside, she said, "I'm going to go get some sleep. I can't even think straight."

"Sure."

She started up the stairs, but turned back a couple of seconds later, staring down at D'Amour with those empty eyes of hers. "By the way," she said, "thank you."

"For what?"

"For what you did on the mountain. I wouldn't be here—Lord . . . you know what I'm saying."

"I know. And there's no need. We're in this together."

"No," she said softly. "I don't think that's how it's working out."

"If you're thinking about what the kid said to you—"

"It's not the first time I've thought about it," Tesla said, "I've been pushing myself to the limits for five years, Harry, and it's taken its toll." He started to say something, but she raised her hand to hush him. "Let's not waste time lying to each other," she said. "I've done what I can do, and I'm used up. Simple as that. I guess as long as I had Raul in my head I could pretend I was making sense of things, but now . . . now he's gone"—she shrugged—"I don't want to carry on any longer." She tried a tiny smile, but it was misbegotten. She let it drop, and turning her back on Harry traipsed up to bed.

*   *   *

Harry brewed himself some coffee, and sat down in the living room among the out-of-date copies of *TV Guide* and the overfilled ashtrays, to think things through. The coffee did its job. He was wide awake, despite the exhaustion in his limbs. He sat staring up at the ceiling and turned over the events that had brought him to this confounded state.

He'd gone up the mountain under the cover of mist and Voight's tattoos to search for Kissoon, but he'd not found the man: at least not in any form he recognized. Children, yes; the Brothers Grimm, yes; a Blessedm'n, three crucified souls, and Tesla Bombeck, yes. But the man who'd murdered Ted Dusseldorf and Maria Nazareno had evaded him.

He thought back to Morningside Heights—to that squalid room where his enemy had slept—wondering if perhaps there'd been some clue to Kissoon's present form that had seemed inconsequential at the time. He recalled nothing useful. But he *did* remember the deck of cards he'd found there. He dug in his jacket pocket and brought them to light. Was there a clue here, he wondered, in these images? He cleared the coffee table and laid them out. *Ape, moon, fetus, lightning—*

Potent symbols, every one.

Lighting, hand, torso, hole—

But if it was a game, then he didn't know the rules. And if it wasn't a game, then what the hell was it?

Barely conscious of what he was doing he arranged and rearranged the cards in front of him, hoping some solution would appear. Nothing did. Despite the power of the symbols, or perhaps because of it, there was no clarity; just a sense that his mind was too lightweight to deal with such issues.

He was in the midst of these musings when the telephone rang. The Cobb household did not believe in answering machines, it seemed, because the ringing went on uninterrupted until Harry picked up.

There was a well-worn voice at the other end of the line. "Is

Tesla there?" the man said. Harry paused before replying, during which time the man said, "It's urgent. I *have* to talk to her."

This time Harry recognized the speaker. "Grillo?" he said.

"Who is this?"

"It's Harry."

"Jesus, Harry. What are you doing there?"

"Same thing Tesla's doing."

"Is she around?"

"She's asleep."

"I have to talk to her. I've been calling all day."

"Where are you?"

"About five miles outside town."

"Which town?"

"*Everville*, for God's sake! Now can I talk to her?"

"Can't you call back in an hour or so—"

"No!" Grillo yelled. Then, more quietly, "No. I need to talk to her now."

"Wait a minute," Harry said, and putting down the phone he went up to wake Tesla. She was slumped on the double bed fully dressed, a look of such exhaustion on her sleeping face he couldn't bring himself to deny her the slumber she so plainly needed. It was a good thing. By the time he got back down into the hallway the line was dead. Grillo had gone.

<hr>

iii

In sleep, Tesla found herself walking on an unearthly shore. Snow had lately fallen there, but she felt none of its chill. Light-footed, she wandered down to the sea. It was thick and dark, its turbulent waters scummy, and here and there she saw bodies in the surf, turning their stricken faces her way as if to warn her against entering.

She had no choice. The sea wanted her, and would not be denied. Nor, in truth, did she want to resist it. The shore was drear and desolate. The sea, for all its freight of corpses, was a place of mystery.

It was only once she was wading into the surf, the waves breaking against her breasts and her belly, that her dreaming mind put words to what place this was. Or rather, one word.

Quiddity.

The dream-sea leapt up against her face when she spoke its name, and its undertow pulled at her legs. She didn't attempt to fight it, but let it lift her off her feet and carry her away like an eager lover. The waves, which were substantial enough at the shore, soon grew titanic. When they raised her up on their shoulders she could see a wall of darkness at the horizon, the likes of which she remembered from her last moments in Kissoon's Loop. The Iad, of course. Mountains and fleas; fleas and mountains. When they dropped her into their troughs, and she plunged below the surface, she glimpsed another spectacle entirely: vast shoals of fish, moving like thunderheads below her. And weaving between the shoals, luminous forms that were, she guessed, human spirits like herself. She seemed to see vestigial faces in their light; hints of the infants, lovers, and dying souls who were dreaming themselves here.

She had no doubt as to which of the three she was. Too old to be a baby, too crazy to be a lover, there was only one reason why her soul was journeying here tonight. Miss Perfection had been right. Death was imminent. This was the last time she would sleep before her span as Tesla Bombeck was over.

Even if she'd been distressed at this, she had no time to feel it. The adventure at hand demanded too much of her attention. Rising and falling, on shoulder and in trough, she was carried on towards a place where the waters, for some reason she could not comprehend, grew so utterly calm they made an almost perfect mirror for the busy sky.

She thought at first she was alone in these doldrums, and was about to test her powers of self-propulsion in order escape them, when she realized that a light was flickering beneath her. She looked down into the water, and saw that some species of fish with luminous flesh had congregated in the deep, and was now steadily rising towards the surface. When she raised her head from the water again she found that she was not alone. A long-haired, bearded man was casually crouching on the water as though it were as solid as a rock, idly creating ripples in the glassy surface. He had been there all along, she assumed, and she'd missed him. But now, as if roused from some reverie by her gaze, he looked up.

His face was scrawny—his bones sharp, his black eyes sharper— but the smile he offered was so sweetly tentative, as though he was a little embarrassed to have been caught unawares, that she was instantly charmed. He rose, the water dancing around his feet, and ambled over to her. His water-soaked robes were in tatters, and she could see that his torso was covered with small, pale scars, as though he'd been wrestling in broken glass.

She sympathized with his condition. She too was scarred, inside and out; she too had been stripped of all she'd worn in the world: her profession, her self esteem, her certainty.

"Do we know each other?" he said to her as he approached. His voice lacked music, but she liked the sound of it nevertheless.

"No," she said, suddenly tongue-tied. "I don't believe so."

"Somebody spoke of you to me, I'm certain. Was it Fletcher perhaps?"

"You know Fletcher?"

"Then it was," the man said, smiling again. "You're the one who martyred him."

"I hadn't thought of it that way—but yes, I guess that was me."

"You see?" he said. He went down on his haunches beside her, while the water buoyed her up. "You wanted connections, and they're there to be found. But you have to look in the terrible places, Tesla. The places where death comes to take love away, where we lose each other and lose ourselves; that's where the connections begin. It takes a brave soul to look there and not despair."

"I've tried to be brave," she said.

"I know," he said softly. "I know."

"But I wasn't brave enough, is that what you're saying? The thing is, I didn't ask to be part of this. I wasn't ready for it. I was just going to write movies, you know, and get rich and smug. I guess that sounds pathetic to you."

"Why?"

"Well, I don't suppose you get to see a lot of movies."

"You'd be surprised," the man said with a little smile. "Anyway, it's the stories that matter, however they're told."

She thought of the child at the crossroads—

We saw your face, and we said: She knows about the story tree.

"What's the big deal about stories?" she said.

"You love them," he said, his gaze leaving her face and slipping down to the water. The glowing forms she'd seen rising from below were within a few fathoms of the surface now. The water was beginning to simmer with their presence. "You do, don't you?" he said.

"I suppose I do," she said.

"That's what the connections are, Tesla."

"Stories?"

"Stories. And every life, however short, however meaningless it seems, is a leaf—"

"A leaf."

"Yes, a leaf." He looked up at her again, and waited, unspeaking, until she grasped the sense of what he was saying.

"On the story tree," she said. He smiled. "Lives are leaves on the story tree."

"Simple, isn't it?" he said. The bubbles were breaking all around them now, and the surface was no longer glacial enough to bear him up. He started to sink into the water; slowly, slowly. "I'm afraid I have to go," he said. "The 'shu have come for me. Why do you look so unhappy?"

"Because it's too late," she said. "Why did I have to wait until now to know what I was supposed to do?"

"You didn't need to know. You were doing it."

"No I wasn't," she said, distressed now. "I never got to tell a story I gave a damn about."

"Oh but you did," he said. He was almost gone from sight now.

"What story was that?" she begged him, determined to get an answer before he disappeared. "What?"

"Your own," he told her, slipping from sight. *"Your own."*

Then he was gone.

She stared down into the bubbling water, and saw that the creatures he'd called the 'shu—which resembled cuttlefish as far as she could see, and were congregated below her in their many millions— were describing a vast spiral around the sinking man, as though drawing him down into their midst. The vortex made no claim on her spirit stuff, however. She felt a pang of loss, watching him disappear into the bright depths. He had seemed wise, and she had wanted to speak to him longer. As it was, she had something to take back with her: the observation that the story she'd told was her own. It meant little to her right now, but perhaps if she succeeded in carrying it into the waking world it would comfort her.

And now, as the spiral of 'shu faded into the depths, there was news from that world. A telephone ringing, and then the sound of footsteps on the stairs.

"Tesla?"

She opened her eyes. Harry had his head around the door. "It's Grillo," he said. "He needs to talk to you. He's called once already." She vaguely remembered hearing a telephone ring as she'd wandered the snowy shore. "Sounds like he's in bad shape."

She got up and went downstairs. There was a stub of pencil beside the telephone. Before she spoke to Grillo she wrote *I told my own story* on the telephone directory, in case the conversation drove the dream from her head. Then she picked up the receiver.

Just as Harry had said, Grillo sounded to be in bad shape; terrible shape, in fact. Like her, like D'Amour, like the water-walker in her dream. It was as though everybody around her was winding down.

"I'm at a place called the Sturgis Motel," he explained, "with Howie, Jo-Beth, and their kid Amy."

"Where?"

"A few miles outside Everville."

"What the hell are you doing there?"

"We had no choice. We had to move quickly, and I knew we were going to need serious help."

"To do what?"

"Tommy-Ray's coming after Jo-Beth."

"*Tommy-Ray?*"

Grillo began to relate to her the events of the last few days. She gave all but five percent of her attention to the account, the remaining portion dedicated to holding onto the dream from which she'd awaken. But the images of terror and flight that spilled from Grillo steadily supplanted her memories of the becalmed sea, and of the man who had known Fletcher.

"I need your help, Tes—" Grillo was saying. She clung to the memory of the water-walker's face for a few desperate moments. "Tes, are you there?" Then she had no choice but to let it go.

"Yeah, I'm here—"

"I said I need some help."

"You don't sound so good, Nathan. Did you get hurt?"

"It's a long story. Look, give me your address. We'll drive into town."

She flashed on the swathe Tommy-Ray the Death-Boy—along with his army of phantoms—had cut through Palomo Grove. Hadn't he brought down his own house in his enthusiasm for destruction, with his mother inside it? If he was unleashed in Everville, especially at a time of mass exodus (which couldn't be far off) the death toll would be appalling.

"Stay where you are," she said. "I'll come to you."

Grillo didn't argue. He was clearly too desperate to have her with him as soon as possible. He gave her the motel's whereabouts and urged her to be quick. That was that.

Harry was in the kitchen, burning toast. She told him all that Grillo had said. He listened without comment, until she got to the part about her leaving.

"So Everville's my baby now?" he said.

"It looks that way."

She wanted to tell him that she'd dreamed her final dream, and that he should not expect her to return, but that sounded hopelessly melodramatic. What she needed was something pithier; a throwaway line that would seem blasé and wise when she was gone. But nothing came to mind. As it was, Harry had a farewell of his own to offer.

"I'm thinking I might go back up the mountain after dark," he said. "If the Iad's coming through I may as well get a ringside view. Which means . . . we probably won't be seeing each other again."

"No. I suppose not."

"We've had quite a time of it, haven't we? I mean, our lives, they've been—"

"Weird."

"Extraordinary," Harry said. She shrugged. It was true, of course. "I'm sure we've both wished it could have been different. But I guess somewhere deep down we must have wanted it this way."

"I guess."

The exchange faltered there. Tesla looked up and saw that Harry was staring straight at her, his lips pinched together as though to keep from weeping.

"Enjoy the sights," she said.

"I will," he replied.

"You take care."

She broke the look between them, went to pick up her jacket, and headed outside. As she reached the front door she almost turned round and went back to embrace him, but she resisted. To do so would only extend the agony. Better be gone, now, and off on the open road.

The parade-watching crowds had long since vacated Main Street, but there were still plenty of people out and about, shopping for souvenirs, or looking for somewhere to eat. The evening was balmy, the sky still cloudless; the party atmosphere a little subdued by the fiasco of the afternoon but not vanquished altogether.

An earlier Tesla might have brought her Harley to a screeching halt in the middle of Main Street and yelled herself hoarse trying to get people to leave before the Iad came. But she knew better than to waste her breath. They'd shrug, laugh, and turn their backs on her, and in truth she could scarcely blame them. She'd caught her reflection in the bathroom mirror just before she'd left Phoebe's house. The lean woman she'd admired a few days before—the woman marked by her journey, the woman proud of her scars—was now a bag of bones and despair.

Besides, what use would such warnings be, even if they were attended to? If the Iad was indeed all it had been promised to be, then there was no escape from it. Perhaps these people, celebrating in the shadow of death and snuffed out before they even knew what force had snuffed them, would be thought the lucky ones in time. Gone too quickly to fear or hope. Worst of all, hope.

Though it was a detour to return to the crossroads, she did so, just to see what clues, if any, remained to the mysteries of the afternoon. Though the streets had been given back to traffic, there were very few cars passing in either direction. There was foot traffic however, and plenty of it. People lingering outside the diner, and in front of the crossroads. A few even had their cameras out to immortalize the spot. Of the people Tesla had last seen on their knees here, praying to the visions they were witnessing, there was now no sign. They'd gone home, or been taken.

As she was putting her helmet back on, she heard a shout from the opposite side of the street, and turned to see her nemesis from Kitty's Diner, Bosley the Righteous, striding towards her.

"What did you do?" he yelled, his face blotchy with rage.

"About what?" she said.

"You had a hand in this *abomination*," he said. "I saw you, right in the middle of it." He halted a couple of yards from her, as though fearful she might infect him with her godlessness. "I know what you're up to."

"You want to explain it to me?" she snapped. "And don't give me some shit about the Devil's work, Bosley, because you don't believe that any more than I do. Not really."

He flinched. And she saw such fear in him, such a profundity of dread that the rage went out of her, drained away from her all at once. "You know what?" she said. "I think I met Jesus this afternoon." Bosley looked at her warily. "At least, he was walking on water, and he had a lot of scars, so . . . it could have been him, right?" Still Bosley said nothing. "I'm sorry, we didn't get round to talking about you, but if we had I'd have said He should drop by your place sometime. Have a piece of pie."

"You're crazy—" Bosley said.

"You and me both," Tesla said. "Take care of yourself, Bosley." And with that she put on her helmet and drove off.

Once she was outside the town limits she gunned the bike, certain that the chief of police and his awestruck deputies would not be watching out for speed freaks tonight. She was right. With an empty road and no law keepers to flag her down she roared on her way as though to meet with Grillo, though the embrace that awaited her at the end of this ride was colder and more permanent than human arms could ever offer.

IX

i

*T*here would be other years, Dorothy Bullard thought as she sat in a mildly sedated haze beside her living room window. Other festivals, other parades, other chances for things to be perfect. She had a mercifully confused memory of what had happened at the crossroads, but she'd been assured by a number of kind folks that it had not been her fault; no, not at all. She'd been under a lot of pressure, and she'd done a fine job, a wonderful job, and next year, oh next year—

"It'll be perfect."

"What did you say, dear?" Maisie had just come in with some fluffy scrambled eggs and a little bran muffin.

"Next year, everything'll be perfect, you'll see."

"Let's not even think about next year," Maisie said. "Let's just take things as they come, shall we?"

For Larry Glodoski, it was not pills that were keeping the memories hazy, it was beer, and plenty of it. He had been propped up at Hamrick's Bar for two and a half hours now, and he was finally getting to feel a little better. It was not what he'd seen at the crossroads he was dulling with alcohol, it was the pain of their departure. The women on the stairs had given him a glimpse of bliss; he'd thought his heart would crack with loss when they faded and disappeared.

"You want another of those?" Will Hamrick asked him.

"Keep 'em coming."

"You want to talk about it?"

Larry shook his head. "None of it makes much sense," he said.

Will passed another bottle down the bar. "I had a guy in here day before yesterday, really spooked me," he said.

"Like how?"

"It was just after Morton Cobb died. He was saying how it was better that he'd been killed that way, 'cause it was a better story."

"A better story?"

"Yeah. An' I was a—what the fuck did he call me?—a disseminator, I think that was it, yeah, a disseminator, and people liked to hear really brutal stories . . . " He lost his way in the midst of his recollections, and threw up his hands. "I don't know, he just seemed like a sick sonofabitch. He had this voice—it was kinda like a hypnotist or something."

The notion rang a bell. "What did he look like?" Larry asked.

"'Bout sixty, maybe. Had a beard."

"Broad guy? Wearing black?"

"That's him," Will said. "You know him?"

"He was there this afternoon," Larry said, quickly. "I think he was the one who fucked everything up."

"Somebody should talk to Jed about him."

"Jed—" Larry growled, "he's no damn good to anyone." He chugged on his beer. "I'm going to talk to some of the band. They were really pissed with what happened this afternoon."

"Be careful, Larry," Will advised. "You don't want Jed on your back for taking the law into your own hands."

Larry leaned over the bar until he was almost nose to nose with Will. "I don't give a shit," he slurred. "Something's goin' on in this city, Hamrick, and Jed's not got a handle on it."

"And you have?"

Larry dug in his pocket and tossed three tens over the counter. "I will have soon enough," he said, pushing off from the bar and heading for the door. "I'll give you a call, tell you when we're ready for action."

Elsewhere in town, a fair appearance of normality had been reestablished. In the town hall the first partners for the Waltz-a-thon were already warming up. At the library annex, which had only been completed two months ago, Jerry Totland, a local author who'd made a nice reputation for himself penning mysteries set in Portland, was reading from his newest opus. In the little Italian restaurant on Blasemont Street there was a line of twenty customers waiting to taste the glories of Neapolitan cuisine.

There were mutterings, of course; rumors and gossip about what had brought the parade to a halt that afternoon, but by and large they simply added a little piquancy to the evening's exchanges. There was little genuine unease, more a mild amusement, especially among the visitors, that the event had gone so hopelessly awry. It would be a story to dine out on, wouldn't it, when they got back home? How Everville had overstepped itself and fallen flat on its ambitious face?

ii

After the horrors of the afternoon, Erwin had not known what to do with himself. He had lost, in one fell swoop, all the friends he'd had, as surely as if they'd been massacred at the dinner table.

He had no real comprehension of what had happened at the crossroads, nor did he really want to know. Death had shown him some strange sights in the last few days, and he'd quickly learned to take them in his stride, but this was beyond him. He wandered the streets like a lost dog for a couple of hours, looking for some place to sit and listen to a conversation that did not remind him of his fear. But everywhere he looked for solace, he found people talking in whispers about the things that discomfited him.

Few of these exchanges were overtly concerned with the events of the afternoon, but all of them had been inspired by it, he was certain. Why else were people confessing their sins to their loved ones tonight, asking for forgiveness or understanding? They had smelled their mortality today, and it had made them maudlin. He passed from one place to another, looking for solace and, finding none, he returned at dusk to the only place he was certain to get some peace and quiet: the cemetery.

There he wandered among the tombs as the sun set, idly perusing the epitaphs, and turning over events that had brought him to this sorry state. What had he done to deserve it? Wanted a little fame for himself? Since when had that been a capital crime? Dug too deep into secrets that should have been left to lie? That was no sin, either; not that he knew of. He'd simply had a patch of bad luck.

He took a seat, at last, on a tombstone close to the tree where he'd first met Nordhoff and the rest. His gaze fell on the stone in front of him, and he read aloud to himself the inscription there.

> What Thomas doubted, I believe:
> That from Death's hand there is reprieve;
> That I, laid here, will one day rise,
> And smell the wind and meet the skies.
> My hope is tender though, and must
> Be kept from harm by those that dust
> Has blinded. So I pray: deliver me from
> The faithless kin of Doubting Tom.

The simplicity and the vulnerability of the words moved him deeply. As he reached the end of the poem his voice thickened and tears came, copious tears, pouring down.

He buried his face in his hands and rocked back and forth, unable to stop weeping. What was the use of living in hope of life after death if all it amounted to was this absurd, empty round? It was unendurable!

"Is the poem so bad?" said a voice somewhere above him.

He looked over his shoulder. The tree was in its last lushness before autumn, its branches thick with leaves, but he caught a glimpse of somebody moving up there.

"Show yourself," he said.

"I prefer not to," came the reply. "I learned a long time ago that there's safety in trees."

"Don't kid yourself," Erwin said.

"What's the problem?"

"I want to be back in the world."

"Oh *that*," said the man in the tree. "It cannot be had, so don't break your heart wanting it." There was a shaking of the canopy, as the man adjusted his position. "They've gone, haven't they?" he said.

"Who?"

"The fools who used to gather here. Nordhoff and Dolan"—he practically spat the word *Dolan* out—"and the rest. I came down the mountain to finish my business with them, but I don't see them and I don't smell them—"

"No?"

"No. All I see is you. Where did they go?"

"It's difficult to explain," Erwin said.

"Do your best."

He did. Described all that he'd seen and felt at the crossroads, though his lawyerly vocabulary was barely adequate. It was the unburdening he'd sought, and it felt good.

"So they were whisked away, huh?"

"That's what it looked like," Erwin said.

"It was bound to happen," the occupant of the tree said. "There was a bloody business started here, and it had to be finished sooner or later."

"I know what you're talking about," Erwin said. "I read a confession—"

"Whose?"

"His name was McPherson."

The man loosed a guttural growl that made Erwin shudder. "Don't speak that name!" he said.

"Why not?"

"Just don't!" the man roared. "Anyway, it's not his atrocities I was referring to. There was another slaughter up on Harmon's Heights, before it ever had a name. And I've waited a long time to see its consequences."

"Who are you?" Erwin said. "Why are you hiding up there?"

"I think you've seen enough strangeness for one day," the man replied. "Without laying eyes on me."

"I can deal with it," Erwin replied. "Show yourself."

There was silence from the tree for a few moments. Then the man said, "As you wish," and the foliage sighed as he clambered down into view. He wasn't so strange. Scarred, certainly, and somewhat bestial, but he resembled a man.

"There," he said, when he reached the bottom of the tree. "Now you see me."

"I'm—glad to know you," Erwin said. "I was afraid I was going to be alone."

"What's your name?"

"Erwin Toothaker. And yours?"

The wounded beast inclined his head. "I'm pleased to meet you," he said. "My name is Coker Ammiano."

PART SIX

The Grand Design

I

*I*t took Musnakaff an hour or more to prepare his mistress for the journey out into the chilly streets of Liverpool, during which time Phoebe was given permission to wander the house. It was a melancholy trek. The rooms were for the most part beautifully appointed, the beds vast and inviting, the bathrooms positively decadent, but there was dust on every surface and gull-shit on every window; a sense everywhere of the best times having passed by. There was no sign of the individuals who had lived in this house; who had admired the view from its windows or laid their heads on its pillows. Had they dreamed? Phoebe wondered. And if so, of what? Of the world that she'd come from? It amused her at first, thinking that the people who'd lived in these fine rooms might have yearned for the Cosm the way she'd yearned for some unreachable dreamplace. But the more she pondered it, the more melancholy it seemed, that people on both sides of the divide lived in discontent, wishing for the other's lot. If she survived this journey, she thought, she would return to Everville determined to live every moment as it came, and not waste time pining for some sweet faraway.

When she emerged from one of the bedrooms she looked into a mirror in the hallway, and told herself aloud, "Enjoy it while you can. Every minute of it."

"What did you say?" Musnakaff asked her, stepping from a doorway along the passage.

She was embarrassed to have been caught this way. "How long have you been watching me?" she wanted to know.

"Only a moment or two," he replied. "You make a fine sight, Phoebe Cobb. There's music in you."

"I'm tone-deaf," she told him, a little sharply.

"There's music and music," Musnakaff replied. "Your spirit sings even if your throat doesn't. I hear drums when I look at your breasts, and a choir when I think of you naked." She gave him the forbidding stare that had terrorized a thousand tardy patients, but it didn't work. He simply grinned at her, his decorated cheeks twinkling. "Don't be offended," he said. "This house had always been a place where people talk plainly about such matters."

"Then I'll talk plainly too," Phoebe said. "I don't appreciate you ogling me when my back's turned, and drums or no drums I'll thank you not to look at my breasts."

"Do you not like your breasts?"

"That's between me and my breasts," Phoebe said, realizing as the words came out how absurd they sounded.

Musnakaff erupted with laughter, and try as she might Phoebe could not help but let go a tiny smile herself, the sight of which only made Musnakaff gush further.

"I'll say it again," Musnakaff told her. "This house has seen many fine women, but you are among the finest, the *very* finest."

It was so nicely said, she could not help but be flattered. "Well . . . " she said. "Thank you."

"The pleasure's mine," Musnakaff said. "Now, if you're ready, the Mistress's bearers have arrived. I believe it's time we all went down to the water."

---

ii

It took less than an hour of traveling on the road to b'Kether Sabbat for Joe to lose most of his sympathy for the refugees flooding in the opposite direction. He witnessed countless acts of casual cruelty in that time. Children more heavily burdened than their parents, whipped along; animals abused and beaten into a frenzy; rich men and women, hoisted up onto the backs of imperious cousins to the camel, cutting a bloody swathe through those careless enough to stumble into their path. In short, all that he might have expected to see in the Cosm.

When these sorry spectacles became too much, however, he simply set his sights on the city itself, and his weary limbs found fresh strength. The people who had lived in b'Kether Sabbat were as petty and barbarous as the citizens of any terrestrial city, but the edifice they were vacating was without parallel.

As for the wave of the Iad, it seethed and divided, but did not advance. It simply hovered over the city like a vast beast, mesmerized by something in its shadow. He only hoped that he could reach the city, and walk its streets and climb its blazing towers before the Iad's interest staled, and it delivered the coup de grâce.

As he came within a quarter mile of the nearest ladders—the city looming like an inverted mountain before him—he heard a shrill shout above the din and an ashen creature dug its way through the throng to block his way.

"Afrique!" he said. "Afrique! You're *alive!*" The creature laid his webbed hands upon Joe's chest. "You don't know me, do you?"

"No. Should I?"

"I was on the ship with you," the man said, and now Joe recognized him. He was one of the slaves Noah had seconded to crew *The Fanacapan*: a broad, burly fellow with sluggish, froglike features. His manner, now that he was once again his own man, belied his appearance. He had a quick, lively quality about him "My name's Wexel Fee, Afrique," he said, covered in smiles. "And I am very glad to see you. Very, very glad."

"I don't know why," Joe said. "You were treated like shit."

"I heard what you said to Noah Summa Summamentis. You tried to do something for us. It's not your fault you failed."

"I'm afraid it is," Joe said guiltily. "Where are the others?"

"Dead."

"All of them?"

"All."

"I'm sorry."

"Don't be. They weren't friends of mine."

"Why did you not die and they did? Noah said when he was done with you—"

"I know what he said. I heard that too. I have very sharp ears. I also have a strong will. I was not ready to die."

"So you heard but you couldn't act for yourself?"

"Exactly so. I'd lost my will to his suit."

"So you *were* hurting."

"Oh yes. I was hurting." Fee lifted his right hand into view. Two of his six fingers were reduced to gummy stumps. "And I would have gladly killed the man, when I woke."

"Why didn't you?"

"He is mighty, Afrique, now he's back in b'Kether Sabbat. While I am very far from home." He looked past Joe now, towards the sea.

"There are no ships, Wexel."

"What about *The Fanacapan?*"

"I saw it sink."

He took the news philosophically. "Ah. So perhaps I did not out-live the others so that I could go home." He made the first smile Joe had seen on this woeful road. "Perhaps I tried to meet you again, Afrique."

"My name's Joe."

"I heard my enemy call you by that name," Fee replied. "There-fore I cannot use it. This is the etiquette in my country. So I will call you Afrique." Joe didn't much like the dubbing, but this was no time to offend the man. "And I will come with you, back to b'Kether Sab-bat. Yes?"

"I'd certainly like your company," Joe said. "But why would you want to come?"

"Because there are no ships. Because I found you in a crowd of ten thousand souls. And because you may be able to do what I could not."

"Kill Noah."

"From your lips, Afrique. From your lips."

iii

The caravan that descended the steep hill from the house on Canning Street was nine souls strong. Phoebe and Musnakaff, both on foot, Maeve O'Connell, traveling in an elaborate sedan chair, borne by four sizable men, plus an individual leading the way and one tagging along behind, both of them very conspicuously armed. When Phoebe remarked upon this Musnakaff simply said, "These are dangerous days. Who knows what's loose?" which was not the most reassuring of replies.

"Come walk alongside me," Maeve said as they went. "It's time you kept your side of the bargain. Tell me about the Cosm. No, forget the Cosm. Just tell me about my city."

"First," said Phoebe, "I've got a question."

"What is it?"

"Why did you dream this city instead of another Everville?"

"I was a child in Liverpool, and full of hope. I remember it fondly. I didn't remember Everville the same way."

"But you still want to know what's happened to it?" Phoebe pointed out.

"So I do," Maeve replied. "Now tell."

Without knowing what aspects of Evervillian life would most interest the woman, Phoebe began a scattershot account of life at home. The Festival, the problems with the post office, the library annex, Jed Gilholly, the restaurants on Main Street, Kitty's Diner, the Old Schoolhouse and the collection it contained, the problems with the sewage system—

"Wait, wait," Maeve said. "Go back a little. You spoke of a collection."

"Yes—"

"It's about the history of Everville, you say?"

"That's right."

"And you're familiar with it?"

"I wouldn't say—"

"Yet you didn't know who I was," Maeve said, her face more pinched than ever. "I find that strange." Phoebe kept her silence. "Tell me, what do they say about the way Everville was founded?"

"I don't exactly remember," Phoebe replied.

Suddenly, the virago started to yell. "*Stop! Everybody stop!*" The little procession came to a ragged halt. Maeve leaned out of her chair and beckoned Phoebe closer.

"Now listen, woman," Maeve said. "I thought we had a bargain."

"We do."

"So why aren't you telling me the truth? Huh?"

"I . . . don't want to hurt your feelings," Phoebe said.

"Mary, mother of God, I've sufferings to my name the likes of which—" She stopped, and started to pull at the collar of her robe. Musnakaff started to say something about not catching cold, but she gave him such a venomous look he was instantly silenced. "Look at this," she said to Phoebe, exposing her neck. There was a grievous scar running all the way around her neck. "You know what that is?"

"It looks like—well it looks like somebody tried to hang you."

"They tried and they succeeded. Left me swinging from a tree, along with my child and my husband."

Phoebe was appalled. "Why?" she said.

"Because they hated us and wanted to be rid of us," Maeve said. "Musnakaff? Cover me up!" He instantly set to doing so, while Maeve continued her story. "I had a very strange, sour child," she said, "who loved nothing in all the world. Certainly not me. Nor his father. And over the years people came to hate him in return. As soon as they had reason to lynch him, they took it, and took my poor husband too. Coker wasn't of the Cosm, you see. He'd come there for my sake, and he learned to be more human than human, but they still sniffed something in him they didn't like. As for me—" She turned her head from Phoebe and peered down the hill.

"As for you?" Phoebe said.

"I was what they wanted to forget. I was there at the beginning—

no, that's not right—I *was* the beginning. I *was* Everville, sure as if it had been built of my bones. And it didn't suit the Brawleys and the Gilhollys and the Hendersons and all the other fine upstanding families to remember that."

"So they murdered you for it?"

"They turned a blind eye to a lynching," Maeve said. "That's murder, I'd say."

"Why aren't you dead?"

"Because the bough broke. Simple as that. My sweet, loving Coker was not so lucky. His bough was strong, and by the time I came out of my faint he was cold."

"That's horrible."

"I never felt love for any creature the way I felt love for him," Maeve said.

As she spoke Phoebe felt a mild tremor in the ground. Musnakaff apparently felt it too. He turned to his mistress with a look of alarm. "Maybe it would be best not to speak of this," he said. "Not out in the open."

"Oh pish!" Maeve said to him. "He *wouldn't* dare touch me. Not for telling what he knows is the truth."

The exchange puzzled Phoebe, but she didn't let it distract her from her questions.

"What about your son?" Phoebe said. "What happened to him?"

"His body was taken by beasts. He always had a stench to him. I daresay he made a better meal than Coker or me." She pondered for a moment. "This is a terrible thing to say about your own flesh and blood, but the fact is, my son was not long for this world one way or another."

"Was he sick?"

"In his head, yes. And in his heart. Something in him had curdled when he was a child, and I thought for the longest time he was a cretin. I gave up trying to teach him anything. But there was malice in him, I think: terrible malice. And he was best dead." She gave Phoebe a sorrowful look. "Do you have children?" she said.

"No."

"Count yourself lucky," Maeve replied.

Then, abruptly shaking off her melancholy tone, she waved Phoebe away, shouting, "Rouse yourselves!" to her bearers, and the convoy went on its way, down the steep hill.

The state of the dream-sea had changed considerably in the hours in which Phoebe had been a guest in Maeve's house. The ships in the harbor no longer lay peaceably at anchor, but pitched and bucked, tearing at their moorings like panicked thoroughbreds. The beacons that had been burning at the harbor entrance had been extinguished by the fury of the waves, which mounted steadily as the party descended.

"I begin to think I'll not be able to keep my end of the bargain," Maeve said to Phoebe once they were on flat ground.

"Why not?"

"Use your eyes," Maeve replied, pointing down towards the beach, where the breakers were ten or twelve feet high. "I don't think I'll be speaking to the 'shu down there."

"Who are the 'shu?"

"Tell her," Maeve instructed Musnakaff. "And you, set me down." Once again, the convoy came to a halt. "Help me out of this contraption," Maeve demanded. The bearers sprang to do just that.

"Do you need help?" Musnakaff asked her.

"If I do I'll ask for it," Maeve replied. "Get on with educating the woman. Though Lord knows it's a little late."

"Tell me who the 'shu are," Phoebe said to Musnakaff.

"Not who, *what*," Musnakaff replied, his gaze drifting off towards his mistress. "What *is* she doing?"

"We're having a conversation here," Phoebe snapped.

"She's going to do herself some harm."

"I'm going to be doing some harm of my own if you don't finish what you were saying. The 'shu—"

"Are spirit-pilots. Pieces of the Creator. Or not. There. Satisfied?" He made to go to his mistress's side, but Phoebe caught hold of him.

"No," she said. "I'm not satisfied."

"Unhand me," he said sniffily.

"I will not."

"I'm warning you," he said, jabbing a beringed finger at her. "I've got more important business than—" A puzzled look crossed his face. "Did you *feel* that?"

"The tremor, you mean? Yeah, there was one a few minutes ago. Some kind of earthquake—"

"I wish it were," Musnakaff said. He stared at the ground between them. Another tremor came; this the strongest so far.

"What is it then?" Phoebe said, her irritation with Musnakaff forgotten.

She got no answer. The man just turned his back on her and hurried away to the spot on the cobbled stones where Maeve was standing. She could not do so without help. Two of her bearers were supporting her, and a third waiting behind in case she should topple.

"We must move on," Musnakaff called to her.

"Do you know what happened on this spot?" she said to him.

"Lady—"

"*Do you?*"

"No."

"This is where I was standing when he first came to find me." She smiled fondly. "I told him, right at the beginning, I said to him: There'll never be anyone to replace my Coker, because Coker was the love of my life—"

At this, the ground shook more vehemently than ever.

"Hush yourself," Musnakaff said.

"*What?*" said Mistress O'Connell. "Hushing me? I should beat you for that." She raised her stick, and swung at Musnakaff. The blow fell short of its mark, and Maeve lost her balance. Her bearers might have saved her from falling, but she was in a fine fury, and kept flailing even as she toppled. The stick struck the bearer to her right, and he went down, bloody-nosed. The man who had been watching over her from behind stepped in to catch hold of her, but as he did so she took another stumbling step towards Musnakaff, swinging again. This time she connected, the blow so hard her stick broke. Then she went down, carrying the bearer to her left—who had not relinquished his hold on her for an instant—down with her.

As she struck the ground, her fall cushioned by the sheer profusion of her shirts and coats, the ground shuddered yet again. But this time, the tremor did not die away. It continued to escalate, turning over the unattended sedan, and sending the guard who had been leading the procession scurrying back up the hill.

"Damn you, woman!" Musnakaff hollered to Maeve as he went to help pick her up. "Now look what you've done."

"What's happening?" Phoebe yelled.

"It's him!" Musnakaff said. "He heard her! I knew he would."

"King Texas?"

Before Musnakaff could reply the street shook from end to end, and this time the ground cracked open. These were not fissures, like those Phoebe had skipped on Harmon's Heights. There was nothing irregular about them; nothing arbitrary. They were elegantly shaped, carving arabesques in the paving, and everywhere joining up, so that within moments the entire street looked like an immense jigsaw puzzle.

"Everybody stay where they are," Musnakaff said, his voice trembling. "Don't anybody move." Phoebe did as she was instructed. "Tell him you're sorry," Musnakaff yelled to Maeve. "*Quickly!*"

With the help of her two conscious bearers the woman had got to her knees. "I've got nothing to apologize *for*," Maeve said.

"God, you are a stubborn woman!" Musnakaff roared, and raised his arm as if to strike her.

"Don't," Phoebe yelled at him. She'd lost most of her patience with Maeve in the last half-hour, but the sight of her about to be struck brought back painful memories.

She'd no sooner spoken than the divided ground shook afresh, and pieces of the jigsaw fell away, leaving holes three, four, even five feet across in a dozen places. The chill out of them made the icy air seem balmy.

"I *told* you," Musnakaff said, his voice dropped to a hoarse whisper.

Phoebe's eyes darted from one hole to the next, wondering

which one the lovelorn King Texas was going to emerge from.

"We should never . . . never . . . have come," Maeve was murmuring. "You talked me into it, woman!" She jabbed her finger in Phoebe's direction. "You're in cahoots with him, aren't you?" She started to struggle to her feet, with the air of her bearers. "Admit it," she said, the words flying from her mouth along with a spray of spittle. "Go on, admit it."

"You're crazy," Phoebe said, "you're all crazy!"

"*Now there's a woman knows what she's talkin' about,*" said a voice from the earth, and from every one of the holes rose a column of writhing dirt, which within seconds had climbed up to twice human height.

The sight was more remarkable than intimidating. Gasping with astonishment, Phoebe turned around to see that on every side the tips of the columns were already sprouting branches like spokes, which spread and knotted together overhead.

"Musnakaff?" Phoebe said. "What's happening?"

It was Maeve who replied. "He's making shade for himself," he said, plainly unimpressed by the display. "He doesn't like the light, poor thing. He's afraid it's going to make him wither away."

"Look who's talkin'!" said the voice out of the ground. "You wrote the book on witherin', love of my wretched life."

"Am I supposed to be flattered?" Maeve said.

"No . . . " the voice from the ground replied. "You're supposed to remember that I always tell you the truth, even when it stings a little. And, sweetness, you look *old*. No, strike that. You look forlorn. Forsaken. Empty."

"That's rich, coming from a hole in the ground!" Maeve snapped.

There was laughter now, out of the earth; soft, ripe laughter.

"Are you going to show yourself," Maeve said, "or are you too ugly these days?"

"I'm whatever you want me to be, my little pussy-rose."

"Don't be crude, for once."

"I'll be a monk for you. I'll never touch myself. I'll—"

"Oh God, how you talk!" Maeve said. "Are you going to show yourself or not?"

There was a short silence. Then the voice simply said "Here," and up out of one of the holes between Maeve and Phoebe came a stream of muddy matter that began to congeal—even before it had finished rising—into a vaguely human form. It had its back to Phoebe, so she had no sense of its physiognomy, but to judge by the dorsal view it was an unfinished thing: a man of dust and raw rock.

"Satisfied?" it drawled.

"I think it's too late for that," Maeve replied.

"Oh no, baby, that's not true. It's not true at all." He raised his arm (his hand was the size of a snow shovel) as if to touch the old lady. But he refrained from contact, his lumpen fingers hovering an inch from her cheek. "Give up your flesh," he said. "And come and be rock with me. We'll melt together, baby. We'll let people live on our backs and we'll just be down there, warm and cosy." Phoebe studied Maeve's face through this strange seduction and knew she'd heard (or read) these words countless times. "You'll never have another wrinkle," King Texas went on. "You'll never have your bowels seize up. You'll never ache. You'll never wither. You'll never die." He ran out of sweet talking there, and seeing that his words were having no effect, turned to Phoebe. "Now I ask you," he said (as she'd suspected, his face was barely sketched in clay), "does that sound so damn bad?" His breath was cold and smelled of the underworld. Caves and pure water; things growing in darkness. It was not unpleasant. "Well does it?" he said.

Phoebe shook her head. "No," she replied. "It sounds fine to me."

"*There!*" said Texas, glaring back over his shoulder at Maeve but almost instantly returning his gaze to Phoebe. "*She understands me.*"

"Then take her. Write your damn letters to her. I want no part of you."

Phoebe saw a wounded look cross King Texas's unfinished face. "You won't get another chance," he said to Maeve, still studying Phoebe as he spoke. "Not after this. The Iad's goin' to destroy your city and you'll go with it."

"Don't be so sure," Maeve replied.

"Oh, wait now . . . " King Texas said, "can you be thinking of going back into business?" He swung his huge head round to peer at Maeve.

"Why not?" she said.

"Because the lad have no feelings. Nor do they have much between the legs."

"So you've seen them, have you?"

"Dreamed 'em," King Texas said. "Dreamed 'em over and over."

"Well go back to your dreams," Maeve said. "And leave me to get on with what's left of my life. You've got nothing I need."

"Oh that *hurts*," King Texas said. "If I had veins I'd bleed."

"It's not just veins you're missing!" Maeve replied.

The King's gigantic form shuddered, and he growled out a warning: "Be careful," he said.

But the words went unheeded. "You're old and *womanly*—" Maeve said.

"Womanly?" Now the street rocked again. Phoebe heard Musnakaff muttering to himself, and realized it was a prayer she knew: *"Mary, mother of God . . . "*

"I'm a lot of things," King Texas said. "And some of 'em I'm none too proud of. But *womanly*—" His head had started to sprout snaky shapes as thick as fingers. Hundreds of them, running from his scalp in writhing streams. "Does this look *womanly* to you?" he demanded to know. His entire body was transforming, Phoebe saw, his anatomy bulging and rippling. As it did so he stepped out of the hole from which he'd risen onto solid ground, detaching himself from the flow of rock. He stood before Maeve like a shaggy titan, with a growl in his throat. "I could take you all down with me," he said, reaching to seize the cobbled street, the way somebody might catch hold of a rug. "Let you see what it's like in my beautiful darkness." He tugged on the street, just a little. Musnakaff was thrown off his feet, and instantly slid towards one of the holes.

"Please God no!" he shrieked. "Mistress! Help me!"

"Just *stop it!*" Maeve said, as though speaking to a fractious child. Much to Phoebe's surprise, the tone worked. King Texas let go of the ground, leaving Musnakaff sobbing with relief.

"Why do we always end up arguing?" Texas said, his tone suddenly placatory. "We should be spending this time reminiscing."

"I've got nothing to reminisce about," Maeve said.

"Not true, not true. We had fine times, you and me. I built you a highway. I built you a harbor." Maeve looked up at him unmoved. "What are you thinking of?" King Texas said, leaning a little closer to her. "Tell me, blossom."

Maeve shrugged. "Nothing," she said.

"Then let me think for us both. Let me love for us both. What I feel for you is more than any man ever felt for any woman in the history of love. And without it—"

"Don't do this," Maeve whined.

"Without it, I am in grief, and you—"

"Why won't you listen?"

"You are forgotten."

At this, Maeve bristled. "Forgotten?" she said.

"Yes. Forgotten," Texas replied. "This city will be gone in a few hours. Our harbor, your fine buildings . . . " He waved his huge hands in the air, to evoke their passing. "The Iad will wipe it all away. And as for Everville—"

"I don't want to talk about that."

"Is it too painful? I don't blame you. You were there at the beginning, and now they've forgotten you."

"*Stop saying that!*" Maeve raged. "*Jesus and Mary, will you never learn? I am not going to be bullied or shamed or tempted or seduced into ever loving you again! You can build me a thousand harbors! You can write me a love letter every minute of every day till the end of the world and I WILL NOT LOVE YOU!*" With this, she turned to the closest of her bearers. "What's your name?" she said.

"Noos Cataglia."

"Your back, Noos."

"I beg your—?"

"Turn around. I want to climb on your back."

"Oh—yes. Of course." The man duly presented his back to Maeve, who with his help began to scramble up onto it.

"What are you doing?" King Texas said quietly.

"I'm going to prove you wrong," Maeve said, grabbing hold of her mount's collar. "I'm going back to Everville."

For the first time in several minutes, Phoebe piped up. "You can't," she protested.

"You tell her," King Texas said. "She won't listen to me."

"You promised to help me find Joe," Phoebe went on.

"I'm afraid he's lost, Phoebe," Maeve said, "so let it go." She pursed her lips. "Look, I'm sorry," she said, though plainly the apology was hard. "But didn't I say to you, don't put your faith in love?"

"If you did I wouldn't believe you."

"Listen to this woman!" King Texas said to Maeve. "She's *wise! Wise!*"

"She's as much a fool for love as you are," Maeve said, her rheumy gaze going from Phoebe to Texas and back again. "You deserve each other!" Then she tugged on her mount's collar. "Move yourself!" she said.

As the poor man started away up the gradient, King Texas looked down at Musnakaff, who had cautiously scrambled to his feet during this exchange. "Woman!" Texas yelled to Maeve. "If you go, I'll kill your little boot-licker."

Maeve cast a glance over her shoulder. "You wouldn't be so petty," she said.

"I'll be whatever I like!" Texas roared. "Now you come back! I'm warning you! *Come back!*" Maeve simply dug her knees into Cataglia's flanks. "He has seconds left to see the sky, woman!" Texas yelled. "I mean it!"

Musnakaff had started to let out a pitiful mewling sound and was retreating from the closest of the holes.

"You are *cruel!*" Texas hollered after Maeve. "Cruel! *Cruel!*"

With that he seemed to lose all patience, and reached down to tug at the ground.

"Don't—" Phoebe said, but her appeal was drowned out by Musnakaff's shriek as he was thrown from his feet. He scrabbled at the cobbles as the street tipped beneath him, but his fingers found too little purchase and he tumbled towards the hole. Phoebe couldn't stand by and watch him go to his death. Yelling to him to hold on, she raced towards him, arms outstretched. He raised his head, a brief glimpse of hope appearing on his ashen face and reached out towards her.

Before her fingers could find his, however, he lost what hold he had and fell. For a fraction of a second their eyes locked and she saw how terrible this was. Then he was gone, screaming and screaming.

She retreated from the hole, letting out a sob of horror—and more, of rage—as she did so.

"Now, *hush*," King Texas said.

She looked up at him. He was just a looming form, blurred by her tears, but that didn't stop her speaking her mind. "You did this for love?" she said.

"Do you blame me? That woman—"

"You just killed somebody!"

"I was trying to make her change her mind," he said, his voice thickening.

"Well you didn't! You just made more grief—"

Texas shrugged. "He'll be safe down there. It's quiet. It's dark—" She heard him sigh, heavily. "All right. I was wrong." Phoebe sniffed hard, and wiped the tears from her eyes. "I can't bring him back," Texas went on, "but please, let me comfort you—"

He raised his vast hand as he spoke, as if to touch her. It was the last thing she wanted. She tried to wave it away, but in doing so lost her balance. She flailed, attempting to recover it, but her foot somehow missed the street completely. She looked down, and to her utter horror saw that the hole where Musnakaff had gone was there beneath her.

"Help," she yelled, and reached out for Texas. But his sluggish body was too slow to catch her. The sky slipped sideways. Then she was falling, falling, the last of her tears whipped from her eyes, but her cleared sight showing her nothing except darkness and darkness and darkness, all the way down.

II

i

As Joe and Wexel Fee emerged from the laddered tunnels of b'Kether Sabbat's belly into the incandescent streets of that city, Joe asked Fee, "What does *b'Kether Sabbat* mean?"

The man shrugged. "Your guess is as good as mine," he replied.

The fact of Fee's ignorance was curiously comforting. Plainly they would both be exploring the city new to its mysteries. And perhaps it was better that way. Better to wander here without hope of comprehending what lay before them, and instead simply enjoy it for the miracle it was. The basic elements of construction were not so different from those of an American city. There was brick and wood, there were windows and doors, there were streets and sidewalks and gutters and lamps. But the architects and the masons and the carpenters and the road-layers had brought to every slab and cornice and threshold a desire to be particular: to find some quality that made that slab, that cornice, that threshold unlike any other. Some of the buildings were of course stupendous, like the towers Joe had first seen from the trees beside the shore, but even when they were of more modest scale, as most were, they'd plainly been built with a kind of tenderness which made each of them a presence unto itself. Though the streets were virtually empty of citizens (and the winged

Ketherians had almost all cleared from the skies) there was a strange sense, more comforting than eerie, that the creatures who had raised this miraculous place were still present, and would live on while their masterworks still stood.

"If I'd built even a little piece of this city," Joe said, "I couldn't leave it for anything."

"Not even for that?" Wexel said, glancing up at the churning wall of the Iad.

"Especially for that," Joe said. He stopped walking, to study the wall.

"It's going to destroy the city, Afrique. And us along with it."

"It doesn't seem to be in any hurry," Joe said.

"True enough."

"I wonder why?"

"Don't bother," Fee said. "We'll never know what's going on inside it, Afrique. It's too different from us."

"I've heard that said about me more than once," Joe replied. "They didn't call me *Afrique*, but that's what they were thinking."

"Did I offend you? If I did—"

"No, you didn't offend me. I'm just saying, maybe it's not as different as we think it is."

"We'll never know which of us is right," Wexel replied. "Because we're never going to see inside its heart."

With that, they moved on, wandering where their noses led, astonished at every corner they turned. In one square they found an immense carousel, turning in the wind without making so much as a creak. In place of carved and painted horses, however, there was a succession of figures that seemed to represent humanity's ascent from apehood and its subsequent return as the carousel spun; a loop of evolution and devolution passed before them. In another spot was a stand of several hundred columns, on the tops of which large geometrical forms that gleamed like polished copper hovered, trembling slightly. Though Joe had made a pact with himself not to ask what couldn't be answered, he here voiced his puzzlement nevertheless, and was surprised to find that Wexel was able to solve the mystery.

"They are the shapes behind our eyelids," he said. "I've heard the Ketherians deem them holy, because they are at the very heart of what we see when the world is shut out."

"Why would anybody want to shut out this place?" Joe remarked.

"Because if you wanted to build something of your own," Fee said, "you'd need to dream it first."

"I'm already dreaming just by being here," Joe said. "Aren't I?"

The complexities of this—being awake in a place his species only visited when sleeping—had baffled him from the outset, and continued to do so. This whole adventure was more than a dream, he knew that; but when he slept here, and dreamed, was he entering yet another reality, beyond this one, where he might also sleep and dream? Or was the Metacosm the other half of the world he'd left; the half people yearned after, prayed for, dreamed of, but only in moments of epiphany dared believe real?

"It's not wise to dwell on these mysteries," Wexel said, a little superstitiously. "Great souls have doomed themselves thinking of such things."

The exchange ended there, and on they went, altogether less voluble now. Indeed they didn't say more than a word or two until their wandering brought them to a bridge that looked to be made of porcelain, which arched over a pool so tranquil it formed an almost perfect mirror.

They gazed down into it awhile, Joe almost mesmerized by the sight of his own face laid against the billows of the Iad. "It looks kinda comfortable," he said to Wexel.

"You would lie on it, huh?"

"Lie on it. Make love on it."

"It would swallow you up," Fee said.

"Maybe that wouldn't be so bad," Joe said. "Maybe there's something wonderful inside."

"Like what?"

Joe thought of their exchange among the columns. "Another dream, maybe," he said.

Wexel didn't reply. Joe looked round at him to see that he was walking back the way they'd come. "Listen to that," he said. There was a murmur of shouts, and what seemed to be the clash of arms. "Hear it?"

"I hear it. You want to stay here or see what's happening?" Wexel asked him. Plainly he was going to do the latter; he was already off the bridge.

"I'll come," Joe told him, and took his reflection from the pool.

The elaborate construction of the streets made the sounds difficult to follow. Joe and Wexel were several times tricked by echoes and counter-echoes before they found the battle they'd heard from the bridge. When they finally turned a corner and came in sight of it they discovered their search had brought them by some obscure route back to the plaza of columns, which had become a battlefield in the little time since they'd walked there. The ground between the columns was littered with bodies, through which the survivors of this fracas fought, most of them armed with short stabbing blades. They were by no means all male. A goodly portion of them were women, fighting with the same mixture of finesse and brutality as their brothers. Overhead, swooping down between the columns to pick off their opponents, were perhaps a dozen winged Ketherians, the first Joe had been close to. They were frail creatures, their bodies the size of a human child of six or so, their bare limbs thin and scaly. Their wings were brilliantly colored, as were their voices, which rose in whoops and squeals and hollers sufficient for half a hundred species.

Like so much else Joe had witnessed on this journey, the scene won a confusion of feelings from him. He'd grown out of his appetite for fighting a long time ago; the sight of wounding and death was simply revolting. But the furious passion of these people could not help but excite him a little; that and the spectacle of the winged Ketherians rising up with their pavonine wings spread against the dark wall of the Iad.

"What are they fighting about?" Joe yelled to Fee over the din of battle.

"The dynasty of Summa Summamentis and that of Ezso

Aetherium have fought forever," he said. "The reason is deeply obscure."

"Somebody must know."

"None of these," Fee said, "that's certain."

"Then why do they continue to fight?" Joe said.

Wexel shrugged. "For the pleasure of it?" he ventured. "There are as many dreams of war as of peace, are there not? It expresses something in the nature of your species that must be *necessary*."

"Necessary . . ." Joe said, looking at the bloodshed in front of him. If it was indeed an expression of human necessity then perhaps his species had lost its way.

"I don't want to watch this any longer," Joe said. "I'm going back to the pool."

"Yeah—?"

"You stay, if it turns you on . . . I just don't want to spend my last minutes watching people killing each other."

"I will stay," Wexel said, a little awkwardly.

"Then I'll say goodbye," Joe said.

The sometime slave extended his hand. "Goodbye," he said.

They shook, and Joe headed back towards the bridge, but he'd gone less than ten yards when he heard a cry behind him, and turned to see Wexel stumbling towards him, clutching his belly. There was blood spurting between his fingers, splashing down his legs.

"Afrique!" he sobbed. "Afrique! He's here—"

Joe started back towards him, but the man shouted for him to keep his distance.

"He's crazy, Afrique! He's—"

At that moment, Noah appeared round the corner behind Fee. In his hands, a stabbing sword, soiled with blood. In his eyes, the pleasure of harm. His time in b'Kether Sabbat had brought him to full flower: his body had thickened, his limbs swelled.

"Joe . . . " he said lightly, as though the dying man did not stand between them. "I *thought* it must be you." He caught hold of Wexel by the back of his neck. "What were you doing with *this*?" he said. "He's probably got more fleas and sicknesses—"

"Leave him alone," Joe said.

"*Run*, Afrique—"

"I think he's afraid I'm going to do you some harm," Noah said.

"And are you?"

"He calls you *Afrique*, Joe. Is that some term of endearment?"

"No, it's—"

"An insult, then?" He pulled Wexel's head back. "I thought so." In an instant he had the blade to Fee's neck. Joe started towards them, an appeal on his lips, but before he could finish Noah slid the sword across Wexel's neck. Blood came. Noah smiled, and let the dying man drop. "There," he said. "He won't insult you any longer."

"He wasn't insulting me!" Joe yelled.

"Oh. Well. No matter. Should I be calling you Afrique?"

"Don't call me anything! Just get the fuck out of my sight."

Noah stepped over Wexel's body and strode towards Joe. "But I want us to go on together," he said.

"Go on where?"

"To get what's owed to you," Noah said. "When I saw you across the plaza, I knew that was why you'd come. We have unfinished business, you and me. I promised you power, and then I lost you—I thought you were dead, Afrique—and now here you are again, in the flesh. I must assume our destinies are interwoven."

"I don't."

Noah strode towards him, until the blade was inches from Joe's belly. "Allow me to prove it to you," he said.

"Isn't it a little late for this?" Joe said.

"Late?"

"The Iad's going to come down on this city any moment."

"I think something's holding it back," Noah said.

"Do you know what?"

"I have a suspicion," he said. "But I'll need you to help me con-firm it." He studied Joe a moment. "Well?" he said. "Do we go as friends, or do I threaten you with this?" He jabbed the sword at Joe.

"We're never going to be friends," Joe said. "But I don't need that either." Noah lowered his sword. "I'll come with you, if you'll tell me something."

"Anything."

"You're promising me?"

"Yes. I'm promising you. What do you need to know that's so important?"

There was a twinge of anxiety in Noah's voice, which Joe took pleasure in hearing. "I'll tell you when I choose," he said. "Now, where are we going?"

ii

On the far side of the plaza of columns stood a building that was in some ways the paradigm of Ketherian aesthetics. It was at first sight a simple two-story structure, but as Noah and Joe approached it, skirting the now-dwindling battle, it became clear that every stone of its unadorned walls had been chiseled to illuminate some particular felicity, so that each was in its simple way a different form of perfection. The sum was breathtaking: like a page of poetry, laid line on line.

But Noah had not time for the study of stone. He led them round to a simple door, and there, taking Joe by the arm, he said, "I promised you power. It's in there."

"What is this place?"

"A temple."

"To whom?"

"I think you know."

"The Zehrapushu?" Joe said.

"Of course. They like you, Afrique. If anybody is allowed access to this place, it'll be you."

"And what's inside?"

"I told you. Power."

"Then why don't you go in?"

"Because I'm not pure enough," Noah said.

Joe found it in him to laugh, even under these grim circumstances. "And I am?" he said.

"You're Sapas Humana, Afrique. *Pure* Sapas Humana."

"And the 'shu like that?"

"I believe they will."

"And if they don't?" Joe said, coming close to Noah now. "What happens?"

"Death happens," he said.

"Simple as that?"

"Simple as that."

Joe looked at the door. Like the wall into which it was set it possessed a physical beauty that took his breath away. What it lacked was a handle or a keyhole.

"If I open the door and don't get killed, you follow. Is that the idea?"

"Always so swift, my friend," Noah said. "Yes, that's the idea."

Joe glanced back at the door, and a wave of curiosity rose up in him to know what lay on the other side. He had looked into the eyes of the 'shu twice now, once on the shore and once in the weed-bed, and each time had felt touched by a mystery that he desperately wanted to solve. Perhaps he could do it here. Concealing his eagerness, he turned back to Noah.

"Before we go in," he said, "answer my question."

"Ask it."

"I want to know what it is the families have been arguing about all these years. I want to know what's made them kill each other." Noah said nothing. "You promised me," Joe prompted him.

"Yes," he said at last. "I did."

"So tell me."

Noah shrugged. "What does it matter now?" he said to himself. "I'll tell you . . . " He looked back towards the battlefield once, then, his voice lowered to a whisper he said: "The dynasty of Ezso Aetherium believe that the Iad exists because Sapas Humana dreamed them into being. That the Iad are the darkness in the collective soul of your species."

"And *your* family?"

"We believe the other way about," Noah said.

It took Joe a little time to realize what he was being told. "You think *we're* something the Iad Uroboros dreamed up."

"Yes, Afrique. That's what we believe."

"Who invented this crap?"

Noah shrugged. "Who knows where wisdom comes from?"

"That's not wisdom," Joe said. "It's fucking stupidity."

"Why do you say so?"

"Because I'm not a dream."

"If you were, why do you suppose you'd know it?" Noah said.

Joe didn't try to get his head around that notion. He simply threw up his hands and said, "Let's just get the hell on with this," and turning his back on Noah he pressed against the door. It didn't swing open, but nor did he remain on the outside of it. Instead he felt a sudden ache through his body, almost like an electric shock, and the next moment he was standing in a buzzing darkness on the inside of the temple. He waited for the ache to subside, and then looked round for Noah. There was a motion in the murk behind him, but he was by no means sure it was his fellow trespasser, and before he could look again he heard somebody call his name.

He looked ahead of him, and saw that the dark ground at the center of the chamber was glittering, the light coming down upon it from a round hole in the roof. Joe crossed the floor to study the phenomenon better, and as he did so realized that he was looking at a pool, perhaps twelve feet across.

It was filled with Quiddity's waters, he had no doubt of that. He could smell the piquancy of the dream-sea, and his skin tingled with the subtle energies it gave off. But as he came to the edge of the pool he had further proof that this was indeed an annex of Quiddity. There, a little way beneath the surface, lurked a 'shu so large it could barely be contained in the pool, but was wrapped around itself in a tangle of encrusted tentacles, from the nest of which one of its eyes—which was from rim to rim a yard across, or more—stared up and out, gleaming gold. Its gaze was not upon Joe, at least not directly. The creature was looking up through the roof of the temple, into the roiling wall of the invader.

"It's holding the Iad . . . " Joe breathed. "My God. My God. It's holding the Iad."

He had no sooner spoken than he heard Noah from somewhere in the dark. "Do you feel it?" he said. "Do you feel the *power* in this place?"

"Oh yeah," Joe said softly. It was so palpable it almost felt like an act of aggression. His flesh ran with sweat, and every bruise and wound his body had sustained—back to the beating he'd taken from Morton Cobb—ached with fresh vigor, as though it had just been sustained. But still he wanted to get closer to the pool; to see what the Iad was seeing, when it gazed into the 'shu's majestic eye. He took another step towards the water, his body wracked with shudders.

"Speak to it," Noah said. "Tell it what you want."

"It doesn't matter what we want," Joe said. "We're *nothing* here. Do you understand? We're nothing at all."

"Damn you, Afrique," Noah said, his voice closer to Joe now. "I've done all the suffering I intend to do. I want to live in glory when the Iad's passed by." He drew closer still. "Now put your hand in the water—"

"What happened to all that talk about being buried in your own country?"

"I'd forgotten how fine it was to be alive. Especially here. There is no finer place in your world or mine than this city. And I want to be the one who heals it, after the cataclysm. I want to be its protector."

"You want to *own* it," Joe said.

"Nobody could ever own b'Kether Sabbat."

"I think you're ready to try," Joe said.

"Well that's between me and the city, isn't it?" Noah said, moving to press the blade against Joe's back. "Go on now," he said. "Touch the waters for me."

"And if I don't?"

"Your body will touch the waters, whether there's life in it or not."

"It's holding the Iad—"

"Very possibly."

"If we disturb it—"

"The Iad finishes its business here and moves on. It's going to happen sooner or later. If you make it sooner then you've changed the course of history, and maybe got yourself power at the same time. That doesn't sound so terrible, does it?" He pushed the blade a little harder. "It's what you came here for, remember?"

Joe remembered. The pain in his balls was a perfect reminder of why he'd made this journey: to never be powerless again. But in the process of coming here—of seeing all that he'd seen, and learning all that he'd learned—the pursuit of power had come to seem like a very petty thing. He'd had love, which was more than most people got in their lives. He'd had physical pleasures. He'd known a woman whose smile made him smile, and whose sighs made him sigh, and whose arms had been an utter comfort to him.

They would not come again, those smiles, those sighs, and it was a worse ache than the sum of his wounds to think of that, but life hadn't cheated him, had it? He could die, now, and not feel his time had been wasted.

"I don't . . . want power," he said to Noah.

"Liar," said the face in the darkness.

"You can say what you want," Joe replied. "I know what's true and that's all that matters."

The words seemed to dismay Noah. He made a little moan, and without another word of warning drove his blade into Joe's gut. Oh God, but it hurt! Joe let out a sob of pain, which only inspired Noah to press the blade home. Then he twisted it, and pulled it out. Joe entertained no hope of doing his killer damage in return. He'd invited this, after his fashion. He put his hands to the wound, hot blood running through his fingers and slapping on the ground between his legs, then he started to turn his back on Noah. The darkness was becoming piebald; gray blotches appearing at the corners of his sight. But he wanted to look at the 'shu one last time before death took him. Just to meet its golden gaze . . .

He started to turn, pressing both hands against the wound now, to keep his body from emptying. There was still pain, but it was becoming more remote from him with every heartbeat. He had just a little time.

"Hold on . . . " he murmured to himself.

He had the gaze in the corner of his eye now, and it was vast. A ring of gold and a circle of darkness. Beautiful in its perfection and in its simplicity. Round and round, gleaming gold, uninterrupted, unspoiled, glorious, glorious . . .

He felt something shifting in his head, as though he was slipping towards the golden circle.

Going, going . . .

And oh, it felt fine. He was done with his wounded flesh, done with bruises and bleeding balls; done with Joe.

He felt his body start to fall, and as it did so—as the life went out of it utterly—he fell into the circle of the 'shu's eye.

He was granted a moment of rest there: but a moment filled with such grace and such ease it wiped all the sufferings of the days that had brought him here, and of the years that had proceeded them.

There was no confusion, nor fear. He understood what had happened to him with absolute clarity. He'd died on the edge of the pool, and his spirit had fallen into the eye of the Zehrapushu.

There, in that gilded round, it stayed for a blissful moment. Then it was gone, up and away along the line of 'shu's sight towards the cloud of the Iad.

In the temple below him he heard Noah let out a cry of rage, and for an instant, though he had neither eyes nor head to put them in, his spirit saw quite plainly what was happening below. Noah had stepped over Joe's corpse and had plunged his blood-stained hands into the pool of Quiddity's waters. The 'shu had responded to the trespass instantly. Its tentacles had started to flail wildly, and one of them—whether by intention or chance Joe would never know—had wrapped around Noah's arm. Enraged and revolted, Noah picked up the sword he'd just set aside and even as Joe watched he plunged the blade into the 'shu's unblinking eye.

A tremor passed through Joe's world. Through the gaze in which he traveled, through the temple below, and out, across the plaza of columns and through the streets of b'Kether Sabbat. He knew on the instant what had happened. The 'shu's hold on the Iad had slipped; and the great wave that had been frozen over the city began to curl.

Joe turned his spirit-sight up towards the Iad, and to his astonishment saw that he was almost upon it, flying like an arrow into its roiling substance.

Below him, the city shook itself into despair, and the island of Mem-é b'Kether Sabbat fell beneath the Iad's shadow.

And he, Joe Flicker, who had given up life but had not perished, flew into the heart of the city's destroyer, and lost himself there as surely as if he had died.

III

i

*T*he Sturgis Motel was a modest establishment, set a quarter of a mile back from the road along what was little more than a gravel strewn track, barely wide enough to allow two cars to pass. The motel itself was a single-story, wooden structure built around two and a quarter sides of a parking lot, the quarter being the office, over which a fitfully illuminated sign boasted that there were NO VACANCIES. Apparently most of the occupants were out having a high time in Everville, because when Tesla drove in, the lot was empty but for three vehicles. One was a flatbed truck, parked outside the office, one a beaten up Mustang, which Tesla assumed was Grillo's, and the third was an even more dilapidated Ford Pinto.

She had not even turned off the engine of her bike when the door of room six opened and a scrawny, balding man in a shirt and pants several sizes too big for him stepped out and said her name. She was about to ask him if they knew each other when she realized it was Grillo. There was no way to conceal her shock. He seemed not to notice, however, or perhaps not to care. He opened his arms to her (so thin! oh, so thin!) and they embraced.

"You don't know how glad I am to see you," he said. The frailty wasn't just in his body. It was in his voice too. He sounded remote, as though his sickness, whatever it was, was already carrying him away.

Both of us, she thought, not long for this world.

"There's so much to tell you," Grillo was saying. "But I'll keep it simple." He halted, as though waiting for her permission to tell. She told him to go on. "Well . . . Jo-Beth's behaving really strangely. Some of the time she's so excitable, I want to gag her. The rest of the time she's practically catatonic."

"Does she talk about Tommy-Ray?"

Grillo shook his head. "I've tried to make her talk, but she doesn't trust me. I'm hoping maybe she'll talk to you, 'cause we need some inside track here or we're fucked."

"You're sure Tommy-Ray's alive?"

"I don't know about *alive*, but I know he's around."

"And what about Howie?"

"Not good. We're all playing some kind of endgame here, Tes. It's like everything's coming together, in the worst way."

"I know that feeling," she told him.

"And I'm too old for this shit, Tes. Too old and too sick."

"I can see . . . things aren't good," she said to him. "If you want to talk—"

"No," he said hurriedly. "I don't. There's nothing worth saying anyway. It's just the way things go."

"One question?"

"All right. One."

"Is this why you didn't want me to come see you?"

Grillo nodded. "Stupid, I know. But I guess we all deal with shit the best way we know how. I decided to hide away and work on the Reef."

"How's it going?"

"I want you to see it for yourself, Tes, if we come out of this." She didn't tell them she wouldn't; just nodded. "I think maybe you'd make more sense of it than I have. You know—make the connections better." He put his arm around her shoulder. "Shall we go in?" he said.

ii

Once, somewhere on the road, Tesla had contemplated setting the story of Jo-Beth McGuire and Howie Katz down for posterity. How in the sunny kingdom of Palomo Grove these two perfect people had met and fallen in love, not realizing that their fathers had sired them to do battle. How their passion had enraged their fathers, and how that rage had erupted into open warfare in the streets of the gilded kingdom. Many had suffered as a consequence. Some had even perished. But by some miracle the lovers had survived their travails intact.

(It was not the first time a story of ill-matched lovers had been told, of course, but more often than not it was the couple who suffered and died, perhaps because people wanted the perfect pair snuffed out before their love could lose its perfection. Better a murdered ideal, which at least kept hope alive, than one that withered with time.)

While making her notes for this story Tesla had several times wondered what happened to the golden lovers of Palomo Grove. Here, in room six, she had her answer.

Despite the warning Grillo had given, she was not prepared to find the couple so changed: both gray-faced, their speech and action devoid of any spark of vitality. When, after some wan greetings had been exchanged, Howie began to describe for Tesla the events that had brought them to this sorry place and condition, the pair scarcely glanced at each other.

"Just help me kill the sonofabitch," Howie said to Tesla, the subject of the Death-Boy's dispatch rousing a passion in him absent until now. She told him she didn't have any answers. Perhaps the Nuncio had bestowed some form of invulnerability upon him (after all, he'd escaped the conflagration in the Loop).

"You think he's beyond death, right?" Grillo said.

"It's possible, yes—"

"And that's from the Nuncio?"

"I don't know," Tesla said, staring down at her palms. "I have a taste of the Nuncio myself, and I'm damn sure I'm still mortal."

When she looked up at Grillo again, she saw such despair in his eyes she could only hold his gaze for a moment before looking away.

It was Jo-Beth, who had added little to the exchange so far, who broke the silence. "I want you to stop talking about him now," she said.

Howie threw his wife a sour, sideways glance. "We're not done yet," he said.

"Well, I am," Jo-Beth said a little more forcibly, and crossing to the bed she picked up the baby and headed for the door.

"Where are you going?" Howie said to her.

"I'm going to get some air."

"Not with the baby you're not."

There was a litany of suspicions in these few words.

"I'm not going far—"

"You're not going *a-a-a-anywhere!*" Howie shouted. "Now put Amy back on the bed and *sit down!*"

Before this escalated any further, Grillo stood up, "We all need some food in our stomachs," he said. "Why don't we go get some pizza?"

"You go," Jo-Beth said. "I'll be fine here."

"Better still," Tesla said to Grillo, "you and Howie go. Let me and Jo-Beth sit and talk for a few minutes."

There was some debate about this, but not much. Both men seemed relieved to have a chance to escape the confines of the motel for a few minutes, and from Tesla's point of view it offered an opportunity to speak to Jo-Beth alone.

"You don't seem very afraid that Tommy-Ray's coming to find you," she said to Jo-Beth when the men had left.

The girl looked across at the baby on the bed. "No," she said, her voice as pale as her face. "Why should I be?"

"Well . . . because of what might have happened to him since you saw him last," Tesla replied, trying to put her point as delicately as possible. "He's not the brother you had in Palomo Grove."

"I know that," Jo-Beth said with a tinge of contempt in her voice.

"He's killed some people. And he's not sorry. But . . . he's never hurt me. He wouldn't ever do that."

"He might not know his own mind," Tesla replied. "He might hurt you, or the baby, without being able to help himself."

Jo-Beth simply shook her head. "He loves me," she said.

"That was a long time ago. People change. And Tommy-Ray's changed more than most."

"I know," Jo-Beth replied. Tesla didn't reply. She just waited in silence, hoping that Jo-Beth would talk about the Death-Boy a little. After a few moments, she did just that. "He's been all over," she said, "seeing the world . . . now he's getting tired—"

"He told you that?"

She nodded. "He wants to be quiet for a little while. . . . He says he's seen some things that he needs to think over—"

"Did he say what?"

"Just things," she said. "He's been traveling around, working for a friend of his."

Tesla hazarded a guess. "Kissoon?" she said.

Jo-Beth actually smiled. "Yeah. How'd you know?"

"It's not important."

Jo-Beth raked her fingers through her long-unwashed hair, and said again, "He loves me."

"So does Howie," Tesla pointed out.

"Howie belongs to Fletcher," Jo-Beth said.

"Nobody *belongs* to anybody," Tesla replied.

Jo-Beth looked at her, saying nothing. But the look of utter abjection in her eyes was chilling.

Would nothing be saved? Tesla thought. There was Grillo, playing his endgame, thinking of the Nuncio as some last reprieve (but not truly believing it); D'Amour climbing the mountain to spend his last hours where the crosses stood; and this poor girl, who had been so blithe and so effortlessly beautiful, ready to be taken by the Death-Boy because love had failed to save her.

The world was turning off its lights, one by one. . . .

A gust of wind shook the windowpane. Jo-Beth, who had turned from Tesla to tend to the baby, looked round.

"What is it?" Tesla said softly.

There was another gust now, this time at the door, as though the wind was systematically looking for some way in.

"It's him, isn't it?" Tesla said. The girl's eyes were glued to the door. "Jo-Beth, you have to help me here—" Tesla crossed to the door as she spoke, and gingerly turned the key in the lock. It was a pitiful defense, she knew (this was a force that brought down houses), but it might earn them a second or two's grace, and that might be the difference between saving a life or losing it. "Tommy-Ray's not going to solve anything," Tesla said. "You understand me? He's not."

Jo-Beth was bending to pick up little Amy. "He's all we've got," she said.

The wind was rattling both the window and the door now. Tesla could smell it as it gusted through the keyhole and the cracks. Death was here, no doubt of that.

Amy had begun to sob quietly in her mother's arms. Tesla glanced down at the child's tiny, knotted face, and thought of what such innocence might rouse in the Death-Boy. He'd probably be proud of infanticide.

The floor was shaking so hard the key was rattled from its slot. And somewhere in the gusts there were voices, or the fragments of same, some speaking in Spanish, some, Tesla thought, in Russian, one of them nearly hysterical, one of them sobbing. She caught only a smattering of their words, but the gist of it was plain enough. *Come outside*, they were saying. *He's waiting for you . . .*

"Doesn't sound all that inviting," Tesla whispered to Jo-Beth.

The girl said nothing. She just stared at the door, gently rocking the troubled baby, while the voices of dead pined and moaned and muttered on. Tesla let them speak for themselves. To judge by the look on Jo-Beth's face they were doing a far better job of dissuading her from stepping over the threshold than Tesla could have done.

"Where's Tommy-Ray?" Jo-Beth said at last.

"Maybe he didn't come," Tesla replied. "Do you . . . maybe want to slip out the bathroom window?"

Jo-Beth listened for a few second longer. Then she nodded.

"Good," Tesla said. "Make it fast. I'll keep them busy."

She watched Jo-Beth retreat to the bathroom, then she turned and went to the door. The ghosts on the other side seemed to sense her approach, because their voices dropped to a murmur.

"Where's Tommy-Ray?" Tesla said.

There was no coherent response, just more distressing din, and a further rattling of the door. Tesla glanced over her shoulder. Jo-Beth and Amy were out of sight, which was something. At least now it the ghosts tried to break in—

"Open . . . " they were murmuring, "open . . . open," and while they murmured they escalated their assault on the door. The wood around the hinges began to splinter, and around the lock too.

"It's okay," Tesla said, fearful that their frustration would make them more dangerous than ever. "I'll unlock the door. Just give me a moment." She stopped and picked up the key, slid it into the lock, and turned it. Hearing this, the ghosts were quieted, the gusts hushed.

Tesla took a deep breath and opened the door. The cloud of phantoms retreated from her in a dusty wave. She looked for Tommy-Ray. There was no sign of him. Closing the door after her, she walked out into the middle of the lot. She'd written an execution scene in one of her failed opuses— a terrible screenplay called As I Live and Breathe. This walk put her in mind of it. All that was missing was the warden and the priest.

She started to turn, looking for the Death-Boy, and her eyes came to rest on an area of stunted trees and ambitious weed on the far side of the lot. There were lanterns hanging in the branches, she saw, giving off a sickly phosphorescence. And somebody standing in their midst, more than half hidden. Before she could start towards the place a voice behind her said, "What the hell's goin' on out here?"

She looked back to see the motel manager appearing from his

office. He was sixty or more, with a bald pate, a gravy-stained shirt, and a can of beer in his hand. By his staggering step it was plain he was the worse for its influence.

"Go back inside," Tesla told him.

But the man had seen the lights in the thicket now, and he strode on past Tesla towards them. "You put them up?" he demanded.

"No," Tesla said, following after him. "Somebody very—"

"That's my property. You can't just go hangin'—"

He stopped in mid-stride, as he came close enough to see exactly what these lanterns were. The can of beer dropped from his hand. "My God . . . " he said.

The branches of the trees and bushes had been hung with horrific trophies, Tesla saw. Heads and arms, pieces of a torso, and much else that was not even recognizable. All of them shone, even the scraps, charged up with a luminescence she assumed was the Death-Boy's gift.

The manager, meanwhile, was stumbling back the way he'd come, his throat loosing a series of panicked animal noises. Instantly, the cloud of phantoms rose up, excited by his terror, and moved to intercept him. He was swept off his feet and pitched ten yards or more, coming to rest a little way from his office door.

"Tommy-Ray?" Tesla yelled back into the thicket. "Stop them!" Getting no response, she strode towards the bushes, haranguing the Death-Boy. "Call them off, damn you! Hear me?"

Behind her, the manager had started to shriek. She looked back in time to glimpse the man in the midst of the swarming cloud, sinking to the ground. He went on shrieking for a little longer, while they tore at his head. It was twisted left, then right, then left again with such violence his neck ripped. The shriek stopped. The head came off.

"Don't look," the man in the thicket said.

She turned back and stared into the mesh of twigs, trying to see him better. The last time she'd laid eyes on Tommy-Ray McGuire, back in Kissoon's Loop, he'd been a shadow of his former glory, wasted and crazed. But it seemed the years had been kinder to him than anybody else in this drama. Whatever duties he'd performed for Kissoon, and whatever he'd witnessed (or perpetrated) along the way, his blond beauty had been preserved. He smiled at her out of his grove of lanterns, and it was a dazzling smile.

"Where is she, Tesla?" he said.

"Before you get to Jo-Beth—"

"Yes?"

"I just wanted to talk a moment. Compare notes."

"About what?"

"About being Nunciates."

"Is that what we are?"

"It's as good or bad as any."

"*Nunciates* . . . " He turned the word on his tongue. "That's cool."

"Being one seems to suit you."

"Oh yeah, I feel fine. You don't look so good yourself. You need to get some slaves, like me, 'stead of wandering around on your own." His tone was completely conversational. "You know a couple of times, I almost came to find you."

"Why would you do that?"

He shrugged. "I guess I felt close to you. Both of us having the Nuncio. Both of us knowing Kissoon—"

"What's he doing here, Tommy-Ray? What does he want with Everville?"

Tommy-Ray took a step towards her. She had to fight the instinct to retreat before him. Any sign of weakness, she knew, and her status as fellow Nunciate would be forfeited. As he approached, he answered the question. "He lived there once," Tommy-Ray said.

"In Everville?"

He was almost free of the thicket now. There were blood stains on his jeans and T-shirt, and on his face and arms a gloss of sweat. "Where is she?" he said.

"We were talking about Kissoon."

"Not any more we're not. *Where is she?*"

"Just give her a little time," Tesla replied, glaring back towards the room as though she expected Jo-Beth to emerge at any moment. "She wanted to look her best."

"She was excited?"

"Oh yes."

"Why don't you go fetch her?"

"She won't be—"

"Fetch her!"

There was a murmur from the ghosts, who were still attending upon the headless body. "Sure," Tesla said. "No problem."

She turned back towards the motel and started across the lot, taking her time. She was about five yards from the door when Jo-Beth stepped into view, with Amy cradled in her arms.

"I'm sorry," she said to Tesla under her breath. "We belong to him. It's as simple as that."

From the lot behind her, Tesla heard the Death-Boy sigh at the sight of his sister.

"Oh baby," he said. "You look so fine. Come here."

Jo-Beth stepped over the threshold. Tesla made no attempt to stop her. She'd only lose her head for her troubles. Besides, by the look on Jo-Beth's face it was plain she was happy to be going into her brother's embrace. The wind, whether natural or no, had died away completely. Night birds had started to sing, and crickets to chirp in the grass, as though conspiring to celebrate this reunion.

As she watched Tommy-Ray open his arms to welcome his sister, Tesla caught sight of a pale form out of the corner of her eye, and looked round to see Buddenbaum's little girlfriend, the avatar, still dressed in white from bow to shoes, staring down at the manager's corpse. She didn't peruse it for long, but wandered in Tesla's direction, leaving her two companions—the clown and the idiot—to study it in her stead. The latter had found the dead man's head, and had it tucked up under his arm.

The girl in white, meanwhile, was now close enough to Tesla to murmur, "Thank you for this."

Tesla looked down at her with a mixture of confusion and disgust. "This isn't a game," she said.

"We know."

"People have died."

The girl grinned. "And there'll be more, won't there?" she said lightly. "Lots more."

As though her words had pressed the drama into a higher gear, the sound of a badly tuned engine reached Tesla's ears and Grillo's Mustang appeared on the dirt road leading into the lot.

Before it had even come to a halt the passenger door was flung open and Howie was out, gun in hand, screaming at Tommy-Ray, "*Get away from her!*"

The Death-Boy unglued his eyes from his sister and lazily stared in Howie's direction. "No!" he said.

Without further warning, Howie fired. His aim was pitifully poor. The bullet struck the ground closer to Jo-Beth than Tommy-Ray. Amy, who had been hushed so far, started to bawl.

A flicker of concern crossed the Death-Boy's sweaty face. "Don't shoot," he yelled to Howie, "you'll hurt the kid!"

At Tesla's side the girl in white murmured a long *oh*, as though she had new comprehension of what was happening here, and like two members of an audience, one prompted by the other into recognition of some wit or irony, Tesla saw a connection here she had not vaguely suspected. A breath of something like to pleasure caressed her nape, seeing this bud on the story tree, ready to burst.

"What next?" the little girl said.

A little part of Tesla simply wanted to stand back and see. But she couldn't. Never had; never would.

"Howie . . . " she said, "come away—"

"N-n-no-not without m-m-my *wife*," Howie said.

"You did good," Tommy-Ray said, "watching over 'em for me, but you're out of the picture now. They're coming with me."

Howie dropped his gun in the dirt, and raised his hands. "Look at m-m-me, Jo-Beth," he said. "I'm n-n-not going to m-m-make you do anything you d-d-don't want to—but baby, it's me—it's H-H-Howie—"

Jo-Beth said nothing. She simply looked down at the baby, as if deaf to Howie's appeals. He tried again, or began to, but he'd got no further than her name when Grillo put his foot down and drove directly towards Jo-Beth. Howie flung himself aside, going down hard, as the car skewed around, kicking up a fan of dirt. The Death-Boy let out a yell to his legion, but before they could come to order Grillo had brought the car to a halt and hauled Jo-Beth and Amy into the vehicle. Tommy-Ray made a move towards it, arms outstretched, and might have somehow checked Grillo's escape had Howie not risen from the dirt and flung himself at the Death-Boy. His fingers went to Tommy-Ray's perfect face, and gouged at his eyes.

Grillo, meanwhile, was backing the vehicle up, yelling to Tesla, *"Get in! Get in!"*

She waved him on. *"Go!"* she hollered. *"Quickly!"*

She caught a glimpse of his face through the insect-spattered windshield: There was exhilaration in his eyes. He offered her a tight, grim smile, then he swung the car round and drove off.

Howie, meanwhile, had done some superficial damage to Tommy-Ray, gouging several furrows down the side of his face and neck. There was no blood. There was instead a brightness beneath the flesh, like the phosphorescence with which he'd lit his lanterns. And it was to the thicket where those lanterns hung that Tommy-Ray now headed, casually pushing Howie to the ground as he did so.

Howie started to get to his feet again, plainly intending to assault the Death-Boy afresh, but Tesla held him back. "You can't kill him," she said. "He'll just end up killing you."

On the fringe of the thicket, Tommy-Ray turned back. "That's it. You tell him." He looked at Howie. "I don't want to kill you," he said. "In fact, I swore to Jo-Beth I wouldn't, and I don't break my word." Again, to Tesla, "Make him understand. She's never coming back to him. Not tonight. Not ever. I've got her now, and that's where she wants to be."

With that he stepped into the thicket, whistling for the cloud of ghosts to come to him. They came, gushing across the lot, and entering the thicket to conceal the Death-Boy from view.

"He's going to go after her," Howie said.

"Of course."

"So we have to get to her first."

"That's the theory," Tesla said, already heading for her bike. Howie stumbled after her.

As she crossed the lot the girl in white called to her. "What's next, Tesla? What's next?"

"God knows," Tesla said.

"No we don't," said the girl's idiot companion, which much entertained all three.

"We like you, Tesla," the girl in white said.

"Then stay out of my way," Tesla said, climbing onto the bike. Howie hopped on behind.

As she turned the key in the ignition there was another gust of wind, and the Death-Boy's legion rose up out of the thicket, taking the lanterns and the man who'd lit them away in its billows. Tesla caught a glimpse of Tommy-Ray as the cloud passed by. He seemed not to be walking, but to be borne up by the cloud, and carried. As for his face, it was already healing, the wounds closing to conceal the brightness that blazed behind.

"He's going to get to her first," Howie said, sounding close to tears.

"Hold on," Tesla told him. "It's not over yet."

IV

i

orgive me Everville—"

"That's what he wrote?"

"That's what he wrote."

"The hypocrite."

They were walking, Erwin and Coker Ammiano, along Poppy Lane. It was a little before nine o'clock in the evening, and to judge by the noise from every bar and restaurant along the lane, festivities were in full swing.

"They forget so easily," Erwin said. "Just this afternoon—"

"I know what happened," Ammiano replied. "I felt it."

"We're like smoke," Erwin said, remembering Dolan's first lessons in ghosthood.

"We're not even that. At least smoke can make people weep. We can do _nothing_."

"That's not so," Erwin told him. "You'll see when we find this woman Tesla. She can _hear_ me. At least she could once. She's quite a woman, believe me. The way she acts, it's like she couldn't give a damn whether she lived or died."

"Then she's a fool."

"No, I mean, she's brave. When she was at my house, I told you, about Kissoon—"

517

"I remember, Erwin," Coker said politely.

"I never saw anything braver."

"You're talking like you're in love, my friend."

"Nonsense."

"I believe you're quite enamored. Don't be embarrassed."

"I'm . . . I'm not."

"You're blushing."

Erwin put his palms to his cheeks. "It's so absurd," he said.

"What is?"

"That I have no blood in my body—don't even have a body—yet I blush."

"I've had a lot of time to try and puzzle that out," Coker Ammiano said.

"And did you come to any conclusions?"

"A few."

"Tell me."

"We invented ourselves, Erwin. Our energies belong to some great oneness—I don't care to give it a name or I'd be trying to invent that too—and we've used them, these energies, in the re-creation of Erwin Toothaker and Coker Ammiano. Now those men are dead, and much of that power has returned to its source. But we hold on to a bit of it, just to keep our fictions alive a little longer. And we clothe ourselves in what's familiar, and we fill our pockets with things to comfort us. But it can't go on forever. Sooner or later"—he shrugged—"we'll be done."

"Not me," said Erwin. "I saw what happened to Dolan and Nordhoff and—"

"What things look like from the outside and what they *are* on the inside can be very different, Erwin. Perhaps all that was happening at the crossroads was that Dolan was going back where he came from."

"Into your *oneness?*"

"It's not mine, Erwin." He paused, musing on this. Then he said, "No, I take that back. I think it *is* mine. And you know why?"

"No. But I think you're about to enlighten me."

"Because once I'm there, I'm everywhere." He smiled, well pleased by this. "And the oneness is mine as much as it is anybody else's."

"So why haven't you just given in to it?" Erwin wanted to know.

"I wish I had an answer to that. I think sometimes it must be some *evil* in me."

"Evil?"

"As in something done in error. Against what's good. I know—"

Erwin interrupted him in mid-flow. "That man!" he said, pointing across the street.

"I see him."

"He was with Tesla. His name's D'Amour."

"He's in quite a hurry."

"I wonder if he knows where she is."

"There's only one way to find out."

"Follow him?"

"Precisely."

ii

D'Amour had put in a call to New York before he left the Cobb house. Norma had been pleased to hear from him.

"I had a visitor yesterday," she said, sounding more unnerved than Harry could ever remember her sounding before. "She just came in through the window, and sat down in front of me."

"Who the hell was it?"

"She said her name was Lazy Susan. At least at first. Then it changed its mind, and God knows probably its sex as well, and started calling itself the Hammermite—"

"Then Peter the Nomad?"

"It got round to him after a while," Norma said. "So is this thing what it claims it is?"

"Yes."

"It killed Hess?"

"He was one of many. What did it want?"

"What do these things ever want? It crowed a bit. It did a dump on the floor. And it asked to be reminded to you—"

"How exactly?"

Norma sighed. "Well . . . it started talking about how the Devil was coming, how we'd all be *crucified* for what we'd done. It harped on that quite a bit. Gave me a brief history of crucifixion, which I could have done without. Then it said: *'Tell D'Amour—'*"

"Let me guess. *'I am you and you are love—'*" He didn't bother to finish.

"That's it," Norma said.

"Then what?"

"Nothing. It told me I had very lovely eyes, and it was sure they were all the prettier because they were useless. Then it left. I still can't get rid of the smell of its shit."

"I'm sorry, Norma."

"It's okay. I got some air-freshener—"

"No. I mean the whole damn thing."

"I tell you what, Harry. It made me think."

"About—?"

"About our conversation on the roof, for one."

"I've thought a lot about that myself."

"I'm not saying I was completely wrong. The world does change, and it keeps changing, and I don't think it's going anywhere soon. But this *thing*, this Lazy Susan . . . " The words fell away for a moment. All Norma could find to say was: "Horrible." Harry said nothing. "I know what you're thinking," Norma said. "You're thinking, why doesn't the old cow make up her mind?"

"No I wasn't."

"Truth is, I don't know anymore."

"Don't let it get you crazy."

"Oh it's too late for that," Norma said, the laughter coming back into her voice. "What is it with these demons anyhow? Why are they so damn *excremental?*"

"'Cause that's what they want the world to be, Norma."

"Shit."
"Shit."

They'd talked on for a while, but it had been little more than chatter. Only at the end, when Harry said he had to be going, did Norma say, "Where?"

"Up the mountain," he told her. "To see what the Devil looks like, face to face."

Now, an hour after that conversation, he was climbing, the trees so dense he was almost blind as Norma, and after all the pursuits and losses of recent times—Dusseldorf's death, the massacre of the Zyem Carasophia, the events in the Badlands, and the murder of Maria Nazareno—it was a relief that things were coming to an end.

He thought of the portrait Ted had made—*D'Amour in Wyckoff Street*, with that black snake crushed under a hero's heel. How simple that seemed. How blissfully simple. The demon writhes. The demon withers. The demon is gone.

It had never been that way, except in stories, and despite what the child at the crossroads had said (*leaves on the story tree*), Harry had no expectation of a happy ending.

iii

Despite his hectoring and cajoling, only four members of the band had turned up at Larry Glodoski's house: Bill Waits, Steve Alstead, Denny Gips, and Chas Reidlinger. Larry broke out the scotch, and laid out his interpretation of events.

"What we've got here is some kind of mind manipulation," he said. "Maybe chemical, maybe something put in the water—"

"Least it's not in the scotch," Bill said.

"This is serious," Larry said. "We've got a catastrophe on our hands, gentlemen."

"What did everyone see?" Gips asked the room.

"Women," said Alstead.

"And light," Reidlinger added.

"That's what they wanted us to see," Larry said.

"Who's they?" Waits wondered. "I mean, we got over the Red Menace, we got over UFOs. So what the hell is it? Don't get me wrong, Larry, I'm not saying you're crazy, 'cause I saw some shit too. I'd just like to know what we're up against."

"We're not going to find out sitting here," Alstead replied. "We have to go look for ourselves."

"And what are we going to defend ourselves with?" Waits wanted to know. "Trumpets and drumsticks?"

At this juncture, Bosley Cowhick appeared at Glodoski's front door, wanting to be included in the ranks. He'd heard about the gathering from his sister, who was a close friend of Alstead's wife Rebecca. None of the five were at ease with Bosley's brand of glassy-eyed fervor, but with their ranks so woefully thin it was impossible to say no. And to be fair, Bosley did his best to restrain his apocalyptic talk, limiting it to a few remarks about how they were all in danger of losing the town to forces, terrible forces, and he was willing to die in its defense.

Which remark brought them back to the business of the guns. It was not a difficult problem to solve. Gips's brother-in-law up on Coleman Street had been fixated on what he called "killing sticks" since he'd first got his tongue around the words, and when the six-man posse turned up on his doorstep a little before ten, practically requisitioning the damn things, he was pathetically happy to oblige. Glodoski felt it only polite to invite the brother-in-law along on the venture. The man declined. He was sick, he said, and would only slow things down. But if they needed more guns, they knew where to come.

Then it was off to Hamrick's Bar (this at Bill Waits's suggestion) to toast the venture with a scotch. Reidlinger was against it. Couldn't they just get on with doing whatever they were going to do (there was still debate as to what that might be), then they could all go home and sleep? He was out-voted. The posse headed down to Hamrick's, and even Bosley was talked into a shot of brandy.

"People just don't care," Bosley remarked, staring around the bar. It was about as full as the fire department would allow, and everyone seemed to be having a good time.

"Thing is, Bosley," Bill Waits said, "nobody's quite sure what they saw. I bet if you asked people what happened this afternoon, they'd all say something different."

"That's the way the Devil works, Mr. Waits," Bosley replied, without a trace of self-importance. "He wants us to argue among ourselves. And while we're arguing, he gets on with his work."

"And what work would that be?" Bill said. "Exactly?"

"Leave it alone, Bill," Chas said. "Let's just get out there and—"

"No," Bosley said, his words a little slurred. "It's a legitimate question."

"And what's the answer, Bosley?"

"It's the same work the Devil's been doing since the beginning of time." While Bosley talked, Alstead put a second brandy into the man's hand, and Bosley, barely aware that he was doing so, drank it in one, then went on, "He wants to take us from God."

"I left a long time ago," Waits said. He wasn't joking.

"I'm sure God misses you," Bosley replied, with equal sincerity.

The two men stared at each other for a long moment, saying nothing.

"Hey, Bosley, give it a rest," Alstead said. "You're creepin' me out. And have another brandy."

iv

The bullet in Buddenbaum's brain had done nothing to subdue his fury.

"They are the most ungrateful, hypocritical, petty, paltry, witless, chicken-brained sons of bitches it's ever been my misfortune to work for," he raged, his hand clamped to his healing head. '*Oh, lay on*

another show for us, Owen. A nice assassination. A little crime pas-
sionelle. *Something with children. Something with Christians.'* He
turned to Seth, who had been standing at the window overlooking
the crossroads listening to this tirade for the better part of thirty
minutes. "And did I ever say *no?*" He paused, waiting for an answer.

"Probably not," Seth said.

"Damn right! Nothing was too much trouble for them. They
wanted to see a president die? No problem. They fancied a massacre
or two? It could be arranged. There was nothing they asked for I
didn't supply. *Nothing!*"

He strode to the window now, casually fingering the wound. "But
the moment I fumble—just a little, tiny mistake—then they're sniffing after that cunt Bombeck, and it's, *'See you later, Owen. We'll take
her off and talk about the fucking story tree.'*"

He stared at Seth, who stared back.

"You've got a question on your face," Buddenbaum said.

"And you've got blood on yours," Seth said.

"Has something changed between us?"

"Yes," Seth said simply. "The fact is, every hour, every minute, I
think something different about you."

"So how would you have it between us?"

Seth pondered a moment. "I wish we could start again," he said.
"I wish you were just coming up to me under the stars and I was
telling you about the angels." Another pause. "I wish I still had the
angels."

"I took them away from you; is that what you're saying?"

"I let you do it," Seth replied.

"The question—"

"Huh?"

"You had a question on your face."

"Yeah . . . I was just wondering about the story tree, that's all."

"There *is* no tree, if that's what you're asking," Buddenbaum
said. Seth looked disappointed. "It's just a phrase some lousy poet
came up with."

"What does it mean?"

Owen's voice had lost its venom now. He leaned back against the wall beside the window from which he'd fallen two days before. "What does it mean?" he said. "Well . . . it means that stories are seeds. Stories are blossoms. Stories are fruit, picked and pressed and eaten. Then we shit out the seeds—"

"Back into the ground?"

"Back into the ground."

"On and on."

Buddenbaum sighed. "On and on," he said. "With or without us."

"You don't mean us," Seth said softly. There was no accusation in this, just a melancholy statement of fact. Buddenbaum started to speak, but Seth cut him off short. "I was down there, Owen," he said, nodding at the street. "You were going to go without me, wherever it was."

"I got distracted," Owen said, "that's all. I've waited so long for this; I couldn't afford to let it slip."

"It slipped anyway," Seth reminded him.

"It won't happen again," Owen replied tersely. "By God it won't."

"How will you prevent it?"

"I need your help, Seth," Buddenbaum said. "And I promise—"

"Don't promise me anything," Seth said. "It's better that way."

Buddenbaum sighed. "It's taken us so little time to grow apart," he said to Seth. "It's as though we've had half a lifetime together in forty-eight hours."

Seth gazed out of the window. "What do you want me to do?" he said.

"Find Tesla Bombeck, and make peace with her. Tell her I need to see her. Say whatever you have to say to bring her here. No, not here . . ." He thought of Rita, hair piled high. "There's a little cafe I went to. I don't remember the name. It had a blue sign—"

"The Nook."

"That's it. Bring her there. And tell her to keep the avatars out of earshot, huh?"

"How will she do that?"

"She'll find a way."

"Okay. And you want me to bring her to the Nook?"

"If she'll come."

"And what if she won't?"

"Then it will all have been for nothing," Owen said. "And I'll be wishing I had your angels to listen for."

---

v

When Harry emerged from the trees the night had become completely still. There was not a murmur in the air, nor in the grass, nor in the cracks of the rocks. Once he'd climbed far enough to be able to see over the tops of the trees, he looked back down at Everville half-expecting that some order to evacuate had gone out, and he would see the town deserted. But no. The lights still burned; there was still traffic in the streets. It was simply that the mist that covered the door at the top of the slope soaked up every sound, leaving the area so hushed he could hear his own heart, beating in his head.

"This is where it happened," Coker Ammiano said to Erwin as they followed D'Amour across the slope towards the mist.

"The hangings?"

"No. The great battle between the families of Summa Summamentis and Ezso Aetherium. A very terrible day brought about by a child."

"You were there?"

"Oh yes. I was there. And I married the child, a little later. Her name was Maeve O'Connell, and she was the most miraculous woman I ever encountered."

"How so?"

"Everville was her dream, passed down to her by her father, Harmon O'Connell."

"Harmon as in Heights?"

"The same."

"Did you know him too?"

"No. He was dead before I met her. She was wandering here alone, and she came where she was not welcome. It was a simple mistake."

"And just by coming here she caused a slaughter?"

"By coming here and speaking."

"*Speaking?*"

"There was a wedding, you see, being celebrated up there"—he pointed towards the mist—"and it was the belief in the world from which the families came that silence was sacred, because it preceded the beginning. Love was made in silence. And anyone who broke such a silence was counted the enemy."

"So why didn't they just kill the girl?"

"Because the families were old enemies, and each thought the child was an agent of the other. As soon as she spoke, they massacred each other."

"Right here?"

"Right here," Coker said. "If we wanted to, I'm sure we could sink into the earth and find their bones."

"I'll stay where I can see the sky," Erwin said.

"It *is* very beautiful tonight," Coker said, throwing back his head to study the stars. "Sometimes it seems I've been alone for a hundred lifetimes, and sometimes—tonight, for instance—it's as if we only parted glances a few hours ago." He let out a strange sound, and when Erwin looked at him he saw that tears were spilling down his cheeks "Hers were the last eyes I saw. I felt them on me, as I was dying. And I tried to hold on to life, just a while. Tried to keep looking at her, to comfort her the way she was comforting me. . . ." He had to stop for a moment to recover himself. "But the life went out of me before it went out of her. And when I came into *this*"—he opened his hands in front of him—"this life after death, her body had been taken, and so had my son's."

"No wonder you hated Dolan so much."

"Oh, I hated him. But he was human. He couldn't help himself."

"Were your people so perfect then?" Erwin said.

"There's no difference between my people and yours," Coker

replied. "Give or take a wing or a tail. We're all the same in our hearts. All sad and cruel." He paused, wiping the tears away, and as he did, glanced up the slope. "I think our friend D'Amour is having a problem," he said.

In the last few minutes, during their tearful exchange, Erwin and Coker had dropped maybe fifty yards behind D'Amour, who was within a few strides of the mist. Plainly he had sensed the enemy, because he now fell to the ground behind a boulder, and lay still. Moments later, the problem Coker had spoken of emerged from the mist in the form of not one but four individuals, each of them of competitive ugliness: one a sliver, one obese; one bovine, one bilious.

The thinnest of them was also the most eager, and came down the slope twenty yards (passing by the place where D'Amour lay) sniffing the air.

"I think maybe it's *us* they're after," Coker said.

"What the hell are they?"

"Creatures of Quiddity," Coker replied.

"Appalling."

"I'm sure they'd say the same about you," Coker remarked. The thin creature was heading on down the incline, and it did indeed seem that he was closing on the ghosts.

"What do we do?" Erwin said. The closer the creature got the more distressing he appeared to be.

"He can't do us any harm," Coker said. "But if they see D'Amour—"

The rake-thin creature seemed to be staring right at Erwin, which he found deeply disquieting. "It sees me," Erwin said.

"I doubt it."

"*It does*, I tell you!"

"Well you were carping about being invisible on the way up. You can't have it—Damn!"

"What?"

"They've found him."

Erwin looked past the thin man, and saw perhaps the most brutal of the creatures catching hold of D'Amour and dragging him to his feet. "This is our fault," Coker said. "I'm damn sure it's us they came looking for."

Erwin was not so certain, but there was no doubt that D'Amour was in serious trouble. One of the quartet had disarmed him, another was beating him about the face. As for the creature that had come down the slope, it had turned from Erwin and Coker, and was making its way back to join its companions, who were now dragging their prisoner into the mist.

"What do we do?" Erwin said.

"We follow," Coker said. "And if they kill him we apologize."

Last time Harry had climbed the Heights, Voight's tattoos had allowed him to reach the very threshold undetected. But the trick hadn't worked this time. He didn't know why, and in truth it didn't matter. He was in the hands of his enemies—Gamaliel the stick-insect, Bartho the crucified, Mutep the runt, and Swanky the obese. There was nothing to be done about it.

He didn't attempt to resist them, in part because he knew it would only invite violence, and in part because after all he'd come up the slope to see what the Devil looked like and they were taking him to the door through which it would come, so why resist?

And there was a third reason. These creatures were cousins of the demon that had taken Father Hess's life. He didn't understand the genealogy of it, but he knew by their chatter and their frenzy and their stench that they were somehow connected. Perhaps then, in the final minutes before the lad's arrival, he might learn from one or other of these horrors what the message from Lazy Susan meant.

"*I am you and you are love*—"

Even at the end, *was love what made the world go round?*

V

*I*t wasn't dark in the belly of the Iad Uroboros, nor was it light. There was only an absence—of light and dark, of height and depth, of sound and texture—that might have passed for oblivion itself had Joe not been able to list all that it lacked. The oblivion, he was sure, would be a thoughtless condition.

So what was this place, and he in it? Was he a ghost of some kind, haunting the Iad's head? Or a soul, trapped in the flesh of the beast, until it puked him up or perished? He felt no threat to his existence here, but he suspected his hold on who he was would quickly become slippery. It would only be a matter of time before his thoughts lost coherence, and he forgot himself completely.

That prospect had seemed attractive enough when he'd been standing by the pool in the temple. He'd lived his life and was ready to give it up. But now, as he floated (if a thing without substance could be said to float) in the emptiness, he wondered if perhaps his presence here had been planned or predicted by the Zehrapushu. He remembered how hungrily the first 'shu he'd encountered, on the shore outside Liverpool, had studied him. Had it, or the mind of which it was part, been sizing him up for some role in events to come, peering *beyond* the flesh of him to see if he'd be worth a damn in the belly of the Iad?

If so—if there was indeed a purpose in his being here—then it was his duty to the 'shu, whose gaze was without question one of the most wonderful experiences of his travels, to preserve whatever part of him remained—his memory, his spirit, his soul—and not succumb to forgetfulness.

Name yourself, he thought. At least remember that. He had no mouth, of course, nor tongue nor lips nor lungs. All he could do was think: *I am Joe Flicker. I am Joe Flicker.*

Doing so had an instant effect. The featureless state convulsed, and forms began to become available to his soul's senses.

He had no way of knowing his true scale here, of course. Perhaps he was tiny in this formless form—like a mote seen in a shaft of sunlight—in which case all that was congealing around him was not titanic, as it seemed, but he, its witness, a fleck. Whichever was true, he felt insignificant in the presence of these cohering shapes. He turned his sight around, and in every direction, rising to the domed darkness above him, where ragged shapes moved as though it were the breeding place for men-o'-war, down to the pit—lined with heaving abstractions—below him, was a latticework of encrusted matter.

He was by no means certain that these sights were real the way the body lying beside the temple pool below had been real. Perhaps they were simply thoughts in the head of Iad Uroboros, and he was present in the midst of some Iadic vision of heaven and hell: a firmament of unfinished angels, a pit of nonsenses and in between a sprawling and infinitely complex web of knotted and corrupted memories.

There were places, he saw, where the strands seemed to become clotted, forming large, almost egg-shaped masses. His curiosity as to their nature was enough to propel him; he'd no sooner puzzled over them than his spirit was moving towards the largest in his immediate vicinity. The closer he came to it the more its appearance distressed him. Whereas the encrustations on the web were organic, the surface of the egg was of another order completely. It was a mass of overlapping forms, like the pieces of a lunatic jigsaw, each failing to quite mesh with the one below, and each worked with an obsessively complex design.

Nor was its appearance the only source of distress. A sound was emanating from it; or rather, several sounds, swarming together. One was like the whispers of children; one was a slow, arrhythmical throb, like the beat of a failing heart. And the third was a whine that wormed its way into Joe's thoughts as if to disconnect them.

He was tempted to retreat, but he resisted, and pressed his spirit on, more certain with every moment that there was great pain here; nearly unendurable pain, in fact. The surface of the form was a catalogue of lunatic motions: tics and spasms and twitches, the jigsaws pieces coming away in a hundred places like shed scales, while others, thorny and raw in their budding form, unfurled.

Off to his left, something iridescent caught his eye, and he looked its way to see that the shedding had momentarily revealed what lay *beneath* this maddened, whispering mass. He moved towards it, and for the first time since approaching the egg had the sense that his presence had been noted. The motions became more fevered the closer to the sliver of iridescence he came, and all around the place the scaly pieces oozed a dark fluid, as if to conceal the spot while they bred a more permanent cover. Joe was not deceived. He closed on the sliver, certain there was some vital mystery here, and in response the motions became more frenzied until suddenly the tremors seemed to reach critical mass and a dozen shapes rose from the surface, surrounding him.

None of them made much literal sense. He could not distinguish a limb, or a head, much less an eye or a mouth. But they gaped and twitched and swelled in ways that evoked a parade of abominations. Something gutted, but living; something aborted, but living; something decayed into muck, but living and living. Though he'd left his body behind him and thought himself free of it, these horrors reminded him of every wound he'd ever suffered, of every sickness, of every weakness.

He had come too close to the iridescence to be frightened off, however. Turning his sight from these manifestations he slipped through their net, and into the midst of whatever secret they concealed.

He was delivered into a curving channel, down which he flew. It rapidly began to narrow, and narrow, as though he were in an ever-closing spiral. The light that had called him here did not diminish as he traveled, but remained steady as the curves tightened, the channel so narrow now he was certain a hair could not have been threaded through it. And still it grew narrower, until he began to think it would wink out of existence completely, and perhaps take him along with it. He'd no sooner formed this thought than his progress seemed to slow, until he was barely moving. Even at a creeping pace, however, the spiral was here so tight he kept turning and turning on himself, until at last all motion ceased. He waited in the gleaming channel, puzzled. And then, slowly, the realization rose in him that he was not alone. He looked ahead, and though he could see nothing, he was aware that something was staring back at him.

He returned the gaze, without fear, and as he did so images began to erupt among his thoughts: beautiful, simple images of the world he'd left behind.

A field of lush grass, through which a tidal wind was moving. A porch, overgrown with scarlet bougainvillea, where a child with white-blonde hair was laughing. A doughnut shop at dusk, with the evening star above it, set in a flawless blue.

Somebody was dreaming here, he thought; yearning for the Helter Incendo. And it was someone who had been there and seen these sights with their own eyes.

Human. There was something human here. A prisoner of the Iad, he assumed, trapped in this gleaming spiral, and guarded by reminders of flesh and its frailties.

He had no way of questioning it; no way of knowing if it had simply folded him into its visions, had comprehended that it was no longer alone. If the latter, then perhaps he could liberate it; lead it out of its dreaming cell.

He turned his curious spirit around, and began to make his way back along the channel, hoping that the prisoner would follow. He was not disappointed. After a few seconds of travel, the channel widening once more, he glanced back and felt the eyeless stare upon him.

The escape, however, was not without consequence. Even as he picked up his pace, fractures appeared in the walls around them, and the fluid he'd seen ooze between the scales when he'd first approached the channel trickled into view. It was not, he now comprehended, the blood of the Iad, but rather its raw stuff, turning even as it appeared into the same wretched, sickening forms.

But for all their burgeoning vileness, there was something about their spread that smacked of desperation. Did he dare believe that they, or the mind that directed them, was *afraid?* Not of him, perhaps, but of whatever came on his spirit-heels; the dreamer he'd woken with his presence?

The further the two spirits traveled, the more certain he became that this was so. The fractures were fissures now, the Iad's mud spilling into their path. But they were quicksilver. Before the Iad could block their path with atrocities they were escaping the spiral, dodging between the entities that had risen from the prison in all directions. Some seemed to have fashioned wings from their flayed hides, others had the appearance of things turned inside out; others still were like flocks of burned birds, sewn into a single anguished form. They came after the escapees in a foul horde, their whispers rising to shrieks now, their bodies colliding with the strands and dragging them after, so that when Joe glanced back the web was shaking in all directions, and sending down a rain of dead matter, which beat upon his spirit like a black hail.

It rapidly became so thick, this hail, that he lost contact with the dreamer completely. He tried to turn back and find his fellow spirit, but the horde had grown apace, and came at him like a raging wall, pressing a gust of hail ahead of it. He felt himself struck over and over, each assault beating him back and blinding him as it did so, until he could no longer see the dome or the pit, or anything between. He reeled in darkness for a few moments, not knowing which way he had come, and then, to his astonishment, a blaze of light enveloped him and he was falling through the empty air.

Below him he saw the dream-sea churned into a frenzy by the Iad's approach, and beyond it a city in whose harbor the ships were lifted so high they would soon be pitched into the streets.

It was Liverpool, of course. In the time he'd adventured in the Iad's head or belly the creature had strode across Quiddity, and was almost at the threshold between worlds. He had time, as he fell in the midst of Iad's hail, to look along the shore towards the door. It was still wreathed in mist, but he could see the dark crack, and thought perhaps he glimpsed a star gleaming in the sky over Harmon's Heights.

Then he struck the waters amid a hail of Iadic matter, and before he could free his spirit of its weight a wave rose beneath him, and bearing him up amid a raft of detritus, carried him on towards the city streets, where it left him, stranded in the shadow of the power that had shat him out.

VI

*L*ucky Joe," said the face looming over Phoebe. It was as cracked as Unger's Creek in a drought.

Phoebe raised her head off the hard pillow. "What about him?"

"I'm just saying, he's damn lucky, the way you talk about him."

"What was I saying?"

"Mostly just his name," King Texas replied.

She looked past his muddy shoulder. The cave behind him was vast, and filled with people, standing, sitting, lying down.

"Did they hear me?" she asked Texas.

He smiled conspiratorially. "No," he said. "Only me."

"Have I broken any bones?" she said, looking down at her body.

"Nothing," he said. "I'd never let a woman's blood be spilled down here."

"What is it? Bad luck?"

"The worst," he said. "The very worst."

"What about Musnakaff?"

"What about him?"

"Did he survive?" King Texas shook his head. "So you saved me but not him?"

"I warned her, didn't I?" he said, almost petulantly. "I said I'd kill him if she didn't turn back."

"He wasn't to blame."

"And neither am I," Texas said. "She's the trouble. Always was."

"So why don't you just put her out of your mind? You've got plenty of company."

"No I don't."

"What about *them?*" she said, pointing to the assembly on his back.

"Look again," he said.

Puzzled, she sat up, and scanning the assembly, realized her error. What she had taken to be a congregation of living souls was in fact a crowd of sculptures, some set with fragments of glittering ore, some roughly hewn from blocks of stone, some barely human in shape.

"Who made them?" she said. "You?"

"Who else?"

"You really are alone down here?"

"Not by choice. But yes."

"So you made these to keep you company?"

"No. They were my attempts to find some form that would win Mistress O'Connell's affections."

Phoebe swung her legs off the bed and got to her feet. "Is it all right if I look at them?" she asked him.

"Help yourself," he told her, standing aside. Then, as she walked past him he murmured, "I could forbid you nothing."

She pretended not to hear the remark, suspecting it would only open a subject she was not willing to address.

"Did she ever see any of these faces?" she asked him, wandering between the statues.

"One or two," he replied, somewhat mournfully. "But none of them made any impression upon her."

"Maybe you misunderstood—" Phoebe began.

"Misunderstood *what?*"

"The reason she doesn't care for you any longer. I'm sure it's nothing to do with the way you look. She's half-blind anyway."

"So what does she want from me?" King Texas wailed. "I built her highways. I built her a harbor. I leveled the ground so that she could dream her city into being."

"Was she beautiful?" Phoebe said.

"Never."

"Not even a little?"

"No. She was antiquated even when I met her. And she'd just been hanged. Filthy, foul-mouthed—"

"But?"

"But what?"

"There was something you loved."

"Oh yes . . . " he said softly.

"What?"

"The fire in her, for one. The appetite in her. And the stories of course."

"She told good stories?"

"She's got Irish blood, so of course." He smiled to himself. "That's how she made the city," he explained. "She told it. Night after night. Sat on the ground and told it. Then she'd sleep, and in the morning what she'd told would be there. The houses. The monuments. The pigeons. The smell of fish. The fogs. The smoke. That's how she made it all. Stories and dreams. Dreams and stories. It was wonderful to watch. I think I was never so much in love as those mornings, getting up and seeing what she'd made."

Listening to his reverie, Phoebe found herself warming to him. He was probably a fool for love, just as Maeve had said, and clearly that had made him a little crazed, but she understood that feeling well enough.

There was a rumbling now, from somewhere up above them. A patter of dust fell from the cracked ceiling.

"The lad has arrived," he said.

"Oh my God."

His pebble eyes rolled in his sockets. "I think it's overturning her city," he said. There was a calm sadness in his voice.

"I don't want to be buried down here."

"You're not going to die," he said. "What I told Maeve is true. The Iad will pass over, but the rock will remain. You're safe here with me." The tremors came again. Phoebe shuddered. "Come into my arms if you're nervous," Texas said.

"I'm okay," she replied. "But I would like to *see* what's going on up there."

"Easy," he replied. "Come with me."

As he led her through the labyrinth of his kingdom—on the walls of which he'd configured and reconfigured his face ten thousand times, rehearsing it for a love scene he'd now never play—he meditated aloud about life in the rock. But with the turmoil from above escalating with every stride she took, and the walls creaking and stones pattering down, she caught only fragments of what he was saying.

"It's not solid at all," he said at one point, "everything flows, if you watch it for long enough . . . "

And a little later: "A fossil heart, that's what I've got . . . but it still aches and aches . . . "

And later still: "San Antonio is the place to die. I wish I had flesh still, to lay down in the Alamo . . . "

Finally, after maybe ten minutes of such bits and pieces, he led her into a sizable chamber, the entire floor of which was raked and polished. There, in the very ground beneath her feet, was a periscopic reflection of what was going on above ground. It was an awe-inspiring sight: the seething darkness of the Iad's body invading the streets of the city she'd been walking in just hours before, carrying before it remnants of the places it had laid waste on its way here. She saw a head lopped from some titanic statue rolling down one of the streets, felling entire buildings as it went. She saw what looked to be a small island deposited in the middle of a city square. Several ships had come to rest among the spires of the cathedral, and their sails had unfurled as if to bear it away before the next wind.

And among this debris, in numbers beyond counting, were creatures trawled from the depths of the dream-sea by the Iad's passage.
The least of them were fantasias on the theme of fish: gleaming
shoals of visionary life, thrown up in waves above the city's roofs,
then falling in glorious profusion. Far more extraordinary were the
creatures drawn up, Phoebe supposed, from Quiddity's deepest
trenches, their forms inspired by (or inspirations for) the tales of
mariners the world over. Was that glistening coil not a sea-serpent,
its eyes burning like twin furnaces in its hooded head? And that
beast wrapping its arms around the masks of a grounded cutter, was
that not the mother of all octopi?

"Damn it," King Texas said. "I never liked competing with that
city of hers for her attention, but this is no way for it to end."

Phoebe said nothing. Her gaze had gone from the debris to the
Iad itself. What she saw put her in mind of a disease—a terrible,
implacable, devouring disease. It had no face. It had no malice. It
had no guilt. Perhaps it didn't even have a mind. It came because it
could; because nothing stopped it.

"It's going to destroy Everville," she said to Texas.

"Maybe."

"There's no *maybe* about it," she protested.

"Why should you care?" he said. "You don't love it there, do
you?"

"No," Phoebe said. "But I don't want to see it destroyed either."

"You don't have to," Texas said. "You're here with me."

Phoebe pondered this a moment. Plainly she wasn't going to get
him to intervene on her behalf. But maybe there was another way.

"If I were Maeve—" she began.

"You're too sane."

"But if I were—if I'd founded a city the way she'd founded
Everville, not with dreams but with plain hard work—"

"Yes?"

"And somebody protected it for me, kept my city safe—"

She let the notion trail. There was fifteen seconds of silence, while Liverpool shook and trembled under their feet. Then he said, "Would you *love* that somebody?"

"Maybe I would," she said.

"Oh my Lord—" he murmured.

"It looks like the Iad's giving up on the city," she said. "It's starting to move along the shore."

"*My* shore," King Texas said. "I'm the rock, remember?" He crossed the mirror to where she stood and laid his mud hand upon her cheek. "Thank you," he said. "You've given me hope." He turned from her, saying, "*Stay here.*"

"I don't—"

"Stay, I said. And *watch.*"

ii

During the voyage to Mem-é b'Kether Sabbat, Noah Summa Summamentis had spoken of the Iad Uroboros's power to induce terror by its very proximity, but until now—when Joe entered the streets of Liverpool—he had seen no evidence of that power. In b'Kether Sabbat the Iad's malevolence had been held in thrall to the 'shu, and by the time it had been unleashed Joe was a spirit, and apparently immune to its influence. But the survivors who wandered through the shaking desolation were plainly victims, shrieking and sobbing for relief from the madness overwhelming them. Some had succumbed to it, and sat in the rubble with blank faces. Others were driven to terrible acts of self-harm to stop the horrors, beating their heads against stones, or tearing at their chests to still their hearts.

Powerless to help them, Joe could only wander on, determined to at least be a witness to what the Iad perpetrated. Perhaps there was some higher court in which its crimes would be judged. If so, he would testify.

There was a large bonfire burning in the street ahead, its flames brightening the filthy air. Approaching, he saw that it was attended by perhaps twenty people, who were circling it hand in hand, praying aloud.

"You who are divided, be whole in our hearts—"

Surely they were appealing to the 'shu, he thought.

"You who are divided—"

Their prayer apparently went unheard, however. Though the Iad had left off its destruction of the city there were remnants of its shadow presence haunting the streets, and one such portion, no more than a dozen feet tall, and resembling a pillar of darkness, was approaching the fire from the far end of the street. One of the group, a young woman with a mouth that resembled a fleshy rose, broke the circle and started to retreat from the fire, shaking her head wildly. The worshipper to her left caught hold of her hand and proceeded to haul her back to the fire.

"Hold on!" he said to her. "It's our only hope!"

But the damage had been done. The circle, once broken, had lost any charm it might have possessed, and now each of the worshippers succumbed to the Iad's baleful influence. One of the men pulled out a knife and proceeded to threaten the air in front of him. Another reached into the flames, searing his hand and yelling for some horror or other to keep away from him.

As he did so, he looked up through the fire, and his agonized face suddenly cleared of its confusions. He pulled his hand out of the fire and stared at Joe.

"Look . . ." he murmured.

Joe was as astonished as the man witnessing him. "You see me?" he said.

The man failed to hear him. He was too busy yelling for his fellow worshippers to "*Look! Look!*"

Another had seen him now; a woman whose face was a mass of bruises, but who at the sight of him broke into an ecstatic smile.

"Look how it *shines*—" she said.

"It heard," somebody else murmured. "We prayed and it heard."

"What are you seeing?" Joe said to them. But they made no sign of hearing him. They simply watched the place where his spirit stood, and wept and gaped and offered up thanks.

One of their number looked back down the street towards the approaching Iad. It was approaching no longer. Either it had been recalled into the body of its nation, or else it had retreated from the force of joy that suddenly surrounded the fire.

The young woman who had first broken the circle now approached Joe. There were tears running down her cheeks, and her body was shaking, but she was fearless in her desire to touch this vision.

"Let me know you," she said as she raised her hand towards Joe. "Be with me forever and ever."

The words, and the need in her eyes, disturbed him. Whatever had happened here, it was nothing he comprehended, much less sought. He was still Joe Flicker. Still and only.

"I can't . . ." he said, though he knew they couldn't hear him, and willed himself away from the place.

It was harder to leave than it'd been to arrive. Their gazes seemed to slow him, and he had to struggle to free himself from them.

Only when he was fifty yards away down the street, and their desire no longer held a claim over him, did he dare look back. They were in each other's arms, weeping for joy. All except the woman who'd tried to touch him. She was still looking down the street in his direction, and though he was too far from her to see her eyes he felt her gaze upon him, and knew he would not readily be free of it.

iii

"*Texas!*" Phoebe yelled. "Damn you, can you hear me?"

She had long ago vacated the mirror chamber for the very good reason that it was close to collapse. Now, in a tunnel lined with his faces, she stood and demanded his presence. He didn't come, however. Remembering how much the thought of a woman's blood being spilled here had distressed him, she dug through the rock shards underfoot until she located something sharp, pulled up her sleeve, and without giving herself time to think twice, opened a four-inch cut just above her wrist. Her blood had never looked redder. She squealed with the pain of it, but she let it flow, and flow, sinking back against the wall as her head spun.

"*What are you doing?*"

Almost instantly he rose before her in the form of liquid rock, raging.

"I told you: *no blood!*"

"So get me out of here," she said, chilly with a sudden sweat "or I'll just keep bleeding."

The shaking was getting worse by the moment. In the walls there was a grinding sound, as though some vast engine was slipping its gears.

"I am the rock," he said.

"So you keep saying."

"If I said you were safe, then safe you were."

The wall behind her shook so violently several of his rejected faces cracked and fell to the ground. "Are you going to take me up, or not?" she said.

"I'll take you," he said, unknitting his feet from the floor of the passage and approaching her. "But you must come with me on my terms."

She looked at him through a throbbing haze. "What . . . are . . . your terms?" she said. His face was cruder than she'd previously seen it, she realized, like a mask hewn with a dull axe.

"If I take you," he said, "then it must be here." He opened his arms. "For your safety, you must be cradled in the rock. Agreed?"

She nodded. It was not such a terrible idea. He was a King, he was a rock, and he had a heart for love, even if it was a fossil. "Agreed," she said, and clamping her hand to her cut arm to stem the flow, let him gather her into his embrace.

VII

i

Grillo was no expert when it came to babies but he was damn
sure the sound coming from the child in Jo-Beth's arms
wasn't healthy.

"What's wrong with her?" he said.

"I don't know."

"It sounds like she's choking."

"I think maybe you should stop."

The baby seemed to be having minor convulsions now, and with
every bump in the road they were worsening. Grillo slowed down a
little, but Jo-Beth wasn't satisfied. "Stop!" she said. "Just for a
minute or two."

He glanced down at little Amy, who was making a pitiful sobbing
sound. Reluctantly, he pulled over and brought the car to a halt.

"She wants her Daddy," Jo-Beth said.

"He'll catch us up."

"I know," the girl went on. The child's sobs were subsiding now.
"Why don't you leave us here?" she said. "He won't come looking for
you, as long as he's found us."

"What the hell are you talking about?"

"I know you did what you thought was right. But it *wasn't*. Amy
knows it and so do I."

"You're talking about Tommy-Ray—" Grillo said softly.

"We have to be together," she said. "Or we'll die. We'll all of us die."

Grillo looked back down at the child in her arms. "I don't know whether you're mixed up, fucked up, or just plain crazy, but I'm not trusting you with Amy any longer." He reached down to take the baby from her. She instantly drew the child tight to her body, but Grillo wasn't about to be denied. He dug his arm down around the bundle and pulled Amy out of her mother's arms.

To his surprise, Jo-Beth didn't attempt to reclaim her. Instead she glanced back down the road.

"He's coming," she said, reaching for the handle of the door.

"Stay inside."

"But he's *coming*—"

"I said—"

Too late. She had the handle down, and was pushing open the door. He grabbed for her arm, and caught it momentarily, but she slipped him and stumbled out into the road.

"Get back in here!" he yelled.

A gust of wind rocked the car. Then a second, more violent than the first. Jo-Beth was standing in the middle of the road now, turning on her heels, and lightly touching her breasts. Again, the car rocked. This time Grillo knew he couldn't wait for her. If he got out to fetch her, she'd outrun him, and all the time her beloved Death-Boy was getting closer, closer.

He gently laid the child on the passenger seat and was reaching over to pull the door closed when a blast of bitter, dirty air hit him in the face, sending him sprawling across the seat. The back of his skull hit the window hard, but grabbing the wheel he started to haul himself up again, reaching for the baby with his free hand as he did so. The dust was filling the interior, forming fingers to scrabble at his eyes, and reaching down into his throat to choke him.

Blinded, he kept reaching for the child, as the car's rocking became steadily more violent. He found the blanket, and began to pull it towards him, but as he did so the ghosts pushed the car over onto two wheels, where it teetered, its metalwork creaking. He inched the blanket towards him, fearful that at any moment the dusty dead would claim the baby from its folds, while the legion threw its will and wind against the car, plainly determined to overturn it. Perhaps some of his tormentors had been summoned to help, because the fingers tearing at his eyes and throat had retreated. He wiped his face against his shoulder to clear his sight, and opened his eyes only to find that the blanket in his hand was empty. Grabbing the dashboard he hauled himself up towards the open door, determined to get Amy back. The windshield shattered as he climbed, and through the dust he saw the abductors' faces, four or five of them, carved of the dirty air, and leering at his desperation.

"*Bastards!*" he yelled at them. "*Bastards!*"

The sound of his voice brought a sob, not from the ghosts but from Amy. They'd not taken her after all; she'd slipped between the front seats, and was lying, as yet unharmed, on the floor behind him.

"It's okay," he said to her, forsaking his handhold to reach for her. As he did so the car's teeterings reached the point of no return, and it was flung over onto its side. Through the din of breaking glass and concertinaed metal he heard the voice of the Death-Boy, roaring, "*Stop!*"

The order came too late. The car was pushed over onto its roof, which buckled under the impact. The remaining windows blew inwards, the glove-compartment spilled its contents. Tumbling in a hail of trash, Grillo's instincts overtook his conscious thought, and he drew the baby into his arms as he fell. His frail body snapped and tore. He felt something in his belly and chest, like a sudden dyspepsia.

Then the vehicle rocked to a halt, and there was something close to silence. For a moment he thought the child was dead, but it seemed she was simply shocked into silence, because he heard her ragged breathing close to him in the darkness.

He was upside-down, his legs akimbo, and something hot was running down his body from his groin. He smelled it now, sharp and familiar. He was pissing himself. Very gingerly he tried to shift himself, but there was something preventing him doing so. He reached up to his chest and his fingers found a spike of wet metal sticking out of his body a few inches behind his left clavicle. It gave him no pain, though there was little doubt he was skewered from back to front.

"Oh Lord . . . " he said to himself, very softly, then feebly reached out towards the source of Amy's breathing. The motion seemed to take an age. He had time, while he reached and reached, to think of Tesla and hope she would be spared the sight of him like this. She had endured so much and after all her searching and suffering had gained so very little.

His fingers had found Amy's face, and inch by inch he passed his hand over her tiny body. His hand was becoming numb, but as far as he could gather she was not bloodied, which was some comfort. Then, as he once again reached up to her face she took hold of his finger and grasped it. He was astonished at her strength. Delighted too, for it surely meant she'd not sustained any significant harm. He demanded his body draw a little extra breath, and his muscles obliged him. He drew a sip of air into his seeping lungs, enough for a word or two.

He used it wisely.

"I'm here," he said to Amy, and died so quietly she didn't know he'd gone.

ii

Even before they rounded the corner Tesla heard the ghost's cacophony: a rising wail of complaint. She pulled the bike over, and parked on the curve, just out of sight.

"Whatever we find around that corner," she told Howie as they dismounted, "keep control of yourself."

"I just want my wife and baby back."

"And we'll get them," Tesla said. "But Howie, brute force isn't going to do us any good. One word and we're both dead. Think about that. You're not going to be much use to Jo-Beth and Amy dead."

Point made, Tesla headed off round the corner. There were no streetlights along the road, but there was enough light from moon and stars for the scene to be plain enough. Grillo's car sat battered and overturned. Jo-Beth was standing clear of it, apparently unharmed. There was no sign of either Grillo or the baby.

As for Tommy-Ray, he was disciplining his troops, the ghosts gathered around his feet like a pack of beaten curs.

"Fucking stupid!" he yelled at them. "*Stupid!*"

He reached down into their shifting substance and hauled two ragged handfuls of it up towards his face. It hung from his fingers in tatters.

"Why don't you *learn?*" he raged.

The murmurs of the ghosts grew more panicky. Some of them turned their wretched faces up towards him in supplication. Others hid their heads, apparently knowing what was coming.

Tommy-Ray opened his mouth, wider than any natural anatomy allowed, and put the muck-laced ether between his teeth. Then he literally inhaled it, sucking the dirty air into his body. Tesla saw two phantom faces, sobbing and gasping, disappear down the Death-Boy's gullet, while the next in line scrabbled to avoid joining them. But the lesson was apparently over, because now he grabbed the strands of matter that hung from the corners of his mouth and bit down on them, grinding them between his teeth. The ether dropped away from either side of his chin. He let the severed ends drop.

The survivors murmured their gratitude and shrank away.

The whole episode had taken perhaps fifteen seconds, during which time Tesla and Howie had halved the distance between the corner and the wreckage. They were now no more than twenty-five yards from the car, and in danger of being seen if Tommy-Ray chanced to look in their direction. Luckily, he had another distraction: Jo-Beth. He had gone to her and was speaking to her face to face. She didn't retreat from him. Even when his hands went up to her face—stroked her cheek, her hair, her lips—she stood unmoving before him.

"Christ . . . " Howie murmured.

Tesla glanced over her shoulder. "There's something alive in there," she said, nodding back at Grillo's car.

Howie looked. "I don't see anything," he said, his gaze returning to the dalliance between the twins.

"He can't do that," he growled, and pushing past Tesla, started towards them. He was gone so fast Tesla had no choice but to act out at the same time. She moved off towards the car, scanning the dark snarl of metal for further evidence of life. She found it too; a tiny motion. She was perhaps a dozen yards from the car now, the stinging smell of gasoline filling her head. Bending low and moving fast she moved round the far side of the vehicle, putting the wreckage between her and Tommy-Ray. Though she tried to tune out his voice, snatches of what he was telling Jo-Beth drifted her way.

"There'll be more . . . " he murmured. "Lots more . . . "

She knelt in the pooled gasoline and peered into the wreckage, using Tommy-Ray's talk to cover her calling: "Grillo—?"

As she spoke her eyes began to make sense of the tangled forms in front of her. There was an upturned seat; a litter of maps. And there among them, oh God, there, was Grillo's arm. She reached out and touched it, whispering his name again. There was no response. Ducking her head through the broken window she started to pull at the debris blocking her way to him. A drizzle of oil fell in her hair and ran down her face. She wiped it away from her eyes with the back of her hand and attacked the wreckage afresh. A portion of the seat came away this time, which she shoved to the side, offering her a fuller view of him. His face was half-turned towards her, and seeing him she said his name again, knowing in the same moment that her breath was wasted. He was dead, pierced by a spike of metal. Despite the horror of this it seemed from his expression that he'd not died in anguish. His worn face—which she had reached up to touch—was almost serene.

As her fingers grazed his cheek, something moved in the darkness beyond him. Amy; it was Amy! Tesla inched into the creaking wreckage until her face was inches from Grillo's pierced chest and peered over him. There was the baby, her eyes wet and wide in the murk, her hand clutching the index finger of Grillo's left hand.

There was no hope of moving the dead man, Tesla was certain; he and the vehicle were inextricably connected. Her only hope—and Amy's—was to reach over the body, past the spike that had skewered Grillo, and ease the child between the ragged metal overhead and the corpse below. She crawled as far into the wreckage as space would allow, and stretched her arms across Grillo's body—her breasts pressed against his sticky torso—to take hold of the infant.

As she did so she heard Tommy-Ray's voice.

"Dead . . ." he was saying.

This time there was an audible response. Not from Jo-Beth, but from Howie. Tesla caught only a few of the words; enough to know he was addressing Jo-Beth, not her brother.

"Keep talking," Tesla murmured. The longer Howie kept Tommy-Ray distracted, the more hope she had of getting the child out.

With some gentle persuasion she succeeded in loosing Amy's hand from Grillo's finger, and now began to lift her over Grillo's body, shimmying backwards as she did so, belly to the roof of the car. The baby was eerily quiet throughout. Shock, Tesla presumed.

"It's okay," she cooed, attempting a smile of reassurance. Amy looked back at her blankly.

They were almost free of the wreckage now. Certain that she would not lay eyes on Grillo again, she took a moment to study his face.

"Soon," she promised him. "Very soon."

Then she knelt up, gathering the baby to her body, and started to get to her feet.

On the other side of the wreckage, Tommy-Ray was yelling. There was a complexity in his voice Tesla had never heard before, as though he had assembled a chorus of the dead he'd devoured, and they were weaving their voices with his.

"*Tell him—*" the voices were saying to Jo-Beth, "*tell him the truth—*"

Clear of the wreckage now, Tesla dared to stand, assuming (correctly) the Death-Boy would be too preoccupied to look in her direction. He was standing a little way behind his sister, his hands on her shoulders.

"Tell him how it is between us," the voices out of him said.

Jo-Beth's features were no longer a blank. Face to face with her husband, whose distress was all too apparent, she could not help but be moved. Tommy-Ray shook her a little. "Why don't you just spit it out!" he said.

Finally, she spoke. "I don't know any more," she said.

At the sound of her voice, the baby in Tesla's arms began crying. Tesla froze, as three pairs of eyes were turned towards her.

"*Amy!*" Jo-Beth sobbed, and breaking from her place between the two men, she started towards Tesla, arms outstretched.

"Give her to me!"

She was a yard or two from the wreckage when Tommy-Ray yelled, "*Wait!*"

There was such vehemence in his voice she obeyed on the instinct.

"Before you touch that kid," Tommy-Ray demanded, "I want you to tell him who it belongs to."

Tesla could see Jo-Beth's face; the men could not. She could see the conflict written on it. "W-w-what are you t-t-t-talking about?" Howie said.

"I don't think she wants to tell you," Tommy-Ray said. "But I do. I want you to know once and for all. I came calling quite a while back, just to see how my little sister was doing, and we—got together, like you wouldn't believe. The kid's *mine*, Katz."

Howie's eyes were on Jo-Beth. "Tell him he's a liar," he said. The girl didn't move. "*Jo-Beth? Tell him h-h-he's a liar!*"

He had taken the gun out of his jacket—Tesla had seen him drop it in the parking lot; he'd obviously snatched it up again before climbing on the back of the bike—and he waved it in Jo-Beth's general direction.

"I w-w-want you t-t-to tell him!" he yelled at her. "H-h-he's a *liar!*"

Tesla's gaze went from his face to the gun to Jo-Beth to the wet ground, and images of the Mall in Palomo Grove filled her head.

Fletcher, soaked in gasoline and eager for death by fire. The gun, clutched in her own hand, ready to strike a spark—

Not again, she prayed. Please God, not again.

Tommy-Ray was still ranting.

"You never had her, Katz. Not really. You thought you did, but she goes deeper than you could ever get." He jiggled his lips as he spoke. "*Real* deep."

Howie looked down at the gasoline around his enemy's feet, and without hesitation, fired. The whole sequence of events—the looking and the firing—could only have occupied three or four seconds, but it was long enough for Tesla to wonder what place synchronicity had upon the story tree.

Then the spark came, and the flame followed, and the air around Tommy-Ray turned gold.

Howie let out a whoop of triumph. Then he turned his gaze on Jo-Beth.

"You still want him?" he yelled.

Jo-Beth let out a sob. "He loves me," she said.

"No!" Howie yelled, striding towards her now. "No! No! No! I'm the one who loves you—" He stabbed at his chest with his finger. "Always did. Before I met you I loved you—"

As he approached her the fire that had bloomed around the Death-Boy moved across the ground in her direction. She didn't see it. She was too busy yelling at Howie to *Stop, please stop—*

"Howie!" Tesla yelled. He looked her way. "*The fire,* Howie—"

He saw it now. Dropped his gun and raced towards Jo-Beth, shouting to her as he went. Before he'd halved the distance between them the flames that had obscured the Death-Boy parted like a curtain, and Tommy-Ray strode into view. He was blazing from head to foot; fire spurting from his mouth and eye-sockets, from his belly, from his groin. His immolation seemed not to concern him overmuch, however. He advanced upon his sister with an almost casual lope.

She had seen his approach, and would surely have run from him, but the ground at her feet was alight, and as she retreated the flames ignited her dress. She began to shriek, and beat at the fire with her hands, but it quickly consumed the light fabric, leaving her nearly naked for its play.

Howie was a couple of yards from the flames now, and without hesitation he plunged into them, arms outstretched to claim his wife. But the Death-Boy was a yard from him, and caught hold of his jacket collar in his fiery fist. Howie half-turned to beat him back, grabbing at the shrieking Jo-Beth with his free hand. The fire had reached her long hair, and it suddenly ignited, a column of fire rising off her scalp. Howie reached for her, plainly intending to carry her out of the fire. Her arms were open, and as he took hold of her, they closed around him.

Tesla had witnessed horrors aplenty along the road that had brought her to this moment, but nothing—not in the Loop, not at Point Zero—as terrible as this. Jo-Beth was no longer shrieking now. Her body was jerking around as though she was in the throes of a fit, her spasms so violent Howie could not carry her out of the fire. Nor could he detach himself. Her blackened arms were molded around him, keeping him a prisoner in the midst of the pyre.

Tommy-Ray had started to shout now: a shrill, lunatic din. He started to tear Howie away from Jo-Beth, or at least tried to, but the fire had spilled from wife to husband, and their bodies had become a single column of flame and flesh. Jo-Beth's spasms had ceased. She was surely dead. But there was life left in Howie still. Enough to raise his hand behind his wife's head, and let it loll on his shoulder, as though the heat were nothing and they were slow-dancing in the flames.

This tender gesture was his last. His withered legs gave out, and he went down onto his knees, carrying Jo-Beth down with him. He made no sound, even to the last. The couple seemed to kneel face to face in the flames, Howie's hand still cradling Jo-Beth's head, Jo-Beth's head still laid upon Howie's shoulder.

As for Tommy-Ray, he now retreated from the bodies towards the far side of the road, where his ghost-legion lingered after their punishment. Whether at his instruction or no, they came to him, and rose around him, blanketing him. The flames were smothered, and he sank down into the midst of his entourage. Sobs escaped him. So did his sister's name, repeated over and over.

Tesla looked back at the fire around Howie and Jo-Beth. With its fuel almost devoured, it had quickly died down. The bodies were shriveled, but it was still possible to make out their arms, wrapped tightly around one another.

Behind her, Tesla heard somebody sob. She didn't bother to turn. She knew who it was.

"Satisfied now?" she said to the little girl. "Going to go home?"

"Soon—" came the reply.

This time it was not the floating voice of the child who replied. Puzzled, Tesla looked round. There was a grassy slope behind her, with perhaps half a dozen large bushes planted upon it, all dead. The three witnesses were perched upon the uppermost branches, but so lightly it seemed unlikely they had any weight whatsoever. They had put off their previous appearances in favor of what Tesla assumed were their real faces. They reminded her of porcelain puppets, their heads small, their features simple, their skin nearly white. They were cocooned, however, in garments of papal excess, layer upon gilded layer. There was very little variation among their appearance, but she assumed the individual closest to her had been little Miss Perfection, by the way she now addressed Tesla.

"I knew we chose well," she, he, or it said. "You are all we hoped you'd be."

Tesla glanced back at Tommy-Ray. He was still blanketed in mist, still grieving. But he'd come for the child sooner or later. This was no time to be quizzing her unwanted patrons in depth. Just a few questions, and she'd have to go.

"Who the hell are you?"

"We are Jai-Wai," the creature replied. "And I am Rare Utu. Yie and Haheh you already know."

"That doesn't tell me anything," Tesla replied. "I want to know what the fuck you *are*."

"Too long a story to tell you now," Rare Utu replied.

"Then I'm never going to hear it," Tesla said.

"Perhaps it's better that way," Yie replied. "Better you go on your way."

"Yes, go on," the third of the trio said. "We want to know what happens next—"

"Haven't you seen enough?" Tesla said.

"Never," said Rare Utu, almost sorrowfully. "Buddenbaum showed us so much. So much."

"But never enough," Yie said.

"Maybe you should try getting involved," Tesla said.

Rare Utu actually shuddered. "We could *never* do that," she said. "*Never.*"

"Then you'll never be satisfied," Tesla said, and turning from them, she started back towards her bike, casting glances at Tommy-Ray now and again. She needn't have worried. He was still smothered in the mists of his legion.

She broke a couple of bungee cords out of the tool box and carefully secured the baby to the back seat. Then she started the engine, half expecting the sound to bring the legion scurrying to find her. But no. When she rounded the corner the Death-Boy and his ghosts had not moved. She drove on past them, glancing back once to see if the Jai-Wai had gone from the slope. They had. They'd had the pleasure of the triple tragedy here, damn them, and moved on to find some other entertainment. She felt nothing but contempt for them. Plainly they were of some higher order of being, but their vicarious interest in the spectacle of human suffering sickened her. Tommy-Ray couldn't help himself. They could.

And yet, for all her rage towards them, the phrase they had repeated over and over kept returning, and would, she supposed, until death deafened her.

What next? That was the eternal inquiry. *What next? What next? What next?*

VIII

i

"A re they planning to crucify you, D'Amour?"

Harry turned from the crosses in front of which he stood, and looked at the monkish fellow who was emerging from the mist. He was a study in simplicity, his dark clothes without a single concession to vanity, his hair cropped until it barely shadowed his scalp, his wide, plain face almost colorless. And yet, there was something here Harry knew, something in the eyes.

"Kissoon?" The man's blank expression soured. "It *is*, isn't it?"

"How did you know?"

"Untether me and I'll tell you," Harry said. He'd been tied to a stake driven into the ground.

"I'm not that interested," Kissoon replied. "Did I ever tell you how much I like your name? Not Harold; Harold's ridiculous. But D'Amour. I may take it, when you're up there." He nodded towards the middle cross. Camalicl and Baitho were in the midst of taking down the woman's body. "Maybe I'll have a hundred names," Kissoon went on. Then, dropping his voice to a whisper: "And maybe none at all." This seemed to please him. "Yes, that's for the best. To be nameless." His hands went up to his cheek. "Maybe faceless too."

"You think the lad's going to make you King of the World?" Harry said.

"You've been talking to Tesla."

"It's not going to happen, Kissoon."

"Are you familiar with the works of Filip the Chantiac? No? He was a hermit. Lived on an island, a tiny island, close to the coast of Almoth's Saw. Very few people dared go there—they feared the currents carrying them past the Chantiac's island and washing them up on the Iad's shore—but those who did came back with fragments of his wisdom—"

"Which were?"

"I'll get to that. The thing is, Filip the Chantiac had been the ruler of the city of b'Kether Sabbat in his time, and he'd been all the things we pray for our leaders to be. But even so there was dissension and violence and hatred in his city. So one day he said, 'I can't deal with the taint of Sapas Humana any longer,' and took himself off to his island. And at the end of his life, when somebody asked him what he wished for the world, he said, 'I dream only of an end to courage and compassion and devotion. An end to human strength, and to human endurance. An end to brotherhood. An end to sisterhood. An end to defiance in grief, and consolation in laughter. An end to hope. Then we may all return to fishes, and be content.'"

"And that's what you want?" Harry said.

"Oh yes. I want an end—"

"To what?"

"To that damn city for one," Kissoon replied, nodding down the mountain in the direction of Everville. He came a little closer. Harry scrutinized his face, looking for some crack in the mask, but he could see none. "I spent a lot of time sealing up *neirica* across the continent," he said. "Making sure that when the Iad finally came through it would be over *this* threshold they came."

"You don't even know what they are—"

"It doesn't really matter. They're bringing the end of things. That's what's important."

"And what'll happen to you?"

"I'll have this hill," Kissoon said, "and I'll look down from it on a world of fishes."

"Suppose you're wrong?"

"About what?"

"About the Iad. Suppose they're pussycats?"

"They're everything that's rotted in us, D'Amour. They're every fetid, fucked-up thing that feeds on our shit, and waits to be loosed when nobody's looking." He came closer still, until he was just out of Harry's range. His hand had gone to his chest. "Have you looked into the human heart recently?" he said.

"Not in the last couple of days, no."

"Unspeakable, the things in there—"

"In you, maybe."

"*Everyone*, D'Amour, *everyone!* Rage and hatred and appetite!" He pointed back towards the door. "That's what coming, D'Amour. It won't have a human face, but it'll have a human heart. I guarantee it."

Behind Harry, the body of Kate O'Farrell was dropped to the ground. He glanced back at her, the agony of her last moments fixed upon her face.

"A terrible thing, the human heart," Kissoon was saying. "A very terrible thing."

It took Harry a moment to persuade his eyes from the dead woman's face, as though some idiot part of him thought he might learn some way to avoid her suffering by studying it. When he looked back at Kissoon, the man had turned away, and was heading up the slope again. "Enjoy the view, D'Amour," he said, then was gone.

ii

As Joe left the city streets to follow the Iad along the shore—to witness, if nothing more, to witness—the ground began to shudder. To his left, the dream-sea threw itself into a greater frenzy than ever. To his right, the highway that ran along the edge of the beach cracked and buckled, falling away in places.

The mass of Iad, which was now within two hundred yards of the door, was apparently indifferent to the tremors. It had resembled many things to Joe in his brief time knowing it. A wall, a cloud, a diseased body. Now it looked to him like a swarm of minute insects so dense it kept every speck of light and comprehension out as it seethed towards its destination.

The door had grown considerably in the hours since he'd first stepped through it. Though its lower regions were still wreathed in mist, its highest point was now several hundred yards above the beach, and rising even as he watched, cracking the heavens. If there were angels on the other side, he thought, this would be the time for them to show their faces; to swoop and drive the Iad back with their glory. But the crack went on growing, and the Iad advancing, and the only response was not from heaven, but from the earth on which his spirit stood—

The rock's convulsions did not go unfelt on Harmon's Heights. The tremors ran through ground and mist alike, causing some measure of alarm amongst Zury's faction. Harry couldn't see them, but he could hear them well enough, their songs of welcome—which they had only recently begun—decaying into sobs of fearful expectation as the violence in the rock escalated.

"Something's happening on the shore," Coker said to Erwin.

"We should stay away," the lawyer counseled, casting a fearful look up at the crosses. "This is worse than I thought."

"Yes it is," Coker said. "But that doesn't mean we should be cowards!"

He hurried on, past the crosses and the tethered D'Amour, up the slope, which was rolling in mounting waves. Reluctantly, Erwin followed, more out of a fear that he would lose his one companion in this insanity than from any genuine urge to know what lay ahead. He wished—ah, how he wished—for the life he'd led before he'd found McPherson's confession. For pettiness, for triviality; for all the little things that had vexed him. Digging through his fridge for something that smelled bad; finding a stain on his favorite tie; standing in front of the mirror wishing he had more hair and less belly. Perhaps it had been a bland life, puttering on without purpose or direction, but he'd liked its banality, now that he was denied it. Better that than the crosses, and the door, and the whatever was coming through it.

"Do you see?" said Coker, once Erwin had caught up with him.

He saw. How could he not? The door, stretching up through the mist as if eager to pierce the stars. The shore on the far side of it, every rock and pebble upon it rising in a solid wave.

And worst of all, the swarming wall of energies approaching across that shore—

"Is that it?" he said to Coker. He'd expected a more palpable manifestation of the harm it brought. A devourer's tools, a torturer's stare, a lunatic's frenzy: something to advertise its evil. But instead, here was a thing he could have discovered by closing his eyes. The busy darkness behind his lids.

Coker yelled something over his shoulder by way of reply, but it was lost in the tumult. The shore beyond the threshold was convulsing, as though it were a body in the throes of a grand mal, each spasm throwing boulders the size of houses up into the air; and up, and up again, the scale of the seizure increasing exponentially as Erwin watched. Coker, meanwhile, strode on, the ground around him growing increasingly insolid, stones, dirt and plant life melted into filthy stew. It had mounted up to his waist now, and it seemed even his phantom body was subject to its currents, because he was twice thrown off his feet and washed back in Erwin's direction.

He wasn't daring the tide simply to get a better view of the quaking shore. There were two other figures in the grip of this liquid earth—an old woman hanging on to the back of a man who looked to be in the last moments of life—and Coker was struggling to reach them. Blood ran from a grievous wound on the side of the man's head, where something—perhaps a rock—had sheared off his ear and opened his scalp to his skull. Why Coker was so interested to study these unfortunates was beyond Erwin, but he strode into the melted dirt himself to find out.

This time he heard what Coker was hollering.

"Oh Mary, mother of God, look at her. Look!"

"What is it?" Erwin yelled back.

"That's Maeve, Toothaker! *That's my wife!*"

The escalating turmoil had not dissuaded Bartho from his task. The more the ground swayed and shook the more attentive to his duties he became, as though his redemption lay in finishing the business of crucifying D'Amour.

He was bending to the task of untethering Harry to bring him to the cross when one of Blessedm'n Zury's acolytes—a creature with a round, piebald face, and the bow-legged gait of a midget—rolled into view and picked up Bartho's hammer. The crucifier instructed him to put it down, but instead the acolyte rushed at him and struck him in the face, the blow so fast and fierce the bigger man was felled. Before he could get up again the acolyte struck him a second and third time. Pale fluid sprayed from Bartho's cracked skull, and he let out a rhythmical whoop. If it was a call for help, it went unanswered, or perhaps unheard, given the din that was shaking earth and air. With his whoop failing him Bartho started to rise, but the hammer was there to meet him, and this time cracked his face from chin to brow. He sank down, the blood gushing from him, and lay twitching under the empty cross.

Harry had meanwhile been working at his knotted wrists with his teeth, but before he could free himself the acolyte tossed the bloodied hammer away, pulled a knife from Bartho's belt and waddled over to free the prisoner.

"Doesn't take much, does it?" the man said to Harry, his voice a nasal whine. "One rope and you're reduced to an animal." He worked at the knot with the blade, his back to the crack. "What's going on over there?" he wanted to know.

"I can't make out." The rope was cut, and fell away. "Thank you," D'Amour said. "I don't know why—"

"It's me, Harry. It's *Raul.*"

"Raul?"

The round face beamed. "I finally got a body of my own," he said. "Well, not quite. There's something else in here with me, but it's virtually cretinous."

"What happened to Tesla?"

"I was separated from her, at the threshold. The power there, it's overwhelming. It pulled me out of her head."

"And where is she now?"

"She went to look for Grillo, I think," Raul said. "I'm going to go look for her, before it's all over. I want to make my farewells. What about you?"

Harry's gaze went back to the maelstrom around the door.

"When the Iad comes—" Raul said.

"I know. It'll take hold of my head and fill it with shit." There were already signs of the Iad's proximity in the air. Harry's eyes were stinging, his head whining, his teeth aching. "Is it the Devil, Raul?"

"If you want it to be," Raul replied.

Harry nodded. It was as good an answer as any.

"You're not coming then?" Raul said.

"No," Harry replied. "I came up here to see what the Enemy looks like and that's what I'm going to do."

"Then I'll wish you luck," Raul said, as another wave of shudders passed through the ground. "I'm out of here, D'Amour!"

With that, he turned and stumbled away between the crosses, leaving Harry to continue his interrupted ascent. There were fissures gaping in the ground around him, the widest of them a yard across, and growing. A viscous mess of liquefied earth was rolling down from the area around the crevices, and running off into them.

And beyond it, the *neirica* itself, which was now fully thirty yards wide, offering Harry a substantial view of the shore. It was no longer the seductive place he'd glimpsed from the chambers of the Zyem Carasophia. The Iad's titanic form blocked out the dream-sea, and the shore itself was a rising hail of rock and dirt. It didn't block the Iad's influence upon his mind, however. He felt a wave of intense self-revulsion taint his thoughts. It was a sickness in him, the taint told him, wanting to see this abomination face to face: a disease from which he would deservedly die.

He tried to shake the poison from his head, but it wouldn't go. He stumbled on with images of death filling his mind's eye: Ted

Dusseldorf's body on a gurney, covered by a sheet; the mangled flesh of the Zyem Carasophia, sprawled around their chamber; Maria Nazareno's corpse, slumped in front of a candle flame. He heard them sobbing all around him, the dead, demanding explanation.

"You never did understand."

He looked off to his right, and there, wedged in a fissure, his arms trapped at his sides, was Father Hess. He was wearing the wound Lazy Susan had given him all those years ago, and they were as fresh as if he'd just received them.

"I'm not here to accuse you, Harry," he said.

"You're not here, period," Harry said.

"Oh come on, Harry," Hess said, "since when did that matter?" He grinned. "It's not reality that causes the trouble, Harry. It's illusions. You should have learned that by now."

That was all this was, Harry knew: an illusion. He was conjuring it up. Every word, every drop of blood. So why couldn't he just tear his eyes from it and move on?

"Because you loved me," Hess said, as though Harry had asked the question aloud. "I was a good man, a loving man, but when it came down to it you *couldn't save me.*" He coughed, bringing up a gruel of bilious water. "That must have been terrible," he said. "To be so *powerless.*" It stared at Harry pityingly. "The truth is, you still are," he said. "Still looking to see the Enemy clearly, just once, just once."

"Are you finished?" Harry said.

"A little closer—" Hess begged.

"What?"

"Closer, I said." Harry approached the martyr. "That's better," Hess said. "I don't want this spread around." He dropped his voice to a growl. "It's all done with mirrors," he said, and suddenly his arms sprang from the fissure and seized hold of Harry's lapels. Harry wrestled to escape the illusion's grip, but it dragged him down, inch by inch, and as it did so the flesh of its face seemed to slide away in ribbons. There was no bone beneath. Just a brownish pulp.

"See?" it said, its mouth a lipless hole. "Mirror-men. Both of us."

"*Fuck you!*" Harry yelled, and pulling himself free of Hess's grip he stumbled backwards.

Hess shrugged and grinned. "You never did understand," he said again. "I told you over and over and over and over—"

Harry turned his back on the pulpy face.

"And over and over—"

And looked back towards the door. He had a second, perhaps two, to realize that the Iad, or some part of it, was no longer in that world but this. Then the ground around the Uroboros rose up in a solid wall and all that had gone before—the din, the tremors, the revulsion—seemed like a dream of perfect peace.

iii

It was the ride of Phoebe's life: cocooned in a stony womb, and carried in the grip of the rock as it rose to block the Iad's way. Texas had promised she'd be safe, and safe she was, her capsule borne through the convulsing ground and up on fountains of liquid rock with such ease she could have threaded a needle had she wished to take her eyes off the sight he was showing her. The rock was a protean face, shaped and driven by his will. One moment she was plunged into grottoes where the Quiddity ran in icy darkness, the next the strata were dividing before her life so many veils, the next she seemed to be in the midst of a vital body, with liquid rock blazing in its veins, and the King's fossil heart beating like thunder all around.

Sometimes she heard his voice in the walls of her womb, telling her not to be afraid.

She wasn't. Not remotely. She was in the care of living power, and it had made her a promise she believed.

The Iad, on the other hand, for all its motion and its purpose, reminded her of death. Or rather, of its prelude: of the torments and the hopelessness she'd seen death bring. As it approached the door, and the earth rose up to block its passage, the rock pierced it and clusters of dark matter, almost like eggs, spilled from it, all the fouler for their glittering multiplicity. Even if they *were* eggs, Phoebe thought, there was death in every gleaming one. When they struck the shore they burst and their gray fluids raced over the stones as if nosing out the darkness beneath.

Wounded though it was, its appetite for the Cosm was not dulled. Besieged by the rock, it continued to advance, though the very shore it was crossing had become a second sea, a surf of stone rising up to drive it back.

It was difficult for Phoebe to make out quite what was happening in the chaos, but it seemed that the Iad had pressed a portion of its body towards the threshold and was in the act of crossing over when Texas raised a wall of earth with such speed that he severed the questing limb from the main. The Iad let out a sound the like of which Phoebe had never heard in her life, and as it was reeling in its anguish the whole landscape laid before her—highway, dunes, and shore—was simply upended. She saw the Iad topple, bursting in a thousand places, spilling its substance, as what had been horizontal moments before rose in a vertical mass above the enemy. It teetered there a long moment. Then it descended upon the Iad—a solid sky, falling and falling—driving the wounded mass into the pit where the shore had been.

Even as this spectacle unfolded, Phoebe felt the cocoon shudder, and she was carried away from the maelstrom at speed, deposited at last close to the city limits, where the shore was still intact. She had no sooner come to rest than the cocoon cracked and deteriorated, leaving her exposed. Though she was perhaps two miles from the doorway the ground was shaking violently and a hail of rock fragments was falling all around, some of the shards big enough to do her damage. Texas had exhausted all his strength, she assumed, to do what he'd done. She could not expect his protection any longer. She got to her feet, though it was difficult to stand upright and, shielding her head with her hands, she stumbled back in the direction of the city.

She returned her gaze along the shore once in a awhile, but the rain of dust and stones went on relentlessly, and she could see very little through the pall.

Nothing of the Iad, certainly, nor of the door through which she'd stepped to come into this terrible world.

Both had disappeared, it seemed: enemy and door alike.

---

iv

The first casualty on the Heights was Zury, who had been standing at the threshold when the shore on the other side erupted. Caught by a blast of fractured rock he was thrown back into the liquefied ground. His acolytes went to dig him out while the Iad's vanguard, severed from the main by the wall, thrashed in its fury, stirring earth and air alike into chaos. Overturned in the dirt, the Blessedm'n's rescuers drowned along with their master. As for the Iad, though it was but a small part of the invader, it was still immense: a ragged, roiling mass of forms, spilling its blood in the *neirica*'s vestibule. The crack convulsed from end to end, as though the violence done in its midst was unmaking it. On the far side, earth and sky seemed to switch places. Then a storm of stones descended, the crack closed like a slammed door, and all that was left on the Heights was chaos on chaos.

Harry had been flung to the shuddering ground before the Iad appeared and, certain he would be flung down again if he attempted to rise, stayed where he was. From this vantage point he saw Kissoon walk on the liquefied rock towards the wounded Iad. He seemed indifferent to the tremors, and fearless, his head thrown back to study the invader in its frenzy. It seemed to be unraveling. Pieces of its substance, ten, fifteen feet in length were spiraling skyward, trailing sinew; other fragments, the smallest the size of a man, the largest ten times that, were circling in the air, as though hungry to devour themselves. Others still had dropped to the fluid ground, and were immersing themselves in the dirt.

Kissoon reached into his coat, and pulled from its folds the rod

Harry had seen him wield in the Zyem Carasophia's chamber. It had been a weapon then. But now, when he raised it above his head, it seemed to offer a point of focus for the Iad. They closed upon it from all directions, their torn bodies spilling their filth upon him. He raised his face to meet it as though it were a spring rain.

Harry could watch this no longer. His head was awash with images of the dead and death, his eyes stinging from the sight of Kissoon bathing in the Iad's filth. If he didn't go now, despair would have him. He crawled away on his belly, barely aware of his direction, until the crosses came in sight, stark against the sky. He had not expected to see them again, and his aching eyes filled with tears.

"You came back," said a voice out of the darkness. It was Raul.

"And . . . you stayed," Harry said.

Raul came to his side and, crouching, gently coaxed Harry to his feet. "I was curious," he said.

"The door's closed."

"I saw."

"And the Iad that's here—"

"Yes?"

Harry cleared the tears from his eyes, and stared up at the cross where he'd come so close to being nailed. "It bleeds," he said, and laughed.

IX

i

*I*n Everville, the denial had stopped, and so had the music. Not even those so drunk with liquor or love they'd forgotten their names could pretend all was well with the world. There was something happening on the mountain. It shook the sky. It shook the streets. It shook the heart.

Some of the celebrants had come out into the open air to get a better look at the Heights and exchange theories as to what was at hand. Some of the proffered explanations were rational, some ludicrous. It was an earth tremor, it was a meteor crashing. It was a landing from the stars, it was an eruption from the earth.

We should get out of here, said some, and began their hurried departures.

We should stay, said others, and see if something happens we'll remember for the rest of our lives...

Alone in the now-vacated Nook, Owen Buddenbaum sat and obsessed on Tesla Bombeck. She had been a late addition to this drama but now she was beginning to look distressingly like its star.

He knew her recent history, of course. He'd made it his business. She hadn't proved herself any great visionary, as far as he could gather; nor had she shown evidence of any thaumaturgical powers. Tenacious she was; oh yes, certainly that. But then so were terriers. And—though it didn't please him to grant her this—she had a measure of raw courage, along with an appetite for risk.

There was one story about her that nicely illuminated those aspects of her nature. It had Bombeck bargaining with Randolph Jaffe in or under the ruins of Palomo Grove. By this stage of events Jaffe had failed in his aspirations as an Artist and was reduced, so the story went, to a volatile lunatic. She had needed his help. He had been loath to give it. She'd goaded him, however, until he'd handed her one of the medallions like that buried under the crossroads, and told her that if she comprehended its significance within a certain time period she would have his help. If she failed, he would kill her.

She'd accepted the challenge, of course, and had succeeded in decoding the cross; thus making the Jaff her ally, at least for a time. The fact that she'd worked out what the symbols meant was not of any great significance in Buddenbaum's estimation. The fact that she'd put her life on the line while she grappled with the problem was.

A woman who would take such a risk was more dangerous than a visionary spirit. If Seth brought her to him, he would have to be ready to dispatch her at the flicker of an eye—

ii

Tesla was halfway down the path to Phoebe's front door before she saw the figure rising from the step.

"I've been looking all over for you," he said. It was the boy from the crossroads; Buddenbaum's sallow apprentice. "I'm Seth," he said.

"What do you want?"

"It's not really what *I* want—"

"Whatever you're selling, I'm not interested," she said, "I've got a baby here needs tending to."

"Let me help," Seth replied. There was something almost pitiful in his appeal. "I'm good with kids."

She was too exhausted to refuse. She tossed the keys in his direction. "Pick 'em up and open the door," she told him. While he did so she cast a glance up at the mountain, which was just visible between the houses opposite. There was a smoking spiral of mist around the summit.

"Do you know what's going on up there?" Seth said.

"I've got a pretty good idea."

"It's dangerous, right?"

"That's an understatement."

"Buddenbaum says—"

"Have you got the door open yet?"

"Yeah." He pushed it wide.

"Put on the light." He did so. "I don't want to talk about Buddenbaum till I'm sure the kid's okay," she said, stepping into the house.

"But he says—"

"I don't give a shit *what* he says," she told him calmly. "Now, are you going to help me or are you going to get out?"

iii

Harry and Raul were almost at the tree line when Raul stopped in his tracks.

"Somebody's talking —" he said.

"I don't hear anything."

"Well I do," Raul replied, looking around. There was nobody in sight. "I heard voices like this before, when I was sharing Tesla's head."

"Who the hell is it?"

"The dead, I think."

"Hmm."

"Aren't you bothered?"

"Depends what they want."

"He's saying something about his wife, finding his wife —"

* * *

"He hears me!" Coker yelled. "Thank God! He hears me!"

Erwin looked back up at the mountaintop, thinking again of what Dolan had said, standing outside his candy store: We're like smoke. Maybe it wasn't so bad as that, being smoke, if the world was going to be overtaken by what he'd seen up there, coming through a crack in the sky.

Coker, meanwhile, was still talking to the creature who'd saved D'Amour, directing him into the trees . . .

There were two people there in the shadows. One a woman of some antiquity, sitting with her back to a tree trunk, drinking from a silver flask. The other a man lying face-down a few yards from her.

"He's dead," the woman said as Harry leaned over to examine the man. "Damn him."

"Are you one of Zury's people?" Harry asked her.

The woman hacked up a gob of phlegm and spat on the ground inches from Harry's foot. "Mary Mother of God, do I *look* like one of Zury's people?" She jabbed her finger in Raul's direction. "*That's* one of his!"

"He may look like one," Harry replied, "but he's got the soul of a man."

"Thank you for that," Raul said to Harry.

"Well, and are *you* man enough to carry me down?" the woman said to Harry. "I'd like to see my city before the world goes to Hell."

"*Your* city?"

"Yes, *mine!* My name's Maeve O'Connell, and that damn place"—she pointed down through the trees towards Everville— "wouldn't even *exist* if it weren't for me!"

"Listen to her," Coker rhapsodized. "Oh Lord in Heaven, listen to her." He was kneeling beside the harridan, his bestial face covered in bliss. "I know now why I didn't go to oblivion, Erwin. I know why I waited on the mountain all these years. To be here to see her face. To hear her voice."

"She'll never know," Erwin said.

"Oh but she will. This fellow Raul will be my go-between. She's going to know how much I loved her, Erwin. How much I *still* love her."

"I don't want your hands on me!" Maeve was roaring at Raul. "It's this man's back I'll be on or I'll damn well crawl down there on my hands and knees." She turned to Harry. "Now are you going to pick me up or not?"

"That depends," said Harry.

"On what?"

"On whether you can shut your mouth or not."

The woman looked as though she'd just been slapped. Then her narrow mouth twitched into a smile. "What's your name?" she said.

"D'Amour."

"As in *love?*"

"As in love."

She grunted. "That never got me any place I wanted to go," she said.

"She doesn't mean that," Coker said. "She *can't—*"

"People change," Erwin said. "How many years has it been?"

"*I* haven't changed," Coker said.

"You can't be the judge of that," Erwin replied. "It's no use breaking your heart over this."

"Easy for you to say. What did you ever *feel?*"

"Less than I should," Erwin replied softly.

"I'm sorry," Coker said. "I didn't mean that."

"Whether you meant it or not it's the truth," Erwin said, turning his gaze from the woman—who was now clambering up onto D'Amour's back—and again studying the Heights. "You think there's more time than there is," he said, half to himself. "And there's always less. Always."

"Are you going to come with us?" Coker said.

"I'm glad for you," Erwin replied. "Seeing your wife again. I'm really glad."

"I want you to be part of it, Erwin."

"That's nice to say. But—I'm better, staying here. I'll be in the way."

Coker slipped his arm around Erwin's shoulder. "What's to see here?" he said. "Come on—they're leaving us behind."

Erwin glanced round. The trio were already twenty yards away down the slope. "Come see the city my sweet lady built," Coker said. "Before it disappears forever."

X

i

*A*fter the tumult, silence.

The rain of stones dwindled to a drizzle and then ceased altogether. The sea calmed its frenzy, and came lisping against the shore, its waters thickened into mud. There was no sign of life moving in its shallows, unless the glistening remnants of Iad's eggs, bobbing in the filth, could be called life. Nor were there birds.

Phoebe sat amid the rubble of what had once been Liverpool's harbor, and wept. Behind her, the ships that had once swayed at anchor here were smashed in the streets; streets that had been reduced to gorges between piles of smoking debris.

What now? she thought. Plainly there was no way home. And little or no hope of finding Joe, now that she'd lost her guides in this wilderness. She could bear the idea of never seeing Everville again—easily—but the thought of being separated from Joe forever was unendurable. She would have to hide that likelihood from herself for a while, or else she'd lose her sanity.

She turned her thoughts to the fate of King Texas. Could rock die, she wondered, or was he simply lying low for a while, to recover his strength? If the latter, perhaps he might show his face again and help her in her search. A negligible hope, to be sure, but enough to keep her from utter despair.

After a time, her stomach began to rumble, and knowing that hunger would only make her weepier, she got up and headed into the devastation in search of sustenance.

Just a couple of miles from where she wandered, Joe stood in the veils of dust still falling where the door had been, and turned over the significance of all he'd witnessed. This was not, he knew, a total victory; not by any stretch of the imagination. For one, some portion of the Iad had found its way over the threshold into the Cosm before the shore rose to annex it. For another, he was by no means certain the greater part, which now lay buried somewhere under his spirit's feet, was dead. And for a third, he doubted the continent from which this force had come was now deserted. The invasion party might have been defeated, but the nation that had sent it out was still intact, somewhere beyond the Ephemeris. It would come again, he knew. And again, and again. Whatever the Iad were—the dreamers or the dreamed—whatever ambitions they nurtured, they had today sent a force into the Helter Incendo, where it would doubtless be able to prepare for a larger, and perhaps definitive, invasion.

Whether he would have any part to play in the defense of the Cosm he didn't know and, for now at least, he didn't much care. He had the more immediate of his own identity to solve. It had been a fine adventure that had brought him in a circle back to this spot: the voyage on *The Fanacapan*, that sweet reunion with Phoebe in the weeds, the journey to b'Kether Sabbat, his final encounter with Noah and his discoveries in the belly of the Iad—all of it extraordinary. But now the journey was over. *The Fanacapan* was sunk; Phoebe was somewhere in Everville, mourning him; b'Kether Sabbat was presumably in ruins; Noah dead; the Iad buried.

And what was he, who had taken that journey? Not a living man, for certain. He'd lost all that he could have identified as Joe, except for the thoughts he was presently shaping, and how certain were they? Was he then some function of the dream-sea? Or a sliver of the Zehrapushu? Or just a memory of himself, that would fade with time?

What, damn it, *what?*

At last, exasperated by his own ruminations, he decided to make his way back into the street in search of the fire watchers who had seemed to see him in the form of their answered prayers. Perhaps if he discovered one among them who understood the rudiments of life after death he might find some way to communicate, and learn to understand his condition. Or failing that to simply come to peace with it.

Phoebe returned to Maeve O'Connell's house on Canning Street more by accident than intention, though when she finally found herself standing before its gates she could not help but think that her instincts had brought her there. The house was in better shape than most she'd passed, but it had not survived the cataclysm unscathed. Half of its roof had fallen in, exposing both beams and bedrooms, and the path to the front door was littered with slate, guttering, and broken glass.

Once inside, however, she found the lower level almost exactly as she left it. With her stomach demanding its due she went straight to the kitchen, where mere hours before she'd got herself tipsy on mourningberry juice, and made herself something to eat. This time there was no judicious sandwich construction. She simply heaped cold cuts and pickles and bread and cheese and a variety of fruits into the middle of the table and set to. Her stomach was tamed after ten minutes or so and she slowed her rate of consumption somewhat, washing her food down with a spritzer made of two parts water to one of the juice. After half a glass of this a pleasant languor crept upon her, and she allowed herself to muse on the subjects that had earlier brought tears.

Perhaps, after all, she had a few things to be grateful for. She wasn't dead, which was a wonder. She wasn't crazy. She'd never again sleep and wake in the bed she'd shared with Morton all those years, nor turn up to work on a drizzling Monday morning and find half a dozen flu-ridden depressives dripping on the step, but was any of that cause for sorrow or self-pity? No. She had followed her best hope for happiness through a door that had slammed behind her. There was no way back, and it was no use sniveling about it.

The wind had risen while she was eating and was blowing dust against the kitchen window, darkening the interior. She got up and found an oil lamp, which she lit and carried upstairs, lighting lamps as she went. It was a little eerie. The empty passageways, the empty rooms, the paintings on the walls—which she'd really not noticed when she'd first explored the house but which were almost all risqué—staring down at her. Every now and again the rock beneath the city would growl and settle. The walls would creak. The windows would rattle.

Eventually she found her way up to Maeve O'Connell's suite, the ceiling of which was still intact, and feeling like a thief (and enjoying the feeling) she examined the contents of the three wardrobes and the chest of drawers. There were clothes in abundance, of course, and hats and books and perfumes and bric-a-brac, endless bric-a-brac.

Had the old woman dreamed all this into being, Phoebe wondered, the way King Texas had described her dreaming the city? Had she spoken the clothes, then slept and woken to find them hanging here, ready to be worn and fitting perfectly?

If so, Phoebe was going to have to learn the trick of it, because nothing in these wardrobes was faintly suitable, and her summer dress had been reduced to filthy tatters. And while she was dreaming things up, maybe she'd supply herself with a few luxury items. A television (would she have to dream the programs too? if so, they'd all be reruns), a modern toilet (the plumbing in the house was primitive), perhaps an ice cream maker.

And maybe, eventually, a companion. Why not? If she was going to live the rest of her life here—and it seemed she had no choice in the matter—then she was damned if she'd spend those years alone. Sure, she'd seen some survivors in the ruins on her way here, but why look for solace among strangers when she could conjure up somebody for herself?

At last, having searched the room from one end to the other, she realized that she hadn't opened the drapes and, with much effort (there were several thicknesses of fabric, and they'd not been moved, she guessed, in many years), she managed to haul the drapes apart. She was not prepared for the splendor of the sight that awaited her. The window that the drapes had concealed was huge. It offered her a panorama of what had once been the harbor, and beyond it, Quiddity, its once-crazed waters placid. Though there was no sun in the sky, there was nevertheless a pinprick clarity to the scene. If she'd had the desire and the patience she could surely have counted every ripple on the face of the dream-sea.

Gazing out over the waters, she remembered with a sigh her meeting with Joe, in the bed of weeds. Remembered how she'd almost lost herself into the bliss of formlessness, while he, and they, had pleasured her. Was it possible, she wondered, to dream Joe? To close her eyes and raise from memory the man she had lost? It wouldn't be the real thing, of course, but better some semblance of him, like a treasured photograph, than nothing at all. Perhaps he might even share a bed with her.

She put her hand to her cheek. She was hot.

"You should be ashamed, Phoebe Cobb," she told herself with a little smile.

Then she dragged a coverlet and a pillow off Maeve's four-poster (she couldn't bring herself to sleep among the litter of King Texas's love-letters) and, making a bed for herself in the glittering light off the dream-sea, she lay down to see if she could bring herself a likeness of the man she loved.

XI

"*T*here's somebody outside," Seth said.

They were in the kitchen, Tesla at the table trying to coax Amy into eating a few spoonfuls of cereal mushed up in warm milk, Seth eating baked beans cold from the can while he gazed out at the dark yard. "You think it's the avatars?"

"Probably," Tesla said. She glanced up and stared out into the gloom. She couldn't see them, but she could feel their gaze.

"Owen told me—" Seth said.

"Owen?"

"Buddenbaum. He says we're like apes to them. When they watch us, it's like us going to the zoo."

"Is that right?" Tesla said. "Well, for what it's worth I've been taught a thing or two by an ape in my time."

"You mean Raul."

She looked at the boy. "How do you know about Raul?"

"Owen told me all about you. He knows everything about who you are, where you've been, who you've hooked up with—"

"Why the hell would I be of any interest to him?"

"He said you were . . . you were— "

"The gist'll do."

"A *significant irrelevancy*," Seth beamed. "That's what he said

— 583 —

exactly. I asked him what that meant, and he said you being here was all an accident, because you don't belong in this story—"

"Fuck the story."

"I don't see how we can," Seth said. "Whatever we do, wherever we go, we're still telling the story."

"Buddenbaum again."

"No. Seth Lundy." He set down his can of beans. "Here," he said. "Let me have a go at feeding her."

Tesla didn't argue. She let Seth relieve her of the baby, who had so far refused her ministrations, and headed out into the backyard, where she guessed she'd have a view of the Heights. The guess was good. She had to wander twenty, twenty-five yards from the house before the summit cleared the roof, but when it came into view there was much to see. The mist circling the summit had become ragged, and when she studied the holes she glimpsed large, clotted forms moving there.

"The Iad's here," she announced.

"We didn't know until now," said a voice out of the darkness.

She didn't bother to look round to find the speaker. It was one of the trio; which one of them was academic.

"Buddenbaum didn't tell you?" Tesla said.

"No."

"Strange."

"We're not certain he *knew*," said another voice. This she recognized as that of the little girl, Rare Utu.

"I find that hard to believe," Tesla said, still studying the mountain. What were they *doing* up there? Nesting? "You're here. The Iad's here. That's no accident."

"You're right," came the reply. "But that doesn't mean it was *planned*. The history of Sapas Humana is filled with synchronicities."

She turned to them now. They were standing on the darkness a dozen yards from her, barely delineated by the light from the kitchen windows. Looking at them now she realized they were not as indistinguishable from one another as she'd thought. Rare Utu stood a little way to the right, her face carrying just a trace of the girlishness she had pretended. Some distance from her was the individual who'd passed himself off as a jug-eared comedian, Haheh. Again, though the signs of his public face were subtle, they were there to be seen. And closest to Tesla, his features the most plainly tainted by his assumed personality, was the moronic child, Yie. Of the three it was he who regarded Tesla with the most suspicion.

"You seem to know human beings very well," she said.

"Oh yes," Haheh replied. "We never tire of seeing the Great and Secret Show played out."

"My God—" she said, "were you in Palomo Grove?"

"Regrettably no," Rare Utu told her. "We missed that one."

"That was the beginning of our discontent with Owen, truth to tell," Haheh said. "We were growing tired of the same old slaughters. We had an appetite for something more—how shall I put it?"

"Apocalyptic," Yie prompted.

"So he arranged *this?*" Tesla said.

"So it seems," said Haheh. "But his genius has deserted him. This afternoon, for instance. It should have been a triumph, but it just fizzled out. We were very disappointed. That's why we came after you. We want another Palomo Grove. People driven mad by their own nightmares."

"Have you no *sympathy?*" Tesla said.

"Of course," said Rare Utu. "We suffer a great deal at the sight of your suffering. If we didn't why would we seek it out?"

"Give me that again," Tesla said.

"Better to show her," Haheh said.

"Are you sure that's wise?" Yie said. His beady eyes had narrowed to slits.

"I trust her," Haheh replied, descending the shadows and bypassing Yie to stand a few yards from Tesla. As he did so his cocooning robes unfolded. They were more magnificent inside than out, the garments freighted with gems whose colors she could put no name to. Some were the size of fruits—peaches and pears—all overripe, all oozing liquid light.

"This one," Haheh said, gesturing to a jewel the size of an egg with his vestigial arm, "I got it in Des Moines, watching the most terrible tragedy. Three generations, or was it four—?"

"Four," Rare Utu said.

"Four generations killed in one night in a gas main explosion. An entire family name, wiped out. Oh, it was pitiful. And this one"—he said, indicating a gem that had more shades of amber than a Key West sunset—"I got in Arkansas, at the execution of a man who'd been wrongly convicted of murder. We were watching him fry, in the knowledge that the true culprit was smothering infants at that very moment. That was *hard,* very hard. Sometimes I see a milkiness in the blebs, you know, and I think it's there to remind me of the babes—"

While he maundered on, Tesla realized that the finery he'd unfurled was not a garment at all: It was his body. The gems, the blebs as he'd called them, were indeed a kind of fruit, grown from flesh and sorrow. Part remembrance, part decoration, part trophy, they were gorgeous scabs, marking the places where he'd been pierced by *feeling.*

"I see you're amazed," Rare Utu said.

"And revolted, I think," Yie said.

"A little," Tesla said.

"Well," Rare Utu replied appreciatively, "that's something to savor." She stared hard at Tesla. "Buddenbaum was always very careful never to let us know what he felt. It's a consequence of his inversion, I think, the ease with which he conceals himself."

"Whereas you—" Haheh said.

"You are so *naked,* Tesla," Utu said. "Simply being with you is a show unto itself."

"We could have such times," Haheh cooed.

"Aren't you forgetting something?" Tesla said.

"What's that?"

"When you first met me, you said you knew I was going to die. And as it happens I know for a fact that's true."

"Details, details," Rare Utu replied. "Life is in our gift, Tesla. Why you've seen for yourself how Buddenbaum outruns death. He took a bullet to the head this very afternoon, and by now he'll be nearly mended."

"We can't confer immortality upon you," Haheh said.

"Nor would we want to," Yie pointed out.

"But we *can* offer you our extended lifespan. *Considerably* extended, if we find our relationship productive."

"So—if I say *yes*, I get to live, as long as I create experiences for you?"

"Precisely. Make us *feel*, Tesla Bombeck. Give us stories to wring our hearts."

While Rare Utu was speaking, two contrary voices raged in Tesla's head. "Take it!" one yelled. "It's what you were born to do! This isn't churning out movies for popcorn-gobbling imbeciles! You'll be *writing life!*" The other voice was equally adamant. "It's grotesque. They're emotional leeches! Work for them and you throw you humanity to the wind!"

"We need an answer, Tesla," Haheh said.

"Explain one thing to me," she said. "Why don't you just do this yourselves?"

"Because we must not become involved," Rare Utu replied. "It would dirty us. Taint us."

"*Ruin* us," said Yie.

"I see."

"Well?" said Haheh. "Do you have an answer?"

Tesla pondered a moment. Then she said, "Yes, I have an answer."

"What?" said Rare Utu.

She thought a moment longer. "Maybe," she replied.

When she got back inside the house she found Seth had taken Amy into the living room, and was sitting on the sofa, gently rocking her.

"Did she eat anything?"

"Yeah," he said quietly. "She's okay." He looked down at Amy fondly. "Sweet little face," he said. "I heard you talking to them out there. What do they want?"

"My services," Tesla said.

"In place of Owen?" Tesla nodded. "He figured that's what they were up to."

"Where is he now?"

"He'd said he'd wait for you at the Nook. It's a little restaurant off Main Street."

"Then I shouldn't keep him waiting any longer," Tesla said.

Seth got to his feet very slowly, so as not to disturb Amy. "I'll come with you. I'll watch over the baby while you deal with Owen."

"You should know something about Amy—"

"She's not yours, is she?"

"No. Her mother and the man I thought was her father are dead. And the guy who may be her *real* father will be coming looking for her."

"Who is he?"

"His name's Tommy-Ray McGuire, but he prefers to be called the Death-Boy." While she was explaining this her eyes went to the cards spread out on the coffee table. "Are these yours?" she asked.

"No, I thought they were yours." She knew at a glance what they represented, of course. Lightning, cloud, ape, cell: all stations of Quiddity's cross. "Must be Harry's," she said, and sweeping them into a little pack pocketed them and headed for the door.

ii

Two-thirds of the way down the mountain slope, passing through a patch of trees more thinly spaced than elsewhere, the woman on Harry's back said, "Stop a moment will you?" She surveyed the terrain. "I swear—this is where my daddy was murdered."

"Was he lynched too?" Raul replied.

"No," she said. "Shot by a man who thought my daddy was a servant of the Devil."

"Why'd he think that?"

"It's a long story, and a bitter one," the O'Connell woman said. "But I found a way to keep his memory alive."

"How did you do that?" said Harry.

"His name was Harmon," she replied, and as they moved on

away from the place she told Harry and Raul the whole bitter story. She told it without melodrama and without rancor. It was simply a sorrowful account of her father's last hours, and of how he had passed his vision of Everville to his daughter.

"I knew it was my duty to build a city, and call it Everville, but it was hard. Towns don't just spring up because people dream them—well, not in this world, at least. There has to be a reason. A good reason. Maybe there's a place on a river where it's easy to cross. Maybe there's gold in the ground. But my valley just had a piddling little creek, and nobody ever found gold here. So I had to find some other reason for people to come here, and build houses and raise families. That wasn't easy even at the best of times, and these weren't the best of times. See, the man who killed my daddy became a preacher in Silverton, and he used the pulpit to spread all kinds of rumors about how there was a hole to Hell right here on Harmon's Heights, and devils flew out of it at night.

"So, after a couple of years of being almost alone here, I decided to take myself off to Salem, where maybe I'd find some people who hadn't heard what the preacher Whitney was saying. And one day, I'm talking to this man in a feed store, and I'm telling him about my valley, my sweet valley, and how he should come look at it for himself, and suddenly he digs out a silver dollar and slaps it on the counter and says to me: *Show me.* And I say to him: *It's quite a ways from here.* And he puts his hand on my leg, and starts to pull up my skirt and he says: *No, it's real near.*

"Then I realized what he was talking about, and I called him every kind of name under the sun and I took myself off in a high old fury. But as I was walking home, I got to thinking about what he'd said, and I thought maybe the best way to bring men to my valley was first to bring *women*—"

"Clever," said Raul.

"Men don't always follow religion. They don't always follow common sense. But women, they follow. Women they'll suffer every kind of privation for. This has been proved, over and over." She tapped Harry on the shoulder. "You've been stupid for women, have you not?"

"It's been known," said Harry.

"So, you see, I had my method. I knew how I would bring men to fill up my valley. And once they were there, they'd start to build my daddy's dream city for me."

"I get the *theory* of it," Raul said. "But how did it work?"

"Well, my father had been given a cross, by a man called Buddenbaum—"

"Buddenbaum?" Harry said. "It can't be the same man—"

"You've heard of him?"

"*Heard* of him? I shot him this afternoon."

"Dead?"

"No. He was very much alive when I saw him last. But like I said, it can't be the same Buddenbaum."

"Oh I think it could," Maeve said. "And if it is—oh, *if it is*—I have some questions I want that bastard to answer."

iii

Larry Glodoski and his soldiers had staggered out of Hamrick's Bar feeling ready to take on anything that crossed their path. They had guns, they had God, and they could all whistle Sousa: What more did an army need?

The civilian population was not so sanguine, however. A lot of people—particularly the tourists—had decided that whatever was happening on the mountain, they'd prefer to see it on tomorrow's news than experience it in the flesh, and they were beating a hasty and disorderly retreat. More than once, as the men made their way down Main Street, they had to step aside to let a carload of vacationers careen by.

"*Cowards!*" Waits yelled after one such vehicle had almost mounted the sidewalk to avoid them.

"Let them go," Glodoski slurred. "We don't need bystanders. They'll only get in the way."

"You know what?" Reidlinger said, seeing a sobbing woman bundling her kids into a RV, "I'm going to have to leave you guys to it. I'm sorry Larry, but I got kids at home, and if anything happened to them—"

Glodoski gave him the fish-eye. "Okay," he said. "So what are you waiting for?" Reidlinger started to apologize again, but Glodoski cut him short. "Just go," he said. "We don't need you." Reidlinger made a shamefaced departure. "Anybody else want to go, while the going's good?" Larry asked.

Alstead cleared his throat, and said, "You know, Larry, we've all of us got responsibilities. I mean, maybe we're better leaving this to the authorities."

"Are you deserting too?" Glodoski wanted to know.

"No, Larry, I'm just saying—"

Bosley interrupted him. "Well now . . . " he said, and pointed down the block at the two people coming in their direction. He knew and despised them both. The woman for her foul mouth, the youth at her side for his sodomitic ways.

"These two are dangerous," he said. "They're accomplices of Buddenbaum's."

"There's not two of them," Bill Waits observed, "there's three. Lundy's carrying a baby."

"Stealing children now," said Bosley. "How low will they stoop?"

"Wasn't she the one at the crossroads?" Larry said.

"She was."

"Gentlemen, we've got work to do," Larry declared, stepping past Bosley. "I'll front this. You just keep your eyes open."

Tesla and Seth had seen the quartet by now, and were crossing the street to avoid them. Glodoski stepped off the sidewalk to intercept them, demanding as he approached, "Whose kid is that?" His inquiry was ignored. "I'm not going to ask again," he said. "Whose baby have you got there?"

"It's none of your damn business," Tesla said.

"What are you going to do with it?" Bosley said, his voice shrill.

"Shut up, Bosley," Larry said.

"They're going to murder it!"

"You heard him, Bosley," said Tesla. "Shut the *fuck* up."

Now Bosley overtook Larry, pulling out his gun as he did so. "Put the baby down," he squealed.

"I said *I'd* deal with this," Glodoski snapped.

Bosley ignored him. He strode on towards Tesla, leveling his gun at her as he did so.

"*Jesus,*" Tesla said. "Haven't you got anything better to do?" She jabbed her finger in the direction of the Heights. "There's something coming down that mountain, and you don't want to be here when it arrives."

As if to punctuate her warning, the streetlamps began to flicker, and then went out. There were cries of alarm from all directions. "Do we run?" Seth murmured to Tesla.

"We can't risk it," she said. "Not with Amy."

A few lights came back on again, but they were dim and fitful. Bosley, meanwhile, had stepped in to claim the baby from Seth's arms.

"You've got no right to do this," Seth protested.

"You're a cocksucker, Lundy," Alstead said. "That gives us all the right we need."

Bosley had a grip on the baby now, but Seth refused to relinquish her.

"Alstead!" Bosley hollered, "give me a hand here."

Alstead didn't need a second invitation. He came around the back of Seth, and grabbed hold of his arms. Larry, meanwhile, had taken out his own gun and had it leveled at Tesla, to keep her from intervening.

"What's going on up there?" he said to her, nodding in the direction of the Heights.

"I don't know. But I *do* know we're all in deep shit when it gets here. If you want to do some good why don't you evacuate the people who need help, instead of baby snatching?"

"She's got a point, Larry," said Waits. "There's a lot of old folks—"

"We'll get to them!" Glodoski blustered. "I got it all planned."

Amy began bawling now, as Bosley wrested her from Seth's arms.

"She's missing your tits, Lundy," Alstead leered, reaching out to paw his captive's chest.

Seth responded by jabbing his elbow in Alstead's belly, hard enough to drive the wind from him. Cursing, Alstead spun Seth around and punched him in the face, twice, three times, solid blows to nose and mouth. Seth stumbled backwards, his legs betraying him, and fell to the ground. Alstead moved in to kick the youth, but Waits held him back.

"C'mon. *Enough!*"

"Little cocksucker!"

"Leave him alone, for Christ's sake!" Waits hollered. "We didn't come out here to beat up kids. Larry—?"

Glodoski glanced over at Waits, and as he did so Tesla ducked beneath his arm and flew at him, intending to disarm him. She failed. There was a brief, ragged struggle—the gun twice discharged into the air—before he caught her a backhanded blow. She reeled before it.

Waits, meanwhile, was hauling the bloodied Seth to his feet, while yelling at Alstead to keep his distance, and Bosley was fumbling for his own gun, which he'd pocketed before snatching the child.

"*Tesla*—" Seth hollered, "*look out!*"

She shook the blotches from in front of her eyes in time to see not one but two weapons being leveled at her.

"*Run!*" Seth told her.

She had a moment only in which to decide, and her instinct carried the day. Before Glodoski or Bosley could get a bead on her she was away, pelting down the block. Behind her she heard Glodoski yelling. Then he fired. The bullet carved a niche in the sidewalk a yard to her right.

"Larry, *stop!*" Waits was shouting. "Are you crazy?"

Glodoski simply fired again. This time the bullet shattered a store window behind her. She made the corner without a third shot being fired, and glanced round to see that Waits had caught hold of Glodoski and was attempting to wrest the weapon from him. She didn't wait for the outcome, but darted out of sight and range.

She bitterly regretted losing Seth and Amy, but the encounter had served a purpose Glodoski and his bully-boys would regret. If there was power to be begged, stolen, or borrowed from Buddenbaum then she'd have it, and damn the niceties.

<hr>

iv

As Harry, Maeve, and Raul crossed Unger's Creek the lights in the streets ahead, which had been flickering for a quarter of an hour, gave up completely. The trio halted for a moment, their other senses attenuated in the sudden darkness. There was no comfort to be had from them, however. They heard only panicked cries from the city, and from the thicket and trees silence, as though every nightbird and insect knew what Sapas Humana did not: that death was coming, and the loudest would be found first. As for the other senses, their news was no better. For all the balm of the summer air, it carried that tang Harry had nosed entering the building at Ninth and Thirteenth: rotten fish and smoking spice. It was on the tongue too, tempting the stomach to rebellion.

"They're coming," Raul said.

"It had to happen."

"Will you hurry yourself, then?" Maeve said. "I want to see my city before we all go to Hell."

"Anywhere in particular?" Harry said.

"Yes, as you're asking," Maeve replied. "There's a crossroads—"

"What is it about those damn crossroads?" Harry said.

"It's where I lived. Where we built our house, my husband and me. And let me tell you, that house was a glory. A glory. Until the sons of bitches burned it down."

"Why did they do that?"

"Oh, the usual. Too much righteousness and too little passion. What I would give for a taste, just a taste, of the way it was at the beginning, when we still had hope . . ."

She fell into silence for a few moments. Then she erupted afresh: "Take me there!" she hollered. "Take me there! Let me see the ground where it all began!"

XII

*T*esla found Buddenbaum sitting in the Nook, as Seth had told her she would. The little coffee shop was deserted, and dark but for the fire Buddenbaum had started on a plate in front of him, feeding it with scraps of menu.

"I was about to give up on you," he said, with a smile that was very nearly sincere.

"I got waylaid."

"By some of the locals?"

"Yes." She came to his table, and sat down opposite him, plucking a napkin from the dispenser to mop the sweat from her face. Then she plucked another and blew her nose.

"I know what you're thinking," Buddenbaum said.

"Oh, do you?"

"You're thinking: Why should I give a shit about these fucking people? They're cruel and they're stupid, and when they're afraid they just become more cruel and more stupid."

"You're exempting *us* from this, of course."

"Of course. You're a Nunciate. And I'm—"

"The Jai-Wai's man."

Buddenbaum grimaced. "Do they know you've come here?"

"I told them I was going walkabout, to think things through."

595

She dug in her pocket, and pulled out the cards. "Ever seen these before, by the way?" She laid them on the table. Buddenbaum regarded them almost superstitiously, his mouth tight.

"Whose are they?" he said, his fingers hovering over them but not making contact.

"I don't know."

"They've been in powerful hands," he said appreciatively.

Tesla went back into her pocket in pursuit of a stray card, and brought out the remains of the reefer she'd confiscated from the crucifixion singer. She sniffed it. Whatever it contained, it smelled appealingly pungent. She plucked a spill of burning cardboard off the plate, and putting the reefer to her lips, lit it.

"Will you work for them?" Buddenbaum said.

"The Jai-Wai?" she said. He nodded. "I doubt it."

"Why not?"

"They're psychotic, Buddenbaum. They get a buzz out of seeing people suffer."

"Don't we all?"

"No." She inhaled, just half a lungful. Held the smoke.

"Oh, come on Bombeck," Buddenbaum replied. "You wrote for the movies. You know what gives people a thrill."

She exhaled a breath of lilac smoke. "The difference is: This is real."

Buddenbaum leaned forward. "Are you going to share that?" he said. She passed the joint over the fire. It had induced some subtle visual hallucinations. The flames had slowed their licking, and the beads of sweat on Buddenbaum had become crystalline. He drew on the joint, and spoke as he held his breath. "What's real to us isn't what's real to the rest of the world. You know that." He turned his gaze towards the dark street. A family of five was hurrying along the sidewalk, the children sobbing. "Whatever they're suffering," he said, exhaling now, "and I don't mean to diminish them in saying this—it's an animal response. That's not real in any absolute sense. It will pass. All things pass, sooner or later."

She remembered Kissoon, in Toothaker's house. This had been his wisdom too.

"The life of the flesh, the animal life, is transient. It melts, it fades away. But what's *hidden* in the flesh—the enduring spirit—that has permanence, or at least the *hope* of permanence. It's up to us to make that hope a reality."

"Is that why you want the Art?"

Buddenbaum drew on the joint again, passed it back to Tesla, and leaned back in his chair. "Ah . . . the Art," he said.

"I was there when the Jaff got it. You know that?"

"Of course."

"He didn't exactly flourish."

"I know that too," Buddenbaum said. "But then he was weak. And crazy. I'm neither. I've lived two and a half lifetimes, preparing for what's about to happen here. I'm ready to handle power."

"So why do you need me?"

Buddenbaum rolled his eyes to the ceiling. "This ganga's good," he said. "The truth is, it's not *you* I need, Tesla."

"It's the Jai-Wai."

"I'm afraid so."

"Do you want to tell me why?"

Buddenbaum considered this for a moment.

"If you want my help," Tesla said, "you're going to have to trust me."

"That's difficult," Buddenbaum said. "I've had so many solitary years, keeping my secrets."

"I'll make it easy for you," Tesla said. "I'll tell you what *I* know. Or what I've guessed." She picked up the cards, and shuffled them in the firelight, her eyes on Buddenbaum as she spoke. "You buried one of the Shoal's medallions at the crossroads, and over the years it's been gathering power somehow. And now you're ready to use it, to get you the Art."

"Good . . ." said Buddenbaum, "go on . . ."

She pushed the fire-plate aside, and started to lay the cards out on the table, one by one. "The Jaff taught me something," she said, "when we were together under the Grove. I was looking at the cross *he* had, trying to work out what the symbols meant—*these* symbols"—she waved the cards. "And he told me: *To* understand *something is to* have *it*. When you know what a symbol means, it's no longer a symbol. You have the thing itself in your head, and that's the only place anything needs to be." She looked down at the cards for a moment. When she glanced back up at Buddenbaum his gaze was icy. "Everything *dissolves* at the crossroads, doesn't it? Flesh and spirit, past and future, it all turns into *mind*." She had found all the cards picturing the body spreadeagled at the center of the cross, and now proceeded to assemble them. "But for you to access the Art, you need to have all the possibilities there in the stew. There at the crossroads. The human pieces. The animal pieces. The dreaming pieces—" She stopped. Stared at him. "How am I doing?" she said.

"I think you know," said Buddenbaum.

"So—where was I?"

"Dreaming pieces."

"Oh yes. And the last pieces, of course. The pieces that complete the pattern." She had the very card in her hand: the symbol at the top of the vertical arm. She turned it to him. "The pieces of *divinity*."

Buddenbaum sighed.

"The Jai-Wai," she said, and tossed the card down onto the table.

There was twenty, maybe thirty seconds of silence. Finally Buddenbaum said, "Can you imagine how difficult it's been to arrange this? To find a place where I had a hope of all these forces coming at some point or other? This wasn't the only spot I buried a cross, of course. I put them all over. But there was something about this place—"

"And what was that?"

He considered a moment. "A little girl called Maeve O'Connell," he said.

"Who?"

"She's the one who buried the cross for me, back before this little burg existed. I remember hearing her father call her name—*Maeve, Maeve*—and I thought, this is a sign. The name's Irish. It's a spirit who comes to men in their dreams. And then when I met the father, I realized how easy it would be to inspire him. Make him build me a honeypot of a city, where every manner of creature came, and there in the middle of it, my little cross could be gathering power."

"Everville's your creation?"

"No, I can't make that claim. The *inspiration* was mine, but that's all. The rest was made by ordinary men and women going about their lives."

"So did you keep an eye on it?"

"For the first three or four years I came looking, but the seed had failed to take. The father had died on the mountain, and the daughter had married a damn strange fellow from the other side, so people kept their distance."

"But the city got built anyway?"

"Eventually, though I'm damned if I know how. I didn't come back here for a long time, and when I did, what do you know? There was Everville. Not quite the Byzantium I'd envisaged but it had its possibilities. I knew that wanderers from the Metacosm came here now and again, for sentimental reasons. And they crossed paths with Sapas Humana, and they went their way, and all the while the medallion gathered its powers underground."

"You waited a long time."

"I had to be ready, in myself. Randolph Jaffe isn't the only one who lost his wits thinking he could handle the Art. As I said before, I've lived several lifetimes, thanks to Rare Utu and her buddies. I've used the years to *rarefy* myself."

"And now you're ready?"

"Now I'm ready. Except that one piece of the puzzle I need has deserted me."

"So—you want me to bring them to you."

"If you'd be so kind," Buddenbaum said, with a little inclination of his head.

"If I succeed you'll help me keep the Iad from destroying the city?"

"That's my promise."

"How do I know you won't just piss off into your higher state of being and let the rest of us go down in flames?"

"You have to believe I won't break the last promise I made as a mortal man," Buddenbaum replied.

It wasn't an airtight offer, Tesla thought, but it was probably the best she was going to get. While she was turning it over, Buddenbaum said, "One more thing."

"What's that?"

"Once you've brought the Jai-Wai to the crossroads, I want *you* to get out of the city."

"Why?"

"Because this afternoon, when I had everything in place, the working failed because of you."

"How'd you work that out?"

"There was no other reason," Buddenbaum replied. "You're a Nunciate. The power couldn't choose which of us to flow to, so it stayed where it was."

"All right. So I'll get out."

"Now I'm the one who needs the promise."

"You've got it."

"Good enough," Buddenbaum said. "Now—why don't you burn the cards?"

"Why?"

"As a . . . gesture of good will."

Tesla shrugged. "Whatever," she said, and gathering them up she tossed them into the slow flames. They caught quickly, flaming up.

"Pretty," said Buddenbaum, rising from his chair. "I'll see you at the crossroads then."

"I'll be there."

ii

She felt the presence of the enemy the moment she stepped out into the street. Memories of Point Zero came flickering back into her head—the desolation, the dust, and the Iad, rising like a seething tide. They would be here soon, bringing their madness and their appetite for madness, turning over this city, whose only crime was to have been founded in the name of transcendence.

And once it was trampled, what then? Out into the Americas, to find new victims, new adherents? She knew from her years of wandering that it would not go unwelcomed. There were people across this divided nation hungry for catastrophe, plotting to welcome the millennium in with bloodshed and destruction. She'd heard them at diner counters, muttering into their coffee; seen them at the side of highways, raging and raging; brushed by them in busy streets (passing for sane, most of them; dressed and polished and civil): people who wanted to murder the world for disappointing them.

Once the Iad arrived they wouldn't need to talk to themselves any longer. They wouldn't need to berate heaven, or put on smiles when all they wanted to do was scream. They would have their day of wrath, and the power she'd seen unleashed at Point Zero would be suddenly inconsequential.

God help her, in her time, she might have numbered herself among them.

She didn't have to go far to find the Jai-Wai. A hundred yards from the Nook she heard a great commotion, and seeking out its source found the chief of police, along with two of his officers, attempting to calm a mob of perhaps fifty Evervillians, all of whom were demanding he do something to protect their city. Many of them had flashlights and had them trained on the target of their ire. Ashen and sweaty, Gilholly did his best to calm them, but circumstances were against him. The Iad's influence was getting stronger as they descended from the Heights, and the already demented crowd was steadily losing its grip of reality. People started to sob uncontrollably or shriek at the limit of their lungs. Somebody in the throng began speaking in tongues.

Realizing he was losing what little grip he had, Gilholly pulled out his gun and fired it into the air. The crowd simmered down a little.

"Now listen up!" Gilholly yelled above the murmurs and sobs. "If we just stay calm we can ride this out. I want everybody to go to the Town Hall, and we'll wait there until help arrives."

"Help from *where?*" somebody asked.

"I got calls out all over, don't you worry," Gilholly replied. "We'll have support from Molina and Silverton in the next half hour. We're going to get the lights back on and—"

"What about what's going on on the mountain?"

"It's all going to get taken care of," Gilholly said. "Now will you *please* clear the streets so when help gets here nobody's hurt?" He pushed through the crowd, beckoning for folks to follow. "Come on, now! Let's get going."

As the mob began to move off Tesla glimpsed a white dress and, making her way towards it, found Rare Utu, her girlish guise as flawless as ever, watching the scene with a smile on her face. It broadened into a grin at the sight of Tesla.

"They're all going to die," she beamed.

"Won't that be fun," Tesla dead-panned.

"Have you made up your mind?"

"Yes," said Tesla. "I accept the offer. With *one* proviso."

"And what's that?" said Yie, stepping out of the retreating crowd wearing his human face.

"I don't want to be the one to tell Buddenbaum. You have to do it."

"Why do we even need to bother?" Haheh said, emerging at Yie's side.

"Because he served you all those years," Tesla said. "And he deserves to be treated with some dignity."

"He's not going to perish the moment we leave," Haheh pointed out. "He'll have a quick decline as the years catch up with him, but it won't be so terrible."

"Then tell him that," Tesla said. She looked back at Rare Utu. "I don't want him coming after me with a machete, because I took his job."

"I understand," the girl said.

Yie scowled. "This is the *first* and *last* time we accede to your desires," he said. "You should be grateful to be serving us."

"I am," Tesla said. "I want to tell you wonderful stories and show you wonderful sights. But first—"

"Where is he?" said Haheh.

"At the crossroads."

iii

"Thank God for the darkness," Maeve said as they made their way through the murky streets. "I swear if I saw this ugliness in the plain light of day I'd weep." She demanded to be set down in front of the Hamburger Hangout, so that she could be appalled. "Ugly, ugly, ugly," she said. "It looks like something made for children."

"Don't break your heart over it," Raul said. "It won't be standing much longer."

"We were going to build a city that could stand *forever*," Maeve said.

"Nothing lasts that long," said Harry.

"Not true," said Maeve. "Great cities become legends. And legends don't die." She scowled at the Hamburger Hangout. "Anything would be better than this," she said. "A pile of rubble! A hole in the ground!"

"Can we get a move on?" Harry said, glancing back towards the mountain. They'd been meandering through the streets for maybe twenty minutes now, with the O'Connell woman confidently giving directions back to the place where she'd lived, though it was increasingly plain that she was lost. Meanwhile Kissoon and his Iadic legion had been descending from the Heights. Their tangled mass was now no longer visible, which surely meant they'd reached the bottom of the slope. Perhaps they were already in the city, and the demolition Maeve so relished underway.

"It's not far now," the old woman said, making her way unaided to the nearest intersection and looking in all directions. "That way!" she said, pointing.

"Are you sure?" said Harry.

"I'm sure," she said. "It was at the very center of the city, my whorehouse. The first house that was ever raised, in fact."

"Did you say *whorehouse?*"

"Of course they burned it down. Did I tell you that? Burned down half the neighborhood at the same time, when the fire spread." She turned back to Harry. "Yes, I said whorehouse. How do you think I built my city? I didn't have a river. I didn't have gold. So we built a whorehouse, Coker and me, and I filled it with the most beautiful women I could find. And that brought the men. And some of them stayed. And married. And built houses of their own. And"—she opened her arms, laughing out loud—"lo and behold! There was Everville!"

—————————————————— **iv** ——————————————————

Laughter? Bosley thought, hearing Maeve's amusement echo through the streets. How pitiful. Somebody had lost their mind in all this chaos.

He was sheltering in the doorway of the Masonic Hall at present, to keep himself (and the baby he was still carrying) out of the way of people and vehicles. Ten yards down the block, Larry had the Lundy kid up against the wall and was interrogating him. He wanted to know where the sodomite Buddenbaum was hiding out, but Seth wasn't letting on. Every time Seth shook his head Larry traded him a blow: a tap sometimes; sometimes not. Waits and Alstead hung around at a distance. Waits had broken into Dan's Liquor Store on Coleman Street, and got himself a couple of bottles of bourbon, so he was quite happy watching the interrogation over Larry's shoulder. Alstead was sitting on the sidewalk, with his shirt hiked up, examining the abrasions he'd suffered during the earlier skirmish with Lundy. He had already told Larry that when the questioning was finished he would be taking over. Bosley didn't give much for Lundy's chances.

Quietly, he began to pray. Not just for his own salvation, and that of the child, but so that he could explain to the Lord that this was not the way he'd intended things to be. Not remotely.

"I just wanted to do your will," he said, doing his best to ignore the sound of Seth's moans, and of the blows that kept landing. "But everything's got so confused. I don't know what's right any more, Lord . . ."

A fresh chorus of cries rose from somewhere nearby, and drowned out his pleas. He closed his eyes, trying hard to keep his thoughts coherent. But with one of his senses sealed he became aware of information the others were receiving. There was a smell in the air; like the garbage behind the diner in a heatwave, only tinged with a sweetness that made it all the fouler. And along with the stench there was a sound, deep in his head, as though somebody was testing a tuning fork against his skull.

He couldn't bear to stay where he was any longer. Without announcing his departure to the others he slipped from the doorstep, and down the block, turning the first corner he came to, which delivered him into Clarke Street. It was completely deserted, for which he was grateful. From here he could get back to the diner, keeping off the main streets. Once there, he'd take a quick rest, then load a few belongings into the back of the car, and get out of the city. As for the baby, he'd take her along; protect her in the Lord's name.

He was crossing the street when a gust of cold wind found him. Instantly, the baby began to sob.

"It's okay," he murmured to her. "Now hush, will you?"

Another gust came, harder and colder than the first. He drew the child closer to his chest and as he did so something moved in the darkness on the opposite side of the street. Bosley froze, but he'd already been spotted. A voice came out of the shadows, as comfortless as the wind that carried it.

"You found her—" it said, and the speaker shambled out of the deepest shadow into plainer view. It was burned, profoundly burned. Black in places, and yellow-white in others. As it approached, a carpet of living dust lay down before it.

Bosley started to pray again.

"*Don't!*" said the burned man. "My mother used to pray. I hate the sound of it." He opened his arms. "Just give me my little girl."

Bosley shook his head. This was the final test, he thought; the encounter for which the incidents with the virago and the sodomites had been preparing him. This was when he discovered what his faith was worth.

"You can't have her," he said determinedly. "She's not yours."

"Yes she is," the burned man said. "Her name is Amy McGuire and I'm her father, Tommy-Ray."

Bosley took a backwards step, making calculations as he went. How far was it to the corner? If he shouted now, would Glodoski hear him above Lundy's moans?

"I don't want to do you any harm," Tommy-Ray McGuire said. "I don't want any more death . . . " He shook his head as he spoke, and flakes of matter dropped from his encrusted face. "I've seen too much . . . too much . . . "

"I can't give her to you," Bosley said, striving to sound reasonable. "Maybe if you can find her mother."

"Her mother's dead," Tommy-Ray said, his voice cracking. "Dead and gone."

"I'm sorry."

"The baby's all I've got now. So I'm gonna find some place where me and my little girl can live in peace."

My little girl. Lord God in Heaven, Bosley thought, take this poor man's insanity from him. Relieve him of his suffering and let him rest.

"Give her to me," the creature said, moving towards Bosley afresh.

"I'm afraid . . . I can't . . . do that . . . " Bosley said, retreating to the corner. Once there, he loosed a yell—"*Glodoski! Alstead!*"—and pelted back down the block, grateful to find them still tormenting Lundy.

"Where the fuck did you go?" Larry demanded.

Bosley felt a chill wind at his back, and glanced over his shoulder to see McGuire rounding the corner, with the carpet of dust rising around him.

"*Christ Almighty!*" Larry said.

"Keep runnin'!" Alstead hollered. "It's closin' on you!"

Bosley didn't need any encouragement. He fled towards the men, the dust swirling around his legs now, as if to trip him up.

"Out of the way!" Larry yelled, racing towards him. Bosley changed direction, and Glodoski fired at McGuire, who stopped in his tracks. The dust kept coming however, flinging Glodoski against the brick wall. He started to sob for help, but he got out no more than a word or two before his pleas were choked off. In an instant the dust had enveloped him, and his body was lifted off the ground, still pinned against the wall.

Alstead, who had only reluctantly given up his assault on Seth, now let the boy slide to the ground and went to Glodoski's aid. But the dust had done its work. In a matter of ten seconds, if that, it had dashed Larry's brains out against the brick; now it turned on Alstead. He started to back away, raising his hands in surrender, but the dust was on him like a rabid dog and would surely have slaughtered him too had Bosley not begged Tommy-Ray to call it off.

"No more death!" he said.

"All right," said McGuire, and called the dust back to his feet, leaving Alstead sobbing on the sidewalk a few yards from Waits, who had passed out in the gutter and remained there comatose.

"Just give me the kid," Tommy-Ray said to Bosley. "And I'm gone."

"You won't hurt her?" Bosley said.

"No."

"Don't—" Seth murmured, hauling himself to his feet. "In God's name, Bosley—"

"I've got no choice," Bosley replied, and proffered the child.

Seth was on his feet, and with a broken cry in his throat stumbled towards Bosley. But his bruised body couldn't carry him fast enough. Tommy-Ray claimed Amy from Bosley's hands and gathering her to his burned body whistled for the killing cloud to follow him down the street.

Seth was abreast of Bosley now, sobbing out his frustration.

"How could . . . you . . . *do* . . . that?"

"I told you: I had no choice."

"You could have *run*."

"He would have found me," Bosley replied, staring blank-eyed into the darkness that already enveloped Tommy-Ray.

Seth didn't waste his breath arguing. He had little enough energy left in his bruised body, and it was a long trek from here back to the crossroads, where all of tonight's journeys were bound to end.

XIII

*A*t the crossroads Buddenbaum stared down into the ground, into the dark where the medallion lay, gathering power.

The end's almost here, he thought. The end of the stories I've made and the stories I've manipulated, and those I wandered through like a bit player and those I've endured like a prisoner. The end of all my favorite clichés: tragic mismatches and farcical encounters; tearful reunions and deathbed curses. The end of *Once upon a time* and *Now we shall see* and *Can I believe my eyes?* The end of final acts; of funeral scenes and curtain speeches. The end of ends. Think of that.

He would miss the pleasure of stories—especially those in which he'd appeared in some unlikely guise or other—but he'd have no need of them very soon. They were solace for the rest of humanity, who were mired in time and desperate to glimpse something of the grand scheme. What else could they do with their lives but suffer and tell tales? He would not be of that tribe much longer.

"*I have nothing but you, my sweet Serenissima,*" he said, turning on his heel, surveying the streets in all directions. "*You are my sense, my sanity, and my soul.*"

The pain in these words had moved him in the past, many, many times. Now he only heard the word-music, which was pretty in its simplicity, but not so pretty he would miss hearing it again.

"*Go from me now and I am lost in the great dark between the stars—*"

As he spoke he saw Tesla Bombeck approaching down the street. And coming after her the girl, the fool, and the cretin. He went on declaiming: "*And cannot ever perish there, for I must live until you still my heart.*"

He smiled at Tesla, at them all. Opened his arms wide in welcome.

"*Still it now!*"

She looked at him with puzzlement on her face, which he rather enjoyed.

"*Still it now!*" he said again. Oh, but it was fine, roaring over the din of screams and sobs, while his victims came wandering towards him.

"*I beg thee, still it now, and let my suffering cease!*"

Doing her best to conceal her nervousness, Tesla looked back in the direction of the Iad. She could see nothing of the invader itself, but two fires had started in the streets closest to the base of the mountain, and flames from the larger of them were leaping up over the roofs, seeding sparks. Whatever their origins—desperate defense measures or accidents that were going unchecked—the fires would surely spread. In which case the invader would be lording itself over a city of charcoal and ash by morning.

She returned her gaze to Buddenbaum, who had given up his theatrics and was now standing in the middle of the crossroads with his hands behind his back. She was still thirty yards from him, and, the only light being that of the distant conflagrations and a few uneasy stars, she could not confidently read his expression. Would he give her a signal, she wondered, when she'd brought the Jai-Wai close enough that she could retreat? A nod? A wink? She silently berated herself for not prearranging some sign. Well, it was too late now.

"Buddenbaum?" she said.

He inclined his head a little. "What are you doing here?" he said.

Not bad, she thought. He was pretty convincing.

"I came to say. . . well, I guess to say goodbye."

"What a pity," Buddenbaum replied. "I'd rather hoped we'd have a chance to get to know each other."

Tesla glanced back at Rare Utu. "It's up to you now," she said, studying the Jai-Wai's face in the gloom. She could see no sign of suspicion, but that didn't mean much. The features were a mask, after all. "Maybe I should just head off and leave you to it," she suggested.

"If that's what you'd prefer," Rare Utu replied, walking on past Tesla to Buddenbaum.

"I think she should stay," Yie said. "This isn't going to take very long."

Tesla looked back at Buddenbaum, who seemed to be staring at his feet. His hands were at his sides now, and tightly clenched. He's holding something down, she thought, he's suppressing some evidence of what's going on here.

He wouldn't be able to do so much longer. Haheh had by now wandered on past Tesla, sloughing off his human form as he did so, and he seemed to have become aware that the street was simmering.

"Do you have some kind of surprise for us, Owen?" he asked mildly.

"I'm . . . always trying my best to . . . to keep you *diverted*," Buddenbaum replied. The stress of his attempts at containment were audible in his voice. It had lost most of its music.

"You've done well for us over the years," Rare Utu said. She sounded almost sorrowful.

"Thank you," Owen replied. "I've always tried my best. I'm sure you know that."

"We also know that great stories have a shape to them," Utu went on. "They bud, they come to flower, and then . . . inevitably—"

"*Get on with it, will you?*" Yie said from behind Tesla. She turned her head an inch or two, just glimpsing him from the corner of her eye. He had also given up his human skin in favor of his fleshy cocoon. Even in the murk, the blebs his empathy had nurtured gleamed. "We don't owe the man any niceties," he continued. "Tell him the truth and let's be done with it."

"What have you come to tell me?" Buddenbaum asked.

"That it's over," Haheh replied gently. "That we have somebody new to show us the wonders of the story tree."

Buddenbaum looked incredulous. "Just like that?" he said, his voice rising a little. "You're replacing me without so much as a word of warning? Oh, that simply breaks my heart!"

Be careful, Tesla thought. The line about his heart breaking sounded a tad phoney.

"It was inevitable," Rare Utu said, taking a couple of steps towards Buddenbaum. Finally she too was giving up the illusion of humanity, her childish body swelling and glistening as it retrieved its strange divinity. "There are only so many stories in one head, Owen, and we've exhausted your supply."

"Oh you'd be *surprised*," Buddenbaum replied. "Amazed, even, if you knew how much I *haven't* shown you."

"Well it's too late now," Haheh said. "Our decision's made, and it's final. Tesla Bombeck will be our guide as we approach the millennium."

"Well, congratulations," Buddenbaum said to Tesla sourly, and as he spoke took a step towards her, sliding between Haheh and Rare Utu. He was close enough now that Tesla could see his face plainly, and she read the look in his eyes. He wanted her gone, and quickly.

She retreated from him, as though his proximity distressed her. "It wasn't planned this way," she protested. "I didn't seek this out."

"Frankly," he replied, "I don't care one way or the other." He reached out and casually caught hold of Rare Utu's frail arm as he spoke. This was plainly an unusual, perhaps even unique, contact, because the Jai-Wai shuddered, staring down at his hand in some distress.

"What are you *doing*, Owen?" she said, the folds of her bejeweled flesh shuddering.

"Just making my farewells," Owen replied. Haheh's gaze was

approaching the spot that Buddenbaum had vacated. The asphalt there was brightening and softening.

"What *have* you been up to?" he said, staring down.

Behind Tesla, Yie murmured, "Keep away . . . " but Haheh was deaf to the warning. He took another step, while the street continued to brighten. Rare Utu was meanwhile attempting to shake off Buddenbaum's hold, but he refused to let her go. Eyes fixed on Tesla, he smiled through clenched teeth and told her, "Goodbye."

She started to turn but as she did so the ground on which Haheh was standing suddenly blazed, and he was enveloped. Rare Utu loosed the word *Owen* like a shriek, and started to pull at her captor, while Haheh's body ran like butter in a furnace, the blebs bursting in wheels of colors and pouring off into the street.

Tesla had already seen too much. It was dangerous to stay, lethal, probably. But she'd never been good at averting her eyes, whatever the wisdom of it. She kept drinking down the scene in front of her, until Buddenbaum screamed, "*Get the fuck out of here!*" and as he did so pitched Rare Utu back into the light that had claimed Haheh. She went shrieking, but her cry was cut short once the light sealed itself around her. Throwing back her head, she opened her arms as though surrendering to the sensation.

"*I said: Go!*" Buddenbaum yelled at Tesla, and this time she tore her eyes from the spectacle and turned, only to meet a rush of sour, cold air, and Yie, coming at her.

"*You tricked us!*" he said, his voice like scalpels. It cut her courage to ribbons. She froze, staring into his doll-like face, while at her back Rare Utu uttered a shivering sigh and murmured, "*This . . . is . . . wonderful.*"

"What have you done to her?" Yie demanded. The questions was directed at Buddenbaum, but he caught hold of Tesla as he asked it, and hauled her close to his body. His limbs were far from strong; she could have broken the hold if she'd wanted to. But she didn't. The influence of this flesh was like peyote. She felt it invade her, lifting her out of her fear.

"Set them free!" Yie said to Buddenbaum.

"I'm afraid it's too late for that," said Owen.

"I'll kill your woman if you don't," the Jai-Wai warned.

"She's not mine," came the reply. "Do whatever you need to do."

Dreamily, Tesla glanced back over her shoulder at Buddenbaum, and by the light pouring from the ground saw him plainly for the first time. He was pitifully cold; his humanity consumed long ago in the effort that had brought him to this place. No doubt all he'd boasted in the Nook was true: The years had made him wiser than the Jaff. But his wisdom would do him no good. The Art would break him the way it had broken Randolph. Snap his reason and melt his mind.

Beyond him, in the blaze, Rare Utu had almost disappeared, but even now, with her substance pouring off into the ground where Haheh had already gone, she spoke.

"What happens next . . . ?" she said.

"Take her out of there!" Yie yelled to Buddenbaum.

"I told you: It's too late," he replied. "Besides, I don't think she wants to go."

Rare Utu was laughing now. "What's next?" she kept saying, her laughter growing insubstantial. "What? What?"

The ground at her feet was as soft as she, ribbons of brightness running off along the streets.

"*Stop this!*" Yie demanded again, his din so brutal that this time Tesla's body simply surrendered beneath its assault. Her legs failed, her bladder gave out, and she stumbled from Yie's grip towards the blaze.

"No you don't!" Buddenbaum snapped, retreating across the incandescent earth to protect the spot where Rare Utu had stood. "The Art's mine!"

"*The Art?*" Yie said, as though it was only now he understood the purpose of this trap. "*Never, Buddenbaum . . .* " his voice was rising with each syllable. "*You will not have it!*"

His lacerating din was too much for Tesla's beleaguered body. She felt something in her head break; felt her tongue slacken in her mouth and her lids fall. Saw, as darkness came, the bright ground divide before her—

And there it was, shining in the dirt: the cross of crosses, the sign of signs. In the long, slow moments of her dying fall, she remembered with a kind of yearning how she'd solved the puzzles of that cross; seen the four journeys that were etched upon it. One to the dream world, one to the real; one to the bestial, one to the divine. And there at the heart of these journeys—where they crossed, where they divided, where they finished and began—the human mystery. It was not about the flesh, that mystery: It was not about hanging broken from a cross or the triumph of the spirit over suffering. It was about the living dream of mind, that made body and spirit and all they took joy in.

Remembering the revelation now the time between that moment and this—the years she'd spent wandering the roads of the lost Americas—folded up and fled. She had glimpsed the vast eternal sitting in the earth beneath Palomo Grove, and now she was dying into it, her lids closing, her heart stopping.

Somewhere far off she heard Yie shrieking, and knew the power here had claimed him as it had claimed the others.

She wanted to tell him not to be afraid; that he was going into a place where the future of being lay in wait. A time out of time when the singularity from which all things came would be whole again. But she had no tongue. No, nor breath. No, nor life.

It was over.

ii

Harry, Raul, and Maeve O'Connell had just come in sight of the crossroads when Tesla slid from Yie's grasp, and stumbled forward. Though they were a hundred yards from the spot or more, the light was exquisitely particular, and kept no detail of the expression on Tesla's face from Harry's eyes. She was dead, or dying, but her slackening features carried a look of strange contentment.

The luminous ground was no longer solid where she fell. It received her like a shining grave, and she was gone.

"Oh Jesus . . . " Harry breathed. "Oh Jesus Christ in Heaven . . . "

He picked up his pace and raced towards the intersection, following the braided rivulets of light that ran in the ground beneath his feet.

Behind him, Maeve had started to shout.

"I know that man!" she hollered. "That's Buddenbaum! My Lord, that's Buddenbaum! That's the bastard started all this!" Wresting herself from Raul's custody, she started to hobble after D'Amour.

"Will you *please* stop her?" Coker yelled in Raul's ear.

Raul was too distressed by Tesla's disappearance to reply. Coker yelled on until Raul said, "I thought you'd gone."

"No, never," Coker replied. "I was simply silenced by her bitterness. Now I beg you, my friend, don't let her be taken from me. I want her to know what I feel for her, just once."

Raul swallowed a sob. So many people already taken, and this last the most unthinkable. Tesla had survived a bullet, Kissoon, and enough drugs to fell a horse. But now she was gone.

"*Please*," Coker said. "Go after Maeve."

"I'll do my best," Raul said, and started in pursuit of the old woman. For all her frailty, she'd already covered quite a distance.

"Wait!" he called after her. "Somebody wants to talk to you!"

As he caught up with her, she scowled. "It's *him* I want to talk to!" she said, nodding in Buddenbaum's direction. "He's the one!"

"Listen to me a moment," Raul said, catching hold of her arm. "It wasn't an accident we found you. Somebody led us to you. Do you understand? Somebody who's here, right now, beside us."

"Are you crazy?" Maeve replied, looking around.

"You don't see him because he's dead."

"I don't give a shit for the dead," Maeve snapped. "It's the living I want answers from! *Buddenbaum!*" she yelled.

It was Erwin who piped up now. "Tell her who you are!" he said to Coker.

"I wanted it to be a special moment," Coker replied.

"I wasted my life waiting for the special moments," Erwin told him. "Now is all we've got!" So saying, he pushed his fellow phantom aside to get access to Raul's ear. "Tell her it's Coker! Go on! *Tell her!*"

"Coker?" Raul said aloud.

Maeve O'Connell stopped in her hobbling tracks. "What did you say?" she murmured.

"The dead man's name is *Coker*," Raul replied.

"I'm her husband," said Coker.

"He says he's—"

"I know who he is," she said, and drawing a gasping breath she said, "Coker? *My* Coker? Can this be true?"

"It's true," Raul said.

Tears came, but she didn't stop saying his name. "Coker . . . oh my Coker . . . my sweet Coker . . ."

Harry heard Maeve sobbing behind him, and looked round to see her with her head flung back, as though her husband was raining kisses on her and she was bathing in them. When he returned his gaze to the crossroads, Buddenbaum had dropped to the ground where Tesla had vanished, and was beating his fists violently against the now-solidified street. He was on the verge of apoplexy, sprays of spittle, sweat, and tears erupting from his face.

"*You can't, you bitch!*" he shrieked at the street. "I won't let you have it!"

Energies were still pouring up out of the ground, spirals and filigrees rising around him. He tried to snatch hold of them in his bloodied hands, as if they might still transfigure him, but his fists extinguished those he caught, and the rest simply climbed on out of his reach and faded into the darkness above him. His fury and frustration mounted. He began to swing around, unleashing a solid scream of rage, "This can't happen! *It can't! It can't!*"

Behind him, Harry heard Maeve O'Connell say, "Do you see this, Coker? At the crossroads?"

"He sees it," Raul replied.

"That's where I buried the medallion," Maeve went on. "Does Coker know that?"

"He knows."

Maeve had come to Harry's side now. Her face was wet with tears but her smile was unalloyed. "My husband's here . . . " she said to Harry, rather proudly. "Imagine that . . . "

"That's wonderful."

She pointed down the street. "That's where we had the whore-house. Right there. It's no coincidence, is it?"

"No," said Harry, "I don't think it is."

"All that light, it's coming from the medallion."

"It certainly looks that way."

Her smile broadened. "I'm going to see for myself."

"I wouldn't if I were you."

"Well you're *not* me," she said sharply. "Whatever's going on there's my doing." She calmed herself a little, and the smile crept back on to her face. "I don't think you know what's going on any more than I do, am I right?"

"More or less," Harry conceded.

"So if we don't know what's to be afraid of, why be afraid?" she reasoned. "Raul? I want you on my left side. And Coker, wherever you are, I want you on my right."

"At least let me go first," Harry said, and without waiting for her permission, headed on towards Buddenbaum, who was once again berating the asphalt. He saw Harry coming from the corner of his eye.

"Keep your distance," he gasped, his breathing raw. "This ground's mine. And I've still got power in me if you try to take it from me."

"I'm not here to take anything," Harry said.

"You and that bitch Bombeck, plotting against me."

"There was no plot. Tesla never wanted to be a part of this—"

"*Of course she did!*" Buddenbaum replied. "She wasn't stupid. She wanted the Art the same as everyone." He looked round at

D'Amour, his fury decaying into self-pity. "But you see I trusted her. That was my mistake. And she lied!" He slammed his wounded palms down upon the solid ground. "This was *my* ground! *My* miracle!"

"Listen to the shit he speaks!" Maeve hollered. Harry stood aside, to let Buddenbaum see her. "*You're* the liar!" she said. "That land was, is, and always will be mine."

Buddenbaum's expression turned from fury to astonishment. "Are you . . . are you what I think you are?"

"Why do you look surprised?" Maeve said. "Sure, I got old, but we can't all do deals with the Devil."

"It wasn't the Devil I dealt with," Buddenbaum said softly. "I might have more to show for it if I had. What are you doing here?"

"I came to get some answers," Maeve said. "I deserve some, don't you think, before we both go to our graves?"

"I'm not going to my grave," Buddenbaum said.

"Oh are you not?" Maeve replied. "My mistake." She waved Raul away, so as to proceed unaided to where Buddenbaum knelt. "Do you want another hundred, hundred and fifty years?" she said to him. "You're welcome to them. I'm off, after this. Somewhere my bones don't ache."

While she was speaking, one of the luminous ribbons rising from the ground strayed in her direction. She reached out towards it and instead of avoiding her grasp it wove between her arthritic fingers.

"Did you ever see the house we built here?" she said, as she watched the ribbon at play. "Oh it was such a sight. *Such a sight.*"

The ribbon went from her fingers now, but several more strands and particles were rising from out of the earth towards her.

"What are you *doing*, woman?" Buddenbaum said.

"Nothing," Maeve shrugged.

"Even if the land isn't mine, the magic is."

"I'm not taking it from you," Maeve said mildly, "I'm too old to be possessive about anything. Except maybe my memories. Those are mine, Buddenbaum . . . " The motes were getting busier all the time, as though inspired by what she was saying. "And right now they're very clear. Very, very, clear." She closed her eyes for a moment, and a new wave of luminosity broke from the street, rising to graze her hands and face before darting off. "Sometimes I think I remember my childhood more clearly than yesterday . . . " she went on, extending her hand. "Coker?" she said. "Are you there?"

"He's right here," said Raul.

"Will you take my hand?" she said.

"He says he's doing it," Raul said. Then, after a moment. "He's got tight hold of you."

Maeve smiled. "You know I believe I can feel it?" she said.

Buddenbaum caught hold of Harry's sleeve. "Is she crazy?"

"No. Her husband's ghost is here."

"I should have seen, I suppose," he said, his voice a monotone. "Final acts . . . they're a bitch . . . "

"Better get used to it," Harry said.

"I never liked the sentimental shit," Buddenbaum replied.

"I think it's more than that," Harry said, looking up at the motes and filaments that had touched Maeve's skin. They were not extinguishing themselves in the night sky as those that had gone before had done, but were roving purposefully, like bees in a field of flowers, mazing the air as they went about their purpose. Where they traveled they left trails of light, which, once loosed, proceeded to elaborate themselves, describing a multitude of forms in the warm night air.

It was Raul who spoke what he saw first. "The house—" he said in amazement. "You see it, Harry?"

"I see it."

"Enough," said Buddenbaum, waving the sight away as if nauseated. "I'm done with the past. Done with it!"

Covering his head with his hands he stumbled off as Maeve's memory raised her whorehouse out of light and air: walls and windows, staircase and ceilings. Off to Harry's left a passageway led to the front door, and the step beyond. To his right, through another door there was a parlor, and through another, a kitchen, and through a third a yard where the trees were blossoming. And everywhere, even as the floors were laid, the rooms were being filled with furniture and rugs and plants and vases, the sheer proliferation of detail suggesting that once the process had been initiated these objects were coming back into being of their own accord. Their solid selves had gone to dust decades since, but these, their imagined forms, remained encoded at the spot where they'd existed. Now they came again, remembering themselves in all their perfection.

None was so solid, however, as to keep Harry's eyes from wandering in any direction he wished. He could see the picket fence that bounded the backyard and the fine Spanish tile on the front step. He could see up the graceful staircase to the second and third floors, each of which boasted two bathrooms and half a dozen well-appointed bedrooms.

And now, even before the roof had appeared on the house, the souls who had occupied it began to appear, gracing its rooms.

"Ah . . . " Raul cooed appreciatively, "the ladies."

They appeared everywhere. On the landings and in the bedrooms, in the parlors and in the kitchen, their voices and their laughter like whispering music.

"There's Bedelia," Maeve said, "and Hildegard and Jennie, oh my dear Jennie, look at her . . . "

It was not such a bad place to be, Harry thought, come the end of the world, surrounded by such memories. Though only one or two of the women would have been judged pretty by current standards, there was an air of ease and pleasure here, of a house as much dedicated to laughter as to erotic excess.

As for the clients who'd patronized the establishment, they were like the ghosts of ghosts, gossamer forms passing up and down the stairs and in and out of the bedrooms and bathrooms, their dress and flesh gray. Once in a while Harry would catch a glimpse of a face, but it was always fleeting, as though the house had conjured the furtiveness of these men, rather than the men themselves; caught them turning from scrutiny, ashamed of their desire.

There was little evidence of shame among the women. They went bare-breasted on the stairs, and naked on the landing. They chatted to one another as they shat or passed water. They helped each other bathe and douche and shave their legs and what lay between.

"There," said Maeve, pointing to a prodigiously ample woman sitting in the kitchen, taking fingerfuls of pudding from a porcelain bowl, "that's Mary Elizabeth. You got a lot for your bucks with her. She always had a waiting list. And up there"—she pointed towards a slim, pale girl feeding a parrot from between her teeth—"that's Dolores. And the parrot, what was the parrot's name?" She glanced round at Raul. "Ask Coker," she said.

The answer came in an instant. "Elijah."

Maeve smiled. "Elijah. Of course, Elijah. She swore it spoke prophecies."

"Were you happy here?" Harry asked her.

"It wasn't what I'd expected my life to be," she said. "But yes, I was happy. Probably too happy. That made people envious."

"Is that why they burned the place down?" Harry said, wandering to the stairs to watch Mary Elizabeth ascend. "Because they were envious?"

"That was some of it," she said. "And some of it was sheer self-righteousness: They didn't want me and my business corrupting the citizens. Can you imagine? Without me, without this house and these women, there wouldn't have *been* any citizens because there wouldn't have been any city. And they knew that. That's why they waited until they had an excuse—"

"And what was that?"

"Our son, our crazy son, who was too little like his father and too much like me. Coker was always gentle, you see. But there was a streak of the lunatic in the O'Connells, and it came out in Clayton. Not just that, but we made the error of teaching him he was special, telling him he'd have power in his hands one day, because he was a child of two worlds. We should never have done that. It made him think he was above the common decencies; that he had the right to be barbarous if he chose, because he was better than everybody else." She grew pensive. "I saw him once, when he was maybe ten or so, looking up at Harmon's Heights, and I said to him: *What are you thinking?* And do you know what he said to me? *One day,* he said, *I'll have that hill, and I'll look down on a world of fishes.* I've thought so many times, that was the sign. I should have put him out of his misery right there and then. But it had taken Coker and me so much pain and effort to get a child . . . "

While part of Harry's mind listened to the story of Clayton O'Connell's begetting—how Coker's charms and suits had kept Maeve preternaturally young, but slowed her ovulations to a trickle; how she was almost seventy when she gave birth to the boy—another part turned over what she'd said previously. The child's notion of looking down from Harmon's Heights on a world of fishes rang some vague bell.

"What happened to Clayton?" he asked her, while he puzzled over the problem.

"He was hanged."

"You saw him dead?"

"No. His body was taken by wolves or bears . . . "

And now, thinking of wild beasts up on the mountain, he remembered where he'd heard the words before.

"Raul?" he said. "Stay here with Maeve, will you?"

"I'm not leaving." Raul smiled, his face flushed with voyeuristic pleasure.

"Don't you go," Maeve said, as Harry left the bottom of the stairs.

"I'll be back," he replied, "you just keep remembering," and heading off down the hallway he slipped through the unopened front door onto the street.

iii

"Lives are leaves on the story tree," the man who walked on Quiddity had told Tesla. To which she'd replied that she'd never told a story she'd given a damn about.

"Oh, but you did," he'd said. "Your own . . . your own . . . "

It was true, of course. She'd told that story with every blink of her eye, every beat of her heart, with every deed and word, cruel and kind alike.

But here was a mystery; that now, though her heart was no longer beating and her eyes could no longer blink, though she would never again say or do anything in the living world, cruel or kind, the story refused to finish.

She was dead; that much was sure. But the pen moved on, and kept moving. There was more to tell it seemed . . .

The brightness into which she had fallen was still around her, though she knew it wasn't her eyes that were seeing it, because she could see her own body some distance from her, suspended in the light. It lay face-up, arms and legs spread, fingers splayed, in a posture she knew all too well. She'd assembled this image in front of Buddenbaum, half an hour ago: It was the pose of the figure at the center of the medallion. Now it was her dead flesh that took that pose, while her mind drifted around it with a kind of detached curiosity, mildly puzzled as to what all this meant, but suspecting the answer was beyond her comprehension.

In the ground a little way beneath her body—the source of the energies that had transformed the solid ground into a kind of incandescent soup—was the cross itself, and when her spirit looked its way it transported her thoughts in four directions at once, out along the bright paths that ran from its arms. In one direction lay the human journey; a record of the countless men and women who had come to and crossed at this intersection, all of them carrying their freight of dreams. In the opposite direction came a procession of creatures who resembled humanity, but only remotely; exiles from the Metacosm, come to Everville as a place of pilgrimage, and led by their prophetic marrow to this spot. From a third route came the animals, wild and domesticated alike. Leashed dogs sniffing for a place to piss; migrating birds wheeling overhead before they turned south; the flies that had been a curse to Dolan in his candy shop, the worms that had massed here in their many millions just the summer before. Aspiring forms, even the lowliest.

And finally, the most remote element in this conjunction: the divinities whom she'd helped ensnare.

"What happens next?" Rare Utu had waited to know as the blaze had consumed her. It was a question that no longer vexed Tesla. She had her bliss here and was perfectly content. If her consciousness finally caught up with the facts of her demise and flickered out, so be it. And if the pen continued to move, and the story continued to be told, she would accept that too, willingly.

Meanwhile, she would hover, and watch, while the ground ran with brightness in every direction, and the steady processes of decay began their work on the body she'd once met in the mirror.

iv

Harry was two blocks from the crossroads, heading off towards the place where the Iad was at work, when he heard Buddenbaum calling to him.

"Help me, D'Amour!" he said, stumbling across the street. He had not, it appeared, left the site of his working completely bereft. A down of luminescence clung to his face and hands, an inconsequential reminder of all that he'd failed to acquire. "I don't blame you," he said, backing along the middle of the street ahead of Harry. "She was a friend of yours, so you had to conspire with her. You had no choice."

"There was no conspiracy, Buddenbaum."

"Whether there was or there wasn't, you can't leave her down there, can you?" He was attempting a tone of sweet reason.

"She's dead," said Harry.

"I know that."

"So wherever she's buried, it's academic. Will you just get the hell out of my way?"

"Where are you going?"

"To find Kissoon."

"*Kissoon?*" Buddenbaum said. "What the Hell good can he do you?"

"More than you can."

"Not true!" Buddenbaum protested. "Just give me a few minutes of your time, and you'll never look back. There'll be no past to look back to. No future either. Just—"

"*One immortal day?*" Harry shook his head. "Give it up, for God's sake. You had your chance and you blew it."

He turned a corner now, and there, at the other end of the street, was the enemy. He halted for a moment, to try and make some sense of what he was seeing, but the closest of the fires was several streets away, and what illumination it offered only confounded his gaze. One thing was certain: The Iad was no longer the chaotic, panicked thing, or things, it had been on the mountaintop. Even from this distance and with so little light he could see that the enemy had sloughed off its ragged coat and moved in the air like a serpentine engine, its immense form in constant, peristaltic motion.

Harry pulled up his sleeves, to expose his tattoos. Who knew what good they'd do him, probably very little. But he needed all the help he could get.

"What are you going to do?" Buddenbaum wanted to know. "Challenge it to a fistfight? You don't have a chance. Not without some power to wield."

Harry ignored him. Drawing a deep breath, he started down the street towards the Iad.

"You think you're being heroic, is that it?" Buddenbaum said. "It's suicide. If you want to do some good, we can help each other. *Dig* for me, D'Amour."

"Dig?"

Buddenbaum raised his hands in front of him. They were a sickening sight. In his frenzy to reclaim what he'd lost, he'd beaten his flesh to a bloody pulp. Several fingers were askew, their bones broken. "I can't do it myself. And by the time they heal it'll be too late."

"It's not going to happen," Harry said.

"What the fuck do you know about what's going to happen and what isn't?"

"If you were going to get the Art it would have come to you back there. But it didn't."

"That was because of Tesla—"

"Maybe. And maybe you just weren't meant to have it."

Buddenbaum stopped in his tracks. "I won't hear that," he said.

"So don't," Harry replied, stepping around him.

"And I won't be denied what's *mine!*" Buddenbaum said, laying one of his broken hands on Harry's shoulder. "I don't have much in the way of suits left in me," he said, "but I've got enough to cripple you. Maybe even kill you."

"And what good would that do you?"

"I would have laid one of my enemies low," Buddenbaum replied.

Harry could feel a pulse of neuralgia pass through his shoulder from Buddenbaum's palm, lending credence to the threat.

"I'm going to give you one more chance," Buddenbaum said.

Harry's tattoos started to itch furiously. His guts twitched. He knew he should run, but the will had gone from his legs.

"What are you doing, Owen?" somebody said.

The itch was an ache now, and the twitches almost convulsions. Harry tried to turn his head towards the speaker, but it wouldn't move. All he could do was shift his eyes, and there on the periphery of his vision he saw the boy from the crossroads. His pallid face was bruised and bloodied.

"Let him go, Owen," he said. "Please."

Buddenbaum made a sound Harry couldn't quite interpret. Was it perhaps a sob? "Stay away from me, Seth," he said.

"What happened?" the boy wanted to know.

"I was cheated," Buddenbaum replied, his voice thickening with tears. "I had it in my grasp—"

"And this man took it?"

"No!"

"So, what? You're just killing anybody who gets in your way? You're not that cruel."

"I will be," Buddenbaum said. "From now on, no mercy, no compassion—"

"No love?"

"No love!" he yelled. "So you stay away from me or I'll hurt you too!"

"No you won't," Seth said, his words a gentle certainty.

Harry felt the pain in his body easing, and the power over his muscles was returned to him. He made no sudden movements, for fear of inflaming Buddenbaum afresh, but slowly turning his head he saw that Seth had lifted the man's hand off Harry's shoulder and had drawn it up to his lips.

"We've all been hurt enough for one lifetime," he said softly, kissing the broken hand. "We've got to start healing, Owen."

"It's too late for that."

"Give me a chance to prove you wrong," the boy replied.

Harry looked round at Buddenbaum. His rage had passed, leaving his face drained of expression.

"You'd better go," Seth said to Harry.

"Will you be all right with him?"

"Sure," Seth replied gently, slipping his arm around Buddenbaum's shoulder. "We'll be fine. We go way back, him and me. Way back."

There was no time for further exchange. Leaving the pair to make what peace they could, Harry headed on down the street. In the minute or so since he'd last looked the Iad's way it had advanced against the largest building in the vicinity: either the courthouse or the Town Hall, Harry guessed. The site was no more than a hundred and fifty yards ahead of him, and now with every step the Iad's pernicious influence grew. He felt its needles at the base of his skull, and the corners of his eyes; heard its witless noise behind the din of the world.

It was almost welcome, that witlessness, given the alternative: the shrieks and screams coming from those trapped in the besieged building. He was puzzled as to why the victims didn't escape out the back until he saw Gamaliel running down the side of the building with something that looked like a human head in his hand. If Gamaliel was here, so were his brothers, and probably the surviving members of Zury's clan too: all here to enjoy the spectacle.

So where was Kissoon? He'd masterminded this night of retribution; he was surely here to witness it.

Shouting for Kissoon as he went, Harry broke into a run. It sounded strange to be calling a man's name in the midst of such utter bedlam, but hadn't it been Kissoon himself who'd said that whatever the Iad looked like they'd have a human heart? Men were not nameless. Every one of them had a past; even Kissoon, who had spoken so fondly of being nobody: just eyes on a mountain, looking down on a world of fishes . . .

The walls of the Town Hall were cracking, as the great wheel of the Iad pressed against it. The closer Harry came to the place, the more the Iad's name made sense. Uroboros, the self-devouring serpent, encircling the earth while it ate its own tail. An image of power as a self-sufficient engine: implacable, incomprehensible, inviolate.

This time there were no hallucinations in its proximity—no Father Hess accusing from a makeshift grave, no demon spouting enigmas—just this ring of malice, cracking the shell that kept it from its victims. He saw it more clearly all the time. It seemed to him it was displaying itself, tormenting him with the fact that despite the clarity there was no comprehension to be had; no place where its intricacies resolved themselves into something recognizable; a head, a claw, an eye. Just shapes in nauseating abundance, flukes and scraps and scabs; hard forms of indeterminate color (bluish here, reddish there, or neither, or nothing); all soulless, all passionless.

There was, of course, no human face here either. Only repetition, like a scrawl caught between mirrors, its echoes looking like order, like meaning, but being neither.

He had to find the heart. That was his only hope: *Find the heart*.

The noise in his head had grown so loud now he was sure it would burst his skull, but he kept walking towards its source, and the closer he came—sixty yards, fifty, forty—the more clearly he heard a whisper beneath the din. It was calm, this whisper.

It's nothing to be afraid of . . . he was telling himself.

He was surprised at his own courage.

Nothing you haven't seen before . . .

Surprised and reassured.

Just let it embrace you . . .

Wait, he thought; where did that idea come from?

There'll only be the two of us, very soon . . .

That isn't me. It's the Iad.

Oh, but there's no way to divide us . . . the whisper replied, receding now that it had been identified, *you know that, in your heart* . . . it said, *in your human heart* . . .

Then it was gone, and he was ten yards from the vast, slow wheel, the screams from the building drowned out by the mindless noise in his head. Off to his right he saw Gamaliel striding in his direction. It would slaughter him on the instant, he knew. No prayer, no hesitation. Just the killing stroke.

He had seconds to live. Seconds to bring Kissoon to him.

He drew a deep breath, and though he could no longer hear his own voice, yelled into the bedlam.

"I'm looking for Clayton O'Connell!"

There was no response at first. The wheel kept moving, senseless form upon senseless form passing in front of his exhausted eyes. And then, with Gamaliel a yard from him, its hands stretched to rip out his throat, the Iad's motion began to slow. Some unheard order must have gone out, because Gamaliel stopped in mid-stride, and then retreated a little way.

The din in Harry's head retreated too—though it didn't disappear—and he stood before the Iad gasping like a prisoner whose restraints had been loosened enough to let him breathe.

There was some movement amid the Iad's anatomy. It unknotted itself, parted. And there, enthroned in its entrails—which were the same incomprehensible stuff of its outward appearance—was Kissoon.

He looked much as he had on the mountain: simple and serene.

"How did you work out who I was?" he said. Though there was a considerable distance between them, his voice sounded as intimate as the Iad's whispers.

"I didn't," Harry said. "I was told."

"By whom?" Kissoon wanted to know, rising and stepping out of the living sanctum down onto the street. "Who told you?"

"Your mother."

The face before him remained impassive. Not a twitch. Not a flicker.

"Her name's Maeve O'Connell, in case you've forgotten," Harry said, "and she was hanged on a tree, alongside your father and you."

"You talk to the dead?" Kissoon said. "Since when?"

"She's not dead. She's very much alive."

"What kind of trick is this?" Kissoon said. "You think it's going to save anybody?"

"She escaped, Clayton. The bough broke, and she found a way through to Quiddity."

"Impossible."

"The door was always up there, open just a crack."

"How could she have got through it?"

"She had suits of her own, didn't she? And the will to make them work. You should see what she's done at the crossroads." Harry glanced back over his shoulder. "That light . . . " he said. There was a noticeable glow in the sky around the region of the whorehouse. "That's her handiwork."

Kissoon gazed at it a moment, and Harry had the satisfaction of seeing a flicker of doubt upon his face. A tiny flicker, to be sure, but it was enough.

"I . . . don't know . . . about you, D'Amour. You keep surprising me."

"You and me both."

"If you're lying about this—"

"What would be the point?"

"To delay me."

"Why would I bother?" Harry replied. "You're going to do what you're going to do sooner or later."

"And I still will," Kissoon said. "Mother or no mother." He stared on at the glow in the sky. "What's she doing?" he said.

"She reconstructed the whorehouse," Harry said. "For old times' sake."

Kissoon mused on this for a few moments. Then he said, "Old times? Fuck old times," and without further word he strode off down the street towards the crossroads, leaving Harry to follow after him.

Harry didn't need to look back to know that the Iad had left off its assault on the Town Hall, and was also trailing after Kissoon, as though for all its legendary malevolence it didn't have the will—or perhaps the desire—to act without instruction. The noise in Harry's head had dwindled to a murmur, and he took a moment to turn over the options that lay ahead, assuming that the Iad was by now indifferent to his thought processes.

Plainly, the possibility of his mother's survival had done nothing to mellow Kissoon. He was going to meet her, it seemed, more out of curiosity than sentiment. He had his agenda; he'd had it since childhood. The fact that the woman who'd brought him into the world had survived her lynching would not dissuade him from wanting that world filled with fishes. Harry entertained a remote hope that in the midst of the reunion Kissoon might lay himself open to attack, but even if he did, what weapon would touch him? And while an attempt upon his life was being made, would the Iad simply stand by and let it happen? Unlikely, to say the least.

"It's not what you expected, is it?" Kissoon said as they turned the corner. "The Iad, I mean."

Harry watched the great wheel appear behind them, its forms spilling and curling as it came, like a wave perpetually threatening to break. It seemed almost to usurp and transfigure the air on its way, turning the very darkness to its own purpose.

"I don't know what I expected," Harry replied.

"You had any number of Devils to choose from," Kissoon pointed out. "But I don't think this was one of them." He didn't wait for confirmation or denial. "It will change, of course. And change. And change. The one thing it will never be is dead."

Harry remembered Norma's wisdom about the world. Was that true of the Iad too? Changing, but inextinguishable?

"And of course it's just a tiny part of what's waiting on the other side."

"I'm glad I won't be here to see it," Harry said.

"Are you giving up then? That's wise. You don't know up from down any longer, do you, and that fills you with terror. Better to surrender. Go watch TV until the end of the world."

"You hate the world that much?"

"I was taken from a tree by wolves, D'Amour. I woke up in the dark with a rope around my neck being fought over. And when I'd gutted them—when I was standing among the bodies, drenched in their blood—I thought: These were not my enemies. These were not the creatures that took me naked from my bed, and hanged me. It's *their* blood I have to bathe in. It's *their* throats I have to take out. The question was: How? How was a half-crazy nobody, with a brothel-keeper for a mother and a drunken freak for a father to find a way to *take out the throat of Sapas Humana?*" He stopped. Turned. Smiled. "Now you know."

"Now I know."

"One question for you, D'Amour, before we get there."

"Yes?"

"Tesla Bombeck."

"What about her?"

"Where is she?"

"Dead."

Kissoon studied Harry for a little time, as if looking for some sign of deception. Finding none, he said, "She was quite remarkable, you know. I look back on our time together in the Loop almost fondly." He made a tiny smile at the foolishness of this. "Of course finally she was a featherweight. But disarming, in her way." He paused, staring past Harry at the Iad. "Do you know why it eats its own tail?" he said.

"No."

"To prove its perfection," Kissoon replied, and turning his back on Harry strode on to the next intersection. Turning it, they finally came in sight of the crossroads, and of the house that Maeve had built there. It looked almost solid; like a drawing made of light, worked over and over and over again, obsessively. A figure added here, a window there; some steps, some guttering; memory upon memory. Kissoon made no audible response to the spectacle, but proceeded towards it, his stride somewhat slower than it had been.

"Where's my mother?" he wanted to know.

"Somewhere inside, I suppose," Harry replied.

"Go fetch her for me. I don't want to go in."

"It's just an illusion," Harry said.

"I know that," Kissoon replied. Was there a subtle tremor in his voice? Again he said, "I want you to go fetch her for me."

"Okay," Harry replied, and walked on past Kissoon to the front steps.

The door before him seemed to stand open, and he slipped through it into a kind of erotic wonderland. The walls were covered with brocade now, and hung with paintings, most of them titillative works passing themselves off as classical subjects: *The Judgement of Paris, Leda and the Swan, The Rape of the Sabine Women*. And all around him, the feminine flesh so lovingly daubed on these canvases rendered in light, seemingly more real than when he'd left. Women in their camisoles and knickers, chattering in the parlor. Women with their hair unbraided, bathing their breasts. Women lying in bed, their hands between their legs, toying and smiling for their phantom clients.

Moving down the thronged passageway in search of Maeve, Harry's spirits rose, despite all that reason dictated. Doubtless life had been hard here. There had been disease and brutality and bastard children. Doubtless these women had endured the contempt of the very men who'd paid for their services, and longed, while they plied their trade, to escape. But that was not recorded here. It was the joy of this house Maeve had chosen to remember, and though Harry knew none of this was permanent it didn't matter. He accepted the pleasure this illusion offered him with gratitude.

"*Harry?*"

There, in the kitchen, idling in the midst of a group of chattering women, was Raul. "Where did you get to?"

"I went to find Maeve's offspring. Where is she?"

"She's out back," Raul said. "Did you say *offspring?*"

"Kissoon, Raul," Harry said, heading on towards the back of the house. "He's Clayton O'Connell." Raul came after him, forsaking the company of the women.

"Does he *know?*" he said.

"Of course he knows! Why wouldn't he?"

"I don't know, it's just . . . it's difficult imagining Maeve's kid being the one who murdered the Shoal, or created the Loop—"

"Everyone begins somewhere," Harry said to him. "And everyone has their reasons."

"Where is he now?"

"At the front of the house," Harry replied, "with the Iad." He was out the back door now, into the garden. Maeve had remembered it the way it must have looked some distant spring, the cherry trees heavy with blossom, the air as heady as liquor. She wasn't alone out here. One of the women was sitting on the grass, star-watching.

"Her name's Christina," Maeve said. "She knows all the constellations."

"I've found Clayton," Harry told Maeve.

"You've what?"

"He's here."

"Impossible," she said. "*Impossible*. My son's dead."

"It might be better for us all if he was," Harry replied. "He's the one who brought the Iad through, Maeve. It's his revenge for what happened to you all."

"And . . . are you expecting me to teach him some compassion?"

"If you can."

She looked away. First to the star-watcher, then up to the stars. "I was having such a time out here. It was almost as though I'd never left—"

"He wants me to bring you to him."

She looked towards Raul, who was standing on the back doorstep. "Is my Coker here?" Raul nodded. "So he knows?" Again, Raul nodded. "And what does he think?"

Raul listened for the dead man to speak. "He says be careful; the boy was always wicked."

"Not always," Maeve said quickly, moving back towards the house. "He wasn't wicked in my belly. We taught him, Coker. Lord knows how, but we taught him."

She stepped inside, her face stony, and refusing Harry's aid made her way back through the kitchen and the parlor towards the front door.

It was still open. Kissoon was at the threshold, and by the stare on his face it was clear he'd been watching his mother for some time, through the veils of the whorehouse. The monkish face he'd worn was tainted now. He looked pinched and bitter.

"Look at you," he said, as Maeve approached the door.

"Clayton?" she said, halting to study him.

"How sick you look," the sight of her frailty apparently giving him courage. He stepped inside. "You should be dead, Mama," he said.

"So should you."

"Oh," he cooed, "I *am*, Mama. All that's left alive is the hate in me." He was picking up his speed, raising his left hand as he closed on her. In it, the rod he'd wielded twice before, the murderous rod.

Yelling a warning, Harry raced to intercept the blow, but Kissoon was too quick. He struck his mother's head with the rod, and down she went, an arc of blood splashing on the carpeted ground.

In the bright grave below, Tesla felt the murder like a second death. Her spirit shaken, she looked up to see a stain spreading across her sky, while a woman's voice unleashed a sob of agony. . . .

Harry caught hold of Kissoon's arm, and tried to pull him away from his mother, but the man was too strong. With a simple shrug he flung Harry off him, sending him stumbling through the gossamer walls to land on his back beneath the kitchen table. As he got to his feet he saw Raul throw himself upon Kissoon, but his assault was of such little consequence Kissoon didn't bother to dislodge his attacker. He simply fell to his knees beside Maeve, his rod raised to finish his matricide. Once, twice, three, four times the weapon fell, the house shaking with each blow as the mind that had conjured it was snuffed out.

By the time Harry reached Kissoon it was over. Spattered with Maeve's blood, his eyes spilling tears, he hauled himself to his feet. He wiped his nose like any backstreet thug, and said to Harry, "Thank you. I enjoyed that."

Tesla didn't want to hear. Didn't want to move. Didn't want anything but to float here as long as this limbo would have her.

But the cruelty came down from above, loud and clear, and try as she might she couldn't keep the anger from burgeoning in her. Her agitation informed the ground around her, and its motion drove her back towards her floating body. The closer she came to it the more frenzied the energies surrounding her became. They were eager for this reunion, she realized; they wanted her returned into her flesh.

And why? She had the answer the moment she slid back into the space behind her eyes. It wanted to make her heart leap. It wanted to make her lungs draw breath. And most of all, it wanted to come into her living body, and let that body be the crux of all that flowed here. A place where the mind could make sense of the flesh's confusions. A place where beasts and divinities could be dissolved, and get about the work of oneness.

In short, it wanted to give her the Art.

And there was no refusing it. She knew the moment it passed into her that the gift was also a possession. That she would be changed in ways that were presently unimaginable to her, changes that made the difference between life and death look like a nuance.

There was perhaps a moment between the first heartbeat and

the second, when she might have rejected the gift, and fled her body. Let it die again, and wither. But before she quite realized the choice was hers, she'd chosen.

And the Art had her.

"What is this?" Kissoon said, watching as the ground on which his mother's body lay was pierced and a thousand pinprick shafts of light broke from it.

Harry had no answers. All he could do was watch while the spectacle escalated, the old woman's corpse withering where it lay, as if the light—which gave off no discernible heat—was cremating it. If so, it was as adept a creator as destroyer, for even as Maeve O'Connell's corpse went to ash, another form, another woman, was resurrected in the midst of her pyre.

"Tesla?"

She looked like a tapestry sewn from fire, but it was her. God in Heaven, *it was her!*

Harry heard the drone of the Iad in his skull turn to the lowing of a fretful animal. Kissoon was retreating towards the front door, clearly as spooked as his faceless ally, but before he could reach the threshold Tesla called to him by name. Her voice was no more mellifluous for her transfiguration.

"This is unforgivable," she said, the fire threads embers now; her body almost her own. "Here, of all places, where both of us were born."

"Both of us?" said Kissoon.

"I am born here and now," she said. "And you are a witness to that, which is no little honor."

The troubled din of the Iad was continuing to escalate through this exchange, and now, staring past Kissoon into the darkness beyond the faltering walls, Harry saw its abstractions unknitting, its wheel fragmenting.

"Are you doing that?" Harry said to Tesla.

"Maybe," she said, looking down at her body, which was more solid by the moment. She seemed particularly interested in her hands. It took Harry only an instant to work out why. She was remembering the Jaff, whose hands had blazed with the Art. Blazed, then broken.

"Buddenbaum was right," Harry said.

"About what?"

"You and the Art."

"I didn't plan it this way," she said, her tone a mingling of puzzlement and distress. "If he hadn't shed blood—"

She looked up from her hands, back at Kissoon, who had retreated to the place where the door had once stood. Its conjured memory was barely visible now. As for the Iad, its forms turned in the air behind him, drawing the darkness into their loops as they circled, sealing themselves in shadow. Soon, they were just places where the stars failed to shine. Then not even that.

"This is the beginning of the end," Kissoon said.

"I know," Tesla replied, with a ghost of a smile on her face.

"You should be afraid," Kissoon told her.

"Why? Because you're a man capable of killing his own mother?" She shook her head. "The world's been full of scum like you from the beginning," she said quietly. "And if the end means there's no more to come, then that's not going to be much of a loss, is it?"

He stared at her for a few seconds, as if searching for some riposte. Finding none, he simply said, "We'll see . . ." and turning into the same darkness that had taken the Iad, he was gone.

There was another silence then, longer than the one before, while the walls of the whorehouse grew ever more insubstantial. Harry went down on his haunches, his eyes pricking with tears of relief, while the last dreg of the Iad's drone faded and disappeared from the bones of his head. Tesla, meanwhile, wandered a few yards from the place where she'd appeared—which now looked like any other spot in the street—and stared towards the fires. There were sirens whooping in the distance. The saviors were on their way with hoses, lights, and words of reason.

"How does it feel?" Harry asked her.

"I'm . . . trying to pretend nothing's happened to me," Tesla replied, her voice a gravelly whisper. "If I take it slowly . . . *very* slowly . . . maybe I won't get crazy."

"So it's not like they say—?"

"I can't see the past, if that's what you mean."

"What about the future?"

"Not from where I'm standing." She drew a deep breath. "We haven't told that story yet. That's why." There was a peal of laughter from the direction of the garden. "Your friend sounds happy," she said.

"That's Raul."

"Raul?" A tentative smile appeared on Tesla's face. "*That's* Raul? Oh my Lord, I thought I'd lost him . . . ." She faltered, as her gaze found Raul, standing among the last of the blossoming trees. "Look at that," she said.

"What?" said Harry.

"Oh, of course," she said, "I'm seeing with death's eyes." She pondered for a moment. "I wonder . . . ?" she said finally, raising her hand in front of her, index and middle fingers extended. "Do you want to try something?"

Harry got to his feet. "Sure."

"Come here."

He came to her, a little trepidatiously. "I don't know if this is going to work or not," she warned. "But who knows, maybe we'll get lucky."

She laid her fingers lightly against his jugular. "Do you feel anything?" she said.

"You're cold."

"That's all, huh? Okay, let's try . . . *here*." This time, she touched his forehead. "Still cold?" she said. He didn't reply. Just winced a little. "You want me to stop?"

"No," he said. "No, it's . . . just . . . *strange*—"

"Take another look at Raul," she said.

He turned his eyes in the direction of the trees and a gasp of delight escaped him.

"You can see them?"

"Yes," he smiled. "I can see them."

Raul was not in the fading garden alone. Maeve was standing close by him, no longer wrapped in drear and mist but clothed in a long, pale dress. The years had fallen from her. She was in her prime; a handsome woman of forty or so, standing arm in arm with a man who surely had lion in his lineage. He too was dressed for a summer evening, and gazed upon his wife as though this was the first hour of their courtship, and he hopelessly in love.

There was a fourth member of this unlikely group. Another phantom—Erwin Toothaker, Harry supposed—dressed in a shapeless jacket and baggy pants, watching from a little distance as the lovers exchanged their tender glances.

"Shall we join them?" Tesla said. "We've got a few minutes before people start to come sightseeing."

"What happens when they do?"

"We won't be here," Tesla replied. "It's time for us all to put our lives in order, Harry, whether we're dead, living, or something else entirely. It's time to make our peace with things, so we're ready for whatever happens next," she said.

"And you don't know what that'll be?"

"I know what it *won't* be," she said, leading the way into the garden.

"And what's that?" he asked, following her through a spiraling shower of petals.

"Like anything we've ever dreamed."

PART SEVEN

Leaves on the Story Tree

I

*E*verville's weekend of portents and manifestations did not go
unnoticed. In the days immediately following the events of
Festival Saturday and Sunday morning the city came under
the kind of scrutiny usually reserved for communities that have produced mass murderers or presidential candidates. Something of
strange consequence had happened there, nobody contested that.
But nor could anybody quite decide what, not even those who'd
been in the thick of it. In fact the people who should in principle
have been the most reliable witnesses (those who'd been at the
crossroads on Saturday afternoon; those trapped in the Town Hall
around two on Sunday morning) were in one sense the least useful.
Not only did they contradict one another, they contradicted themselves from hour to hour, recollection to recollection, their talk of
quakes and fires and rock falls mingled with details so farfetched as
to turn the story into tabloid fodder within a week.

No sooner had these details found print—along with the
inevitable comparisons to other sites of outlandish bloodshed like
Jonestown and Waco—than the city came under scrutiny from a
very different selection of examiners— psychics, UFO-ologists, and
New Age apocalyptics—their vocal presence further damaging the
legitimacy of the story. Television coverage that had been sympa-

thetic on Tuesday was getting wary or even cynical by the end of the week. *Time* magazine pulled a cover piece on the tragedy before it reached the presses, replacing it with a story inside that implied the whole event had been a publicity stunt that had spiraled out of control. The piece was accompanied by an unfortunate, and deeply unflattering, portrait of Dorothy Bullard, who'd been persuaded to be photographed in her nightgown, and was immortalized standing behind her screendoor looking like a lost soul under home arrest. The piece was entitled: *Is America Losing Its Mind?*

There was no denying that people had perished the previous weekend, of course, many of them horribly. The body count finally reached twenty-seven, including the manager of the Sturgis Motel and the three bodies discovered on the road outside the city, two of them burned beyond recognition, the third that of a sometime-journalist called Nathan Grillo. There were autopsies; there were overt and covert investigations by the police and FBI; there were public pronouncements as to the various causes of death. And of course there was gossip, some of which made it into the tabloids, much of which did not. The story that two skins made of some imitative alien substance were found at the motel did make the pages of the *Enquirer.* The rumor that three crosses had been found close to the summit of Harmon's Heights, with bodies crucified on two of them and a body of some unearthly creature slumped at the foot of the third did not.

In the second week of reporting, with the loonier opiners and witnesses ever more voluble, and the *Time* interpretation of events gaining adherents daily, the story took on a new lease of life with the suicide of one of Everville's most beloved citizens: Bosley Cowhick.

He was found in the kitchen of his diner at six-fifteen on Wednesday morning, a week and three days after Festival Weekend. He had shot himself, leaving, beside the cash register, a note, the contents of which were leaked to the press the following day, despite Jed Gilholly's best efforts to keep Bosley's last words under wraps.

The note bore no address. There were just a few rambling and ill-punctuated lines scrawled on the back of a menu.

I hope the Lord will forgive me for what I'm doing, he'd written, *but I can't go on living any more with all these things in my head. I know people are saying I'm crazy, but I saw what I saw and maybe I did wrong, but I did it for the sake of the baby. Seth Lundy knows that's true. He saw it too and he knows I had no choice, but I keep thinking that God put her into my hands to test me and I was not strong enough to do His will even if I did it for the best. I don't want to live any more thinking about it all the time. I have faith that the Lord will understand and be with me because He made me and He knows that I have always tried to do His will. Just sometimes it's too much. I'm sorry for hurting anybody. Goodbye.*

Inevitably, the mention of Seth Lundy in this pitiful missive set a whole new trail of inquiries in motion, as Lundy was one of the people who was listed as missing after the weekend. Bill Waits admitted witnessing the Lundy boy being assaulted by two of his fellow musicians, but that story remained uncorroborated. One of those two men, Larry Glodoski, was dead under highly suspicious circumstances, while the other, Ray Alstead, was in custody in Salem, suspected of his murder. He was being kept sedated, to minimize his eruptions of violence, which seemed to be associated with a fear that the deceased would be coming to find him because he'd seen more than he was supposed to see. Quite what he'd witnessed he would not say, but his obsession with the vengeful dead strengthened the belief among the police psychiatrists that he might well have been responsible for a number of the slaughters that night. He had gone on a rampage, the theory went, and was now in terror that his victims would come to claim him. Waits explicitly denied this—he'd been with Alstead most of the evening, he pointed out—but he'd also been in a highly intoxicated state for much of that time so he was not the most reliable of witnesses.

Now, with the death of Bosley Cowhick, the authorities lost a potentially useful witness and were left with another collection of puzzles. What had happened to Seth Lundy? Who exactly was this child that the God-fearing Bosley had felt so guilty for relinquishing? And, if the baby had even existed, to whom had he relinquished her?

There were no answers to any of these questions forthcoming in the short term. Bosley Cowhick was buried in the Potter Cemetery, alongside his mother, father, and maternal grandmother; Ray Alstead remained in a cell in Salem, while his lawyer fought to have him released on grounds of insufficient evidence; and as nobody came forward to report a missing baby, the child remained unidentified. As for the disappearance of Seth Lundy, it opened up what was in a sense to be the last of the Everville Mysteries to reach the eyes and ears of the general public, and that surrounded the figure of Owen Buddenbaum. Unlike the baby, nobody doubted Buddenbaum's existence. He'd been seen falling from a window, he'd been examined at Silverton Hospital, he'd been in the midst of events on the afternoon of Festival Saturday, which had ended in such turmoil, and he had still been in the city after nightfall, his presence noted and reported by several people. Indeed, he seemed to have been a constant factor in the weekend's events, so much so that in some quarters he was suggested to have been at the center of the whole cycle of events: the grand master, lording it over what was either a misbegotten hoax, a paranormal phenomenon, or a case of mass hysteria, depending on your point of view. If he could be found, it was widely believed, and persuaded to speak, he would be able to solve most, if not all, the unanswered questions.

A passable artist's likeness was made and appeared in several national magazines, as well as in both the *Oregonian* and the *Everville Register*. Almost immediately, the reports began to come back in. He had been seen in Louisiana two years before; he'd been sculling around a pool in Miami, just last week; he'd been spotted at Disneyland, moving through the crowd watching the Electric Parade. There were literally dozens of such sightings, some of them going back more than a decade, but even when the witness had had occasion to interact with the mysterious Mr. Buddenbaum there was little hard evidence about him. He certainly didn't speak of miracles or Mars or the secret workings of the world. He came and went, leaving behind him the vague sense of somebody who didn't belong in this day and age.

These reports, numerous though they were, were not weird enough to keep Everville's story in the public eye. Once all the funerals were over, and the photographers had been up Harmon's Heights to see the summit (which had been so thoroughly scoured by the authorities there was nothing left to photograph but the view); once the Bosley Cowhick suicide had been recounted, and the Owen Buddenbaum sightings run, the tale of Everville ran out of fuel.

By the end of September it was stale, and a month later it was the stuff of Halloween tales, or forgotten.

ii

I am born here and now, Tesla had said to Kissoon as she'd stood in the dwindling remains of Maeve O'Connell's house, and that had been the truth. The very ground which she'd assumed would be her grave had proved to be a womb, and she'd risen from it remade. Little wonder then that the weeks that followed resembled a second childhood, far stranger than her first.

As she'd told D'Amour, she felt little sense of revelation. The gift that she'd inadvertently received, or—and she did not discount this possibility—unconsciously *pursued*, had not given her any great insights into the structure of reality. Or if it had she was not yet resilient enough to open herself up to their presence. Even the minor miracle she'd worked in the whorehouse that night—allowing Harry to see with the eyes of the dead—now seemed foolhardy. She would not be tempted to go around bestowing such visions on people again; not until she was certain she had control of what she was doing, and that certainty, she suspected, would be a long time coming. Her mind felt more closed down now than it had before her resurrection, as though she had instinctively narrowed her field of vision when the prospect of infinite horizons loomed for fear her thoughts would take flight and she would lose her grip on who she was completely.

Now she was back in her old apartment in West Hollywood, where she had headed immediately after leaving Everville, not because she'd ever felt ecstatically happy there—she hadn't—but because she needed the comfort of the familiar. Many of the neighbors' faces had changed, but the comedies and dramas that surrounded her were essentially the same after five years. Every Saturday night the pre-op transsexual in the apartment below would get maudlin and play torch songs until four in the morning; at least twice a week the couple in the next building would have screaming matches ending in verbally explicit reconciliations; every day somebody's cat was sick on the stairs. It was less than glamorous, but it was home, and there in that cramped apartment with its cheap furniture and its cracked plaster walls she could pretend, at least for a time, that she was a normal woman living a normal life. Not perhaps the kind of normality Middle America would have recognized, but a reasonable approximation. She'd nurtured her hopes here and wasted time she could have used realizing them. She'd tended her wounded ego when a piece of work had been rejected. Tended it too when love had dealt her a blow. When she'd caught Claus cheating; when Jerry had left for Miami and never come back. Hard times, some of them. But the memories helped remind her of who she was, scars and all. Right now that was more important than the pleasures of self-deception.

Of course this was also the apartment where Mary Muralles had perished in the coils of Kissoon's Lix, and where she and Lucien—poor, guiltless Lucien—had talked about how people were vessels for the infinite. It was a phrase she had never forgotten. She might have thought it a kind of prophecy had she not believed what she'd told D'Amour: that the future always remained untold and thus untellable. Prophecy or no, the fact remained that she had become a kind of vessel for what had always been touted as an infinite power. Now she had it, she was determined not to be destroyed by it. She would learn to use the Art as Tesla Bombeck, or let it lie fallow inside her.

Once in a while during this period of restoration she would get a call from Harry in New York, checking in to see that all was well. He was sweetly considerate of her tender condition, and their exchanges were for the most part determinedly banal. They never quite stooped to talking politics, but he kept his side of the conversation light and general, waiting for her to deepen the exchange if she felt resilient enough. She seldom did. Most of the time they chatted about nothing in particular and left it at that. But as the weeks went by she started to feel more confident of her strength, and dared to talk, albeit tentatively, of what had happened in Everville, and its long-term consequences. Had he heard anything of the whereabouts of the Iad, for instance? Or of Kissoon? (The answer to both these questions was no.) What about Tommy-Ray, or Little Amy? (Again, the answer was no.)

"Everybody's keeping their heads down's my guess," Harry said. "Licking their wounds. Waiting to see who moves first."

"You don't sound all that bothered," Tesla said.

"You know what? I think Maeve had it right. She said to me: If you don't know what's ahead of you, why be scared of it? There's a lot of sense in that."

"There's also a lot of people gone, Harry, who had good reason to be scared."

"I know. I'm not trying to pretend it's all sunshine and flowers. It isn't and I know it isn't. But I've spent so much of my life looking for the Enemy—"

"And now you've seen it."

"Now I've seen it."

"And it sounds like you're smiling."

"I *am*. Shit, I don't even know why, but I am, I'm smiling. You know, Grillo used to tell me I was being simpleminded about all this shit, and we kinda fell out about it, but I hope to God he's hearing me, because he was right, Tes. He was right."

The conversation more or less petered out there, but Harry's mention of Grillo started her thinking of him, and once she'd begun there was no stopping. Until now she'd actively feared the thought of dealing with her feelings for him, certain she risked her hard-won self-possession if she was drawn into those troubled waters. But caught off-guard like this, obliged to let the memories snowball or be mowed down trying to halt them, she surrendered herself, and after all her trepidation, it was not so bad. In fact it was rather comforting, bringing him to mind. He'd changed radically in the eight years she'd known him: lost most of his idealism and all of his certainties and gained an obsession in their place. But under his increasingly prickly exterior, the man she had first met—charming, childish, irascible—remained visible, at least to her. They had never been lovers, and once in a while she'd regretted the fact. But there had never been a man in her life so constant as Grillo, or in the end so unalloyed in his affections. Even in more recent times, when she'd been traveling, and sometimes months would go by without their speaking, it had never taken more than a sentence or two between them before they were talking as though minutes had passed since their last exchange.

Recalling those long-distance conversations from truckstop diners and backroad gas stations, her thoughts turned to the labor that had consumed Grillo in the half-decade since Palomo Grove: the Reef. He had described it to her more than once as the work which he'd been put on the planet to perform, and though it demanded more energies and more patience than he had sometimes feared he was capable of supplying, he had kept faith with it, as far as she knew, to the end.

Now she wondered: Was it still intact? Still gathering tales of unlikely phenomenon from across the Americas? And the more she wondered, the more the notion of seeing for herself this collection of things out-of-whack and out-of-season intrigued her. She remembered Grillo giving her a couple of numbers to call if ever she wanted to access the system and leave her own messages, but she'd lost them. The only way to find out whether the Reef was still operational was to go to Omaha and see for herself.

She didn't want to fly. The idea of relinquishing control of life and limb to a man in a uniform had never appealed to her; and did so now less than ever. If she was to go, it would be on two wheels, like the old days.

She duly had her bike thoroughly overhauled, and on the sixth of October she started the journey that would take her back to the city where many years before Randolph Jaffe had sat in a dead-letter office gathering clues to the mystery that now bided its time in her cells.

II

Despite her best intentions, Phoebe had failed to dream of Joe that first night lying under Maeve O'Connell's bedroom window. Instead she'd dreamed of Morton. Of all things, Morton. And very unpleasant it proved to be. In this dream she was standing on the shore as it had looked before King Texas had overturned it, down to the birds who'd almost brought her adventures to a premature halt. And there, standing among the flock, dressed only in a vest and his Sunday best socks, was her husband.

Seeing him she instinctively covered her breasts, determined he wasn't going to lay his hands on them ever again, either for pleasure or punishment. As it was, he turned out to have other ideas. Producing a dirty burlap bag from behind his back, he said, "We're going to go down together, Phoebe. You know that's right."

"Down where?" she said to him.

He pointed to the water. "There," he said, approaching her while he reached into the bag. There were stones in it, gathered from the shore, and without another word he proceeded to thrust them into her mouth. Such was the logic of dreams that she now found her hands were glued to her breasts, and she couldn't raise them to prevent his tormenting her. She had no choice but to swallow the stones. Though some of them were as large as his fist, down they went, one after the other; ten, twenty, thirty. She steadily felt herself growing heavier, the weight carrying her to her knees. The sea had meanwhile crept up the shore and plainly intended to drown her.

She started to struggle, doing her choking best to plead with Morton. "I didn't mean any harm to come to you—" she told him.

"You didn't care," he said.

"I did," she protested, "at the beginning, I loved you. I thought we were going to be happy forever."

"Well, you were wrong," he growled, and started to reach into the bag for what she knew would be the biggest stone of the lot, the stone that would tip her over and leave her struggling in the rising water.

"Bye, bye, Feebs," he said.

"Damn you," she replied. "Why can't you ever see somebody else's point of view?"

"Don't want to," he replied.

"You're such a fool—"

"Now, we get to it."

"*Damn you!* Damn you!" As she spoke she felt her innards churning, grinding the stones in her belly together. She heard them crack and splinter. So did Morton.

"What are you doing?" he said, leaning over her, his breath like an ashtray.

In reply she spat out a hail of fractured stones, which peppered him from head to foot. They struck him like bullets, and he stumbled back into the surf, dropping his burlap bag as he did so. The wounds were not bleeding. The shrapnel she'd spat at him had simply lodged in his body and weighed him down. In seconds the eager waters had covered him and he was gone, leaving Phoebe on the shore, spitting up stone dust.

When she woke up the pillow was wet with saliva.

The experience dampened her enthusiasm for dreaming things into being. Suppose she hadn't killed Morton in her dream, she thought; would he have appeared on the doorstep the following day, with his burlap bag in hand? That wasn't a very comforting notion. She would have to be careful in future.

Her subconscious seemed to get the message. For the next little while she didn't dream at all, or if she did she remembered nothing of it. Time went by, and she determined to settle into the O'Connell house as best she could. She was assisted in this process by the arrival of a strange, tic-ridden little woman called Jarrieffa, who introduced herself as Musnakaff's second wife. She had been in service at the house, she explained, cleaning and cooking, and wished to be reemployed, happy to work in order to have a roof over her family's head. Phoebe agreed gladly, and the woman duly moved in, along with her four children, the eldest an adolescent called Enko, who was—he proudly explained—a bastard, got upon his mother by not one but two sailors (now deceased). The children's shouts and laughter quickly enlivened the house, which was big enough that Phoebe could always find a quiet spot to sit and think.

The presence of Jarrieffa and brood not only distracted her from the pain of being without Joe, it also helped to regulate the passage of time. Until their arrival Phoebe had pretty much been driven by a mixture of need and indulgence. She'd slept whenever the whim had taken her; eaten the same way. Now, the days began to recover their shape. Though the heavens still refused to offer any diurnal regularity—darkening without warning, brightening just as arbitrarily—she quickly trained herself to ignore these signs. And the increasing good order of the house was echoed in the city streets when she went out walking. Restoration was underway everywhere. Houses were being rebuilt and the harbor cleared; ships were being repaired and relaunched. Plainly these people didn't have Maeve's ability to dream things into being or they wouldn't have needed to sweat so much, but they seemed happy enough in their work. A few of her neighbors got to recognize her after a while, and would greet her with a surly look when they saw her out and about. They made no attempt to engage her in conversation, however, and her attempts to chat with them were always shortlived.

Isolation, she began to realize, could became a problem if she didn't find some way to be accepted into the community, and she started to make a list of possible ways to ease that process. A party, held in the street outside the house, perhaps? Or an invitation to the house for a few choice neighbors to whom she could tell her story.

While she was turning these options over she made a discovery that was to prove strangely influential. She found a cache of reading matter—books and newspapers—stuffed at the back of one of the closets. She realized as soon as she'd started to sort through the volumes that they had not been dreamed up by Maeve. More likely they'd been smuggled over into the Metacosm (or carried accidentally) by flesh-and-blood trespassers like herself. How else to explain the presence of a book of higher mathematics beside a treatise on the history of whaling beside a water-stained edition of the *Decameron*?

It was this last that most appealed to her, not for the text—which she found dry—but for the black and white etchings scattered throughout it. Two of the artists—the pictures were rendered in three distinct styles—had chosen episodes of great drama to depict, but the third was only interested in sex. His style was far from slick, but he made up for that by dint of his sheer audacity. The people in his pictures were caught in the throes of sexual frenzy, and none of them shy about it. Monks sported huge erections, peasant women lay on bales of hay with their legs in the air, a couple were fucking in mud: all in bliss.

One illustration in particular caught Phoebe's fancy. It pictured a woman kneeling in a field with her dress hitched up so that her amply endowed lover could come into her from behind. As she studied it, a ripple of pleasure passed through her, her flesh remembering what her mind had tried so hard to forget: Joe's hands, Joe's lips, Joe's body. She felt his palms against her breasts and belly; felt the pressure of his hips against her buttocks.

"Oh God . . . " she sighed at last, and pitched the book back into the closet, slamming the door on it.

That wasn't the end of the story however; not by a long way. When she retired a couple of hours later, the image and its consequences still lingered. She would not be able to sleep, she knew, unless she pleasured herself a little, so she lay there on her mattress—which was still where she'd first set it, in front of the window—and with her eyes on the undulating sky she played between her legs until sleep found her.

She dreamed; of a man. But this time it was not Morton.

Joe had never found the fire watchers who had believed him a manifestation of the 'shu, nor—in all his wanderings around the city—did he encounter anybody else whose eyes were acute enough to make him out. Was whatever visible presence he possessed—the shred of self the fire watchers had seen—dwindling still further? He feared so. If they were to see him now he doubted they'd be quite so worshipful.

Several times he decided to leave Liverpool altogether—he didn't find the sights and sounds of reconstruction comforting; they only reminded him of how removed from life he'd become—but something kept him from leaving. He tried to attach some rationale to his reluctance (he needed time to recuperate, time to plan, time to understand his condition), but none of these explanations touched the truth. Something was holding him in the city, an invisible cord around his invisible neck.

Then, one gloomy day while he was loitering down by the harbor watching the ships, he felt something tug at him.

At first, he dismissed the sensation as wish-fulfillment. But it came again, and again, and on the third try he dared allow himself a measure of excitement. This was the first time since the fire watchers he'd felt some interaction with the world outside his thoughts.

He didn't resist the summons. Up from the harbor he went, following the unspoken call.

Phoebe dreamed she was back in Dr. Powell's office, and Joe was out in the hallway, where she'd first seen him, painting the ceiling. It was raining hard. She could hear the deluge slapping against the window of the empty waiting room, and beating on the roof.

"Joe?" she said.

Her lover-to-be was perched on the top of a ladder, naked to the waist, his broad back spattered with pale green paint. Oh, but he looked so fine, with his hair cropped close to his beautiful head, and his ears jutting out, and that patch of hair at the small of his back disappearing under his belt into the crack of his ass.

"Joe?" she said, hoping she could get him to turn around. "I've got something to show you."

As she spoke she went to the low table in the middle of the waiting room and, clearing off all the dog-eared magazines with one sweep of her arm, she lay on it facing him. For some reason the rain had started to come through the ceiling, and it fell on her in sharp, straight drops. They did more than drench her; they began to wash the clothes from her body as if her blouse and dress had been painted on, the colors running off her limbs and pooling around the table, leaving her naked, which was exactly how she wanted to be.

"You can turn round now," she said to him, putting her hand down between her legs. He always liked to watch her play. "Go on," she said to him, "turn round and *look at me.*"

He'd passed by this house on the hill before, and wondered who lived here. He would soon find out.

He was moving down the path to the steps, up the steps to the door, through the door to the staircase. Somebody at the top of the flight was murmuring: He couldn't quite hear what. He paused a moment to listen. The speaker was a woman, he could make out that much, but he couldn't yet grasp the words, so he started to ascend.

"Joe?"

He had heard her; there was no doubt of that. He'd put down his paintbrush and was wiping his hands, taking his time, knowing it only made the moment when their eyes met all the more intense if it was delayed a little.

"I've waited a long time for this . . . " she told him.

* * *

He didn't dare believe what he was hearing. Not the words them-selves, though they were wonderful: the voice that spoke them.

Phoebe *here?* How was that possible? She was in Everville, the world he'd left and lost forever. Not here; not in this musty house, calling to him. That was too much to hope for.

"Oh, Joe . . . " the woman was sighing, and God in Heaven, it sounded like her, so very like her.

He went to the door, knowing whoever was speaking was on the other side of it and suddenly afraid to enter, afraid to know it wasn't her. He paused a moment, preparing himself for the pain to come, then slipped inside. The room was huge and chaotic. His gaze instantly went to the bed at the far end. It was piled high with pil-lows and scattered with pieces of paper, but there was nobody lying there.

Then, from the tangle of sheets on the floor, the voice, *her* voice, warm with welcome.

"Joe . . . " she said. "I've missed you so much."

He was looking at her. Finally, he was looking at her. She smiled at him, and he smiled back, descending the ladder and sauntering in from the hallway to the table where she lay, her body wet with rain.

"I'm all yours," she said.

It was her. God in Heaven, it was her! How she came to be here didn't matter. Nor did why. All that mattered was that here she was, his Phoebe, his glorious Phoebe, whose face he'd despaired of ever seeing again.

Did she know he was close?

Her eyes were shut, her pupils roving behind her lids, but he didn't doubt she was dreaming of him. There was sweat on her face, and on her legs, which were bare. He longed for the fingers to pull away the sheet that lay between; for the lips to kiss that place and the cock to pleasure it. To make again the love they'd made those afternoons in Everville, bodies intertwined as though they'd never be separated.

"Come closer," she said in her sleep.

He did so. Stood over the bottom of her bed and looked down on her. If love had weight, she'd feel it now. Or if a scent, smell it, or if a shadow, know it was cast upon her. He didn't care how she came to realize his presence, as long as somehow she did; somehow understood that after the dream of him she would find his spirit waiting close by, ready for the moment when she opened her eyes and made him real.

He was standing between her legs now, covered in paint. Flecks and splashes of it, all over his face and in his hair, on his shoulders and down over the chest. She reached up towards him.

In dreams, and out of them, reached up . . .

He felt her touch. Though he had no skin, he felt the contact nevertheless, where his belly had been.

"Look at the state of you," she said, her fingers moving up from his stomach to the muscle of his chest, brushing his invisible presence, now with her fingers, now with her thumb. And wherever she'd touched him, he saw the air begin to seethe and knit, as though— dared he even hope?—she was dreaming him back into being.

The paint was coming off, bit by bit. She brushed a little from his cheek and from the bridge of his nose, from his left ear, and from around his eyes. Then, though the job of paint-removal was far from finished, she went back down to his belt and unbuckled it. He smiled conspiratorially, and let her unbutton and unzip his pants, which despite their bagginess could not conceal his arousal. It seemed her finger had learned the trick of the rain, because the fabric around his groin now ran off as her dress and blouse had done, fully exposing him. He put his hands on his head, and thrust his hips forward, grinning while she ran her fingers over his cock and balls.

* * *

There were no words for this bliss, seeing his flesh knitting together as she stroked it; his balls remade unwounded, his cock as fine as she remembered it, perhaps finer.

And then—dammit!—from somewhere in the rooms below, the sound of children shouting. Phoebe's hand stopped moving, as though the din had reached into her dream.

Children? What were children doing in the doctor's offices? Oh Lord, and here was she, stark naked. She froze, hoping they would go away, and for a few moments the hollering faded. She waited, holding her breath. Five seconds, ten seconds. Had they fled? It seemed so.

She started to reach for Joe's arm, to draw him down onto her and into her, but as she did so—

They began again, pounding up the stairs, shrieking in their games. He would gladly have strangled them both at that moment and there wouldn't have been a lover alive who'd have blamed him for it. But the damage was done. Phoebe's hand dropped back down onto her breast. She let out a soft, irritated moan.

Then her eyes flickered open.

Oh, what a dream; and what a way to be woken from it. She'd have to tell Jarrieffa that in future the children—

Something moved in front of her, silhouetted against the window. For a heartbeat she thought it was outside—some shreds of cloth or litter, rising in a gust of dusty wind—but no. It was *here*, in the room with her: something ragged, retreating into the shadows.

She would have screamed, but that the thing was plainly more afraid of her than she of it. And no wonder. It was a tattered, twitching thing, wet and raw; it posed no threat.

"Whatever the fuck you are," she told it, *"get the hell out of here!"*

She thought she heard a sound from it, but with so much noise from the kids, who were now just outside the door, she couldn't be certain.

She called "Stay out!" to them, but they either ignored her or missed the warning, because no sooner had she spoken than the door opened and in Jarrieffa's youngest pair tumbled, brawling.

"*Out!*" she yelled again, fearful that even if the interloper was beyond harming them it would still give them a fright. They ceased their hullabaloo, and the littler of the two, catching sight of the thing in the shadows, began to shriek.

"It's all right," Phoebe said, moving to usher them out of the room. As she did so the creature emerged from the murk and headed for the open door, pausing only to look in Phoebe's direction. It had eyes, she saw; human eyes attached by trailing threads of dark flesh to an ear and a piece of cheek, the air in which the fragments hung buzzing, as though it was some way of solidifying itself.

Then the creature was gone, out past the panicking children into the hallway.

Phoebe heard Jarrieffa on the stairs, demanding to know what all the noise was about, but her words were cut short, and by the time Phoebe was out onto the landing the woman was clinging to the banisters sobbing with fear, watching the creature retreating down the flight. Then, recovering herself, she began up the stairs afresh, yelling for her kids.

"They're okay," Phoebe told her. "Just frightened, that's all." While Jarrieffa gathered the children with her arms Phoebe went to the top of the stairs and looked down after the intruder. The front door stood open. He'd already slipped away.

"I'll fetch Enko," Jarrieffa said.

"It's all right," Phoebe said. "He wasn't going to—"

The rest of the words failed her, as halfway down the flight— halfway to closing the door to lock the creature out—she realized whose gaze she had met in that instant before the creature had fled.

"Oh God," she said.

"Enko'll shoot it," Jarrieffa was saying.

"No!" Phoebe shouted. "No—"

She knew already what she'd done: half-dreamed him, then driven him away incomplete. It was unbearable.

Gasping for air, she stumbled on down the stairs, and across the hallway to the front door. The sky was murky, and the light drear, but she could see that the street was empty in both directions.

Joe had gone.

ii

Despite the fact that Grillo's body had been identified, it seemed he had confounded any trail that might have led the authorities back to the Reef in the event of his demise. When Tesla got to the house in Omaha it was untouched. There was dust on every surface and mold on every perishable in the fridge, drifts of mail behind the front door, and a backyard so overgrown she could not see the fence.

But the Reef itself was in good working order. She sat in Grillo's stale, windowless office for a few minutes, amazed at the amount of equipment he'd managed to pile into it: six monitors, two printing machines, four fax machines, and three walls of floor-to-ceiling shelves, all loaded down with tapes, cassettes, and box-files of notes. In front of her the messages continued to fill up the screens as they had presumably been doing since his departure. Getting a grasp of the system, and of all the information it contained, was not going to be a simple matter. She was here for days, at least.

She headed back out to pick up a few essentials from the local market—coffee, milk, bagels, peaches, and (though she hadn't touched alcohol since her resurrection) vodka—then sorted out a few domestic details (the house was freezing, so she had to turn on the heating; and the contents of the fridge and the garbage can in the kitchen had to be dumped to clear the sickening smell) before settling down to familiarize herself with Grillo's masterwork.

She'd never been particularly adept at handling technology. It took her the best part of two days to teach herself how to operate everything, working slowly so as not to accidentally wipe some invaluable treasure from the files. She was aided in her exploration by Grillo's handwritten notes, which were pinned, glued, and taped to both the machines and shelves. Without them, she would have despaired.

Once she had a basic grasp of both the system and his methodology, she began to make her way through the files themselves. They numbered in the thousands. The names of some were self-evident— *Dog-Star Saucers*; *Seraphic Visions*; *Death by Animal Ingestation*— but Grillo had titled most of them for his own amusement, obliquely, and she had to call them up one by one in order to find out what they were about. There was a kind of poetry in some of the titling, along with Grillo's love of puns and a playful obscurantism. *The Devouring Song, Zoological Pardons, The Fiend Venus, Neither Here nor There, Amen to That*; the list went on and on.

What soon became apparent was that while Grillo had assiduously collected and collated these reports, he had not edited them. There was no distinction made within each file between a minor bizarrity and something of cataclysmic scale; nor any between a lucid, measured account and a scrap of babble. Like a loving parent, unwilling to favor one child over another, Grillo had found a home for everything.

Increasingly impatient, Tesla scrolled page after page after page, still hoping for come clue to the mystery in her cells. And while she dug, the reports kept pouring in from all directions.

From Kentucky a woman who claimed she had been twice raped by "the Higher Ones," whoever they were, checked in to report that her violators were now moving south-southeast towards the state, and would be visible tomorrow dusk in the form of a yellow cloud "that will look like two angels tied back to back."

From New Orleans a certain Dr. Tournier wanted to share his discovery that disease was caused by an inability to speak "with a true tongue," and that he had cured over six hundred patients thought terminal by teaching them the basic vocabulary of a language he dubbed Nazque.

From her home town of Philadelphia came a piece of psychotic prose from one who signed himself (it was surely a man) the Cockatrice, warning the world that from Wednesday next he would be in glory, and only the blind would be safe—

For three days she remained hostage to the Reef, like an atheist locked in the Vatican library, contemptuous, repulsed even, but going back and back to the shelves, morbidly fascinated by the dogmas she found there. Even in her most frustrated moods she could not quite shake the suspicion that somewhere amid this wilderness of insanities were gems she could profit by—knowledge of the Art, knowledge of the Iad—if only she could find them. But it became increasingly clear that she might very well have passed over them already, their form so garbled or their code so dense she'd failed to recognize them for what they were.

At last, in the middle of the afternoon of the fifth day, she told herself: If you do this much longer you'll be as crazy as they are. Turn it off, woman. Just turn the damn thing off.

She flicked back to the file list, and was about to kill the machines when one of the names caught her eye.

The Ride Is Over, it read.

Perhaps she'd passed over these four words before, and not recognized them, but now they rang bells. *The Ride Is Over* had been the headline Grillo had wanted for his last report from Palomo Grove; he'd told her later she could use it for a screenplay if she wanted, as long as the movie was cheap and opportunistic. It was probably just a coincidence but she called up the file anyway, determined it would be the last.

Her heart jumped at the words that appeared on the screen.

Tesla, Grillo had written, *I hope it's you out there. But whether it is or it isn't, I guess it doesn't matter much now, because if you're reading this—whoever you are—I'm dead.*

It was the last thing she'd expected to find, but now that it was there in front of her, she wasn't so surprised. He'd known he was dying, after all, and though he'd always hated farewells, even of the casual variety, he was still a journalist to the bone. Here was his final report then: intended for a readership of one.

It's the middle of June right now, he'd written, *and the last couple of weeks I've been feeling like shit. The doc says things are moving faster than he's seen before. He wants me to go in for tests, but I told him I'd prefer to use the time working. He asked me on what, and of course I couldn't tell him about the Reef so I lied and said I was writing a book.*

(It's strange. While I'm typing this I'm imagining you sitting there, Tes, reading it, hearing my voice in your head.)

She could; she could hear it loud and clear.

I tried to write once, when I first got the bad news. I'm not sure it was ever going to be a book, but I did try and put down a few memories, to see how they looked on the page. And you know what? They were clichés, all of them. What I remembered was real enough—the feel of my mother's cheek, the smell of my dad's cigars; summers in Chapel Hill, North Carolina; a couple of Christmases in Maine with my grandmother—but there was nothing that you couldn't find in a million autobiographies. It didn't make the memories any less meaningful to me, but it did make the idea of writing them down redundant.

So I thought: Okay, maybe I'll write about the things that happened in the Grove. Not just what went on at Coney Eye, but about Ellen (I think of her a lot these days) and her kid, Philip (I don't remember if you met him or not), and Fletcher in the mall. But that plan went to shit just as quickly. I'd be writing away and some report would come in from Buttfuck, Ohio, about angels or UFOs or skunks speaking in tongues, and when I got back to what I'd been writing the words were like week-old cold cuts. They just lay there, stale and tasteless and gray.

I was so pissed with myself. Here was me, the wordsmith, writing about something that had actually happened in the real world, and I couldn't make it sing; not the way these crazies who were putting down whatever wild shit came into their heads could do it.

Then I began to see why—

Tesla leaned forward at this juncture, as if she and Grillo were debating over a couple of glasses of vodka, and now he was getting to the crux of his argument.

"Tell me, Grillo," she murmured to the screen, "tell me why."

I wouldn't let the truth go. I wanted to describe things just the way they'd happened (no, that's not right; the way I remembered them happening), so I killed what I was doing trying to be precise, instead of letting it fly, letting it sing. Letting it be ragged and contradictory, like stories have to be.

What really happened in Palomo Grove doesn't matter anymore. What matters is the stories people tell about it.

I'm thinking while I'm writing this: None of it makes much sense, it's just fragments. Maybe you can connect it up for me, Tes.

That's part of it, isn't it? Connecting everything.

I know if I could just let my mother's skin and Christmas in Maine and Ellen and Fletcher and the talking skunks and every damn thing I ever felt or saw be part of the same story and called that story me, instead of always looking for something separate from the things I've felt or seen, it wouldn't matter that I was going to die soon, because I'd be part of what was going on and on. Connecting and connecting.

The way I see it now, the story doesn't give a shit if you're real or not, alive or not. All the story wants is to be told. And I guess in the end, that's what I want too.

Will you do that for me, Tes?

Will you make me part of what you tell? Always?

She wiped the tears from her eyes, smiling at the screen, as though Grillo was leaning back in his chair, sipping his vodka, waiting for her to reply.

"You've got it, Grillo," she said, reaching out to touch the glass. "So . . . " she added, "what happens next?" The age-old question.

There was a breathless moment while the glass trembled beneath her fingers. Then she knew.

III

S eptember had been a month of recuperation for Harry. He'd made a project of tidying his tiny office on Forty-fifth Street; touched base with friends he hadn't seen all summer; even attempted to reignite a few amorous fuses around town. In this last he was completely unsuccessful: Only one of the women for whom he left messages returned his call, and only to remind him that he'd borrowed fifty bucks.

He was not unhappy then, to find a girl in her late teens at his apartment door that Tuesday night in early October. She had a ring through her left nostril, a black dress too short for her health, and a package.

"Are you Harry?" she said.

"Yep."

"I'm Sabina. I got something for you." The parcel was cylindrical, four feet long, and wrapped in brown paper. "You want to take it from me?" she said.

"What is it?"

"I'm going to drop it—" the girl said, and let the thing go. Harry caught it before it hit the floor. "It's a present."

"Who from?"

"Could I maybe get a Coke or something?" the girl said, looking past Harry into the apartment.

The word *sure* was barely out of Harry's mouth and Sabina was pushing past him. What she lacked in manners she made up for in curves, he thought, watching her head on down the hall. He could live with that. "The kitchen's on your right," he told her, but she headed straight past it into the living room.

"Got anything stronger?" she said.

"There's probably some beers in the fridge," he replied, slamming the front door with his foot and following her into the living room.

"Beer gives me gas," she said.

Harry dropped the package in the middle of the floor. "I've got some rum, I think."

"Okay," she shrugged, as though Harry had been the one to suggest it and she really wasn't that interested.

He ducked into the kitchen to find the liquor, digging through the cupboard for an uncracked glass.

"You're not as weird as I thought you'd be," Sabina said to him meanwhile. "This place is nothing special."

"What were you expecting?"

"Something more crazy, you know. I heard you get into some pretty sick stuff."

"Who told you that?"

"Ted."

"You knew Ted?"

"I more than knew him," she said, appearing at the kitchen door. She was trying to look sultry, but her face, despite the kohl and the rouge and the blood-red lip gloss was too round and childlike to carry it off.

"When was this?" Harry asked her.

"Oh . . . three years ago. I was fourteen when I met him."

"That sounds like Ted."

"We never did anything I didn't want to do," she said, accepting the glass of rum from Harry. "He was always real nice to me, even when he was going through lousy times."

"He was one of the good guys," Harry said.

"We should drink to him," Sabina replied.

"Sure." They tapped glasses. "Here's to Ted."

"Wherever he is," Sabina added. "Now, are you going to open your present?"

It was a painting. Ted's great work, in fact, *D'Amour in Wyckoff Street*, taken from its frame, stripped off its support and somewhat ignominiously tied up with a piece of frayed string.

"He wanted you to have it," Sabina explained, as Harry pulled back the sofa to unroll the painting fully. The canvas was as powerful as Harry remembered. The seething color field in which the street was painted, the impasto from which his features had been carved, and of course that detail Ted had been so proud to point out to Harry in the gallery: the foot, the heel, the snake writhing as it was trodden lifeless. "I guess maybe if somebody had offered him ten grand for it," Sabina was saying, "he would have given you something else. But nobody bought it, so I thought I'd come and give it to you."

"And the gallery didn't mind?"

"They don't know it's gone," Sabina said. "They put it in storage with all the other pictures they couldn't sell, I guess they figured they'd find buyers sooner or later, but people don't want pictures like Ted's on their walls. They want stupid stuff." She had come to Harry's shoulder as she spoke. He could smell a light honey-scent off her. "If you like," she said, "I could come back and make a new support for the canvas. Then you could hang it over your bed—" she slid him a sly look, "or wherever."

Harry didn't want to offend the girl. No doubt she'd done as Ted would have wished, bringing the picture here, but the notion of waking to an image of Wyckoff Street every morning wasn't particularly comforting.

"I can see you want to think about it," Sabina said, and leaning across to Harry laid a quick kiss beside his mouth. "I'll stop by sometime next week, okay?" she said. "You can tell me then." She finished her rum and handed the empty glass to Harry. "It was really nice meeting you," she said, suddenly and sweetly formal. She was slowly retreating to the door as if waiting for a sign from Harry that she should stay.

He was tempted. But he knew he wouldn't think much of himself in the morning if he took advantage. She was seventeen, for God's sake. By Ted's standards that was practically senile, of course. But there was a part of Harry that still wanted seventeen year olds to be dreaming of love, not being plied with rum and coaxed into bed by men twice their age.

She seemed to realize that nothing was going to come of this, and gave him a slightly quizzical smile. "You really *aren't* the way I thought you'd be," she remarked, faintly disappointed.

"I guess Ted didn't know me as well as he thought he did."

"Oh it wasn't just Ted told me about you," she said.

"Who else?"

"Everyone and no one," she replied with a lazy shrug. She was at the door now. "See you, maybe," she said, and opening the door was away, leaving him wishing he'd kept her company a little longer.

Later, as he trailed to the john at three in the morning, he halted in front of the painting, and wondered if Mimi Lomax's house on Wyckoff Street was still standing. The question was still with him when he woke the following morning, and as he walked to his office, and as he sorted through his outstanding paperwork. It didn't matter either way, of course, except to the extent that the question kept coming between him and his business. He knew why: He was afraid. Though he'd seen terrors in Palomo Grove, and come face to face with the Iad itself in Everville, the specter of Wyckoff Street had never been properly exorcised. Perhaps it was time to do so now: to deal once and for all with that last corner of his psyche still haunted by the stale notion of an evil that coveted human souls.

He turned the notion over through the rest of the day, and through the day following that, knowing in his gut he would have to go sooner or later, or the subject would only gain authority over him.

On Friday morning, he got to his office to find that somebody had mailed him a mummified monkey's head, elaborately mounted on what looked suspiciously like a length of human bone. It was not the first time he'd had such items come his way—some of them warnings, some of them talismans from well-wishers, some of them simply ill-advised gifts—but today the presence of this object, its aroma stinging his sinuses, seemed to Harry a goad, to get him on his way. What are you afraid of? the gaping thing seemed to demand. Things die, and spoil, but look, I'm laughing.

He boxed the thing up, and was about to deposit it in the trash when some superstitious nerve in him twitched. Instead he left it where it lay in the middle of his desk and, telling it he'd be back soon, he headed off to Wyckoff Street.

ii

It was a cold day. Not yet New York–bitter (that was probably a month, six weeks from now), but cold enough to know that there'd be no more shirtsleeve days this side of winter. He didn't mind. The summer months had always brought him the most trouble—this summer had been no exception—and he was relieved to feel things running down around him. So what if the trees shed, and the leaves rotted and the nights drew in? He needed the sleep.

He found that much of the neighborhood around Wyckoff Street had changed drastically since he'd last been here, and the closer he got the more he dared hope his destination would be so much rubble.

Not so. Wyckoff Street remained almost exactly as it had been ten years before, the houses as gray and grim as ever. Rock might melt in Oregon, and the sky crack like a dropped egg, but here earth was earth and sky was sky and whatever lived between was not going to be skipping anywhere soon.

He wandered along the littered sidewalk to Mimi Lomax's house, expecting to find it in a state of dilapidation. Again, not so. Its present owner was plainly attentive. The house had a new roof, a new chimney, new eaves. The door he knocked on had been recently painted.

There was no reply at first, though he heard the murmur of voices from inside. He knocked again, and this time, after a delay of a minute or so, the door was opened a sliver and a woman in late middle-age, her face taut and sickly, stared out at him with red-rimmed eyes.

"Are you him?" she said. Her voice was frail with exhaustion. "Are you De Amour?"

"I'm D'Amour, yes." Harry was already uneasy. He could smell the woman from where he stood; sour sweat and dirt. "How do you know who I am?" he asked her.

"She said—" the woman replied, opening the door a little wider.

"Who said?"

"She's got my Stevie upstairs. She's had him there for three days." Tears were pouring down the woman's cheeks as she spoke. She made no effort to wipe them away. "She said she wouldn't let him go till you got here." She stepped back from the door. "You gotta make her let him go. He's all I got."

Harry took a deep breath, and stepped into the house. At the far end of the hallway stood a woman in her early twenties. Long black hair, huge eyes shining in the gloom.

"This is Stevie's sister. Loretta."

The young woman clutched her rosary, and stared at Harry as though he was an accomplice of whatever was upstairs.

The older woman closed the front door and came to Harry's side. "How did it know you were coming here?" she murmured.

"I don't know," Harry replied.

"It said if we tried to leave—" Loretta said, her voice barely a whisper, "it'd kill Stevie."

"Why do you say *it?*"

"Because it's not human." She glanced up the flight, her face fearful. "It's from Hell," she breathed. "Can't you smell it?"

There was certainly a foul smell. This wasn't the fish-market stench of the Zyem Carasophia's chamber. This was shit and fire.

Heart cavorting, Harry went to the bottom of the stairs. "You stay down here," he told the two women, and started up the flight, stepping over the spot on the fifth stair where Father Hess's head had been resting when he expired. There was no noise from upstairs, and none now from below. He climbed in silence, knowing the creature awaiting him was listening for every creaking stair. Rather than let it think he was attempting to approach in silence and failing, he broke the hush himself.

"Coming, ready or not," he said.

The reply came immediately. And he knew within a syllable what thing this was.

"Harry—" said Lazy Susan. "Where have you been? No, don't tell me. You've been seeing the Boss Man, haven't you?"

While the demon talked, Harry reached the top of the stairs and crossed the landing to the door. The paint was blistered.

"You want a job, Harry?" Lazy Susan went on. "I don't blame you. Times are about to get *real bad.*"

The door was already open an inch. Harry pushed it, lightly, and it swung wide. The room beyond was almost completely dark, the drapes drawn, the lamp on the floor so encrusted with caked excrement it barely glimmered. The bed itself had been stripped down to the mattress, which in turn had been burned black. On it lay a youth, dressed in a filthy T-shirt and boxer shorts, face-down.

"Stevie?" Harry said.

The boy didn't move.

"He's asleep right now," said Lazy Susan's curdled voice from the darkness beyond the bed. "He's had a busy time."

"Why don't you just let the kid go? It's me you want."

"You overestimate your appeal, D'Amour. Why would I want a fucked-up soul like yours when I could have this pure little thing?"

"Then why did you bring me here?"

"I didn't. Sure, Sabina may have planted the thought in your head. But you came of your own accord."

"Sabina's a friend of yours?"

"She'd probably prefer mistress. Did you fuck her?"

"No."

"Ah, *D'Amour!*" the Nomad said, exasperated. "After all the trouble I went to getting her wet. You're not turning queer on me, are you? No. You're too straight for your own good. You're boring, D'Amour. Boring, boring—"

"Well maybe I should just piss off home," Harry said, turning back to the door.

There was a rush of motion behind him; he heard the bedsprings creak, and Stevie let out a little moan. "*Wait,*" the Nomad hissed. "*Don't you ever turn your back on me.*"

He glanced over his shoulder. The creature had shimmied up onto the bed and now had its bone and muck body poised over its victim. It was the color of the filth on the lamp, but wet, its too-naked anatomy full of peristaltic motions.

"Why's it always *shit?*" Harry said.

The Nomad cocked its head. Whatever features were upon it all resembled wounds. "Because shit's all we have, Harry, until we're returned to glory. It's all God allows us to play with. Maybe a little fire, once in a while, as long as He isn't looking. Speaking of fire, I saw Father Hess the other day, burning in his cell. I told him I might see you—"

Harry shook his head. "It doesn't work, Nomad," he said.

"What doesn't work?"

"The fallen angel routine. I don't believe it any more." He started towards the bed. "You know why? I saw some of your relatives in Oregon. In fact, I almost got crucified by a couple of them. Brutish little fucks like you, except they didn't have any of your pretensions. They were just in it for the blood and the shit." He kept approaching the bed as he talked, far from certain what the creature would do. It had disemboweled Hess with a few short strokes and he had no reason to believe it had lost the knack. But, stripped of its phoney autobiography, what was it? A thug with a few days' training in an abattoir.

"Stop right there," the creature said when Harry was a yard from the bed. It was shuddering from head to foot. "If you come any closer, I'll kill Little Stevie. And I'll throw him down the stairs, just like Hess."

Harry raised his hands in mock-surrender. "Okay," he said, "this is as close as I get. I just wanted to check the family resemblance. You know, it's uncanny."

The Nomad shook his head. "I was an angel, D'Amour," it said, its voice troubled. "I remember Heaven. I do. As though it were yesterday. Clouds and light and—"

"And the sea?"

"The sea?"

"Quiddity."

"No!" it yelled. "I was in Heaven. I remember God's heart, beating, beating, all the time—"

"Maybe you were born on a beach."

"I've warned you once," the creature said. "I'll kill the boy."

"And what will that prove? That you're a fallen angel? Or that you're the little bully I say you are?"

The Nomad raised its hands to its wretched face. "Ohh, you're clever, D'Amour," it sighed. "You're very clever. But so was Hess." The creature parted its fingers, exhaling its sewer breath. "And look what happened to him."

"Hess wasn't clever," Harry said softly. "I loved him and I respected him, but he was deluded. You're pretty much alike, now that I think about it." He leaned an inch or two closer to the entity. "You think you fell from Heaven. He thought he was serving it. You believed the same things, in the end. It was stupid to kill him, Nomad. It's not left you with very much."

"I've still got you," the creature replied. "I could fuck with your head until the Crack of Doom."

"Nah," Harry said, standing upright. "I'm not afraid of you any longer. I don't need prayers—"

"Oh don't you?" it growled.

"I don't need a crucifix. I just need the eyes in my head. And what I see—what I see is an anorexic little shit-eater."

At this, it launched itself at him, shrieking, all the wounds in its head wide. Harry retreated across the filthy floor, avoiding its whining talons by inches, until his back was flat against the wall. Then it closed on him, flinging its arms up at his head. He raised his hands to protect his eyes, but the creature didn't want them, at least not yet. Instead it dug its fingers into the flesh at the back of his neck, driving its spiked feet into the wall to either side of his body.

"Now *again*, D'Amour—" the creature said. Harry felt the blood pour down his spine. Heard his vertebrae crack. "Am I an angel?" Its face was inches from Harry's, its voice issuing from all the holes at once. "I want an answer, D'Amour. It's very important to me. I was in Heaven once, wasn't I? Admit it."

Very, very slowly, Harry shook his throbbing head.

The creature sighed. "Oh, D'Amour," it said, uprooting one of its hands from the back of Harry's neck and bringing it round to stroke his larynx. The growl had gone from its voice. It was no longer the Nomad; it was Lazy Susan. "I'll miss you," it said, its fingers breaking the skin of Harry's throat. "There hasn't been a night when I haven't thought of us"—its tone was sultry now—"here, in the dark together."

On the bed behind the creature, the boy moaned.

"*Hush* . . . " Lazy Susan said.

But Stevie was beyond being silenced. He wanted the comfort of a prayer. "Hail Mary, full of grace—" he began.

The creature glanced round at him, the Nomad surfacing again to shriek for the boy to shut the fuck up. As it did so, Harry caught hold of the hand at his neck, lacing his fingers with the talons. Then he threw his weight forward. The Nomad's feet were loosed from the wall and the two bodies, locked together, stumbled into the middle of the room.

Instantly, the creature drove its fingers deeper into Harry's nape. Blinded by pain, he swung around, determined that wherever they fell it wouldn't be on top of the boy. They reeled wildly, round and round, until Harry lost his balance and fell forward, carrying the Nomad ahead of him.

Its body struck the charred door, which splintered under the combined weight of their bodies. Through his tear-filled eyes Harry glimpsed the misbegotten face in front of him, its hands slack with shock. Then they were out onto the landing. It was bright after the murk of the bedroom. For the Nomad, painfully so. It convulsed in Harry's embrace, hot phlegm spurting from its maws. He seized the moment to wrest its talons from his neck, then their momentum carried them against the banisters, which cracked but did not break, and over they went.

It was a fall of perhaps ten feet, the Nomad under Harry, shrieking still. They hit the stairs, and rolled and rolled, finally coming to rest a few steps from the bottom.

The first thing Harry thought was: God, it's quiet. Then he opened his eyes. He was cheek to cheek with the creature, its sweat stinging his skin. Reaching out for the spattered banister he started to haul himself to his feet, his left arm, shoulder, ribs and neck all paining him, but none so badly he could not enjoy the spectacle at his feet.

The Nomad was in extremis, its body—which was even more pitiful and repulsive by the light of day than in the room above—a mass of degenerating tissue.

"Are . . . you . . . there?" the creature said.

It had lost its growl and its silkiness too, as though the selves it had pretended had flickered out along with its sight.

"I'm here," Harry replied.

It tried to raise one of its hands, but failed. "Are you. . . dying?" it wanted to know.

"Not today," Harry said softly.

"That's not right," the creature said. "We have to go together. I . . . am . . . you . . . "

"You haven't got much time," Harry told it. "Don't waste what you've got with that crap."

"But it's true," the thing went on. *"I am . . . I am you and . . . you are love . . . "*

Harry thought of Ted's painting; of the snake beneath his heel. Clinging to the banister, he raised his foot.

"Be quiet," he said.

The creature ignored him. *"You are love . . . "* it said again. *"And love is . . . "*

Harry laid his heel upon its head. "I'm warning you," he said.

"Love is what . . . "

He didn't warn it again, but ground his foot down into its suppurating face as hard as his weary body would allow. It was hard enough. He felt its muck cave in beneath his heel, layers of wafer-bone and ooze dividing under his weight. Small spasms ran out along the creature's limbs to its bloodied fingertips. Then, quite suddenly, it ceased, its schtick unfinished.

In the hallway below, Loretta was murmuring the prayer her brother had begun above.

"Hail Mary, full of grace, the Lord is with thee, blessed art thou among women—"

It sounded pretty to Harry's ears, after the shrieks and the threats.

"And blessed be the fruit of thy womb, Jesus—"

It would not turn death away, of course. It would not save the innocent from suffering. But prettiness was no insignificant quality, not in this troubled world.

While he listened he pulled his heel out of the Nomad's face. The creature's matter, stripped of the will that had shaped it, was already losing distinction and running off down the stairs.

Five steps to the bottom, Harry saw. Just like Hess.

The victory had taken its toll. In addition to his lacerated neck and punctured throat Harry had a broken collarbone, four cracked ribs, a fractured right arm, and mild concussion. As for Stevie, who had been the Nomad's hostage for three days, his traumas were more psychological than physical. They would take some time to heal, if they ever did, but the first step on that journey was made the day after the creature's death. The family moved out of the house on Wyckoff Street, leaving it to the mercy of gossip. This time there would be no attempt to redeem the house. Untenanted, it would fall into disrepair through the winter months, at what some thought an uncanny speed. Nobody would ever occupy it again.

One mystery remained unsolved. Why had the creature plotted to bring him back to Wyckoff Street in the first place? Had it begun to doubt its own mythology and arranged a rematch with an old enemy to confirm its sense of itself? Or had it simply been bored one September day and taken it into its head to play the old game of temptation and slaughter for the sheer hell of it?

The answer to those questions would, Harry assumed, join the long list of things he would never know.

As for Ted's magnum opus, after a few days of indecision Harry elected to hang it in the living room. Given that he was presently one-handed, this took him the better part of two hours to accomplish, but once it was up—the canvas nailed directly to the wall—it looked better than it had in the gallery. Unbounded by a frame, Ted's vision seemed to bleed out across the wall.

Of the lovely Sabina, who had presumably been obeying the Nomad's instructions when she'd delivered the painting, there was no further sign. But Harry had two new deadbolts put on the front door anyway, just in case.

A little less than a fortnight after the endgame in Wyckoff Street, he got a call out of the blue from a fretful Raul.

"I need you to get on a plane, Harry. Whatever you're doing—"

"Where are you?"

"I'm in Omaha. I came looking for Tesla."

"And?"

"I found her. But . . . not quite the way I thought I would."

"Is she okay?" Harry said. There was a silence down the line. "Raul?"

"Yeah, I'm here. I don't know whether she's okay or not. You have to see for yourself."

"Is she at Grillo's place?"

"Yeah. I tracked her from L.A. She told her neighbors she was heading out to Nebraska. That's proof of insanity in Hollywood. How soon can you get out here?"

"I'll catch a flight today, if I can find one. Will you pick me up at the airport? I'm not in the best of shape."

"What happened?"

"I trod in some shit. But it's dead now."

IV

*P*hoebe didn't tell Jarrieffa that she knew the identity of their visitor. It was too painful, for one thing, and for another she was afraid the result would be to scare the woman and her children out of the house. She certainly didn't want that; not just for their sakes, but for her own. She had become used to their mess and their ruckus, and it would make the recognition of what she'd done all the more unbearable if she was left alone in the O'Connell mansion as a consequence.

Jarrieffa had a lot of questions, of course, and she was less than satisfied with some of the answers Phoebe furnished. But as time slipped by, and the children's nightmares and spontaneous bursts of tears diminished in frequency, the house returned to its former rhythm, and whatever doubts Jarrieffa still had she kept to herself.

Phoebe, meanwhile, had begun a systematic search of the city, looking for some clue as to Joe's whereabouts. Assuming he had not simply evaporated upon departing the house (this she doubted; rudimentary he'd been, but still solid), his escape through the streets could not, she reasoned, have gone completely unnoticed. Even in this city, the streets of which boasted more strange forms and physiognomies with every new vessel that dropped anchor, Joe's appearance had been to say the least noteworthy. Somebody must have seen something.

She soon came to regret that she'd been so tardy warming up relations with her neighbors. Though most of them were reasonably polite to her when she came asking questions, they were all wary of her. As far as they were concerned she remained an outsider, and she feared that even if they *had* answers to her questions they would not be forthcoming. Several days in a row she returned to the O'Connell house frustrated and exhausted, having traipsed from door to door (on some streets from construction site to construction site) asking for information, the parameters of her search steadily expanding, along with her sense of desperation. She lost her appetite and her sense of humor. Some days, having skipped two consecutive meals, she'd wander the streets lightheaded and close to tears, calling Joe's name like a crazy woman. Once, finding herself at the end of the day lost and too weary to discover a way home, she slept in the street. On another occasion, wandering into the middle of some territorial dispute between two families, she almost had her throat cut. But she continued to journey out every day, hoping for some clue that would eventually lead her to him.

As it turned out, the sliver of information she'd been searching for came from a source close to hand. Preparing to step into her bath one day, having walked the city for twelve hours or more, there was a knock on her bedroom door, and upon her invitation Enko entered, asking to speak to her for a few moments. He had always been the least friendly member of Jarrieffa's brood; a gangly boy, even by adolescent standards, his face human but for the symmetrical patches of mottling upon his brow and neck, and the vestigial gills that ran from the middle of his cheeks down to his neck.

"I've got a friend," he explained. "His name's Vip Luemu. He lives down the street two blocks. The house with the boarded up windows?"

"I know it," Phoebe said.

"He told me you'd been round asking about . . . you know, that thing that was here."

"Yes I was."

"Well . . . Yip knew something about it, but his mother told him not to speak to you."

"That was neighborly," Phoebe remarked.

"It's not you," Enko replied. "Well . . . it is and it isn't. It's mainly what happened here, you know, in the old days, and with the ships coming back in again, they think you're going to start up business like Miss O'Connell."

"Business?" said Phoebe.

"Yes. You know. The women."

"I'm not following this, Enko."

"The *whores*," the boy said, the mottling on his face darkening.

"Whores?" said Phoebe. "Are you telling me this house . . . used to be a brothel?"

"The best. That's what Vip's father says. People came from all over."

Phoebe pictured Maeve, sitting in regal splendor amid her pillows and her billet-doux, opining on the imbecility of love. And no wonder. The woman had been a madam. Love wasn't good for business.

"You could do me a great service," Phoebe said, "if you'd tell Vip to spread the word that I have no intention of reopening this house for business any time soon."

"I'll do that."

"Now . . . you said he knew something?"

Enko nodded. "He heard his father talking about a *misamee* that was seen down at the harbor."

"*Misamee?*"

"Oh, that's a word the sailors use. It means something they find out at sea that's not really made yet."

Half-dreamed, she thought. Like my Joe; my *misamee* Joe.

"Enko, thank you."

"No trouble," the boy replied, turning to go. Hand on the door, he glanced back. "You know, Musnakaff wasn't my father."

"Yes, I had heard."

"He was my father's cousin. Anyway, he told all about how he used to go out and find women for Miss O'Connell."

"I can imagine," Phoebe said.

"He explained everything. Where to go. What to say. So—"

Enko halted and stared at his shoes.

"So if I ever go back into business—" Phoebe said.

The boy beamed.

"I'll bear you in mind."

She let the bathwater go cold, and began to get dressed again, putting on several layers of clothing against the wind, which had been bitter the last couple of days and was always keener close to the water. Then she went to the kitchen, filled up one of Maeve's silver liquor flasks with mourningberry juice, and headed down to the harbor, thinking as she went that if she failed to find Joe after a year or so, she'd reopen the brothel just to spite the neighbors who'd given her so little help, and like Maeve grow old and sour in luxury, profiting from lovelessness.

---

ii

As Raul had promised, he was waiting at Eppley Airport, though at first Harry failed to recognize him. He'd warmed up the somewhat eerie pallor of his host body with a little pancake, and was sporting a fancy pair of tinted glasses to conceal his silvery pupils. Covering his bald pate, a baseball cap. The ensemble wasn't particularly fetching, but it allowed him to move unnoticed through the crowds.

On the way back to Grillo's house, with Raul tucked behind the wheel of the antiquated Ford convertible (which he confessed he had no license to drive), they exchanged accounts of their recent adventures. Harry told Raul about all that had happened in Wyckoff Street, and Raul reciprocated by telling of the journey he'd made back to the Misión de Santa Catrina, on the Baja Peninsula, where Fletcher had first discovered and synthesized the Nuncio.

"I built a shrine up there a long time ago," he said, "which I tended till Tesla found me. I was sure it would have disappeared. But no. It was still there. The village women still go up to the ruins to pray and ask Fletcher to intercede if their children are sick. It's quite touching. I saw one or two women I knew, but of course they didn't know me. There was one woman though—God knows she must be ninety if she's a day—and I did go seek her out and tell her who I was. She's blind now, and a little crazy, but she swore to me she'd seen him, the day before she lost her sight."

"You mean Fletcher?"

"I mean Fletcher. She said he was standing on the edge of the cliff, staring up at the sun. He used to do that—"

"And you think he's still up there?"

"Stranger things are true," Raul pointed out. "We both know that."

"The walls are getting thinner, right?" Harry said.

"I'd say so."

They drove on in silence for a while. "I thought I'd maybe make another pilgrimage," Raul said after a minute or so, "while I'm here in Omaha."

"Let me guess. The Dead-letters Office."

"If it's still standing," Raul said. "It's probably a deeply uninteresting piece of architecture, but we'd neither of us be here if it hadn't been built."

"You believe that?"

"Oh, I'm sure the Art would have found somebody to use if it hadn't been Jaffe. But we might never have known anything about it. We could have been like them"—he nodded out through the window at Omaha's citizenry, going about their business—"thinking what you see's what you get."

"Do you ever wish it were?" Harry asked him.

"I was born an ape, Harry," Raul replied. "I know what it's like to evolve." He chuckled. "Let me tell you, it's wonderful."

"And that's what this is all about?" Harry said. "Evolving?"

"I think so. We're born to rise. To see more. To know more. Maybe to know everything one day." He halted the car outside a large, gloomy house. "Which brings us back to Tesla," he said, and led Harry up the overgrown driveway where Tesla's bike was parked, to the front door.

The afternoon was drawing on, and the house was even gloomier inside than out, its walls bare, its air damp.

"Where is she?" Harry asked Raul, struggling out of his jacket.

"Let me give you a hand."

"I can do it," Harry said, impatient now. "Just take me to Tesla, will you?"

Raul nodded, his mouth tight, and ushered Harry through to the back of the house. "We have to be careful," he said, as they came to a closed door. "Whatever's going on in here, I think it's volatile."

With that, he opened the door. The room was packed to capacity with all the paraphernalia of Grillo's beloved Reef, the sight of which put Harry in mind of Norma's little sanctum, with its thirty screens busily keeping lost souls at bay. Here, he knew, the reverse process was at work. Here the lost and the crazy found refuge; a place to unburden themselves of all that obsessed them. Their reports were on the screens now, scrolling furiously. And sitting in front of them, her eyes closed, Tesla.

"This is how she was when I got here," Raul said. "In case you're wondering, she's breathing, but it's *very* slow." Harry took a step towards her, but Raul checked him. "Be careful," he said.

"Why?"

"When I tried to get close to her I felt some kind of energy field."

"I don't feel anything," Harry said, advancing another step. As he did so something grazed his face, oh so lightly, like the tremulous wall of a bubble. He made to retreat, but he was too slow. In one paradoxical moment the bubble seemed to suck him in and burst. The room vanished, and he flew like a bullet fired into the blaze of a scarlet sun, its color pure beyond expression. A moment there, and he was gone, out the other side and into another, this one blue; and on, into a yellow, then green, then purple. And as he traveled, sun succeeding sun, vistas began to open to left and right of him, above and below, receding from him to the limit of his sight. Forms erupted on every side, stealing their incandescence from the suns he was piercing, the blaze of which was retreating now, as the forms claimed his devotion. They came at him from every direction, bombarding him with images in such numbers his mind failed to grasp a single one. He started to panic as the assault intensified, fearing his sanity would abandon him if he didn't find a rock in this maelstrom.

And then, Tesla's voice: "*Harry?*"

The sound fixed a vision for an instant. He saw a scene of vivid particulars. A patch of scarred ocher ground. A hole and a bitch mutt sitting beside it, chewing at her rump. A hand with bitten fingernails emerging from the hole, tossing a shard of pottery out onto the cloth laid beside it. And Tesla—or a fragment of her—somewhere beyond the hole and the hand and the mutt.

"Thank God," Harry said, but he'd spoken too soon. The picture slid away, and he was off again, yelling for Tesla as he flew.

"*It's okay,*" she said, "*hold on.*"

Again her voice pulled him up short. Another scene. More particulars. Dusk, this time, and distant hills. A wooden shack in a field of swaying grass, and a woman running towards him with a bawling baby in her arms. Behind her, three dark, diminutive creatures in eager pursuit, their heads huge, their eyes golden. The woman was sobbing in terror as she fled, but the child was weeping for very different reasons, its skinny arms reaching back towards the pursuers. And now, as the babe turned to beat at its mother's head, Harry saw why. Though it appeared to be a human child, its eyes were also golden.

"What's happening here?" Harry said.

"*Anybody's guess,*" Tesla replied. As she spoke he saw another piece of her in the vicinity of the shack. "*It's all part of the Reef.*"

And now, as the child started to slip from its mother's arms, the scene slid away like the first, and on he flew, his mind starting to snatch hold of some of the dramas he was piercing. Never more than a piece—a flock of birds in ice, a coin bleeding on the ground, somebody laughing in a burning chair—but enough to know that every one of these innumerable images was part of some greater scheme.

"Amazing—" he breathed.

"*Isn't it?*" Tesla said, and again her voice brought him to a halt. A city, this time. A lowery sky, and from it flecks of silvery light dropping lightly, like mirrored feathers. On the sidewalks below, people went about their business blind to the sight, except for one upturned face: an old man, pointing and hollering.

"What am I seeing?" Harry said.

"*Stories . . .* " Tesla replied, and hearing her, Harry glimpsed another piece of her mosaic, in the crowd. "*That's what Grillo gathered here. Hundreds of thousands of stories.*"

The street was slipping. "I'm losing you—" Harry warned.

"*Just let go,*" Tesla replied. "*I'll catch up with you somewhere else.*"

He did as she instructed. The street fled, and he moved on at breath-snatching speed while the stories continued to fly at him from all directions. Again, he caught only glimpses. But now he had some way to interpret the sights, however brief. There were epics and chamber pieces here; domestic dramas and quests to the end of the world; Old Testament splendors and nursery-tale terrors.

"I'm not sure I can take much more," Harry said. "I feel like I'm going to lose my mind."

"*You'll find another,*" Tesla quipped, and again he stopped dead in the midst of a tale.

This time, however, there was something different about it. This was a story he knew.

"*Recognize it?*" Tesla said.

Of course. It was Everville. The crossroads, Saturday afternoon, with the sun pouring down on a scene of farce and lunacy. The band on their butts; Buddenbaum digging for glory; the air laced with visions of whores. It was not the way Harry remembered it exactly, but what the hell? It held its own with anything he'd witnessed so far.

"Am *I* here?" he asked.

"*You are now,*" Tesla replied.

"What?"

"*Grillo was wrong, calling it a reef,*" Tesla went on. "*A reef's dead. This is still growing. Stories don't die, Harry—*"

"They change?"

"*Exactly. Your seeing all this enriches it, evolves it. Nothing's ever lost. That's what I'm learning.*"

"Are you going to stay?" Harry said, watching the drama at the crossroads continue to elaborate.

"*For a while,*" she said. "*There are answers here, if I can get down to the root.*"

She reached out towards Harry as she spoke, and he saw that the fragments he'd glimpsed on the way here were before him still. Part of her was carved from a patch of ocher ground, and part from the hole dug there. Part resembled the shack in the field, and part the golden-eyed child. Part was made of mirror-flakes, part was the old man, pointing skyward.

And part, of course, was made from that sunlit afternoon, and from Owen Buddenbaum, who would be at the crossroads raging for as long as stories were told.

Finally, though he could not see this sliver, he knew she was also made from *him*, who was in this story somewhere.

I am you . . . the Nomad murmured in his head.

"*Do you understand any of this?*" Tesla asked him.

"I'm beginning to."

"*It's like love, Harry. No; that's not right. I think maybe it is love.*"

She smiled at her own comprehension. And as she smiled the contact between them was broken. He flew from her, back through the blazing colors, and was returned in the bursting of a bubble to the stale room he'd departed.

Raul was there, waiting for him, trembling.

"God, D'Amour," he said, "I thought I'd lost you."

Harry shook his head. "It was touch and go for a moment there," he said. "I was visiting with Tesla. She was showing me around."

He looked at the body sitting in the chair in front of the monitors. It seemed suddenly redundant: the flesh, the bone. The true Tesla—perhaps the true Harry, perhaps the true world—was back where he'd come from, telling itself in the infinite branches of the story tree.

"Will she be coming back?" Raul wanted to know.

"When she's got where she wants to go," Harry replied.

"And where's that?"

"Back to the beginning," Harry said. "Where else?"

iii

That first trip down to the harbor proved fruitless; Phoebe found nobody who knew anything about the *misamee*. But on the second day her relentless questioning bore fruit. Yes, one of the Dock Road bar owners told her, he knew what she was talking about. Some creature in an agonized and unfinished state had indeed been seen down here several weeks before. In fact, if his memory served, some attempt had been made to corral the abomination, for fear it had murderous appetites. To his knowledge the creature had never been caught. Perhaps, he suggested, it had been driven back into the sea, from which everybody had assumed it emerged. In which case the tide had carried its misbegotten body away.

There was both good news here and bad. She had confirmation that she was at least searching in the right quarter of the city; that was the good. But the fact that Joe had not been sighted of late suggested that perhaps the bar owner's theory was correct, and he had indeed been lost to the waters. She now went in search of somebody who had been a member of the pursuit party, but as the days went by it became more and more difficult to keep track of her progress. There were new ships docking daily, from single masted vessels to the plethora of fishing boats that plied in and out of the harbor, leaving light and returning heavy with their catch. Often she found herself neglecting her inquiries and listening, half enchanted, to the talk exchanged by the sailors and the stevedores: stories of what lay out beyond the tranquil waters of the harbor, out in the wilds and wastes of the dream-sea.

She had heard of the Ephemeris of course, and from Musnakaff of Plethoziac and Trophetté. But there were far more than these; countries and cities whose names conjured glories. Some were real places (their goods being unloaded at the dock), others in the category of fables. Into the former group went the island of Berger's Mantle, where crews were apparently lost all the time, preyed upon by a species so exquisite the victims died of disbelief. Into the latter went the city of Nilpallium, which had been founded by a fool, and which was ruled over—justly and well, so legend went—by its founder's dogs, who had devoured him upon his decease.

The story that most engaged her, however, was that of Kicaranka Rojandi. It was reputedly a tower of burning rock, which rose straight-sided out of the sea, climbing to a height of half a mile. The species that crawled and climbed upon it were not consumed by its flames, but had to constantly fling themselves down into the steaming waves to cool their bodies, only to begin the ascent afresh when they could bear to, desperate to court and fertilize their queen, who lived encased in flame at the very summit.

The more preposterous of these stories were a healthy, indeed vital, distraction from her misery, and the true ones were curiously encouraging, evidence as they were of how many miraculous states of being were plausible here. If the citizens of b'Kether Sabbat had the courage to live in an inverted pyramid, and the fire climbers of Kicaranka Rojandi the devotion to climb their tower, believing they would one day reach their queen, should she not keep looking for her *misamee?*

And then came the day of the storm. It had been predicted by the retired mariners along the quayside for some time: a tempest of notable ferocity that would have all manner of deep-sea fish rising in shoals from their trenches. For those enterprising fisherman willing to risk their nets, their boats, and very possibly their lives in open waters, a haul of prodigious proportions was predicted.

Phoebe was warming herself in front of the kitchen fire when the winds started to rise, the children sitting eating stew nearby, their mother kneading bread.

"I hear a window slamming," Jarrieffa said, as the first rain pattered on the kitchen sill, and hurried away to close it.

Phoebe stared into the flames, while the gusts whooped and howled in the chimney. It would be quite a spectacle down by the Dock Road, she suspected. Ships tossing at anchor and the sea throwing itself against the harbor wall. Who knew what a storm like this would drive up onto the shore?

She rose as she formed the thought. Who knew indeed?

"Jarrieffa?" she yelled, as she fetched her coat from the closet. "Jarrieffa! I'm going out!"

The woman was coming down the stairs now, a look of concern on her face. "In this weather?" she said.

"Don't worry. I'll be fine."

"Take Enko with you. It's cruel out there."

"No, Jarrieffa, I can stand a little rain. You just stay in the warm and bake your bread."

Still protesting that this was not a wise thing to be doing, Jarrieffa followed Phoebe to the door, and out onto the step.

"Go back inside," Phoebe told her. "I'll be back in a while."

Then she was off, into the deluge.

It had cleared the streets as effectively as the Iad. She encountered scarcely a soul as she made her way down through the warren of minor streets and back alleys that were by now as familiar to her feet as Main Street and Poppy Lane. The closer she got to the water, the less cover she had to shield her from the fury of the storm. By the time she reached the Dock Road she was leaning into the wind, and more than once had to grip a wall or railing to keep herself from being thrown off her feet.

The quayside and the decks of the ships were a good deal busier than the streets she'd come through, as crews labored to secure sails and lash down cargo. One of the single-masted vessels had slipped its mooring and as Phoebe watched it was dashed against the harbor wall. Its timbers splintered, and a number of its crew jumped into the water, which was frenzied. She didn't wait to see if the vessel sank, but hurried on, past the harbor and through the warehouse district adjacent to it, out onto the shore.

The waves were tall and thunderous, the air so thick with spray and rain she could not see more than a dozen yards ahead of her. But the grim fury of the scene suited her mood. She stumbled over the dark, slick rocks, daring the waters to reach high enough to claim her, yelling Joe's name as she went. The gale snatched the syllable from her lips, of course, but she strode on doggedly, her tears mingling with the rain and the spume off the dream-sea.

At last her fatigue and her despair overcame her. She sank down onto the stones, soaked to the skin, her throat too hoarse and lungs too raw to call his name again.

Her extremities were numb with cold, her head throbbing. She raised her hands to her mouth to warm her fingers with her breath, and was thinking that if she didn't move soon she might very well freeze to death when she caught sight of a figure in the mist further along the beach. Somebody was approaching her. A man, his few clothes less than rags, his body a strange compendium of forms and hues. In places he was purplish in color, his skin scaly. In others he had small patches of almost silvery skin. But the core of him—the flesh around his eyes and his mouth, down his neck and across his chest and belly— was black. She started to rise, the name she had been yelling to the wind too much for her astonished lips.

It didn't matter. He had seen her; seen her with the eyes she herself had dreamed into being. He halted now, a few yards from her, a tiny smile on his face.

She could not hear his voice—the waves were too loud—but she knew the shape of her name when he spoke it.

"Phoebe . . . ?"

Tentatively, she approached him, halving the distance between them, but not yet coming within reach of his arms. She was just a little afraid. Perhaps the rumors of murderous intent were true. If not, where had he found the pieces of flesh to finish his body?

"It is you, isn't it?" he said. She was close enough to catch his words now.

"It's me," she said.

"I thought maybe I'd lost my mind. Maybe I'd imagined it all."

"No," she said. "I dreamed you here, Joe."

Now it was he who approached, looking down at his hands. "You certainly put some flesh on me," he said. "But the spirit—" one of those hands went to his chest, "what's in *here*—that's me. The Joe you found out in the weeds."

"I was certain I dreamed you."

"You did. And I heard. And I came. But I'm not some fantasy, Phoebe. This is Joe."

"So what happened to you?" she said. "Where did—"

"The rest of me come from?"

"Yes."

Joe turned his gaze towards the water. "The 'shu. The spirit-pilots." Phoebe remembered Musnakaff's short lesson on that subject well enough: *Pieces of the Creator*, he'd said, *or not*. "I threw myself into the water, hoping I'd drown, but they found me. Surrounded me. Dreamed the rest of me into being." He raised his hand for her scrutiny. "As you can see," he said, "I think they put a little of their own nature into me while they were doing it." The limb was more strangely fashioned than she'd first realized; the fingers webbed, the skin full of subtle ripples. "Does it offend you?"

"Lord, no . . . " she said. "I'm just grateful to have you back."

Now at last, she opened her arms and went to him. He gathered her to his body, which was warm despite the rain and spray, his embrace as fierce as hers.

"I still can't quite believe you followed me," he murmured.

"What else was I going to do?" she replied.

"You know there's no way back, don't you?"

"Why would we want to go?" she said.

*   *   *

They stayed there on the shore for a long while, talking sometimes, but mostly just cradling one another. They didn't make love. That was for another day. For many days, in fact. Now, just embraces, just kisses, just tenderness, until the storm had exhausted itself.

When they returned along the quay, several hours later, the heavens clearing, the air pristine, scarcely a gaze was turned in their direction. People were too busy. There were damaged hulls to be repaired, torn sails to be mended, scattered cargoes to be gathered up and restowed.

And for those audacious fishermen who'd dared the violence of the storm, and returned unharmed, prayers offered up on the quayside as the boats were unloaded. Prayers of thanks for their survival and for the dream-sea's largesse. The prophets who'd predicted the tempest had been proved correct: The frenzied waters had indeed thrown up an unprecedented catch.

While the lovers wandered unnoticed to the house on the hill (where they would with time come to a certain notoriety), the contents of the nets were heaped on the dock. Up out of Quiddity, from its unfathomed places, had come creatures strange even to the fishermen's eyes. They were like things made in the first days of the world, some of them; others like the scrawlings of an infant on a wall. A few were featureless, many more bright with colors that had no name. Some flickered with their own luminescence, even in the daylight.

Only the 'shu were thrown back. The rest were sorted, put in baskets, and carried up to the fish-market where a crowd had already gathered in anticipation of this bounty. Even the ugliest, the least of the infant's scrawls, would nourish somebody. Nothing would be wasted; nothing lost.